THE
TOM DUGAN
OMNIBUS

Thrillers by

R. E. McDermott

DEADLY STRAITS

For Andrea

"Whosoever commands the sea commands the trade;
Whosoever commands the trade of the world
commands the riches of the world, and consequently the world itself."

—Sir Walter Raleigh, October 1618

CHAPTER ONE

OFFICES OF PHOENIX SHIPPING
LONDON
10 MAY

Alex Kairouz turned from the screen and swiveled in his chair to bend over his wastebasket, barely in time. He vomited as his nausea crested, then slumped head down and sobbing over the basket. A hand appeared, holding a tissue.

"Wipe your bloody face, Kairouz," Braun said.

Alex did as ordered.

Braun continued.

"Mr. Farley, please be good enough to refocus our pupil on the task at hand."

Alex tensed against the pain as he was jerked upright by his thick hair and spun around to once again face the computer screen. He closed his eyes to blot out the horrific sight and tried to put his hands to his ears to escape the tortured screams from the speakers, but Farley was quicker, grabbing his wrists from behind and forcing them down.

"Open your bloody eyes and cooperate, Kairouz," said Braun, "unless you want a ringside seat at a live performance."

Alex looked not at the screen but at Braun.

"Why are you doing this? What do you want? If it's money—"

Braun moved his face inches from Alex's.

"In due time, Kairouz, all in due time." Braun lowered his voice to a whisper. "But for now, you need to finish our little lesson. I assure you, it gets much, much more amusing."

M/T *WESTERN STAR*
EASTERN HOLDING ANCHORAGE
SINGAPORE
15 MAY

Dugan moved through the humid darkness of the ship's ballast tank, avoiding pockets of mud. At the ladder he wiped his face on a damp sleeve and turned at muttered Russian curses to shine his flashlight on the corpulent chief mate struggling through an access hole. The man's coveralls, like Dugan's own, were sweat soaked and rust streaked. The Russian pulled through the access hole with a grunt and joined Dugan at the ladder. Sweat rolled down his stubbled cheeks as he fixed Dugan with a hopeful look.

"We go up?" he asked.

Dugan nodded and the Russian started up the long ladder, intent on escaping the tank before Dugan had a change of heart. Dugan played his flashlight over wasted steel one last time, grimacing at the predictable result of poor maintenance, then followed the Russian up the ladder.

He emerged on the main deck at the tail end of a tropical thundershower so common to Singapore. His coveralls were already plastered to his skin by sweat, and the cool rain felt good. But the relief wouldn't last. The rain was slackening, and steam from the deck showed the negligible effect of the brief shower on the hot steel. Two Filipino seamen stood nearby in yellow slickers, looking like small boys dressed in their fathers' clothing. One handed Dugan a wad of rags as the second held open a garbage bag. Dugan wiped his boots and tossed the rags in the bag, then started aft for the deckhouse.

He showered and changed before heading for the gangway, stopping along the way to slip the steward a few dollars for cleaning his room. The grateful Filipino tried to carry his bag, and, when waved away, ran in front, holding doors as an embarrassed Dugan made his way to the main deck. Overtipped again, thought Dugan, making his way down the sloping accommodation ladder to the launch.

He ducked into the launch's cabin and settled in for the ride ashore. Three dogs in six weeks. He didn't look forward to telling Alex Kairouz he'd wasted his money inspecting another rust bucket.

***

An hour later, Dugan settled into an easy chair in his hotel room. He opened an overpriced beer from the minibar, then checked the time. Start of business in London. May as well give Alex a bit of time to get his day started before breaking the bad news. Dugan picked up the remote and thumbed on the television to Sky News. The screen filled with images of a raging refinery fire in Bandar Abbas, Iran. Must be a big one to make international news, he thought.

***

Alex Kairouz sat at his desk, trembling, his eyes squeezed shut and face buried in his hands. He shuddered and shook his head, as if trying to physically cast out the images burned into his brain. Finally he opened his eyes to stare at a photo of his younger self—black hair and eyes in an olive face, and white even teeth, set in a smile of pure joy as he gazed at a pink bundle in the arms of a beautiful woman. He jerked at the buzz of the intercom, then struggled to compose himself.

"Yes, Mrs. Coutts?" he said into the intercom.

"Mr. Dugan on line one, sir."

Thomas! Panic gripped him. Thomas knew him too well. He might sense something wrong, and Braun said if anyone knew—

"Mr. Kairouz, are you there?"

"Yes, yes, Mrs. Coutts. Thank you."

Alex steeled himself and mashed the flashing button.

"Thomas," he said with forced cheerfulness, "how's the ship?"

"Junk."

"Damn."

"What'd you expect, Alex? Good tonnage is making money. Anything for sale now is garbage. You know how it works. You built your own fleet at rock-bottom prices in down markets."

Alex sighed. "I know, but I need more ships and I keep hoping. Oh well, send me an invoice." He paused, more focused now, as he glanced at a notepad on his desk. "And Thomas, I need a favor."

"Name it."

"*Asian Trader* is due into the shipyard there in two days, and McGinty was hospitalized yesterday with appendicitis. Can you cover the ship until I can get another superintendent out to relieve you?"

"How long?"

"Ten days, two weeks max," Alex said.

Dugan sighed. "Yeah, all right. But I may have to break away for a day. I got a call from Military Sealift Command this morning. They want me to inspect a little coaster for them sometime in the next few days. I can't ignore my other clients, even though sometimes it seems I'm on your payroll full-time—"

"Since you brought that up—"

"Christ, Alex. Not again."

"Look, Thomas, we're all getting older. I mean, you're what, fifty now—"

"Forty-seven my next birthday."

"OK, forty-seven. But you can't crawl through ships forever. And it's a waste of talent. Plenty of fellows can identify problems. I need someone here to solve them."

"OK, OK. I'll think about it. How's that sound?"

"Like what you always say to shut me up."

"Is it working?" Dugan asked.

"All right, Thomas. I give up. For now. But we'll talk again."

Dugan changed the subject.

"How's Cassie?"

"Ah…she's…"

"What's wrong?" asked Dugan.

"Sorry, my mind was just wandering a bit, I'm afraid. Cassie's fine, just fine. Looking more like her mother every day. And Mrs. Farnsworth says she's making remarkable progress, considering."

"And how is the Dragon Lady?" Dugan asked.

"Really, Thomas, I think you two would get on if you gave it a chance."

"I don't think I'm the one who needs that advice, Alex."

"Well, if you were around more and Mrs. Farnsworth got to know you, I'm sure she would warm to you," Alex said.

Dugan laughed. "Yeah, like that's going to happen."

Alex sighed. "You're probably right. At any rate, I'll have Mrs. Coutts e-mail you the repair specifications for *Asian Trader* straightaway. Can you get up to the yard in Sembawang tomorrow morning and begin preparations for her arrival?"

"Will do, pal," Dugan said. "I'll call you after she arrives and I get things started."

Alex thanked Dugan and hung up. He'd maintained a good front with Dugan, and, for that matter, everyone else. But it was draining. The everyday minutia of running his company he'd so enjoyed just a few days ago seemed pointless now—there'd likely be no Phoenix Shipping when this bastard Braun was finished. But that didn't matter. Only Cassie's safety mattered. His eyes went back to the photo of his once-complete family, and he shuddered anew as the images from Braun's video flashed through his memory.

MIRAFLORES PALACE
CARACAS, VENEZUELA
18 MAY

Ali Reza Motaki, president of the Islamic Republic of Iran, stood at the window, gazing out at the well-manicured grounds. He tensed as his back spasmed. Even in the comfort of the presidential jet, the long flight from Tehran to Caracas had taken its toll. He massaged his lower back and stretched to his full five foot five.

"And is this Kairouz controllable?" asked a voice behind him.

Motaki turned to the speaker, President Hector Diaz Rodriguez of the Bolivarian Republic of Venezuela.

"He is devoted to his daughter," replied Motaki. "He will do anything to keep her from harm. Don't worry my friend, Braun has it well in hand."

Rodriguez smiled. "And what do you think of Braun? Is he not everything I promised?"

"He seems…competent."

Rodriguez's smile faded. "You seem less than enthusiastic."

"I am cautious, as you should be. Acting against the Great Satan is one thing. Duping China and Russia simultaneously is another. We cannot afford mistakes," Motaki said.

"But what choice do we have?" Rodriguez asked. "For all their fine words of friendship, neither the Russians nor the Chinese have acceded to our requests. If we must maneuver them into doing the right thing, so be it."

Motaki shrugged. "I doubt the Russians and Chinese would view it as mere maneuvering."

Rodriguez nodded as Motaki moved from the window to settle down in an easy chair across from the Venezuelan.

"And now it is even more critical that we succeed," Motaki continued. "The damage at the Bandar Abbas refinery is worse than reported in the media. Iran will have to import even more of our domestic fuel requirements, just as the Americans are pressing the UN for tighter sanctions. It is strangling our economy, just as your own lack of access to Asian markets for Venezuelan crude cripples your own."

"That's true," Rodriguez said. "And to be honest, I am concerned we're using only one company. We are putting all our eggs in one basket, as the *yanquis* say."

Motaki shook his head. "No, Braun is right about that. With widely separated attacks, the plan is complicated. Braun's selection of Phoenix was astute—a single company with ships trading worldwide, controlled by one man without outside directors. Control Kairouz, control Phoenix, no questions asked."

Rodriguez nodded. "So we proceed. When will Braun confirm the strike date?"

"I got an encrypted message this morning through the usual channels," Motaki said. "July fourth looks promising. Perhaps we can, as they say, rain on the Americans' parade."

"Excellent." Rodriguez rubbed his hands together. "That will allow me to include some sympathetic remarks in my speech on our own Independence Day on July fifth. Perhaps I can even get an early start in laying these terrible deeds at the feet of the Americans."

Motaki smiled and nodded. And, perhaps in so doing, become the sacrificial lamb should things go awry, he thought.

CHAPTER TWO

M/V *ALICIA*
EASTERN ANCHORAGE, SINGAPORE
20 MAY

Jan Pieter DeVries scratched his bare belly and looked down from the bridge wing. He wore dirty khaki shorts and a wrinkled shirt hanging open from missing buttons, and was shod in flip-flops. A dark tan and tangle of long brown hair made the thirty-year-old look more like an itinerant fisherman than a captain and ship owner, but M/V *Alicia* was his free and clear.

At just over two hundred feet, fifteen hundred tons deadweight, and a shallow draft, she was a trim little ship. She'd been well maintained in prior years, when she was named *Indies Trader* and operated by his stiff-necked family back in Holland. She'd been a "parting gift" of sorts—a convenient way for the family DeVries to prune one of their less desirable branches. It was a parting that suited Jan Pieter as well. Even with no maintenance, *Indies Trader* could trade years before cargo surveyors questioned her seaworthiness—longer in remote ports of Asia, far from the disapproving oversight of the family DeVries. She was perfect for his plan—just as he'd promised a broker named Willem Van Dijk.

He renamed the ship *Alicia*, after a girl whose last name he'd forgotten but whose sexual appetites and flexibility were vivid memories. He moved his first cargo for Van Dijk and never looked back. The broker handled everything, and each voyage included clandestine calls at remote anchorages where illicit goods changed hands, with revenue split between the partners.

As crewmen left on vacation, Van Dijk arranged Indonesian replacements, among the first a competent chief mate named Ali Sheibani. Soon Sheibani was running the ship, and DeVries became a pampered passenger, spending little time on the ship in port and sea passages in his cabin, listening to music through state-of-the-art headphones, smoking dope, and reviewing his burgeoning account balances. M/V *Alicia* had perhaps five years of life left, assuming breakdown maintenance, then he would scrap her and retire a rich man.

But first he must satisfy the US Navy. He peered down into the open cargo hold, where Sheibani escorted three men, two in blue coveralls and a third in white. A blue-clad figure looked up and DeVries nodded, receiving a return wave before the man lowered his gaze and turned to speak to his companions. The other men laughed. At least they were in a good mood.

***

Dugan watched as Petty Officer First Class Doug Broussard US Navy, returned the Dutch captain's nod with a wave.

"Captain Flip-Flop reached the bridge," Broussard said. "So much for his participation."

Dugan and the third man in his party, Chief Petty Officer Ricardo "Ricky" Vega, USN, laughed.

"Probably just as well," Vega said, nodding to a small man in coveralls talking to a crewman nearby. "The chief mate there seems to be running the show."

Broussard nodded. "Yeah, he seems OK. But I wish his English was better." He leaned closer. "But what about the ship?"

Vega shrugged and turned to Dugan.

"What about it, Mr. Dugan?" Vega asked. "You're the expert."

Dugan shook his head and looked around. "She's not quite in the crapper yet, but she's on the way down. Give Flip-Flop up there a few years and you'll be wearing snowshoes to keep from crashing through the frigging deck." He paused. "Tell me again why we're inspecting this greyhound of the seas."

Vega grimaced. "Mainly because we got no choice. We got a SEACAT exercise scheduled off Phang-Nga, and our boats and gear got off-loaded here in Singapore by mistake, instead of up in Thailand. If we don't pre-position the boats so the Royal Thai Navy guys get some hands-on with us prior to the exercise, it's gonna be a cluster fuck. We can't run up under our own power, 'cause the Malaysians and Indonesians have a hard-on about unescorted foreign gunboats in territorial waters." Vega paused. "*Alicia* here is all that's available that can meet our time frame."

Vega looked around the cargo hold again and shook his head. "Thing is," he continued, "she falls outside our normal chartering criteria. That's why MSC wanted a third party to give her a clean bill of health before we take her."

"So basically," Dugan said, "the MSC chartering pukes want someone to blame if the fucking thing sinks."

Vega grinned. "Pretty much, yeah."

Dugan sighed and looked pensive. "OK, look," he said, "her inspections are current, and the firefighting equipment was serviced last month. We're talking a two-day run in good weather and sheltered water, never out of sight of land, with a dozen ports of refuge. She's not the Queen Mary, but I guess she'll do."

Dugan finished as Sheibani, the chief mate, approached. "You like ship, yes? You want us fix something? You tell me, no problem."

"We'll need some pad eyes welded to the deck for securing gear. You have chalk we could use to mark the locations?" Dugan pantomimed marking.

"You wait," Sheibani said, palms outward in the universal sign for "wait" as he shouted up to a crewman on main deck who scurried away.

As they waited, Broussard pointed at the booms. "Those look way too small, Chief."

Vega turned to Sheibani. "Your booms. How many tons?"

"Three tons," Sheibani said. "Both booms same. Three tons."

Vega nodded. "The boats with cradles weigh twenty tons. We'll need shore cranes at both ends."

"No problem here in Singapore," Broussard said. "I'll get on the horn to Phang-Nga."

Sheibani looked up at a shout and stretched with easy grace to catch a piece of chalk sailing down from main deck. He turned. "You show. I mark."

Dugan unfolded a sketch, and they started through the hold.

***

Chief Mate Ali Sheibani, AKA Major Ali Sheibani, Iranian Revolutionary Guard Corps Navy, seconded to Qods Brigade for the work of Allah, praised be His Name, in Southeast Asia, watched the infidels' launch depart as he attempted to ignore the nervous captain beside him.

"This is too risky, Sheibani," DeVries repeated.

Sheibani sneered. "A bit late to develop an interest," he said in perfect English.

DeVries bristled. "I'm the captain and owner. I'll cancel the charter."

"Try, DeVries, and both your captaincy and your ownership will come to an unpleasant end." Sheibani glanced at nearby seamen. "You might, with a little help, fall into the hold. A tragic, but not infrequent, occurrence. Go now. Go play your music and smoke your dope."

He turned his back, and Captain DeVries, master after God of M/V *Alicia*, slunk away.

SEMBAWANG MARINE TERMINAL
SINGAPORE
22 MAY

Dugan stood on *Alicia*'s main deck and glanced at his watch. Balancing two clients simultaneously was always a challenge, but he had a bit of time before Alex's ship was high and dry and the shipyard was only five minutes away. He looked down into the hold through the open hatch, watching as the second boat landed beside her already-secured twin. Longshoremen swarmed, unshackling the slings and securing the boat. Dugan nodded approval as Broussard supervised the process.

"Sweet boats, Chief," Dugan said to Chief Petty Officer Vega, who stood beside him. He pointed to a steel container secured aft of the boats. "Firepower in the container?"

"Can't have a gunboat without guns," Vega said.

"Isn't that risky?" Dugan asked. "I mean, with all these people involved."

Vega shook his head. "We couldn't keep this quiet, anyway. We figure to let everyone see her leave with our guys riding shotgun. The raggedy-ass pirates in the strait like softer targets. We've hidden tracking transponders in each of the boats with a backup on the ship, and Broussard will report in every six hours."

Dugan nodded and extended his hand. "OK. It looks like everything's in hand here. I have one of Phoenix Shipping's tankers going on drydock this morning, and she should be almost dry, so I'll head back to the yard. When will *Alicia* sail?"

Vega took Dugan's hand. "At this rate, they'll finish by midnight and sail at first light." He grinned. "Presuming they can drag Captain Flip-Flop out of whatever whorehouse he's in."

Dugan laughed. "OK. I'll stop by tomorrow morning and see she gets off all right. It's on my way to the yard, anyway."

"See you then," Vega said.

Neither noticed a crewman squatting behind a winch, pretending to grease it.

Third Mate Ronald Carlito Medina of the Phoenix Shipping tanker M/T *Asian Trader* pushed his way down the narrow gangway, ignoring the protests of oncoming workers as he squeezed past. He paused on the wing wall of the drydock, captivated by the controlled chaos unfolding far below. Mist filled the air as workers blasted the hull with high-pressure water, and he watched the American Dugan race into the bottom of the dry dock, the shipyard repair manager in tow. Dugan stopped and pointed up at the hull as his voice cut through the din of machinery, demanding more manpower. The yardman responded with that patient Asian nod indicating not agreement but "Yes, I see your lips moving." Medina smiled as he turned to move down the stairs to sea level and dry land beyond.

Dodging bicycles, trucks, and forklifts, he made his way to the main gate and a cab for the Sembawang MRT station, and minutes later sat in a train car, backpack between his feet as he leaned back and dozed. He could have been a student or civil servant on his day off—anything but a Jihadist intent on Paradise. But then little was as it seemed.

He was born to a Christian father and Muslim mother, and official records listed him as Roman Catholic but orphaned in his infancy, he was adopted by his Muslim grandparents. A fiercely proud man, his grandfather called him Saful Islam, or Sword of Islam, and set about bringing the boy up properly, intent on erasing the stain on the family name left by his daughter's marriage to an infidel.

At the age of twelve, and with his grandfather's blessing, young Medina joined the Abu Sayyaf freedom fighters in the service of Allah, where his non-Moro appearance and official identity were considered gifts from Allah to blind the infidels' eyes. He was a resource, and a valuable one, and the leaders of Abu Sayyaf reckoned he would be more valuable still if he had a legitimate cover to roam the world. When the time was right, Ronald Carlito Medina entered the Davao Merchant Marine Academy.

***

Medina started awake as the train jerked to a stop in Novena station. He dashed off the train and up the escalator into Novena Mall, past chain stores and fast-food outlets to settle at a terminal in an Internet café. The meeting with his contact the previous day had been troubling, providing a mission but few resources. And the American Dugan's almost constant presence aboard *Asian Trader* was another unanticipated complication. But Allah would provide. He moved the mouse and clicked on a link for the website of the Panama Canal Authority.

CHAPTER THREE

Dugan stood on the dock and watched as Sheibani, the chief mate, manned *Alicia*'s bridge wing and spoke into a walkie-talkie, and the crew took in mooring lines in response. They got to a certain point and stopped.

"What the fuck's going on?" asked Chief Petty Officer Vega beside him. "They singled up lines fore and aft and then just stopped, and the friggin' gangway's still down."

In answer to his question, a cab raced onto the dock and skidded to a stop near the gangway. A disheveled Captain Flip-Flop exited the cab, shoved a wad of money through the driver's-side window, and lurched up the gangway in an unsteady trot. He reached the top to derisive cheers from the crew and disappeared into the deck house, as the crew set about taking in the gangway.

"Christ if that doesn't look like standard operating procedure," Vega said as he watched the crew take in the final lines.

"Yeah, I'd have to agree that doesn't look like it was unexpected," Dugan said as they watched a tug warp *Alicia* away from the dock.

"Well," Vega said, "thank God it's only two days and that the chief mate seems to have his shit together."

Dugan nodded silent agreement as he stood beside the navy man and watched *Alicia* move into the channel. One ship away and one to go, he thought as his mind drifted to *Asian Trader* sitting on drydock less than a mile away. That was a strange one. *Asian Trader* had been in the yard over a week and Alex Kairouz hadn't called once. Alex was a hands-on guy, and though Dugan knew he had Alex's complete trust, he also knew Alex was incapable of staying aloof from the myriad details of his business. At least he had been that way.

"I guess that's it then," said Vega beside him, pulling Dugan back to the present. "Thanks for the help, Mr. Dugan." Vega extended his hand.

"My pleasure, Chief," Dugan said, as he shook Vega's hand. "I guess I'd better get on over to the yard and see what latest crisis is brewing on *Asian Trader*."

Broussard looked out from the bridge wing over the waters of the strait and suppressed a yawn. His attempt at sleep off watch had yielded catnaps between sweaty awakenings, as the decrepit air conditioning of the four-man cabin he shared with his team had labored in vain. The sun was low now, so maybe nightfall would lessen the strain on the antiquated cooling system. Perhaps Hopkins and Santiago, now off watch, would have better luck sleeping than he and Washington had.

He'd just begun his second six-hour watch, but he was already sweating. The body armor was hot, and he was restrained from shedding it only by Chief Vega's graphic description of what he would do to anyone who did. Broussard's single concession to comfort was his helmet strapped to his web gear instead of on his head.

"How do you copy?" asked Washington's voice in Broussard's ear, as his subordinate checked in from his position on the stern.

"Five by five," Broussard said.

He looked up as Sheibani approached with his ever-present smile. Nice little guy, he thought, though he talked like an Asian in a crappy TV movie.

"Mr. Broussard," Sheibani said, "you sleep very good, yes? Cabin OK?"

"Just fine," Broussard lied, "thanks for your hospitality."

"Good," Sheibani said, squinting into the distance. "What that?"

Broussard followed Sheibani's gaze and said over his shoulder, "I don't—"

A light burst behind Broussard's eyes as he dropped, equipment clattering. Sheibani pocketed the sap and knelt to bind the American's wrists before rising to move away, his smile now genuine.

***

Broussard awoke to a throbbing head, the scuffed blue tile of the officers' lounge cool on his cheek and filling his vision. He was gagged and bound hand and foot, the night sky through the portholes telling him the sun had set.

"Ah, Broussard," said a strangely familiar voice, "you decided to rejoin us."

He ignored his pounding head and twisted to look up, then tried to twist away as Sheibani pried his eye wide with thumb and forefinger and a bright light obliterated his vision. He squirmed as Sheibani repeated the process on the other eye.

"Good," Sheibani said. "Pupils equal and reactive. I feared a concussion. I don't normally use nonlethal force. It was a learning experience."

Broussard's curse emerged as an irritated grunt through the tape covering his mouth.

"Patience, Broussard," Sheibani said. "I want to hear what you have to say, but first you must listen."

He barked orders and two crewmen manhandled Broussard into a chair. Hands bound behind, he balanced on the edge of the seat, feet pressed to the deck. Hopkins and Santiago perched nearby, similarly restrained. All were barefoot and stripped to their utility trousers. Broussard's hope surged at Washington's absence then died as quickly.

"While you napped," Sheibani said, "Washington and I chatted."

Sheibani nodded and his subordinates stepped into the passageway and dragged in a plastic-wrapped bundle, leaving it in front of the three Americans and throwing back the plastic. Washington was face up, blood pooled in empty eye sockets. The severed fingers of one hand, his genitals, and his eyeballs were piled in the center of his massive chest. Ebony skin was flayed in wide strips and blood wept from raw flesh to pool on the plastic. Broussard screwed his eyes shut and fought rising vomit. Hopkins did the same, but Santiago made strangling noises, vomit pulsing from his nose. Sheibani ripped the tape from Santiago's mouth as the sailor retched on the corpse and then coughed wetly before managing a ragged breath.

***

Washington had told Sheibani nothing. He had, in fact, spit in Sheibani's face, sending the Iranian into a rage that ended in Washington's death. Sheibani regretted his loss of control, but, after some thought, decided Washington would serve him in death as he'd refused to in life. As horrible as the mutilations to the big man's body appeared, they occurred when he was beyond feeling pain.

"I suspected," Sheibani lied, "there were tracking devices. Washington provided the locations, maintaining to the end there were three. But I'm a suspicious fellow. I could question each of you, but that would be tedious. Instead, Broussard, I will question you. You don't know which locations Washington divulged, so you must reveal them all. If you refuse, I kill your colleagues and resort to more painful techniques. Understood?"

Broussard glared.

Sheibani sighed. "I see you need convincing."

He drew a pistol and shot Santiago in the head. The man fell, twitching across Washington's corpse, blood pumping out in a widening circle as Broussard's screams were muffled by the tape and his attempts to stand thwarted by Sheibani's underlings. Hopkins stared down in shock, attempting to move his feet out of the spreading blood pool.

Sheibani ripped the tape off Broussard's mouth. "Now! The locations!"

Broussard tried to spit in Sheibani's face, but his lips were still glued shut from the adhesive, and spit leaked down his chin. Sheibani laughed and put his gun to Hopkins's head.

"Wait," Broussard croaked, forcing his lips apart.

Sheibani prodded Hopkins's head. "The locations!"

"In each boat," Broussard gasped, "behind the fire extinguishers, and one in the forward storeroom."

Sheibani smiled as one of his underlings rushed out. Only then did Broussard understand.

"You didn't know."

"I knew the number, not the locations," Sheibani said, grinning. "You saved us a great deal of time and may be of further use. Cooperate and you two live. Fail to do so and Washington's death will seem merciful. Consider that as you wait."

***

Sheibani left the room and moved up the stairway to the bridge. He passed the captain's cabin and saw DeVries through the open door, sprawled on his bunk with his headphones, in a funk of blue smoke. He sneered and climbed the last flight to the bridge.

On the bridge wing, he watched in the moonlight as a Zodiac inflatable matched *Alicia*'s speed and moved alongside. Lines were passed as a rope ladder dropped from main deck, and the transponders were transferred. He confirmed everything was going to plan and rushed back down to the lounge, where two men stood guard.

"Listen well, Broussard," Sheibani said, producing a small recording device.

Sheibani pushed a button and Broussard's voice came from the speaker, giving an earlier position report.

"You two," Sheibani said, "will be placed in a small boat and report in as expected. If you try anything, Hopkins will be killed and you will be taken to a secure location, where it will take you a long, long time to die. Understand?"

Broussard nodded and Sheibani continued.

"Your previous reports were identical. Keep them so. My men have memorized these recordings, both words and tone. If you deviate in the slightest, they terminate the call and shoot Hopkins." Sheibani smiled. "And you will envy him."

The crewmen's smirks confirmed their command of English.

Using the Americans to buy a bit more time was a calculated risk. If his men had to disconnect, and could do so cleanly, Singapore would suspect technical problems, given that the Zodiac was on *Alicia*'s agreed course. But even if Broussard managed a warning, Sheibani's men would have plenty of time to kill the Americans and dump their bodies and the transponders before disappearing into the mangrove swamps along the Malaysian coast. And *Alicia* would be well concealed before the Americans even mounted a search.

First the stick, thought Sheibani, now the carrot.

"We don't need you, Broussard, but if your help buys us a bit of time, I will spare you both. You will be hostages, eligible for exchange in time. Will you cooperate?"

Broussard nodded.

"Excellent," Sheibani said as he ordered his men to get the Americans to the boat.

Minutes later, Sheibani stood on the bridge as the Zodiac maintained *Alicia*'s original course and speed, and *Alicia* inched to port. When the separation was sufficient, he set a new course and increased speed for his hideout, eight hours away.

***

Broussard lay on the plywood floorboard as the boat bounced along. They were still bound, their arms in front and their ankles bound more loosely, changed to allow them to inch down the rope ladder into the boat. He faced Hopkins, dumped there after the midnight call, when his resolve to warn Singapore had melted at the sight of the gun to Hopkins's head. After that, the terrorists had relaxed, dumping the hostages on the floorboards, not bothering to retape Broussard's mouth. He whispered to Hopkins in the moonlight.

"Donny, can you hear me?"

Hopkins nodded.

"Donny, you know they're gonna kill us, right?"

Another nod.

"I'm warning Singapore on the next call. You with me?"

Hopkins stared at Broussard. He nodded.

"We got one shot," Broussard said, and he whispered his desperate plan.

Broussard's ears rang from a slap. "No talking," screamed the closest hijacker, rolling Broussard so that his back was to Hopkins and taping his mouth. Something hard dug into Broussard's thigh, and he smiled beneath the tape moments later as he slipped bound hands beneath his leg and felt the shape of his small folding Ka-Bar knife through the fabric. Tiny in the cavernous pocket, his captors had missed the knife. He adjusted his plan.

***

The outboard stopped, and Broussard was dragged upright and the tape ripped away. The two *Alicia* crewmen flanked him as opposite the two hijackers that had arrived in the Zodiac held Hopkins up, a gun to his head. The Americans sat across from each other, their bound feet flat on the plywood floorboard as they leaned back against the inflation tubes forming the boat's sides. One of Broussard's captors punched speaker mode on the sat phone and dialed Singapore, nodding to Broussard as the duty officer answered.

"*Alicia*—" began Broussard as Hopkins shot bound hands up to deflect the gun and jammed bound feet down to propel himself straight up, breaking the terrorists' holds as he flew backward over the side. As anticipated, the men hesitated to fire with Singapore listening, and a heartbeat after Hopkins's escape, Broussard duplicated his move, screaming "Mayday, terrorists" as he flopped overboard.

The original plan had been to escape in the darkness, with death by gunshot or drowning the likely outcome. The knife changed things.

Broussard stroked downward with bound hands, ignoring muffled shouts and gunfire. At ten feet he fumbled for the knife, forcing himself calm as he put it between his teeth and opened it with his hands. Blade open, he grabbed the knife in both bound hands and slashed the ankle binding to kick for the surface, the knife point extended above him.

The Zodiac was a dark shadow on the moonlit surface, and he kicked for the starboard tube. Just before impact, he lowered his hands, then thrust upward, relying on momentum and arm strength to pierce the tough skin. A maelstrom of bubbles erupted.

The boat listed to starboard as panicked terrorists rushed to stare at the roiling water. Broussard moved under the port bow, farthest from the disturbance, to break the surface with his face, sucking in sweet air. The men were shouting as he floated, hidden by darkness and the overhang of the inflation tube. He submerged again and clenched the knife handle between his teeth, sawing his wrist binding against the blade. With his hands free, he surfaced, unsure of his next move.

The list worsened as the men argued. Broussard had decided to puncture another air chamber when he heard splashes as the terrorists dumped the transponders, followed by the rumble of the awakening outboard. He dove deep, surfacing as the outboard faded to the east, and called out to Hopkins.

"Here. I'm hit bad, " came a weak reply.

"Hang on, and keep talking," Broussard shouted, swimming toward the voice. He arrived as his friend slipped below the surface, and he dove, groping until he grabbed an arm. He kicked them to the surface and gulped air as he made out Hopkins's face in the moonlight, tape dangling from a cheek. Hopkins coughed.

"C'mon, buddy. You can make it. Hang in there."

"I'm all sh…shot up," Hopkins said, "… got a full clip into m…me."

"Knock that shit off, Hopkins. You gotta make it, or Vega will kill me," Broussard said.

Hopkins rewarded him with a feeble smile before he closed his eyes and spoke no more.

Broussard ran hands over Hopkins's body, confirming by touch the accuracy of Hopkins's diagnosis, as he struggled to apply pressure to more wounds than he had hands. The lightening sky found them bobbing in a circle of bloodstained water as Hopkins stared through lifeless eyes. Near exhaustion, Broussard checked for a pulse one last time, then blinked back tears of anger and grief as he closed Hopkins's eyes and let his friend sink.

***

An hour later aboard a Super Lynx helicopter of the Royal Malaysian Navy, vectored to the last-known coordinates of the *Alicia* by the Singapore Operations Center, Broussard looked over the straits. Sheibani's smirking face rose unbidden.

"Keep smilin', asshole," he said, "payback's gonna be hell."

CHAPTER FOUR

US Embassy
Napier Road, Singapore
26 May

Christ. What an ugly building. Dugan walked up the rise to the embassy entrance. Singaporean civilian guards confirmed his identity and business, and he moved through a metal detector and bombproof doors, past a Marine guard to passport services. Minutes later, he stood in a windowless conference room as Jesse Ward appeared, trailed by a younger man.

Dugan hadn't seen Ward in person in some time. The man's wiry black hair was thinner and flecked with gray now, and his dark face lined. Intellect still sparkled behind the soft brown eyes, but in khakis and a rumpled blue blazer, he looked ordinary and forgettable. The perfect look for an intelligence agent.

"Good to see you, Tom," Ward said, pumping Dugan's hand as he nodded toward his companion. "This is my boss, Larry Gardner."

Quite a contrast, thought Dugan, shaking Gardner's hand. Gardner was much younger, with a flawless tan, movie-star looks, and black blow-dried hair. His suit had never graced a store rack, high-end or otherwise, and his silk tie sported a perfect knot. The cuff of his snowy dress shirt protruded from his jacket to reveal monogrammed initials, and a gold Rolex advertised resources beyond a government salary. He looked like a lawyer. Dugan disliked him on sight.

"OK, what gives?" Dugan asked as they sat. "It must be important to get you all the way from Langley to Singapore."

Ward opened his mouth, but Gardner cut him off.

"What's your relationship with Phoenix Shipping, Dugan?" he asked.

Dugan shot Ward a questioning look, then shrugged. "Alex Kairouz is my biggest client and a good friend. I'm taking one of his ships through yard period up in Sembawang right now." He paused. "Why? What's this all about?"

"Would it surprise you to know Kairouz has links to terrorists?"

Dugan's face registered surprise before his eyes narrowed in anger.

"Alex Kairouz? Terrorists? Bullshit. He hates those Muslim fanatics."

"Who said anything about Muslims, Dugan?"

Dugan glared at Gardner. "It was a wild guess. The IRA and the Popular Front for the Liberation of Kansas haven't blown anyone up lately."

Gardner colored and opened a folder, pretending to study the contents. "He's given you a lot of money."

"He hasn't 'given' me a damn thing. He paid me for services rendered."

"Perhaps," Gardner said, "but your association, and other things, put you under a cloud. Ward here speaks well of you, but until we're sure where your loyalty lies—"

"Where my loyalty lies?" Dugan interrupted, looking first at Ward, then refocusing on Gardner. "You know, if I were sensitive, this would hurt my feelings."

"Look, Dugan," Gardner said, "lose the attitude. Your duty as an American citi—"

"Mr. Gardner. Larry. May I call you Larry?" Dugan asked, continuing without waiting for a response. "Larry, I assure you, I will cooperate."

Gardner flashed Ward a smug smile.

"However," Dugan went on, "cooperation is about relationships. For example, the bond Agent Ward and I enjoy. But Larry, I don't feel that same chemistry here. I'm sure it's my fault, but I think I should continue with one of your associates." He paused. "Is Moe or Curly Joe available?"

Gardner's smile faded. "You son of a bitch," he said, rising to stalk out, then slamming the door behind him.

Ward shook his head. "You could get me canned, Tom."

"Nah. Even the government needs a few competent people around. Why don't you buy me dinner while you brief me on my duty as a loyal American?"

Ward nodded.

"Great. See you in the lobby of Trader's at eight. And grab a nap. You look like shit."

"Thanks," Ward said.

"Seriously," Dugan said. "If you drop dead, I might have to deal with that asshole."

***

Ward drained his mug. Crab shells overflowed a plate, surrounded by mostly empty dishes of fried noodles and other Singaporean delicacies. Dugan lifted a pitcher of Tiger beer and raised his eyebrows, but Ward declined. Dugan refilled his own mug and looked around. They sat alone on the roof terrace of the restaurant, above the bustle of open-air eateries that lined Boat Quay. Access via a cramped spiral staircase made service difficult, but Dugan's status as an old customer and generous tipper allowed secluded dining.

"Secure enough for you?" Dugan asked.

Ward nodded.

"So tell me, Jesse, how'd you end up with that asshole as your boss?"

Ward shrugged. "The agency occasionally buys in to the 'nutty management theory of the week,' in this case, 'leadership candidates' rotating through supervisory positions. Ops is usually exempted, but not this time. Gardner's our first. I got him because maritime terrorism isn't as sexy as falling planes."

"Surely everyone sees through him. He's got the personality of a dose of clap."

"He can be slick when he wants to, and he's connected. He has political aspirations." Ward grinned. "Maybe you shit on a future president."

Dugan shuddered. "God help us."

"Anyway, I'll handle him."

"Handle him while we do what exactly?" Dugan asked.

23

Ward looked Dugan straight in the eye. "Tom, I need you to accept Kairouz's offer."

Dugan looked puzzled. "How did…"

Then he understood. "Son of a bitch. You bugging my phone?"

Ward didn't blink. "Of course you're bugged. And so am I, and so is everyone else. You might not have read it, but you signed that waiver a long, long time ago. Way back when you agreed to keep your eyes and ears open and to take some pictures for us now and again. How could it be otherwise? There's too much at stake not to monitor ourselves."

After a long moment, Dugan nodded. "All right, point taken. That doesn't mean I like it. So what's the deal with Phoenix? Oh yeah, and what the hell did Gardner mean when he said my association with Alex 'and other things' put me under a cloud. What other things?"

"You inspected a ship for MSC last week," Ward said.

Dugan nodded. "The *Alicia*, but how's that relevant?"

"She was hijacked en route to Thailand."

"Hijacked? No way," Dugan said. "What about the navy protective detail?"

"Three dead," Ward said. "The only survivor was the team leader, a young petty officer named Broussard. He managed to get off a warning and was picked up floating in the strait by the Malaysians."

Dugan grew quiet. "I met him," he said at last. "Seemed like a nice kid."

Ward only nodded, and Dugan continued. "But I still don't see what that has to do with Phoenix…or me."

"MSC chartered the ship through Willem Van Djik in Rotterdam," Ward said. "Van Djik was told about the job by a call from someone at Phoenix. He was under surveillance by the Dutch for unrelated smuggling issues. The phone conversation itself was secure, but they heard his side through bugs in his office and traced the source to Phoenix in London. They only put two and two together after the hijacking.

"Thing is," Ward continued, "MSC chartered *Alicia* because she was the only available tonnage, and that was no accident. Backtracking it, Van Djik spent a lot of money chartering other suitable tonnage though a variety of fronts just to take the other ships out of play."

Ward looked Dugan in the eye. "People don't jack gunboats to water ski, Tom, and you're tied to this from both ends. There's your connection to Phoenix and the fact that you inspected the ship before she was hijacked and knew the cargo—"

"Along with about a thousand other people," Dugan said.

Ward held up his hands. "I'm not saying I think you're involved, Tom, but it is a coincidence, and folks in my business don't much like coincidences. I've known you a long time, but for someone like Gardner, you look a lot like a suspect. I'm sticking my neck out here bringing you in. To be honest, I probably wouldn't, except for our long relationship and the fact that, with your relationship with Kairouz, you're our best shot at getting inside Phoenix quickly."

"Jesse, I'm not trained for this."

"Mainly you'll be helping us place a British agent," Ward said.

Dugan hesitated, toying with the idea of telling Ward about Alex Kairouz's recent strange behavior. No, he thought, best leave that for now. "I just don't feel right spying on Alex," Dugan said instead.

"What's better for Kairouz? Having you there or a stranger?"

Dugan grew quiet. "All right, I'll do it," he finally said.

"Good. Assuming you accept the possibility Kairouz is guilty."

"Like you accept the possibility that I'm guilty?" Dugan asked.

Ward changed the subject.

"Tell me what you remember about *Alicia*."

Dugan shrugged. "Not much to remember. She's a little one-hatch coaster owned by her skipper, a Dutch guy who's running her into the ground. Chief mate's name is Ali something—Sheboni, I think. He seems to be running the show."

"Sheibani," corrected Ward. "According to Broussard, Sheibani orchestrated the hijacking and murdered three of Broussard's guys in the process. Two at point-blank range in cold blood."

Dugan's face hardened. "That little fucking puke. Do you have any leads?"

Ward shook his head.

"We had the strait blanketed by satellite coverage within hours of the news, with no sighting. *Alicia* couldn't have cleared the strait by then. We're assuming she's on the Indonesian side, and given her last-known position and maximum speed, she could be anywhere along two hundred miles of coastline—a thousand miles, counting islands and inlets. Hundreds of good hiding places."

Dugan nodded. "I see the problem. You can't really even rule out too many places due to water depth. As I recall, *Alicia* draws fourteen feet fully loaded. That's fifteen hundred tons. Those boats and associated gear totaled less than fifty. She can get pretty light."

"That's right," Ward said. "But the real priority is recovering the boats, and we don't figure the hijackers will waste any time getting them off *Alicia*. The boats alone will be much easier to hide and move through the mangrove swamps."

"There's your answer," Dugan said.

Ward looked confused, and Dugan continued. "*Alicia*'s gear can't handle the boats. They need a crane. And shore cranes need strong docks, and big floating cranes are few and far between."

TWO DAYS EARLIER
M/V *ALICIA*
INDONESIAN COAST

Sheibani moved from bridge wing to bridge wing as he calmly issued helm orders, conning *Alicia* up the shallow, twisting passage through the mangrove swamp in the moonlight and on a rising tide. He had his best man on the helm, and he'd lightened *Alicia* to seven feet. The rest of the crew manned the rails with powerful handheld lights and called warnings of obstacles.

With the propeller and rudder only partially submerged, the ship handled poorly, but each time he grounded in the soft mud, he waited for the tide to lift her, then backed off to continue his cautious transit. He regretted no one would know of *Alicia*'s final resting place and appreciate his skill, but duping the infidels was satisfaction enough.

As the sky lightened in the east, he spotted his objective ahead in the predawn: a crumbling concrete dock by a pool of still water. Trees rose from gaping cracks in the dock, some a foot in diameter with tops higher than *Alicia*'s deckhouse, and thick limbs spread over the water. Sheibani shouted a warning, and the crew scurried into the deckhouse as he retreated to the wheelhouse and increased speed. He pushed the helmsman aside and took the wheel himself to slam *Alicia*'s port side toward the dock, her momentum forcing her superstructure, booms, and masts through the foliage. Stout limbs snapped like cannon shots and fell across the deck as the little ship slowed abruptly. *Alicia* listed slightly to starboard as she fought her way through the obstacle, then Sheibani heard the screech of steel on concrete. He killed the engine and *Alicia* shuddered to a stop.

Seconds later, Sheibani stood on the starboard bridge wing, watching as his crew boiled from the deckhouse and went about their prearranged tasks. Some climbed to the dock and began passing mooring lines, while others fired up chain saws and began clearing the deck of broken limbs, tossing the debris over the offshore side of the ship. In minutes, the ship was secured, overhanging limbs shielding most of the vessel. The camouflage netting would do the rest.

He'd first come to this place on a dirt bike, guided by an old man who'd worked here long ago. All that remained was a crumbling dock and dilapidated Quonset hut, its rusted sides covered in vines, the open end a black cave in the greenery. Convincing the International Development Fund to finance a port miles from deep water must have been difficult, even years ago, but the developers had been well connected. They slapped down a dock and dredged a thirty-five-foot-deep hole along it to collect a hefty progress payment. Months later, when a survey party found the site abandoned and overgrown and the deepwater channel into the dock to exist only on paper, the government feigned outrage, the IDF shrugged, and everyone forgot the site until Allah guided Sheibani to it thirty years later. He'd used the site as a smuggling depot for three years, anchoring *Alicia* in deep water miles away and approaching by Zodiac. Both the ship and this place had served his needs well, but it was time to move on.

M/V *ALICIA*
25 MAY

Sheibani nodded to himself as he moved through the hold, pleased at the progress. He watched as men swarmed the boats, removing the securing straps and lashing heavy vinyl tarps over the cockpit openings before sealing the boats completely with industrial stretch wrap. Soon they would be as buoyant and unsinkable as corks.

In the aft end of the hold, men emptied the weapons container, hoisting its contents over the main deck to the crumbling concrete dock, while forward, the chief engineer squatted on the deck, cutting through plating. The hissing torch changed pitch, and a neat circle of steel tumbled into the water of the ballast tank below, hot edges belching steam. Sheibani glanced up through the hatch at patches of blue sky through overhanging tree limbs and camouflage netting, then moved to the ladder, reviewing preparations as he climbed to the main deck. All that remained was rigging a web of wires around the hold, tight between the pad eyes at the bottom of the hold and the top of the hatch, to corral the boats directly under the open hatch. God willing, he could sink his prison at dawn. He would not miss *Alicia* or the heat or the Indonesian monkeys.

***

The sky was lightening as Sheibani stood with the crew on the dock. *Alicia* was below the dock now, and a short, steep gangway led down to main deck. The camouflage netting was gone and the hatch open to the sky as the chief engineer climbed the gangway.

"It is done, Major," he said. "She's down past her marks with the bow a bit deeper. I've started flooding the cargo hold through the broached ballast tanks. The water will run to the forward end and speed the sinking of the bow. The engine space aft will flood last. By the time the water shorts out the pumps, she will be free-flooding." He paused. "God willing, she will settle straight down."

Sheibani nodded and watched. Water rose in the hold, and the boats floated free, rising as the ship sank beneath them. Then *Alicia*'s deck went under, and water poured over the hatch coaming, cascading down on the boats from all sides like a waterfall. The boats bounced and bobbed under the torrents, and within seconds *Alicia* fell out from under them with a great bubbling swirl. A relieved grin split the chief engineer's face as the boats bobbed to the surface unharmed, and a spontaneous shout of "*Allahu Akbar*" rose from the throats of *Alicia*'s former crewmen.

***

The tile was cool on DeVries's cheek as he lay trussed hand and foot. His head throbbed from the beating, and he felt the deck tilt beneath him as the hull moaned under unfamiliar stresses. The lights winked out and he closed his eyes and wished for an end to the bad dream, opening them as water wet his cheek. He flopped about in the deepening flood, cursing ships and the sea and his stiff-necked family. In the end, his grave was marked by a section of the bridge deck and the tops of the masts and king posts, rusted brown and blending with the surrounding jungle, the only sign that Captain Jan Pieter DeVries, master after God of the good ship *Alicia*, had gone down with his vessel.

CHAPTER FIVE

Dugan sat in the same conference room, waiting. When Ward appeared, Dugan raised his eyebrows. "Where's the Boy Wonder?"

"Gardner flew back to Langley this morning," Ward said. "Management conference."

Dugan snorted, then continued. "Any news on *Alicia*?"

Ward shook his head. "Negative. The Indonesians are being their usual noncooperative selves, but we have our own assets on the ground tracking down every available crane. And we've tasked the satellites to collect imagery of every dock capable of supporting a large crane and every anchorage deep enough to support a floating crane. We still got bubkes."

"Crap."

Ward shrugged. "It's still our best lead. Obviously they've found a hiding spot, but, sooner or later, they'll have to come to a crane or a crane has to come to them. Intelligence is a game of patience, Tom."

Ward changed the subject. "You call Kairouz yet?"

"Since you're bugging my calls, you know the answer to that."

"Make the call."

"So," Dugan asked, "what happened to 'intelligence is a game of patience'?"

Ward scowled.

"Don't get your bowels in an uproar. My relief arrived last night, and I showed him around *Asian Trader* and gave him my turnover this morning. Alex will be expecting a call. I was just waiting until it seemed natural."

"No time like the present," Ward said.

Dugan sighed and pulled out his cell phone.

Alex's stomach boiled from too much coffee, even at this early hour, and he was tense and irritable from lack of sleep. Nothing had been the same since Braun's arrival with his thug Farley. He eyed his overflowing in-box. His productivity had suffered as well, and he'd instructed Mrs. Coutts to hold all calls while he attempted to clear the backlog.

He looked over, annoyed, as the intercom buzzed.

"Yes, Mrs. Coutts?"

"I'm sorry to disturb you, sir, but Mr. Dugan is on line one."

He smiled despite the tension. Trust Dugan to charm his way past Mrs. Coutts. He mashed the flashing button.

"Thomas. How are you? Did Guido arrive?"

"I'm fine, Alex," Dugan said. "I picked him up at Changi airport last night, and we walked the ship together this morning. She's off the dry dock now and should shift to the ExxonMobil refinery to load sometime next week. Guido's got it."

"Excellent, Thomas, and thank you for helping me out in a bind."

"No problem, Alex, but there's something else I want to discuss. I think I'm ready to take you up on your offer and come to work for you full-time."

Alex sat stunned. Thomas couldn't come. Not now. If he sensed something wrong and went to the authorities—

"Alex, are you there?"

"Yes, yes, Thomas. I'm just…surprised. Why the change of heart after all these years? Are you serious? What about your consulting practice?"

"Serious as a heart attack," Dugan said. "As to why, I guess you've finally convinced me I should spend more time behind a desk. And since you're seventy percent of my billings anyway, I'm not concerned about the practice. If it doesn't pan out, we'll just go back to the way it was. You know money's not an issue for me anyway, thanks to Katy's financial wizardry."

"What about Katy?" Alex asked. "Won't she be upset if you move to London?"

Dugan laughed. "Let's face it, Alex, I'm traveling most of the time anyway, and just because my kid sister lets me crash in her pool house between trips, doesn't mean I'll be missed that much. I'll still get back home for holidays, which is about as much as they see me now, anyway." Dugan paused. "But what's with all the objections? You trying to talk me out of something you've spent ten years talking me into?"

"No, no, not at all. It's just unexpected, and the timing is a bit…awkward. You see, I just hired a fellow as director of operations," Alex lied on the fly, "with the understanding that he'll eventually move into a newly created general-manager slot. I had no idea you'd reconsider, but if I bring you on now as general manager, he'll take it as bad faith."

"I see your problem, Alex. How about this? I don't mind competing for the GM spot, so why don't you hire me for a trial period as this guy's equal, say director of engineering. Then after a while, you decide who's the best fit. If I later decide to leave, you have this new guy in place. If we decide I should continue, you'll have a choice. It will be no hardship for me to resign later if necessary."

The logic was unassailable. Alex stalled again.

"You've really caught me by surprise, Thomas. May I call you back?"

"Sure, Alex," Dugan said, "take your time."

"Fine, Thomas. Talk to you soon."

Alex Kairouz disconnected and buried his face in his hands.

***

"Captain Braun, Mr. Kairouz is not to be disturbed," Mrs. Coutts said.

Braun stood in Alex's door, hand on the knob as he glared back over his shoulder.

Mrs. Coutts gave Alex a look of helpless apology.

"It's fine, Mrs. Coutts," Alex said.

She nodded and retreated to her desk.

Braun shut the door and moved to Alex's favorite armchair.

"You should sack that old bitch, Kairouz, and get someone easier on the eyes," he said, pointing to the sofa. "But come sit. I don't have all day."

Alex stood, stiff with rage. "I'm cooperating, Braun, so don't abuse my staff. Clear?"

"That's *Captain* Braun, and you're *not* cooperating, or that old hag wouldn't interfere. She'll have an accident if she isn't careful. Is *that* clear? Now sit," Braun said, pointing again.

Defeated, Alex complied.

"Now," Braun said, "who is this American?"

"Thomas Dugan, a consultant and friend. I'll get rid of him."

"Won't that arouse curiosity, given his rather logical offer?"

"Perhaps," conceded Alex, "but I can hold him off. Long enough for you to finish whatever this business is and be gone."

Braun shook his head. "I think not. I don't want some curious Yank starting to ask questions. Better to keep him close and watch him. Besides, he may prove useful."

"I'll just get rid of him," Alex repeated.

"On the contrary," Braun said, his voice hardening, "offer him the job, effective immediately."

"No. Best keep him away."

Braun sighed. "How tiresome."

He rose from the chair to snatch Cassie's photo from the desk and toss it into Alex's lap. Alex set the picture on the end table and glared.

"Time for a reminder, Kairouz? Must we review the videos?" Braun paused. "Then again, she does look like your dead wife. Perhaps you've already begun her education. Bedding the retard are you, Kairouz? Perhaps I can help. Have her broken in by a dozen big fellows while you watch. Sound appealing?" Braun laughed and awaited the expected response.

Alex charged, but Braun was younger, fit, and well trained. In seconds, Alex was face down, his right arm twisted behind him, as Braun ground his face into the carpet.

"I grow tired of these lessons, Kairouz. The next time you cross me, Farley will rape the retard in front of you as a down payment. Understand?"

Alex nodded and Braun released him. "Good. Now phone Dugan." He sneered. "After you pull yourself together, of course. You're pathetic."

Alex heard Braun leave as he lay unmoving, and tears of impotent rage stained the carpet.

"That's great, Alex," Dugan said into the cell phone. "I'll e-mail Mrs. Coutts my flight information. I assume I can stay at your place as usual until I find a place of my own?"

"Of course, Thomas," Alex said. "Cassie will be excited when I tell her."

"I look forward to seeing you all. Bye now," Dugan said and hung up.

He sat silent for a moment until Ward spoke.

"So what do you make of that, Tom?"

"I honestly don't know," Dugan said. "He...he has been acting a bit strange lately, and he definitely seems a bit less enthusiastic than I anticipated."

"Yeah, something's up, all right," Ward said.

Dugan didn't respond.

"Having second thoughts?" Ward asked.

"I don't know if I can do this, Jesse. I may have taken a few photos and snooped around for you a bit, but I'm not a spy, and I sure as hell can't learn to be one in twenty-four hours."

"Don't worry. The Brits will backstop you. MI5 is putting together a team now."

"I sure hope you know what you're talking about, pal," Dugan said.

Offices of Phoenix Shipping
London

Karl Enrique Braun, freelance "problem solver," formerly of the East German Ministry for State Security (Stasi), returned to his spacious new office, the former home of three disgruntled ship superintendents now displaced to the cubicle farm. He was sated from an excellent lunch, courtesy of his new Phoenix Shipping credit card, and he smiled at the sign on the door: Captain Braun—Director of Operations. The "captain" was a nice touch and as real as his name, after all. He'd been many people in service to the state. When the end had come, he'd forecast it a bit more clearly than his former colleagues and arrived in Havana hours after the wall fell. The Cuban Ministry of the Interior (MININT) was a Stasi clone and always in need of talent, especially talent with fluent Spanish and Cuban roots. He touched his face. The Cubans had excellent plastic surgeons.

His Nordic good looks and native fluency in a half a dozen languages provided the Cubans an asset of incalculable value, and he parlayed that to his own advantage. He'd become a "consultant" and then a free agent, protected by the Cubans in exchange for sharing intelligence. Capitalist by default now, he worked for anyone with his fee, from drug lords to African dictators. His best clients to date were Latin American demagogues, champions of a failed model, buying the votes of the dispossessed with promises no economy could make real, especially not the bungled economics of the neo-socialism.

Braun smiled again. No client had been as malleable and oblivious to fees as that idiot Rodriguez in Venezuela. It would be a shame to lose the cash flow should it prove necessary to sacrifice him as damage control. Then again, the Iranian had proven to be more than generous and deserved his fire wall. Braun was looking forward to a very comfortable retirement.

He settled in behind his desk and contemplated the latest turn of events. He didn't like this American lodging with Kairouz, but it was apparently an arrangement of long standing; best to keep to routine. Besides, Kairouz was thoroughly cowed, and this Dugan was one more American he could throw into the mix to make things all the more believable.

Willingly to the slaughter. Braun could hardly believe his good fortune.

CHAPTER SIX

Mohammad Borqei stood, balled fists in his back as he stretched to ease the stiffness of the old shrapnel wound. American shrapnel, for the Great Satan had been generous in aid to Saddam when the madman had been murdering Iranians. Borqei swallowed his anger. He moved from the window to his desk and picked up the message from Tehran.

A wistful smile crossed his bearded face at thoughts of Iran, a home he'd never see again. It had taken years to craft his "legend" as a moderate, advancing viewpoints he despised in mosques across Tehran, enduring the hostility of colleagues, and finally imprisonment for seditious acts. Then he'd "escaped" to the US via Canada, and the foolish Americans had tugged the Trojan horse through the gate.

He'd settled in Dearborn, with its large Muslim community, joining interfaith groups and preaching tolerance. When the Imam of the House of Islamic Knowledge died in a car crash, he was the logical choice to assume leadership of the community's preeminent mosque. Able to count Islamic voters, the local congressman fast-tracked Borqei's citizenship application and stood smiling as he took the oath. Indeed, Borqei's public "assimilation" was so convincing that it undermined his mission. His inner circle of the faithful was small and resistant to all efforts at expansion.

For, despite cynicism about American ideals as preached and practiced, the Muslims of Dearborn were optimistic. Conflicts with their "real" American neighbors were frequent but waged with words during meetings, not by stone-throwing mobs or suicide bombers. Each grudging compromise was a small victory, as their sons played American football and ate *halal* pizza, and they built new lives, much better than those they'd left behind.

Borqei had faced the paradox. His need for "assimilated" Americans would never be met by American-born Muslims, who were corrupted beyond redemption. Hezbollah had come to his aid, trolling teeming refugee camps for orphans. While they trained in Iran, Borqei prepared the ground, helping the faithful of his inner circle get citizenship, allowing them in turn to use the Child Citizenship Act to adopt "foreign-born children," all graduates of Hezbollah training. They arrived, committed to serving Islam by becoming ever more American in appearance. He had a dozen now, and the first was the finest.

Yousif Nassir Hamad, or "Joe" Hamad, was finishing college, with honors, on a US Navy ROTC scholarship. Fluent in Arabic, he was courted heavily, and Borqei had been helping him review his options, deciding just where in the navy he could best serve Islam. Now it had been decided for them. Borqei gazed at the message with distaste.

DEADLY SRAITS

"No!" Cassie glared defiance, flopping the hair bow on the table. "This dorky uniform is bad enough. Please, Papa, tell her I don't have to wear it."

Alex studied the bow over his cup, remembering Cassie's delight when Mrs. Farnsworth first made it. As Cassie, at age fifteen, struggled between her physical and mental ages, conflicts had become frequent—difficult for Cassie, but harder still on Mrs. Farnsworth.

"Cassie, the bow makes you even prettier," he said.

"I hate it, I hate it," Cassie spoke into her cereal, pouting.

"Cassie," Mrs. Farnsworth said, "a proper young lady does not pout. People respond to courtesy, not petulance or angry demands. Would you like to ask me again, young lady?"

Alex stiffened. The proper-young-lady campaign was difficult for him, but Mrs. Farnsworth was insistent that repeated challenge strengthened Cassie's abilities. He accepted the theory but was incapable of causing Cassie discomfort. He bit his tongue and left correction to Mrs. Farnsworth, thankful she was made of sterner stuff.

"Please, Mrs. Farnsworth, must I wear it?" Cassie asked, barely audible.

"Not if you don't wish to," Mrs. Farnsworth said. "Now go up and tidy your hair. It's almost time to go."

"Oh thank you, thank you," Cassie cried, rushing to the door. She stopped midstride and turned. "Oh. I almost forgot. When will Uncle Thomas be here, Papa?"

Alex smiled. "He arrives this evening, Cassie. He'll have dinner with us."

"Cool," Cassie said, then bolted for the door.

"Don't…." Mrs. Farnsworth said at Cassie's retreating back, "… run."

Alex chuckled as Cassie disappeared. "A bit late, I'm afraid."

Mrs. Farnsworth smiled. "She's coming along nicely."

"You expected that?"

The housekeeper nodded. "Self-assertion. Notice how she tried to play us against each other? A good sign."

Alex deferred to her judgment. She'd cared for Cassie since infancy, and the shelves of her bedroom overflowed with books on development, special needs, and remedial teaching techniques. Many nights he saw her through the open doorway, pouring over arcane tomes.

He sighed. "I have mixed emotions at seeing innocence replaced by manipulation."

"Loss of innocence is inevitable, sir, if she's to achieve independence. We won't be around forever."

Alex nodded as they sipped coffee in silence. Mrs. Farnsworth seemed uneasy, on the verge of speaking several times, then studying her coffee.

"The coffee isn't that interesting. Speak your mind, Mrs. Farnsworth. If it's about Thomas—"

Mrs. Farnsworth shook her head. "I resigned myself to your friendship with the boorish Mr. Dugan some time ago. It's this Farley I'm concerned with. He's not working out, sir."

Alex stiffened. "Go on."

"I can't understand why, without notice, you engaged him as our driver, replacing Daniel after years of loyal service. I've managed to keep Daniel busy with other tasks, but he feels wronged. He may leave us."

"You're quite right, Mrs. Farnsworth, and I do apologize. The need arose suddenly and for reasons I can't discuss, but I've handled it badly."

"'Need,' sir? What need? Farley's reckless and unsavory in the extreme, hanging about the kitchen, offending Mrs. Hogan with crude humor, and calling Daniel an 'old kike' to his face." She lowered her voice. "And he ogles Cassie with undisguised lust. The lout must go."

Alex tried to speak several times before succeeding.

"He'll leave soon," he said. "Until then, make sure Cassie is never alone with him."

"Did you understand what I said, sir?"

"Perfectly," Alex said through tight lips, "but I can't discharge him yet. He's a bodyguard. There have been…kidnap threats against Cassie."

"Good Lord. From whom? Have you notified the police?"

"Anonymous e-mail threats," Alex lied, reciting the story Braun invented. "The police are investigating. I hired Farley at their recommendation."

Mrs. Farnsworth digested the news but focused on the imminent threat.

"Understood, sir. But I still don't trust Farley. We must replace him."

"Impossible," Alex said.

"But surely the agency you engaged—"

"God damn it, woman!" he said, red-faced. "I'll thank you to stop meddling and do as you're told!" He glared at her, then seemed to deflate as he sat, elbows on the table and face buried in his hands, as if hiding from his own outburst.

Mrs. Farnsworth sat shocked until Alex spoke again, his head down, avoiding her eyes.

"That was unthinkable. Please forgive me, Mrs. Farnsworth. I'm overwrought with concern about Cassie."

She stiffened. "As am I, sir. Will that be all?"

"I'll hire another car and use Daniel to run errands around the office. That will salve his feelings and spare him contact with Farley."

She rose. "Whatever you decide, sir. I must check on Cassie."

Alex called her name as she reached the door, and she turned.

"About your…suspicions. Please watch Cassie closely."

"I always do, sir. I always do," she said softly.

***

Alex smiled as he watched Dugan rub his stomach in mock distress.

"It's clear I'll have to find my own place quickly, Mrs. Hogan," Dugan said to the cook. "If I stay here too long, I'll be needing a new wardrobe."

The cook beamed as she poured coffee. "Sure, and it was nothing fancy, Mr. Dugan," she said, retreating to the kitchen.

Another Dugan conquest, thought Alex. Thomas had even managed to defrost Mrs. Farnsworth a bit this evening. He noticed the housekeeper's approving glance as Cassie chatted happily with their house guest.

"Cassie, you have homework, so say good night," Mrs. Farnsworth said.

"Please, please, may I do it in the morning?" Cassie pleaded.

"No, dear. I'm sure your father and Mr. Dugan have matters to discuss."

"Oh, all right," Cassie said, standing to hug Dugan. "I'm so glad you're here, Uncle Thomas."

"Me too, Cassie," Dugan said. "We'll talk tomorrow after school. Daniel will be driving you home before you know it."

"Not Daniel, Farley," Cassie said.

"We've a new driver," explained Mrs. Farnsworth, her distaste obvious.

"And he's really creepy, Uncle Thomas," Cassie said. "But Papa says he'll go away."

Dugan looked at Alex, confused.

"I'll explain later, Thomas," Alex said. "Now Cassie, where's my kiss?"

Cassie hugged Alex and pecked his cheek as Mrs. Farnsworth stood.

"Will that be all, sir?" the housekeeper asked.

Alex smiled and nodded, hoping to hide the sudden tension, but the look on Dugan's face signaled he'd been unsuccessful.

"So, what's up?" Dugan asked, after Cassie and Mrs. Farnsworth left.

Alex hesitated, then lowered his voice. "There have been kidnapping threats against prominent families."

"You've been threatened?"

"Not directly," Alex lied, "but I was concerned. I engaged Farley as a bodyguard. Turns out he's not the most personable chap."

"But why's Mrs. Farnsworth upset?"

Alex sighed. "I didn't consult her. You know how proprietary she is regarding Cassie. Farley being a lout made things worse."

"I see," Dugan said, but the look on his face said he didn't see at all. Tactfully, he changed the subject.

"Fill me in on the work situation," Dugan said. "What about this other guy? How do you envision the work split?"

"His name is Braun, Captain Karl Braun," Alex said. "He's director of operations—scheduling, crewing, fuel purchases, payroll, that sort of thing. You'll be technical director—maintenance, yard repairs, and so on. We'll play it by ear on overlaps."

"Sounds fine," Dugan said. "I'm eager to start."

Alex hesitated. "There's really no rush, Thomas. Why don't you work half days a few weeks to settle in, hunt for a flat, and get your feet on the ground?"

"I want to earn my keep."

"Of course, of course," Alex said, "but it's a marathon, not a sprint."

"OK…I guess," Dugan said. "Easy does it" was not Alex Kairouz's style at all.

"It's settled then," Alex said, rising. "Join me for a nightcap?"

Dugan yawned. "No thanks. I'm jet-lagged as hell. See you in the morning."

∗∗∗

Two hours later, Dugan lay awake in the dark, mulling Alex's strange behavior. From what he knew, Alex failing to involve Mrs. Farnsworth in any matter related to Cassie was unthinkable. However, even if he had, Dugan didn't think Mrs. Farnsworth would nurse a grudge when Cassie's safety was concerned. Something was definitely not right.

PENTHOUSE, PLAZA ON THE THAMES
LONDON
28 MAYBE

"How is it you're livin' like a fuckin' Saudi prince, and I'm in a bloody closet over a garage?" Ian Farley asked, glaring from the sofa. At six foot and two hundred pounds, he looked like a muscle-bound skinhead, full of quiet menace. If he would only stay quiet.

Braun took a sip of brandy, then held the snifter to his nose, savoring the aroma as the liquid slid down his throat. He looked from the dancing fire to the glass wall of the huge living room with its view of Parliament across the Thames. Rain on the glass refracted the lights to dazzling effect. Cuban weather was better, but he couldn't enjoy the finer things in the worker's paradise, and Braun was making the most of London. At Kairouz's expense, of course. He looked at Farley and sighed. No more than his due, given the fools he had to endure.

"Because, Farley, your cover is a servant. You live in servant quarters."

Farley started to speak, but Braun's look chilled him.

"And don't leave the girl's proximity again, unless she's at school or elsewhere your presence would be suspicious. Understand?"

"Yeah, yeah, I got it."

Braun sipped again and studied Farley over the rim of his glass. For all his faults, Farley had the necessary skills—and he was expendable. The rest of the operation was equally lean, his only other operative a techno-geek eager to keep past work for foreign governments secret. Blackmail wasn't Joel Sutton's only incentive. Braun had dismissed the IT staff and contracted Sutton at a huge fee, again with Kairouz's money.

Sutton had bugged Kairouz's office and phones—office, home, and mobile—and now controlled the company computers. Braun monitored the work phones in real time and other phones via recording. He'd avoided bugging Kairouz's home; the daily chatter would be tedious to sort through and reveal little. Dugan's presence might change that.

"With Dugan around, spend time in the house," Braun said. "Keep your ears open."

"For what?" Farley asked.

"Signs Dugan is suspicious, of course." Idiot.

"Not so easy, guv. That bloody Irish bitch hates me. She'd poison me tea given the chance, and that snooty cunt Farnsworth stares holes in me. I ain't exactly Mr. Invisible."

Braun sighed. "All right. Do the best you can."

"OK." Farley rose to go. "When do I get a go at the retard? Remember our deal."

"Keep it in your pants, Farley. I'll tell you when. And you can't damage the goods. She'll bring a fortune in the Middle East. The wogs love blonds."

Farley leered. "I'll be a regular bleedin' Sir Galahad. She'll be cryin' when she has to leave me, she will."

CHAPTER SEVEN

Offices of Phoenix Shipping
1 June

"How many more?" Dugan asked into the intercom.

"Just one, sir," Mrs. Coutts said. "A Ms. Anna Walsh in ten minutes."

"Send her straight in, please," Dugan said.

He was worried. Had he missed a signal? Ward had told him he'd recognize the agent when she appeared and just to "follow her lead," whatever that meant. If the last applicant wasn't the agent, Dugan had screwed the pooch big time.

He looked out the big windows at the Thames just across Albert Embankment and wondered again at Alex's insistence he use his office. Strange, given Alex's resistance to hiring a new secretary and his irritation when Dugan pressed the point.

***

Braun sat in his office across the hall multitasking, checking schedules and listening with one ear. The interviews were in Kairouz's office at his insistence. He wanted a feel for the American, and it was far easier to move Dugan than to bug his temporary office in the conference room. He was pleased Dugan demanded a secretary. The more he fixated on such details, the less time to meddle. And perhaps he'd hire something one might actually want to get a leg over. Braun had shelved his own plan for a playmate with regret. Someone close by was a liability unless they were in on the operation, and he didn't want to expand the team. He smiled. Maybe Dugan would help him out.

***

"Come in, Ms. Walsh," Dugan said, leading the final job seeker to the sofa.

She was five four with shoulder-length auburn hair, green eyes, a freckled nose, and looked much younger than the thirty-eight years on her resume. A well-tailored wool skirt stopped above the knee, accentuating legs encased in dark silk. The neckline of her designer blouse was revealing, and she exuded sexuality.

She smiled. "My updated CV," she said, handing Dugan several pages.

He settled in his chair as he read the note attached.

We may be under audio or video surveillance. Follow my lead. Must convey impression I am a tart you are hiring for looks. Conclude by hiring me on the spot.

Dugan nodded. "Ah, well, Ms. Walsh. Tell me about yourself."

Her recitation was captivating. At typing speed, she crossed and uncrossed her legs; at spreadsheets and software, she leaned in and smiled. By then he was beyond listening. He only belatedly realized her lips had stopped moving.

"Yes… very impressive, Ms. Walsh," he said, befuddled, turning a page to stall.

"Pardon my digression, Mr. Dugan," she said, "but your office is beautiful."

"Actually, I'm borrowing it from the managing director while mine is completed."

"Well, it's lovely. And the sofa so comfy." She smiled. "Will you have one like it?"

"Why don't I hire you and you can make sure I do?"

"I'd love to," she said, "depending on salary, of course. The range indicated is below expectations, I'm afraid. Might there be flexibility?"

"We could go a bit higher," Dugan said. "How's 10 percent sound?"

"I suppose I could start there until you're satisfied with my… services." She smiled. "Then I'll expect a 25 percent increase."

Dugan stood and extended his hand. "Welcome aboard, Ms. Walsh."

Anna rose, moving closer as she took his hand. "Anna, please."

"All right, Anna. Let's get the ball rolling."

***

Mrs. Coutts gave Anna a withering look before turning to Dugan.

"And when is she to start, sir?" she asked, ice in her voice.

"Tomorrow if possible," Dugan said. "We'll put her on outfitting my new office."

Mrs. Coutts looked as if she'd been slapped.

"Under your supervision, of course," Dugan added, but the damage was done.

"Very good, sir. Come along, Ms. Walsh," Mrs. Coutts said, moving into the hallway as Anna hurried after.

Dugan watched them disappear and wondered how to patch things up with Mrs. Coutts.

***

Braun stood in his doorway and watched Anna's retreating backside. Bloody well perfect. And more than enough to distract Dugan. And when Dugan was out of the way, he'd double the slut's salary if she was accommodating. It was only Kairouz's money, after all.

M/T *Asian Trader*
Sembawang Shipyard, Singapore
1 June

Medina leaned on the rail, mentally hurrying his shipmates down the steep gangway in their "goin' ashore" clothes. The ship floated at a wet berth now, the main deck high above the dock, her tanks mostly empty. The second mate smiled and waved up at Medina, then said something to the man beside him, who shook his head and laughed, undoubtedly at a joke at Medina's expense. Let them laugh, thought Medina; the last laugh would be his.

He'd volunteered for night watches, citing his desire to explore Singapore by day. He spent those days in internet cafés and, as plans evolved, the electronics shops of Sim Lim Tower, returning to nap each afternoon in preparation for evenings alone on board. Or almost alone. The yard night shift was populated by the sick, the lame, and the lazy—they topped the gangway in search of a sleeping place, never to be seen again except as man-hours on the yard invoice. It had been dicey at first when the American Dugan was around. He'd had an unfortunate tendency to show up at all hours, checking on progress. But with the yard period almost over and the little Italian in charge, things were more predictable on the night watch.

Medina entered the deckhouse, climbed the stairs to the bridge deck, then began a slow deck-by-deck descent, walking each passageway to ensure everyone was ashore. He continued into the engine room, where he found yard workers dozing in scattered corners, and then walked the main deck from bow to stern, finding no one. Satisfied, he went to his cabin and locked the door behind him before rooting in his wardrobe locker.

He placed two items on his bed, and then sat in his desk chair and looked at them, still amazed that he'd been expected to strike a mighty blow with such meager weapons. An ancient Makarov pistol with a single clip and a martyr's vest, now disassembled, were his entire arsenal. His contact had given him the things, said "Allah will guide you," and left, leaving Medina uncertain and trembling at the prospect of failure.

He smiled now, thinking of his initial doubt, for Allah had been generous in His guidance. Had not Allah given him the interest in electronics years before, and had He not opened Medina's eyes to the canal's weak point? And did not the Holy Quran tell of David slaying Goliath with a single stone?

Medina unlocked a desk drawer and pulled out two plastic-wrapped bundles, the last two of twelve to be placed. Each was the size of a cigarette pack, and a length of antenna wire extended from each. They contained plastique, scavenged from his martyr's vest, and each held a detonator, a tiny remote-ignition circuit of his own devising, a nine-volt battery to power it all, and a small but powerful magnet. Their destructive force was minimal, but each would produce a significant flash, and that was all he needed.

Medina's mouth was dry. Tomorrow the ship shifted to the refinery loading berth. He had made great progress since Dugan's departure, but he had to finish tonight. He slipped a charge in each front pocket, donned a fanny pack, and went down to the main deck.

The yard was quiet save distant shouts and welding flashes from the dry docks, but Medina felt exposed in the glare of deck lights. He breathed deep and forced himself to an unhurried walk, up the deck to the vent for number one port ballast tank. Near the vent, he scanned the deck, then pulled a spool of wire and cutters from his fanny pack. He fed the fine wire into the vent pipe slowly to prevent kinks, and when an ample length dangled into the tank below, clipped the wire and bent the free end under the vent opening and wrapped it securely around a bolt head, almost invisible.

He moved to the manhole and stared down into the black void. They'd removed the temporary lights. He pulled an elastic headband from the fanny pack and donned it, slipping a small flashlight into it like a headlamp to free his hands and light his way down the ladder. He left the ladder at the uppermost horizontal stringer plate and moved forward through the tank, one of twelve forming the double hull between the cargo tanks and the sea, counting the frames forming the ship's ribs as he went. When he reckoned himself in position, he looked up and smiled as his light illuminated the vent opening near the shipside, the fine wire he'd placed dangling out, almost invisible.

Structural members marched up the outer hull like widely spaced shelves or rungs of a giant ladder, and Medina climbed, stretching and straining to pull himself up to the underside of the main deck. At the uppermost member, he clung one-handed, his feet on the next member down as he reached toward the ship's side with a charge. He gave a relieved grunt as the magnet sucked the charge to the steel, and then examined the placement. It sat on the uppermost member, like a box at the back of a high shelf, invisible unless someone scaled the structure as Medina had.

He groped under the vent and pulled the dangling wire to the charge antenna and twisted the two together, locking them with a tiny wire nut with trembling fingers. Sweat stung his eyes and soaked his coveralls, and he wiped his eyes with the back of his free hand to study his work in the beam of his little light. Perfect, he thought, and began to inch his way down.

Clang. The sharp ring of steel on steel sent Medina's heart into his throat, and he clung motionless, listening as more noise indicated activity on the main deck above him. He recovered and continued his descent, faster now. Back on the horizontal stringer, he moved aft toward the ladder with no clear plan. Should he go up? He still had to drill and plug a tiny hole near the top of the common bulkhead between this tank and the adjacent cargo tank. But what was happening on main deck? What if they were bolting the manhole? No one knew he was here. He'd be trapped until he starved to death or drowned when they flooded the ballast tank.

Medina took a deep breath and controlled his fear. His hand fell on the fanny pack, and he felt the small cordless drill through the fabric. He gathered his resolve and moved across the tank to the cargo-tank bulkhead.

Twenty minutes later, Medina eased his head out of the manhole and surveyed the main deck. Whoever had been there was gone, and he pulled himself from the manhole and stood on deck. His legs ached from climbing, but he felt the weight of the remaining charge in his pocket and pressed on. A half hour later, he exited the last ballast tank, sweating and dirty but exultant. He entered the deckhouse and went to the Cargo Control Room, where he walked to a control panel labeled "Mariner Tek—Model BT 6000—Ballast-Tank Gas-Detection System."

He extracted a pair of needle-nose pliers and a spool of wire from this fanny pack, then secured the power to the panel and opened it. This was the easy part. He'd studied the schematic in the technical manual for days and knew it cold. His fingers flew as he wired in jumpers, then arranged them within the existing wiring so that nothing looked amiss. He stepped back and admired his handiwork before closing the panel and powering up the system.

Green lights glowed, showing all ballast tanks safe and gas-free. He smiled again, knowing those lights would stay green, regardless of conditions in the tanks. He powered down the system and hummed a little tune as he climbed to his cabin for a shower.

OFFICES OF PHOENIX SHIPPING LTD.
LONDON
3 JUNE

Dugan wrinkled his nose at the faint smell of fresh paint and watched through the door as Anna scooped up folders from her own desk and maneuvered around a ladder in the outer office. Over Alex's objections, Dugan was working full days, even though his new office was a work in progress. Conversion of the storeroom to office space was all but complete, and throughout the process, Anna deferred to Mrs. Coutts completely. She'd managed to assuage the older woman's antipathy by following suggestions to the letter, including counsel as to proper dress. Unfortunately, Anna's sensuality defeated even Mrs. Coutts's wardrobe hints. The elderly secretary concluded the poor child was destined to look a tart, with no help for it.

"Last of the lot, Tom," Anna said, dumping folders on his desk.

"Thanks," Dugan said. "Computers?"

Anna sighed. "I've been on to Sutton four times today."

"OK. Keep on him," Dugan said.

As Anna left, Dugan stole a glance at her well-shaped backside before forcing himself back to work. He opened the folder on top of the stack to find a note.

Dugan, ask me to dinner tonight. We must talk.

Dugan pocketed the note. About time. Ward said contact would be through Anna. So far, there hadn't been any. He felt isolated, and for the first time, ill at ease in Alex's presence.

He pressed the intercom.

"Yes, Tom," Anna said.

"Can you stay late? I may need you to pull more files for me. I'll make it up with dinner. You pick the place."

She laughed. "Quite the best offer I've had all day. Bring your gold card."

"No problem. Thanks," Dugan said, picking up the phone to call Alex.

"Yes, Thomas," Alex answered, looking at his caller ID.

"Alex, I'm working over. Please give Mrs. Hogan my regrets."

Alex paused. "I've things to do as well. She'll put something back for us."

"Alex, that's not necessary. I've made—"

"No problem, Thomas. I'll just call home—"

"Alex. I have other plans."

A silence grew. "Very well," Alex said at last. "I'll see you tomorrow then."

Dugan hung up, troubled by his friend's behavior. He sighed and returned to the file he was studying.

***

"It's seven," Anna said from the doorway. "Starving me is nonproductive. I'm more agreeable on a full stomach."

Dugan stood and walked to the door. "Sorry. Lost track. You picked a place?"

Anna nodded and gathered her things. As they walked out, she pointed to light leaking beneath a door. "Captain Braun's working late."

Dugan shrugged. "He's always here when I leave."

***

43

About bloody time, thought Braun, irritated at Kairouz's failure to control Dugan. Not that he was too concerned. Working late was an obvious ploy to have a go at the slut. Took him long enough. Braun smiled. If they became lovers, bugging her flat might be worthwhile.

***

Anna listened as Dugan talked. After deflecting his attempts to discuss business with a quick hand squeeze and almost imperceptible head shake, she'd hung on to his every word. She deserved an Oscar. Despite knowing it was an act, he was enjoying himself.

"Dessert?" the waiter asked.

Dugan gave Anna a quizzical look.

"I'm stuffed," she said. "How about coffee at my place?"

Dugan asked for the check.

In the cab, Anna crawled onto his lap and kissed him, keeping at it all the way to her building. Dugan exited the cab, unable to hide his arousal from the smirking cabby, as Anna pulled him into the lobby for a smoldering kiss and kept at it in the elevator, kissing his neck and giggling. She dragged him to her door and fumbled with the key before pushing him in, lips on his, and closing the door behind them with her foot. Then she stopped.

"Sit." She pointed to a sofa as she threw the bolt, then moved to a chair.

Dugan stood in the entryway, his confusion complete.

"Surely you knew that wasn't genuine," she said.

He glanced down. "Part of me was hopeful."

Her face turned cold. "Yes, well, hope springs eternal. Sit."

Dugan complied. "OK. What now?"

She softened. "First, I'm sorry if I overdid it. We don't yet know how closely we're being watched. I was unsure you could fake it. So I aroused you."

"Superbly," Dugan said.

Anna colored. "Understand, Mr. Dugan, I'm happily married. I will deal with you professionally and expect no less."

"Married? Really?" Dugan said. "Must be tough."

"That's none of your business."

"You're right. Sorry," he said. "Let's just consider this, for the purposes of our cover only, our first spat and put it behind us?"

She ignored the sarcasm. "Tonight we set our cover. We can speak freely here. This place will be swept daily. Assume you're under surveillance elsewhere, for sure at the office."

"Are you sure?" Dugan asked.

"We put an undercover on the janitorial staff to do a sweep. Our offices and Kairouz's are bugged. From Braun's office."

"So Braun's running things. And he's bugging Alex, so Alex isn't involved."

"He's involved. Maybe he's using Braun to create deniability."

"I can't believe Alex is a willing party to terrorism."

Anna was noncommittal. "We'll see. Anyway, this is where we communicate. As lovers, it'll be natural to come here evenings or even to sneak off for afternoon trysts. We'll raise eyebrows but not suspicions."

"But won't whoever it is just bug this place?"

"We'll handle that. I'll tell you about it if and when necessary."

Dugan bristled. "Do let me know when I'm deemed trustworthy."

"Tom, we compartmentalize. You needn't be so touchy."

He considered that. "Yeah, I understand. Sorry I overreacted. Let's put the hostility behind us and go back to being Tom and Anna."

"Fine by me. Provided you stop being so damned cheeky."

Dugan smiled. "But that's my most endearing quality."

She shook her head and moved to the kitchen to brew coffee. When she returned, they settled down to discuss strategy.

"This is going to be harder than I thought," Dugan said. "I must admit Alex is behaving strangely. Like he's going out of his way to minimize my office time. We arrive late every day, then he has me out the door at the dot of five. Totally out of character for him; the guy's a workaholic. Braun must be coercing him somehow, maybe through threats to Cassie."

Anna looked skeptical. "I've seen Kairouz's file. He isn't someone easily intimidated. After his entire family was killed in the Lebanese civil war, he came to London as a penniless teen with no prospects and managed to build a major shipping company from scratch. Now he's wealthy and connected. If he's being threatened, why wouldn't he turn to the authorities?"

"I don't know. But Alex Kairouz is no terrorist."

Anna sighed. "Let's start with what we do know. This Farley arrived on the scene right after Braun's employment. We can assume he's a player, and the computer guy is in on it for sure. Word among the clerical staff is that Braun dismissed the IT people and brought Sutton on right after he joined the company. I suspect Hell will freeze over before we get any sort of reliable computer access."

"The biggest problem," Dugan said, "is how to snoop without raising suspicion if we're caught. If Braun's somehow squeezing Alex, he's pretty damn smart. We don't want to put his guard up."

Anna smiled. "We just need a believable motive. You have one made-to-order."

Dugan looked confused.

"Think about it," Anna said. "You and Braun are rivals. We style our snooping as an attempt to uncover some incompetence or malfeasance on Braun's part, so you can undermine him with Alex. Even if we're caught, it will look like corporate politics."

Dugan nodded, impressed. "Pretty sharp."

Anna smiled at the compliment and spent the next half hour briefing Dugan on how they would develop their cover relationship. At midnight, she let him out.

"Must keep up appearances," she whispered at the doorway, sending him off with a smoldering kiss.

***

Braun slumped in the driver's seat. He'd just decided the Yank was making a night of it when Dugan exited the building and turned up the walk. *I overestimated him*, thought Braun. *When he's gone, I'm sure the bitch will enjoy having a real man.*

CHAPTER EIGHT

M/T *Asian Trader*
ExxonMobil Refinery
Jurong, Singapore
4 June

The chief mate tensed at the console, focused on the rising level in the last cargo tank.

"Stop," he barked into his radio, commanding the terminal to stop pumping. The load was complete, and at a nod from the chief mate, Medina left to check the drafts.

It was a relieved Medina that rushed down the gangway. They'd taken minimal ballast for the short transit to the refinery; water hadn't even risen to his plugs. The ballast tanks were empty now, and the plugs had held as powerful fans pushed inert gas into the empty cargo tanks, displacing oxygen-rich air before gasoline surged into the tanks.

He'd been terrified that the gas pressure—slight though it was—would unseat the shredded bits of Styrofoam cup he'd packed into the tiny holes. He'd paced the deck, alert to telltale whiffs from ballast-tank vents or the loud keening of gas whistling through an unplugged hole.

But they all held, praise be to Allah, high on the bulkheads, submerged now under a foot of gasoline on the cargo-tank side. It wouldn't take long for the cargo to dissolve them.

But it would be long enough.

Offices of Phoenix Shipping
London

Braun smiled. Sutton had hacked backdoor access to several porn sites, making tracking his communications like looking for a needle in several thousand haystacks. Only the logic of the method had convinced Motaki to disregard his revulsion at accessing the sites. Braun's smile widened. Perhaps this might expand the Iranian's horizons a bit.

He opened an encrypted file. Motaki had done well. The Chechens looked European, and below each picture was age, height, weight, and hair and eye color. Braun printed the pictures and erased the file before typing the Web address of the Baltic Maritime Job Exchange, to begin his search for unemployed ex-Eastern Bloc mariners resembling the Chechens.

ANNA WALSH'S APARTMENT BUILDING
8 JUNE

Joel Sutton, dressed in a British Telcom uniform and with toolbox in hand, rang Anna Walsh's doorbell. Showing his face was a risk, but he'd confirmed Dugan and the bitch were at work, and no one else would know him. When no one answered, he picked the lock and went to work.

He hid transmitters in the phones and throughout the small apartment and a tiny receiver on a high closet shelf, tapped into a spare circuit in the existing phone wiring. Satisfied, he left things as he'd found them and rode the elevator to the lobby, leaving his toolbox there as he went to the van. He returned with a heavy shopping bag, its handles biting into his hand, to collect his toolbox and ride the elevator to the basement.

The telephone box was well marked and he set to work, stepping back twenty minutes later to survey the results. Concealed under a stack of boxes and connected to the panel by a hidden wire sat a lead-lined wooden box with a near-invisible antenna wire run to a high window. The box was soundproof, with a speaker inside echoing any sound from the apartment. Inches away was a cell phone, voice activated to dial at any sound. There was no connection between the devices but sound waves, eliminating a trace. The outgoing cell signal was detectable, but isolating it would be difficult. Difficult became impossible as the audio was relayed through two identical boxes, both hidden far away in high-cell-traffic areas.

All the phones were untraceable, purchased for cash, and modified with long-life batteries. Each box held enough plastic explosive and white phosphorus to destroy the contents and anyone opening them without first calling the phone inside and entering a disarming code.

Sutton dialed Anna Walsh's number on another throwaway phone and let her voice mail greeting play without responding. In the basement of the Iranian embassy, another cell phone disconnected after Anna's words were recorded, and a technician phoned his superior. His superior walked to a window of his second-floor office and smoothed his hair with his right hand in full view of another man standing across the street pretending to read a newspaper. The man walked to a public phone and dialed a number from memory.

"Hello," Sutton said.

"I'm sorry. I was ringing George McGregor. I misdialed," the man said and hung up.

Sutton disconnected and reached for his toolbox. Surveillance was established for whoever the hell was running it. He left the building to ditch the van.

OFFICES OF PHOENIX SHIPPING

Dugan cursed as his monitor went black for the third time. He checked his watch. Might as well pack it in. Ever since he and Anna had begun their "affair," they'd stayed late every night to establish a pattern of being in the office after hours. They left together every evening, and twice Dugan slept on her sofa, arriving the next morning in the same clothes—a fact noted by office gossips. What Dugan had failed to anticipate was the impact of his relationship with Anna on his other relationships.

Mrs. Coutts registered disapproval in every icy glance, addressing him with cold formality, while Anna was somehow transformed in Mrs. Coutts's view into a poor innocent led astray by her lustful boss, a sexual predator. It got worse. Daniel, the driver, shared the gossip with Mrs. Hogan, the cook, who, certain he was wrong, passed it on to Mrs. Farnsworth. After admonishing Mrs. Hogan on the evils of gossip, Mrs. Farnsworth phoned Mrs. Coutts so that she might find the source of the malicious rumor and squash it, only to learn the rumor was true.

Mrs. Farnsworth, never one of Dugan's fans, now addressed him, when she spoke at all, as if he was only slightly less unpleasant than something she couldn't get off her shoe sole. Mrs. Hogan registered disapproval in her own way. His eggs this morning had been rubber, served with black toast and orange juice with a half-inch layer of seeds in the bottom of the glass.

The only female in the house who still liked him was Cassie, but she was in bed when he got home now, and his first morning absence had not gone unnoticed. Her inquisition the following morning had been curtailed only by a "proper young lady is not nosy" dictum from Mrs. Farnsworth, accompanied by an icy stare at Dugan.

It had come to a head on the ride in this morning, with Alex's repeated throat clearing.

"You better spit it out before you get a sore throat, Alex," Dugan said.

"It's… awkward, Thomas. Your involvement with this Walsh woman is upsetting the household."

"Agreed," Dugan said, "but I'll be damned if I know why. My private life's my own."

"True, Thomas. But the ladies"—Alex smiled—"except Mrs. Farnsworth, of course, all held you in high regard. I'm sure they didn't think you a monk, but assumed you would choose a more… appropriate partner. Hiring a woman for her looks just to bed her is just so… unsavory."

"Anna's a damn good secretary."

"Indeed," Alex said, "a fortunate accident according to Mrs. Coutts."

"How about you, Alex? Do you share the ladies' opinion?"

Silence answered.

"That's the pot and the kettle, old friend," Dugan said. "Kathleen was your secretary."

He regretted the words immediately. Alex purpled.

"Don't you dare imply my marriage was the product of some cheap office dalliance. Kathleen worked for me for years before we dated. I am your friend, but if you ever, ever repeat that, I will be no longer. Is that clear?"

"That was a cheap shot, Alex. I'm sorry. I guess I'm just confused by everyone's reaction. I certainly don't want to upset your household. Should I move out?"

"Perhaps that's best," Alex said, still angry. "But where? In with Miss Walsh?"

"That's my business, Alex," Dugan said, and they'd ridden the rest of the trip in silence.

***

And now I'm homeless in London, thought Dugan as Anna popped her head in the door.

"How about dinner?" she asked.

"I'm with you," Dugan said, standing to leave. "We've weighty matters to discuss."

"Oh?"

Dugan smiled. "How'd you like a roommate?"

***

Perfect, thought Braun as Dugan and Anna left. The timing on Sutton's visit had been spot on, and if the Yank moved in, perhaps they'd spend more time in the apartment, and he could off-load some of the surveillance. A celebration was in order. A nice dinner courtesy of Kairouz and some entertainment. He dialed his cell as he left the office.

"Send me the little brunette at ten," he said into the phone. "I forget her name."

"Yvette," a voice said, "and the price is triple. You bloody near killed her last time. I couldn't work her for days. I expect payment for lost time."

"No problem," Braun said. "Make sure she brings the toys."

He hung up and hailed a cab, smiling as he settled in the seat—things were going well.

***

Dugan and Anna stepped out into a beautiful evening, pleasantly full and mellow from wine. He'd recounted his trouble with Alex over dinner as Anna feigned delight at the prospect of cohabitation. Dugan played along, though less than eager to exchange a good bed for a lumpy sofa. Anna clung to him now, head against his shoulder as he started to hail a cab.

"No, don't," she said. "It's lovely. Let's walk."

Foot traffic was light, but as they reached Anna's building, a short, bald man, head down and phone to his ear, rushed down the steps to collide with Anna, moving on without slowing. Dugan glared after him.

"Easy, Tarzan," Anna said, a restraining hand on Dugan's arm. "I'm fine. Let it go."

Anna tugged Dugan's arm and they moved inside.

In the safe haven of the apartment, Dugan relaxed, but before he spoke, Anna clamped a hand over his mouth.

"I think I'll shower. Care to wash my back, Tiger?" she asked.

"Sounds delightful," Dugan said, nodding as she removed her hand.

He stood in the bathroom in mute confusion as Anna arranged the showerhead so the water drummed loud against the plastic curtain. She removed her shoes and motioned him to do the same, then led him on tiptoe through the small kitchen and out the back door of the apartment. There were two apartments per floor, all with front entrances served by the residents' elevator and rear entrances with a common service elevator. As she closed her own door, a tall man in a rumpled suit beckoned from the open back door of the next apartment. Anna entered the apartment with Dugan in tow and followed the man into the living room.

The tall man grinned. "And how is our Phoenix Shipping slut?"

"Sod off, Harry," Anna said. "Lou back yet?"

"Any minute," Harry said as a key rattled in the front door and Lou entered.

"You're the guy who ran into us," Dugan said, still confused.

"Guilty," Lou said. "I had to let Anna know about the bugs."

Anna nodded at the new arrival. "Tom, this is Lou Chesterton and"—she indicated the tall man—"Harry Albright. My colleagues in the Anti-Terrorism Unit."

Dugan shook hands as she continued. "Who wired us?" she asked.

"Sutton," Lou said. "Professional job. Multiple booby-trapped relays. Untraceable."

"Christ," Dugan said, "there goes our time outside the fish bowl."

"Welcome to our world, Yank," Lou said, turning to Anna. "Shower running?"

"Less than five minutes, but we don't have long." She turned to Harry. "Cover audio?"

Harry smiled. "Some of the finest sex sounds the Internet has to offer."

"Voices?" she asked.

"Not a problem," Harry said. "Talk is minimal and a bit… repetitive. I distorted it, and you can put on music to help mask it. It'll do for tonight."

"What's after the sex sounds?" Anna asked.

"Snoring in an endless loop. To buy time for you two to come back and do some recordings for alternative sound feeds."

"I don't snore," Dugan said.

"Actually, you do. Like a bloody train," Anna said. "At least on my sofa."

"Actually, you both do. At least on my recording," Harry said as Dugan smirked.

"Right," Lou said, "we best get to it. Harry, get Anna the portable CD player while she briefs Mr. Dugan here."

Minutes later, they crept into Anna's apartment. She turned off the water and gave a sensuous moan as she placed the CD player by the bedside phone. Dugan, per instructions, grunted sexual sounds, looking so self-conscious Anna was hard-pressed not to laugh. She put music on her sound system and started the sex sound track on the portable player. Satisfied, they slipped out the back door and into the other apartment.

CHAPTER NINE

Braun read the decrypted message and cursed. He pulled the sat phone from a drawer. The encryption algorithm was unbreakable, and calls were routed through random and changing links, but still, he preferred to minimize voice contact. He sighed; anxiety was to be expected, he supposed, when one dealt with amateurs. He dialed. In Tehran, an identical phone rang.

"Yes," Motaki answered.

"I got your message," Braun said. "All is proceeding. *Asian Trader* sailed from Singapore on schedule, and I chartered a VLCC named *China Star* to the Iranian National Oil Company. She must depart Kharg Island no later than 21 June to arrive in the Malacca Straits as *Asian Trader* reaches Panama. Please ensure there are no loading delays in Iran."

Braun had learned that giving his principals some simple task within their control always had a calming influence.

"I will see to it," Motaki said. "But what about Panama? I'm concerned we do not have sufficient control. Rodriguez might be a problem if his pet project goes awry."

"Our man on *Asian Trader* has minimal resources. It is not a problem."

"All right," Motaki said. "And this man Richards?"

"On standby pay. He knows nothing yet. I'll move him to Jakarta when the time is right."

"So, the sideshows move ahead. What of the main attack?"

"The Chechens are at the training facility. They can't become experts, but they will learn enough to serve our purposes."

"Their Russian is better than their English," Motaki said. "I still think a facility in Eastern Europe would have been better."

"Chechen-accented Russian," Braun replied. "Chechen seamen are rare, Mr. President. Here in UK their accents are unrecognizable, and if they say something that reveals them to be other than seamen, it can be covered as language misunderstanding."

"And what of these men whose identities you've stolen? What if one of them should make an inconvenient appearance?"

Braun smiled. "Those men are being well paid to stay home. I employed them for fictitious ships under construction in China and put them on full pay to stand by, ready to fly at moment's notice. The seamen get paid for nothing, and the agency gets their commission. All courtesy of Kairouz. Everyone is happy."

"Very well," Motaki said, his acknowledgment grudging, "and the last ship?"

"I have several options, but it's too early to—"

"Mr. Braun, need I remind you—"

"You need remind me of nothing, Mr. President, but the main attack is the most difficult. Runs from Black Sea ports to the target are short, with no chance to manipulate arrival time. Additionally, the ports involved are not the most efficient, and there may be lengthy delays. There are many things that can go wrong," Braun said. "With respect, sir, too many cooks spoil the broth. Please leave this to me."

"Very well," Motaki said, "but keep me informed."

"Of course."

ANNA WALSH'S APARTMENT BUILDING
1915 HOURS LOCAL TIME
9 JUNE

Dugan sat with the Brits in the apartment next to Anna's. Dugan and Anna had returned there the first night, to work with Harry recording scripts for additional cover audio, including, to their discomfort and Harry's amusement, breathless sexual audio. Anna had colored and pointed a smirking Harry from the room as she moaned "Yes, yes, yes," into the mike.

Dugan had been skeptical.

"How do you turn a few hours into days of fake audio?" he'd asked.

"Bloody magic, Yank, and the wizardry of British intelligence," Harry had replied. "But we don't need 'days.' You spend nights there, and most of that sleeping. Sex will occupy some time and Internet tracks laced with your recordings will work there." Harry had shrugged. "That leaves hours, and conversation varies little day to day. Our lads have software to assemble daily dialogues, then they review and tweak it. Mornings, you'll need to mind what you say, but we'll craft evening dialogues for you to play at Anna's while you stay here. We'll add sex as it seems to fit, and that will be that."

And so it had. To his delight, Dugan traded Anna's lumpy sofa for the bed in the surveillance apartment, creeping into her place each morning to begin the daily charade. The surveillance apartment became their center of operations, a meeting place by day, and a refuge where Dugan and Anna could escape the bugs for a while each evening while the fake audio ran.

***

"I smell a rat," Dugan said, holding up a copy of the daily ship-position report.

"What do you mean, Yank?" Lou asked.

Dugan tapped the page. "This ship. The *China Star*. She's a VLCC Phoenix chartered from a competitor, then subchartered to the Iranian National Oil Company. I can't see any way we can make money on that sort of deal at prevailing rates."

Harry looked confused. "A vee bloody what?"

"Sorry," Dugan said. "VLCC is short for 'very large crude carrier.' Supertanker to you."

"But what's it mean?" Anna asked.

Dugan shrugged. "Maybe nothing, but it might be a lead. At any rate, it's the only thing I've been able to turn up so far. If I can get a look at the charter agreement, I might be able to make some other connections."

"Can you get at it?" Anna asked.

Dugan shook his head. "That's another thing that makes me suspicious. There's neither a copy of the agreement on the server nor is it in the hard-copy files. I could just ask for it, but if I'm right, that might set off all sorts of alarms."

"So how are you going to get it?"

"I've got an idea," Dugan said.

HEAD HILL TRAINING CENTER
SOUTHAMPTON, HAMPSHIRE, UK
11 JUNE

Khassan Basaev's monitor flashed a congratulatory message and a prompt to move to the next training module. He yawned and arched into a stretch, rubbing his blue eyes before he reached out of habit to stroke a nonexistent beard. He grimaced at his unfamiliar reflection in the monitor and hoped he looked "European" enough. His three companions were also freshly barbered, with lighter lower faces stark against tanned necks and foreheads, a difference fading under application of the sunlamp. All the men's hair was light, blond to brown, and they looked Nordic rather than the mujahideen they were.

"Ah. Another milestone," Shamil whispered in Russian from his seat next to Basaev. "Quite impressive for a mountain peasant."

Basaev gave a brief smile as Aslan and Doku chuckled. "Joke as you will, Shamil," Basaev said, "but don't forget our mission."

"I never do," Shamil said, serious now, as all the men turned back to their terminals.

Basaev looked around the computer training lab, empty on a Saturday except for the four men. The instructor had been surprised at Basaev's request to use the training facility on the weekend for review, declining an opportunity to relax in town with the rest of the class after a grueling week of instruction. The Chechens had no desire to mix with the other—mostly British and Western European—students. Basaev's men were known collectively as "the Russians" by the others, an insult not normally tolerated. Now it comforted him. The infidels couldn't tell a Chechen from an Eskimo.

Shamil's joke aside, they were no peasants, but university graduates, fluent in several languages. They'd met in university in Grozny a lifetime ago, before Russian aggression drove them to the Cause of Allah and Free Chechnya. They escaped the city just before the Russians encircled it, fleeing to a mountain village, where weeks had grown to months and then years as their war ground to a fitful stalemate, neither side capable of victory. In time, they were ignored, and if it was not victory, it was better than living under the Russian heel. The village became home, and they started families. Life had been simple but full.

So much so that Paradise for Basaev was not a place of willing virgins but a vision of his village. A place to hold his wife, as she whispered he would be a father once more, as he watched his toddler move around a modest hut. A place gone forever when the guns of a helicopter gunship tore his family into bloody refuse, identifiable only by shreds of clothing.

He'd been away at the time, leading a dozen others on a routine patrol. They returned to bury their dead and move into hiding, asking Allah only for Russians to kill, a wish come true as Russians arrived in force to crush the holdouts. It became a long, hard war of attrition, and they killed many Russians, but there were always more. Iranian agents were frequent guests in his mountain hideaway, asking nothing in return for their aid. Until last month.

"We are not seamen," Basaev had protested, "and why strike our Muslim brothers? Killing Russians is pleasing in the sight of Allah."

"You do the work of Allah," the Iranian said, "but there are tasks more urgent. We can teach you the skills required but cannot make our other brothers look European."

"And the Faithful who die?"

"Most casualties will be infidel tourists, and the Faithful who die will be gathered into Heaven. And ask yourself this, Basaev: are those that whore themselves to gawking tourists really our brothers? Are the governments that fawn on the Americans in return for military aid really true Muslims? When was the last time you saw a Saudi or Egyptian or a Turk or anyone but an Iranian in these mountains, bringing you guns and ammunition and medicine?" The Iranian had paused. "You should reflect upon who stands by your side during your darkest hour."

Basaev had conceded the point but continued to resist. "We know how to kill Russians and should continue until Allah calls us to Paradise."

"Look around you," the Iranian said. "Four left. And in these mountains, groups of two or four or seven fight on, growing fewer as the Russians grow stronger, financed by the sale of oil. If, God willing, you sell your lives for a hundred Russians each, there will be four hundred infidels in Hell. A drop in the ocean. Take my offer and slay infidel tourists by the thousands and bring down the Russian economy. Think, my brother."

"I have," Basaev said, "and it is clear to me this will raise oil prices and enrich Iran."

The Iranian smiled. "The better to support world Jihad," he said.

In the end, Basaev had acquiesced, and now he slipped into silent prayer, asking for Allah's favor, for he thought himself a godly man and sought divine approval often. The self-deception was so complete he never understood he'd converted to a more elemental faith, kneeling among the bloody remains of his family at the altar of vengeance. His religion was the destruction of all things Russian.

Basaev pulled himself back to the present and clicked his mouse to bring up the next module, "Cargoes and Possible Ignition Sources."

OFFICES OF PHOENIX SHIPPING
11 JUNE

Dugan got off the elevator and walked through the deserted offices, illuminated by the morning sun filtering through hallway windows. He left the overhead lights off and made his way past the cubicle farm to an office marked CHARTERING. He looked around nervously, then opened the door and entered, turning to ease the door closed.

"May I help you, Mr. Dugan?"

Dugan spun to see Abdul Ibrahim sitting at his desk with a perplexed expression. Even on a Saturday, the little Pakistani wore a well-tailored suit and a perfectly knotted silk tie.

"Uh… Mr. Ibrahim. Forgive me for not knocking. I didn't know you were here. I was uh… just going to leave a note on your desk to call me. I would have messaged you, but I'm having some problem with my e-mail."

Ibrahim smiled and gestured to a chair. "No apology necessary. Please. Sit and tell me how I may be of service."

Dugan took the chair, his mind racing. Shit.

"I'm just curious," he said. "I saw a VLCC on the position report… *China Star*, I think her name is. I noticed she was subchartered to lift a cargo to Japan. I figure if rates are good enough to charter in, then subcharter on that route, I should check it out. If that trade picks up, it means I can get our ships positioned in the Far East much more cheaply for repairs. That will really help our maintenance budget."

Christ, thought Dugan, pretty smooth. That even sounded believable to me.

Ibrahim looked uncomfortable. "I have only a vague recollection of the details, but I will look into it and get back with you Monday, if that's all right."

He'd hit a nerve. Dugan started to back off, then realized that any damage was already done. He may as well find out what he could. In for a penny, in for a pound.

"You're head of chartering," Dugan said. "This is a big-money deal that went down three days ago."

Ibrahim was sweating. "I… I…"

"Mr. Ibrahim," Dugan said, "I've known you almost ten years and know you're honest. If you've somehow caught up in something illegal—"

Ibrahim shook his head. "Not me," he said, lowering his voice. "Braun put together the charters. I went to Mr. Kairouz, but—"

He stopped and looked around, then lowered his voice further. "I will not speak of it here. But I know you are Mr. Kairouz's friend, and something is very, very wrong. I will tell you what I know. Meet me near the entrance to Vauxhall tube station in one hour."

Dugan nodded and rose to leave. He opened the door quietly and looked around before slipping out and down the corridor to his own office. He closed his office door just as the elevator doors opened down the hall.

***

Braun stepped off the elevator and swiveled toward the quiet click of Dugan's office door closing. What the bloody hell was Dugan doing here?

VAUXHALL TUBE STATION
LONDON

Braun watched Dugan and Ibrahim from a distance as they stood on the platform, staring straight ahead as they pretended to be disinterested strangers waiting for a train. He couldn't see their faces but noted tension in their postures. They were obviously conversing. Amateurs.

Braun mulled the possibilities. Dugan's fumbling attempts to catch him in some malfeasance or incompetent action were apparent and concerned him not at all. Nor did Ibrahim know anything except the barest financial essentials of the *China Star* deal, and Braun had arranged those to look like a kickback scheme. So even if Dugan learned of *China Star*, he couldn't go to the authorities without implicating his friend Kairouz.

Braun considered killing them both, just to be sure, but dismissed the idea. Two dead executives from the same company were bound to attract unwanted attention. But there was the problem of perception. He'd promised Kairouz that if he couldn't control the little Pakistani, the man would die, along with his family. Braun hated breaking promises. Kairouz had to understand Braun was a man of his word. Otherwise, when things got really challenging, Kairouz might feel insufficiently motivated.

It was a conundrum, and he now regretted the specificity of his threat. Killing the Paki and his entire family would be far too sensational and sure to attract media attention. Braun sighed. How tedious. He continued to mull things over as he waited until the men boarded separate trains. He had no need to follow. He knew where Ibrahim lived.

ANNA WALSH'S APARTMENT BUILDING
1615 HOURS LOCAL TIME
11 JUNE

"He's really stressed out," Dugan said. "Apparently Braun handled the charters of *China Star* personally. The first Ibrahim learned of it was when the ship appeared on the position report. Like me, he thought it looked hinky and started asking questions." Dugan paused. "That's when it got interesting. He went to Braun, who blew up. When he failed to get satisfaction there, he approached Alex, who told him if he didn't back off, he'd be fired."

"More proof of Kairouz's involvement," Lou said, "but what's Ibrahim make of it?"

"He doesn't know what to think," Dugan said. "On the surface it looks like some sort of kickback deal. His main fear is personal. He believes Braun has somehow forced Alex to enter a shady deal, and he's afraid that he will somehow become the fall guy if the deal goes sour. He's pretty conflicted. He's worked for Alex a long time and knows he's scrupulously honest. On the other hand, Alex seems to be deferring to Braun completely, and Ibrahim thinks he's screwed no matter what he does. I guess that's why he opened up to me so easily."

"You're sure no one saw you?" Harry asked.

"I can't see how," Dugan said. "We left the office separately and met off site."

"Still," Anna said, "I wish you had consulted us before the meet."

"No time," Dugan said, "Ibrahim seemed to be in a talkative mood, and I didn't want to give him time to think about it."

"Well, your instincts were probably right on that," Anna said.

"I guess that's it then," Lou said. "*China Star*'s not even at the load port yet, so I doubt there's an immediate threat. We'll just keep an eye on it and see what develops. Is there anything else, Anna?"

Anna shook her head, and Harry and Lou stood up. Anna followed them to the door. Just as they reached the door, Lou turned. "By the way, good work, Tom," he said.

Dugan nodded as Anna let the pair out and locked the door behind them.

"Let me second that," Anna said as she returned. "It was good work."

Dugan sighed. "Something's obviously up with Alex, but I know he's a victim."

"Given the evidence, Tom, I can't understand your certainty."

"I just am," Dugan said. "I know him."

"You seem unlikely friends, really."

"How so?"

"Well, you're just… different, that's all. Alex is so… so 'European' I guess is the word. Tactful, multilingual, almost courtly, and…" Anna stopped.

"And I'm what…" Dugan deadpanned. "Blunt? Monolingual? Abrasive?"

"Tom, please, I didn't—"

Dugan grinned. "How 'bout 'American'… will that sum it up?"

Relieved, she smiled. "Quite nicely, you bloody annoying Yank. But seriously, whatever do you and Alex Kairouz have in common?"

"Dead wives," he said softly and looked away.

He lapsed into silence, and she thought he'd said all he intended. Then he went on.

"Years ago, Alex hired me to inspect a ship. He liked my work and became a regular client. Later I was working a short project in his office that got delayed. I tried to extend my hotel, but they were booked, as were most hotels in London, so Alex invited me home."

Dugan smiled. "Cassie was just a toddler. Mrs. Hogan served a great meal, and after Mrs. Farnsworth took Cassie to bed, Alex and I had brandy and coffee." He smiled again. "Mostly brandy. That's when he told me his wife had died of cancer two years earlier. His wounds were raw, and it was obvious he was burying his grief in work and raising Cassie."

"The more we drank, the more we opened up. My wife had been dead awhile, but it all came back." He paused. "Because I had suppressed it too. My kid sister was a rock after Ginny's death, but some things I couldn't share even with her, but Alex and I connected. We drank and talked and vented. About good things and bad and things we missed most. We got shitfaced and maudlin and toasted lost loves, and sober and hungover and finally"— Dugan gave a sheepish smile—"embarrassed by our behavior. We never spoke of it again. But I know Alex Kairouz, and Alex Kairouz is no terrorist."

Anna nodded, understanding and intrigued.

"Will you tell me about Ginny?"

She was afraid she'd offended him, but slowly his face softened.

"The love of my life," he said with a wistful smile. "Her name was Virginia."

"How'd you meet?"

Dugan chuckled. "I ran into her. Literally. I bashed my old pickup into her brand-new Mustang convertible in a parking lot."

"You met in a car crash?" Anna asked, incredulous.

"More like a fender bender. She was livid. The first words she ever said to me were 'Why don't you watch where the hell you're going, you big jerk?'"

Anna smiled. "Not a terribly auspicious beginning."

"Oh, but it was. There she was, green eyes flashing and the wind in her red hair, ready to kick my ass, all five foot two inches of her, the most beautiful woman I'd ever seen. She calmed down and we traded contact info, and then she called the next day. She was having trouble with the insurance because the accident happened on a private lot with no police report. I told her just to get her car fixed and I would pay for it, provided she let me buy her dinner to apologize. Long story short, we married a year later."

"What did she do?" Anna asked.

"She was a teacher. First grade. She loved kids," Dugan said.

"Did she die of cancer too?"

"Accident," Dugan said. His face clouded, and he looked away. Anna moved closer and took his hand.

"I'm sorry," she said, "it was wrong of me to pry."

"No. It's OK," he said, turning back to her. "I want to tell you, though I don't know why. It's just… difficult to get out." She squeezed his hand, and he went on. "We were both off for the summer when I was offered some relief-chief work. Since the only way to a permanent chief-engineer job was to start as relief, I jumped at it. We postponed a planned trip, and I went back to sea.

"It was a container ship on a North Europe run. Sat phones were new, and the ship didn't have one. I called Ginny from pay phones on the dock in US ports, but in Europe then you had to go to the phone company or a hotel to call the US. I couldn't always get away from the ship, but I did call from our last European port with our ETA in New York so she could meet us, and we could spend a few hours together before the next trip."

Dugan paused. "When I called, she told me she had a surprise for me in New York, but I couldn't drag it out of her. Then we just talked about everything and nothing, like you do when you're in love, just feeling connected. She was talking about visiting her sister in upstate New York when we got cut off. I kept trying back but kept getting a German recording. I got through a half hour later, but there was no answer, and I had to get back to the ship.

"We hit a storm coming back, lost some containers overboard and took minor damage. We were delayed, but I knew Ginny would call the company for an updated ETA before she left home. When we docked, the Coast Guard and a crowd of insurance surveyors boarded to inspect the damage. When the crowd cleared and I hadn't seen Ginny, I grabbed my coffee can of quarters and headed for the pay phone. I got no answer at home, so I called Ginny's sister." Dugan paused. "That's when I found out.

"We had a renovated apartment, hardwood floors and rugs everywhere, all sizes. Ginny loved the damned things. She slipped on one and smashed her head on the coffee table. When she didn't show up and her sister couldn't reach her, she called the police. They found Ginny.

"Ginny wasn't great with administrative details. Her sister was still listed as next of kin, and she didn't know how to reach me or when I'd return. After the autopsy, she went ahead with the funeral. Ginny was buried the day before I arrived. I didn't even get to say good-bye."

Anna squeezed his hand and nodded, not trusting herself to speak, as Dugan went on.

"I know now her sister did the best she could, but I wasn't rational. I said terrible things to her. I apologized later, but scars remain. I don't hear from her."

"Oh Tom, I'm—"

He ignored her, as if having started, he couldn't stop.

"My shipmates found me crying on the dock. The first thing I remember is my sister, Katy, packing up my stuff. She took me home and moved in and commuted to school. I drank. She tried to help, but she was a college kid with no idea how to handle a morose, nutty drunk. I got it in my head Ginny was murdered. I needed a target for my hate, I guess. I went down and demanded a copy of the autopsy report."

Dugan took a ragged breath as a tear leaked from his eye. "It took a bottle of Wild Turkey to get through it, but I found Ginny's surprise. She was pregnant."

"Oh God. Tom, I'm so sorry."

"I was in a drunken rage, still convinced someone had killed her. I read it all again and again—date, time, and cause of death—until I understood. Until I found the bastard." He turned, his anguish unbearable, as he revealed a dark secret he'd shared with no one, not even Alex, in twenty years.

"It was me," he whispered. "I killed them."

Anna sat entranced as it poured out. His realization that Ginny died near the time of their last call. His image of Ginny irritated at the disconnection. Of an impatient wait for a callback and a slip on the rug as she rushed to answer.

"If I hadn't kept trying," he said, "Ginny and our baby would be alive."

Anna sat, unsure how to respond, but knowing grief, survivor's guilt, and failure to share these terrible thoughts had solidified this horrible notion. No words could heal this. She hugged him awkwardly as he hid his face in her shoulder, ashamed of his horrible secret.

After a while, he lifted his head. "Sorry," he said with an embarrassed smile.

She kissed him tenderly, and he tensed. She stood and tugged him to his feet.

"Anna, wait."

She placed a finger on his lips and pulled him toward the bedroom. Sex was slow and tender as they explored each other with the wonder of new lovers, mingled with an inexplicable familiarity. Afterward, Anna lay in the crook of his arm as she toyed with his chest hair.

"A penny for your thoughts?"

"I'm wondering why women always ask that after sex."

He jumped as she jerked his chest hair. "Ouch. That hurt, damn it."

"Serves you right for spoiling the moment."

Dugan hugged her close. "Lady, it would take a lot more than that to spoil this moment."

They lapsed into silence, each thinking their own thoughts.

"Ah… actually," Dugan said, "I may spoil it. What about Mr. Walsh?"

"Who?" She raised her head, confused.

"You know. Your husband."

Anna began to laugh. "My God, Dugan. You are a bloody Boy Scout, aren't you? Ex-husband, Tom. I'm long since divorced."

"But you said—"

"Cast as a slut," she said, "I needed to discourage you. Actually, I was pleasantly surprised I wasn't forced to use a knee to the groin."

"So what happened?" Dugan asked.

"Not much to tell. We met in school, both studying forensic accounting. You know, finding people 'cooking the books' as you Yanks say. We married, and I joined MI5 and David went to a private firm. After training, I joined a firm supplying temps, basically a front to place me in companies under investigation. In time," she continued, "my job seemed to upset David. I guess it was emasculating, like he was a stodgy accountant and I was a spy. He hinted and then demanded I quit, but I quite liked my job."

She sighed. "Perhaps I was selfish. I might have dealt better with his insecurity, but I didn't. He grew cold and had frequent—and open—affairs, as if advertising he was a stud. We divorced, and last I heard, he was married for the third time and living in the Midlands."

"Is the offer of a penny for my thoughts still open?"

"Sure."

Dugan hugged her tight. "David was a fucking idiot."

Anna smiled into his chest.

"I've often thought so myself," she said.

CHAPTER TEN

Offices of Phoenix Shipping
13 June

Braun sat in Alex Kairouz's favorite chair and watched over steepled fingers. Alex sat on the sofa, ashen faced and trembling as he digested the news. Ibrahim's body was found in an alley, throat slashed and wallet missing. Metro Police considered it a random street crime, as did the media. There was a small story on an inside page of *The Daily Telegraph* and a thirty-second mention on the morning news shows. Braun was pleased.

"Quit sniveling, Kairouz," Braun said. "It's your own bloody fault."

"M… my fault. You basta—"

"Of course it's your fault," Braun said. "Didn't I warn you what would happen if you didn't control Ibrahim? As a matter of fact, please note I spared his wife and children. For now. I'll remedy that if you don't quit whining and get back in the game."

"What do you want?"

"Your renewed participation. Does it surprise you to know your friend Dugan has been snooping about? He and Ibrahim became fast friends, unfortunately for Ibrahim. Dugan is out of control, and I'm holding you responsible for putting him back in the box."

"I warned you this would happen," Alex said. "How can I possibly control Thomas?"

"To start, get closer to him," Braun said. "Play on his friendship and find a way to keep him ignorant and out of the picture. You're a clever fellow. I'm sure you'll come up with something. I don't care how you do it, but contain him."

"And if I can't?"

"Then Mr. Dugan and the family Ibrahim will all meet with accidents. Are we clear?"

Alex gave a stiff nod, and Braun rose and walked out.

He was pleased with his solution. Delegation was the mark of a good manager, and surely Kairouz could control Dugan for a week or two. After that, it wouldn't matter.

Anna Walsh's Apartment Building

Anna awakened and lifted her head from Dugan's chest to peer at the lighted alarm clock. Dugan stirred, his soft snoring interrupted as he shifted in his sleep. Anna smiled down at his sleeping face, barely visible in the light of the clock. She had never before mixed her professional and personal lives. She knew she should regret it. She didn't.

She shook his shoulder.

"Wh… time is it?" Dugan's voice was thick with sleep.

"Ten thirty. Almost bedtime."

He smiled. "Again?"

Anna poked him in the ribs. "*Separate* bedtimes, I mean. Come on. Get up. We need to go over a few things before I go back my place."

Dugan pulled her close. "What's wrong with staying right here? We seem to communicate just fine."

Anna laughed and pulled away. "You're too easily distracted. Up."

Dugan sighed and sat up to grope for his boxer shorts.

"I'm gonna grab a beer. Get you anything?"

"Just a glass of wine," Anna said. "I'll be out after I visit the loo."

***

Anna came in, wrapped in a silk robe, and joined him on the sofa. Dugan was staring at his beer bottle, lost in thought.

"It's not your fault, you know," she said.

He shook his head. "Yeah, it is. Ibrahim trusted me, and it got him killed. I should have left it to you guys."

"Tom, you have no idea what tipped Braun off or even if Braun killed him. It could have been a common robbery/homicide, just like it appears."

"You don't really believe that?"

Anna sighed. "Actually I don't, but what I do believe is that you can't second-guess yourself in this business. Otherwise you'll go loopy."

"'Loopy'?"

Anna smiled. "I believe that's 'nuts' in Yank speak."

"I'm not too far from that now," Dugan said, "and Alex is closer. Did you see him when he came into my office today?"

"He looked horrible," Anna agreed. "What did you two talk about?"

"Ibrahim mostly," Dugan said. "Alex is really taking it hard, but in a crazy sort of way, he's more like the old Alex. He asked us to dinner on Wednesday. I put him off until we could discuss it. What do you think?"

"We should go. Reestablishing closer contact can only help."

"Yeah, well, it's likely to be strained," Dugan said. "Apparently all the ladies of the house except Cassie are convinced I'm a lecherous toad."

Anna smiled. "Just shows what remarkable instincts they have."

KAIROUZ RESIDENCE
15 JUNE

"Oh. I'm ever so sorry, Mrs. Hogan," Gillian Farnsworth said as she bumped into Mrs. Hogan bustling out of the pantry.

62

The cook smiled. "No harm done. Did you see Cassie safe to school?"

Mrs. Farnsworth shook her head. "Barely. That Farley is a menace."

"Aye, he's a bad 'un. I'd like to poison his bloody tea and bury him in the back garden."

Mrs. Farnsworth smiled at the image of portly Mrs. Hogan dragging Farley across the lawn; thoughts of Farley rarely brought a smile. His hulking presence upset their routine, and his driving was deliberately reckless, provoking tirades from Gillian to which he responded with insincere "Sorry, ma'ams" and smirks in the mirror.

The women fell quiet as Farley came in the back door.

"Hello, luv," he said to the cook, ignoring Mrs. Farnsworth. "How 'bout a cuppa?"

"You've a kitchen in your quarters, Farley. Take your tea there," Mrs. Farnsworth said.

"Well, ain't we all high and mighty? The old kike took his tea here."

"You aren't Daniel," Mrs. Farnsworth said. "And do not call him that. It's not teatime, in any event. Stop loafing. Wash the car."

"I did it yesterday," Farley said.

"Then do it again."

He glared at her, barely under control, and a chill ran through her before he slammed out. She felt Mrs. Hogan's arm on her shoulders.

"Don't you worry, dearie," the cook said. "He lays a hand to you or Cassie, I'll gut 'im like a pig, I will." She held open a capacious apron pocket to display the handle of a kitchen knife. Suddenly, burying Farley in the lawn didn't seem so far-fetched.

Mrs. Farnsworth smiled. "An appealing thought, Mrs. Hogan, but if you're arrested, where ever would we find a cook as good?"

"Hah. Nowhere, that's where, me girl."

"Right you are." Mrs. Farnsworth composed herself. "Now, where were we?"

"Oh, I almost forgot. Mr. Kairouz rang to—"

"He did? Is anything wrong? He's been very upset about Mr. Ibrahim."

"Aye, that he has," Mrs. Hogan said, "but he seemed a bit better just now. In fact, he rang to tell me we'll have guests tonight."

"Who?"

Mrs. Hogan made a face. "Mr. Dugan and his tart."

"Her name is Anna Walsh, Mrs. Hogan, and Alice Coutts tells me she's a lovely girl."

"Aye," the cook said, "and what else do you call a 'girl' fancyin' a rich gent old enough to be her father? She's a tart, right enough." She sighed. "But it's him that's the letdown. Men. Even the best of 'em thinks with the wee head down below. Mr. Kairouz excepted, o'course."

Mrs. Farnsworth stifled a smile. "Mr. Dugan isn't quite old enough to have sired Ms. Walsh. Do try to keep an open mind."

"Oh, aye. I'll give the little tart every benefit of the doubt, I will."

Hiding her amusement, Mrs. Farnsworth moved down the hall to sit in her tiny office under the stairs. She'd turned the former closet into a neat and efficient workspace, with a small desk and chair. A corkboard was covered with schedules and "to do" lists, and an under-desk computer fed a flat monitor and keyboard. A photo collage of Cassie filled the opposite wall.

As always, the photos brought a smile, one that faded a bit at her tired reflection in the monitor. She had fine features and soft brown eyes, but her hair was as much salt as pepper now, and there were lines that hadn't existed even weeks ago. Not that she cared. Physical beauty had only brought her pain. Her plain, matronly image and the "proper" world she created was a safe haven, not only for her, but for Cassie as well.

She smiled at the photos again. Cassie—her great treasure—bequeathed by a dying woman who had seen through her lies and trusted her anyway. A woman who squeezed her hands and extracted a promise. A promise Gillian fully intended to keep. Progress was uneven and success unsure, but Cassie would have a good life. Gillian would see to it.

TWENTY-SEVEN YEARS EARLIER
HER MAJESTY'S PRISON HOLLOWAY
NORTH LONDON

When the prison gates clanged shut behind Daisy Tatum, she was terrified. Not of freedom, but of failure and slipping back into her old life. She was twenty-two and had never had a job or a bank account or a credit card. She'd taken every course prison offered but knew it wasn't the same. A charity had gotten her a job, but she'd never waited tables.

The first day was bad. She mixed up every order and dropped a tray. But the café owner, an ex-con himself, was patient. Two weeks later she walked home to her tiny apartment, her first ever paycheck in her pocket. She was unlocking the door when strong arms encircled her.

"Hullo, luv. Don't we look smart? A regular stunner," Tommy's beery breath wafted over her as he pushed her inside into the tiny kitchenette.

"Right hurtful it was, you not comin' round to see dear ole Dad. But I kept tabs on ya. She's busy, I sez to me self, so I'll just pop round and see her." He glared. "So 'ere I am."

Daisy stared, mute, tears streaking her cheeks.

"There, there now," Tommy said. "No need to carry on, though I'm a bit misty me self. Prison suited you, I see. You ain't near the washed-out hag you was. Do a fair business among the lads what fancies older birds, I'll wager. Matter of fact, we'll have our own little family reunion in a bit, but first you can say hello to an old friend."

He put the drug paraphernalia on the kitchen bar, and Daisy's terror turned to rage as he ignored her to melt heroin in a spoon, humming a tune to himself, her own aspirations irrelevant. Memories came flooding back: the nightmare of being strapped spread-eagle on a filthy mattress when Tommy sold her virginity to a fat pedophile with halitosis; of turning tricks for "special clients" in the back of Tommy's "gentleman's club" until she looked old enough to be put on the streets. She remembered rebellion and attempted escapes and beatings. And more beatings when she failed to make enough or to induce miscarriages or just because Tommy bloody well felt like it. Beatings until all the fight was out of her and the pain dissolved into a dull blur of the drugs, Tommy's "little pick-me-ups" to keep her ambulatory and producing. She remembered his sneer when he visited her in jail to tell her she was worth neither bail nor a lawyer and to warn her to keep her bloody mouth shut and do the time.

Tommy's tune ended abruptly as the kitchen knife entered his chest to the hilt, propelled by 120 pounds of hatred fueled by thirteen years of rage. He died surprised, unable to believe his kindness was so unappreciated.

Daisy panicked. She gathered her meager belongings and fled, stopping to make a call from a pay phone. A short bus ride later, she sat on Gloria's sofa.

***

"Served the bastard right," Gloria said, "but Daisy's history. We have to reinvent you. And you can't stay here, luv. They know we were cell mates. This is the first place they'll look. But not to worry. Auntie Gloria's on top of it."

Gloria found Daisy a place to hide with a trusted friend of a friend and reappeared two weeks later, in disguise and carrying a shopping bag.

"Sorry, luv," she said, hugging Daisy. "The coppers were all over me for a while, but I think they've given up. Just to be safe, I came here by tube and transferred a half-dozen times." She grinned and led Daisy to the sofa. "I wanted to deliver your new life in person."

Daisy looked on, confused, as Gloria fished a newspaper from the shopping bag. She saw a photo of a woman resembling herself above a story titled "War Widow Dead in Car Crash."

"Wh… what is this?" Daisy asked.

"Your new life, luv," Gloria said. "Gillian Farnsworth, age twenty-four. Died three weeks ago in a crash. Widow of Leading Seaman John Farnsworth, Royal Navy. Poor sod. Died in the Falklands when the Argies sank his ship. No kids and both John and Gillian are only children of dead parents." Gloria smiled. "It's bloody perfect."

"I… I don't know Gloria. How can I—"

"Daisy. Luv," Gloria said. "We couldn't ask for more. Widow of some poor enlisted sod blown up by an Argie bomb. Anyone asks, you tear up. It's too painful to discuss. It's perfect."

"But… but how can I pretend? I don't know anyth—"

"You don't pretend, luv," Gloria said, "you become."

She pulled a thick file from her bag.

"It's all here. Parents' names, important dates, schools, teachers, everything. With that mind of yours, in two weeks you'll know Gillian better than she knew herself."

"But surely there's a record of her death."

Gloria nodded. "In Oxford, where she died in a crash while passing through, and which is not at all cross-referenced to Reading, where she was born and lived her whole life. Only a search at Oxford will turn up Gillian's death certificate, but someone would need to know first, that she was dead, and second, that she died in Oxford. But no one is likely to be looking. She has no family, and all her friends live in Reading. If they should cross your path in London at some point, they'll just assume it's a coincidence. Many people share names."

"But how will I live? I'm not even a very good waitress, and I'm sure she worked at something I couldn't possibly do."

Gloria smiled. "Perfect again. She worked as a nanny to a family that returned to the US just before her death. She was between jobs. I phoned the American family, pretending to be a prospective employer. They didn't know of her death and gave a glowing reference."

"I don't even know what a nanny does."

"She wipes noses and bums and says 'there, there' a lot," Gloria said. "You'll pick it up. We'll position you with an arriving American family. They'll likely be clueless and over-the-top with the whole idea of having a 'real British' nanny. That'll give you a chance to get Kings Cross out of your speech. Most of the Yanks can't seem to tell a Yorkshireman from an Aussie anyway. Anyone who isn't North American sounds like Sir Lawrence Olivier to them." Gloria patted her hand. "You'll do fine, luv."

And so she had, finding she'd a real aptitude for the work. She worked for a succession of families, receiving glowing references from them all. Twelve years later, there was no better nanny in London than Gillian Farnsworth.

Kathleen Kairouz had hired her on the spot, and Gillian soon fell in love with the gentle woman and flawed child. When Kathleen was diagnosed with cancer, Gillian took on Kathleen's care without a second thought but began to have misgivings. She'd grown to love Cassie and worried about the impact on the child if she were found out and arrested.

She found Alex Kairouz in his study one evening, staring into the fire. He looked up and motioned her to a chair across from his desk.

"How is she?"

"Resting comfortably. They increased her dosage. I hope she'll have an easy night."

Alex nodded as Gillian went on. "Mr. Kairouz, when Mrs. Kairouz... no longer needs me, I will be tendering notice."

"But why, Mrs. Farnsworth? Cassie needs you. I need you. If it's money—"

"No, no, sir. That's not it at all. There are... things. Personal reasons I can't discuss."

Alex persisted. "You can't just leave us in our hour of greatest need. Please, tell me what's wrong. We can work something out."

"I can't say, sir. But I will stay until you've found someone."

Alex stared at her a long moment and then nodded, almost to himself, as if he'd made a decision. He unlocked a drawer and handed her a file.

"Does it concern this?"

The file held a photo of Daisy Tatum stapled to her arrest report. There was a copy of her prison record, an article about Tommy Tatum's death, and a copy of Gillian Farnsworth's death certificate.

"When did you know?" she whispered.

"The second week," Alex said. "Kathleen was supposed to wait for the report before hiring." He smiled. "I didn't sack you because she wouldn't have it. She's an uncanny judge of people, you know. I often included her in business dinners for her opinion of potential clients or associates. She's never wrong.

"Anyway," he continued, "she made me reread the damned report line by line as she stood at my shoulder, pointing out you were victim, not villain. So I didn't turn you in. A decision for which I'm most thankful." He held out his hand, and she returned the folder.

"But I won't compel you to stay, though our need is great." He paused. "I'm not without connections. Two months ago, the body of a street person was fished from the Thames, a drowning victim. Her fingerprints were a match to Daisy Tatum, allowing the police to close that file." He paused again. "I also understand that when the records office in Oxford moved last month, several death certificates were misfiled. Just simple clerical errors, but I doubt Gillian Farnsworth's death certificate will be located in a hundred years."

He walked to the fireplace and tossed the file into the flames. "So Daisy Tatum is dead and Gillian Farnsworth very much alive. You've a place in my home as long as you wish, but the decision is yours. The file burning brightly is, I assure you, the only copy."

Tears streaked her face as she watched her past disappear up the chimney.

"Thank you, sir. I should like very much to stay."

"Then so you shall, Gillian. Welcome home."

Kathleen passed ten days later. The death hung over the household, but Gillian refused to let Alex bury himself in work. "The child has lost her mother and shouldn't lose her father as well," she said, insisting he spend an hour with Cassie each morning and evening. He soon cherished his time with the laughing child and spent most of his free time with her.

Cassie was their salvation and their bond.

CHAPTER ELEVEN

"You're sure the house isn't bugged?" Dugan asked for the third time.

"Swept it myself after Anna alerted us to the dinner," Harry said. "Showed up this afternoon as a meter reader while the cook was at market and the Farnsworth woman and driver were collecting the girl at school. I had time alone in the house. Things are unchanged; phone taps to a recorder in Farley's quarters but no bugs in the house. Makes sense. Cuts out a lot of idle household chatter."

"Not that it matters, Tom," Lou said. "If Kairouz is under duress, he'll assume he's being monitored and say nothing. And if he's a player, which seems likely, he'll lie. The best you can hope for this evening is a return to a closer relationship that we can use to watch him for slipups. You may not like that, but it's a fact."

Dugan said nothing, frustrated he'd convinced no one of Alex's innocence. His only partial convert was Anna, and her support was tepid at best.

"Tom. We best go if we're to reach Alex's by half seven," Anna said.

Kairouz Residence

Dugan and Anna arrived shortly after Mrs. Farnsworth and Cassie had reached home from choir practice. Cassie was still in her school uniform. She hugged Dugan and smiled at Anna.

"You're beautiful," Cassie said, her sincerity evident.

Anna was in a dark skirt and white silk blouse with lace at neck and wrists, simple but stunning. She blushed. "Why thank you, Cassie, you're quite lovely yourself."

"I look like my mom. She died, but I have pictures. Want to see them? They're in my room." Cassie took Anna's hand.

"Dinner's almost ready, Cassie," Mrs. Farnsworth said.

Cassie sighed. "Oh OK," she said, releasing Anna's hand. "After dinner, OK?"

Anna smiled. "I shall look forward to it, Cassie."

Cassie insisted on sitting between Anna and Dugan, and dinner conversation was unforced, as Cassie chattered and Anna listened with unfeigned interest. Mrs. Farnsworth said little, but watched with grudging approval. By meal's end, even Mrs. Hogan was smiling, serving coffee and nodding. During dessert, Anna gave Cassie's hand an affectionate squeeze, but as she withdrew her own hand, the lace at her cuff tangled in Cassie's charm bracelet and separated with an audible rip.

"Oh dear," Anna said, inspecting the dangling lace with an embarrassed laugh.

"I'm really sorry," Cassie said, "it was an accident."

"My fault entirely," Anna said. "No harm done. I'll get it mended."

"I can do it," Cassie said, folding up the edge of her jumper to reveal a needle wrapped with thread stuck into the underside of the hem.

"A proper young lady," she intoned in an unintended but accurate mimic of Mrs. Farnsworth, "prepares for any eventuality."

Anna looked confused.

"At one time," Mrs. Farnsworth explained, "young ladies always kept needles and thread near at hand. It seemed practical."

"Yes," Cassie said, "and that's not all—"

"Cassie," Mrs. Farnsworth said, "Ms. Walsh may wish to have it mended elsewhere."

"Oh no," Anna said. "I accept with thanks, Cassie. Then perhaps I can see the photos."

"OK," Cassie said. "We can go up now, and you can take your blouse off while I mend it. I don't want to stick you. That hurts."

"Excellent idea," Mrs. Farnsworth said, rising. "I'll get Ms. Walsh a robe."

Alex smiled. "Seems we're to be left on our own, Thomas. Join me in the study?"

"Thought you'd never ask."

Minutes later, they sat in the study, brandy in hand. Dugan watched Alex over the rim of his glass. Alex looked older, much older. The gray at his temples spread through his black mane now, and dark-circled eyes topped pale, hollow cheeks. Dugan was reminded of those "before and after" pictures of past US presidents.

"I haven't enjoyed a meal or the company as much in some time," Alex said. "Thank you for joining us. And Thomas, I'm sorry for my earlier behavior. Anna is wonderful." He smiled. "Cassie obviously likes her, and she has her mother's sense of people. So if Anna passed muster with Cassie, defrosted Mrs. Coutts, and in one evening charmed both Mrs. Hogan and Mrs. Farnsworth, she is exemplary indeed. I toast your good fortune." He raised his glass.

Dugan smiled and raised his own glass.

"Thomas, I've been thinking. We have a number of dry-dockings scheduled next year. We could save a great deal of money if we confined them to a single yard and negotiated a volume discount. I think it would be a good idea if you spent a week or two touring the Far East yards and discussing it with them." Alex smiled over his brandy glass. "Anna wouldn't have much to do while you were away. You could take her along. Make it a bit of a holiday."

Son of a bitch, thought Dugan. He's trying to get rid of me.

"Good idea," Dugan said, trying to sound casual, "we'll probably have most of our ships in the Far East trade if the *China Star* deal is any indication of market trends."

Alex stiffened. "Whatever do you mean, Thomas?"

"Ibrahim mentioned the *China Star* deal to me. He seemed concerned, actually."

"*China Star* is just some deal of Braun's. I don't really know the details."

"The Alex Kairouz I know could recite every word of every charter agreement from memory," Dugan said. "C'mon, Alex. What's goin' on?"

"Just drop it, Thomas. Please." Alex's eyes darted about the room.

Lou was right, Dugan thought, Alex thinks we're bugged. A catch-22. He needed Alex to confide in him, but the man would never do so if he thought he was monitored. Dugan considered his half-formed plan and decided to take a risk.

"You can speak freely, Alex," he said. "We're not being bugged."

"What? What do you mean?" Alex asked.

"I know something's wrong, so I hired an investigator," Dugan lied. "He came in at night and swept the office. I know Braun is bugging our offices and phones. He swept your house today. Phones are bugged but not the house. Talk to me, Alex."

Alex buried his face in his hands. Dugan waited for Alex to unburden himself or, if he was wrong, explode into angry denial. Either way, Dugan's lie cast him as a concerned friend, not a covert agent. But when Alex looked up, his face held neither relief nor anger but terror.

"Thomas. What have you done?" Tears ran down ashen, stubbled cheeks.

"What do you mean, Alex? What's wrong?"

"Cassie," Alex said, "he'll… wait, I'll show you."

He stood and locked the study door before moving a laptop from his desk to the low table beside Dugan. The computer booted as Alex opened his case and thrust a CD at Dugan.

"Look at it," Alex ordered, and Dugan slid the disk into the computer.

The clip began with a narrator, a woman speaking French as she walked the streets of a Third World village to a rude hut. Inside, a young girl was held spread-eagle by a group of women. One produced a knife and began to cut at the girl's genitals, in full view of the camera and explaining as she performed the butchery. Even with the volume turned down, the girl's screams carried through the narration. The screen morphed to a new scene: large, dirty men sodomizing a blond girl of no more than six. Dugan slapped the computer closed and swallowed hard to keep Mrs. Hogan's meal from ending up in the wastebasket.

"Good God, Alex, where did you get that filth?"

"Braun," Alex said. "He says it will all happen to Cassie if I disobey. You watched seconds, but it's over an hour and gets worse, much worse. I'm forced to watch it regularly."

"But surely you contacted the police?"

Alex nodded. "I pretended to go along with Braun, then phoned Scotland Yard. I was on hold when a live video of Cassie walking up the school steps filled my computer screen, filmed through a sniper scope with crosshairs on her head. The message was clear. I hung up. Braun called at once, warning me not to try it again."

He paused. "Even then, I didn't give up, but I realized I couldn't alert the police until Cassie was safe. I knew my phones were tapped, so while dining with a customer that night, I excused myself to visit the loo and ducked into the restaurant office to use the phone. I called a contact at the security firm I use and set up a meeting in St. James Park the following day at two. Time was short, so I told the man I would provide details at the meeting.

"I assumed Braun couldn't watch everyone, so I intended to send written details to the park via Daniel, with instructions for a bodyguard and safe house. I would string Braun along until the security people whisked Cassie to safety. I never got that far. Braun rang the next morning and said he'd 'taken the liberty' of canceling my appointment. He said he wouldn't do anything to Cassie immediately to lessen her hostage value, but if I continued my efforts, Mrs. Farnsworth would have a fatal accident."

"But… but how did he find out about the park?" Dugan asked.

"He either anticipated whom I might call and bugged them or bugged the phones of my usual restaurants; there aren't many. I only know he blocked me everywhere. I was terrified."

"Wasn't the guy you contacted suspicious at the cancellation?"

Alex shook his head. "He rang to confirm an e-mail cancellation Braun sent in my name. I confirmed and apologized. He probed a bit, but had no reason to suspect duress."

"So," Alex continued, "I hired Braun and Farley. Braun forces me to watch the video weekly. 'Motivational sessions' he calls them. He stands over my shoulder as I watch, detailing additional things Cassie will face if I resist in any way. I had a session this afternoon."

Dugan sat stunned. It was a wonder Alex wasn't dead of a heart attack.

"What does he want, Alex?"

"Not money. I tried to buy him off. He needs the company for something."

"What's he done so far?" Dugan asked.

"I haven't a clue," Alex said. "He made me sign blank contracts and give him carte blanche on all accounts. For the most part it seems to be business as usual, but he's doing things at the margins in my name, and perhaps yours. *China Star* is a case in point. When Ibrahim got curious, Braun told me that unless I kept him quiet, he would kill the man and his entire family. I had to threaten to sack poor Ibrahim and order him to refer inquiries to Braun.

"He's dangerous, Thomas, and very, very good. Your investigator may already be dead and Braun listening to our every word." He paused. "Initially I feared you'd endangered Cassie, but I realize now nothing's changed. Braun still needs me, and she's his guarantee. But if Braun is listening, you'll be dead by morning. And if your efforts have somehow escaped his attention, you should go. Take my offer to visit the yards and keep going. You can't help us, Thomas. I have to see it through and hope Braun spares Cassie. Save yourself and tell no one so Cassie isn't endangered further."

Dugan realized any promise to safeguard Cassie would seem unbelievable to Alex. If Alex Kairouz, with all his connections, had been unable to do so, what chance did Dugan have alone? And Alex thought Braun was listening, despite Dugan's assurances. Suddenly Dugan realized Alex was playing to the bugs, assuring Braun of continued cooperation while, if there were no bugs, warning Dugan to escape. Alex might be cowed, but his brain was working.

The revelation was more disquieting than encouraging. Alex was stretched to the breaking point, and Dugan was concerned for his health, mental and physical. He had to let his friend know the situation wasn't hopeless, and he would never have a better opportunity.

"Alex, I know Braun isn't listening because the house was swept with much better equipment than is available commercially. I'm working with US and British intelligence."

Alex listened as Dugan explained and assured him Cassie would be protected. They stood and Alex hugged Dugan with a ferocity born of relief. For the first time in months, Alex Kairouz did not feel he was alone, staring into a black abyss.

And Dugan wondered how to tell the others about the newest member of the team.

CHAPTER TWELVE

Constrained by the driver's presence, Anna was quiet during the cab ride as Dugan pondered a way to break the news. He hadn't found one by the time they walked into the apartment.

"So, how'd it go?" Lou asked.

"Well, I think," Anna said, turning to Dugan. "Tom, did you learn anything from Alex?"

He tried to ease into it. "We discussed *China Star*. He thinks—"

"Bloody hell, Dugan," Lou said. "How did that come up? You weren't supposed to—"

Anna waved Lou to silence and gestured for Dugan to continue. He took a deep breath and made a clean breast of it, finishing to dead silence.

"Bloody unbelievable," Lou said. "You revealed an operation to a prime suspect."

"He's a victim," Dugan said. "How much evidence do you need?"

"More than a bloody fairy tale," Lou said.

"Bullshit. He made up a story complete with video, then waited weeks to present it? No way. We can use him, and I decided to enlist him."

Anna exploded. "YOU decided! On whose bloody authority? I'm lead agent, not you. You might have at least discussed it before charging in on a white horse to save the bloody day."

"Things were happening fast," Dugan said. "I wasn't sure I'd have another chance. Maybe I should have discussed it first, but what's done is done."

"Yes, Tom. Maybe you should have," Anna said, ice in her voice.

"Actually," Harry said, "we can verify Kairouz's story. Phone records will confirm calls to Scotland Yard and from the security firm, and we can question the security firm under the Official Secrets Act. If that checks out, I doubt it's a fairy tale. British Telcom has a night shift. We can confirm the calls straightaway."

Dugan shot Harry a grateful look.

"Do it," Anna said, and Harry dialed. Moments later, he hung up and nodded.

"Phone records corroborate Kairouz's story," Harry said.

"OK," Anna said, "we'll deal with the security firm tomorrow. Perhaps this can be salvaged. But we have to tell Ward." She gave Dugan a withering look. "I believe that will be your job, Tom."

Dugan gave a resigned nod, pushed a preset on his sat phone, and set it on the coffee table in speaker mode.

***

Five time zones away, Ward's phone trilled as he worked late. He saw Dugan's number on the display.

"Hold one, Tom," he said into his own sat phone as he reached for the office phone.

Gardner wanted in on field agents' calls, but in reality, disturbing him after hours incurred his wrath. Ward protected himself by leaving voice mail on Gardner's office number to verify attempted contact. Gardner was seldom there after hours, so Ward preferred to talk with field agents then just to avoid his boss's interference.

"Gardner," came the answer. Shit, Ward thought.

"Yes, Larry," Ward said, "I've got Dugan. You want in?"

"Damn. Yeah, OK. Come down here." Gardner hung up without awaiting a reply.

Ward told Dugan he'd call him right back and went down the hall to Gardner's office. Gardner was in a tux.

"Don't you look spiffy," Ward said.

"I'm due at the symphony with the Gunthers in twenty minutes. This better be good."

Ward understood. Image enhancement. Senator Gunther chaired the Senate Intelligence Committee, and Gardner would spin a tale of having to stop by the office to handle a problem. The indispensable man.

Gardner pointed at the conference table. "Use the speakerphone," he said.

"Hello, Tom," Ward said as Dugan answered, "Larry Gardner is with me on speaker."

Dugan paused. "Hello, Jesse. Hello, Larry. I have—"

"Cut to the chase, Dugan," Gardner said. "I'm running late."

Dugan hadn't expected Gardner. He led with *China Star* again, stalling.

"We have suspicious activity on a ship named *China Star*, now loading at Kharg—"

"Where?" Gardner asked.

"Kharg Island, Iran," Ward said. "Go ahead, Tom."

"If there's anything to it," Dugan continued, "the mostly likely target would be the Malacca Strait near Singapore."

"When does she sail?" Ward asked, scribbling.

"Unknown," Dugan said. "I'll keep on it, but you might initiate satellite surveillance—"

"Just worry about your end, Dugan," Gardner said. "What else? Or did you call just to alert us to a ship which 'might' be suspect and may be days away from leaving port?"

There was a long pause, then Dugan spoke in a rush, as if eager to finish his recitation of the events of the last few hours before he was interrupted. He needn't have worried; both Ward and Gardner were shocked speechless. Gardner recovered first.

"YOU FUCKING DID WHAT?" Gardner screamed, launching an abusive tirade punctuated with a list of Dugan's violations of the Patriot Act. Then he turned on Ward.

"God damn you, Ward, where the hell is that limey cunt you had sitting on this idiot?"

Dugan interrupted before Ward could respond.

"Look, Larry, calm down," Dugan said. "I've explained that Alex Kairouz is not—"

"That's not your call, asshole. Leave that to the intelligence professionals."

Dugan lost it. "'Intelligence professional'? And that would be you? You couldn't track a fucking elephant through ten feet of snow."

The Brits regarded their shoes in the sudden silence.

"You're done, asshole," Gardner's voice whispered through the speaker. "You've killed the operation. I'll have the Brits arrest you. You and Kairouz can be cell mates in Gitmo."

"Actually, Mr. Gardner," Anna said, "the operation is far from compromised."

"Who's that?" Gardner demanded. "Damn it, Ward, this line was supposed to be secure."

"We're perfectly secure," Anna said. "I'm Agent Anna Walsh, AKA the 'limey cunt.'"

Oh shit, can this get any worse, Ward thought as Gardner gaped at the phone.

"I do not intend to end this operation," Anna continued, "and expect your continued support. Of course, we're recording now as standard procedure, as, I'm sure, are you. Should you proceed with action against Mr. Dugan, I will ask for an official review, including this conversation. Dugan's remarks were intemperate, but he was provoked, and your language was equally foul. On that subject, while I admire your ability to malign my nationality, gender, and character in the space of two words, your terminology was most objectionable. I believe our superiors will agree, should it come to that. So let's just move on, shall we?"

"Yes, of course," Gardner said. "Uh… what do you propose?"

"We'll work out a way to communicate with Kairouz, and I'll detail assets to shadow the girl and her nanny and to intercede if necessary," Anna said.

"Why? You might tip off Braun."

"Risks are minimal. It will reassure Kairouz, and it's the right thing to do," she said.

"Still, it seems a waste of assets," Gardner said.

"British assets, protecting British subjects, at the discretion of Her Majesty's representative. That would be me," Anna said.

"Uh, OK, your call. Anything else?"

"No," Anna replied, "unless you or Agent Ward have anything."

"No," Gardner said, disconnecting without looking at Ward, who had a great deal to add but nothing he wanted to say in front of Gardner.

***

"That was amazing, Anna. Thank you," Dugan said.

"Yes, well, everything's relative," she said. "This Gardner twit infuriated me even more than you, something I scarcely thought possible twenty minutes ago."

Harry grinned. "I dunno, I think the Yank redeemed himself. I rather enjoyed the 'ten feet of snow' bit. I woulda loved to have seen the wanker's face."

The men laughed as Anna struggled to suppress a smile.

CIA HEADQUARTERS
LANGLEY, VIRGINIA

"How in hell did you let this get so out of control, Ward? Dugan just blew the whole operation, just to protect his raghead buddy. He's dirty. Get the finance guys on this: bank accounts, e-mails, phone records, foreign-held companies, the lot."

"We've had Dugan's complete financials for years," Ward said. "He doesn't need money. I share your concern about his actions, but if Walsh and her team are comfortable, we have to respect that. Besides, if Dugan wanted to scuttle us, he'd do it quietly."

"Just because he's fooled the crumpet munchers doesn't mean he's not a traitor."

"OK, OK, I know you're upset, but try to calm down. Go enjoy your evening."

The reminder of the social engagement worked as intended. Nothing was more important to Gardner than a chance to rub shoulders with the power elite.

Gardner nodded and rose. As they walked out and Gardner locked his door, Ward got in a subtle dig.

"Enjoy the ballet with Congressman Gaynor," he said.

"It's the symphony with Senator Gunther," Gardner said.

Ward shrugged. "Whatever."

Gardner stalked off, appalled at Ward's ignorance. No wonder he was still an agent.

Minutes later, Ward sat at his computer, requesting a flyover of Kharg Island, Iran, with a specific request for updates on the *China Star*. He'd refrained from mentioning satellite coverage to Gardner, fearing the man might object because it was Dugan's idea. If you didn't ask, no one could say no.

CHAPTER THIRTEEN

M/T *Asian Trader*
South China Sea
Bound for Panama
16 June

Medina jogged down the deck, his routine well established after two weeks at sea. The afternoon sun was warm on his back as he moved along the deck and dropped to do push-ups near a ballast-tank vent. His exercise attracted no notice now other than jokes about his sanity. It was the perfect way to keep check on events unfolding unseen below the deck at his feet.

The gasoline had eaten through the Styrofoam by now, he was sure of it. In his mind's eye, he envisioned the gasoline weeping down the bulkheads of the empty ballast tanks, evaporating in the process. As the sun warmed the deck each day, the expanding air in the empty tanks whispered out the vents, and at night, sea water rushing past the outer hull cooled the air and reversed the process, sucking in oxygen-rich sea air. Fumes would escape each day, but most would remain, slowly filling each tank from the bottom up as it "breathed" through each cycle, mixing its contents into explosive vapor.

He put his nose near the deck as he did push-ups and smelled the faint odor wafting from the nearest vent to lie invisible along the deck before being swept away by a breeze. He smiled. The tanks were ripening and chances of discovery slight as the wind dissipated the fumes. His plan would work, *inshallah*.

Sterling Academy
Westminster, London
17 June

The car lurched to a stop, and Farley watched Gillian Farnsworth's face in the mirror, disappointed that she was ignoring his provocation. She got out and went into the school, returning with a glum-looking Cassie in tow.

"Take us to the doctor's and wait," she said. "We should be out by half two."

Farley grunted and shot off with squealing tires, pondering the change in the woman over the last two days. She'd never hidden her disdain or hesitated to challenge him, but always with an undercurrent of fear, despite her brave words. She was different now, more confident. A subtle change, felt rather than spoken. Should he tell Braun? He dismissed the notion, sure he'd get a scornful response.

He curbed the tires in the waiting area of the doctor's building, bringing the car to a rocking halt. The housekeeper ignored it as she exited the car, hurrying Cassie along with her. She'll get hers, he thought as they bustled into the building. Maybe he'd make the old bitch watch while he shagged the retard. Now wouldn't that be sweet.

***

"Why do I have to get a jab?" Cassie whined as the elevator opened on the third floor.

"It's a flu shot," Mrs. Farnsworth lied. "Now out you go."

They were expected and led to an exam room, where a nurse took Cassie's vital signs and directed Mrs. Farnsworth to the doctor's office. Anna Walsh sat across from the doctor. She motioned Mrs. Farnsworth to an empty chair.

"Doctor," Anna said, "might I speak to Mrs. Farnsworth alone?"

He smiled. "Certainly. I'll check on Cassie."

"You do know what's going on?" Anna asked as the doctor left.

"I know you're MI5. Mr. Kairouz told me. I assume you'll take Cassie to safety."

"It's not that simple," Anna said. "Removing Cassie makes it obvious Alex is cooperating, but we don't have enough evidence to hold either Braun or Farley. You would all likely still be targets." She leaned closer and lowered her voice. "We have to play this out, making the best of the hand dealt us. Here's what we're going to do…."

TEHRAN, IRAN
17 JUNE

Motaki was anxious. Gasoline shortages ate at his support like a cancer. Former allies grew distant, rumors abounded, and even Imam Rahmani was under pressure. How ironic, he thought, that he had been so successful in importing material for his nuclear program, only to be undone by something as prosaic as gasoline. But, God willing, that would soon change. The intercom buzzed.

"Yes, Ahmad?"

"Sorry to disturb you, sir, but President Rodriguez is calling."

He sighed a thanks.

"Mr. President. Nice to hear from you."

"Good day, my friend," Rodriguez said, "are you well?"

Motaki curbed his impatience. "Yes, thank you. How may I help you?"

"It's about the… our project. I've heard no reports and—"

Camel shit for brains, thought Motaki. Not on an open line.

"Yes, the petrol shipments," Motaki said. "I will arrange an update via secure means."

"All right… fine," Rodriguez said. "It's just I've heard little and—"

"Never a bother, my friend," he said as he silently cursed Braun. "Anything more?"

"No. No. Thank you," Rodriguez said before saying a polite good-bye.

Motaki frowned as he tapped out a terse message on his computer.

Braun returned from lunch to find a telltale spam message. He downloaded a video clip from the porn site and decrypted the embedded message.

CONTACTED BY OUR FRIEND. UPDATE HIM TO PREVENT REPETITION.

That bloody Venezuelan. Like Motaki, Rodriguez had a secure sat phone, but to preclude overuse, Braun first locked it into receive-only mode. Anticipating problems, Braun also allowed Rodriguez backdoor access to a single porn site, used by him alone to isolate him from the real operation. He'd still been a pest, deluging Braun with frequent inane messages and suggestions to the point the German no longer even downloaded them. The idiot must have contacted Motaki on a landline. He'd underestimated the Venezuelan's stupidity.

Rodriguez answered the sat phone on the sixth ring.

"Mr. President," Braun said, "forgive me. I was awaiting updates before reporting."

"You do well to remember who is in charge, Braun. Now report."

Braun stifled a laugh. "Yes, sir. *China Star* arrived at Kharg, and our Chechen friends—"

"Yes, yes," Rodriguez said, "what of Panama?"

"*Asian Trader* is en route from Singapore. All is according to plan."

"Remember," Rodriguez said. "Minor damage. And we must not be implicated."

"Don't worry, sir. Our man can kill himself and those around him, but little more. And even if he survives, he knows nothing."

"Are we still on schedule for July 4?"

"Yes, Mr. President," Braun said. "Is there anything more, sir?"

"No. That is sufficient, Karl, but do not fail to keep me informed."

"You may rest assured I will, sir."

"Thank you, Karl. That will be all."

Braun shook his head and hung up. Bloody pompous fool.

"Caught any bad guys today?" asked a familiar voice.

Ward chuckled into the phone. Mike Hill worked for NSA, tasked with global electronic snooping. "Not yet, Mike, but the day's young. Whatcha got?"

"You know that London site the Brits are monitoring and sharing intel on with us?"

"Yeah, Phoenix Shipping. What about it?"

"Well, we also have ongoing surveillance on that nut job in Caracas," Hill said, "and El Presidente received a scrambled sat phone call this morning from guess where?"

"Phoenix Shipping?"

"Bingo, brother. The Brits had the outgoing, too, but not the Caracas end. We aided our cousins who were pathetically grateful, though they covered it with British reserve—"

Ward grinned. "OK, OK, Hill. I get the picture."

"Jeez, nerds are never appreciated. Anyway, the bad news is we couldn't unscramble it."

"Well, even the connection is a breakthrough," Ward said.

"Ah, but our legerdemain continues," Hill said. "Earlier El Presidente called Iran, rather stupidly in the clear. We recorded one President Motaki shitting his pants at the mention of a 'project,' and El Presidente's failure to be updated on same. Motaki says not to worry, and presto, El Presidente gets a call from London." Hill paused. "A reasonable man might conclude a connection between Iran and Venezuela running through Phoenix Shipping."

"Outstanding," Ward said. "When next we meet, my friend, drinks are on me."

"Don't be cheap. You have an expense account. I want dinner."

"Done," Ward said.

CHAPTER FOURTEEN

"It's been a friggin' week since Jesse made the Iran/Venezuela link," Dugan said, "and we've still got squat."

Anna shrugged. "That's not surprising. Braun's smart, and we probably got a bit lucky on the *China Star* thing. With increased electronic surveillance here and in Caracas and Tehran, something will break soon."

"Yeah," Dugan said, "but until then, all we have is *China Star*, and only suspicions at that. I wish there was some way we could be sure."

"But we have some time there as well, Yank," Harry said. "She just sailed. She'll be in the middle of the ocean for a while, out of harm's way."

Dugan nodded, then seemed to think of something. He opened up his briefcase and pulled out his laptop to punch at the keyboard. He brought up the Searates.com Web site and began entering information.

"Shit," Dugan said.

"What is it?" Anna asked.

"At her current speed, *China Star* should be in the middle of the Straits of Malacca on the Fourth of July. Now what are the odds of that?"

Steven "Bo" Richards slouched in a chair with his feet on an ottoman, clad in boxer shorts and nursing a hangover. He'd woken at noon and roused the whore to deal with his morning erection before shoving her into the hall, throwing money after her and slamming the door as she struggled into her clothes. He drained the beer and dropped the bottle on the carpet before scratching his stomach. The bed lay in tangled disarray, and a cart held the remains of a room-service breakfast. The room needed tidying, an event deferred by the Do Not Disturb sign on the doorknob outside.

He checked the time and stood to slip on a pair of jeans and pull on a tee shirt. He was tying his shoes when he heard a knock.

***

Sheibani stared at the *Do Not Disturb* sign, calming himself. The scum inside was a thug of the Great Satan, and Sheibani longed to kill him sight unseen. But the deception required Americans, and Richards's citizenship and record were documented. He forced a smile as the door opened a crack.

"Yeah?"

"Mr. Richards, I am Ali. May I come in?"

Richards opened the door and stood aside, nodding toward the sitting area. Sheibani entered and took a seat with his back to the wall as Richards settled across from him.

"Your accommodations are to your liking?" Sheibani asked.

"Yeah, yeah, everything's fine," Richards said. "What's the job?"

How American. Sheibani struggled with anger.

"In a week or so," Sheibani said, "a ship named *China Star* will transit the Malacca Straits, escorted by a security force comprised of private contractors and US Navy personnel. Or rather, men disguised as US Navy personnel. You will lead that force."

"Why me?" Richards asked. "I'm no sailor, and the pay is far beyond anything offered for a straight security job."

"In good time, Mr. Richards. For the moment let's just say—"

"You plan to sink the ship and block the strait," Richards guessed.

Sheibani once again swallowed his ire. "On the contrary. We will avoid blocking the strait, while appearing to attempt just that. We will ground in Indonesian waters and escape."

"Won't that be obvious to the crew?"

"The crew will be dealt with," Sheibani said.

Richards nodded. " Resources? How many in our team? Weapons?"

"The makeup and armament of the team will be as you require; in fact, I want you to recruit some of the team. The goal is deception. We will be joined by a young Arab-American naval officer."

"So why do you need me?"

"Insurance," Sheibani said. "Survivors will report an attack led by Americans."

"But you have an American."

Sheibani shook his head. "The ship is Liberian flag, but the senior officers are American. We will present them with an unusual situation. We must gain control fast, before they have a chance to think too much about it. Our young mujahideen is untested, and he looks like the Arab-American he is. They will likely be less suspicious of a countryman who shares their ethnicity."

Richards smirked. "So I'm your token white man."

Sheibani nodded. "I suppose you could say that. Questions?"

Richards shook his head. "No questions," he said, then smiled. "But seeing as how I'm such a valuable commodity, I think we need to renegotiate."

Sheibani suppressed a smile. So predictable. He feigned resistance and then yielded to Richards's exorbitant demand. After all, he'd never live to collect the money.

"Make your course one seven five," said Captain Dan Holt of the VLCC M/T *China Star* over his shoulder as he squinted out at the ship traffic.

"One seven five, aye," the helmsman repeated, then a moment later, "Steady on one seven five, sir."

Holt watched as the Strait of Hormuz widened and ships spread out in the increased sea room. He walked over to study the radar.

"OK, put her on the mike," he said to the helmsman.

"Aye, sir. Steering one seven five. Transferring control to the mike," the sailor said, switching control to the autopilot, or "Iron Mike," and watching the gyrocompass repeater a moment before he stepped away from the wheel.

"OK, Ortega," Holt said to the second mate, "call me if necessary. And don't let me catch you with your nose glued to the radar. Visibility's good, so use the radar to confirm a bearing or distance, not as a substitute for your goddamned eyes."

"Yes, Captain," Ortega said.

"OK. You have the conn. Helm's on the mike, steering one seven five."

"I have the conn, sir. Helm's on autopilot, steering one seven five," Ortega said.

Holt gave a curt nod and strode out the door, down the single flight to his office. He settled into his chair and glanced at a printed e-mail before reaching for the phone.

"Engine Room. Chief speaking," Jon Anderson said.

"Chief, can you come up?"

"OK," Anderson said. "I'm buttoning up the transfer pump. Give me a minute."

Ten minutes later the chief stood at Holt's door in oil-stained coveralls and carrying a clean piece of cardboard. He slipped off dirty work shoes to avoid staining the carpet and moved to the sofa in stockinged feet, placing the cardboard down to protect the fabric before sitting.

"Jesus H. Christ," Holt said, "aren't you friggin' engineers ever clean?"

Anderson grinned. "Some of us work for a living instead of sitting on our ass. You said come, so here I am. Want me to leave?"

Jon Anderson was one of Captain Daniel Holt's very few friends, a relationship rooted in mutual respect and the fact that Anderson took no crap from Holt.

"No, God damn it," grumbled Holt as he sat. "Coffee?"

"Nah. I've had my quota." Anderson smiled as the ship rolled. "God it's good to be out of there and back at sea."

"That's for sure," Holt said. "I'm just surprised they didn't give us a big ration of shit when they boarded and found Americans aboard. I can't say I was happy to be there."

Anderson shrugged. "Maybe we had a guardian angel. Anyway, what's up?"

Holt handed Anderson the e-mail and waited while he read it.

"What the hell is Maritime Protection Services?"

"Just what it says," Holt said. "Hired guns to protect us through the Malacca Straits."

Anderson looked skeptical. "Are we talking gunmen running all over the ship?"

"I don't think so. I think they just shadow us in a boat."

"Still sounds hinky," Anderson said. "I'll bet they know jack about tanker safety. We get all sorts of training about no matches, cigarette lighters, no spark-producing equipment, et cetera, et cetera, and now we're supposed to be OK with a bunch of trigger-happy assholes circling the ship with machine guns?"

"I agree," the captain said, "but the charterer hired them, and our owner agreed, so that's that. As long as they keep their distance, it should be all right."

"Yeah, well, like you say, there's nothing we can do about it." Anderson grinned. "Besides, I bet somebody's getting a kickback. They'll get an invoice for a hundred grand, and we'll be escorted by an old guy in a canoe with one tooth and a pellet gun."

Holt laughed. "I wouldn't doubt that for a minute."

CHAPTER FIFTEEN

CIA HEADQUARTERS
LANGLEY, VIRGINIA
25 JUNE

Gardner glared at Ward. "No. And stop beating a dead horse, Ward. The answer was no two days ago, and it's still no."

"We should notify MALSINDO," Ward persisted, using the acronym for the alliance of Malaysia, Singapore, and Indonesia policing the Malacca Strait.

"And tell them what? Your boy Dugan and his terrorist buddy have a gut feeling?"

"Listen, Larry—"

"No, YOU listen, Ward. Me, chief. You, Indian. Understand?"

Ward bit back a sharp reply. "At least let's notify our own guys."

"Ward. It's a goddamned VLCC," Gardner said. "It will check into the traffic system, so I see no need to cry wolf and look stupid. You've screwed this up enough, so let's just lie low and avoid embarrassment."

Great, Ward thought, all this asshole is worried about is image. There was a huge difference in the scrutiny *China Star* would get if the authorities suspected trouble.

"Look, Larry. You have to understand—"

"No, YOU look. I haven't handed you your ass for your boy Dugan fucking things up by the numbers, but if you mention *China Star* to Singapore, I will HAVE YOUR ASS! Clear?"

Ward managed an angry nod.

"Fine. We're done. I'm invited to a congressional prayer breakfast, and I'm late."

Ward stifled an impulse to suggest Gardner pray for some fucking brains and stalked to his own office. After a moment of indecision, he glanced at his watch and called London.

***

"The bloody wanker," Lou Chesterton said. "So what now?"

"I follow orders and hope you'll do the same, but I know you Brits are blabbermouths."

"Yes, we are a loose-lipped lot," Lou said. "Why, given that the British High Commission is next door to your embassy, I suspect our Singapore lads gossip over the fence like old hens."

"No doubt," Ward said. "However, I hope if they do somehow hear about *China Star*, that they keep their efforts low-key. My ass is hanging out here a bit, Lou."

"Understood," Lou said. "I'm sure things will work out."

Medina frowned. The sun had pounded the deck for a week, and the steel deck grew hotter each day. He wore gloves now for push-ups, and even the wind rebelled, veering astern and matching their speed to leave the deck becalmed. He watched a nearby thunderhead and willed it closer, with its promise of cooling rain and concealing wind.

His eyes moved toward the bow as the bosun descended from the forecastle with a grease gun. He knew fumes were thick on deck just aft of the raised forecastle and watched the bosun for a reaction. Sure enough, upon reaching the deck, the man tilted his head, and Medina saw cognition in his eyes. The sailor squatted and sniffed at a tank vent. He rose to find Medina beside him.

"We have a bulkhead leak. We must tell the chief mate," the bosun said, starting aft.

"Wait," Medina said. "I smelled it before on the starboard side too. Let's check it out before we get everyone excited."

Unwilling to appear an alarmist while a green third mate remained calm, the bosun followed Medina under the centerline pipe rack, out of sight of the bridge watch high above.

Medina stopped under the pipes. "There's the problem," he said, pointing to a rising stem valve, the spiral threads of its stem protruding vertically from its center.

The bosun scoffed. "How can that be the problem?"

"Look closely," Medina said.

The bosun hid his amusement as he bent low over the irrelevant valve. Junior officers became senior officers and were to be humored. He was about to straighten when strong hands on the back of his head slammed his face toward the valve, and he lost his balance, adding to his downward momentum. His last memory was the tip of the valve stem rushing toward him and a searing pain as it mangled his left eye and pushed into his brain.

Medina kept his full weight on the bosun's head until the flailing stopped. He removed the man's shoe and dabbed the sole with grease from the man's grease gun, then pressed the shoe to the deck, simulating a slip in grease. He put the shoe back on the bosun's foot and laced it.

A freshening wind cooled Medina's face as he ran aft for help. A cooling rain was washing the bosun's blood into the sea by the time he returned with that help two minutes later.

"Why does anyone have to go?" Braun demanded. "For that matter, why even have a damned inquiry? The captain logged it as an accident."

Alex gritted his teeth. "Because it's the law, Braun. Whenever—"

"Captain Braun."

"All right. Captain Braun. Whenever there's a death at sea, international law requires an inquiry at the next port of call with a company representative in attendance."

"Well, I'm sure as hell not letting you go, and I'm not going." Braun smiled. "Wait a minute. Send Dugan."

"I don't think—"

"Didn't Dugan take *Asian Trader* through the yard in Singapore just last month?"

"He started her through, yes," Alex said. "But I don't think—"

"I don't care what you think, Kairouz. He knows the ship. He's available. Send him. Now get out."

Alex stiffened and left Braun's office as the German reflected on how often adversity is opportunity in disguise. He was a bit concerned that the accident might draw unnecessary attention to *Asian Trader*, but that effort was a sideshow anyway. He was sure the expendable lunatic there would manage to kill himself in spectacular fashion. Now, with luck, Dugan would be there to take the fall after it happened. Braun hummed a little tune as he brought up the Web site of the National Bank of the Caymans and opened a new account in Dugan's name.

ANNA WALSH'S APARTMENT BUILDING
2135 HOURS LOCAL TIME
28 JUNE

Dugan and Anna's team sat around the coffee table in the surveillance apartment, his sat phone open in speaker mode on the table.

"Braun's adamant," Dugan said. "Alex called me into his office and told me I was going to Panama. We carried on a conversation for Braun's benefit while we scribbled notes back and forth. I made the expected excuses—said it was Braun's job, I was too busy, et cetera, and Alex made a show of forcing me."

"But why is Braun so keen for you to go?" Anna asked.

Dugan shrugged. "After the *China Star* deal, I guess he wants me out of the way."

"It makes sense," Ward's voice from the speaker said. "He isn't likely to allow Alex out of his control, and Tom knows the ship. I don't think we should read too much into this."

"I agree with Ward," Lou said. "He has *China Star* under satellite coverage, and we still have Anna in the office to keep an eye on things. If Dugan pushes back at this point, it may make Braun suspicious."

Anna nodded. "OK, let's keep Braun happy then. Between *China Star* and the Caracas intercept, we're finally getting somewhere. We don't want to upset him now."

"I'll pack a bag," Dugan said.

CHAPTER SIXTEEN

Borqei stared at the message, sighed, and dialed the phone. He had a conversation in Farsi, including code words. An hour later, Yousif's adoptive mother went to her doctor, who admitted her to his private clinic and called her clergyman, Borqei, of course. Borqei informed the navy that Ensign Hamad's mother was gravely ill, along with the doctor's number for verification. In hours, Hamad was on a plane from San Diego, with connections in Los Angeles.

***

In a toilet stall in LAX, a man slipped Yousif an envelope under the divider. He opened it to find a ticket to Jakarta, a forged passport, and a wallet holding cash, a driver's license, and credit cards. The hand reappeared under the divider, and Yousif passed over his own boarding pass and ID. His seat on the plane to Detroit would be occupied by a man looking very much like him. It wouldn't do for the airline to record him as a no show.

An hour later, Yousif sat in the international terminal, in civilian clothes with boarding pass in hand, baffled at his trip to Indonesia but trusting Imam Borqei.

Sheibani stood with Richards, watching in the growing light as his men spread netting over the boats moored fifty meters away under overhanging limbs. A good staging point, he thought, where the Andaman Sea narrowed into the Malacca Strait. Sheibani felt secure in Aceh Province. Holy Jihad had strong support here, where Islam first arrived in Indonesia.

"Is the cover sufficient?"

Richards nodded. "Between the trees and net, they'll be invisible to the satellites."

"And you have everything you need?"

Richards grinned. "Enough C4 to blow 'em and enough clay to fool your bomber boys."

"Do not ridicule them," Sheibani snapped. Deceiving brave men was regrettable. He hoped they would be welcomed in Paradise, and he would not allow them to be mocked by this infidel.

"I leave tomorrow to collect our American in Jakarta," Sheibani said. "You must finish before we return tomorrow night."

"What? Why? We got four days."

"The others will not understand, but this man may. Finish and cover it."

"Shit," Richards said.

Sheibani left Richards to his work, and the next morning as he got into his SUV, the American had the material stacked next to the boats.

"Gonna be broilin' under that camo net," the American said.

"Just make sure you finish before I return."

Sheibani left Richards cursing, as he drove off down the jungle track, the American soon forgotten. Success was only a matter of degree. Even if they failed to dupe China into believing the attack was an American ruse to justify seizing control of the strait, the attack alone was enough to raise oil prices and divert suspicion from Iran. Sheibani smiled and mulled his plans for "spontaneous" street demonstrations once American treachery was discovered.

JUDICIAL INVESTIGATIVE DIRECTORY HQ
PANAMA CITY, PANAMA
1 JULY

The chair groaned as Lieutenant Manuel Reyes reached for a file.

"One day, Manny," Sergeant Juan Perez said, "your fat ass is gonna hit the floor."

"You're just jealous, shrimp," Reyes said, with some truth. At six four and powerfully built, Reyes towered over his diminutive partner. Perez stifled a reply as Captain Luna approached and handed Reyes a folder.

"What's this?" Reyes asked.

"You boys are taking a little boat trip," Luna said. "Fatality on a tanker."

"Shit. Why us? Why not those SMN assholes?" Perez asked, referring to the Servicio Maritimo Nacional. "Wait. Let me guess. She arrives on a weekend."

"You know the drill, Perez," Luna said. "Suspected foul play comes here."

"Foul play?" Perez asked, interested now.

"Looks like it," Reyes said, looking up from the file. "You read this, Captain?"

Luna nodded. "No witness except the guy that reported the accident. Victim a skilled seaman in good health. Good weather. Yeah, it warrants a look."

Reyes continued, "Says he fell on a valve stem that pierced his brain through the eye."

"No way," Perez said. "With his hands free? I can see a broken arm or jaw, or even losing an eye. But the thing couldn't go into his brain unless he came straight down on it with force. Sounds like he had help."

Reyes and Luna nodded.

"Any bad blood between the victim and the witness?" Perez asked.

"Nothing in the file," Luna said. "Her agent will update you on the ETA. Keep me posted." He grinned. "Perez has time to stock up on seasick pills."

Reyes smiled. His partner's aversion to anything that floated was a department joke. Perez got violently ill, even riding a launch in the smooth water of the harbor. Reyes decided to let him stew for a bit before volunteering to work the case solo. Served him right for that fat-ass remark.

"This'll screw up the weekend for sure," Perez muttered at Luna's retreating back.

"I hope not," Reyes said, nodding at a framed photo of his eight-year-old twins in soccer uniforms. "The boys have a game this weekend, and I don't want to miss it."

OFFICES OF PHOENIX SHIPPING
2 JULY

Braun smiled as he read. He was managing message traffic for both *Asian Trader* and *China Star* now, sending or modifying messages in Dugan's name. The ruse wouldn't work long, but the attacks were imminent. *Asian Trader* had increased speed per "Dugan's" earlier orders, with a new ETA of 0100 hours on July 4, ready to start canal transit at first light. The ship would arrive a full twenty-four hours before anyone else in the office had a clue it had reached Panama.

He accessed the Panama Canal Authority webpage auctioning transit slots, signing in as Dugan. Bidding for the July 4 slot was heavy. He doubled the current bid and grinned as no challenger emerged. The slot secured, he pulled up an outgoing message he'd intercepted and held, asking the agent to arrange a hotel and airport pickup for Dugan. He added orders to advise the authorities that *Asian Trader* had transit priority and to request the inquiry be postponed until after transit. Braun hit send and leaned back, satisfied.

Dugan would arrive after the attack—in time to be detained. An investigation would reveal Dugan's Cayman Island account, owned through a series of fronts, with recent transactions totaling a million dollars from sources with known terrorist links. The money had stayed in the account just minutes before Braun whisked it away, causing it to vanish through another series of skillful transfers. A frame was one thing, but a million dollars was not something he abandoned lightly.

Things were progressing, despite a few hiccups. *China Star* and *Asian Trader* were on schedule, and the Chechens were in position for the final act. He could hardly ask for more.

PARIS, FRANCE
2 JULY

Basaev paced the room. He was impatient, as they all were. They'd been in the seedy transient hotel a week, keeping to themselves as they studied their course notes and identity documents, preparing to board the ship as a riding repair crew. Their weapons waited in the load port, concealed among the tools to be loaded aboard for the "riding crew" to use during the voyage. They would take the first flight from Paris to the load port as soon as they received word the ship had moved to the loading berth. They would board the ship just before sailing, when they would receive less scrutiny.

Allah make it soon, prayed Basaev.

CHAPTER SEVENTEEN

M/T *China Star*
Andaman Sea
East of Banda Aceh, Indonesia
3 July

Holt peered into the predawn gloom as *China Star* crept along at dead slow. He muttered and moved to the radar, his escort's late arrival just the latest irritation. He still chafed at the peremptory e-mail from this Dugan, ordering him to board the "escort team leader" for a "pre-transit conference." And his own company hadn't backed his protest.

The VHF squawked. "*China Star*, this is MPS team leader. Do you copy, over?"

"I copy, MPS," the captain said. "I have two targets to starboard. Is that you, over?"

"Affirmative, *China Star*. Five minutes out. Are you rigged for boarding, over?"

"Starboard side. I'll light it up." He walked over and threw a breaker, and floodlights bathed the boarding area and the adjacent sea in a circle of light.

"Thank you, *China Star*. I have a visual on the ladder. See you in five, out."

"Bonifacio," Holt barked. "Make yourself useful. Go meet our guest and escort him to the bridge." Third Mate Bonifacio scurried out, cursing the curiosity that led him to hang around after he was relieved.

Holt heard the engines now, a growing roar that subsided as the boats cut speed, one paralleling the ship as the second moved crab-like into the light to the pilot ladder. I'll be damned, he thought, looking at the flag. US Navy. Then he cursed as not one but six black-clad figures scrambled aboard. He waited until an agitated Bonifacio arrived with visitors in tow.

Holt looked at the group. "You seemed to have lost a few, Bonifacio."

"Captain, I told them—"

"Not his fault, Captain. We deployed," said the leader of the group, an American.

Before Holt could respond, the man extended his hand.

"I'm Bo Richards, MPS." He nodded at a second man. "This is Ensign Hamad, US Navy."

Holt shook their hands, glancing at a third man who hung back, gripping his weapon.

"By helping private firms," Richards said, "the US can protect the strait without upsetting local governments."

"Riding around under the Stars and Stripes isn't low profile," Holt said, not buying it. "What the hell is going on here?" he asked just as the phone rang.

The second mate held up the phone. "It's the chief," he said. Holt took the phone.

"Three GI Joe-lookin' assholes are in my engine control room. What the hell's goin' on, Cap?" Anderson demanded.

"Hold one, Chief," he said, looking at Richards. "The chief engineer's none too pleased with your 'deployment,' nor am I. So just get back in your little boats and follow us."

"Apologies, Captain," Richards said. "We'll do it any way you want. However, we do need a meeting with you and the chief before we leave."

Holt hesitated. "Fine," he said at last. He spoke into the phone. "Chief, can you come up to the D Deck conference room?" He nodded at the response and hung up.

"Mr. Ortega, you have the conn," he said to the second mate. "Course is one two five. Steering is on hand."

Holt listened to the man's confirmation before turning to the third mate. "Mr. Bonifacio, get some rest, but first ask the steward to bring coffee to the conference room."

Holt led the group down to the conference room, swallowing his irritation at the belated realization that the third man, the silent one, had remained on the bridge. Jon Anderson joined them in the conference room, fit to be tied. As before, Richards diverted the engineer with introductions as the smiling steward arrived with coffee. As the steward served, Anderson sank into a chair beside the captain as Richards closed the door.

Without warning, Richards slammed the steward down on the table and with one fluid movement pulled a silenced sidearm and fired twice into the man's face. Holt and Anderson watched horrified as the steward's blood and brains pooled on the table. They looked up to see Richards's steady smile and dead, dead eyes.

"Now gentlemen," Richards said, "let's discuss our little cruise, shall we?"

M/T *China Star*
Malacca Strait
Due West of Port Klang, Malaysia
Local Time 4 July

Richards watched the bridge crew in the glow of console instrument lights. With a gun at their heads and the dead steward in front of them, the senior officers had been understandably cooperative. Most of the crew was now captive in the crew lounge. The gear had been brought aboard, and the gunboats ran dark, hugging the ship's starboard side, their return masked by the huge ship's own radar signature.

The captain was on the bridge, along with Second Mate Ortega, Third Mate Bonifacio and Urbano, the helmsman, all dead tired, allowed no rest in over twenty-four hours. Richards, Yousif, and Sheibani shared guard duty, two at a time with the third napping as needed. The three hijackers in the engine room followed the same two-watching-one-resting pattern, guarding Anderson and First Engineer Benjamin Santos. By design, only the seamen on watch knew the hijackers' numbers, and ignorant of the odds, the others captive in the crew lounge would be less inclined toward heroics.

Not that it mattered. The thick lounge windows were all but unbreakable, and the handles of the lounge doors were lashed to the storm rail in the passageway, precluding worries of hidden keys. The steward's body dumped in the lounge and a warning the doors were booby-trapped further discouraged resistance, enhanced by the cook's report of grenade-festooned doors when he returned under guard with sandwiches, water, and buckets for "sanitary needs."

∗∗∗

Holt squinted at the radar through watery eyes, his stomach boiling from endless coffee.

"Southbound VLCC," squawked the VHF, "this is Klang VTS. Report. Over."

He felt the gun at the back of his head.

"OK, nice and businesslike," Richards said.

"Jesse," Mike Hill said, "two calls in two weeks. People will talk."

Ward chuckled. "Whadda ya got, Mike?"

"You know that boat we been tracking? *China Star*?"

Ward sat up, interested. "Yeah."

"Well, she picked up admirers. Two Malaysian boats as escorts."

Christ, that was fast, thought Ward. "Malaysians? You sure?"

"Not positive," Hill said, "but the two guys in each boat are Asian, and they're flying red-white-and-blue flags. A stern wind is keeping the flags limp, but they're red-and-white striped. That means US or Malaysia. I know it's not us, so it must be them. The boats look a lot like our Dauntless 34s, but that's a pretty common design."

"Two guys per boat is a bit light. Our crews are bigger."

"Lemme look again. Shit, there's a ladder rigged. They're on board. I should have caught that."

"Actually, I'm relieved," Ward said. "We passed a back-channel warning to the locals but got no response. Any other friendlies in the area if they need help?"

"There's a CARAT exercise on to the south," Hill said, using the acronym for the Cooperation Afloat Readiness and Training exercise. "A multinational cluster fuck. Us, Singapore, Malaysia, and Indonesia. I'd hate to lead that parade."

Ward laughed. "Sounds like everything's OK. Thanks for the update."

"No sweat, pal," Hill said and hung up.

∗∗∗

For all his relief that his backdoor warning had paid off, Ward couldn't shake an uneasy feeling. He was in the supermarket two hours later, shopping for his Fourth of July cookout, when it hit him. He rushed through the checkout to his car and began punching numbers into his sat phone, praying his gut feeling was wrong.

Sheibani moved through the chart-room curtains onto the darkened bridge.

"We're close," he whispered. "Best deal with the excess crew as they sleep."

"It'll make the others more difficult," Richards protested.

"They will hear nothing in the engine room," Sheibani said, "and we tell these their shipmates tried to escape, and a few were injured by booby traps, and the rest gave up after warning shots. It will calm them long enough. Soon we'll be in Indonesian waters and no longer need them. Any fool can ground a ship."

"OK. Will you do it?"

"Yes. I will take Yousif."

"No," Richards said. "That leaves me too thin here."

"You do well to remember who is really in charge, Richards."

The comment hung in the air until Richards broke the silence.

"All right," he whispered, "but go quietly and hurry back."

Sheibani smiled in the dark as he moved away. He'd included Yousif as an afterthought to salve his pangs of conscience. He would not let the young man die without dipping his sword in the blood of the infidel.

***

Sheibani peeked in a window. Men slept sprawled on sofas and armchairs or the deck. Three insomniacs played cards in the light of a lamp. He moved back and targeted the window, nodding for Yousif to take another. They opened fire, stitching holes around the edge of the thick glass before directing fire into the center, sending a maelstrom of shards inward, followed by grenades as they ducked low. Sheibani rushed to the window after the explosions, unmoved by the carnage, firing at anything that twitched. He looked over at Yousif bent over a puddle of vomit.

"Control yourself and rejoice in the blood of infidels. Come, a few still squirm. We will toss in two grenades each and finish it."

Yousif shook his head, mute.

"Beard of the Prophet, you are a woman. I will finish alone. Go."

Yousif stumbled up the stairs to the bridge as explosions sounded behind him. Sheibani arrived on the bridge moments later to find Yousif trembling in the dark, wiping vomit from his chin. Sheibani's foul mood was tempered by the ease with which his captives accepted his tale of attempted escape. If they noticed the patterns of shots and explosions didn't match the story, it hadn't registered. A comforting lie was more palatable than a terrifying truth.

***

Sheibani erred in thinking his act went unnoticed below. Engineers are attuned to sound and vibration, for unexpected noises invariably herald problems. In the control room, Anderson and Santos felt the shocks through their feet, though their guards were oblivious.

Anderson paced in front of the control console. Unlike Holt, preoccupied with conning the ship, his automated engine room allowed him time to think. With Americans among them, he figured the hijackers nonsuicidal. He was partially right; Yousif and the men in the boats were eager martyrs, while Richards and Sheibani planned escape. The three guards in the engine room were also unenthusiastic martyrs, Burmese mercenaries hired by Richards.

No one seemed intent on destruction; they had neither stopped the inert-gas system nor ventilated the cargo tanks into the explosive range. They were either intentionally leaving the ship in a safe condition or were inept. They didn't seem inept.

Anderson didn't figure he and Santos were there by accident. Their captors anticipated a possible need for a senior engineer, and while they might kill one to coerce the other, if either escaped, the other likely wouldn't be killed. But he sensed they were nearing some climax, perhaps connected to the shocks he'd felt. Time was getting short.

He watched the guards out of the corner of his eye. The engineers were accustomed to long periods in the windowless control room and at least had the distraction of monitoring the main engine and engineering plant. Their guards had no mental stimulation whatsoever, and being confined in a box had taken its toll. They were noticeably less alert than they had been when the ordeal started over twenty-four hours before. Anderson took a chance.

***

Santos watched as Anderson turned toward him and repeatedly arched his eyebrows to get his attention. He stared silently as Anderson looked at the CO_2 alarm on the bulkhead then pointed at him with a finger shielded by his body. Santos grew more puzzled as Anderson then looked pointedly toward a rack of emergency-escape masks used for tank entry and discreetly pointed to himself. The chief obviously had a plan, but what? He was still trying to piece it together when Anderson turned to the senior of the three guards.

"I'm hungry," he said. "We're not going to escape aft, so how about bringing down more sandwiches before I find another way out of here?"

The hijacker looked confused. "You no talk."

"Santos can go with one of your guys," Anderson pressed. "They can leave and shut that door tight." He pointed to the door leading to the deckhouse stairs.

"No. No eat. Shut up now."

Suddenly, Santos understood, but the hijacker wasn't cooperating. Anderson turned back to the console, disappointment on his face, but Santos was elated. He caught Anderson's eye and nodded. He'd plotted his own escape for hours. The only thing stopping him had been his fear of retaliation against Anderson. Now it seemed the chief had a plan of his own.

***

"Toilet." Santos hugged his stomach and moved toward the door.

The nearest hijacker leveled his weapon. "You stop."

Santos moaned. "Must go toilet."

The man spoke and the others laughed, obviously at Santos's expense. The head man nodded, and the underling escorted Santos out the door to the engine-room toilet and the deckhouse stairs beyond. As the control-room door shut behind them, Santos hurried across the narrow vestibule to the toilet. He tried to close the toilet door, but as expected, his captor shook his head, so Santos shrugged down his coveralls and sat, glaring out at the man. Minutes later, he pulled up his coveralls and moved to the small sink, his back to the hijacker. He turned on the water and extracted a fistful of powdered hand soap from a container on the sink, his actions hidden by his body. He murmured a prayer and turned off the water.

Surprise was complete as soap flew into the guard's face. His weapon hung slack as he jammed fists to burning eyes. In one fluid motion, Santos plucked a pen from his pocket and drove it into the man's throat. Blood covered Santos as he grabbed the man's wrists and pinned him against the bulkhead, praying no sounds of the struggle reached the control room. The man gasped and bled out, powerful spurts soaking Santos's face and front. It took an eternity before the flow dwindled, and a stench filled the space, signaling loss of sphincter control. He let the body slide down the bulkhead and stood trembling, willing the face from his memory.

Santos cleaned himself as best he could with paper towels from the toilet. A mop from the cleaning-gear locker became his improvised lock, jammed across the narrow passageway between the outward-opening control-room door and the opposite bulkhead, its tangled head compressed tight against the door just above the knob. He grabbed the hijacker's gun and hurried up the stairs.

USS *Hermitage* (LSD-56)
Malacca Strait
North of Riau Island, Indonesia

Captain Jack Leary, USN, sat in his ready room with the sat phone at his ear.

"Captain Leary, this is Jim Brice from the embassy in Singapore. I'm conferencing in Jesse Ward from Langley. We need your help. Go ahead, Jesse."

Leary listened. When Ward finished, Jim Brice spoke.

"Port Klang has nothing unaccounted for near *China Star*, and they didn't send out any escorts," he said.

"Are they following up?" Ward asked.

Brice sighed. "I suspect they'll drag their feet until she's out of their waters."

"That's not gonna hack it," Leary said. "Any threat needs to be handled before the passage narrows at Phillip's Strait. But what can *we* do about it?"

"Can you check it out?" Ward asked.

"I'm running a multinational effort planned for months. I can't just head north."

Ward persisted, "Maybe one vessel—"

"Look, Ward," Leary said, "I can't go into territorial waters without consulting my counterparts. And they'll request instructions, and we'll get no decision until the tanker is in flames or safe and halfway to Japan. See my problem here?"

Ward sighed. "Yes, I do, Captain, but what *can* we do?"

After a long silence, Leary replied. "I guess we take a risk. I can get a chopper over her without being too obvious. If there's a problem, we close, and if that ends well, we call it a multinational effort and all take a bow. If not… well, I never wanted to be an admiral anyway."

"Thanks, Captain," he said. "By the way, is that sailor from the hijacking with you?"

"Broussard? Yeah, he's one of our referees."

"Might be a good idea if he was on that chopper."

M/T CHINA STAR
MALACCA STRAIT

"Where the hell have you been?" Richards demanded.

"Preparing our escape," Sheibani said. "Allah smiles on the prepared."

"Good," nodded Richards, mollified. "How much longer?"

"We turn into the western channel now and ground off Rupat Island in an hour, maybe a bit longer. I will reduce speed. I don't want to ground hard enough to breach both the outer and inner hulls." He smiled. "It is difficult to swim in crude oil."

Richards returned the smile, heartened by mention of escape. Sheibani moved to where Ortega stood near the helmsman.

"Make your course one seven oh," Sheibani said.

Holt stepped in from the wing just as the second mate protested. "The western channel is too shallow. We cannot!"

Sheibani shot Ortega in the head, and Holt recoiled as wet bits of brain hit his face and slid from his chin to fall beside Ortega's twitching corpse.

"One seven oh," Sheibani repeated, and the terrified helmsman spun the wheel.

"Half ahead," Sheibani said.

Bonifacio stood on the far side of the bridge, waiting, but the captain stood frozen, staring down at Ortega's body, barely visible in the predawn light. Bonifacio raced to the console.

"Half ahead, aye, sir," he shouted.

Such a pity, Sheibani thought. Just when I get these monkeys trained I have to kill them.

***

Anderson stole a glance at the clock, willing Santos to hurry.

The head man said something, and his underling started for the door. Anderson's mind raced, desperate to buy Santos time, when unexpected motion caused him to grab the console storm rail as the ship turned.

The head man reached the console just as the engine control changed to half ahead.

"What you do?"

Clueless, thought Anderson, looking past the head man to the second man, halfway to the door, unsure what to do given the new development.

"I do nothing," Anderson said. "We don't control here. Bridge do." He pointed to the phone. "You talk friends. They tell you."

The hijacker picked up the phone, and when he hung up, Anderson launched into a stream of technobabble.

"OK, OK. You shut up now." The hijacker stuck the gun in Anderson's face, Santos forgotten for the moment. Anderson sneaked a look at the time. Damn it, Ben, what's taking so long?

***

Santos stood in the CO2 room, racked with indecision. Was he really meant to trigger the CO2? He had a gun now. Should he try to rescue Anderson? He felt the ship turn and slow and decided to trust his instincts. He crossed himself, pulled the release, and raced aft.

***

"What you do?" the senior terrorist demanded, gun to Anderson's chest.

"Not me. Bridge do," Anderson screamed over the alarm. "Big mistake. Someone started gas to put out engine-room fire. Gas comes in twenty seconds!" He pointed to the raucous alarm and the large red sign beneath it.

DANGER—CO2 RELEASE—WHEN ALARM SOUNDS VACATE IMMEDIATELY.

The head man reached for the phone.

"No time! We stay, we die!" Anderson moved toward the engine-room door.

The head man dropped the phone and leveled his gun. "Stop," he ordered, as the other hijacker struggled with the most obvious exit, the door leading to the deckhouse.

"No," Anderson lied, pointing to the blocked door, "that door locks automatically to keep people out of engine room. Don't worry about your friend. He'll escape with Santos. We must go this way." Anderson pointed through the control-room window to a large sign stenciled on the engine room bulkhead, reading EMERGENCY ESCAPE ROUTE, with an arrow pointed down.

The underling rushed to Anderson's side, and an argument broke out between the hijackers. Anderson grabbed three masks from the rack, keeping one and setting the others on the deck to allay the men's suspicions. The men didn't notice that the two he'd set out for them came from a shelf of discharged masks, awaiting recharge.

Anderson slung the mask around his neck and fled into the engine room, with the men on his heels, juggling masks and guns. He raced down the steep stairs sideways in a controlled fall, right hand gripping the rail behind as he steadied himself with his left on the opposite handrail in front, feet hitting every third step. It was an acquired skill, and he was soon well ahead, increasing his lead on each flight of stairs as he spiraled downward. The hijackers could do nothing to stop him, for they dared not kill their guide out of the maze.

He planned to lead them to the emergency escape trunk, sure that when they saw the vertical ladder out, they'd push past him in their panic. When they were on the ladder, he planned to fade back into the engine room and escape by a different route with his mask. The hijackers wouldn't know Santos had locked the hatch until they were at a dead end, on top of the ladder, with no escape.

The warning horns continued their plaintive wail as Anderson reached the lower engine room and rushed aft beside the giant turning shaft. He hadn't figured on such a lead. They would be suspicious if he stopped now. He decided to lie on the deck at the foot of the ladder, feigning a pulled muscle. He stepped into the escape trunk and looked up.

To a square of black sky and stars. Shit. Ben hadn't closed the hatch.

OK, change of plans. He'd try to make it out and lock the hatch down behind himself. He started up the long ladder at breakneck speed as the alarm horns began to fade. Halfway up, the CO_2 began to roar through distribution nozzles, and he looked down. The expanding gas sucked heat from the humid space, condensing moisture in the air. His terrified pursuers emerged from the thick white fog, climbing toward him for all they were worth.

***

Santos stood on the main deck looking at the hatch. Was he really meant to close it? What else could the chief have meant by the "not going to escape aft" clue? But what if he misunderstood and cut off the chief's escape? But no, the clue could mean nothing else. Santos grabbed the cantilevered counterweight that held the heavy cover open just as the horns stopped wailing below. He hesitated. One quick look, then he'd close it for sure.

He peeked over the hatch coaming to see Anderson climbing fast with the hijackers right behind, all eyes on the ladder and none looking up. Santos braced himself and waited until Anderson began to emerge.

"Jump, boss," he yelled as he hooked his arm under Anderson's and heaved, their combined strength sending Anderson over the hatch coaming to land in a heap. Santos pulled up on the counterweight with all his strength, and the heavy cover crashed shut. He slapped one of the threaded dogs in place and spun the wing nut to screw it down tight. No one else was coming out.

Below, the junior hijacker was in the lead, and he balanced himself on the ladder and loosed a burst up at the hatch cover in spite of his boss's screams of protests. The protests died quickly, as did the men, as ricochets caromed through the close confines of the steel escape trunk.

The shots were faint outside, swallowed by the myriad sounds of a ship underway.

"What now, Chief?" Santos asked, helping Anderson to his feet.

"Damned if I know, Ben," Anderson gasped.

CHAPTER EIGHTEEN

M/T *China Star*
Malacca Strait
North of Rupat Island, Indonesia

"*China Star, China Star*. You are out of the main channel. Repor—"

"Change," Sheibani said into the mike, twisting the knob to a new channel. He keyed the mike rapidly and nodded at responding clicks from the boats, confirming compliance via a prearranged code.

"Too late to stop us, and their babbling might disrupt contact with the boats," he said as Richards nodded. An unfamiliar alarm shrieked and they looked across the bridge to where Holt stood at a flashing panel.

"What are you doing?" Richards said as he rushed over, gun raised.

Holt seemed beyond caring, as if being forced to dump Ortega's body overboard had erased any illusions of survival.

"I'm trying to silence this friggin' alarm if you'll get the fuck out of the way."

Surprised, Richards complied. "What is it?" he asked, lowering his gun.

"CO_2 release. Probably a false alarm."

Sheibani frowned. He was reaching for the phone when the ship blacked out. He heard the distant muted roar of the emergency generator.

"Main-engine trip!" Bonifacio cried.

In the engine room, the generator engines had coughed to a halt as the CO_2 rose to the level of the generator flat and the engines sucked in CO_2. With no power, safety devices shut down the main engine and everything else, and the remotely located emergency generator sprang to life automatically to power limited emergency services.

Richards leveled his gun. "False alarm, my ass. Fix this. Now. Or you're dead."

"There's no fast fix, you ignorant asshole," Holt said. "The CO_2 has to be purged. That means resetting dampers and starting fans. Takes time."

"So how do you do that?" Richards asked.

Holt smirked. "I call the chief engineer."

Richards knocked him to the deck.

"Enough!" Sheibani yelled as Bonifacio helped Holt.

Sheibani started to call the engine control room, then realized the futility of that action. Anyone still there would be dead.

"Yousif," he said, "go down and check. Cautiously. If you have difficulty breathing, return at once."

Yousif nodded and left as Sheibani moved to the chart and stepped off the distance with dividers. By the time Yousif returned, Sheibani was reassured. They were near Indonesian waters, and momentum would take them there.

"Gas," Yousif said, breathless from his climb. "I got halfway down but saw the body of one our men. The control-room door is jammed close with a mop."

"The man's gun?"

Yousif shook his head. "Gone."

Sheibani nodded. "Yousif, watch these three. Richards, join me on the wing."

"This is bad," Richards said when they were alone.

The Iranian shrugged. "She will ground with or without us. The VHF is on the emergency circuit, so we can communicate with the boats. If the Burmese died, it saves us killing them, and if any survived, they will report being led by an American. If the engineers are alive and armed, they will hide in a defensive position and wait for help."

"But they know what went on."

"They were in a windowless box and know nothing," Sheibani said. "There are many hiding places, and time is short. And they are armed. Why risk being shot? We leave them."

"OK. Let's finish these guys, blow the boats, and get the hell out of here."

"A half hour more," Sheibani said, smiling at the lightening sky. "The farther we drift, the shorter our swim."

***

Anderson studied his blood-covered subordinate in the growing light.

"Christ, Ben, are you hurt?"

"Not… not mine," Santos said, suddenly drained. He looked down, as if seeing the gore for the first time, then bent and retched, as Anderson stood near, unsure what to do.

Santos straightened, wiping his mouth on a sleeve.

"We got a gun," he said, retrieving it from the deck and thrusting it at Anderson.

Anderson accepted the unfamiliar weapon.

"What now, boss?" Santos asked again.

"A drifting VLCC will bring help," Anderson said. "There's three hijackers left aboard for sure, and even with a few more from the boats, they lack manpower to rig a tanker this size with enough charges to sink it, and they can't use the cargo because we're still inert. With a dead ship, the pumps are down, so they can't even jettison cargo. And they seem like pirates, not terrorists, so why don't they just clean out the safe and haul ass?"

Santos nodded as if equally baffled.

"Let's assume the worst," Anderson said. "If the murdering assholes aren't gone before help arrives, the hostages become bargaining chips. If we can free at least some of them, they can scatter and hide." He looked at the sky. "Let's move before full light."

Santos nodded and trailed Anderson around the machinery casing, into the deckhouse and the glow of emergency lighting. Anderson eased the stairwell fire door open and peeked up the first flight to the A Deck landing and started up. A putrid smell washed over them as they left the stairwell on A Deck.

"Christ," Anderson whispered, "smells like somebody shit in a meat market."

Santos's face contorted, and he rushed forward, stopping short at the rope lashing the lounge door and the sight of grenades hung from the door frame. The metal door was peppered with dents, as if attacked inside by hundreds of screwdrivers. Scattered fragments had penetrated to smash into the steel bulkhead across the hall and fall mangled to the deck. Stench wafted from the holes.

"We have to go in, Ben," Anderson said softly. "Some might live."

Santos untied the rope as his boss studied the grenades. Pins in place. Window dressing. Anderson was careful nonetheless as he pulled the grenades from their magnetic clips and set them aside.

The battered door refused to budge, and Anderson leaned into it. It yielded suddenly, with a wet sucking sound, as the partial torso blocking it slid away, and Anderson pitched forward on his hands and knees. Gore squished between his fingers and soaked the legs of his coveralls as he stared at body parts in a horrifying jumble. The reek of open bowels was overpowering. He tried to rise and slipped, then scrambled backward on his hands and knees through the gore to draw himself up against the far bulkhead of the passageway, fighting down vomit and wiping his hands furiously on his coveralls.

Santos stared into the room. After a moment, he crossed himself and closed the door before sliding down the bulkhead to sit opposite Anderson.

"No one alive there, boss," he said quietly.

"They mean to kill us all, Ben. I have to try to help whoever's left, but we only have one gun. Hide, Ben. Survive to testify against these bastards."

Santos shook his head. "In that room," he said, "are two cousins and my sister's husband, and others from my town. What will I say to their families? That I hid only so I could live to testify? Who will believe it? I would not be alive, boss. Only waiting to die. We go together."

USS HERMITAGE (LSD-56)

Chief Petty Officer Ricky Vega passed the backpacks to Broussard and scrambled aboard the SH-60 Sea Hawk as the younger man stowed them.

"Welcome to Malacca Air," said the pilot into his helmet mike. "I do believe this is the earliest I've ever seen boat people vertical and ambulatory." He grinned over his shoulder.

Vega grinned back. "Fuck you… sir."

"I see rising in time to actually put in a day's work has made you cranky, Chief Vega."

Vega just grinned. He waited until they were well clear of *Hermitage* before speaking.

"So what's up, sir? They told me to get Broussard here ASAP. I decided to tag along."

"Milk run," the pilot said. "Gotta eyeball some gunboats shadowing a tanker."

Broussard and Vega exchanged looks.

"How are you armed?" Vega asked.

The pilot laughed. "In the middle of a multinational exercise? Not a chance. It's not great PR to kill your allies while you're training 'em."

Vega moved his backpack so his Beretta M9 was in reach. Broussard did the same. Neither had gone unarmed since the *Alicia* incident. Another "milk run."

101

"Got it on the scope yet?" the pilot asked.

"Christ, yes," said the copilot. "She's huge. Be over her in twenty."

M/T CHINA STAR
0618 HOURS LOCAL TIME
4 JULY

The boats were visible now and Rupat Island a dark slash ahead. Sheibani looked into the wheelhouse at the captives, wondering which would foul themselves when the boats exploded. It would be amusing when they found themselves unharmed. Like killing them twice. And Yousif. He would be denied even the illusion of martyrdom and understand before he died just how he had been used.

"Chopper." Richards pointed.

"Sooner than expected," Sheibani said, unconcerned. "Very well. Let us end it."

He smiled on his way to the VHF. "We'll soon be in Paradise, Yousif. *Allahu Akbar!*"

"*Allahu Akbar!*" Yousif parroted with a nervous grin.

Sheibani keyed the mike, and the roar of engines split the air as the boats rocketed away. Five hundred yards out and they turned, and the crews shouted encouragement to each other before speeding at *China Star*, rooster tails behind them.

***

"Boats moving away," the pilot said, swinging the chopper to frame the boats in the open side door. As Vega and Broussard watched, the boats turned, their crews shouting and gesturing before the sea behind the boats boiled and the boats shot forward.

"Those are our boats!" Broussard screamed into his mike. "They're gonna ram the tanker! Suicide bombers!"

"Get closer," Vega said. "Put us right on their asses and keep them in the door."

"Roger that," the pilot said as he descended and closed on the boats sideways. Vega and Broussard left their seats and gripped grab rails as they opened fire.

Firing pistols from an unstable platform at a bobbing target was a long shot. They hoped to get lucky. They didn't. The boats separated, making it impossible to target both, and the second man in each boat manned a .50-caliber machine gun. The pilot turned to present a minimal target and fled.

Broussard and Vega watched fireballs erupt at the ship's side, followed by booming thunderclaps as water and debris rained down. They awaited secondary blasts that never came.

***

Sheibani and Richards emerged from behind the drawn curtains of the chart room, where they'd sheltered against the possibility of flying glass. Sheibani walked toward a confused Yousif as Richards stepped out on the wing.

"Just burn marks on the hull and debris in the water," Richards said as he returned. "The chopper's hovering a mile off, probably reporting. Let's go."

"In good time," Sheibani said and smiled at Yousif.

"I… I don't understand," Yousif said. "Why didn't we explode?"

Sheibani shrugged. "Our brothers' sacrifice was a regrettable but necessary subterfuge."

"You had men martyr themselves for… some sort of… of trick?"

"Just so," Sheibani said. "Now, as far as you are concerned—"

"For Christ's sake," Richards said. "If you wanna give speeches, run for Congress." He shot Yousif in the face.

"I told you no head shots!" Sheibani yelled, looking down at Yousif's ruined face.

"So they ID him with DNA and fingerprints," Richards said. "He's wearing armor, genius. Should I have shot him in the foot and waited for gangrene? Let's finish and go."

"Very well," Sheibani said. "Since you're so eager, you do the honors."

Without hesitation, Richards shot Urbano in the head, but as he turned the gun on Bonifacio, Holt shoved the third mate, and Richards's burst went wide, shredding the man's ear and shoulder. As Bonifacio fell, Holt charged, aiming a left-handed haymaker at Richards while deflecting the gun with his right hand. Richards slipped the punch and it glanced off his head. Unable to raise his gun, he fired a burst across Holt's thighs and twisted like a matador as the captain's momentum carried him wounded to the deck.

Richards scrambled backward and felt his ear, cursing as his hand came away bloody.

"Why the hell didn't you shoot him?" he demanded over his shoulder.

"I assumed you could kill unarmed men. Now if you're done mucking about, we can—"

Sheibani jerked at an explosion to port.

***

The chopper hovered, with orders from *Hermitage* to "continue at discretion," which the pilot figured meant he was screwed no matter what.

"Whadda ya think, Chief?" he asked. "Not much damage."

"I concur, sir," Vega said.

"Get closer," Broussard urged. "We need to know what we're facing."

"Listen, Rambo," said the pilot, "our entire arsenal is your unauthorized peashooters."

"C'mon, Lieutenant," Broussard said. "The .50s are gone, and they're not likely to take us down with small arms. We can get closer."

"*We* aren't flying this bird, sailor. That would be *me*."

"The orders *are* to continue surveillance, sir," Vega said. "Can't see much from here."

"Shit. All right, we'll circle fast, then dart out of range."

He tilted the chopper toward *China Star*.

Anderson waited to dash up the exterior stairway to the starboard bridge wing. The sea was littered with debris, and he stood parsing this latest development. They had one gun, limited ammunition, and grenades taken from the lounge. A search of the workshops had yielded no weapons but led to the discovery that inspired their plan. They'd found scuba gear and two underwater scooters on the starboard side of main deck.

The plan was to get between the hijackers and the hostages and leave the escape path clear. They had crept to D Deck, one level below the bridge, and Anderson waited on the starboard exterior stairs for Santos to creep through the deckhouse and toss a grenade overboard to port as a diversion. With the hijackers focused on the port side, Anderson hoped to rush onto the bridge from starboard and get between the hostages and hijackers, keeping them at bay until Santos joined him. He hoped that, faced with resistance, the hijackers would run.

But the explosion of the boats confused things, and Anderson crouched against the side of the house, unsure. He flinched at gunfire above. God damn it, they were killin' 'em. He rushed up the stairs just as an explosion sounded from the far side of the ship.

***

Sheibani rushed to the port wing. Richards glanced at the unmoving men, then backed after him. "What's going on?" he demanded over his shoulder.

He reached the port door just as Anderson charged in from starboard, firing. Outside, Sheibani dived aft for cover. Richards began to return fire just as a poorly aimed bullet from Anderson caromed off a window frame into his armor with stinging force. He backed outside through the door and ducked down beside Sheibani.

***

All for nothing, Anderson thought as he took cover. The bastards killed everyone.

"Christ," Holt growled. "You couldn't hit a bull in the ass with a fucking bass fiddle."

Relief washed over Anderson. "You OK, Dan?" he asked over his shoulder.

"Of course I'm not OK, you dumb ass," Holt snarled. "The son of a bitch shot me." He went on with a catch in his voice. "And they killed the others."

Anderson fired at movement, striking the doorway near where he'd aimed, just as Santos burst through the starboard door and dropped down beside Bonifacio.

"Boney is alive," Santos said. "Not too much blood. I think he will live."

The third mate groaned as Santos dragged him to cover.

"Thank God," Holt said from behind the steering stand, crawling to retrieve Yousif's gun and then forward to help Anderson.

"Ben," Anderson said, "encourage them to leave with one of those grenades."

***

"Fuck this," Richards said. "Like you said, let's leave them and get out of here."

"That was the engineers. The bridge crew heard things. And may live, thanks to you."

They bickered. Sheibani was considering shooting Richards himself when a grenade clanged down beside them on a crazy bouncing path, past them and over the edge of the deck to explode below on top of the lifeboat.

"Beard of the Prophet," Sheibani said, "how I wish we'd kept some grenades."

"Uh… I have one," Richards said, groping in a side pocket.

Allah deliver me, Sheibani thought.

"Then throw it, you idiot. And make sure to pull the pin."

Sheibani raised his head at a sound as the chopper loomed toward them.

"Our toothless friends are coming to watch, Richards. Please don't disappoint."

***

The chopper was running in fast from starboard when the pilot pulled up at muzzle flashes inside the wheelhouse. Something exploded on the far side of the ship, and a large armed man in bloody coveralls bolted up the starboard stairs and into the wheelhouse. More shooting.

"Folks aren't playing nicely," the pilot said.

"Good guys and bad guys, but who's who?" Broussard asked as a small man dashed up the stairs and into the wheelhouse.

"Company coveralls," Vega said. "Must be crew. Bad guys must be to port."

The pilot circled far to the port, in time to see a grenade explode on top of the lifeboat. Broussard trained binoculars on black-clad figures crouched just aft of the open bridge door. One looked up.

"Sheibani!" Broussard screamed. "That murdering bastard! Get us closer!" He loaded a full clip as Vega did the same.

The pilot slowed and studied the weapons in the hands of the terrorists.

"Lieutenant," Vega said, "that scumbag killed three of my men. Skinned one of 'em alive. We can't hover with our thumb up our ass and do nothing… sir!"

"Roger that, Chief," the pilot said as he slipped the chopper sideways at the ship.

"OK, junior," Vega said, sitting on the deck with feet toward the door, "let's improve our odds." He rolled on his side and raised his knees, the Beretta between them in a two-handed grip, pointing out the door. "Squeeze your knees together for support," he said, and Broussard copied. "We'll be stable and smaller targets. Course, if they drill us, we'll be singing soprano."

"Lieutenant," Vega continued, "keep us a little high so we don't take friendly fire from inside and vice versa, and angled down a bit so we can see the targets."

"Roger that, Chief. Good hunting."

Broussard was trying not to think about a bullet in the balls.

"Target left," Vega said, indicating he would take Richards.

"Sheibani is mine," Broussard confirmed.

"Let's do it, junior," Vega said.

***

A bullet ricocheted beside Sheibani and whined away. He aimed at the black square of the chopper door but saw nothing except an indistinct mass near the bottom of the square.

"Hurry, fool," he said. "We must kill them and get inside."

Richards rose to his knees, the door to his left. To minimize exposure, he would throw left-handed. He flinched as a bullet whined off a bulkhead, pulled the pin, and twisted to his left.

***

Vega knew the range was absurd. They were shooting downward, so they didn't have to worry too much about the bullets dropping over the ridiculous distance, but all they could really do was put rounds in the general vicinity and hope. He shot economically nonetheless, adjusting as the pilot closed the range. He was thankful his target was not returning fire until he saw the man draw back to throw. In a heartbeat, Vega evaluated the situation and emptied the clip as fast as he could pull the trigger.

None of Vega's fusillade struck his target directly, but a ricochet clipped the man's ankle midway through his throw. He jerked and released the grenade prematurely. It sailed forward over the wind dodger, tumbled to the main deck far below, and bounced over the side to explode harmlessly. Broussard, hearing Vega's fire and deluged by ejected casings, also changed to rapid fire.

***

"I'm outta here," Richards said as bullets struck around them. He rose to a crouch and limped aft. Sheibani moved in concurrence, passing him to rush ahead down the stairs and into the shelter of the deckhouse.

***

Anderson's joy at the retreat was brief.

"The Chartroom door," he shouted and rushed through the curtains with Santos.

Santos held the door open and stood aside, giving Anderson a clear shot at anyone topping the stairs. They tensed as a door opened below, followed by hurried footfalls descending the stairs, away from them.

"They're running," Anderson whispered. "It's over, Ben."

"Not yet, boss," Santos said, plunging through the door.

***

The stairs were solid plate, and Santos knew a blast at one level would be contained. At D Deck he tossed a grenade, banking it like a billiard ball off the bulkhead of the next landing down, so it bounced down the stairs after the fleeing hijackers.

"For Paco and Juni," he said his cousins' names as he ducked back and covered his ears.

***

Sheibani heard the clatter and leapt the last steps to the B Deck landing, grabbing the handrail to slingshot around the landing and continue his plunge, feet hitting every third step. He was well out of the kill zone when the grenade detonated at limping Richards's back.

His ears rang as he resumed his downward rush, thankful he'd delayed killing Richards. He'd planned to leave the American's body on the bridge, his gambit of preparing two sets of escape equipment a ruse. But Allah had preserved the American as a shield. He pushed Richards from his mind. He had to get out of the stairwell. One more deck to go.

***

Santos hit the landing fast, slipping in Richards's slimy remains and crashing to his knees. He tossed the grenade from his knees, banking it once again off the lower-landing bulkhead. "For Victor," he invoked his brother-in-law's name before ducking back. He covered his ears just as he heard the main-deck fire door open. Missed him, he thought, as he awaited the blast.

***

The main-deck fire door slammed behind Sheibani as he ran down the passageway and clamped hands over his ears just before the blast. After the blast, he straightened, training his gun on the fire door. "Come out, come out, my foolish friend," he whispered.

The engineer threw open the fire door, then ducked back to the safety of the stairwell as bullets bit through the metal cladding of the door as it swung closed. Sheibani cursed himself for falling for the ruse and reflected. If the monkey had grenades left he would have tossed one, and if armed, he couldn't fire without exposing himself. Sheibani watched the door and stripped off his armor one-handed, dumping it on the deck while backing toward the starboard door. Outside, he closed the heavy steel watertight door behind him, twisting the handle of a closing dog with a solid clunk as the door seated, then jamming all six dogs to delay pursuit. He grinned as he donned the scuba gear. The chopper still hovered to port, and the monkey trembled in the stairwell, no doubt pleased at slaying the idiot Richards. They would still be searching the ship when he was halfway ashore.

***

Santos slipped back up the stairs to retrieve the dead hijacker's gun. When he returned to main-deck level, he heard a door slam and the dogs of a watertight door being engaged. He threw the fire door open for a look, darting his head out near the deck, where it wouldn't be expected. Seeing no threat, he moved into the passageway, not to starboard after Sheibani but to port, to exit the house on the opposite side and circle astern, aft of the machinery casing. He moved deliberately, in no hurry now.

***

Sheibani laughed aloud as he hefted the sea scooter by its handles, its weight pressed against his thighs as he lugged it to the ship's side. Five feet from the rail, his world went black.

***

The booby traps were Santos's idea. Anderson had lifted each sea scooter as Santos used duct tape from the bosun's shop to tape a grenade in the recess just in front of the propeller cowling. He left the grenade handle pointing downward, held against the deck by the weight of the unit, and then taped the grenade handle to the deck so it wouldn't fly off and alert the terrorists when they lifted the units. Finally, he had pulled the pins.

Santos waited out of sight. He feared the booby traps would be seen and had pressed the hijackers hard down the stairwell to keep them distracted. If the remaining man did disarm the trap, Santos intended to charge forward as he splashed into the water and rain the remaining grenades down on him.

Santos flinched at the explosion and then raced past the blackened remains of the sea scooter to where Sheibani lay unmoving. His upper body was intact, shielded by the heavy body of the scooter, but both legs were severed above the knees. Bright arterial blood pumped from the stumps and puddled on the deck. Sheibani groaned.

Santos squatted, bringing his face close.

"Can you hear, you fatherless son of a whore?" Santos asked.

Sheibani nodded.

"Then know this is for the men you murdered today." Santos spit in Sheibani's face.

The Iranian looked up with a mocking grin as spittle ran down his cheek.

"And this," Santos whispered, rising and unzipping, "is from their families. Do you think Allah will gather you into Paradise reeking of piss?"

Sheibani's smile vanished as urine stung his eyes.

***

Santos sat in bloody coveralls, staring at the body, hugging his knees, and crying. Tears of mourning for his family, friends, and shipmates. Tears of release from terror. But mainly tears of relief that when the mothers and fathers and women and children of his shipmates mourned their men, they would know their men had been avenged, and that Benjamin Honesto Santos had not hidden like a frightened rabbit, waiting to testify.

***

The chopper hovered, its occupants staring down at the sobbing man. They had arrived in time to watch in shocked silence as the scene played out below them.

"Who the hell is that guy?" the pilot asked.

"I don't know his name yet," Broussard said, "but he's my new best friend."

"Amen to that," Vega said.

CHAPTER NINETEEN

Ward pulled into his parking spot. Traffic before daylight on a holiday had been almost nonexistent, but he knew that would change. If he didn't get home ahead of the jam sure to follow the Fourth of July parade, his ass would be in a crack. He smiled as he got out and headed into the building; after twenty years of long hours and blown holidays, the "I'm busy saving the world" excuse no longer cut much ice with Dee Dee.

Brice had few details when he'd called earlier. He'd promised Ward an e-mail update as soon as he learned more. True to his word, Ward found an e-mail waiting. Christ. Twenty-four dead seamen. Four survivors. Two wounded. Ten dead bad guys, but no one to interrogate. None of it made sense. Ward picked up the phone.

"Jim Brice."

"Jim. Jesse Ward."

"I've been expecting your call," Brice said. "It's confusing as hell, isn't it?"

"I'll say. It looks like it was over before we got there," Ward said.

"Essentially it was," Brice said. "The bad guys murdered most of the crew, and the four survivors took out the bad guys with an able assist from our surveillance chopper."

"Political fallout?"

"I think we dodged a bullet," Brice said. "Captain Leary was masterful. He planted the seed with his Indonesian counterpart on the exercise that Jakarta was unlikely to throw bouquets to anyone who got them involved. Simultaneously, he got the Singaporeans to convince the Malaysians it would be a coup if they saved the day. When the Indonesian waffled about *China Star*'s position, the Malaysian promptly agreed she was in Malaysian waters and accepted Leary's offer of choppers for a boarding party of Malaysian marines. Leary then arranged a tow to the anchorage off Jurong, where the Singaporeans will fend off the press and sequester survivors."

Ward smiled. "Good for him. I guess he's still in the running for an admiral's star then. But tell me, how is it two explosive-laden boats blow up against a loaded tanker and only leave a dent and scratch the paint?"

"Only way we can figure," Brice said, "is that the boats held shape charges directed back on the boats themselves, away from the ship. We'll know more when forensics gets through with the pieces of the boats we salvaged."

"Strange."

"That's not the half of it, Jesse. What I didn't put in the report, because I just found out, was the composition of the assault team."

"Go on."

"Three Burmese rent-a-thugs," Brice said, "and four Indonesian villagers longing for Paradise. It's the remaining three that are interesting. One was the ex–chief mate off *Alicia* and the guy that masterminded the hijacking of the boats. Broussard and Vega ID'd him, but we have no idea who he really is. Then there's a rogue American named Richards: ex–US Army, ex–private-security contractor, in our files as a known bad actor. We used him on some low-level stuff a time or two, but he was way too volatile and unstable. He was cut off the company Christmas-card list some time ago." Brice hesitated.

"You're one short," Ward prompted.

"Yeah, the last guy could be a problem. Yousif Nassir Hamad AKA Joe Hamad, Ensign USNR. The cream of the latest crop of NROTC graduates, allegedly on compassionate leave in Dearborn, Michigan."

"Oh shit," Ward said.

"Shit is right. This kid's the poster child for Arab-American assimilation. The navy was ready to put his picture on recruiting posters." Brice paused. "Like I said. A problem."

"You got a solution?" Ward asked.

"We're working on it."

"Need any help?" Ward asked.

"We're good. But we'd like the body to stay 'unidentified' a while. Do what you can to make sure no one at Langley gets hot to trot to run down the identities of every single assailant. I need a little breathing room here."

"Done," Ward said and wished Brice luck.

***

Three hours later, Ward was still at his desk, trying to piece together the strange parts of the puzzle. Should he call Gardner? He didn't look forward to that conversation. Ward smiled. Screw it. He'd been right about *China Star*, so Gardner couldn't come down too hard. And since his boss was going to be pissed anyway, he might as well combine the chewing out for disobeying orders along with one for failing to keep Gardner informed. Two transgressions for the price of one.

Ward glanced at the time and shut down his computer. He might have time to get home and spend the afternoon hosting his holiday cookout before he got an irate call from Gardner. That would get Dee Dee off his back, at least.

Ward was locking his door when Gardner appeared.

"Where the hell do you think you're going?"

"Home," Ward said.

"Not before we talk. I'll call you in when I'm ready." Gardner stomped off without waiting for a reply.

Ward glared at Gardner's back.

***

As it turned out, Gardner did get a call—from the deputy director of the CIA. The Old Man received a morning briefing report 365 days a year. In a slight nod toward relaxation, on holidays he delayed perusing the report until after a late breakfast and most of a pot of coffee, but when something attracted the Old Man's interest, he inquired. *China Star* qualified.

Blindsided, Gardner had panicked at mention of *China Star*, weighing his options. Just before he threw Ward under the bus, the Old Man offered a gruff "well done."

"Just doing our job, sir," Gardner had replied before a polite good-bye.

He was enraged at Ward's disobedience, all the more so since the man had apparently been right. His first instinct was to pick up the phone, but he quickly had second thoughts. If he could get into the office and ahead of Ward on the information curve, maybe he could paint Ward as out of touch and not doing his job. He might not be able to openly punish the man for disobeying orders, but there was more than one way to skin a cat.

Gardner's plan had fallen apart when he found Ward in the office. His only outlet for petty retribution was to keep Ward waiting as he skimmed the intel from Singapore and simmered. After a cursory review, he decided to kill a bit more time by checking his e-mail, and his eyes were drawn to a flashing "high priority" icon. As he read the message, his frown morphed into a smile. He printed the e-mail and punched his speed dial.

"Ward. Get in here."

***

Ward controlled his anger as Gardner waved him to a chair.

"So, you were right," Gardner said. "I guess even a blind pig finds the odd acorn."

You're welcome, asshole, Ward thought.

"But don't go getting too smug"—Gardner shoved a paper across the desk—"because your instincts about Dugan are a bit further off the mark."

Ward studied the printout detailing transfer of a million dollars through several accounts with terrorist associations into and out of a new Cayman Island account, held by a series of dummy corporations and trusts that led back to Thomas Dugan.

"Dugan's under financial surveillance?"

"You're god damned right," Gardner said.

"Larry, we've had his financials forever. Dugan's not for sale, and if he was, it'd take a lot more than this. This is chump change."

Gardner scoffed. "So someone wasted a million bucks to set up your buddy?"

"Not really. The money's gone. What's that tell you?"

"That Dugan's smart. He made it disappear."

"Yet dumb enough to leave a trail in the first place? I don't think so, Larry."

"Whatever. Dugan and Kairouz are still our prime suspects. Clear?"

"Crystal," Ward said.

"Good. Get out." Gardner shut down his computer as Ward rose.

"Wait a minute," Gardner said. "Where's your pal now? I don't want him to disappear."

Ward stifled his anger and looked at his watch. "He's on his way to Panama. He's not going to disappear."

"Whatever. At least the asshole is out of the way for a while." Gardner also checked the time. "I'll be at the parade," Gardner said. "Senator Gunther invited me to sit with him on the reviewing stand. Call me if there are any developments."

Ward nodded and walked down the hall, dreaming of putting a bullet into Gardner's head.

CHAPTER TWENTY

JUDICIAL INVESTIGATIVE DIRECTORY HQ
PANAMA CITY, PANAMA
4 JULY

Reyes hung up the phone. Something was very strange. *Asian Trader* hadn't delayed on the Pacific side even long enough to off-load the dead seaman's body. A death at sea was traumatic for all concerned, and usually the company involved was eager to land the remains and put the event behind them. The ship's agent had also seemed surprised, saying only that he was following orders from a Señor Dugan that nothing should prevent the ship from meeting her priority transit slot.

Given the accelerated transit, Reyes had expected pushback when he told the agent that since *Asian Trader* wouldn't anchor at Cristobal until early evening, the inquiry would start the following morning in daylight. The agent had seemed unconcerned, allowing that was expected, and in any event, Señor Dugan himself would attend the inquiry and was not arriving until later this evening.

Now why would an owner pay dearly for early transit and then so easily accept delay? He had many questions for this Señor Dugan. But that was tomorrow.

He looked at the stack in his in-box and sighed. He'd actually been looking forward to getting out of the office for a while. He glanced at the time and considered calling Maria to meet him for lunch later. Then he remembered. She was helping with the field trip to the locks today. He smiled as he remembered the twins' excited chatter at breakfast about seeing the big ships.

His smile faded as he looked back at the in-box. He sighed again and picked up a file.

OBSERVATION DECK
MIRAFLORES LOCKS VISITOR CENTER
PANAMA

"*Aiee! Miguelito. Cuidado.*" Maria Reyes grabbed her son. "No climbing. That means you too, Paco," she added to his brother about to join his twin on the rail.

"*Si, Mama,*" said the boys in sullen unison before the ship in the lock recaptured their attention. Maria smiled and stepped back where she could keep an eye on all the children.

The passengers on the big white ship waved back at the excited children until the vessel moved away toward Pedro Miguel, replaced by a container ship, stacked high with colored boxes. With a mother's eye, Maria noticed the onset of boredom as here and there children began to act out. She grabbed a boy racing by, hugging him close.

"Is this Alejandro I have captured, running when he knows not to do so?"

"*No, señora,*" the boy said with an impish grin.

"You are not Alejandro? You look just like him. Well, if you see him, please remind him not to run."

"*Si, señora,*" said not-Alejandro.

"Good." She released him with a playful swat. "Behave yourself and earn a treat."

As not-Alejandro spread news of treats, Maria glanced at Señora Fuentes, who mimed eating. Maria nodded and herded the children toward the stairs. She hoped they liked her cookies. She knew two of them would. She smiled as she watched her sons, little copies of their father. If Manny returned from Cristobal early, she thought, they might work on their little "project." A daughter would be nice this time.

M/T ASIAN TRADER
APPROACHING PEDRO MIGUEL LOCK
PANAMA

The detonator felt heavy in Medina's pocket as *Asian Trader* stood second in line at Pedro Miguel Lock, ships stretched behind her through Miraflores back to the Pacific. He watched the gates close on the leader, a tanker whose bright paint marked her as fresh from the builder's yard, and glared at the American flag hanging limp above the name M/T *Luther Hurd* painted on her stern.

The captain relayed an engine order from the pilot, and Medina moved the joystick, inching *Asian Trader*'s port side along the center guide wall projecting from between the double locks. Heaving lines flew to drag aboard wires to attach the ship to the mechanical "mules" that would pull her through the lock, and Medina watched the *Luther Hurd* complete her vertical journey and inch from the lock ahead of them toward Gaillard Cut and Gatun Lake beyond.

Allah had been generous since the bosun's death, cooling the deck with daily showers, but today the sun hammered the steel, and Medina worried about fumes. His target was Gatun Locks across Gatun Lake, where even a blast failing to breach the lock could destroy several ships and plug the locks with scrap. His secondary target was here at Pedro Miguel, which like the upper lock at Gatun, held back the lake. Destruction of either would drain the lake and destroy the canal, with catastrophic secondary damage. Allah guide me, Medina prayed as the ship inched forward amid clanging bells, the mules tugging her into the lock.

CRUISE SHIP *STELLAR SPIRIT*

The second mate of *Stellar Spirit* stood among the passengers lining the rail as a tanker crept into the east lock and his own ship prepared to enter the west. Mingling was required of the ship's officers, not a chore on "fun runs" with willing young females eager for romance, but deadly dull on canal runs populated by oldsters and honeymooners who surfaced only for meals. The newly wed and the nearly dead, he thought, looking over gray heads to the gates closing behind *Asian Trader* as he debated slipping away.

M/T ASIAN TRADER
IN PEDRO MIGUEL LOCK, PANAMA

In the end, Medina's decision was made for him.

"Bridge, this is the bow," squawked the radio. "I smell strong gasoline fumes, repeat, strong gasoline fumes on deck. Over."

Medina pulled his gun and was moving even before the control pilot keyed his radio to respond, rushing to the port bridge wing to shoot both the control pilot and captain in the head before returning to the wheelhouse to meet the confused assisting control pilot coming in from the starboard wing. He ended the man's confusion with a bullet. The terrified helmsman fled the wheelhouse, down the outside stairs. Medina didn't bother to chase him. He was calm now as he returned to the starboard wing, sure that when the people of his grandfather's village spoke now, it would be of Saful, Sword of Islam, not Faatina, Whore of the Infidel.

"Allahuuuuu Akbaaaaar!" he screamed as he thumbed the remote.

***

The blast was beyond imagination, amplified by Medina's design. Twelve blasts actually, grouped in pairs and separated by milliseconds, starting aft to build into a directional force, battering the gates that held the lake at bay.

The canal's designers were no strangers to redundancy, and the locks had double, massively overdesigned gates, the twin leaves of each mitered pair meeting in a point upstream so the weight of water pressed them closed as a lock drained. A good design, but unequal to a blast of near nuclear strength. The gates crumpled like tinfoil and ripped free, their useless remains undulating in the rushing torrent, impeded only by the debris from *Asian Trader*.

Constrained by the lock walls and the incompressible water beneath the ship, the blast forced an escape upward, ripping the entire cargo-tank section free of the ballast tanks and tossing it into the air to crash down at an angle, one end landing on *Asian Trader's* bow and the other on *Stellar Spirit* as the passenger ship nosed into the western lock. Checked at either end but unsupported in the middle, the cargo section split like an overripe fruit, ruptured tanks gushing tons of gasoline into the torrent now rushing through the open lock.

In the lock, watertight integrity vanished from *Asian Trader's* battered remains as the forward collision bulkhead collapsed into the forepeak tank, and her after pump-room machinery was driven through the engine-room bulkhead. She sank, pushed by the torrent as she settled but restrained by remnants of the outer hull blasted tight against the lock walls. The steel screamed like a living thing as it yielded, a huge friction brake holding the mass upright as it settled to the lock floor.

The end of the ruptured cargo block resting on *Asian Trader's* bow dropped as the bow sank beneath it until the middle of the cargo block rested on the wall separating the locks. There the section teetered, the high end on *Stellar Spirit*, the middle on the wall between the locks, and the low end dangling unsupported over the ruined lock, as spilled gasoline ignited, turning the entire scene into a maelstrom and sucking air from passengers still alive deep in the cruise ship. The flames rushed southward on the flood, a fiery wall of death moving toward Miraflores, Balboa, and the wide Pacific beyond.

M/T *Luther Hurd*
Gaillard Cut
North of Pedro Miguel Lock
Panama

"Christ. What was that?" asked Captain Vince Blake as he hung on the windowsill and stared out through the cracked glass of the bridge windows. The pilot shook his head and raced to the wing, Blake on his heels. Blake could see men down on *Luther Hurd*'s bow, some beginning to stir. He moved to the back of the bridge wing and saw a similar scene on the stern.

"Everyone's down," Blake said, "will you take the conn while I organize help?"

"Do it," the pilot said, moving to the opposite wing as Blake raced to the phone.

"Engine Room. Chief," Jim Milam answered.

"You OK down there, Chief?"

"I think so. What happened, Cap?"

"Explosion ashore. The mate's down on the bow, and I can't see the second. We're in the cut, and I can't leave the bridge. Can you—"

"We're on it," Milam said.

"Thanks, Jim," Blake said, hanging up to join the pilot on the starboard wing.

He followed the pilot's gaze ashore, confused.

"We've slowed down?"

The pilot shook his head. "There's a current," he said, pointing at eddies and flotsam moving along the bank.

Oh shit, Blake thought.

"Full ahead," the pilot said.

"Full ahead," Blake relayed the order to the third mate at the joystick.

The pilot stared ahead, fear in his eyes.

Miraflores Locks Visitor Center

Maria pushed herself up from the sun-heated tiles, relief washing over her at the sight of her sons nearby, stunned and crying but unhurt. Señora Fuentes's timing had been fortunate, placing them in the patio area behind the building before the blast. The teacher herself was less so. She lay on the tile in a growing circle of blood, the back of her head smashed on the corner of a concrete bench. Maria fought down panic and crossed herself before closing the teacher's sightless eyes.

The other mothers had recovered and were calming the terrified children, dabbing at scrapes with napkins wet with bottled water. Outside their sheltered corner, the ground was dotted with bodies and sparkled with broken glass. A big blond man staggered onto the bridge wing of the ship in the lock and peered upstream.

Suddenly, Maria stood in water and the man screamed, pointing as she splashed from her corner to look. Water poured over the lock gate. What didn't fall into the lock fanned out in shallow waves, lapping at buildings to slosh back and fall into the lock from the sides. Mule wires moaned as the ship rose, operators dead or unconscious, unable to slack the wires. One by one, the mules were pulled from their tracks and overturned. Upstream, beyond the colored boxes of a container ship, she saw a yellow blur.

"Fire!" the blond man screamed. "Go inside! High! Away from the windows!"

Maria called to Isobel and Juanita, and the three mothers started the group up the outside steps to the observation deck, Maria clutching her boys' hands as she brought up the rear, counting heads. The first level was littered with bodies and glass crunched underfoot as the mothers ignored scattered moans and herded their charges upward. They had to save the children.

The children were all crying by the time they reached the next level. Maria could feel the heat.

"No time to go higher," she shouted, trying a door. "We must get inside!"

The door was locked. The building was controlled access with entrance from the ground floor only. Doors relocked behind people as they exited to the observation decks at each level.

"The toilets," she yelled, and the women herded the children toward three doors near the end of the observation deck.

"There is no room," Maria said as the other mothers divided the children between the two small restrooms. "I will put my boys in the janitor's closet."

Isobel nodded as the door closed, and Maria was left alone with her sons. She dragged them to the tiny closet, faint with relief to find a janitor's sink filling the small space. She lifted her boys into the big sink and turned on the cold water, stilling their protests with slaps.

"Listen to me," she said. "Do not turn the water off. Keep your heads under and only stick your noses out. Understand?"

"Don't leave, *Mama*," Paco pleaded.

"If I stay, we cannot close the door. I'll be fine with the others," she lied. "Remember I love you, *hijos*," she added softly.

"*Si, Mama*," the boys sobbed as she closed the door.

God, protect my sons, she prayed, moving through the heat.

"Your boys aren't here," Juanita said as Maria pushed in. "They must be in the other toilet with Isobel."

Maria forced a smile and prayed God would forgive her for putting her own children in a more sheltered location. "Yes, but there's no more room there," she lied. "I'm your new roommate."

Juanita nodded as Maria fished out her cell phone—to find it dead. An image flashed of Manny chiding her for not keeping her battery charged. Oh *Mi Amor*, she thought, I hope you know what a wonderful life you have given me.

"Do you have your cell?" she asked Juanita.

Juanita shook her head. "I left my purse in the excitement."

Maria nodded as the roar and heat increased.

"Oh Maria, what can we do?" Juanita asked.

"It's in God's hands, Juanita," Maria said. "We should pray."

Juanita nodded, unable to speak, as Maria turned to the children.

"Children, we will talk to God. Please hold hands and help each other be brave."

They joined hands as she prayed. *"Padre nuestro que estas en el cielo, santificado…"*

CNN CENTER
ATLANTA, GEORGIA

The blast enlivened a slow news day in the US with newsrooms on holiday staffing. In moments, a CNN staffer discovered the Internet camera feed from the Canal Authority, with real-time photos of ships in transit. Five minutes later, he dreamed of a bonus as he e-mailed photos of the final feed of the Centennial Bridge camera: one of a man on the bridge of the M/T *Asian Trader,* mouth open in a shout, a gun in one hand and a remote in the other; the second showed the explosion. The photos were aired in two minutes flat, and within five, all the networks had them. Talking heads speculated, and executives screamed at people to get some goddamned facts or to make them up if necessary.

PEDRO MIGUEL LOCK
PANAMA

Breach of an upper lock was an event long feared, for the canal's designers had respect for the forces of God and nature, an outlook validated just months before the canal's opening when the "unsinkable" Titanic plunged to the bottom. But fears faded with decades of safe operation until they seemed as quaint as high button shoes. Gone were safety chains to restrain runaway ships, removed in 1980 in admission that ships were now so big as to make them useless. Eliminated earlier were the emergency dams meant to seal a breach; removed in the fifties after years of disuse. Only the double gates had survived, now blasted to scrap; for what design could anticipate the deluded fanaticism of *Jihad*?

***

The chopper hovered above Pedro Miguel as Juan Antonio Rojas, administrator of the Autoridad del Canal de Panama, watched gasoline drain from wrecked tanks, not a gush now but gurgling belches as air bubbled up to break vacuums. Each burp flared, but the gas burned near the source now, with only scattered islands of flame floating southward.

"It's burning out," he said into his mike.

"I pray you're right," said Pedro Calderon, ACP operations manager, from the seat behind Rojas.

"How fast are we losing the lake?" Rojas asked.

"Hard to say," Calderon said. "I'll know more after the next depth reading, but the lake was already low. If that plug fails…" He pointed at the wreckage partially blocking the lock.

As if in response, gasoline gushed anew from the ruined tanks, sending up a fireball and disturbing a precarious balance. For the ruptured tanks had not disgorged their contents evenly, and most of the gasoline remaining in the mangled mass was trapped in the lower, unsupported end. As the last of the cargo drained from the higher end, the cargo block pivoted on the central lock wall like a huge seesaw, the lighter end rising from *Stellar Spirit* as the lower end dipped toward the waters of the lock. The upper end of the cargo block was inches off the cruise ship when the fire-weakened steel buckled in the middle, dropping the higher end back down across *Stellar Spirit* as the lower end plunged into the lock. Water rose behind the new obstacle, forcing it down the lock and tearing it free of the remaining wreckage ashore. At the moment of separation, the portion of the cargo block in the lock shifted, filling the lock wall to wall as it slammed into the face of the ruined deckhouse.

***

The men in the chopper watched helplessly as the cargo section hit the deckhouse and shifted it several feet, then in grateful amazement as the water compacted the mass. Water gushed through in a dozen places and ran over the top inches deep on either side of the deckhouse, but the debris was damming the flood more effectively than before.

"*Gracias a Dios,*" Rojas whispered. "It holds."

"*Y Jesus y Jose y Maria,*" Calderon added as he crossed himself.

"Move over Miraflores," Rojas ordered the pilot, and in moments they were there.

Water swirled over the locks and down the slope a foot deep, carrying pools of burning gasoline, the flames dancing over the new rapids and around overturned mules on the lock walls as if they were rocks in a river roaring out of Hell. The operations building and visitors center smoldered, and a blackened container ship bobbed in a lock, surging against the gates astern in great hollow booms. But even as they watched, the flow ebbed and soon barely overtopped the complex.

"Get men here by chopper," Rojas ordered. "If we crack open the lock valves, we can drain off the water upstream from below the surface and contain floating gasoline north of Miraflores."

As Calderon spoke into his radio, Rojas looked southward. Gasoline burned in places, and nearby was a burning hulk, her bow hard aground, the first ship to meet the flames south of Miraflores. Faced with certain death, the pilot had warned those behind and bought them time by swinging his ship across the canal like a gate, slowing the flames and preventing his ship from drifting down on Balboa like a flaming battering ram.

Nor was that pilot the only hero, Rojas thought, squinting downstream where the busy docks were unharmed. After the pilots had turned their ships, they released their tugs to speed seaward under ships' power. The masters of the freed tugs had taken initiative, nosing into the bank at strategic points and using their propeller wash to divert the fire from the docks at Balboa, La Boca, and Rodman across the harbor.

"A crew is on the way, *jefe,*" Calderon said. "I should return to the operations center."

"One stop more," Rojas said. "Gatun Locks," he said to the pilot.

"So, old friend," Rojas said as they flew north, "how long will the miracle hold?"

Calderon shrugged. "An hour… or a year. It's in God's hands."

Rojas nodded and fell silent until they hovered over Gatun Locks.

"I ordered everything out of the lake," Calderon said. "Seven client vessels came up from Cristobal before the attack. We will send them back down to Cristobal, along with the one northbound vessel that reached the lake. Eight ships total."

"Priorities?"

"Two tankers and three container ships all laden and with no way to reduce their drafts will go first. Then two passenger ships, with a tanker in ballast last. We'll get the deep-loaded vessels over the sill of the upper lock while we still have water. We'll lighten the others in the lake if necessary."

"The ballasted tanker is the new American ship?"

"*Si*. Her maiden voyage."

"Is that her?" Rojas pointed.

"*Si*," Calderon said, and Rojas motioned the pilot to circle the anchorage.

"So, Pedro. Who, do you think, was *El Señor Luther Hurd*?"

"No idea, *jefe*," Calderon said.

"Nor do I," Rojas said, "but perhaps we can make him famous. Leave the *yanqui* in the lake. I have an idea."

CHAPTER TWENTY-ONE

The photos on Ward's monitor seemed as unreal now as when they'd flashed on TV, prompting his return to work. Gardner had called to vent outrage Ward hadn't notified him immediately, hanging up as soon as he learned what little Ward knew. Ward knew little more now, hours later. The focus now was on Panama, but the spotlight would swing his way soon enough; and the spotlight was a bad place for a spook with no answers. He lifted the phone.

"Carlucci."

"Frank, Jesse Ward."

"Well," said Frank Carlucci, Panama Station Chief, "one of three people at HQ who hasn't called, besides the janitor and the snack-bar lady. How may I disappoint you?"

"That bad, huh?"

Carlucci sighed. "You don't wanna know."

"Yeah, I do. Can you update me?"

"Jesus H. Christ. Didn't that pompous asshole you work for fill you in? I spent twenty minutes answering his dumb-ass questions. Don't you people talk?"

"Gardner? When?"

"Over two hours ago," Carlucci said.

Ward stopped, embarrassed.

"Ah… I'm sorry, Frank. Could you…"

Carlucci relented. "OK, Jesse. The short version: Five ships toast, one a cruise ship, everyone dead. All three Pacific locks out of commission, with all ACP personnel dead. A hundred visitors at a visitors center, including a school group, all presumed dead. A bunch of American expats missing from a barbecue at Pedro Miguel Boat Club. Hospitals swamped with related casualties. The death toll is a guess. Pedro Miguel lock is breached but partially plugged by debris, and they're losing the lake. A total disaster."

"Shit," Ward said. "OK. I'm on the way. Keep Dugan with you when he arrives."

"Who?"

Christ. Gardner didn't tell him. Ward summarized the operation.

Carlucci exploded. "You knew about this and didn't warn us!"

"No, we didn't know. Look, Frank, it's a long story. I'll explain when I arrive."

"I hope you know what you're doin' here, Jesse."

Yeah, me too, Ward thought.

MIRAFLORES PALACE
CARACAS, VENEZUELA

Rodriguez awoke, savoring the silk sheets and Eva's skin as she lay atop him, tense and unmoving. He slapped the teenager's butt, laughing as she flinched.

"You let me oversleep. I should imprison you for treason." He chuckled as she leaped up, trembling.

He was still smiling minutes later as he entered his spacious outer office, gesturing to his secretary for coffee before nodding to his waiting chief of staff, who followed Rodriguez into his private office.

"What news?" Rodriguez asked, thumbing the TV remote.

"Excellency, there have been… developments…"

Rodriguez shushed him and raised the volume as scenes of devastation filled the screen.

"…over five thousand dead, including passengers of a cruise ship. Photos obtained by CNN show the attacker moments before the blast." A photo of a man with upraised arms appeared. "…unconfirmed reports of a link to a similar attempt yesterday near Singapore…"

"This is a disaster! Why was I not informed immediately?" Rodriguez screamed.

"Forgive me, Excellency. But I have strict orders not to disturb your… *siestas*."

"Could you not see this was an exception, imbecile?"

"I was not sure—"

"Out! Everyone out!" Rodriguez screamed as his coffee arrived, and his terrified secretary fled with the chief of staff, clutching the undelivered coffee.

His mind raced. If he was exposed, who knew what the Americans or Chinese might do. The Chinese might even be the greater threat, since any retaliation would likely be blamed on the Americans. He took the sat phone from a drawer, his single link to Braun. He smiled as his rage subsided and summoned his chief of staff.

"Come in, Geraldo," Rodriguez said agreeably as the man returned, still shaking.

"Destroy this phone within the hour and incinerate the debris. Also, due to the tragedy, our own Independence Day celebration tomorrow will be muted. Cancel the fireworks and other events. I will speak of our shared sorrow and announce the money saved will be added to our Panamanian Relief Fund."

"But Excellency, the money is spent. There will be no savings."

"Nor is there a relief fund, you idiot." Rodriguez shook his head at the man's inability to grasp the nuance of diplomacy.

OFFICES OF PHOENIX SHIPPING

"Hello," Basaev said in Paris.

"It's a go. Good luck," Braun said.

"Understood," Basaev said and hung up.

Braun was improvising in response to the unexpected. *China Star* was in Singapore, and coverage was limited while Panama dominated the news. Blow-dried anchormen had descended on the isthmus and hired every available helicopter at exorbitant rates, screaming "cover-up" at the Panamanian authorities' fruitless efforts to restrict air traffic over the canal. But things weren't all negative. The Black Sea vessel had berthed at last, allowing him to unleash Basaev. He just needed to wind things up while his luck still held.

He studied a CD, a dialogue pieced together from recordings of Rodriguez, Dugan, and Kairouz, with Rodriguez detailing the attacks and the others agreeing. Initially he'd been concerned with the focus on Panama, for Rodriguez talked of little else and he had to use what he had, but the unexpected severity of the Panamanian attack strengthened the ruse. The recording would be more credible still when Kairouz confirmed it, on pain of unspeakable horrors to befall Cassie. Things were coming together despite the unexpected.

He tapped out a message to Motaki.

RECENT EVENTS NO PROBLEM. FINAL PHASE INITIATED. TIDYING UP.

He encrypted the message and piggybacked it on to the porn-site video, then lingered on the site, aroused. He hated to celebrate alone. Perhaps sweet little Yvette had recovered.

PRESIDENTIAL RESIDENCE
TEHRAN, IRAN
0130 HOURS LOCAL TIME
5 JULY

Motaki stared at the monitor, bleary-eyed. US markets were closed for the holiday, and it was after market hours in Europe and Asia, but from Toronto to Sao Paulo gold and oil spiked. The panic was sure to roil Asian markets at the open. But where was Sheibani, and why was there no coverage of *China Star*? And more to the point, would the unintended disaster in Panama heighten global security and jeopardize the final strike?

He calmed himself. Everything was Allah's will. Panama was necessary to recruit Rodriguez, who provided Braun, who so cleverly blinded the infidels to Iran's role. Motaki slipped a hardware key into a port to allow access to his office e-mail. He expected the spam message but rose to ensure none of his sleeping family stirred before accessing the porn site.

He read Braun's message with relief. Soon now, he thought, glancing at the time. He wouldn't wait up for the Asian markets. He needed his rest.

HOSPITAL DEL NIÑOS
PANAMA CITY, PANAMA

Doctors scurried by, heads bent in urgent exchanges, struggling with disaster beyond even the worst postulated by planners of never-held emergency drills. Reyes reentered the room he'd fled when Miguelito had stirred and cried for Maria. Telling the boys terrified him because first he must accept it himself, abandoning the lies he'd told himself when he couldn't reach her. But truth lay nearby in a makeshift morgue.

He met the sad gazes of his parents and in-laws. One grandmother sat at each bedside, holding the boys' hands as the men stood nearby quiet in their grief. Reyes's mother rose and took his face between her hands.

"You should rest, *hijo*. We will call if the little ones wake."

Reyes shook his head. "There is no rest for me, *Mama*."

"I know, *hijo*, I know. But you need this time to grieve. The boys need your strength."

Reyes folded her in a hug, then nodded and left. He was near the visitors lounge, crowded with people glued to a TV, when he heard his name.

"Manuel," Maria's father said, hurrying after him. "Do you know yet who did this?"

He shook his head. "No. I left the office when—"

He stared past his father-in-law and charged into the lounge to the TV.

"…confirmed the explosion of the M/T *Asian Trader* was the work of a suicide bomber, as shown in this photo obtained by CNN. At present, no group has claimed responsi—"

Reyes stared. After the blast, the search for his family had taken precedence. Only now did he hear the familiar name. He ran for the stairs.

BEIJING, PEOPLE'S REPUBLIC OF CHINA

President Zhang Wei waited until the steward poured tea and bowed from the room.

"So, gentlemen. What of these attacks?"

"They seem linked," Premier Wang Fei said.

"But motives are unclear," added Li Gang, Minister for State Security. "Malacca alone could be a US ruse to justify increased US Navy presence in the strait, but Panama makes no sense in that context."

Wang nodded. "We must consider it. Your instructions, Mr. President?"

"Tread cautiously," Zhang said. "Offer Panama our help while assuring the US our help is based on mutual interest and not to exert influence. The lie will be recognized, but reducing the burden on US taxpayers will make it palatable. Simultaneously, signal our resolve to protect our own interests in the Malacca Straits by rotating our new destroyers through to visit our friends in Myanmar on a regular basis."

"At once, Mr. President," Wang said. "Further thoughts?"

"Just one," Zhang said. "Not so very long ago, our Venezuelan friend petitioned us to lend financial support to a second canal in Nicaragua. As I recall, one of his main arguments was that it would reduce our vulnerability to trade disruption at Panama." He paused. "President Rodriguez was quite prescient, it seems."

"Almost clairvoyant," Wang agreed.

"Explore that," President Zhang said.

GARDNER RESIDENCE
ALEXANDRIA, VIRGINIA

Gardner cursed the Panamanians. He was on hold. Christ, what a day. He was at post-parade drinks at the Gunthers' when the news hit. He'd immediately called the DDCI and volunteered to "coordinate intelligence." That had backfired. Ward had been useless, and that territorial asshole Carlucci in Panama was worse. First he copped an attitude, and then tried a brush-off.

Gardner had soldiered on, working from home to dress up what little he knew into some semblance of a briefing. Then after all that, the Old Man rejected his offer of a personal Power Point presentation, insisting on a phone report—a mediocre recitation at best, and one it seemed the DDCI had already heard.

"Thanks, son," the Old Man said when he finished. "What's Ward's ETA in Panama?"

Carlucci had sandbagged him, obviously with Ward in on it. Blindsided, he'd played along. "This evening, sir. I'll call back with an updated ETA."

"Unnecessary. Just inform me of anything significant."

He'd found himself listening to a dial tone.

Ward left without so much as a "by-your-leave," and everyone knew but him. And Ward was apparently still unconvinced Dugan was dirty, even after finding the offshore account and the ship he was babysitting in Singapore blew up. Just how many "coincidences" was Ward going to swallow? And now the insubordinate bastard wasn't answering his phone.

Gardner fumed for hours, racking his brain for ways to reestablish control. He had to be careful though. Dugan's involvement was a problem. He'd documented his own suspicions of Dugan by initiating the financial probe, but he hadn't overridden Ward about involving Dugan in the first place, so he wasn't completely in the clear. It could get even messier if Ward continued to insist on the traitor's innocence. What was required was a clear, unambiguous confession, sooner rather than later.

Inspiration came after his third Glenfiddich. All it took was a word to the Panamanians. When Dugan confessed, Gardner's doubts were on record. If he didn't—well, Gardner could hardly be held responsible for the excesses of foreign police.

He smiled and poured another scotch, thinking pleasant thoughts as he waited.

***

Like everyone in Panama, Sergeant Juan Perez was working late, trying to wrest order from the chaos. He looked down at the flashing button on his phone, surprised at the gringo's persistence. He'd classified this Gardner as an asshole about ten seconds into the first call and lapsed into Spanish before hanging up. When multiple hang-ups failed to discourage him, Perez put him on "perpetual hold." True, it tied up one of his lines, but he had three and could only talk on one at a time anyway.

Perez looked up as Captain Luna emerged from his office, pointed at his watch, and mimed eating. Perez nodded and stood, giving his phone one last look before leaving. Perhaps the gringo asshole would give up before he returned from dinner.

***

Reyes waited outside until Captain Luna and Juan Perez left for dinner. He wanted no awkward condolences and feared he might be sent home. The squad room fell quiet as he entered, warning his colleagues away with body language and a grim face.

As he sat, he noticed the blinking "hold" light on one of the lines he shared with Perez.

"*Teniente Reyes. Quien habla?*"

"You speak English?" a voice blurted, obviously startled.

"Yes, I speak English. This is Lieutenant Reyes. Who is this?"

"Gardner, Lieutenant. Lawrence Gardner. I'm with the Central Intelligence Agency in Washington. I have confidential information regarding the *Asian Trader* situation."

Reyes bristled. Not a "situation," gringo. Murder. Who was this drunken asshole?

"Information, *señor*?"

"A man named Thomas Dugan arrives there this evening. You should question him."

Reyes sat bolt upright.

"Interesting, *señor*," he said. "This implies advanced knowledge of the attack, yet we had no warning from the CIA." His words held unmistakable menace.

"We knew nothing of the attack," Gardner sputtered, "but Dugan works for us. I mean he's supposed to, but I… that is, some of us… feel he's been turned. A great deal of money recently appeared in his offshore account, and he supervised repairs to *Asian Trader* in Singapore last month."

Gardner lowered his voice. "Please understand. Not everyone agrees with me. I'm warning you as a brother in arms. I appreciate your discretion."

"I will treat you as a confidential informant," Reyes lied.

"Thank you," Gardner said, relief in his voice.

"On the contrary, *señor*, thank you."

Reyes hung up without waiting for a response and thumbed through his notebook for Dugan's flight number and arrival time.

CHAPTER TWENTY-TWO

IBERIA AIRLINES FLIGHT 6307
APPROACHING PANAMA CITY, PANAMA
2125 HOURS LOCAL TIME
4 JULY

Lights brightened and Dugan stirred, trying to focus on the announcement.

"…attack. The airport is closed. We are cleared to refuel and will depart for Miami, where agents will meet us. Nonresidents attempting to deplane here will be reboarded."

A stewardess knelt beside him. "*Señor Dugan*?"

He nodded.

"You are to deplane. You will be met."

Met by whom, he wondered minutes later in the immigration line.

"*Señor Dugan*," a big man said, taking Dugan's passport. "Come with me please."

"What's this about?" Dugan asked as he complied.

The man slammed Dugan against a wall and cuffed him, before dragging him toward an exit. A man approached, speaking unaccented Spanish.

"*Teniente Reyes*. I'll take Mr. Dugan now. Thank you."

"Regrettably, *Señor Carlucci*, he is under arrest," the big man said. "Unless, of course, he has immunity?"

He smiled at Carlucci's head shake.

"Then I will wish you good evening," he said.

JUDICIAL INVESTIGATIVE DIRECTORY HQ
PANAMA CITY, PANAMA

Reyes towed Dugan inside, rushing between glass walls through which could be seen rows of occupied desks. A small man gave a puzzled wave as Reyes shook his head and hurried by, hustling Dugan downstairs to an unmarked door. Dugan found himself in a concrete cube. Pipes crisscrossed the ceiling and cast odd shadows. The walls and floor were stained, as was a battered wooden table. Reyes shoved him into the single chair.

"Look," Dugan said, half turning, "I think there's some misunderstanding—"

Reyes slapped the back of his head.

"Yes, *Señor Dugan*. You misunderstand. You are here to answer questions. Clear?"

Dugan nodded.

"Good," Reyes said. "Tell me of *Asian Trader*."

"I'm here to attend an inquiry aboard. I was to board her at the Pacific anchorage. Why? Was she damaged in the attack?"

Reyes's eyes narrowed. "Why do you say that?"

"The pilot announced an attack. You asked about the ship. Seems logical."

Reyes changed tacks.

"Why did you buy a priority transit slot?" he asked.

"I… I don't know what you're talking about," Dugan said.

Reyes slammed Dugan's face into the table and raised him by his hair.

"Enough lies," Reyes whispered. "The truth. Or you will not leave here alive."

Blood ran down Dugan's face as he turned to Reyes with a cross-eyed stare.

"Fuck you, asshole."

Under the circumstances, an ill-considered remark.

***

"*Digame*," Luna said.

"*Capitán Luna*. Frank Carlucci."

"What can I do for you, *Señor Carlucci*?" Luna asked.

"Tell me what you know about Thomas Dugan."

"Not much. *Señor Dugan* was to attend an inquiry on *Asian Trader*," Luna said. "Reyes was to meet with him tomorrow, but now…" He paused. "You know of Reyes's loss?"

"What loss?" asked Carlucci.

"Maria died today at Miraflores, and his boys were hurt. He is with them at the hospital."

"*Capitán*," Carlucci said, "Reyes arrested Dugan at the airport less than an hour ago."

"You are misinformed," Luna said.

"I saw him myself," Carlucci said, "there is no mistake."

"I will get back to you," Luna said, hanging up to rush into the squad room.

"Perez," he said. "Where's Reyes?"

Perez looked uncomfortable.

"God damn it, Juan! Tell me!"

"With a gringo," Perez said. "In the Hole, I think."

Luna ran with Perez on his heels. They found Dugan lying on the concrete, Reyes above him, fists clenched, red faced with rage.

"Manny! No!" yelled Luna as they wrestled him away.

"Juan," Luna ordered as he knelt beside Dugan, "get Manny out. Call a doctor."

He touched Dugan's face. Dugan winced and cracked an eye.

"Is he gone?" Dugan asked weakly, relieved when Luna nodded.

"Lie still," Luna said. "A doctor is coming."

"He's not so fuckin' tough," Dugan croaked. "I was beat up worse than this by three guys outside a bar in Naples."

M/T LUTHER HURD
GATUN LAKE ANCHORAGE, PANAMA

"Seize my ship," Captain Vince Blake said. "That's piracy, by God."

"Goddamned right," agreed Chief Engineer Jim Milam, glaring defiance.

Rojas looked at Calderon and nodded. Calderon dialed his cell phone as Rojas turned back to the American captain.

"*Capitán Blake*," he said, "to be clear, this was approved by your president."

"Ray Hanley?" Blake asked, unable to picture the irascible president of Hanley Trading and Transportation parting with his brand-new ship.

"I refer," Rojas said, "to the president of your country. You will, of course, need to confirm this. We have your embassy on the phone."

Rojas nodded to Calderon, who passed Blake the phone. Blake put the phone to his ear and listened, thunderstruck, grunting an affirmation before hanging up and looking at the chief engineer.

"Son of a bitch. It's true, Jim," Blake said. "The president approved this."

"And I voted for that asshole," Milam muttered.

It was a done deal, thanks to Rojas's preparation. He'd briefed the Panamanian president promptly, and when the inevitable phone call from the American president had come, asking "how can we help," the answer had been "give us *Luther Hurd*." The interests of one shipowner paled beside potential loss of the canal.

Blake took one last shot.

"But surely you have other ways to block the lock?"

Calderon shook his head. "Our temporary caisson gates are in Balboa. Even if we could somehow get them up into the lake, the damaged gates are obstructing placement. But a tanker just upstream of the damaged lock will work. We will ballast her until she grounds and build an earthen dam against her upstream side. Your ship is the ideal size, empty and clean. No danger from pollution or fire and explosion."

"Hanley will do well," Rojas added. "Above market rate during use, and a return to service at our expense plus five years revenue, guaranteed."

Blake sighed. "When do we start?"

Rojas look flustered. "I'm sorry; I was unclear. There is nothing to start. We will remove the crew and place the ship with tugs."

"You've discussed this with your pilots?" Blake asked.

"We've moved dead ships before," Calderon said.

"Smaller vessels," Blake said, "in still water with mules. We barely fit the lock; there'll be current, no mules, and little room for tugs to maneuver. You'll need the engine."

"And you'll need the plant up to ballast her down once in place," Milam said.

"We'll find a way, gentlemen," Rojas said. "There are seamen among our employees."

"Look, pal," Milam said, "nobody's gonna learn this ship in a few hours."

"The chief's right," Blake agreed. "We'll ask for volunteers. We won't need many."

The room grew quiet. "You would do this?" Rojas asked.

Blake shrugged. "We're your only shot."

TOCUMEN INTERNATIONAL AIRPORT
PANAMA CITY, PANAMA

"Long day," Ward said, shaking Carlucci's hand.

"Not over, I'm afraid," Carlucci said. "Let's talk while we walk."

Ward followed him away from the Gulfstream toward his car.

"Dugan was arrested on arrival. I couldn't spring him and smelled a rat because a cop named Reyes drove off with him solo." He paused. "I called his boss, who said Reyes wasn't working because his wife died in the attack and his kids are in the hospital. I filled him in, and he hung up and called back five minutes ago saying Dugan had an 'accident' but is OK. Translation—he got there before Reyes killed Dugan."

Carlucci continued as they got in his car.

"We're headed there now. I expect Dugan's a bit worse for wear."

Ward groaned. "Jesus H. Christ. Does it get any worse?"

"Yeah, it does," Carlucci said. "Seems Reyes got a 'confidential' call from that asshole Gardner that Dugan was dirty and hinting he should be questioned aggressively."

"That stupid son of a bitch," Ward said.

"My sentiments exactly," Carlucci said.

JUDICIAL INVESTIGATIVE DIRECTORY HQ
PANAMA CITY, PANAMA

The Americans sat across the table from Luna, Reyes, and Perez.

"You can see Dugan," Luna repeated, "when you explain your failure to warn us."

Damn Gardner, Ward thought, trying again.

"Captain, we didn't know. Just let us see Dugan, and I'll tell—"

"No," Luna said. "Tell us now. Or we resume questioning Dugan. File your protest. We will know everything before it works through channels."

Ward sighed and nodded at Carlucci, who addressed Luna in Spanish.

"*Capitán*. We have your word this remains confidential?"

Luna nodded. "Juan," he said to Perez, "go turn off the recorder."

He turned back to Carlucci. "Is that sufficient, *Señor Carlucci*, or would you like to accompany *Sargento Perez*?"

"Your word is more than sufficient, *Capitán*," Carlucci said as Perez left the room.

Luna nodded his thanks, and Ward began the briefing, including Dugan's role in the operation.

"So," he concluded minutes later, "we thought this trip to Panama was a ruse to get Dugan out of the way. We didn't suspect the attack."

"I am confused," Reyes said. "You do not deny the truth of the information provided by Gardner—the money in Dugan's offshore account and the fact Dugan was involved with *Asian Trader* just before she departed Singapore for Panama. And yet you seemed convinced of Dugan's innocence. Why?"

"Because," Ward said, "I've known him for over ten years and know he would never do this. And even if I'm wrong about that, I know he is far too smart to leave such obvious evidence to be found. Also, Lieutenant, ask yourself this: If you were Dugan and you *had* committed this heinous act, would you board a plane for Panama and land in the middle of the chaos? Only God and good fortune are holding the lake back. If things had gone a bit differently, Dugan could have deplaned in Tocumen just in time to be washed into the Pacific."

Reyes and Luna nodded. After a long pause, Luna spoke.

"Very well, gentlemen," he said. "You can see Dugan. Beyond that, I promise nothing."

"Captain Luna," Ward said, "as devastating as this attack was, I don't think it is the final objective. Braun is still in place in London, and that tells me he has more attacks planned. I need to go there, and I need Dugan. His expertise may be vital in preventing another attack."

Luna looked Ward in the eye.

"Agent Ward," he said, "my concern is bringing the murdering bastards that did this to justice. I am not yet convinced *Señor Dugan* is not one of them, despite your assurances. He will remain our guest for the time being."

M/T *Luther Hurd*
Gatun Lake Anchorage, Panama
0120 Hours Local Time
5 July

Blake sat at the loading computer in the Cargo Control Room, cursing.

Milam turned from the window. "The magic box giving you trouble, Cap?" he asked.

Blake sighed. "No, but it's anybody's guess how much water we'll have on the way in. I go in too deep and we ground before we get there. Go in light and risk getting sucked into the lock before we can get her down."

"We need to get her down fast, all right," Milam agreed.

"But how?" Blake asked. "We'll need water in the cargo tanks, and the emergency storm ballast crossover's way too slow."

Milam looked thoughtful. "How 'bout some new connections."

"Breach the bulkheads?"

Milam nodded. "I got two cutting rigs. We can drop the water level in the ballast tanks enough to get into the top of the tanks, and the cargo tanks aren't inert yet, so that's no problem. The First and I can cut holes between each ballast tank and the adjacent cargo tank, then drop into the cargo tanks and open holes between them. We'll make her one great big cargo tank. Open the sea valves and throw on the all ballast pumps, and you're done."

Blake frowned at the notion of intentionally destroying the watertight integrity of his brand-new ship. "But I won't be able to control draft and trim en route," he said.

"Yeah, you will," Milam said. "We'll cut the ballast-tank bulkheads up high. The ballast tanks won't spill into the cargo tanks until they're almost full. Trim her any way you want, then overflow the ballast tanks into the cargo tanks when we're in position."

Blake sighed. "Do it," he said.

Milam moved for the door but stopped as he glanced out the window.

"We got company," he said to Blake.

Blake moved to the window. "God damn it," he said. "What are they doing back? Anyone the hospital released was supposed to go to a hotel."

Second Mate Lynda Arnett was walking up the deck, trailed by three crewmen and a sheepish looking Pedro Calderon. Arnett's right hand was in a cast, and the three men following her sported a variety of bandages. She entered the Cargo Control Room moments later with Calderon as the three sailors waited in the passageway, out of sight but within earshot.

"Arnett," Blake said, "you OK? How're the others?"

"I'm OK. A broken wrist is all. Chief Mate's got a concussion, and the bosun's leg is broken. Alvarez, Green, and Thornton are with me—minor injuries."

Blake's face hardened. "Why are you here?"

"It's all over the news. We came to help."

Blake looked a question at Calderon.

"Panic was rising," Calderon said. "We released the plan to calm things a bit."

Blake turned back to Arnett. "But I told that goddamned agent—"

Calderon interrupted. "*Señorita* Arnett can be quite… persuasive. She threatened to remove certain anatomical features to which the agent is very attached should he fail to provide transport. She was very convincing. I authorized the boat, hoping you might reason with her."

Blake and Milam smiled as Arnett reddened.

"I appreciate this, Lynda," Blake said, "but we got it covered."

"The chief mate's down and the third mate's green. I'm staying."

"God damn it, woman," Blake said, "you got a busted arm, for Christ's sake."

"Wrist," she corrected, "and what's this 'god damn it, woman' shit? Pissant chivalry? Or discrimination? Put me off and I'll sue your freakin' socks off."

Chief Steward Dave Jergens spoke from the doorway, breaking the tension.

"Lynda," he said, "Cookie put supper back. Y'all come on in, and I'll warm it up." He inclined his head to include the three sailors in the passageway.

Blake shot Jergens a grateful look.

"Thanks, Dave," he said. "Go on, Lynda. Go eat. I'll think about it, OK?"

She left with a stiff-necked nod. Jergens stood aside to let her pass but hung back.

"Something else, Dave?" Blake asked.

"Cap," Jergens said, "my guys want to help, too. We'll handle lines or… something."

"Christ on a crutch—" Blake caught himself.

"Look, Dave," Blake said, "I appreciate it, I really do, but you can't stay."

"Ain't right, Cap'n," Jergens said. "We got as much right as anybody to help."

Blake stalled. "OK. OK. I'll get back to you. All right?"

Jergens nodded and left. When he was out of earshot, Blake turned to Milam.

"Did I just hear the chief steward volunteer to work on deck?"

"Same with the engine gang," Milam said, "right down to the wiper. They're all ready to whip my ass if I even suggest puttin' them off."

"Christ, what's goin' on?" Blake asked.

"Maybe it's understandable," Milam said. "Remember how you felt on 9/11?"

Blake grew quiet.

"Stunned, outraged, but mostly helpless," he said finally.

"I figure everyone did," Milam said. "Now we *can* do something. Nobody wants to be left out. We should let them help."

"I can't risk their lives unnecessarily," Blake said.

"Just let 'em contribute. They can haul gas cylinders, pull hoses, rig lights, whatever, then ride until just before the lock."

"Might work, and it's better than a mutiny," Blake said, turning to Calderon.

"Can you arrange a launch to remove nonessential crew before the lock?" he asked.

"*Por supuesto, Capitán,*" Calderon said, "it would be my honor."

"Thank you, *señor,*" Blake said, turning back to grin at Milam.

"What the hell you waiting for?" he said. "You got holes to cut. And I have to convince Arnett to disembark with the rest."

"Glad I got the easy part," Milam said, heading for the door.

Judicial Investigative Directory HQ
Panama City, Panama

Dugan kept moving so he didn't stiffen up. The old doctor had been thorough and seemed competent, though his English was limited.

"Is OK. I see much worse," he'd said, leaving as Perez arrived with rice, beans, and strong, sweet coffee. Despite the beating, Dugan was starved. He'd wolfed down the food, slowed only by swollen lips. The empty plate sat on the table as he limped around it.

He looked up as the door opened and read Ward's face.

"Christ, Jesse," Dugan said, "I can't look that bad."

"You OK?" Ward asked.

"Well, a guy who might be a doctor told me I was just peachy."

Ward nodded as Dugan glanced at Carlucci, who stuck out his hand.

"Frank Carlucci," he said. "We almost met at the airport. You look better than I expected. Reyes is tough."

"I cleverly lapsed into unconsciousness," Dugan said. "Even a psycho doesn't get off beating an inert body. What's up with that asshole?"

"A dead wife and injured kids, thanks to *Asian Trader*," Ward said. "Figure it out."

"Son of a bitch," Dugan said softly. "I didn't know."

He listened, subdued, as Carlucci summarized the attack.

"There's more," Ward added when Carlucci finished. "You were set up—fake e-mails, a Cayman account, your authorization on a priority transit slot, all very elaborate."

Dugan nodded and looked thoughtful.

"If Braun went to that much trouble to set me up, that means he's looking to deflect attention and maybe buy a little time. And if he's still in London," Dugan continued, "odds are he has more attacks planned."

"I think so, too," Ward said. "I'm going straight to London."

"What about me?" Dugan asked.

Ward looked at Carlucci.

"We're working on it," he said.

***

Luna sat with his subordinates in a room nearby. He'd promised not to record the earlier conversation but said nothing about future surveillance.

"So, *señores*. What do you think?"

"Their words follow the earlier story," Juan Perez said, "but they may suspect we listen."

"True. Manny?" Luna prompted.

Reyes shrugged. "If Dugan is dirty, he's our only lead."

"Emotion aside," Luna asked, "what does your gut tell you?"

Reyes shrugged again. "Ward's logic seems sound, and this Gardner is an obvious idiot. I think it is possible Dugan is innocent, or at worst, a dupe."

Luna nodded. "We must face facts. We lack resources to operate overseas. Our only real hope lies with the *yanquis* and the English."

Reyes's face clouded. "And so we let Dugan go and hope our kindly Uncle Sam will come back later to pat our heads and tell us what is going on? This is an atrocity against Panama, and we have a suspect in custody. I do not think we should release him so easily."

"And what if Ward is right?" Luna asked. "What if this Dugan's expertise is required not only to prevent more attacks but to bring the perpetrator of this one to justice?"

"I did not say Dugan should not be allowed to go with Ward, *Capitán*," Reyes said, "only that he should not leave our custody."

Tocumen International Airport
Panama City, Panama

Reyes settled back in the leather seat of the Gulfstream and glared at Dugan in the seat across from him. The man was already snoring, thanks to heavy-duty painkillers courtesy of Carlucci.

"Thank you for releasing him," Ward said from the seat beside him.

"To be clear, Agent Ward," Reyes said, "we did not release him. He is traveling in my custody. I can return with him to Panama at any time. I expect both your government and the British to abide by the terms of our agreement in that regard."

Ward looked as if he were about to speak and then seemed to think better of it. He nodded instead and turned to stare out the window, leaving Reyes to his own thoughts.

His sons were both awake now, and the doctors said there was no great physical injury, but they were confused and frightened. Leaving them had been hard, made possible only by the presence of his parents and in-laws. It had taken all his resolve, but he knew in his heart his sons would want him to bring Maria's murderers to justice.

For all his bluster with Ward, his mission was anything but "official." It was an arrangement hammered out between Ward and Luna, with the Walsh woman on the telephone from UK. Reyes was not even officially assigned to the task. Things were too chaotic in Panama to hope to get such an arrangement approved quickly. Reyes had merely put in for his annual leave, with a promise from Luna that he would clean up the paperwork after the fact.

As the Gulfstream leveled out at cruising altitude, Reyes unbuckled his seat belt and leaned toward Dugan. The man stirred but didn't wake as Reyes unlocked the handcuffs and slipped them into his jacket pocket.

"Thank you," Ward said. "I'm sure he will appreciate that."

Reyes shrugged. "I don't think he's going anywhere."

***

The watchman at Pedro Miguel Lock raised his eyes as the Gulfstream passed overhead. As he watched the lights fade, he heard a muffled screech and then a gigantic groan as the mass in the lock shifted.

"Central Control. This is Pedro Miguel. The plug is shifting. Repeat, the plug is shifting."

CHAPTER TWENTY-THREE

M/T *Luther Hurd*
Gatun Lake Anchorage, Panama
0325 Hours Local Time
5 July

Calderon stood at the rail. Deck lights made *Luther Hurd* a bright pool on the dark surface of the lake. Sailors swarmed, rigging hoses and lights into tanks with shouts and curses and rough humor, to the din of impact wrenches loosening tank manholes. A launch scraped against the shipside, and he watched two men climb the accommodation ladder toward him.

The shorter man shook his head. "It is not good," he began.

"Wait, Carlos. The *capitán* should hear," Calderon said, leading the men to where Blake stood with Milam, checking off breached bulkheads on a tank layout.

"Go ahead," Calderon said, nodding at the senior of the two pilots.

"The plug shifted," said Captain Carlos Sanchez. "The current is increasing. And we have only thirty-feet depth before the lock. It will be difficult, even now."

"We need to move then?" Blake asked.

"We should heave anchor in an hour to start into the cut at first light," said the second pilot, Captain Roy McCluskey.

Milam nodded. "I can finish in transit. ETA at the lock?"

"About 0700," Sanchez said. McCluskey nodded agreement.

Milam checked the time. "OK, we can make that."

Sanchez raised a hand. "There's more. We must modify our approach. *Señor Milam*, may I?" Milam passed him the clipboard. The pilot flipped the paper to draw on the back.

"We block the east lock," he said, "with the starboard stern against the center guide wall and the bow against the east bank. The problem is here"—he tapped his sketch—"where the east bank narrows to the lock at this diagonal wall. If we cannot hold the bow against the bank while you ballast, it will be pushed down onto the angled wall and funneled into the lock." He paused. "We must ground the bow fast and hard so it cannot shift. Then the current and tugs will hold the stern to the wall while you ballast down."

Blake nodded. "What's the depth near the bank?"

Sanchez and McCluskey exchanged glances. "Ten feet and falling."

"Christ," Blake said. "Chief, what do we need aft to immerse the prop?"

"Twenty-one feet, minimum," Milam said. "And we lose some power at that draft."

"I can get the bow up to eight feet," Blake said, "but we'll be like a fat man in the stern of an empty canoe. She'll handle—"

"Like a pig," McCluskey finished.

"It will be difficult," Sanchez conceded. "The current is over four knots now. We must go in at speed, two to three knots faster than that."

Blake stared. "You want to put a forty-thousand-ton ship in the worst possible condition, then try to ground at a specific spot at an over-the-ground speed of eight knots?"

Sanchez nodded.

"And if we miss? Or a pressure wave forces the bow to shear? Then we go into the lock 'at speed,' with the weight of the whole lake behind us. This is… this is…" Blake stopped, speechless.

"Total lunacy," Milam finished. "I unvolunteer."

The pilots exchanged looks. "Gentlemen," Sanchez said, "there is no alternative. It is not now a case of slowly losing the lake. If the plug fails, thousands will die downstream. We must attempt this. With or without you."

"You can't do it without us," Blake said. "There is no time."

"Quite a choice," Milam said. "Risk death or spend the rest of our lives looking at news footage of floating corpses. I'll go, god damn it, but I'm not happy about it."

"I agree," Blake said, "but we're only speaking for ourselves."

"Thank you, gentlemen," Sanchez said, his relief evident.

"Tugs?" Blake asked.

"Only room for two," Sanchez said. "One to push the stern into the wall while the other pulls back from our port bow to help turn us into the bank."

"OK," Blake said, "but I'm going to hang off the port anchor. If necessary, we'll drop it to help turn. Warn the bow tug to stay clear."

"Given the depth," McCluskey said, "we might run over it if we drop it."

"If we end up having to use it, that'll be the least of our worries," Blake said.

Calderon looked at the two pilots, who nodded agreement, conceding the point.

"Very well," Calderon said to Blake and Milam, "it is decided. I leave you gentlemen to your work. *Capitáns* Sanchez and McCluskey remain. If you need anything at all, just ask."

Handshakes were exchanged, and the group parted. Milam flipped the paper on his clipboard and studied the diagram.

"Shift ballast anytime," he said to Blake. "I'll be out of the last ballast tank before the water reaches me."

"You sure?" Blake asked. "I don't want to get your feet wet."

"Might be better to drown early and get it over with," Milam growled.

M/T *LUTHER HURD*
NORTH OF CENTENNIAL BRIDGE
PANAMA

Blake gazed at Pedro Miguel, visible in the distance below Centennial Bridge, as the engine labored astern to hold *Luther Hurd* in the current, and the crew descended to the waiting launch. They'd all volunteered, but he kept a minimum, all unmarried except for himself and Milam. Despite his efforts to put her ashore, Arnett had asserted her prerogative as ranking deck officer to man the bow. She was there now, with three seamen to handle lines and run the anchor windlass. Green, Blake's best helmsman, manned the wheel. Milam kept his three engineers.

Blake had refused ACP help. There were enough grieving families in Panama. For the same reason, the pilots had refused offers of their colleagues. The plan would work or fail regardless of the number of pilots aboard.

The second engineer began tugging hoses from the last tank as Milam emerged and flashed a thumbs-up. Blake waved in reply as the engineers started aft.

"I should get forward," McCluskey said, starting for the stairs.

"God be with you, Roy," Sanchez said softly.

"God be with us all, Carlos," McCluskey replied.

The launch with the crew moved away, Blake silently wishing he was aboard. A chopper approached, cameraman perched in the door. Wonderful, he cursed.

M/T *Luther Hurd*
Centennial Bridge, Panama

Blake watched the crew scramble to safety on the west lock wall before stowing the binoculars. Arnett's group passed a line to the bow tug, which moved away, connected and ready to match the tanker's speed. The tug at a safe distance, he saw Arnett signal Alvarez at the windlass, then peer down over the bulwark to watch the port anchor. Alvarez eased the anchor out, the massive chain clunking in the hawse pipe, until Arnett's balled fist shot up and Alvarez stopped the wildcat. She barked an order, and he spun the brake tight and disengaged the wildcat, leaving the anchor dangling, ready for release. Blake felt quiet pride at McCluskey's approving nod.

***

Sanchez spoke into his radio, alerting both tugs.

"Dead slow ahead," he said.

"Dead slow ahead, aye," Blake repeated, at the engine controls.

"Steer one two five," Sanchez ordered.

"One two five, aye," Green said.

"Slow ahead," Sanchez ordered, then after a moment asked, "How's she answering the helm?"

Sweat rolled down Green's dark face. "She wants to do as she pleases, Cap'n."

"Half ahead," Sanchez ordered.

"Half ahead, aye," Blake replied as they increased speed to gain steerage way.

Soon they were moving fast. Too fast. Sanchez felt like a man on his first ski jump, deciding halfway down it was a bad idea. They accelerated as the cross section of the channel decreased and the laws of physics took over. The same volume passing a smaller opening in the same amount of time must move faster. He couldn't control her at this speed. Better to use the tugs.

"Dead slow ahead," he barked.

"Dead slow ahead, aye," Blake confirmed, concern in his voice.

On the bow, McCluskey raised his radio, then lowered it without speaking. There could be only one command pilot.

***

The stern crabbed to port, and Sanchez barked an order to the tugs, overcorrecting into a series of wider and wilder swings as he struggled for control. With the bow pointed dead center at the lock, he ordered an all-out pull to port by the bow tug.

Water frothed as the tug strained. The line snapped taut and parted with a crack, recoiling in both directions, a huge rubber band. It killed one tug hand instantly and knocked a second overboard. On the ship, the other end struck McCluskey and men near him at knee height, slamming them into the steel bulwark, before whipping around a fairlead to strike Alvarez at the windlass controls. Only Arnett was spared, and she stared down at Alavarez's bloody remains.

***

"LET GO THE ANCHOR!" her radio screamed, and she clawed at the brake, panic rising as it didn't budge. She bent to pull a wheel wrench from beneath Alvarez's corpse as she heard Sanchez shouting tug orders into the radio.

***

Sanchez ordered the bow tug back to push the stern to starboard and the stern tug forward to push the bow to port. The stern tug captain hesitated, then dashed forward through the rapidly closing gap between the ship and the guide wall, all too aware of the risk.

***

Arnett had the wrench now, gripped in her left hand and multiplying her leverage. The wheel broke free, and the anchor splashed as the giant chain surged through the spinning wildcat. She closed her eyes as the shower of dirt from the running chain peppered her face. The chain slowed as the anchor hit the bottom, then paid out in jerks as the ship's motion dragged the chain out.

"SNUB IT UP! NOW!" her radio squawked.

She tightened the brake with her good hand. The chain stopped, only to break free again as the ship's motion lifted links off the bottom and the weight overcame the brake. She cursed as the wrench slipped from her hand and bounced under the windlass, then gripped the wheel with both hands and pulled, screaming as bones separated. She collapsed over the wheel with a relieved sob as the brake held at last.

A muffled boom mocked her as the anchor jerked free to crash into the hull, and *Luther Hurd* continued her headlong rush.

***

Carlos Sanchez was a vigorous sixty, respected and near retirement. If unequal to the task at hand, he was by seniority the "least unqualified," and both honor and pride had precluded his refusal when the task arose, despite the dull chest pains he'd suffered for days without complaint. Only a coward would hide behind such trivial discomfort in the face of his responsibilities. But the pain struck again as he started the run at the lock, exploding this time, clouding his judgment during the most stressful minutes of his life. The final sledgehammer blows induced visions of floating bodies, each staring up as if they knew they'd been sacrificed to an old man's pride, as pain stole his breath and speech. He turned apologetically to Blake, sure in his last moments he was the architect of a great failure, shamefully grateful he wouldn't live to see it.

***

Blake knew Sanchez was dead before he reached him.

"Oh shit," Green murmured as Blake searched for a pulse.

Blake moved on instinct, ignoring the tugs as he rushed back to the console and jammed the stick to full ahead. The ship shuddered as the big propeller bit.

"The Lord is my shepherd. I shall not want…" Green prayed, hands tight on the wheel.

"Ten left," Blake barked, praying himself that they had enough speed to steer.

"Ten left, aye." Green spun the wheel. "…lie down in green pastures…"

They turned, Blake timing the rate of swing against a landmark ashore. Too slow, he thought, we're done. But due to luck or Green's fervent prayer, *Luther Hurd* caught a break. The anchor, bouncing through the mud and periodically holing the hull, drove its flukes under a buried boulder. Momentum ripped it free, but not before it jerked the bow, hastening the turn to port. The bulbous bow crumpled and rode up the bank, pushing a huge pile of mud, while the ship pivoted on the bow like a gigantic door in a draft. The starboard stern smashed against the guide wall in a din of screeching steel on concrete and a cascade of sparks, as momentum and current drove *Luther Hurd* tightly into place.

***

Upstream, the channel calmed abruptly, and the captain of the tug now astern cruised in circles, calling Sanchez on the radio. Downstream, unsure what was happening when the ship started to turn, the captain of the second tug had sheltered in the narrow lock entrance. He hovered there now, his bow upstream, holding on his engines as his little boat road atop the dropping water. He made for an escape ladder recessed into the lock wall. The boat was lost, but the crew might escape.

***

Blake rose from where he'd been thrown over the console.

"Thank you, Jesus!" Green cried, clinging to the wheel. "We fuckin' did it, Cap'n!"

The pair were grinning at each other so hard their faces hurt when a terrible screech sounded from the lock. They watched in horror as the changing conditions in the lock disturbed the equilibrium of the debris plug. A creeping crack in the weld between the deckhouse and ruined main deck accelerated through the last few feet of its length, and the mass came undone, tumbling from the lock with a huge splash. Water boiled through the lock, overturning the captive tug just moments before it reached the escape ladder. Then

Luther Hurd shifted, and the stern screeched against the wall as she settled. Blake rushed to the phone.

"Engine Room. First Engineer," a shaky voice said.

"First. Where's the chief?"

"In the Cargo Control Room," the first said.

Blake heard the hydraulic ballast pumps winding up. Thank you Milam, he thought as he hung up. He started for the stairwell.

"C'mon, Green. Let's get to the bow."

***

Arnett groaned as she struggled upright. Her fingers protruded from the dirty remnants of the cast like painful purple sausages. A moan reached her. Someone's alive, she thought, staggering toward the sound.

The deck forward of the windlass was slick with blood. She stepped over a severed foot laced in a work boot. Thorton and Billingsley were dead against the bulwark, and Roy McCluskey lay moaning between them, his left leg missing below the knee. The stump spurted blood.

She knelt in the gore and removed his belt. He moaned.

"Hang on, Captain," she said.

She wrestled the belt onto his stump with her left hand and twisted. The blood flowed unabated. She held tension with her throbbing right hand and repositioned her left to twist tighter. He was unconscious when she got the blood stopped.

"Don't you fucking die on me!" she screamed, all the pain and horror of the last moments pouring out. She repeated it between sobs as she rocked on her knees in the gore, clutching the twisted belt. They found her there, and it took all Green's strength to pry her fingers away.

M/T *Luther Hurd*
Pedro Miguel Lock, Panama
1135 Hours Local Time
5 July

Only Blake and Milam remained aboard. Water leaked by the hull in slackening streams as workers packed earth against the port side. From the bridge, Blake watched trucks on the east bank dumping rocks and broken concrete. The hull rang with repeated clangs as small dozers pushed the rubble out into the water against the ship's side, followed by sand and dirt to fill in the voids and create a solid road against the shipside. The next loads were dumped farther out. They were already fifty or sixty feet along.

Blake winced as rocks and dozer blades scraped new paint and dust billowed over the pristine deck. He shook his head and moved down the stairs. The Engine Control Room was empty, but he saw Milam through the window standing on the walkway looking down into the engine room. His engine room. A spotless place, bright with new paint and full of new equipment. An engineer's wet dream, Blake thought not unkindly.

He moved through the door quietly and stood behind Milam, hesitant to disturb him. The only sounds were the muted drone of the emergency generator and the hollow booms of rocks against the hull. Finally, Blake cleared his throat.

Milam looked back with a sad smile. "What brings a rope choker to the realm of the honest working man?"

"They're burying our ship, Jim. I couldn't watch anymore."

Milam shook his head. "I've been at sea almost twenty-five years. Mostly rust buckets older than me I kept running with duct tape, baling wire, and whatever I could make with a lathe and a welding machine. I finally get the engine room of my dreams"—he sighed—"and it's a friggin' dam." He changed the subject. "We about wrapped up?"

"Yeah," Blake said, "I talked to the office on the satellite, right to Hanley himself. He's chartering a jet to fly us all to Houston, including the injured folks and our… casualties."

Milam nodded. "How's McCluskey?"

"Calderon says he'll make it," Blake said, "thanks to Arnett."

"She's got sand, that one," Milam said, and Blake nodded agreement.

They both stood, reluctant to leave, flinching as a rock boomed against the hull.

"OK," Milam said. "I'll go kill the emergency generator."

Neither moved.

"Look, Vince," Milam said. "You saved our asses. You're a hero."

"I don't feel like a hero," Blake said. "I feel like an asshole who couldn't even get his brand-new ship to the first load port and who got good men killed in the process."

Milam squeezed Blake's shoulder. "Yeah, I guess this hero stuff's overrated."

CHAPTER TWENTY-FOUR

Dugan drifted toward consciousness, feeling better after a five-hour nap, his headache reduced to a dull throb. He heard voices through the fog and opened his eyes.

"It's motive I can't understand," Ward said to Reyes. "What can Iran and Venezuela possibly gain by targeting Panama and Malacca?"

"Obviously the canal was the prime target," Reyes said.

Ward shook his head. "Not from the allocation of resources. There were ten attackers in Malacca, and they hijacked *Alicia* and stole the boats to set it up. To say nothing of chartering *China Star* and timing her arrival in the straits. All very elaborate. Compare that to the attack on your country. As effective as it was, it seems to be the work of one man, acting alone."

"There may have been others in the crew," Reyes said.

"No way," Dugan interjected. "That crew worked for Phoenix for years. Medina was the only unknown. The regular third mate was due back from vacation but was injured in a car wreck in the Philippines. Medina was a last-minute relief, and the captain was pissed about going through the yard with a green man. He was happy when Medina turned out to be a capable worker." Dugan paused. "Evidently a bit too capable."

"Which brings us right back to why," Ward said. "Closing Malacca would hurt Iran, so a failed attempt there might deflect blame. But destroying the canal wouldn't greatly impact Iran, and I don't see how either act would help Venezuela."

Reyes shrugged. "Oil prices are sure to spike."

"Temporarily, yeah," Dugan said. "But Malacca's still open, and tanker traffic through the canal is minimal. Prices will settle in a week or so. That alone can't be the motive."

Reyes looked pensive. "I do not know about Iran, but Rodriguez is no friend of Panama. He supports the FARC guerrillas in Colombia, who are an increasing problem on our border. Also, it is no secret he is upset our current canal expansion will be insufficient to allow the transit of loaded VLCCs. He openly advocates a second, larger canal in Nicaragua, and there are rumors that he urges the Chinese to pledge to send half their trade though a new canal so that his friends in Nicaragua can secure financing in the international market."

Ward sighed. "That may be part of it, but my gut tells me the worst is yet to come. And we're playing a man down. Tom obviously can't go back into the office. The ship's agent will have reported his arrest by now, so Braun thinks he's in Panama."

"Alex can help Anna inside," Dugan said.

Ward chose his next words with care.

"Alex isn't out of the woods, Tom."

"Bullshit. You know he's being coerced."

"I do. But we have no hard evidence. Closures at either Panama or Malacca increase distances and soak up capacity. Freight rates will skyrocket and Kairouz stands to profit. Money equals motive. A nice, uncomplicated motive. People like things simple, even if they're wrong. And between your relationship with Alex and your own involvement with *Alicia, Asian Trader,* and an offshore bank account, you both look pretty hinky. With Gardner beating that drum in Langley, my support might mean squat. Unless I miss my guess, he's already on the horn, pressing for the Brits to arrest you when we land."

Dugan looked worried. "So how do we play it?"

Ward looked at Reyes and smiled. "Well, since you're officially, or at least semiofficially, in Panamanian custody, it's really out of our hands. That'll throw Gardner a curve, and he'll hesitate to escalate things until he's sure they won't blow up in his face. But make no mistake. This is high profile. The holiday weekend means it'll take a bit longer for a critical mass of political assholes to form, but in forty-eight hours tops, we enter the never-never land of congressional hearings. When the shit hits the fan, I'm the goat and you and Alex are prime suspects. Two days. After that we're toast."

CIA HEADQUARTERS
LANGLEY, VIRGINIA

The *Luther Hurd* at Pedro Miguel dominated the news. Gardner watched on his office television, the graphic gore roiling his stomach. He'd arrived at work at six thirty, sleep denied him by a pounding head and quivering gut. He chased Tylenol with tepid coffee and considered how what he'd learned in the last three hours impacted Larry Gardner. Throwing Dugan to the Panamanians was still promising, presuming Ward hadn't screwed it up. He tried Ward again and hung up at the voice mail. He dialed Panama.

"Carlucci."

"Gardner here," he said. "Ward with you?"

"I'm not at liberty to say."

"Do the Panamanians have Dugan in custody?"

"Who is Dugan, and why do you think he's in custody?"

"Ah… I saw his name in the briefing notes."

"Funny," Carlucci said, "I write those. I didn't mention a Dugan."

"What the hell difference does it make? Where is he?"

"I'm not at liberty to say."

"Look, Carlucci, you're hindering an ongoing operation. If you don't want to end up somewhere even less important than Panama, start being helpful."

"Fuck you."

Gardner burst into obscenities at the dial tone and slammed the phone down. Still cursing, he picked it back up and dialed.

"Flight Operations."

"Gardner here. What do you have on Ward?"

"Let's see, looks like he left Panama for Heathrow this morning at 0215, refueling in Miami. I show his ETA in London as 2015 local; that's 1515 our time."

Hair rose on Gardner's neck. "He alone?"

The man paused. "Nope. Manifest shows Ward, a Thomas Dugan, and a Panamanian national named Manuel Reyes."

Gardner hung up. Son of a bitch. Reyes. With Ward and Dugan. No good could come of this. He needed some cover, just in case. He was parsing the possibilities when Senator Gunther appeared on television, standing at a bank of microphones in front of the Capitol. Gardner raised the volume.

"…will leave no stone unturned in fixing the blame for these intelligence failures. To that end, I've convened a special Senate investigation…"

Gardner smiled. It was about to rain shit, and he'd just found a raincoat.

OFFICES OF PHOENIX SHIPPING

Braun frowned. "Be here, Sutton. That's final."

"But I can upload the virus now and trigger it remotely. I don't need to be here."

"What if it's discovered?" Braun said. "Besides. I want you here tonight to ensure every system is running. Complete destruction. No file remnants on local hard drives."

"You're burning the bloody building. What's the point?"

Braun's stare was ice. "The point, Sutton, is you'll do as told. Now. Backups?"

"Held off-site. Only Kairouz and I have decryption keys." Sutton handed Braun a flash drive. "This one works but his doesn't. Without this, the backups are useless."

Braun slipped the drive into his pocket. "Good. Is the safe house set up?"

Sutton nodded. "I tested the cable and Internet yesterday."

"And I drove the route," Farley said. "Looked fine."

"Any trouble renting the place with the cover identity?" Braun asked.

"Didn't have to," Sutton said. "It's my aunt's place in Kent."

Braun exploded. "You bloody idiot! A place connected to one of us will be obvious!"

"Bu… but there's no connection," Sutton stammered. "It's in her name. She's in the loony bin. Alzheimer's."

"What's her name?" Braun demanded.

"Married name's Lampkin. Husband's dead. I don't even visit. I got the key when me mum passed last year. It's safer than a rental."

Braun considered it. No time for other arrangements.

"All right," he said. "But Sutton. Don't disappoint me again. Clear?"

Sutton nodded as Braun continued. "Everything ready on your end, Farley?"

"Yeah. I checked out the school. Like you figured, it's all girls with no males on staff except a custodian. I slipped in last night to check the setup. One gent's toilet, off a side corridor to a supply storeroom. It's at the back of the building with a window opening on to the alley. It's perfect. We'll be halfway to the safe house before anyone knows she's gone."

Braun nodded. "That's it then," he said, dismissing them. As they left, he moved to his desk and took a pair of pliers from a drawer. He crushed the flash drive beyond recognition and slipped the remains back into his pocket for later disposal, then dialed his phone.

"Sudsbury and Smythe," a pleasant female voice answered.

"Mr. Carrington-Smythe, please. Captain Braun calling."

"He's been expecting your call, Captain. I'll put you right through."

After a great deal of persuasion, Reyes agreed not to cuff Dugan upon landing. However, the big Panamanian kept Dugan close as the pair trailed Ward across the tarmac to Lou Chesterton and Harry Albright. The Panamanian's introduction to the Brits was perfunctory—both men were staring at Dugan.

"Bloody hell, Yank," Harry said. "You hit by a lorry?"

Dugan glanced at Reyes, who remained expressionless.

"You OK, mate?" Lou asked.

"I'm fine," Dugan said. "What's the plan?"

Lou looked at Ward. "A bloke from your embassy called and urged us to detain you. I patiently explained to him that MI5 is intelligence, not law enforcement, and without arrest powers. He then suggested that I convey you, and particularly Dugan here, to the US embassy for 'debriefing.'"

Ward shook his head. "Mr. Dugan is in the custody of Lieutenant Reyes. He will not be going to the embassy, though perhaps the lieutenant and I should go to the embassy and explain the situation while you take Dugan to Anna's building."

"Go where you will, Agent Ward," Reyes said. "I stay with Dugan."

Ward sighed. "All right. Lou, can you take me to the embassy while Harry drives these two to Anna's?"

ANNA WALSH'S APARTMENT BUILDING

"My God, Tom," Anna said, "are you all right?"

Dugan's smile faded. "I can't tell you what a confidence builder that was. I'm beginning to feel like the Elephant Man."

"There's a resemblance, mate," Harry said, "but he was quite intelligent."

145

Reyes smiled, and Dugan laughed, his pain made tolerable by the pills he'd taken on landing.

"They didn't beat the cheekiness out of you I see," Anna said, then turned to Reyes.

"But I'm forgetting my manners. May I offer you something to drink, Lieutenant Reyes?"

"Coffee, if it would not be too much trouble," Reyes said.

"No trouble at all," Anna said. "Tom? Harry?"

Both men nodded and followed Anna into the small kitchen and watched her prepare the coffee. When it was ready, they all moved to the living room.

"Cassie OK?" Dugan asked.

Anna nodded. "Well covered. Two men at all times."

"And Braun?" Dugan asked.

"Quiet. But up to something," she said. "That's my gut anyway."

"Mine as well," Harry agreed.

"Then it's unanimous," Dugan said. "But damned if I can figure his next move."

They fell into frustrated silence, but soon Anna smiled.

"I've seen that look," Harry said. "What are you on to, Anna?"

"We can assume the next attack will be by a Phoenix-owned or -chartered tanker, right?"

"So what?" Dugan said. "We can't check them all without alerting Braun."

"Bear with me," Anna said. "Targets?"

Dugan shrugged. "Suez, the straits of Hormuz and the Bosphorus, maybe the Cape of Good Ho—" He stopped and looked at her.

"Exactly," she said.

Harry and Reyes looked confused.

"Would you two mind sharing?" Harry asked.

"We concentrate on tankers near choke points," Anna said. "That's the short list."

"Braun will only manipulate communications for attack ships," Dugan added. "It'd be noticed if he tried that for every ship in the fleet."

"Tom can call the short-listed ships on a pretext," Anna continued. "Alex can't do it because Braun is watching him closely, and a call from me would seem strange. The captains might call back to see what's going on and alert Braun in the process. But no one in the fleet knows Tom's not in the office."

"And if Tom senses something amiss," Harry finished, understanding, "that's the ship. Bloody brilliant."

"One problem," Anna said. "My computer crashed again, as did Tom's. And Sutton was his usual helpful self. I can't access the position report. Tom, you have a hard copy?"

"Not a current one," Dugan said. "Get word to Alex. He can slip it to you somehow. By the way, does he know I'm here?"

"He thinks you're in custody in Panama. And let's keep it that way. He's reacting as Braun would anticipate. Knowing you're here could change his demeanor and alert Braun."

"But he—"

"You have to trust me on this, Tom," Anna said, ending discussion of the issue.

"Now," she continued, "I have to see him out of the office. I'll call and say I'm worried about Tom and want to talk. I'll suggest we meet tomorrow morning for coffee."

"Wrong motive," Harry said. "Braun thinks you're a tart. Come on to Kairouz—imply you're worried about your position with Dugan gone. Offer to discuss 'serving his needs.'"

"Won't that shock him?"

"He'll get it," Dugan said. "And if he's initially shocked, so much the better."

Anna nodded and called. As predicted, Alex played along and agreed to meet Anna at eight thirty the next morning.

She snapped the phone shut. "My reputation as a slut is secure. Now what?"

Harry yawned. "I'll update Lou and Ward and piss off home to the little woman."

"Do that," Anna said. "Let's all get some sleep."

Harry stood up. "I'll let myself out," he said.

Reyes kept his seat, and Anna shot Harry a surprised look.

Harry shrugged. "Lieutenant Reyes is quite diligent in his custodial duties," Harry said and moved to the door.

The door clicked shut behind Harry, followed by a few seconds of awkward silence.

"Well then," Anna said. "I guess I'll just pop off to bed."

She gave Dugan a rueful look and moved through the kitchen and out the back door to her own apartment.

Dugan glared at Reyes.

"Looks like you're my new roommate, so let's get something straight. There's only one bed, and it's mine. You got the sofa."

***

Twenty minutes later, Dugan stepped out of the bathroom in his boxer shorts, showered and ready for bed. Reyes waited in the bedroom with handcuffs.

"I'm not into that, Reyes," Dugan said, "and you're not really my type."

The Panamanian controlled his temper. "I intend to cuff you to the bed."

"Seriously?" Dugan asked.

"Your colleagues' faith in you is touching, *Señor Dugan*, but I am not a believer just yet. Do you think I would risk waking with my own gun in my face?"

"What if there's a fire?" Dugan asked.

"Unlikely," Reyes said.

"What if I have to piss?"

Reyes shrugged. "Then you will be uncomfortable."

"What if—"

"What if you shut up and extend your hand before I am forced to become unpleasant?"

***

Just before dawn, Reyes rose from the lumpy sofa and moved to a chair by the window. Sleep had been a disjointed series of catnaps, separated mostly by hours of thoughts of

Maria and the boys. When he could bear the pain no longer, he had forced his thoughts to the situation at hand.

That was equally troubling. He could hardly contain his disdain for the methods being employed. He had learned enough to be convinced this Braun was key, and yet the *hijo de puta* was being handled with kid gloves while Ward and the Walsh woman's team gathered "hard evidence."

Where, he wondered, were the secret CIA planes standing by to whisk this Braun to some accommodating country where he could be questioned "aggressively"? Perhaps he should offer the services of his agency? He was sure that after a few hours in the Hole, *El Señor Braun* would be most cooperative.

He sighed. The gringos needed him to keep Dugan at large, just as he needed to remain close to the investigation. He would play their game, as they played his, until he learned who was really behind the death of his Maria and so many others. Then things would be different.

OFFICES OF PHOENIX SHIPPING LTD.
2315 HOURS LOCAL TIME
5 JULY

"That's it. Kairouz's was the last." Sutton looked up from Alex Kairouz's desk.

"Thank you, Sutton," Braun said as he pulled a silenced pistol and shot his surprised underling in the head.

He returned the gun to his waistband and moved to his office, where he opened a small fireproof lockbox and checked the contents: cash, several false passports with Sutton's photo, and the CD of conversations between Rodriguez, Kairouz, and Dugan. He locked the box and carried it to Sutton's office, hiding it in a drawer just as Farley entered.

"All done," Farley said. "I wedged open the stairwell fire doors and set incendiary charges on both the Phoenix Shipping floors. The main sprinkler supply valve is jammed shut. The place will go up in seconds."

"It's all concealed? I want no slipups."

Farley shrugged. "Someone might close the fire doors, but it won't matter. I've rigged both floors. The charges are out of sight."

"And you're sure Sutton's and Kairouz's offices will survive?"

"They should. They're on the outer wall, away from the charges. The fire trucks will pump water through the windows first." He looked around. "Sutton done?"

"Mr. Sutton has, and is, finished," Braun said, "and as promised, his bonus money is now available to augment your own."

Farley smiled. "Right then," he said. "That leaves the timer. When you want to pop?"

Braun had struggled with timing until the Walsh slut's call to Kairouz. Cassie had to be in their control to ensure Kairouz's cooperation, but snatching her at home involved too many witnesses to silence. Authorities might believe Kairouz had the girl snatched, but not that he'd sanctioned the murder of his entire domestic staff. They had to grab the girl at school, and timing was key. It wouldn't do for Kairouz to die in the office fire, but he normally

148

arrived at the office about when Cassie reached school. Kairouz's eight-thirty meeting with the slut was perfect. He'd even have a ringside seat to the destruction of his life's work.

"Set it for eight forty," Braun said.

STERLING ACADEMY
WESTMINSTER, LONDON
6 JULY

Farley accelerated. The retard would dawdle, this of all mornings. If the old bitch had to sign her in as tardy, it would cock things up proper.

"SLOW DOWN, FARLEY," demanded Gillian Farnsworth as he rocketed around a corner. He ignored her, lurching to a stop moments later before Sterling Academy, relieved to see the headmistress still atop of the steps. He leaped out, opening Cassie's door. He grabbed her arm as she scrambled out.

"I gotta use the loo," he said through the open door.

"Get back in this car at once," Gillian Farnsworth said.

"I'll be a while," he grinned. "Don't get your knickers in a knot, luv."

He slammed the door and moved up the long steps, still gripping Cassie's arm. He bobbed his head politely to the surprised headmistress, looking embarrassed as he whispered his need and brushed past before she could object. Inside, he feigned ignorance.

"Where's the loo?"

"Down there," Cassie pointed. "Now let me go. I'll be late."

"Show me first."

"Oh, all right. But hurry." She led him down an empty side hall.

At the toilet door, he clamped a hand over her mouth and pushed her in, her jerks exciting him as he pressed against her. He pinned her head against his chest, fished out a syringe, removed the cap with his teeth, and jabbed her neck. She went limp, and he lowered her to the floor to open the window.

"Right on time," Braun said, framed in the window. Farley passed her out and then grabbed the top of the window frame to swing through the small opening feetfirst. He landed atop a panel truck painted in the livery of the International Parcel Service, backed up to the wall beneath the high window in the deserted alley. Braun was already scrambling to the ground, clad in an IPS uniform. Farley closed the window and lowered Cassie into Braun's waiting arms, then jumped down beside them.

"I'll put her in back," Braun said. "Change and get behind the wheel."

At 8:36, the truck turned onto Victoria Street.

CASTLE LANE
500 YARDS FROM STERLING ACADEMY

"Nanny. Control. Over," squawked the radio.

"We copy, Control. Over."

"Nanny, be advised subject is moving east on Victoria. Over."

The driver pulled around the corner. The two men in the car shared a look of relief at spotting the stationary Kairouz car.

"Negative, Control. Subject's vehicle has not moved. Over."

"I show the subject in motion, Nanny. Eastbound on Victoria. Over."

"Control, I say again. Subject's vehicle is stationary. Check your equipment. Over."

"Nanny, DO YOU HAVE A VISUAL ON SUBJECT? Over."

"Negative, Control. But the vehi—"

The operator abandoned protocol. "The bloody CAR may be there, but the SUBJECT is in motion, now southbound on Artillery Row and getting farther away by the minute. DO YOU COPY?"

"Bloody hell," the driver said.

"Control. We're on it," said the second agent as the driver whipped the car onto Victoria, heading east.

Anna and Alex both arrived early and sat now in the Starbucks near the office, empty cups between them. She studied Alex. Panama and Dugan's arrest had taken its toll.

"All those deaths. Thomas arrested," he said. "If I'd just alerted you sooner… maybe you could've prevented it. I was just so afraid for Cassie." His voice broke. "I am still."

Anna took his hand. "She's safe now. I promise."

He sat, eyes downcast, and squeezed her hand before looking up.

"Right then," he said. "Back to business. I'll get you a position report, but how can you contact ships without alerting Braun?"

"We're working on that," Anna said vaguely.

"Well, you're the expert. I'll have Mrs. Coutts slip you a copy."

Anna looked through the window. "You can tell her now."

Alice Coutts was emerging from Vauxhall tube station. They went out to intercept her.

"Why good morning," Mrs. Coutts said. "What a pleasant surp—"

A blast slapped them, followed so closely by a second it seemed like an echo. Shock waves cracked windows. They turned to see smoke billow above a familiar building, and the blood drained from Alex's face as he watched the enterprise he'd built with years of blood, sweat, and tears go up in smoke.

Braun heard the explosions as they neared Lambeth Bridge. He'd chosen to cross the Thames at Lambeth for visual confirmation of the fire. Once on the bridge, he saw smoke billow on the far bank and heard the distant wail of fire engines. Gawkers jammed the walk south of the burning building.

He jumped at the sound of a horn. Farley was gawking too and almost hit a taxi.

"Keep your eyes on the bloody road," Braun barked.

Farley muttered under his breath as Braun ignored him and dialed his cell phone. Alex Kairouz answered.

"Ah, Kairouz. Enjoying the bonfire?"

"You bastard. I'll see you hang."

Braun laughed. "I think not, Kairouz. But I'll forgive that outburst. I'm sure you'll be more respectful since I'm entertaining Cassie. Remember the videos?"

"Liar! She's at school," Alex said as the "call waiting" tone buzzed.

"Do take that, Kairouz. No doubt it's the Farnsworth bitch. You have ten seconds to deal with her before I disconnect and Cassie disappears. Ready? Go."

"Look, Braun—"

"Nine seconds, Kairouz. Tick. Tick. Tick."

Alex switched calls.

***

"Mr. Kairouz! Thank God!" Gillian Farnsworth said. "That brute Farley has somehow taken Cassie fr—"

"I know. I'll call back," Alex blurted, reconnecting with Braun.

***

"What do you want?" he asked, shaken.

"Much better," Braun said. "Speak to no one. Take the tube to Sudsbury and Smythe on Lombard Street. Do you know the firm?"

"I know of it."

"Ask for Mr. Carrington-Smythe, the managing director. You're expected. He'll give you a case with cash and bearer bonds. Take receipt quickly and leave. Is that clear?"

"Yes."

"Take a cab to Heathrow, the Global Air Charter counter. There's a jet waiting to take you and Cassie to Beirut, your old home. Board and wait."

Alex's hopes rose. To be dashed.

"Cassie, of course, will never arrive," Braun said.

"But, what—"

"Shut up and listen!" Braun said. "When the police arrive, confess you and Dugan conspired to blow up *China Star* and *Asian Trader* to manipulate freight rates, but that when Dugan was arrested in Panama, you panicked and fled. When Sutton discovered your plan to leave him as scapegoat, you killed him and torched the office to cover the murder. You arranged for Farley and me, mere cogs in your evil plan, to collect Cassie as you couldn't trust the upright Mrs. Farnsworth. You will speculate we saw police and, fearing arrest, disappeared with her."

"And if I refuse?" Alex asked.

"Surely you can guess, Kairouz. We've reviewed the video often enough."

A strangled sob told Braun he'd won.

"One more thing, Kairouz," Braun said. "While in custody, kill yourself."

Alex gasped.

"Oh, don't carry on," Braun said. "It's a trade, Kairouz. Your pathetic life in exchange for sparing Cassie."

"You think I trust you?"

"I appeal not to your trust, you fool, but your logic. If Cassie reappears unharmed, it supports what I want believed: that we panicked, dumped the girl, and escaped. They won't waste resources on minor players after they've captured you, the ringleader. But if she disappears or is found dead, she becomes a sympathetic victim and the authorities will keep looking. And if you confess and die, I can release her without fear you'll recant. It's in my interests to do so."

"But how am I supposed to… to…"

"Inmates manage to kill themselves daily, Kairouz. I have every confidence in you. But don't think a halfhearted effort will satisfy me. I need commitment, old boy. Clear?"

"Yes," Alex said, barely audible.

"Excellent. On with it then. And remember, contact no one. In fact, remove your phone battery. I'll know if you don't and might allow Farley a go at darling Cassie."

Braun hung up and smiled. "That went well."

"How are you bugging his phone from here?" Farley asked.

"I'm not, obviously," Braun said with forced patience. "But he's too frightened to do anything but follow orders."

"You think he'll off himself?"

"Of course," Braun said. "But just as importantly, he'll implicate Dugan now. He'll unconsciously compare his own noble sacrifice against a prison term for Dugan. Dugan's fate will seem acceptable." Braun smiled. "Kairouz's suicide will make his confession irrevocable and dovetail nicely with the evidence found in Sutton's desk."

Farley frowned. "So we let the girl go?"

Braun laughed. "Of course not, you idiot. You think I care if some bumbling oafs are looking for me? By the time they suspect anything we'll be long gone."

CHAPTER TWENTY-FIVE

"Bloody hell," Anna said into the phone. "What about the protective detail?"

"On his tail," Lou said, "but quite a ways behind."

She sighed. "All right. Air support?"

"A chopper's en route. Control has Cassie eastbound on Lambeth Bridge, near you. Vehicle unknown."

"I need transport," Anna said.

"It looks like the chase car will be coming right by you," Lou said. "Can you be at the corner of Lambeth Road and Pratt Walk in ten minutes?"

"Affirmative."

"All right," Lou said. "I'll have the chase car call when they near the intersection and start another car en route from HQ as a backup in case the chase moves abruptly in another direction. Harry, Dugan, Reyes, and I are leaving from Askew Road. I'll call Ward, but we've no time to collect him. We'll get her back, Anna."

We better, Anna thought, hanging up and pushing through the crowd to Mrs. Coutts at the mob's edge checking off arriving employees to start a list of missing colleagues. Anna looked around.

"Mr. Kairouz?"

Mrs. Coutts pointed to Alex some distance away, his back turned as he pocketed his phone. He turned as she approached, his face red.

"So much for your bloody promises."

"Alex?... But how—"

"From Mrs. Farnsworth, who is apparently more competent than the whole of Her Majesty's bloody Security Service. Where the hell was the protection?"

"We've a strong signal," Anna said, "and I'm going after her. But you shouldn't be alone now. Wait here while I get Mrs. Coutts."

Anna hurried away. When she returned with Mrs. Coutts, Alex was gone.

***

Alex skirted arriving firefighters to walk north along the river, crossing Westminster Bridge to the tube station. He'd been wrong to entrust Cassie's safety to others. Braun was too smart. He had no choice now but to play Braun's game.

Even now, pursuit endangered Cassie, but he knew he couldn't stop it. Braun was the real target now, whatever Anna said, for only he held the key to the attacks. And if Braun did escape, it would mean he'd found and disabled the implant and knew he was compromised. In that scenario, Alex was Cassie's last chance. Braun the desperate fugitive would kill her and flee. Unless Alex provided an option. Unless his confession and suicide made the news in time for Braun to hear. Braun couldn't even be charged with kidnapping if acting on Alex's orders. Assuming he left Cassie unharmed.

Alex embraced that fragile hope and marched toward a date with death.

BRIDGE STREET
APPROACHING WESTMINSTER BRIDGE

"Any luck?" Lou asked over his shoulder as Dugan dialed again, unaware Alex was entering the tube station only yards away.

"Another 'unavailable' message," Dugan said from the backseat next to Reyes, glaring out at traffic. Assuming Lambeth Bridge would choke first, Lou had diverted to Westminster Bridge, along with most of the rest of London it seemed.

"Try the Farnsworth woman," Harry suggested.

Dugan nodded and dialed. She answered at once.

"Mr. Dugan," she said, "thank God you're here. Farley has kidnapped Cassie. I called Mr. Kairouz straightaway, but he hung up and hasn't rung back. When I call, I get a bloody recording. The headmistress called the police, but Ms. Walsh's 'protection' is nowhere to be seen. What should I do?"

She was coming unwound. Dugan tried to calm her.

"Mrs. Farnsworth—Gillian. You need to be calm for Cassie's sake. Anna's people are tracking her and have a rescue plan." He hoped. "I can't reach Alex either, but I'll keep trying and call you when I do."

"All right," she said, perceptibly calmer.

"We don't want the media involved. Suggest to the headmistress it's likely a kidnapping for ransom. Swear her to silence. Can you do that for me?"

"Of course. You needn't speak to me as if I were a child, Mr. Dugan."

"You're right. Forgive me," he said, relieved at the steel in her voice.

"Anna's guys will deal with the police," Dugan said, looking at Harry, who nodded and dialed his own phone. "You best go home. I'll call when I know anything."

"See that you do," she said, again in control. "Good-bye, Mr. Dugan."

Dugan hung up and waited for Harry to finish his call.

"Cops say they went out the toilet window," Harry said as he hung up. "A two-man job. Braun must be along."

"His plan is in motion," Dugan said. "Burning the office cuts him off from the attack ship or ships and prevents us from searching for it. Which means—"

"We have to take the bastard alive," Lou finished from behind the wheel.

They sat, digesting that. Harry broke the silence.

"You handled the Farnsworth woman well, Yank."

"Maybe in gratitude you can describe the rescue plan I assured her we had," Dugan said.

LAMBETH ROAD EASTBOUND

Farley laid on his horn.

"Are you *trying* to attract attention, you idiot?" Braun said.

Farley sulked. Traffic was worse than anticipated. They had cutout vehicles in multiple locations, but they'd yet to reach the first one. Braun decided to forgo multiple switches and go to the safe house after the first change.

The shadow flickered again, and Braun leaned out to see a helicopter high overhead. He drew in and studied the traffic. The left lane was moving well as cars turned left to escape the accident ahead.

"Turn left on Saint Georges Road."

"But we're almost past the jam."

"Do it."

LAMBETH ROAD AT PRATT WALK

The car pulled to the curb in front of Anna. The agent in the front passenger seat jumped out and got in back, yielding his seat to Anna. Anna got in, and the driver laid on his horn and forced his way back into traffic.

"This is a bloody balls-up," Anna said. "Was watching one young girl too taxing for you two?"

The driver shot a sheepish glance over his shoulder, deferring to his partner in the back. After a long pause the man in back spoke. "Anna—"

"Stow it. There is absolutely nothing you can say to help yourselves. Now give me the damn radio," she said, holding out her hand.

The agent in back passed over the radio, and Anna took charge.

"Control. This is Walsh. I'm now in the chase car at Lambeth Road and Pratt Walk. Do you have the link with all units yet?"

"Affirmative, Walsh. You're Chase One. Chesterton is Chase Two. Chopper is Air One. Target is east of your position on Lambeth, near the War Museum."

"Chase One to Air One. Do you have an ID?"

"Negative, Walsh. I can't separate him yet," the chopper pilot said.

"Chase Two, did you copy? What's your location, Lou?" Anna asked.

"I copy Anna," Lou said. "We're across the bridge, east on Westminster Bridge Road. We'll parallel you in case he breaks north. Where do you want the police?"

"Out of sight," she said. "When the chopper IDs him, we'll fake an accident in his path. When he stops, we'll surprise him."

"Got it," Lou said, then added, "Anna, have you seen Kairouz?"

"Negative. He's disappeared."

"Understood," Lou said.

She wondered briefly about Alex, then cursed traffic. At least Braun was trapped too.

Saint Georges Road Northbound

Traffic moved faster on Saint Georges Road, most turning east on to Westminster Bridge Road back toward Saint Georges Circus.

"Make the right. Stay with the eastbound traffic," Braun said, leaning out again.

As Farley complied, Braun pulled his head in. "Still there," he said.

"Who?"

"The helicopter that's tracking us."

Farley tried to look up through the windshield.

"Eyes on the road," Braun snapped.

Farley shot Braun a glare, then stared ahead.

"Interesting," Braun said. "The police couldn't have found us. Even if someone saw an IPS truck at the school, there are hundreds in the city; that's why I chose it. They're tracking us somehow. It can only be the girl. She must have a tracking device or an implant."

"Christ, the flu jab," Farley said. "It seemed legit. She whined all the way home. Even missed school the next day, which now that I think on seems a bit of a carry-on for a jab."

"Right under your bloody nose," Braun started, then contained himself. First things first.

"All right," he said. "Let's take stock. Our opponents coerced a doctor, have remote surveillance and a helicopter. That says authorities."

"Shit. Cut out the implant and toss it. Better yet, toss her out as a diversion."

"And do what, you idiot? Magically speed through the snarl in this brightly colored shoe box? No, I have plans for our little simpleton. They obviously haven't identified us, or they'd have attempted something. We're still only a signal. Just drive while I think."

It came to him as they neared Saint Georges Circus.

"Take London Road to New Kent," Braun said. "Most of these cars will stay with us, and an IPS van headed to the terminal is normal." He laid out the rest.

Later on New Hope Road, Farley purposely caught the light near a B&Q Super Center.

"OK," Braun said, "the loading dock in ten minutes. And Farley, do act like you belong."

Farley gave an affirmative grunt as Braun left the truck to melt into the crowd.

LAMBETH ROAD
APPROACHING SAINT GEORGES CIRCUS

Anna swore. Braun's lead had widened.

"Target is stationary at New Kent Road and Balfour Street," Control said.

"Copy that," the chopper pilot said. "An IPS van and two cars caught the light. It's one of those. Wait; someone is leaving the van. Damn. I lost him in the crowd and—"

"Air One, stay on the signal," Anna said. "We're a mile back. Lou, location?"

"A quarter mile behind you, Anna."

"The cars are turning," the chopper pilot said, "but the van's going straight for the terminal."

"This is Control. Signal is still on New Kent Road."

"Bingo!" the pilot said. "Positive ID on IPS truck."

"Brilliant," Anna said. "Lou, have the police close to two blocks while we work out how to engage."

"Will do, Anna."

She leaned forward as if to speed traffic by force of will just as squealing tires preceded a loud bang ahead, and a wave of flashing brake lights rippled toward her.

SUDSBURY AND SMYTHE
PRIVATE BANKERS
LOMBARD STREET, LONDON

Clive Carrington-Smythe, managing director and majority shareholder of Sudsbury and Smythe, stared at the case uneasily. If generations of Smythes and hyphenated Smythes had learned anything, it was that one's reputation was all, and this felt dodgy. But he couldn't refuse. Thanks to Braun's appearance months ago, Phoenix Shipping was his largest account, and Braun never questioned charges. Almost like halcyon days of old when family fortunes were managed by gentlemen far too polite to question fees. But it was a great deal of money, he thought again, looking at the oversize case.

"Mr. Kairouz, sir," his secretary said, showing a man in.

"Mr. Kairouz, at long last. I've so enjoyed dealing with Captain Braun. I am sorry your own schedule has precluded our meeting."

The man nodded but looked puzzled. The banker was puzzled as well. His visitor was disheveled, with circles under his eyes and a vacant look.

"Coffee or tea?" Carrington-Smythe asked, waving his guest to a sofa.

"Nothing, thank you. I'm pressed, I'm afraid."

"Of course," the banker said, moving the case to the coffee table. "Nasty buggers, these pirates. The Royal Navy should hang the lot, like the old days."

He opened the case. "Had to be creative to fit it all in, I'm afraid. Dollars, pounds, and bearer bonds." He offered a paper. "If you'll verify and sign, we're done."

"I'm sure it's all in order." Kairouz scrawled his signature.

"But… but… my God, sir, that's twelve million doll—"

"I'm sure it's fine." Kairouz closed the case and rose, hefting it in his left hand and extending his right. "Do forgive my rush, but as I said, I am pressed."

"Of course," the banker said. "Is there anything else?"

"No, I… Actually, yes. My phone battery is flat. Could you call a cab?"

"Absolutely. Where to?"

"Heathrow. The private terminal."

B&Q Super Center
New Kent Road
Near IPS Main Terminal, London

Braun left the B&Q with a long box on his shoulder. He dashed for the terminal, slowing as he reached the gate to wave to a bored guard and get a nod in return. He spotted Farley at the far end of the covered loading dock next to another truck, both backed in with only their fronts visible from above. He crossed the distance and climbed in, motioning Farley to follow him to the back.

"Tape her up so she can't flail about," Braun said, tossing Farley a roll of duct tape.

Farley worked quickly, glancing over as Braun opened the box.

"Data Shield—Window Film," he read aloud. "What the bloody hell is that?"

"This, Farley, will make our guest invisible. Help me wrap her."

Minutes later, Cassie was encased in a silvery cocoon.

"OK," Braun said, "when you hear my tap, be ready to carry her to the next truck."

"But why—"

"JUST DO IT," Braun said, raising the rear door to exit, then closing it after himself.

He moved into the back of the next truck. The driver was stacking boxes, his back turned. He turned as the van shifted with Braun's weight and got a bullet in the forehead, the soft pop of the silenced pistol lost in the dock noise. Braun moved boxes to the dock, building a wall behind the two trucks, then tapped the back of his own truck and ripped up the roller door. Farley carried Cassie into the next truck unseen.

Braun looked in, nodding at the dead driver. "Get the keys and be ready."

"Where are you going?"

Braun smiled. "To arrange a little distraction," he said and rolled the door down.

The break room was empty, its worn furniture littered with newspaper. Vending machines lined a wall across from a counter holding small appliances. In a corner, Braun found a utility closet with a gas water heater. He moved to the counter and stuffed newspaper into a toaster oven, leaving the oven door ajar before returning to the utility closet. Gas hissed as he unscrewed the connection. He turned the oven on and left.

NEW KENT ROAD
HALF MILE WEST OF IPS TERMINAL

"Control. This is Chase One. We're moving again on New Kent Road," Anna said.

"I copy, Chase One. Target is... wait... no signal, repeat, no signal."

"Air One," Anna said, "do you have visual?"

"I can see the front of the truck," the pilot said. "He hasn't moved."

"Control, is your equipment OK?" Anna asked.

"We're fine, Chase One. The transmitter has been disabled."

The bastard's made us, Anna thought. "Lou. Status?"

"A half mile back," Lou said, "Harry's on with the police. They're hamstrung by jams; they need more time to close."

"Chase One," the chopper broke in, "movement in the terminal."

"Braun's van?" Anna asked.

"Negative. But four others are queuing to leave."

Braun was taking Cassie, Anna realized, else he would've left the signal as a decoy. He was moving, but not his van, and men afoot dragging a girl could hardly escape notice.

"All units," Anna said, "Cassie's in one of those trucks."

"This is Air One. All four are eastbound on New Kent. Whom do I tail?"

"Air One," Anna said, "they have to take the Great Dover roundabout. That leaves four trucks with three possible exits. Stay over the largest group. Chase Two and I will tail trucks that split off. Keep as many in sight as long as possible to vector in police cars. All units confirm."

"Understood, Chase One," the pilot said, doubt in his voice.

"We copy," Lou said. "Harry's called a second chopper, and the police are ordering IPS to ring all of their drivers to stop. Even if he slips us, he'll be the only truck moving."

"Brilliant, Lou," Anna said. "I see the back of the last truck ahead of us now."

"We have you in sight as well," Lou said. "We'll get the bastards, Anna."

Your lips to God's ears, Anna thought, focusing on the truck ahead.

NEW KENT ROAD EASTBOUND

Farley drove third of four.

"Which way?" he asked.

"One chopper can't follow us all. We'll go wherever the others don't," Braun said, watching the trucks ahead and glancing in the side mirror at the truck behind.

The lead truck and the last truck moved left as the second truck edged right.

"Good," Braun said. "Two look to be heading northbound on Great Dover, and the one behind us is going south on Old Kent Road. We'll take Tower Bridge Road. Odds are the chopper will follow the two northbound trucks. And"—he peered back at the terminal in the side mirror—"we should get a little help right about... now."

He grinned as flame bloomed behind them, followed by a low rumble.

Tower Bridge Road

"We've lost them," Braun said. "Time to dump the truck."

Farley nodded. "Our closest cutout is in the car park on Saint Thomas."

"Think, Farley. We stick out like a sore thumb. Duck into the next covered parking. I'll sit on the girl while you change and take a cab to bring the car from Saint Thomas."

Farley nodded, and minutes later, was pulling into a space on the second floor of a parking garage. He changed into street clothes. As he left, Braun dialed his phone.

"Mr. Carrington-Smythe, please. Captain Braun calling," he said.

A moment later, Carrington-Smythe was on the line.

"Good morning ,Captain Braun. How may I—"

"Please," Braun whispered, "you must help me. Has he been there yet?"

"Who? Kairouz? Why yes, some time ago. I did just as you asked."

"Only under duress. Kairouz threatened my family. Poor Sutton resisted, and the monster shot him and torched the office to cover it. He's looting the company and fleeing."

"Good Lord, man! You must go to—"

"I can't. His goons are watching. Notify the authorities, but please, please, leave my name out of it for the sake of my children. Wait! Someone's coming. I must—"

Braun hung up, smiling. That should do it.

CHAPTER TWENTY-SIX

"I'm fine, Tom," Anna repeated.

The IPS terminal had exploded just before her car passed it, wreaking havoc and bringing traffic to an immediate halt. Caught accelerating into the melee, her driver had rear-ended a taxi despite his best efforts. Double black eyes from the exploding air bag left her with a racoonish look, prompting Dugan's unwanted solicitude. She'd insisted on returning to HQ, and the paramedics hadn't argued, having had more serious injuries to attend.

Destruction of the terminal halted efforts to stop the trucks. The police were searching, but she knew they'd find an abandoned truck and cold trail.

"Harry, where's Lou?" she asked. "He and Ward should be here by now."

"He called. They stopped by New Scotland Yard. Didn't say why. I'll give him a call." He was raising his phone when Lou walked in with Ward.

"Christ," Ward said. "Anna, are you—"

"I'm fine."

"Welcome to the Elephant Man Club," Dugan said, earning a glare from Anna.

Dugan ignored the glare and turned to Ward. "So, Jesse. Did the police have something?"

Ward glanced at Lou.

"Metro arrested Alex Kairouz at Heathrow with $12 million in cash and negotiables," Lou said. "He confessed to engineering the attacks. Says he panicked at your arrest and decided to escape."

"Bullshit. How can anyone believ—"

Lou held up a hand. "There's more. He also confessed to killing Sutton and setting the firebombs in the office to cover it. Metro confirmed Sutton's death." Lou paused. "And he named you as coconspirator, Tom."

"Braun coerced him. He's trying to save Cassie. Who can blame him when we screwed up by the numbers? Did you tell that to Scotland Yard?"

"I did," Lou said. "But his story's tight. Says he ordered Braun to grab Cassie for fear Mrs. Farnsworth wouldn't play along. He speculates Braun didn't bring her to the plane because he had an observer who saw the police and warned him off. Rubbish, but credible."

"We need to talk to him," Dugan said.

"We did, Tom," Ward said. "When he learned we'd lost Cassie, he said, 'It's always been up to me—tell Thomas I'm sorry,' and asked to return to his cell."

"Christ on a crutch. Am I under arrest, Jesse?"

"Of course," Ward said, nodding toward Reyes, "you're in Panamanian custody. And Agent Chesterton was most creative in explaining to the Financial Crimes folks at New Scotland Yard both the arcane aspects of international law that allowed you to be in Panamanian custody on British soil and just how they should go about requesting transfer of custody."

Lou Chesterton smiled. "I also assured our law-enforcement colleagues we're keeping close tabs on you and that you had information that is key to our operation. How much time that buys us, I don't know."

Dugan shot Lou a grateful look.

"All right, let's get cracking," Anna said. "Parallel objectives—thwart the attacks and find Braun and Cassie. Tom, you're our ship expert. Thoughts?"

"I'll have Mrs. Coutts check the off-site backups, but I'm sure they're compromised. That leaves my week-old position report and some educated guessing.

"Braun's departure," he continued, "suggests imminent attacks, say within two days. If I exclude Panama and Malacca and draw circles around other choke points with a radius equal to two days' steaming time, we have probable attack-ship envelopes. With the old report, I'll try to weed out tankers that can't possibly have reached these areas."

Anna nodded. "A short list, like before."

"More like a 'much-longer-than-I-want list.' Working with week-old data will complicate things." He sighed. "But I don't have a clue what else to do."

Anna nodded. "Get started straightaway. Tell Harry what you need. This will be our ops center. The IT people will have us up and running within the hour. Braun's escape was improvised, and he's probably reassessing. We'll keep pressure on. I released his photo, along with Farley's and Cassie's, to the media. Moving will be difficult.

"He'll be close," she went on. "We'll check rentals and utility hookups in a fifty-mile radius and cross those against known aliases and family and associates for Farley and Sutton."

Anna saw skepticism. Ward voiced it.

"That's a big area, Anna. There must be a thousand possibilities."

She sighed. "Several thousand. We best get started."

17 SAXON WAY
GRAVESEND, KENT

Braun opened the pantry. "Bloody fuck all."

"Here either," Farley said, standing in front of the open refrigerator.

Braun cursed Sutton as an incompetent fool. First the balls-up about renting the safe house and now this. How difficult could it be to lay in food and supplies? He now understood Sutton's sudden insistence on sabotaging Kairouz's computers via phone link. He'd put off stocking the safe house and intended to do it while Braun and Farley were in the office. He must have been sweating bullets while he sabotaged the computers, rushing to finish so he could get away and stock the place before they arrived. He died before he had the chance, and now Braun regretted not killing the fool slowly.

Braun sighed. "I'll go to the market we passed. But let's check the news first. Assuming that bloody idiot actually got the cable connected."

They moved to the living room and turned on the television.

"…Alexander Kairouz was taken into custody at Heathrow."

Braun smiled.

"Kairouz's daughter is missing, abductors thought to be Karl Braun and Ian Farley, whose photos are shown here along with the girl's. Anyone seeing…"

"Bloody hell," Farley said as Braun's smile faded.

"We'll adapt," Braun said. "You stay here. I'll disguise myself and go. But first, let's take care of the girl."

***

Cassie lay in her silver cocoon on the bedroom floor as they transformed the big closet, taping film to the walls and ceiling and spreading it on the floor, covering that with a rug. Finally they lined the door and hung a film curtain inside, a barrier when the door opened.

Farley carried Cassie in, and Braun squatted on the closet floor beside her as Farley unwrapped the girl. A bloody implant. He fingered her scar. It was deep, but he could get it. No need to rush. They'd be here a while. If she became a great liability, he'd have his fun and slit her throat. He ripped the tape off her mouth and rose, leaving her bound and unconscious.

"I'm going to get ready. Stay in the bedroom and call me if she wakes."

"There ain't a telly in the bedroom. I'll hear her fine in the living room."

"So might the neighbors, you bloody fool," Braun said.

"Oh, all right, but at least let me watch the porn on your laptop."

***

"Just at the best part," muttered Farley as Cassie whimpered.

"Wher… where am I?" she asked as he pushed through the silver curtain.

"In the bosom of your new family."

She lowered her voice. "I have to pee."

"Go ahead," he whispered back, laughing as he left.

He exited the closet to come face-to-face with a stranger, and his hand flew to his shoulder holster.

"It's me, you idiot."

Farley stared. Black hair, not blond. Gray at the temples with a salt-and-pepper mustache. Oral inserts made Braun's face fuller.

"Bloody magic."

"I'll bask in your admiration later, Farley. Is she awake?"

"Yeah." He smirked. "Said she had to piss. I told her go ahead."

"Brilliant. Did you tell her you'd clean it up? She'll be in there several days. Get a pot from the kitchen and a toilet roll from the bathroom."

Chastened, Farley started off as Braun entered the closet.

"Who are you?" Cassie asked.

"Call me 'Uncle Karl.'"

"Please. I have to go to the bathroom really, really bad."

Braun fished out a pocketknife to slice her restraints. He helped her stand as Farley entered and set the pot and toilet paper in the corner.

"I can't use *that*," Cassie whined.

Braun twisted her arm.

"You're hurting me. OK, I'll do it," she said, staggering to the pot.

"Go on," Braun said as she hesitated.

"No. You both leave."

Braun suppressed his anger and motioned for Farley to follow him.

"Goin' soft, are we?" Farley asked outside.

"Slapping a retard with a full bladder is ill-advised, Farley. I'll attend to her before I go."

"I'll do it, guv." Farley rubbed his groin. "I need some fun."

"Forget it, Farley. If you're randy, have a wank."

"But you said—"

"I lied. Live with it."

Farley's nostrils flared. Braun mollified him. He needed Farley. For now.

"Look, Farley, she wasn't part of your original deal. I went along later because your interest terrified Kairouz, but the wogs will pay a fortune for a blond virgin. We'll split it. And if she gets too hot to move, we'll both have a go, then kill her. Fair enough?"

Farley nodded, and Braun beat on the closet door.

"Get a bloody move on, princess. Sixty seconds."

***

Cassie swayed as she rose on stiff legs. She steadied herself on the wall, shifting a strip of film. She watched, terrified, as it curled down from the ceiling in a growing triangle. They'd hurt her again even though it was an accident. She pushed at the tape, smoothing it as far up as she could reach. It looked OK, then the unattached corner resumed its slow crawl downward.

She jumped at the pounding on the door, then calmed herself. A proper young lady did not go flibbertigibbet at setbacks. A young lady rose above difficulties. She slipped out of one shoe, grasped it by the toe, and squatted to explode upward, stretching to push the errant corner in place with the shoe heel. She was slipping back into the shoe as the door opened.

***

Braun pushed her down.

"Tape wrists and ankles again, Farley, wrists in front," Braun said, nodding as Farley complied.

"That's good. Now stand her up and hold her from behind. And pay attention, Farley. You might learn something."

Braun got in her face. "You did a very bad thing, Cassie."

She shook her head, wide-eyed. How did he know?

"You defied me, Cassie. Told me to leave. Now I must punish you."

She was trembling. Farley chuckled.

"Now Farley," Braun said, "with market value a factor, avoid knuckle damage. Use a flatty." He slapped her with his open hand, snapping her head to the side. He went on, ignoring her sobs. "An alternative is the backhand flatty, but it requires care. Jewelry that might leave scars should be removed and nails well trimmed." He pocketed a ring and wiggled manicured fingers.

"The backhand flatty is delivered thus."

He snapped Cassie's head to the opposite side, then pinched her chin between thumb and forefinger, turning her face from side to side.

"Observe, Farley. Only soft-tissue damage. Painful but fast healing. The only scars are mental. The most useful sort.

"Now Cassie," Braun said, "do you understand you must never be bad again?"

She squeezed her eyes shut and nodded.

"Say it."

"I... I wo... won't b... be ba... bad."

"Good, Cassie. But"—he feigned regret—"I'm not sure you're sincere." He slapped her again, twice to each side of her face, and signaled Farley to drop her.

"I'll be back in an hour or so. Leave her in the dark and stay in the bedroom."

SECURITY SERVICE (MI5) HQ
THAMES HOUSE, LONDON

"How's it coming?" Ward asked, passing Dugan a cup of coffee.

"Just peachy. Too many prospects already."

Dugan sighed and looked around. Reyes sat nearby, sipping coffee and watching. Technicians manned terminals. Harry was on the phone with London Metro's Specialist Fire Arms Command, also known as CO19, the hostage rescue unit. Anna and Lou sat, heads together, in the corner.

His phone rang, and Dugan saw Gillian Farnsworth's number on the caller ID. He considered letting it go to voice mail again. He answered on the fifth ring.

"Mr. Dugan. At last. What news?"

"Ahh, there have been... setbacks."

"Setbacks?"

"We lost her signal. We... we've lost her."

Anna hurried over and motioned Dugan to put the call on speaker.

Gillian's voice exploded into the room. "... failed to keep me informed, and those fools with whom you're associated lost Cassie as well. This on top of the lies about Mr. Kairouz in the media—"

"Gillian, this is Anna Walsh. Where are you?"

"On my way to New Scotland Yard. I am—"

"Gillian, I think—"

"I bloody well don't care what you think. I've had quite enough of you all. After I speak with the police, I'm going to the media. With everything in the open, Braun may see there's no advantage in—"

"Gillian, stop behaving like a bloody twit. Your anger's justified, but don't be rash. Come here to Thames House. See what we're doing. Then go to the media if you wish."

"Very well. Daniel is driving me. I'll be there in fifteen minutes."

"I'll have you met in the lobby."

"See that you do." The speaker hummed with a dial tone.

"Anna, you can't be serious?" Ward said.

"Hopefully she'll understand," Anna said. "But if not, we'll have to detain her."

***

"I'm here, Ms. Walsh. Just what am I to see?" Gillian Farnsworth asked.

"The resources we're devoting to Cassie's recovery. Suggestions are appreciated."

"Really? After you ignored my suggestion to move Cassie out of harm's way?"

Anna's response was cut off by a loud beeping.

"Hit on the implant!" a technician screamed.

Anna rushed to his side.

"East. In Kent," he continued. "Yes, North Kent. Let's zero in."

The screen refreshed with agonizing slowness.

"There. Gravesend. Now the address… damn… lost it."

Anna turned. "Sarah. Filter rentals and hookups. Gravesend only. John. Search on Sutton and Farley with Gravesend as primary filter."

"Over a hundred recent hookups," Sarah said quickly.

"Damn. Still too many," Anna said as John hooted.

"Bingo. An obit, two years ago." He read, "'Margaret Sutton. Survived by son, Joel Sutton, of London, and sister, Mary Lampkin, seventy-eight, of Gravesend, Kent.'"

"Address?"

"Checking… got it," John said. "Seventeen Saxon Way, Gravesend. Taxes current. But National Health shows her widowed and resident at a nursing home with senile dementia."

"But planning a recovery," Sarah added. "A new cable hookup at that address was paid for by Joel Sutton."

"Brilliant," Anna said. "Nearest police station?"

Sarah pulled up a map. "There. The North Kent Station."

"Helipad?" Anna asked.

"No," Sarah said. "But there's a car park."

"Lou," Anna said. "Ring North Kent Police to cordon off their car park. They should expect a landing in fifteen minutes."

"On it," Lou said.

"Harry. Ring the CO19 lads with the site. Request a chopper for us as well."

Anna turned back to the technicians. "Sarah, send the—"

"Maps and photos to your phone. Done," Sarah said. "I sent it to the CO19 lads as well."

Anna nodded thanks and turned. "All right, people, let's get to the roof."

They raced out the door. As they rushed down the hall, Anna turned to speak to Ward and stopped in her tracks.

"Gillian, what are you doing?"

"Following you, obviously."

"Out of the question."

"Now you listen—"

"I'm sorry, but this isn't negotiable, and I've no time for argument. You're staying here."

Anna turned and called to a young man walking down the hall. He hurried over.

"Wentworth," Anna said, "escort Mrs. Farnsworth back to the command center and place her in Sarah's care. Tell Sarah Mrs. Farnsworth is to stay there until she hears otherwise from me."

The young agent nodded as Anna turned back to Mrs. Farnsworth.

"Gillian, the command center will be in touch with us at all times, so you'll know what's going on. That's the best I can do," Anna said, then turned and led the team away.

Gillian stood enraged, watching their backs. They'd bungled things and now had the cheek to suggest she wait patiently to be "informed," as if they hadn't bungled that as well. Sod that.

"Ma'am? Mrs. Farnsworth?"

Gillian roused and stared at the young man.

"Please come with me," he said, taking her arm.

Gillian saw a door marked Women nearby. She faked a stumble, then bent slightly at the waist and clutched her midsection.

"Ma'am? What's wrong?" Wentworth asked.

"All the... stress and exci... excitement..." Gillian gasped, moving toward the toilet. "I... I'm ill."

Wentworth allowed Gillian to lead him through the door and stood uncomfortably in the center of the women's restroom as Gillian stumbled into a stall and let the door swing shut behind her. She made horrible retching sounds.

"Ma'am? Are you all right?" Wentworth asked.

"I... I... think you better get... get help. Ge... get... Sarah. Ple... please hurry."

Wentworth raced to the door of the toilet and looked out at the closed door of the command center, down the corridor. He looked about for help, but it was lunch hour, and the hallway was deserted. He called Sarah's name several times, then reached for his cell phone just as another strangled cry came from the stall. The command center was only fifty feet away. He pocketed his phone and raced for the door.

***

167

Gillian was on her feet and out of the stall as soon as she heard the toilet door swinging closed. She caught it just before it closed and held it open a crack, watching Wentworth's back as he rushed away. She timed her exit as he reached the control room door, bursting from the toilet and across the hall to the stairwell. The stairwell door opened with a loud clunk, and Gillian heard Wentworth's angry shout through the closing stairwell door as she rushed down the single flight to the ground floor.

The ground-level exit was prominently marked EMERGENCY EXIT ONLY—ALARMED DOOR. Gillian burst through it without slowing, and the piercing wail sent her already racing pulse even higher. She raced around the building to find Daniel in the waiting area where she had left him only minutes before.

"How far to Gravesend?" she gasped, out of breath as she slid into the rear seat.

"Are you all right, mum?" Daniel asked, his concern obvious.

"I'm fine, Daniel. But quickly. Gravesend?"

"Do you have an address?"

"Seventeen Saxon Way, Gravesend."

The old driver nodded. "Me wife used to visit a friend out that way before she passed. It's maybe three-quarters of an hour. A bit less if I push."

"See that you do. We're off to get our Cassie."

He turned to the wheel, and she was thrown back in her seat as tires squealed.

17 SAXON WAY
GRAVESEND, KENT

Farley watched porn, pants bulging as he debated a wank. Bloody Kraut. Leading a bloke on. He got up and stalked to the living room, parting the drapes. Slip a taste and slap her quiet? If Braun twigged, what would he do? Cut his bloody bonus, that's what. Bugger. He let the curtains fall and moved back to his porn.

***

"We can't worry about her now, Sarah," Anna said into the phone as she peered between the blinds at the house across the street. "And I don't think she'll go to the media given that she knows we're closing on Cassie's kidnappers."

Anna's radio crackled. "One to Walsh. Positive ID on Farley."

"I have to go, Sarah," Anna said into the phone, hanging up to key the radio mike.

"I saw him, One. Anyone else?"

"Negative. Infrared shows one heat signature. Our lads have a good angle on the window in the back of the garage. There is no vehicle."

"Hold positions; I will advise."

The front door and attached garage of Braun's safe house faced the street, with the backyard enclosed by a fence. Throughout the neighborhood, service alleys separated residents' backyards from those of their neighbors on adjacent streets. Fourteen Saxon Way, diagonally across from the safe house, was vacant, and Anna's team had entered unseen from the service alley. She stood now in the living room, a sniper in the bedroom above and an assault team in the alley directly behind number seventeen.

Anna stepped back from the window as Lou moved to take her place.

"They must have shielded the implant," she said. "We got the flicker when that was somehow compromised. But if they shielded a whole room, Cassie and Braun might be inside. But where's their car?"

"Farley stared one way," Ward said. "He's expecting someone. My bet's Braun."

Standing nearby, Reyes grunted agreement.

"Take Farley out," Dugan said. "Save Cassie and wait for Braun."

Anna looked doubtful. "Braun may have some sort of prearranged "all clear" signal before he returns. If Cassie's with him, we risk losing them both. Taking out Farley's not worth the risk of losing both Cassie and any chance of sweating Braun."

"I don't think we have to worry about Farnsworth going to the media," Lou said from the window.

"Bloody hell," Anna said as she joined him to see a poorly disguised Gillian Farnsworth approach a nearby bus stop.

"What can we do now?" Dugan asked.

"Nothing," Anna said. "If we try to pull her in, Farley will spot us for sure, especially if she makes a fuss. All we can do is pray Braun develops myopia. Harry," Anna said over her shoulder, "when it hits the fan, go collect Mrs. Bloody Farnsworth."

***

Gillian Farnsworth sat at the bus stop in a head scarf and dark glasses. Sufficient, she was sure. She'd be the last person Braun expected.

They'd arrived before Daniel's projection, and it had taken all her persuasive powers to get the driver to agree to drop her and park well away to await her call. She was unsure what to do but trusted it would become obvious. She peeked over her shades. She could hardly do worse than the "professionals," after all. It was obvious their priority was Braun, not Cassie.

***

Braun returned the clerk's smile, though he hardly felt cordial. The selection was abysmal, and his cart was piled with food he detested. He rolled it out to the van, parked between the supermarket and the chemist shop where he earlier bought supplies for removing the implant.

Braun loaded the supplies and pulled out of the parking lot, turning away from the safe house to trace a meandering path through the surrounding neighborhood, alert to anyone following. Good tradecraft was always necessary, even when one was sure of no surveillance. He smiled. Or perhaps especially when one was sure of no surveillance.

He completed a series of random turns and was just about to head for the safe house when he passed Kairouz's car. It was parked in plain sight on the side of the road, the driver leaning against the side and smoking his pipe. What the hell was the old kike doing here? Coincidence? He didn't believe in coincidence. But if it was some sort of trap, why was he parked in the open? Braun continued, scanning his surroundings with even more care than usual.

***

Farley rubbed himself through his pants. Braun would likely dawdle, picking wine and other Frenchified crap. Not like a proper bloke who'd grab a few cases of Guinness and some grub. Farley had time. And he'd thought on the virgin thing. No problem. She could give him a gobble, then take it up the bum.

She blinked up at the light.

"You need a stretch." He smiled as he cut the tape on her wrists and ankles.

"Th… thank you."

"We should be friends, Cassie. Nice to each other, like."

"I… I guess so."

"Good," he said, unbuckling.

She drew away, but he grabbed a fistful of hair with one hand and pushed down his pants with the other.

"Here's a new friend then. Come on. Give him a kiss."

***

Braun continued his circuitous route, confidence returning as each unnecessary detour failed to reveal a tail. Then he spotted Gillian Farnsworth at the bus stop. How'd she find them? That idiot Sutton must have let something slip to the Coutts hag, who then told Farnsworth. Sitting in plain sight in that ridiculous disguise was proof enough she was acting alone. Even the police weren't that incompetent.

However she'd found him, she was a complication, bound to call the police when she spotted him. But he had to get the laptop and take care of Farley and the girl. She turned toward him, then looked away without recognition. Good. She'd be confused when he turned into the drive and likely delay calling the police. He'd finish his business inside and be gone, two minutes tops. He'd put a bullet in her head on the way out. Even if she'd already called, he'd have plenty of time before the cops showed up.

He turned into the drive, his plan in place, to be undone by an earsplitting scream from 17 Saxon Way.

CHAPTER TWENTY-SEVEN

Cassie tried to stay calm, remembering the secret things Mrs. Farnsworth taught her. She chanted to herself in the dark, comforted by the words and the rigid sliver concealed between cupped palms. Then he was there—all kind words and a mean smile. She felt a sharp pain as he yanked her by the hair and shoved her face toward his ugly, swollen thing. She fought down her terror and lived the rhyme:

Jab it in deep
Right to the end
Knickers to knees
Then run like the wind

Farley screamed when she drove the needle through his penis. He groped himself with both hands, and Cassie jerked his pants down and scooted away. Farley lunged and fell forward, his clawing fingers just brushing her as the needle snagged the carpet, tethering him in place by his member.

Cassie burst from the closet and raced through the house. She found the front door locked tight with a keyed dead bolt and retraced her steps, racing past the bedroom where Farley bellowed. She rushed through the kitchen toward the door to the garage, but the sound of the garage-door opener brought her up short. She darted into the pantry, making herself small against shelves to squeeze the door closed to a crack just as Uncle Karl burst in from the garage, gun drawn, rushing toward Farley's voice.

As Uncle Karl disappeared into the hallway, Cassie bolted through the open kitchen door just as the big garage door kissed the concrete. The windowed back door was also locked with a keyed lock. Heart pounding, Cassie mashed the wall control and raced to the big garage door. She fell to her hands and knees as the door inched upward, intent on the widening opening.

***

Farley held up bloody pants with one hand and gripped his Glock with the other.

"You get her?" he asked.

"You lost her? You bloody imbecile."

"She stabbed me. You must—"

Braun heard the garage-door opener and cursed as he raced back through the kitchen and around the van. The rising door was eighteen inches off the concrete, and Cassie's feet disappeared beneath it. He thought quickly. The Farnsworth bitch would rush to the girl. He'd drop them both and drag the bodies inside. Then he'd deal with Farley and be away before the cops arrived. There was time still. He dropped to one knee, waiting for the rising door to reveal his targets.

TWO MINUTES EARLIER
ACROSS THE STREET AT 14 SAXON WAY
GRAVESEND, KENT

"One. Can your man wound him?" Anna asked into her throat mike as the van turned in.

"If he gets out before the door closes. And the house?"

"Have your lads crash it on your shot."

"Roger," he said.

A scream split the air, and Anna watched Gillian Farnsworth stand and rush forward.

"God damn it," Anna said. "Stand down, One."

Anna turned, but Harry was already moving.

***

Harry overtook her in the drive as the garage door closed. He grabbed her arm.

"Come along, luv. Off the street."

Gillian turned. "Let me go, you bloody fool. Cassie's in there."

"And we'll save her if you don't muck it up," Harry said, pulling her along.

They both turned at the sound of the rising door to see a blond head appear. Cassie wriggled free, and Gillian flattened Harry's nose with an elbow worthy of an NBA point guard and bolted. He rushed after, blood pulsing from his nose as he drew his gun and focused on the door, alert to pursuit.

"Get her across the street!" Harry yelled to Gillian, moving to shield them. He saw Braun's feet and fired, cursing as the feet disappeared and the big garage door reversed course. He backed after his charges, gun trained toward the threat.

***

Mrs. Farnsworth held Cassie, whispering reassurance. Despite her outward calm, Gillian Farnsworth simmered. Anna saw it in her eyes as she touched the girl's bruised face. Only Cassie's need was containing that rage. Anna turned back to the task at hand.

"Good work, Harry," Anna said. "They've no leverage now, and they'll be rattled."

"What's the plan?" Ward asked.

"We'll let them stew a bit until they're ready to deal," Anna said. "With any luck, they'll surrender, and we can separate them—play one against the other."

The men nodded, then everyone looked toward the windows at the sound of gunfire from Braun's hideout.

"Bloody hell," Anna said. "Now what?"

"I think, Agent Walsh," Reyes said, "someone is securing a monopoly on marketable information."

"Crash the house," Anna yelled into her mike.

***

Braun was angry but not rattled. He fully intended to surrender—after he'd taken care of things. The laptop was on the living-room coffee table, with the programmed destruction of the hard drive in progress.

"I finally got it out," Farley said as he limped in. "Where is that little bitch?"

Farley was oblivious, having left Cassie's pursuit to Braun to sequester himself in the bathroom, preoccupied with his punctured dick.

"She escaped, you idiot. And we're surrounded."

"What?" Farley limped to the window as Braun mulled options.

With the girl free, he had only information to trade. He had a bit of negotiating time, perhaps as much as twenty-four hours before the next attack, then the value of his information would plummet as the body bags were stacked. Farley knew little, but the authorities wouldn't know that. They might waste valuable time on the idiot, a costly delay for Braun. He drew his gun. He had to clarify the situation for them.

Farley peered out, his back turned. "I don't see—"

He dropped as he saw Braun's reflection in the windowpane, just before the *sphut, sphut* of the silenced pistol and the sound of breaking glass. Farley scrambled, popping up behind the sofa to return fire, his Glock booming. Braun crawled unseen behind an armchair and covered the only door just as Farley fired at Braun's last position and ran. He was framed in the doorway when Braun's bullet shattered his spine. He pitched forward, his Glock clattering on the hardwood as Braun stepped into the hall and shot him twice in the head.

Braun returned to find the computer done, the screen black, just as projectiles crashed through the windows. How unnecessary, he thought, tossing his gun to the floor and flopping down on the sofa, hands over his ears, eyes shut. The flash bangs were followed by splintering wood. So bloody predictable it was hardly a challenge.

"I'm unarmed. I surrender," he called.

***

"What now?" Dugan asked.

Farley sprawled in a bloody pool. Braun was perched on a straight-back chair in the dining room, bound hand and foot and under guard.

"With a firearm-related fatality," Anna said, "the locals will document the scene. Our request for Braun will go through channels, but we can question him now, while we wait."

Ward walked in. "Where's Harry?"

"With Cassie and Mrs. Farnsworth," Anna said. "He'll see them home."

Ward nodded as she turned to the uniformed officer guarding Braun.

"You can go, Constable," Anna said. "Thank you."

"Glad to help, Agent Walsh," said the cop as he left.

"*Agent* Walsh is it?" Braun said. "And you played the slut so well. Experience? And Dugan's an agent as well? Bravo. I've never been outfoxed before."

Anna smiled. "Yet here you sit, trussed up like a bloody Christmas goose."

173

"A temporary setback."

"Oh really?" she asked.

"Don't be tedious, Anna. You know you need my help, and I'm not unwilling to give it."

"In exchange for what?"

"Immunity and a private jet, of course."

"Not bloody likely," Anna said.

Braun shrugged.

"Let's just beat it out of him," suggested Dugan.

Braun laughed. "You pathetic amateur. I'm trained to tolerate harsher methods than you lot are allowed. By the way, when can I see a lawyer?"

Ward grabbed Dugan as he lunged, and tugged him into the hall.

***

Reyes thought Dugan's suggestion was eminently sensible, and he followed as Ward wrestled Dugan into the hallway. Ward gave Reyes a look over his shoulder and then ignored him to concentrate on Dugan.

"Tom. Control yourself or leave," Ward said.

"That son of—"

"Like it or not, we play by the rules," Ward said. "We don't beat suspects or hook jumper cables to their balls. Remember that."

"Suspect? He's not a suspect. We know the bastard's behind this, and people—more people—are gonna die if he doesn't talk, so maybe we just need to remember red is positive and black is negative."

"God damn it, Tom. We don't—"

Dugan held up his hands in surrender. "All right. All right. I'll control myself," he said.

Ward gave him an appraising look, then nodded, leading Dugan back into the room. Reyes followed. He was beginning to like this Dugan.

***

The three men returned to the dining room, trailed by a local policeman.

"Harry Albright?" asked the cop, directing his query at the group.

"Across the street," Anna said.

The cop keyed his mike. "Colin. George here. Is Albright, the MI5 bloke, near you?"

"Right here," came the reply.

"A friend of his at Metro called," the cop said into his radio. "He hasn't been able to get through on his cell but asked us to pass the word that some bugger named Kairouge hung himself. Said he figured Albright would want to know."

"He heard, George."

"OK. Thanks, mate." As George left the room, a peal of laughter shattered the silence.

"Now this makes the cheese more binding," Braun said. "Kairouz dead. In a fit of remorse, no doubt. I'm sure my lawyer—"

Dugan was faster than Ward this time. He knocked Braun to the floor and was over him in a flash, cocking his fist again as Ward and Lou wrestled him away. Dugan screamed abuse and kicked at Braun with adrenaline-fueled rage as he struggled in the men's grasp. Lou pressed a hard knuckle behind Dugan's ear, and he slumped.

"Wha… what the hell was that?" Dugan asked a moment later as Ward helped Braun to the chair.

"Subjection pressure point," Lou said. "We need the bastard conscious, Tom."

Braun grinned up with bloody teeth. "Enjoy that, Dugan? It changes nothing. Kairouz hung himself up like a fat, rotten Christmas ornament, and now I'm untouchable. And the price of information has risen. Take a few minutes to consider a reasonable offer, why don't you all? But not too long. Tick. Tick. Tick."

14 SAXON WAY
GRAVESEND, KENT

Cassie clutched Gillian's hands. "Is Poppa all right?"

"I'm sure he is, dear. I'll just go straighten this out," Gillian said, gently freeing her hands. "Agent Albright," she called.

Harry entered tentatively, unsure if they'd overheard the radio.

"Agent Albright. Stay with Cassie. I need a word with Agent Walsh."

"Ah… I don't know—"

"Thank you," Gillian said.

She maintained her composure until she got outside, then tears blurred her vision as she crossed the street in a stumbling run, praying she'd misunderstood. She walked into number seventeen and stopped, staring at Farley's body in a pool of blood, his gun nearby on the hardwood floor beside a numbered marker as technicians photographed the scene. Then she heard Braun's odious, mocking voice from a doorway down the hall, so like another she'd silenced long ago.

"…changes nothing. Kairouz hung himself up like a fat, rotten Christmas ornament, and now I'm untouchable. And…"

In that horrible moment, she knew it was true that Braun had somehow killed the noblest man she'd ever known. Suddenly she knew what she must do, drawn to the door like a mongoose to a cobra, scooping up Farley's gun from the floor on the way.

"You bloody arsehole!" she screamed as she rushed into the room.

She was Daisy now, firing point-blank, the round punching into him. Recoil spoiled her aim, and the next shot went wild as the slide popped open, the Glock empty. She charged, the gun a club, and it took both Ward and Lou to restrain her.

The next thing Daisy remembered was Anna's voice in her ear.

"Cassie needs you now," said the voice, and rage abated, replaced with a strange emptiness. Daisy searched for Gillian as she was led away between two constables, afraid her wonderful life was lost forever.

***

Braun lay faceup, frothy blood bubbling from his bare chest. He was blue.

"Sucking chest wound," Lou said. "No exit. Hit a rib maybe. Gotta seal it."

"Tom," Ward said. "The bedroom. I saw some duct tape there."

Dugan rushed out as Anna called medevac. When he returned, Ward taped the wound, and they sat Braun up against the wall. He quickly improved—and sneered.

"Bravo," Braun said. "Is this where I'm overcome by gratitude and tell all?"

Lou looked at the others and jerked his head toward the door.

"ETA on the chopper?" he asked in the hall.

"Fifteen minutes," Anna said. "Will he make it?"

"Probably," Lou said. "Not that it matters much now."

She nodded. "By the time he gets out of surgery, we'll be up to our bums in lawyers. And it may be too late anyway."

"Unless he has a change of heart," Lou said, "near-death experience and all. Pity we can't ask, seeing as how we must help the locals prepare a landing area for the chopper."

Lou turned to Dugan. "Can you ask him, Tom? Now mind you, he's not to be mistreated—though he may well claim you did, there being no witnesses and all."

Anna objected. "It should be one of us. Tom's not a trained interrogator."

Ward shook his head. "No, Anna. Lou's right. Braun's not worried about us, but Tom's a credible threat."

Anna looked at Dugan. "Can you do it?"

Dugan's eyes left no doubt. "Oh yeah," he said softly.

Reyes spoke for the first time. "May I suggest that it may seem more credible to Braun if it appears that *Señor Dugan* has slipped away to question Braun on his own?"

Moments later, Anna cleared the house by requesting all the local police to help cordon off the landing zone. As people trooped into the street, Ward hung back a bit, his hand on Dugan's shoulder. They locked eyes.

"I guess sometimes maybe it has to be red is positive and black is negative," Ward said.

Dugan nodded, and Ward moved off with the others.

***

"Where did everyone go, and what are you doing here?" Braun demanded.

Dugan locked the door and squatted by Braun, forearms across his knees. He smiled.

"I slipped back for a chat about the next attacks. It'll help at your trial."

"What trial? Kairouz confessed. Worry about your own trial, you idiot."

Dugan changed tacks. "Think of the thousands that will die."

Braun's laugh finished in a bloody cough.

"They mean nothing to me," he said as he recovered. "You look ridiculous, squatting there like some movie cowboy. Say something appropriate. Yippee tie yie yay, perhaps?"

Dugan rose and grabbed Braun's ankles, jerking the man from the wall so fast his head bounced on the hardwood. Dugan ripped the tape off the wound and got in Braun's face.

"Yee haa," he said, spraying spittle. "How's that, asshole?

"You've fucked me all right," Dugan continued. "Maybe a little too hard. I got nothing left to lose. You think I give two shits about your evil masters or your motives. News flash. I don't. I can use info about the attacks to save my own ass. If you won't provide it, I've no reason to keep you alive. I'll watch you drown in your own blood, then slap the tape back and sit you up. There's no downside, Karl. I can't be any worse off than I am."

Braun gasped, and Dugan patted his shoulder.

"I know it hurts. And I want you to know, I'm still open to a trade. But don't take too long, because you're looking a little blue." He paused. "What was that phrase you like? Oh yeah. Tick. Tick. Tick."

Braun's lips moved. "O… OK," he said.

"Great, Karl. Let's start easy. How many more attacks? I'll say numbers, and you nod or shake your head. OK?"

Braun nodded.

"Here we go. Three or more?"

Braun shook his head.

"Good," Dugan said. "Two more attacks?"

Again, Braun shook his head.

"Great, Karl. So there's one more attack?"

Braun nodded. Eyes closed. Face a blue mask. Dugan slapped his cheeks.

"Stay with me, Karl. Where?"

Braun's lips moved, and Dugan put his ear close. "Is… Is… Ista…"

"Istanbul? The Bosphorus Straits?"

Braun managed a nod.

Dugan slapped him harder. "What ship? What load port? Talk to me."

Braun opened his eyes and tried to speak as frothy blood whistled from his wound. "O… o…" he began. His head fell to one side.

Dugan slapped the tape back and dragged Braun upright just as paramedics entered the house. Dugan ran outside.

"One more attack," Dugan shouted over chopper noise. "Istanbul."

Anna shouted back. "We've good news too. Alex survived, but he's in serious condition."

Dugan closed his eyes and nodded as Ward gripped his shoulder. He opened them to see paramedics rush Braun to the chopper.

Anna had called in their own chopper, and as they flew back to Thames House, Dugan's thoughts turned eastward to Istanbul, city of thirteen million astride the winding Bosphorus.

CHAPTER TWENTY-EIGHT

Dugan looked up as Anna entered the waiting room.

"How's Braun?" he asked.

"Still under from the surgery," Anna said. "And Alex? What's the doctor say?"

"That he's lucky to be alive," Dugan said. "The activation bulb in the sprinkler head he rigged the rope to fractured and set off the sprinklers. They got to him fast, but we won't know about brain damage unless… until… he wakes up."

"Have you been in?"

Dugan shook his head. "Visitation's limited. I didn't want to deprive Cassie and Mrs. Farnsworth of any time in case…"

Anna nodded, and Dugan fell silent, composing himself before continuing.

"Thank you for Gillian. She couldn't bear being locked away now."

Anna shrugged. "She was bringing the gun to us, and it accidentally discharged."

"You're OK with that?"

"When the law is at odds with justice, I'll take justice."

"Thank you," he said again. Then added, "I have to get to Russia."

"Why? It's up to the Russians and Turks now."

A known target had cut Dugan's list to six ships, and he'd called each with news of the office fire and updated their positions in the process. Only the M/T *Phoenix Orion*, loading crude at Novorossiysk, Russia, was close enough. Braun's "'O… o…'" had meant "Orion."

"Someone has to protect Alex's interests. Liability from the *Asian Trader* alone could ruin him, and you can count on the underwriters denying claims on the premise of criminal activity."

"But what's that have to do with the next attack?"

"Because he'll need all his assets to survive this. *Orion* is a profitable ship, and I need to be on the ground to persuade the Russians not to impound her after they stop the attack. And there's the crew. Remember that school incident? The Russians killed half the kids along with the terrorists. You think they care about our crew?"

"But what can—"

"Ingratiate myself. Offer advice. Whatever. I'll play it by ear."

Ward walked in during Dugan's discourse and was nodding.

"Can you even get there in time?" Anna asked.

"I need help," Dugan admitted. "Commercial flights are via Moscow with long layovers, but it's only five hours by business jet. The airport is daylight only, but if I leave by eleven, I'll be there at dawn."

Anna stared. "Aren't you forgetting something? You're still in 'Panamanian custody,' and even if you weren't, with Alex's confession, Scotland Yard considers you a suspect. We can look the other way, but neither Jesse nor I can openly provide transport."

Ward cleared his throat. "I don't think the Panamanian custody thing will be too big a problem. Being a good cop, Reyes has figured out where the bodies are buried. He's sticking to Braun like glue. He seems to have lost interest in Tom."

"And I don't expect either of you to provide transport, Anna," Dugan said. "I'm betting Braun prepaid that charter outfit to take Alex to Beirut. How would they react to a call from MI5 questioning their involvement?"

"Nervously, at the very least," Anna said.

Dugan smiled. "Now suppose you implied Her Majesty's Government would be grateful if the forfeited payment were used to take me to Russia?"

She nodded. "Devious, Dugan, but it might work."

She pulled out her phone, then noticed a No Mobile Phone sign and moved to an exit.

Dugan turned to Ward.

"So Jesse, how are things at the Langley Puzzle Palace?"

"Shaky. With these latest developments, Gardner's back up on the fence ready to hammer us or take credit, depending on the outcome. But he hates your guts. I'm concerned about you going to Russia solo."

"Come with me."

Ward shook his head. "I need to stick near Braun. He's still the key. But I'll try to watch your back. With Gardner involved, anything could happen."

Dugan nodded as Anna returned.

"Air Dugan departs tonight at ten thirty," she announced.

AIRBORNE EN ROUTE TO RUSSIA

Dugan jerked awake.

"Dugan," he said into the phone.

"Tom. Jesse."

"Is Alex—"

"No change there, but Braun talked. But we had to cut a deal—"

"We've got the ship. Why rush to cut a deal with that—"

"No, we don't. He was saying 'Odessa,' not 'Orion.'"

"We got nothing loading in Odessa. I couldn't—"

"An unrecorded charter. Not your fault, Tom."

Dugan sighed. "OK. Let's hear it."

"*Contessa di Mare*, owned by Fratelli Barbiero Compagnia di Navigazione, loading gasoline in Odessa for Genoa. Four Chechen terrorists aboard."

"I'll divert."

"Too late. She sailed yesterday. ETA at the Bosphorus pilot station is 1100 local today. Langley notified everyone, but the Turks seem skeptical. Our earlier misstep didn't reassure them. And the Russians are still involved. They won't ignore a threat to the Bosphorus."

"Christ. What should I do?"

"Nothing. Things are too unstable. Langley, Moscow, Ankara, and God knows who else are in the act. Land, refuel, and leave before the shit hits the fan. If you're met, give what advice you can and leave."

"Got it," Dugan said. "By the way, what's the target? The strait's pretty long."

"Unknown. Braun was having problems. The docs made us stop. We'll try later."

"OK, pal. See you soon," Dugan said.

M/T *Contessa di Mare*
BLACK SEA DUE NORTH OF ISTANBUL
0130 HOURS LOCAL TIME
7 JULY

Khassan Basaev's gut knotted from weeks of stress, but it was almost over. The Chechens and their weapons, boxed as "ship spares in transit," sped through the airport behind liberal bribes. The midnight boarding had gone equally well.

Awakened from his attempt at a few hours rest before a predawn sailing, the chief engineer was predictably confused by the forged work order. He'd ordered no riding gang. On cue, Basaev suggested riding to Istanbul, a day away, confirming the orders in transit. If there was a mistake, he promised his team would disembark at no cost. Happy to avoid spending the rest of the night on the phone to Genoa, the captain and chief engineer agreed.

They seized the bridge just after departure, Basaev holding the captain at gunpoint as his comrades corralled the crew in the aft rope locker. The Chechens freed a few crewmen at a time to raise cargo-tank covers and remove the steel blanks from the manifold discharge flanges as Doku and Shamil rigged charges along deck.

Then they used their recent training, and fumes boiled from the hatches as they ventilated the cargo tanks with fresh air. Inert gas hung above the deck in a cloud, changing to an explosive mix of air and gasoline as the inert gas was purged. Finally, they concealed their work, stopping the fans and moving the hatch covers almost, but not quite, closed. The wind dissipated the explosive cloud, but the fans would force it from the tanks again when the time was right.

Basaev touched the detonator in his pocket. He'd increased speed to claim the first morning transit slot. Soon he would be in Paradise, and the Russian scum would be choking on their oil. He thought of his loved ones' deaths and wrapped himself in hate like an old, familiar blanket. A poor substitute for love, but it was all he had.

"Welcome to Mother Russia," the copilot said from the cockpit door as the plane rolled to a stop. "We'll refuel and stand by, but I think you'll have a welcoming committee. They asked for you by name when we requested clearance."

Not good, Dugan thought.

Three men waited on the tarmac: two in black behind a short man in a baggy brown uniform. Shorty glanced over his shoulder before turning back to Dugan and extending his hand.

"Passport," he said, exhausting his English. Dugan surrendered his passport, and Shorty passed it to the larger of the men behind him.

Mr. In Charge studied the passport and Dugan's battered face as Dugan reciprocated, ignoring Shorty. The others were tall, midthirties, with old faces. They wore tailored combat utilities with the Russian tricolor on the shoulder.

Mr. In Charge pocketed the passport and barked at Shorty in Russian, and the little bureaucrat scurried away without a backward glance.

"You come," Mr. In Charge said as he and his subordinate turned.

"Wait," Dugan said, "I'm returning to London."

"Nyet," the Russian called back, walking away.

Dugan hustled past them to stop in their path, his arm extended palm outward. Soon it pressed against Mr. In Charge's chest.

"OK, let's try that again. Give me my damned passport and tell me who the hell you are. If I like your answer, we'll talk."

The Russian glared at the hand until Dugan removed it. Then he nodded.

"I am Major Andrei Borgdanov, and this is Sergeant Ilya Denosovich. We belong to Federal Security Service, Special Operations Detachment, Krasnodar, Directorate V, Counterterrorism Unit." He paused. "And your plane leaves when I say. So if you want me to authorize this, you come. Or plane will be here long, long time."

The Russians resumed their walk toward a Humvee-like vehicle. Left with no choice, Dugan followed. The sergeant pointed to the rear seat before crawling behind the wheel, as Borgdanov took shotgun. They roared away, Dugan groping for a nonexistent seat belt, up the taxiway to a service area and a helicopter surrounded by men in the same black uniforms.

The sergeant braked hard, dumping Dugan on the floorboard to jeers from the waiting Russians. The major yelled something, stifling the jeers if not the smirks. The sergeant grinned over the seat at Dugan.

Eight of the Russians were dressed like the sergeant, but three had different uniforms, Dugan saw as he got out. Aircrew, he thought, not full members of the Crazy Commando Club. Borgdanov wrapped a big hand around Dugan's bicep and steered him toward the chopper.

"We must get ready," he said.

Dugan jerked his arm free. "So what can I tell you?"

"What? Nyet. Get ready." The major nodded toward black utilities and body armor the sergeant was unloading.

"Whoa. I'm an advisor. I'm not going with you."

"You are Agent Thomas Dugan of American CIA, here to help us as agreed." Borgdanov nodded, and the sergeant approached, intent on undressing Dugan, by force if necessary.

Dugan backed away, alarms clanging at "Agent Dugan."

"Look. I'll just be in the way."

"*Da,* but you are American. We go to extreme range and must land in Turkey after, but Turks deny permission because we are Russians. So, we become multinational force, *da*? Turks are in NATO and will accept American-led force. You are only American close enough, so"—he smiled—"you are leader."

"I'm not CIA," Dugan insisted.

"Gardner explained you have to say this, but do not worry, Dugan. Now you work with us. This man Gardner agreed on conference call. Is his idea. He is your CIA superior, *da*?"

"Shit," Dugan said, pulling out his phone. The sergeant snatched it, smirking. Dugan swallowed his anger, his judgment improved since Panama.

"Communications blackout," Borgdanov said, adding, "Dugan, is safe. You are here for show. You stay with chopper."

"I am not getting on that fucking chopper."

Borgdanov's face clouded as he drew his pistol. "Understand, Dugan. Body of CIA man and American passport is enough I think, maybe easier. Our American leader maybe killed during attack on ship. You decide."

Dugan swallowed his heart and nodded.

Borgdanov smiled, holstering his gun and unleashing a burst of Russian that had Sergeant Denosovich and another Russian tugging off Dugan's jacket.

"But why do I have to wear this shit?"

"Must look good for Turks, and armor is in case terrorist bastard shoots at chopper."

So much for safe, Dugan thought as he struggled with the unfamiliar gear and the sergeant's running commentary drew chuckles from the others.

"I'd feel better if Sarge here didn't say 'dead' every second sentence."

"Not 'dead,' Dugan. '*Dyed.*' Short for '*dyedushka,*' or grandfather."

Dugan glared at the sergeant, who grinned back and spit out a stream of Russian.

"What did he say?" Dugan asked, still glaring.

"He says that from looks of grandfather's face, he has seen recent combat, but he doesn't think you win this fight."

Borgdanov struggled to keep a straight face.

"Actually, Dugan," he added, "*dyed* is term of great respect."

I guess that explains the shit-eating grins, Dugan thought.

The sergeant looked him over. Satisfied, he ripped the Russian Federation tricolor from Dugan's shoulder and pressed an American flag patch onto the Velcro. He moved beside Borgdanov, and to Dugan's amazement, both came to attention and saluted.

"Agent Thomas Dugan of American CIA. I greet you as American component and Commander of Multinational Strike Force One." Borgdanov snapped his hand down.

"Now get in chopper."

***

Dugan sat beside the major, facing backward at the others. A man pointed, and Dugan saw another helicopter. He looked quizzically at Borgdanov, who produced a headset, miming for Dugan to put it on as he did the same with another.

"Is Captain Petrov's team. They assault. We are support and backup. Always we send two teams. How you say? Redundancy?"

Dugan nodded. "What's the plan?"

"We attack at sea. Both choppers come in high, then drop and sweep bridge with Gatling guns. Then we circle while Petrov closes. They use ropes. How you say…"

"Rappel?"

"*Da,* rappel. Then Petrov kills fanatics and stops ship. Your CIA says four fanatics on board. We should kill one or two on bridge. Should not take so long for others."

"What about the bridge crew?"

Borgdanov seemed confused. "They die. Of course."

Dugan stared. "That's the plan?"

"*Da.* We have fuel to stay a few minutes only. If ship gets to Bosphorus, many people die, including all crew. We save many people, maybe even some crew. Is better, *da*?"

Brutal, but logical. Dugan nodded without speaking, listening to exchanges in Russian between the choppers. Then came a lengthy burst, the voice strained. Borgdanov responded, triggering an argument. Borgdanov screamed a final "nyet" and a short sentence that ended it.

"What's up?" Dugan asked when his headset grew quiet.

"Other pilot complains of very high headwinds. It means increased fuel consumption, and he claims no way to reach target with such winds. He wants to abort. Always these flyers look for tricks to escape duty. I refuse."

Their pilot glared over his shoulder, obviously an English speaker. Borgdanov glared back, and the man looked away.

"But how can you stop him from aborting?" Dugan asked.

"If he aborts, I say to Petrov to shoot flight crew as soon as chopper lands."

Christ, Dugan thought, this is one scary bastard.

***

An hour and a half later, Dugan roused to the pilot's voice in his headphones. Borgdanov acknowledged the pilot and returned Dugan's passport, motioning the sergeant to return his sat phone as well.

"Point of no return," Borgdanov said, "now we continue to Turkey no matter what. But I need your help. The terrorists have disabled GPS on ship so she is not so easy to find. My plan was to fly to Bosphorus entrance, then north on course for Odessa to find ship, but now pilot says because of wind, fuel is too low for this. He exaggerates, of course, but even so, I think we do not have fuel to waste. With good position, we go straight to ship. I need CIA satellites."

"What about your own satellites?"

"We have not so many now, and they watch US and China, not Black Sea." He smiled. "I think your satellites already look Black Sea, so no need to retask, *da*?"

Dugan nodded, then shed his headset and called Ward, phone jammed against one ear and his finger in the other against the noise of the chopper.

"God damn it, Tom, where the hell are you? The charter plane pilot said th—"

"In a Russian chopper over the Black Sea thanks to your asshole boss."

"Gardner? Son of a bitch. He's screwed this up by the numbers. OK, look. Have the Russians—"

"Too late. We're low on fuel. You have a position on the ship?"

"Christ. Langley was to have updated the Russians an hour ago. I guess Gardner screwed that up too." He paused. "She'll reach the pilot station four hours early. Your best bet is to intercept just before arrival."

"Not good, Jesse. We've got strong headwinds. What about the Turks?"

"Langley's in contact with Ankara, but it's a cluster fuck. I have no clue what's actually filtering down to the locals in Istanbul or to the Bosphorus pilots. We're dancing in the dark."

Dugan sighed. "OK. Got a specific target yet?"

"We're still waiting to resume questioning Braun."

"Ship info?"

"Yeah, Anna's tech wizards converted the vessel particulars sheet to a text message. We'll send it to your phone."

"Thanks, Jesse. Keep me posted."

"Will do, Tom. Watch yourself."

"Like I have a choice," Dugan said.

CHAPTER TWENTY-NINE

M/T CONTESSA DI MARE
BLACK SEA
NORTH OF TURKELI LIGHTHOUSE

Day dawned as Basaev watched radar dots become ships, converging on the Bosphorus. He moved to the bridge wing, his stomach knot tightening at the sight of the tanker overtaking him, a competitor for the first southbound slot. A slot he had to have to arrive when his target crawled with infidel tourists and fawning Turks.

Passage through the Bosphorus "without delay or regulation" had been guaranteed by treaty for decades when the Turks moved unilaterally in 1994 to regulate burgeoning tanker traffic. Her northern neighbors protested still, while many Turks pressed for a total ban. Western Europe, hungry for Russian oil, stayed neutral, and a compromise developed. The Black Sea states refused to accept Turkey's actions, even as they complied, and the Turks let compliant tankers pass. A compromise Basaev would end, God willing. He moved to the radio.

"Turkeli Control, this is the tanker *Contessa di Mare*. Over."

"Go ahead, *Contessa di Mare*."

"Our ETA is oh seven hundred. We request clearance, over."

"You are early, *Contessa*," came the reply, "from your twenty-four hour rep—"

"Control, this is tanker *Svirstroy*," said a Russian voice. "*Contessa* is not at reporting point. I will arrive first and claim first slot. Over."

"*Contessa*, this is Control. You are cleared for transit. Call the Kavak Pilots on channel seventy-one. Use twelve in the strait, but report on thirteen at Anadolu Light. Over."

"Control, this is *Contessa di Mare*. I copy and will—"

"*Svirstroy* to Control. I protest. I was clearl—"

"Control to *Svirstroy*. Go to anchor. You are next in queue. Presuming you comply."

Basaev smiled. "Thank you, Control. *Contessa di Mare*, out."

"Safe transit, Captain. Turkeli Control, out."

∗∗∗

Basaev watched from the bridge wing as the pilot climbed aboard, then moved back into the wheelhouse to wait as Shamil, uniformed as the third mate, escorted the pilot up. He glanced at the helmsman. The young Italian was behaving like the chief engineer in the Engine Control Room, aware the slightest transgression would mean death for their shipmates.

The pilot arrived and introduced himself, giving cards to both Basaev and Shamil. Shamil went into the chart room, ostensibly to record the man's name in the logbook. Basaev stayed with the pilot to review a transit checklist.

In the chart room, Shamil entered the pilot's name into an Iranian-supplied laptop and smiled. He printed out the information, pulling a pistol from a drawer as the printer whirred, then collected the output and stepped onto the bridge behind the pilot. He jammed the gun to the back of the man's head.

"That's a gun, Captain," Shamil said. "Raise your hands. Slowly."

The pilot complied as Basaev relieved him of his radio and cell phone. Then Shamil handed Basaev the information.

"Very good, Captain... Akkaya," Basaev said, glancing through the pages. "And your wife and daughter are beautiful," he said, displaying photos.

"Shamil here made a call," Basaev lied, "and our colleagues ashore are going to visit them. Their safety is in your hands. Will you cooperate?"

The pilot nodded, ashen faced. Basaev gestured he could lower his hands.

"All right," Basaev continued in Turkish. "Proceed and report as usual. No tricks. I speak your language." The man nodded.

"Good. Captain Akkaya. You have the bridge."

The pilot took over, and Basaev lifted the console phone.

"Engine Room," Aslan said.

"Aslan. Start the fans."

IN FLIGHT OVER BLACK SEA
APPROACHING BOSPHORUS STRAITS

Dugan looked toward the Turkish coast as a burst of excited Russian sounded in his headphones, precipitating a three-way exchange between Borgdanov and the pilots of both choppers. Finally, Borgdanov shot a worried look across at the other chopper and gave a resigned "*da*" as the other chopper peeled away and headed away from the coast out to sea.

"What's up?" Dugan asked when he was sure the Russians were finished speaking.

"Low-fuel alarm on other chopper," Borgdanov said. "He has twenty minutes air time, no more. Is no way he will reach Bosphorus with us."

Dugan looked at the nearby coast, confused. "But why is he going out to sea?"

"He has no American aboard," the Russian said, "and would be big problem if he lands in Turkey. I tell him to go well to sea to be sure he is clearly in international waters. He has enough time to get there and hover while crew deploys raft. Then he will ditch. One of our naval vessels is already on way to pick up men."

Dugan was still confused. "Why was he lower on fuel than us?"

"Because he hovers a few minutes at rendezvous point while we collect you," Borgdanov said, "and also as primary strike force he has heavier load—five more men and their weapons. Under most conditions, would make little difference, but with this wind..." The Russian shrugged, leaving the thought unfinished.

Borgdanov spoke in Russian into his mike, and Dugan saw an answering nod from the chopper pilot. The chopper dropped to skim the surface of the water and moved closer to the Turkish coast.

"I think Turkish radar will pick us up soon," the Russian said, "but we will stay as low as possible to delay that. We have you aboard, so we can land if necessary." He smiled. "Assuming Turks don't shoot us down first and ask questions later."

***

Ten minutes later, as Dugan watched the Turkish coast flash past the left side of the chopper, a raucous alarm brought another burst of Russian in his headset.

"Fuel alarm," Borgdanov said. "Pilot says twenty minutes, no more."

"Do we land?" Dugan asked.

"Nyet," the Russian said. "We are close now. We will complete mission."

He smiled at the worried look on Dugan's face.

"Do not worry so, *Dyed*," he said. "Always these pilots exaggerate the danger."

Dugan was about to debate the point when his phone vibrated.

"Jesse. Thank God. Talk to me."

"I called the Turks direct. The Bosphorus pilot boarded an hour ago. A Turkish Coast Guard boat is closing, but chopper response will take time. I informed the Turks the Russians are in route. They want your help."

"An hour ago? She must be halfway through the strait. What's the damn target?"

"Braun just talked. Sultanahmet, between Attaturk Plaza and Eminönü ferry terminal."

Sultanahmet, a dense square of attractions—Topkapi Palace, the Attaturk statue, the Grand Bazaar, Sultanahmet Mosque, all clustered around the bustling ferry terminal, sure to be thronged on a beautiful summer morning.

"The Russians have a plan?" Ward asked.

"Yeah. For an open-sea intercept. Now? Who the hell knows?" Dugan said as the fuel alarm buzzed again.

AIRBORNE
OVER UPPER BOSPHORUS STRAITS

Dugan stared forward as they cleared Fatih Mehmet Bridge.

"There," Dugan pointed. "Stay high and hover."

Southward, almost to First Bosphorus Bridge, was a tanker with a distinctive green hull and BARBIERO in white letters on her side. A boat sped toward a pilot ladder rigged on the ship's starboard side. As the boat neared, a figure appeared on the starboard bridge wing, carrying something.

"RPG," Borgdanov said as the boat disappeared in a fireball. Dugan watched, stunned. The Russian shook his arm.

"Dugan. I said how long to target?"

Dugan looked beyond First Bosphorus Bridge to Topkapi Palace in the distance and did a quick mental calculation.

"Assuming full harbor speed of eight knots, she'll pass the bridge in about ten minutes. Then maybe twenty-five more to target. You have a plan?"

Borgdanov shook his head. "Only that we rappel aboard and try to kill fanatics. If we cannot kill them, we set charges and jump in water. Some people die, but maybe not so many."

"What about RPGs?"

"I think no problem. How far from wheelhouse to bow of ship?"

"Four hundred fifty, maybe four hundred sixty feet, give or take—"

"Nyet. In meters, Dugan. In meters."

"Sorry," Dugan said. "About a hundred and forty meters. Why?"

"Because RPGs accurate to only eighty meters. This we learn in Afghanistan where our choppers have no problem until Americans give savages Stinger missiles."

He glared, then continued. "I know these savages. They will not risk blowing up ship with wild RPG shot over deck this near complete success. We circle wide, hide behind bridge, and drop near front of ship by surprise. After that?" He shrugged.

Hell of a plan, thought Dugan as the fuel alarm buzzed again.

HOVERING
SOUTH OF FIRST BOSPHORUS BRIDGE

The alarm was constant as they hovered behind the span.

"Will they attack when you board?" Dugan asked.

Borgdanov looked up from his preparations. "Nyet. They know we must come to them. Two will probably defend engine room with two on bridge. Maybe some booby traps." He raised his eyebrows. "You have some idea, *Dyed*?"

"Sultanahmet's at the south entrance of the strait. You could override the bridge at the emergency steering station and change course into the Sea of Marmara."

Borgdanov looked doubtful. "Fanatics stop engine," he said.

"But you'll be on a new course. A loaded tanker doesn't stop quickly."

Borgdanov hesitated. "We know nothing of these controls, *Dyed*. For this, you must come. You do this?"

Dugan envisioned charred bodies in the ruins of Sultanahmet as the buzzing fuel alarm defined the limits of his options. May as well go down swinging. He swallowed and nodded.

Borgdanov grinned. "Good. So is unnecessary to have Ilya shoot you in painful but unimportant place. You come with me. How you say… tandem jump."

Oh goody, Dugan thought.

"You are certain, Shamil?"

"I saw him after I fired the RPG but lost him. You think I cannot recognize a Russian?"

"Forgive me," Basaev said, "I was surprised. If the Turks now ally themselves with Russian scum, I strike them with a song in my heart."

Shamil nodded as Basaev lifted binoculars and looked ahead.

He handed Shamil the glasses. "The surface just beyond the bridge."

"I see only ripples," Shamil said, peering through the binoculars.

"Or a downdraft," Basaev said.

Shamil trailed him to the bridge wing. Barely audible through ambient noise was the thump of blades.

"He hides behind the span," Shamil said.

Basaev nodded. "An ambush."

"What now?"

Basaev smiled. "Praise Allah for Russian targets. Get on the wheelhouse with the Stinger. Shoot the tail like the Iranians showed us. He will spin away."

Shamil grinned and rushed inside as Basaev moved in to call the engine room.

"Doku," Basaev said, "we will be attacked. I will transfer engine control to you. They know of us, so we no longer need to follow rules. Go to sea speed, send Aslan to the Cargo Control Room to prepare to discharge, and arm booby traps on all the engine-room doors."

"At once," Doku said and hung up.

Basaev called to Shamil as he hurried past.

"Take time to aim well. A few of them on deck are less a threat than a flaming chopper."

Shamil nodded, annoyed.

Basaev grinned. "Besides, why should you have all the fun?"

Shamil returned his grin and hurried out.

***

Dugan stood terrified as wind and noise blasted him. The major yelled in his ear.

"On 'set,' wrap arms around my neck and legs around my body like lover. On 'go,' I jump. Don't worry. I control everything." Dugan nodded mutely as the Russian continued. "Ilya goes first and will hold rope. When we land, I unclip here"—he put Dugan's hand on the carabiner clip—"and we separate. Fast. Understand?"

Dugan nodded again and was still pondering his lunacy when the sergeant disappeared. Seconds later he was hurtling downward, a death grip on Borgdanov.

"Release my arm, idiot! I cannot control speed," the Russian screamed.

He made his point by smashing his helmet into Dugan's battered face. Dugan's hands flew to his nose, and Borgdanov stopped their plunge abruptly, just above deck. Dugan's legs jerked free, leaving the pair joined by their web gear and spinning. They hit the deck hard, Borgdanov on top. Dugan lay gasping as the Russians clawed at the snarled rope.

Shamil sat, elbows on knees and the Stinger on his shoulder as the bridge loomed. A man dropped into view as the bow cleared the span, the chopper still shielded. The man landed cleanly in a clear area of the main deck just aft of the raised forecastle deck and pulled the rope taut for a pair of men that followed, faster and without grace, landing in a jumble of flailing limbs.

Shamil could see the chopper skids now and waited impatiently. Then it was there, and he locked on to the tail rotor and fired. A fireball bloomed, and he panicked momentarily as a flaming chunk plunged, narrowly missing the bow to splash into the sea. The chopper corkscrewed away, slinging black-clad Russians to their deaths.

"*Allahu Akbar!*" he screamed.

NEAR THE BOW
M/T CONTESSA DI MARE

The sergeant released the rappelling rope and leaped back as the two men slammed to the deck. He watched the rope jerk taut as an explosion rocked the chopper and it twisted away, dragging the mass of tangled limbs and twisted rope toward the ship's rail. He grabbed the rope one-handed, dragged along as he reached into his boot with his free hand and pulled a knife to saw at the rope. Ten feet from the rail, the rope parted, and the men collapsed in a heap.

He recovered first to cut the men apart and hook a hand in Borgdanov's armor and drag him under the protection of the centerline pipe rack. He turned to see the American limping to join them.

***

Dugan was unsure whether his nose or rope-burned leg hurt worse. The Russians seemed indestructible. They conferred, heads together, looking aft with undisguised hatred.

"OK," Borgdanov said. "We go back. Ilya first, then you Dugan, while I give cover fire. Then Ilya covers me. Then repeat."

"Cover fire? Smell that gasoline! A muzzle flash will blow us all to hell."

"But fanatics shot RPG and Stinger."

"Yeah," Dugan said, "up high. Fumes hug the deck. A flash on the bridge won't ignite them. The boat exploded away from the ship, and the chopper was high, plus its downdraft dissipated the fumes."

"You tell me this now? How we kill fanatics?"

"You can't fire here, but you can inside. Air intakes are high, and fans maintain a positive pressure inside so no fumes leak in." Dugan looked at ripples on the water. "And there's a good breeze, so the open deck aft is probably OK as long as you don't shoot forward. A ricochet spark here in the cargo area could be deadly."

"So. We go fast and hope fanatics also do not want sparks."

Borgdanov spoke in Russian, and the sergeant darted aft.

"Wait," Dugan cried. Too late.

NAVIGATION BRIDGE
M/T CONTESSA DI MARE

Basaev raised the binoculars and watched the chopper careen across the summer sky toward Sultanahmet, leaking Russians. He laughed as it splashed down just offshore, and he saw tiny figures ashore rushing to the water's edge to point and gawk like moths to a flame. All the more people in the kill zone.

"Well done," he said as Shamil returned. "Only three got down, one injured. They cringe beneath the pipes."

"I saw. What now?"

"We give them something to think about," Basaev said as he called the Cargo Control Room.

"Aslan," Basaev asked, "ready?"

"I need only start the pumps," Aslan said.

"Defenses?"

"The outside doors on this deck are jammed. They can only get to me by entering the deckhouse on the main deck and coming up the central stairwell, and I have the door from the stairwell on this deck booby-trapped. It will explode in their faces. I will finish any survivors."

"Draw them to you then," Basaev said. "Start the petrol early. They may try to stop it."

"But it will trail us like a fuse."

"Let it cover the strait and increase the destruction," Basaev said. "Nothing is likely to ignite it before we are upon the target, and if then, momentum will complete our task whether we live or not."

"Very well, Khassan," Aslan said, sounding unsure.

"Watch from the window, Aslan. Time the start to catch them between the manifold and the rail. Try to wash them overboard."

"It will be done, my brother," Aslan said.

Shamil yelled a warning.

"Aslan," Basaev said, "be ready. They are coming. Port side."

MAIN DECK
M/T CONTESSA DI MARE

Dugan peeked around the deck locker at the sergeant crouched behind a tank hatch farther aft, then he looked back at Borgdanov sheltering behind a winch. In the interest of speed, the Russians chose the less cluttered route near the rail, over the piping maze inboard. But as Dugan had anticipated, the sergeant had run out of cover, leaving him a long sprint down the rail past the cargo manifold.

The sergeant made his move just as Dugan's neck hair rose at the whine of hydraulics and the rumble of pipelines filling. His warning cry was lost in the growing din of the cargo pumps, and Dugan started after the sergeant in a limping run, screaming. The Russian was even with the manifold when a fluke of acoustics allowed Dugan's screams to reach him. He stopped and turned as Dugan arrived, oblivious to gasoline trickling into the drip pan beside him heralding torrents to come. Dugan grabbed the Russian and heaved himself backward. They hit the deck hard, the sergeant on top, as an eight-inch jet of gasoline rocketed through the space they'd occupied.

"Get off me, you dumb asshole!" Dugan yelled, keeping low as he dragged himself from under the Russian. He struggled backward on his elbows to clear the stream of gasoline that shot above them, splashing the rails and deck on its way overboard. When he was clear, he stood and surveyed the situation. He was looking to starboard as Borgdanov arrived.

"We should've gone inboard in the first place. Now let's try it my way," Dugan said, limping to the cover of the centerline piping without looking back. He plunged aft through the maze, squeezing over and around pipes, scraping his shins and banging his helmet in his rush as the larger Russians struggled to keep up.

NAVIGATION BRIDGE

"I cannot see them."

"Do not worry, Shamil," Basaev said. "Our defenses are good. They are few with little time." He paused. "Depending on their target, you help Aslan or Doku. For now, guard the outside stairways and watch for boats or aircraft. Take a radio. The Turks know we are here, and I doubt they speak Chechen."

He pointed toward Sultanahmet. "We meet in Paradise."

MAIN DECK
PORT SIDE OF DECKHOUSE

Dugan stood by the side of the deckhouse, watching the gasoline spread in the ship's wake.

"Dugan! We must get to the steering place. Now," Borgdanov yelled over the hydraulics.

"We have to stop that gasoline," Dugan yelled back.

"Nyet. Is fanatic delaying trick."

"Look, asshole. They'll cover the strait, and one spark will ignite it. There are hundreds of people out there on ferryboats. We deal with this."

Without waiting, Dugan entered the deckhouse, the Russians trailing. He paused at the central stairwell and motioned the sergeant to guard the stairwell door, then followed his ears down a nearby corridor, Borgdanov in tow. The din in the power-pack room was deafening. Dugan yelled into Borgdanov's ear.

"You booby-trap the door. I stop the power packs. We leave. OK?"

Borgdanov nodded and began taping a grenade above the door. He finished and nodded, and the space fell silent as Dugan pressed buttons and rushed out. Borgdanov followed, looping a string from the grenade over the inside doorknob as he closed the door.

They retraced their steps, the sergeant falling in behind as they passed, walking backward, gun trained on the stairwell door. Outside, gas barely trickled from the manifold.

"That'll distract 'em," Dugan said. "Which is good since we have to run aft in the open. They won't be slow to shoot down at us back here." He started astern in a limping run before the Russians overtook him on either side, lifting him under the armpits to dash aft.

Basaev debated killing his two captives. The Turkish pilot at least understood their intentions by now and might take desperate action. His thoughts were interrupted by the plaintive moan of dying hydraulics. He rushed to the window as the gasoline streams slackened to dribbles.

"Aslan," he said into his radio, "why have you stopped?"

"I did not. They must have stopped the power packs."

"Restart them. We must maximize the fire."

"I tried, but they switched the power packs to local control. They can only be restarted from the power-pack room. Perhaps they try to draw me into an ambush," Aslan said.

Shamil broke in. "All the Russians run aft."

Basaev processed that. Why would the Russians go to the stern?

"Doku," he barked, "you heard?"

"Yes, Khassan," Doku said from the engine room.

"Is the infidel engineer secure?" Basaev asked.

"He is handcuffed to the console."

"Leave him. The Russians will attack you from the Steering Gear Room. Take cover with a clear field of fire to kill any that survive the booby-trapped door. Warn the infidel to keep the engine full ahead, or we kill his shipmates slowly before his eyes."

"Understood," Doku said.

"Aslan," Basaev said, "stopping the power packs was merely a diversion to distract us while the Russians went aft. Get the gasoline going again, then go aft and toss grenades down into the steering gear room. Our Russian friends will be trapped between you above and Doku in the engine room."

"At once," Aslan said.

As Basaev turned, the pilot met his eyes.

"You are fortunate," Basaev said, "to witness the work of Allah."

"The work of Allah is not murder. The god you serve is your own twisted hatred."

Basaev staggered him with a fist, but the Turk straightened. Basaev hocked and spit. "Spoken like a woman, Whore of the Crusaders."

The pilot was calm. "Better that than to be ruled by fanatics. I would prefer death."

"A wish I can grant," Basaev said, drawing his pistol. The Turk smiled.

"Death amuses you?" Basaev asked.

"Your arrogance amuses me. These Russians are smarter than you think."

"What do you mean?"

He smiled again, and Basaev pistol-whipped him, knocking him down. He aimed at the Turk's head, finger quivering, but stayed his hand. Something felt wrong, and he might yet need this Turkish whore.

CHAPTER THIRTY

"Let me go, you asshol—" Dugan stumbled as they released him.

"Careful, Dugan," Borgdanov said, "and do not call me asshole."

Dugan bit off a response, startled by the view ashore over Borgdanov's shoulder. They'd increased speed.

"This is door to steering place?" Borgdanov asked.

Dugan nodded. "There'll be another from the engine room."

"Ilya goes down first," Borgdanov said, nodding to the sergeant. Descending between the Russians, Dugan reflected. At this speed, he'd have no time with the controls, likely in Italian, and if he got control, he'd be steering blind. He'd just concluded this was one of his dumber ideas when the sergeant jerked to a stop at voices below.

Italian voices.

Dugan pushed him down the last few steps and rushed past, around a corner to a wire-cage locker. The crew stood atop piles of mooring lines, cheering his arrival.

"We have to free them," Dugan said. "They can help."

Borgdanov aimed at the padlock, but Dugan pushed the gun down, pointing at the steel bulkheads surrounding them. "Ricochets," he said.

A man pointed through the chain link. "*Martello*—hammer—there."

Dugan limped to a workbench to return with a short-handled sledge. He raised the hammer, but Borgdanov jerked it away and destroyed the lock with one blow. Italians boiled out, laughing and shouting as the captain pumped Dugan's hand, thwarting explanation. The major improvised, grabbing a crewman.

"Silence, or I kill him!" he yelled to instant quiet.

"Captain," Dugan said, "the terrorists will ground the ship and explode her in less than ten minutes, killing thousands. If they succeed, none of us can escape in time. You must help us prevent the grounding."

Pandemonium broke out anew as English speakers translated.

"*Zitto!*" the captain shouted, restoring calm and turning back to Dugan.

"How can we help, *signore*?"

Dugan nodded to the steering gear. "Have the chief engage emergency steering."

"The chief engineer is captive. The first engineer is here." He turned and spoke to the man who'd pointed out the hammer.

"*Si, Commandante*," the man said and rushed to the steering gear.

"What more?" the captain asked.

"Change course to port. And"—Dugan nodded at the engine-room door—"block that door. Maybe wedge it. They might use explosives—"

The captain held up a hand. "*Signore*. May I suggest you let us solve these problems while you concentrate on keeping us alive to do so?"

Dugan nodded, impressed.

"*Grazi*," the captain said, turning to bark orders. In moments, the crew formed a line from the rope locker, passing heavy mooring lines hand over hand and piling them against the door.

Damn smart, Dugan thought. This might work.

"A DECK"
NEAR CARGO CONTROL ROOM

Aslan disarmed his booby trap and descended the stairwell. At the bottom, he crept into the passageway and hurried toward the power-pack room. He was almost inside when the grenade handle clanged against the far bulkhead. He ducked down in the open doorway and looked around, unsure. The grenade took his head off.

STEERING GEAR ROOM

The pile of mooring lines formed a huge Gordian knot from the deck to above the door and ten feet at its base, an impenetrable barrier. Borgdanov nodded approval.

"Fanatics must come over deck now. But we must kill them without big fight." Borgdanov's face clouded. "I worry if, as you say, bullets go forward to make sparks."

Dugan nodded. "Me too, but I have an idea."

They jerked at the thump of the explosion in the power-pack room.

"Now there are three," Dugan said with grim satisfaction.

Borgdanov shot him an appraising look.

"You are not such dumb fellow, *Dyed*." No derision now. "Tell me your idea."

NAVIGATION BRIDGE

"What was that explosion?" Basaev demanded into the radio.

"Nothing in the engine room," Doku reported.

"Understood, Doku," Basaev said. "Aslan, report."

After repeated failures, Basaev addressed the others. "I think Aslan has preceded us to Paradise. Doku, what is your situation?"

"No change. But the door moves a bit, like they push against it."

"Understood, Doku. Shamil. Approaching threats?"

"Nothing," Shamil said, "but what are the infidels doing?"

"Playing foolish games as time slips away," Basaev said. "Soon Allah will vomit on their souls."

ENGINE CONTROL ROOM
M/T *CONTESSA DI MARE*

Sweat dripped off the chief engineer's nose as he hesitated, concerned the *beduino* would return. They didn't resemble Arabs, but who else would blow themselves up? He turned back to working at a screw with the steel ruler from his pocket overlooked by the terrorists and now his makeshift screwdriver. He gripped it tight, willing the screw to turn before the ruler edge bent. If he could remove the rail support, he could free himself.

He had no qualms, despite their threats. Any *cretino* could see the *beduini* intended to blow them all up anyway, and the chief engineer was no idiot. The oxygen meter showed 21 percent in the cargo tanks with the fans running in fresh-air mode. No one would place a loaded tanker in such a condition unless planning an explosion.

The screw yielded, and as he moved to the next, he heard a muffled thump. Would that, whatever it was, draw them back? He swallowed his fear and worked on.

MAIN DECK AT STERN

Dugan looked down at the captain supervising two burly sailors wrestling a square of steel plate up the stairs. *That damn thing weighs over two hundred pounds,* he thought, hoping this wasn't a waste of valuable time.

The Russians stood behind opposite corners of the machinery casing, watching forward with hand mirrors, as volunteers from the crew found cover on the stern. There were eleven Italians plus Dugan divided into six pairs, holding things from tools to fist-size bolts. Dugan nodded to his partner, the second mate, crouched behind a mooring bitt.

Dugan jerked at the shriek of steel on steel as the sailors heaved the plate on deck, skidding it edgewise to the starboard rail. They leaned it against a gooseneck vent, and one dashed back to the shelter of the machinery casing, and the other dropped behind the plate as bullets whined off the steel. The man behind the plate unwound a rope from his waist and, exposing only his arms, flipped a loop over the plate to settle six inches above the deck. He cinched the rope behind the upright vent pipe, securing the plate from slipping.

"*Tutto pronto, Commandante,*" the man shouted.

"*Bravo, Mario,*" the captain replied from the shelter of the machinery casing. "*Uno... Due... Tre... Ora!*"

On three, they exchanged places in a rush. The captain squatted behind the plate and peeked down the starboard side. He nodded back to Dugan.

How the hell is he going to conn the ship from there? Dugan wondered.

Reading Dugan's expression, the captain pointed to the chief mate squatting behind the machinery casing at the small rope hatch. Dugan smiled.

NAVIGATION BRIDGE

"Shamil. Why did you fire?" Basaev asked.

"The Italians are up to something on the stern."

"Fire occasionally. Keep them timid. And do not worry so. Success is near."

MAIN DECK AT STERN

Alarms buzzed up through the rope hatch as the first engineer changed over the steering.

"*Tutti pronti, Commandante!*" yelled the chief mate, squatting at the hatch.

The captain replied with a helm order, relayed by the chief mate to the man in the rope store below, who shouted it through the wire cage to the first engineer.

Dugan smiled at changing vibrations underfoot as the rudder bit.

NAVIGATION BRIDGE

"I… I… do nothing," the terrified helmsman said as the steering alarm buzzed and Basaev jammed the Beretta under his chin.

"Leave the boy alone," the pilot said, silencing the alarm.

Basaev turned on the Turk. "What's happening?"

"Obviously, they activated emergency steering."

"Transfer it back, or you die," Basaev said, "as will your family."

The Turk shrugged. "My family is away on holiday in Cyprus, so I soon realized your threats were empty. And the Russians control steering at the source. I cannot override, even if I wanted to."

Basaev watched the bow creep to port, weighing the Russians' chances of success. Something moved in his peripheral vision.

"Stop!" He froze the fleeing helmsman with raised pistol as the man eyed the door. Then Basaev's arms were pinned.

"Run, boy!" the Turk screamed, bear-hugging Basaev as the sailor fled out the door to vault off the bridge wing.

***

On the bridge wing, Shamil turned at shouts from the wheelhouse and footsteps behind him. He had no time to act as the young sailor raced past him and vaulted the rail. He rushed to the rail and looked down at a widening circle of ripples, the only evidence of the sailor's passing. Shots drew him back inside the wheelhouse, to see Basaev push the gut-shot Turk to the deck.

"A slow and painful death, Whore of the Infidels," Basaev said. "Unfortunately our departure for Paradise will shorten your agony. In the time remaining, petition Allah for enlightenment."

Basaev spit on the dying Turk and moved to the bridge wing.

Shamil followed Basaev outside. "Who's steering?" he asked.

"The Russians." Basaev pointed at the improvised conning station, then looked toward Sultanahmet ahead, the bow now aimed at Attaturk's statue.

"But why so timidly?" he mused aloud, then smiled. "They cannot see well and fear a drastic turn will leave us slipping on the original course. So, we have time to deal with them yet."

"Shamil," Basaev said. "Take the extra grenades. Doku will meet you. You will attack down both sides, coordinating on the radios. They cannot hide from a grenade barrage, and when they retreat down into the Steering Gear Room, we make it their coffin. Multiple grenades down into a closed steel box will finish them.

"Doku can secure the infidel engineer on deck," Basaev continued. "After the attack, we will force the infidel to transfer steering, or time lacking, steer from there. I will lay covering fire to occupy the infidels while you and Doku position yourselves."

"Grenades and bullets at main-deck level will ignite the fumes too soon," Shamil said.

"God willing, wind keeps the stern clear," Basaev said. "And we have no option."

Shamil nodded and moved to collect grenades as Basaev raised his radio.

"Doku," Basaev said. "Meet Shamil on deck. Bring the infidel engineer. Shamil will explain."

"Yes, Khassan," Doku said.

Basaev moved inside for an assault rifle to be met with more buzzing alarms and flashing lights.

"Beard of the Prophet. What now?"

ENGINE CONTROL ROOM

The chief engineer pulled the rail free and slipped the ring of the handcuff off the end just as the buzz of the steering-failure alarm sent his heart into his throat. The alarm fell silent, and status lights on the console blinked to local control. His shipmates.

He stopped, unsure now how his initial plan to black out the ship would impact his shipmates. But he still needed a diversion, something to draw the *beduini* here so he could slip by them.

He stopped the fans to the cargo tanks and smashed the controls with a fire extinguisher snatched from the bulkhead. At the console, he stopped the engine and swung the extinguisher in a roundhouse arc against the upright lever, bending it badly and smashing the housing. Seconds later, he crouched in the engine room, watching the control-room windows.

MAIN DECK AT STERN

The captain was squinting down the starboard side, longing for a glimpse of open sea, when the helmsman hit the water cleanly. Seconds later a head broke the surface, even with the stern.

"*Bravo, Salvatore!*" he yelled, rewarded by an upraised fist.

"*Martucci è sfuggito!*" the captain called to the crew's cheers.

★★★

"What's that about?" Dugan asked as Borgdanov watched forward with his mirror.

The Russian didn't turn. "Their comrade on bridge escaped."

"Good," Dugan said absently. "When will they come?"

"Soon, *Dyed*. You should get in position." Dugan didn't move.

"Remember. Leave the pins in."

"It may be your plan, *Dyed*, but I am not idiot," Borgdanov said, eyes on the mirror. "You should take cover," the Russian repeated.

Dugan nodded and moved starboard to dart behind the minimal shelter of a tank vent. He squatted there, feeling the throb of the great engine through the deck and willing the terrorists to come soon. He was rubbing his injured leg when the vibration stopped.

"Midships!" yelled the captain, adjusting to the engine stoppage with a stream of orders, alternating between midships and slight left rudder, coaxing the bow to port without killing speed. This guy's good, Dugan thought.

NAVIGATION BRIDGE
M/T *CONTESSA DI MARE*
A HALF MILE FROM SULTANAHMET

"He's gone," Doku said. "He stopped everything and destroyed the controls!"

Basaev watched the bow creep to port. The speed log read six knots and dropping.

"What shall I do?" Doku asked.

"Forget him. Join Shamil on main deck. Disarm all the engine-room booby traps except the steering-gear door and bring the grenades."

"Khassan," Shamil's voice interrupted, "how can we change the steering now without the infidel engineer?"

"Kill the others and put the rudder hard right; it cannot be complicated. Allah provides a target we cannot miss. Call me when you are ready to start aft."

199

Dugan cowered behind his cover as automatic fire raked the starboard stern. The fire ceased abruptly, and he tensed at the two-note "get ready" whistle from Borgdanov.

***

Borgdanov was elated. The fanatics' attack route was obvious. External stairways jutted from both sides of the machinery casing, shielding the portion of the bulkheads forward of the stairways from the Russians' view. The fanatics would use that, creeping close along each bulkhead and stopping just forward of the stairs to coordinate the attack. He counted on that. Depended on it, in fact. His nagging concern had been when. Now he knew.

The fire to starboard was obviously meant to keep heads down while a fanatic approached. The third fanatic would provide cover fire for the attacker to port as well, and when that stopped, both fanatics would be in place. Borgdanov smiled. Then the surprise.

As fire stopped to starboard, Borgdanov looked over at the sergeant, who nodded, their thoughts identical. Borgdanov whistled softly to the others and leaned back against the casing, grenade ready.

Starboard Side of Bridge Deck Aft

"Doku," Basaev said. "Shamil is in place. I am coming to cover you."

"Yes, Khassan," Doku said as he prepared to rush aft.

"GO!" shouted Borgdanov as the gunfire died to port. The Russians lobbed grenades, pins in place, to clang on deck beside the terrorists' hiding places. Death at their feet and unable to retreat, the Chechens broke cover just as Dugan and the crew also burst forth, each man screaming as they dashed into the open to trade hiding places with their partners, hurling their missiles as they ran.

The attackers were paralyzed by multiple targets and the clang of what they took for grenades on the deck all around them. From semi-concealment, the Russians dispatched the confused Chechens with single three-round bursts. When Basaev emerged on the starboard bridge wing a moment later, a burst from Borgdanov staggered him and drove him back.

The Italians reemerged cautiously, then cheered before being silenced by the captain, who stood smiling at a growing patch of open sea to starboard.

"*Paolo*," he yelled to the second mate, " *La zattera! Subito!*—The life raft—quickly."

As the man moved to comply, the captain called orders to the chief mate and moved to Dugan's side.

"We will miss the headland, I think," he said, "but the current is tricky, and we can do no more. I ordered the rudder locked amidships and—"

"*Commandante*," the chief mate said, "*il Capo Macchinista viene.*"

The chief engineer rounded the corner, handcuffs dangling from his wrist.

"*Bravo, Directore*," the captain said, embracing the engineer before pointing him aft where the chief mate kept a tally as men leaped overboard to swim toward the bobbing raft.

The captain turned back to Dugan. "If the *beduino* lives, he will explode the ship. We should go, *signori*." Dugan nodded and watched enviously as the captain moved to the rail to follow his men overboard.

Dugan turned to Borgdanov. "You think he's alive?"

Borgdanov shrugged. "I know I hit him. How bad, I cannot say."

Dugan darted from the shelter of the machinery casing to squat behind the Italian's makeshift conning station. He looked down the starboard side toward Sultanahmet and tried to gauge the ship's speed before dashing back to the Russians.

"I can't tell how close we'll pass to the headland," Dugan said, "but my best guess is we'll be as close as we're going to get in five minutes. If the asshole's alive and able to detonate, that's when he'll do it." Dugan added, "My guess is he'll stay on the starboard bridge wing where he can best judge the distance."

"Good, *Dyed*," Borgdanov said, starting up the starboard side, "we go."

"Hold on," Dugan said. "We'll be exposed if you approach up the starboard stairway. Best go to port stairway to the bridge-deck level. You can attack through or around the wheelhouse."

Borgdanov nodded and spoke to the sergeant in Russian. The sergeant started forward along the port side in a crouching run, Dugan close behind.

STARBOARD SIDE OF BRIDGE DECK AFT
M/T CONTESSA DI MARE
0.20 MILES NORTH OF SULTANAHMET

Basaev's head ached where the Russian's bullet creased his scalp. He wiped blood from his eyes and crawled on his belly to the back of the bridge wing to peer down over the edge. The deck was empty save for Shamil's body. Streaks of foam marked the wake, and a raft bobbed astern, Italians pulling themselves aboard. Where were the Russians?

He knew. They were coming. They always came.

Basaev studied the now-straight line of foam marking the wake, then rose cautiously and turned toward Sultanahmet, mentally extending the track. The bow pointed to sea, but the current set the ship to starboard, and she might yet graze the shore. God willing, he would succeed. If he could hold off the Russians.

He put his assault rifle in single-shot mode and ran to the catwalk behind the wheelhouse. He rushed to port on the catwalk and then quickly walked backward, his gun pointed down, as he blasted the metal clips securing the aluminum grating. He retraced his route, ripping up sections of grating as he walked backward this time, tossing them over the rail to clatter on the deck far below. In less than a minute he had created a gaping chasm behind the wheelhouse, blocking the access to both the starboard bridge wing and the single ladder to the top of the wheelhouse.

201

Next he ran through the wheelhouse to the port side and slammed the heavy sliding door and locked it. They couldn't come through, over, or around the wheelhouse now to get at him on the starboard bridge wing. The exterior doors into the deckhouse and the doors of the central stairwell were still booby-trapped on the upper levels, and if they tried to come up the starboard exterior stairway, they would be sitting ducks as he fired down at them through the open treads of the stairway. He could hold them off for an hour here. He needed only minutes.

Basaev positioned himself at the top of the stairway, facing ashore with his back to the wheelhouse. His eyes flickered between the stairwell and the crowded shore as Sultanahmet drew closer.

MAIN DECK
PORT SIDE OF DECKHOUSE
M/T CONTESSA DI MARE
0.10 MILES NORTH OF SULTANAHMET

Dugan jumped at the sound of firing followed by metallic clanging from behind the deckhouse. "OK, I guess he's not dead," Dugan said.

"What is fanatic doing?" Borgdanov asked as the sliding door crashed shut two decks above them.

"I think he's getting ready for us," Dugan said. "Maybe it's time for Plan B. Let's try the stairs inside."

Borgdanov nodded and spit out a stream of Russian. The sergeant moved to the deckhouse door and began to ease it open.

He froze and pointed to a thin wire visible through the narrow crack of the open door.

Borgdanov cursed. "Booby trap."

"Can't you cut the wire? Disarm it?" Dugan asked.

"Da," Borgdanov said, "but it must be done carefully, and if there is one, I think there are others, and there is no time. We must go up. Now," he said and started up the exterior stairs.

STARBOARD BRIDGE WING
M/T CONTESSA DI MARE
SULTANAHMET 100 FEET FROM SHORE

The crowd milled and pointed as the ship approached, the locals long accustomed to the nearness of ships, and the tourists following their lead. Basaev's hopes of grounding died, stillborn, as water trapped between the bank and boxy hull cushioned the ship and she began to sheer away. He raised the detonator, and some in the crowd mistook it for a wave, but those nearest saw the bloody face and rifle and turned to claw through the crowd as his cry pierced the air.

"Aallaaahuuu Aak…"

Basaev's wrist smashed the rail, and the detonator flew overboard. The pilot rolled off his arm and sank to the deck, back against the rail, smiling as he finished the cry, "*Akbar*."

"What have you done, Excrement of Satan!"

"As you... advised... petitioned Allah. For... for... strength to stop murder... in His Name."

Enraged, Basaev fired into the Turk's face until no face remained. He looked back landward and watched the gap widen as ashore the fleeing clashed with the ignorant that were pressing forward for a better look. He reached for a grenade, then remembered Shamil took them all. He rushed forward and leaned over the wind dodger to spray the main deck with bullets, smiling as the rounds sparked through the maze of pipes, until his gun fell silent, magazine depleted on the Turk.

PORT BRIDGE WING

Dugan reached the port bridge wing on the Russians' heels just as a burst of automatic fire rose from the starboard wing. They caught a glimpse of the terrorist through the side windows of the wheelhouse, firing wildly at something at his feet. They ducked down before he saw them, and the sergeant raced forward, keeping low. He tried the sliding door into the wheelhouse, then turned to Borgdanov and shook his head.

Borgdanov nodded and rushed aft, the others at his heels. They turned the corner of the wheelhouse and stopped, brought up short by the gaping chasm where the catwalk had been. They returned to their starting point as gunfire erupted again to see the terrorist leaning forward over the wind dodger, spraying the main deck with bullets.

"Christ. He'll detonate the fumes. Shoot the bastard through the windows!" Dugan yelled.

Dugan backed up from the window with the Russians as the pair opened fire at the terrorist in full auto. The bridge windows were laminated double thicknesses of toughened, tempered glass, designed to withstand hurricane-force winds. The port-side glass spiderwebbed with cracks as the bullets penetrated, then whipped across the wheelhouse and through the starboard-side glass with the same result. Deflected by the double impact, the Russians' fire was wildly inaccurate, and the bullet-riddled glass clung tenaciously in place, obscuring their target.

STARBOARD BRIDGE WING
M/T *CONTESSA DI MARE*
SEA OF MARMARA
1,000 FEET SOUTH OF SULTANAHMET

Basaev reached in his pocket for a fresh magazine and found none, then pulled his Beretta, cursing the infidel engineer for stopping the fans. Wind dissipated the fumes, and igniting the invisible pockets remaining was hit or miss. He fired methodically now, placing shots around the nearest cargo-tank hatch in hopes of igniting the fumes.

Basaev jerked as bullets sprayed through the bridge window, and bits of glass peppered his neck and the side of his face. But no bullets hit him, and he resumed his measured fire, oblivious to the Russian threat.

PORT BRIDGE WING

"I need clear target," Borgdanov said, and he and the sergeant slapped in fresh magazines as the fire continued unabated from the starboard wing.

Borgdanov yelled instructions to the sergeant, who turned his gun to stitch the window perimeter while Borgdanov held his fire. In seconds the glass toppled from the port window, and the sergeant started on the starboard. The glass crashed from the starboard window, and Borgdanov fired a three-round burst. The terrorist jerked and fell out of sight below the window opening.

Relief washed over Dugan, then quickly evaporated as he glanced forward. They were out of the strait, clear of the approach channel and still moving at three knots toward an anchorage crowded with ships awaiting a pilot. He looked astern. They were well clear of Sultanahmet now, with its hordes of tourists. He turned at a babble of Russian as the sergeant started through the ruined window.

"Wait," he called. "Where the hell is he going?"

"Ilya goes to check fanatic," Borgdanov said.

"No time," Dugan said, pointing. "In two minutes, we'll crash into one of those ships, and there'll be plenty of sparks. In this condition, there's no way she won't blow. We need to be as far away as possible."

"But fanatic—"

"Leave him. We missed Sultanahmet and stopped massive casualties. Even if she blows now, she won't block the channel. We've got no engine, no steering, and no time. If we stay here, we're dead," Dugan said. "It's that simple."

The Russian hesitated as Dugan looked over the rail at the long drop to the water. He thought better of that idea and moved toward the stairs.

"But we must do something," Borgdanov said.

"Yeah," Dugan said as he started down the stairway, his injured leg forgotten as adrenalin dulled the pain, "run like hell."

He rushed downward as fast as his legs would carry him, and behind him he heard the Russians' voices raised in argument. He was halfway down to main deck when he heard the Russians' boots clanging on the steel treads above him, coming down fast.

STARBOARD BRIDGE WING
M/T CONTESSA DI MARE

Basaev lay on his back in a pool of blood, his feet toward the wheelhouse and the Beretta in a two-hand grip and pointed at the shattered window. The Russian scum would come soon, and he thanked Allah the Merciful for the opportunity to send another of them to Hell before he died.

But they did not come, and he heard shouting through the shattered windows and then the sound of heavy boots on steel stair treads, loud at first, then growing faint. He smiled. The scum was fleeing. He shoved the pistol into his waistband and reached up to grab the wind-dodger handrail. He bit back the pain as he hauled himself to his feet.

MAIN DECK PORT SIDE

Dugan was already crawling over the rail when the Russians got to main deck. He paused and screamed encouragement.

"Wait, *Dyed*!" Borgdanov screamed back as he rushed toward the rail.

Wait my ass, Ivan, my enlistment is up, Dugan thought, going over the rail.

He hit the water feetfirst and plunged deep, spreading his arms to slow descent, then kicking upward. He rose slowly, sinking if he slacked at all. The armor. Kicking hard, he tore off the helmet and clawed at the vest for straps. He found one and parted the Velcro to free the vest at his waist as he sank, despite his frantic kicking. No time, he thought and dove downward to slip the vest like a tee shirt, with a gravity assist. Hope surged as it slipped, yielding to panic when it trapped his arms.

His lungs were near bursting, and ice picks drove into his ears when he finally fought free to stroke hard for the surface. But he was too deep, too tired, and too old. Unable to suppress the breathing reflex, he sucked in water like life itself, and his larynx spasmed and clamped shut. His panic subsided, almost as if he watched from a safe place, disinterested. He didn't see his life pass before his eyes or a white light, only growing dimness broken by his last conscious thought.

Christ, Dugan. What a dumb-ass way to die.

STARBOARD BRIDGE WING

Basaev leaned against the wind dodger and stared back at Sultanahmet astern, a multicolored tapestry, details indistinct. He was calm now, accepting the Will of Allah. Had the Turk been correct? he wondered. Was hatred now his faith? He felt weary, the Beretta leaden in his hand as he turned and aimed down over the wind dodger at the hatch of the nearest cargo tank.

"*Allahu Akbar*," he said softly and fired. The gun bucked in his hand, and he dropped it and watched it tumble toward the deck, almost in slow motion. He never saw it land because his aim was true at last, and a great explosion rocked the ship, throwing his mangled body skyward and releasing him from the pain in his heart. Was that not indeed Paradise?

CHAPTER THIRTY-ONE

"Always a pleasure, Mr. President. See you soon."

Motaki hung up, elated. What a difference a day made. Knowing the Iranians were pinched, only last week the Russians were cool to the idea of a crude-for-gasoline swap except on outrageously favorable terms, even hinting they might vote in favor of sanctions at the UN. But now, with the cork in the bottle at Istanbul, the Russian president was calling him, seeking an audience. God willing, Iran would be awash in cheap petrol.

He smiled to himself. It was an ingenious plan indeed and succeeded even when it failed. Intelligence was limited, especially since Braun had been apprehended, but it seemed clear the Chechens had failed. How ironic that the Turks, shaken by the near miss, had only to look to the unintended devastation in Panama for a reminder of just how catastrophic the attack could have been. The message was clear, and the Turks had unilaterally closed the strait to all tanker traffic until further notice. With Russian oil off the market, crude prices had doubled overnight, other producers enjoying a windfall as Russian foreign exchange plummeted.

Now the Russians were pinched, and when the Russian gasoline flowed freely into Iran, calm would be restored. Motaki's political opposition would evaporate, along with the foolish calls for the dismantling of his nuclear program and rapprochement with the West.

His single regret was Braun. He could have used the German for future projects. But then again, Motaki always assumed Braun might be captured. That's why he employed a freelancer with no connection to Iran in the first place and hired him through Rodriguez. Any trail would stop in Caracas. He smiled again. The Americans may have invented the term "plausible deniability," but it had taken a Persian to perfect it.

Braun was the single loose end, and he lifted his phone to snip it.

Dugan drifted awake, unable to understand his inability to touch his throbbing nose. He blinked in the fluorescent glare at a man rising from a bedside chair.

"Easy," the man said. "You're in the hospital." He stepped back, replaced by a man in a white coat.

"Mr. Dugan," the doctor said, "you survived a near drowning. We left you intubated as a precaution. I'll remove the tube now. I apologize for the restraints," he continued, freeing Dugan's wrists, "but you kept pulling at the tube. You also," he added, talking as he removed the tube, "have a nasal fracture, aggravated by CPR. I realigned and splinted it. You will feel discomfort for several days."

"Thanks," Dugan croaked when the tube was out.

The doctor nodded. "You're welcome, but in truth you should thank your Russian friends." He checked the time. "I'm due on rounds. Call if you need anything."

His visitor smiled as the doctor left. "Discomfort is doc speak for 'hurt like hell.'"

"Do I know you?" Dugan rasped.

"Wheeler, Jim Wheeler." He extended his hand. "Cultural attaché."

Friend or foe? Dugan wondered as he regarded the hand and thought of Gardner.

"Also a friend of Ward's. I think you got a shitty deal."

"That makes two of us," Dugan said, taking the hand. "What's this about the Russians?"

"They jumped in after you. You were all underwater a hundred yards from the ship when it blew. They got you clear of the burning gasoline and were burned in the process, but not badly. A Turkish chopper brought you all here."

"What's the situation?"

"You've been out two days, and it's bad, but not like Panama. There are thirty dead, counting the Turk pilot and Coast Guard boat and the Russians. The rest were passengers on a ferry that ignited the patch of dumped gas. More were burned, so the death toll's rising."

"The Italians?"

"They all made it," Wheeler said. "Now everything's political. What's left of the ship is still afloat. They've contained the fire and are waiting for it to burn out so they can tow it. The Turks reopened the strait, but they've banned tankers. Globally, radical environmentalists support them, though no one seems to know how Europe is going to run without oil. Russia's vowing intervention, which puts NATO on the spot. It's total chaos."

Dugan nodded. "Where's all this leave me?"

"With a jet standing by. Gardner wants you in Langley for debriefing." Wheeler smiled. "But you refuel in London."

Dugan smiled back. "When?"

"The doc said tomorrow or the next day, but I'll see what I can do," Wheeler said, moving for the door.

"Thanks, Jim. Can I see the Russians?"

"I'll let 'em know you're awake," Wheeler said as he left.

They arrived in minutes, wearing hospital pajamas and grins. Their hands were bandaged, and angry red skin, shiny with ointment, marked patches of their scalps.

"So, *Dyed*, just when I think you are clever fellow you leap into sea with kilos of armor. If Ilya here was not number-one swimmer, I think you are now very dead."

"You're right," Dugan said. He looked at the sergeant. "Thank you."

The sergeant looked embarrassed and said something in Russian.

"Ilya says you save him from washing into sea by petrol, so is even," Borgdanov translated.

Dugan nodded. "Your burns?"

"They are nothing, though Ilya is hoping for a scar to impress ladies when he tells of bravely defeating fanatics," Borgdanov said.

The sergeant grinned.

"What will you do now?" Dugan asked.

The Russian's face clouded. "I do not know. I failed, so nothing good I think."

"But you saved thousands of lives."

Borgdanov shook his head. "The Turks close strait to tankers. I failed at what matters, *Dyed*. There is talk of war."

SURGICAL STEP-DOWN UNIT
SAINT IGNATIUS HOSPITAL
LONDON

The soft whir of the floor buffer whispered down the corridor, lulling the guard toward sleep. He jerked upright and rose to pace as the buffer operator felt the syringe in his pocket and cursed the cop's diligence. The more heavily staffed day shift would begin soon, making it even harder to get at the German.

A piercing alarm sounded, and the cop stepped aside as medical personnel rushed into the room. The killer edged the buffer closer, straining to hear.

"Time of death 5:23 a.m.," he heard at last.

***

"So he's dead then?" the cop asked as a nurse emerged from the room.

She nodded.

"Christ. Couldn't wait now, could he. The brass'll have their knickers in a knot on this one right enough. They wanted to sweat this bugger proper."

The nurse shrugged. "Not your fault."

"Aye, but try telling that to my sergeant." He sighed. "Oh well, I best grab a cuppa tea and get to the bloody paperwork."

***

The killer kept buffing, watching for an opportunity. He was just past the door when a nurse rolled the corpse out, leaving the gurney unattended to go to the nurses' station. He swung close, holding the buffer one-handed and lifting the sheet with the other to compare the pasty face with the photo he'd memorized.

He grinned. Easiest hit ever. His secret, of course, to preclude any quibbling about the remaining fee. He eased the buffer down the hallway and abandoned it near the stairwell door. He raced down the stairs, shucking his coveralls as he descended to reveal street clothes. He jammed the wadded coveralls in a trash bin as he left. Several blocks away, he called to report Braun's death, then tossed the throwaway phone down a storm drain.

SAINT IGNATIUS HOSPITAL
LONDON
11 JULY

When the CIA Gulfstream plane touched down at Heathrow at eight the previous evening, Anna had marched aboard and officially detained Dugan "for debriefing on orders of Her Majesty's Government." She'd then taken him home and "debriefed" him so enjoyably he'd had difficulty getting out of bed this morning. Beat the hell out of water boarding, thought Dugan as they walked toward Alex's room.

"He's doing well, Tom. No brain damage. They say the vocal chords will mend in time, though he'll be hoarse." Anna paused. "Gillian's my concern. She's hasn't left his bedside. She even eats there—when she eats at all. Mrs. Hogan is looking after Cassie. Gillian needs rest, but she acts like he's at death's door."

Dugan saw for himself as they found an unkempt Gillian dozing in a chair under Alex's worried gaze. Alex frowned up at Dugan's nose splint, then relaxed as Dugan smiled.

"Thomas," he croaked.

"The pad, Alex," Anna reminded him, nodding toward a pad and pen on the side table. Gillian roused and jumped up like a soldier caught sleeping on guard duty.

"Mr. Dugan…" She stopped, befuddled.

"Gillian," Anna said, "please go home and rest. Harry's waiting to drive you."

She shook her head. "I can't possibly. He may need something."

"He'll be discharged soon," Anna said, "and when he really needs you, you'll be exhausted. I insist you go rest."

"Oh, *you* insist, do you…" Gillian started, then she sagged, on the verge of tears. "May… maybe you're right. I'm just so confused.…"

Alex held up his pad, a message scrawled in block letters.

ANNA'S RIGHT, LUV. GO REST. I'M FINE.

Mrs. Farnsworth nodded, and Anna embraced her. "Don't worry. We'll look after him," she whispered as she walked Gillian to the elevator.

"Alex," Dugan said as they left, "I'm responsible for this. If we'd leveled with you sooner, you wouldn't be in that bed. And if we hadn't let the bastards grab Cassie—"

Alex scribbled furiously and held up the pad.

DID YOUR BEST. CASSIE SAFE. ALL THAT MATTERS.

Before Dugan could reply, Anna returned, Ward at her side.

"Look whom I found getting off the lift." She smiled as Ward advanced with outstretched hand, shaking first Alex's hand, then pumping Dugan's.

Ward cocked an eye. "How the hell do you break your nose drowning?"

"I had help. Russian this time. I'm an equal-opportunity punching bag."

Ward chuckled, then turned serious. "You know about Braun?"

Dugan nodded. "Can't say it breaks my heart, but where do we stand?"

"If by 'we' you mean you and Alex," Ward said, "I'd say you're in good shape. We got enough out of Braun before he passed to combine with what we knew from other sources to piece together the plot." Ward smiled at Anna. "And using a rather liberal interpretation, we classified the info from Braun as a deathbed confession, which carries legal weight. The Panamanians have dropped the charges against you, and no charges will be filed against either you or Alex in the UK or the US."

"Anna told me," Dugan said, "but is Gardner really signing off on that?"

Ward smiled again. "A lot of folks up the food chain are looking now. Larry Boy wants to take a bow. Given your results in Turkey, he can hardly throw you under the bus again without looking like the asshole he is."

Ward's smile faded. "If only everything had worked out as well."

"What do you mean?" Dugan asked. "You got it figured out. Can't you go public or to the UN or the World Court or someplace?"

"Knowing and proving are not the same, Tom," Anna said. "And for all our efforts, the plotters succeeded."

"Well, not Venezuela," Ward said. "Best we figure there, Rodriguez wasn't trying to destroy the canal, merely spook China into backing a second canal through Nicaragua. One big enough for VLCCs to get his crude to Asian markets without a competitive disadvantage. That literally blew up in his face. Ironically, the disaster in Panama worked to his buddy Motaki's advantage. When the Turks dodged the bullet, it didn't take too much imagination to figure out just how bad it could have been."

"So you can't prove it in court," Dugan said, "so what? Surely you have enough to share with the Russians and the Chinese? I can't believe they'll sit still for this."

"What choice do they have even if we convince them?" Ward asked. "The Chinese won't even openly admit they were victims, because to them, it would be a big loss of face. They'll likely internalize it and make the plotters pay, but it may be years from now. And Motaki's got Russia by the balls. He needs Russia as a safe, overland supplier of fuel—a source we can't use our naval presence to interdict, but now Russia needs Iran's crude even more."

"I don't see how that necessarily makes Iran any more secure," Dugan said. "If our navy can cut off gasoline going into Iran by tanker, surely we can do the same for crude coming out by tank—" He stopped. "Oh yeah."

"Right," Ward said, "no one in the West is going to get too upset if we embargo gasoline into Iran, but the crude coming out to fulfill Russian supply contracts is going to our European allies. The idea of stopping Iranian crude exports is unlikely to get much traction, not with Russian crude off the market."

Dugan looked thoughtful. "Then maybe we should concentrate on getting Russian crude back on the market," he said.

SECURITY SERVICE (MI5) HQ
THAMES HOUSE, LONDON

"That should just about do it," Dugan said, nodding at the pile of maps and intelligence briefing reports piled on the table in front of him. "This was terrific—a hell of a lot more information than I'm used to working with."

Beside him, Harry scratched his head. "So tell me, Yank, how is it a ship bloke knows so bloody much about overland pipelines?"

Dugan smiled. "I'm a graduate of Tanker Trade 101 at the prestigious Alex Kairouz School of Economics. At some point or another, almost all pipelines end at a marine terminal where ships pump something in or take something out. Alex figured that out a long time ago. Pay attention to new pipelines—get a leg up on future trade patterns."

"This is first-rate, Tom," Anna said. "It will take some work on the diplomatic front, but the Russians should go for it. Motaki will be right back to square one—short of fuel and facing domestic unrest."

"Actually," Dugan said, "I've been thinking about that. I think maybe our Russian friends should give Mr. Motaki all the fuel he wants."

"What do you mean?" Ward asked.

"I mean sometimes you should be careful what you wish for," Dugan said.

HEATHROW AIRPORT
LONDON
12 JULY

"Thank you once again, Agent Ward," Reyes said, shaking Ward's hand.

"The pleasure was mine, Lieutenant," Ward said. "Have a safe trip home."

Reyes nodded. "I wonder if I might have a word alone with *Señor* Dugan."

Ward shot Dugan a puzzled frown. Dugan shrugged. "OK by me," he said.

"Ah… fine," Ward said. "I'll just go get the car and meet you at the passenger pickup point, Tom." Ward turned back to Reyes. "I'll be in touch about our joint operation in your area, Lieutenant."

Reyes nodded, and Ward walked away, leaving Dugan alone with the big Panamanian. Reyes waited until he was sure Ward was out of earshot.

"First, *Señor* Dugan, let me apologize for my regrettable behavior during our first meeting," he said.

"Understandable," Dugan said, "given the circumstances."

"Thank you," Reyes said. "I wished to speak to you alone because I have some concerns to which I believe you will be more sympathetic than your colleagues."

"Ah… how's that?"

"I do not know quite how to phrase this," Reyes said, "but I am not completely comfortable with the way things stand. Up to the point of the bastard Braun's death, I was fully involved in the operation. I was napping in the hospital lounge, to be notified immediately when he regained consciousness so that we could resume interrogation, and the next thing I knew he was dead. Since that time, I have been kept a bit at arm's length."

"I'm sure Jesse—"

Reyes held up his hand. "Please, *Señor* Dugan. Do not feel the need to defend Agent Ward. I know he is your friend, and I'm sure he is merely doing his job. But that is my problem."

Dugan looked confused, and Reyes continued.

"You see," Reyes said, "I am a simple policeman, not an intelligence agent. Agent Ward promises a "joint operation" against Rodriguez and assures me I will "participate." However, I suspect my definition of participation will be quite different from his."

"Go on," Dugan said.

Reyes continued. "I want to be present when we deal with Rodriguez, but I strongly suspect that because of my personal loss Agent Ward considers me too emotionally involved—in short, a liability. I believe that the operation timetable might be arranged so that I am otherwise engaged and unable to participate in the main mission."

"Even if that's true," Dugan said, "how can I change that?"

Reyes took a business card from his shirt pocket and handed it to Dugan.

"Not change, *señor*," he said, "merely inform. I know that you are… shall we say "quite close" to Agent Walsh. I need only know the real date and time of the operation. If you learn of this and call me, I will be forever in your debt."

Dugan was noncommittal. "I probably won't know, but if I do, I'll think about it."

Reyes extended his hand. "I can ask no more. Thank you, *señor*."

"So what did Reyes want?" Ward asked as Dugan got in the car.

"He apologized for kicking my ass," Dugan said. "I told him I understood. And the thing is, I really do. When Ginny died, I was ready to find someone to pin it on and kill them on the spot. I can't imagine how much harder it must be to really know who was responsible and have to bottle up your rage. It must be eating the poor guy alive."

Ward nodded. "Well, hopefully the Venezuelan op will bring him some closure."

CHAPTER THIRTY-TWO

"Landing in ten, ma'am."

The secretary of state smiled her thanks up at the steward before stuffing a file into her briefcase and fastening her seat belt. It had been a whirlwind seventy-two hours, with stops in Ankara, Turkey, and Baku, Azerbaijan. She still couldn't quite believe what she'd managed to accomplish in such a short time. She looked at the file and smiled. She was no great admirer of the intelligence community, but the spooks had outdone themselves this time. The plan was masterful.

She thought again about leaving the Chinese out of the plan and again reluctantly concluded it was for the best. She had provided her Chinese counterpart the basic intelligence, enough to assuage any concerns about US duplicity in the Malacca attack. But there were enough moving parts in the spooks' plan as it was; Chinese involvement would just complicate things unnecessarily. Russia was the key.

The Kremlin

The secretary sat with the Russian president and Russian foreign minister, watching their faces as they, in turn, watched the video, their rage barely contained. When it was over, the foreign minister turned to face her.

"This is obviously most disturbing, Madam Secretary," he said, glancing at the Russian president. "We will analyze this and act on it accordingly, but I think it is obvious that nothing can be done in the short term. And as much as we appreciate you bringing it in person, we are puzzled as to your intention in doing so."

The secretary of state looked at the Russians. "I came to seek your cooperation in, to use a Russian proverb, killing the wolf closest to the door."

The Russian president spoke for the first time. "It will be difficult to hide our outrage, but until the strait reopens to tanker traffic, we must play Motaki's game. The first cargoes of Iranian oil to fill our European contracts are in transit to Rotterdam, and payment in Russian fuel is arriving in Iran even now."

"And if the strait does not reopen to tanker traffic?"

His face colored. "Unacceptable! That threatens our entire economy. International law and long-established precedent are on our side. If the Turks persist, military response is inevitable."

"Your points are sound, but the Treaty of Montrose was signed over seventy years ago. Given current world public opinion, I doubt the Turks will respond to ultimatums."

"What would you propose? The Black Sea Straits"—he used the Russian name—"are open to all by treaty. Failure to defend that right puts control of our only warm-water ports in foreign hands. Would the US accept a Cuban blockade of the Florida Strait? And we cannot deal with Iran until our oil flows again."

"Must it flow through the straits?"

The Russian president snorted. "How then? Pipelines? All are inadequate and cross Turkey or Georgia, involving contracts of dubious enforceability. You ask us to abandon legal rights of free passage to place ourselves at the mercy of other countries?"

"Not abandon, Mr. President, merely assert more strategically." She spread a map.

"If I may," she said. "Five percent of Black Sea exports can be moved north to Baltic ports through your own pipelines. Correct?" He nodded.

"As you know," she continued, "Western interests are in constructing a pipeline across Turkey, from Samsun on the Black Sea to Ceyhan on the Mediterranean, projected operational in six months. Completion can be accelerated to six weeks or less, allowing tankers to shuttle between your ports and Samsun. From there the oil can be pumped across Turkey to Ceyhan, bypassing the straits. That can handle half your exports." The Russian listened, nodding.

Her finger moved east. "At Baku in Azerbaijan, the Baku-Novorossiysk line, formerly carrying Azeri oil to your oil port, lies idle as the Azeris now prefer the Baku-Tbilisi-Ceyhan line."

The Russian grunted at the reference to yet another incidence of Western companies undermining Russian influence. "What has that to do with anything?"

"The terminals for the Baku-Novorossiysk and the Baku-Tbilisi-Ceyhan lines are two kilometers apart. There is spare capacity on the Baku-Tbilisi-Ceyhan line, and a connection could be built in days, allowing you to reverse the direction of the Baku-Novorossiysk line and pump your oil from Novorossiysk to the Mediterranean via Baku. These steps combined could see 95 percent of your exports flowing to Western markets in weeks."

"And the remaining 5 percent?"

"Will transit the Bosphorus via tanker, maintaining your right of free passage."

The Russian looked skeptical. "The Turks and Azerbaijanis accept this?"

"They do, pending negotiation of pipeline tariffs. The Turks will accept the tankers with increased security against accidents and terrorism. They want joint inspection teams to include a Russian, a Turk, and a neutral-country observer on a rotating basis. Ships will be inspected before departure from Russian ports, by 'invitation' of your government. No one will be seen as 'conceding.' This arrangement can be publicized as a cooperative international effort to deal with a difficult issue. Mutual cooperation and diplomacy at its best."

The Russian scoffed. "Except, of course, the tariffs. We pay ransom to transport oil that is now moving freely. This is behind the Turks' fine talk of safety and environment."

"The tariff they've agreed to barely recoups their operational costs."

"But it increases our own. And why a low tariff? That alone is suspicious."

"Because, Mr. President," the secretary said, "the Turks know a 95 percent traffic reduction achieved peacefully is a bargain." She paused. "And the tariffs are a pittance compared to the cost of military action against Turkey, which will draw NATO in on Turkey's side."

The Russian glared. "This leaves Turkish hands on our jugular."

"With respect, sir, history and geography placed those hands long ago." Her voice hardened. "Will you fare as well in the grip of Iranian fanatics?"

He sighed, then gave a wan smile. "Points well-taken, Madam Secretary. You are disturbingly familiar with our oil distribution network."

She smiled back. "I take it you concur with our analysis?"

He nodded, his brow furrowed in thought. "Fifty percent in days and full resumption in six weeks seems possible. But perhaps we can be secure much sooner. The Iranians are being quite accommodating. If we press them, I believe we can convince them to export heavily now, and put a six-week reserve on the water beyond their control. We will use the excuse that the recent disruption has us nervous, and that we are renting extra storage capacity in European ports. I think we'll be back to business as usual in a week, or perhaps ten days." He smiled a hard smile. "And then we will see about choking off their fuel."

The secretary of state smiled back.

"Again with respect, Mr. President," she said, "perhaps you might wish to supply them even more."

The Russians looked at each other.

"Another 'suggestion,' Madam Secretary?" the foreign minister asked.

She nodded and presented the rest of the plan.

DEARBORN, MICHIGAN
18 JULY

Borqei limped along on a leg full of Iraqi shrapnel, troubled after a meeting with Yousif's adoptive parents. The couple had been shocked beyond belief when the boy's bullet-riddled corpse was found on the street outside their home, the apparent victim of a drive by shooting. How Yousif got there remained a mystery, and the boy's parents were hardly comforted when Borqei shared with them Motaki's message describing Yousif's death as heroic. He doubted they believed it any more than he did.

The press had lionized "Joe Hamad," all-American boy, and linked his death to a Latino gang, prompting a reprisal. The Defenders of Islam was a motley collection of delinquents of Arab descent, none devout, but nonetheless determined to uphold the honor of Islam. Their single foray into southwest Detroit wounded a member of Los Pumas, the dominant gang, and tensions rose, with calls for calm from all sides. Borqei had been on television twice and received death threats, but that didn't bother him like the loss of his protégé for doubtful ends. He trudged along, thinking of Yousif, praying he was enjoying the rewards of Paradise.

***

Lieutenant Manuel Reyes sat in the front passenger seat. He had suspected Dugan was an honorable man and was thus unsurprised at last evening's phone call. He was equally unsurprised that the little "favor" he was undertaking now for Agent Ward seemed to be planned so that it would be impossible for him to take part in the Venezuelan operations. That is, it *would* have been impossible if he performed the favor tomorrow as requested. That's why he was performing the little favor a day early.

"This is embarrassing, Manny," Perez said from the driver's seat of the lowrider, shouting over the Spanish rap. "If I have to listen to this *pinche* 'music' much longer, the only one I'm going to kill is myself."

Reyes nodded. Both wore blue bandannas of Los Pumas with faded jeans and tank tops exposing garish, but temporary, gang tattoos. They dripped gold chains.

"That him?" Reyes asked, pointing across a vacant lot to a cross street.

Perez followed the finger. "That's him. He looks just like the picture."

"Move into the street," Reyes said, "and raise the front."

Perez nodded. The car lifted with a whine as Reyes silenced the throbbing music. They crept forward, a malevolent predator, high in front with the rear almost dragging.

Borqei was well into the street when they struck him waist high, trapping his body between the pavement and the rear bumper. They striped the street with gore to the end of the block, where Perez raised the rear and sped away, leaving just another gang-related death.

F.A.R.C. TRAINING CAMP
SANTA MARIA DE BARRINOS
VENEZUELA
20 JULY

Manuel Reyes and Juan Perez stood before a crude shack, dressed in sweaty camouflage, eyeing a group of similar buildings. A paved runway lay in contrast to the dirt track providing access to the camp from the Venezuelan interior to the east and the Colombian border ten kilometers west. A man emerged from a building and trotted over.

"The gringos finished, *Teniente*," said Corporal Vicente Diaz, "the camp is secure."

"*Bueno, Vicente,*"—Reyes checked the time—"eat and rest. You too, Juan." He nodded at Perez. "I'll join you in a moment."

As they moved away, Reyes watched with approval. For two years, young Diaz had played a disaffected Panamanian in FARC, the Revolutionary Armed Forces of Colombia. He'd been invaluable, monitoring activity in the Darien, the jungle sprawl between Panama and Colombia used by FARC as safe haven. He wouldn't be able to return undercover, but Reyes and Captain Luna agreed this mission justified the loss.

Reyes turned as the leader of the "gringos" approached and smiled at the term. Sergeant Carlos Garza, US Army Special Forces, and his five men were hardly gringos. Natives of places from Puerto Rico to Texas, they shared Hispanic heritage and a desire to be the best soldiers on the planet. Special Forces had seen to that, then immersed them in language training. Now, whether their native dialect was East LA slang, Puerto Rican Spanglish, or Tex-Mex, they could pass as native in any Spanish-speaking place on earth.

Reyes and Perez had had to scramble to meet "Garza's Gringos" the night before to crash the Venezuelan border with Colombian forces in hot pursuit, bolstering the illusion with a hail of intentionally inaccurate gunfire. The FARC commander had been waiting at the training camp, alerted by the Venezuelans at the border. He saw a truckload of new recruits led by Diaz, a man known to him and trained in that very camp. Such arrivals were not unprecedented, and the FARC leader decided to bed them down and deal with it all in the morning. A day that never dawned for the twenty narco-terrorists in the camp.

"The camp is secure, Lieutenant," Garza said as he reached the shack's porch.

"Diaz told me. What now?"

"We take their places and wait. After the hit we'll place bodies to mimic a firefight, dressing a few with no tattoos or other marks in Colombian uniforms and mangling them with grenades. Make it look like a cross-border action."

"Need help?"

"No, sir," Garza said, "my men are more convincing FARC if we get visitors. Diaz gave us passwords." He paused. "A good man, Diaz."

Reyes smiled. "I agree, *Sargento*, though it is nice to hear from another professional."

Garza hesitated. "Sir, can I ask something, one professional to another?"

"Ask away, *Sargento*."

"I expected Diaz, but not you and Perez." He paused. "Your presence is unplanned, and unplanned is risky. I don't know what numb nut OK'd this, but if it ends up costing casualties, I assure you that individual and I are going to have a discussion."

"Apologies, *Sargento*. There is no 'numb nut' involved, and I suspect your superiors may be equally upset when they learn of our presence. Now that we can't be sent back, I will tell you the truth. We invited ourselves, knowing that you were observing radio silence and gambling that if we just appeared, you would accept us at face value." He shrugged. "I will face any consequences when we return."

Garza stifled a curse, then said, "All right. You're here now, but you're strictly observers. Got that?"

Reyes looked the American in the eye. "I may have to disappoint you there, *Sargento*. I have a promise to keep."

Garza studied the ground. "It's your wife, isn't it?"

Reyes stiffened. "How do you know that?"

"I overheard your men. I can't let your hard-on for Rodriguez compromise the plan."

"The plan is to kill Rodriguez, no? Who has more right to shoot the bastard than myself?"

"Shit," Garza said as he sat on the porch step. "I suspected as much. You only know part of the plan. Sit yourself down, Lieutenant. No one is going to shoot Rodriguez."

***

Rodriguez gazed down as the King Air circled, glad the FARC men were waiting in formation. A quick tirade against the *yanquis* while his people checked the warehouses and he'd be off. His men did the checking, of course, so he could honestly say he saw nothing. Honesty was important.

He sighed. Not everyone was so honest. His deal with FARC called for payment of 10 percent of the value of the cocaine transiting. Amazing how revenue increased after he began these impromptu visits to the camps.

Even without the drug money, the camps were assets, placed to terrorize his opposition. Initially FARC had traded muscle for havens to rest and rearm, but as US aid allowed Colombia greater resources to disrupt drug traffic, FARC moved distribution under Rodriguez's protection. For a fee, of course. Free muscle and cash to boot.

His mood was transformed in the anxious weeks since Panama, with the media diverted by the Bosphorus attack and news of Braun's death bringing the welcome realization that the lone thread linking him to the attacks was severed. Confident now, he was on the offensive, his speeches condemning the attacks as an American plot, a pretext to exert control of global choke points with the ultimate aim of reclaiming the Panama Canal. He ended his speeches with a pledge of "the honor and treasure of the Bolivarian Republic of Venezuela to resisting to the death American hegemony."

Rodriguez scowled, his mood dampened by the close confines of the King Air. Runway length precluded the use of his jet and reduced his security detail to six. But they were his best, and, he thought, smiling back at the last row, there was the sacrificial lamb.

"Navarro," he taunted, "are you ready to take a bullet for your *presidente*?"

The sullen face staring back was a copy of his own, down to the smallest scar. The men were dressed identically in chinos and bright-red open-collared shirts.

"Really, Navarro," Rodriguez said, "so morose. You have a handsome face that required little surgery; I provide a fine life and ask only that you smile and wave. Yet you sulk. Perhaps your daughter would be better company. She is what? Fifteen now?"

"Forgive me, Excellency. I would be honored to fall in your service."

"Much better, Navarro," Rodriguez said, then grinned at the bodyguard next to him.

The man grinned back. "As usual, *Señor Presidente*, Navarro goes first. When we're sure all is secure, he'll reboard and you deplane in his place."

Rodriguez sighed. "If the fool could speak, I wouldn't take these tedious trips at all."

***

Reyes stood at attention as the door opened and six men deplaned, forming a circle into which a red-shirted man emerged. The bogus guerrillas stood at present arms, safeties off their weapons. A shot inside the plane drew the bodyguards' attention as the man in their midst dove to the tarmac. The Americans' guns came up as one, and the six bodyguards were dead before they hit the ground.

Garza and his men circled the plane as Red Shirt's twin stumbled down the steps, followed by the copilot with a pistol.

"The pilot?" Garza asked the copilot.

"Dead," the man replied. "He was loyal to Rodriguez."

"I am not Rodriguez," said the man beside the copilot. "I am Victor Navarro. *He* is Rodriguez," he pointed to his approaching double.

"Really?" Garza asked. "What is the countersign?" The man looked panicked as Garza continued. "The rain in Spain—" Garza stopped. "Complete the phrase."

Rodriguez smiled. "Falls mainly on the plain."

"Actually, I made that up." Garza turned to the second Red Shirt. "Pass phrase, *Señor*?"

Navarro smiled. "Rodriguez is an asshole."

"*Mucho gusto, Señor Navarro*," Garza said, nodding for his men to bind Rodriguez.

"Now," Garza said to the copilot, "I suggest you and"—he smiled at Navarro—"*Señor Presidente* here coordinate your stories. We'll add authenticity with bullet holes in noncritical areas of the plane."

"*Un momento, Sargento*," said Navarro before Garza turned away, "perhaps you should also shoot me in some 'noncritical' area."

"Hardly necessary, *Señor Navarro*."

"To the contrary. I can blame a difference in my voice or gestures on the stress of being shot. In this case, I am only too happy to 'take a bullet' for the president."

Garza shrugged. "OK, then. A grazing wound to the arm. Just before you leave." Navarro nodded, and Garza moved to Rodriguez, kneeling on the tarmac, encircled by two Americans, Reyes, and Perez as the rest of the force staged the bodies.

"What now?" Reyes asked Garza.

"Presidente Rodriguez/Navarro returns, plane shot up. He is enraged, so everyone keeps their heads down. Suspicion will fall on the vice president, who will be allowed to resign and be replaced by an obscure member of Rodriguez's clique, a secret member of the opposition.

"Then," Garza went on, "Navarro will undo the worst abuses: restore term limits, ease press controls, et cetera. In a few months, he'll have a fatal heart attack, and the vice president will take over. Navarro and his family will be smuggled to the US for plastic surgery and new identities. And Rodriguez here"—Garza looked down—"will have a state funeral."

Muffled protests came from Rodriguez's taped mouth as he struggled.

"Good," Reyes nodded. "No assassination. No conspiracy theories."

"An embalming table and cold storage await in Colombia," Garza said.

Rodriguez struggled harder as a soldier produced a syringe. Garza nodded to Reyes.

"You want to do the honors, Lieutenant?"

Reyes hesitated. "For days, I've dreamed of little else but putting a bullet between his eyes, but this… this pathetic piece of shit sickens me. I had not envisioned putting him down like a rabid dog."

"Just remember Miraflores," Perez said softly, "and the many more has he killed just with the filth in these warehouses. He is worse than a rabid dog, Manny, for the dog has no choice in the matter."

Maria's agony filled Reyes's mind, and in seconds, he was over Rodriguez, the needle deep in the man's neck. Long after the body stopped twitching, Perez pried his fingers away.

Motaki smiled as he read. The Russian fuel was flowing, with the state press trumpeting the news, and there was optimism in the streets for the first time in recent memory. He put down the report and pressed the intercom.

"Ahmad," he said, "please have the car brought around."

"At once, Mr. President. May I know your destination to alert security?"

"No place in particular, Ahmad. I just want to go among the people. And no security detail. They intimidate people."

"Are you… are you sure that is altogether… wise, Mr. President?"

Motaki stifled a rebuke. "I'll be fine, my young friend. Like the early days, when I roamed freely. The driver is all I need."

"Very well, Mr. President," Ahmad said.

***

Boron carbide was the perfect contaminant—virtually indestructible, inert, the third-hardest material known to man, and available commercially as a fine powder. Mixed into the paint used on the interiors of the tank trucks and railcars, the hard, tiny crystals were initially harmless and fuel quality hardly compromised during inspection and custody transfer at the border. After all, no one was testing for boron carbide.

As Russian fuel surged through the Iranian distribution system, the impact was cumulative, felt first in smaller towns near the border. Here and there, ancient cars coughed to a halt, and country mechanics scratched their heads, the scattered failures prompting no concern.

The cancer spread to the population centers, reaching critical mass in Tehran in the wee hours of morning as cars coughed and died in increasing numbers. Their drivers shrugged off this latest hardship and pushed their cars to the nearest garage. By dawn, every shop had a line; the drivers clustered in groups, smoking and musing on the cause of the serial breakdowns.

Fuel was the obvious culprit, and admiration of Motaki's Russian coup changed to anger as motorists waited for the bill for his stupidity. The verdict came midmorning as mechanics removed cylinder heads to peer at seized and blackened pistons. Like doctors pronouncing a terminal illness, they folded greasy hands and gave the news: engine replacement required, a diagnosis that doomed most of the stricken cars to the scrap yard.

News spread as waiting drivers crowded round and thumbs flew, sending texts to warn family and friends against refueling. Warnings already too late, as across the city vehicles bucked to a stop, an unmoving mass of blaring horns and angry voices. The battered cars were mobility, one of few remaining freedoms, and a loss not easily endured.

Voices gained purpose and coherence as they coalesced into a chant.

"Death, Death, Death to Motaki!"

***

Motaki stared out the car window, bemused. Cheap fuel meant crushing traffic, but he was enjoying the ride as people did double takes. He wanted to be among people to bask in their approval. He might get out and walk, he thought, since they weren't moving.

The driver stood outside, craning his neck. He got in, shaking his head.

"What is it, Rahim?"

"Bonnets raised everywhere, sir. And distant chanting. 'Death to America,' I think."

Motaki smiled. "Praise Allah for providing our people a target for frustration, though I am not sure the Great Satan creates traffic jams."

Rahim chuckled as Motaki watched a motorist peer under his hood. The man pulled a cell phone from his pocket and stared at the display, scrolling through a text. He grimaced and raised his eyes, recognizing Motaki, then pointing at him as he shouted. A mob surged around the car, tugging at locked doors and pressing angry faces to the windows, picking up the faraway chant: "Death, Death, Death to Motaki!"

The car rocked with the chant as Motaki fumbled for his phone, and was lifted off the ground, crashing back to throw its occupants about like rag dolls. On the next heave, the car rolled over. Motaki dropped the phone, and Rahim was knocked unconscious, a blessing he'd never appreciate. Motaki lay on the ceiling, gazing out at feet and taunting, upside-down faces. He heard glass break and smelled gasoline as the remains of a bottle hit the pavement and clear liquid ran down the outside of the bulletproof window.

"Here's your Russian petrol, Excrement of Satan," a voice screamed. "Drink it. It will not run our cars!"

More gasoline splashed over the car from nearby stations overrun by the mob. They descended with anything that would hold liquid, hurling the tainted fuel and screaming abuse. The fuel pooled around the car, finally igniting from a stray spark and setting a dozen rioters alight with it to run screaming through the mob like human torches.

A warning was transmitted by text message as motorcycle police wound their way through unmoving cars, and the mob scattered. The police rushed to the charred limo, the more foolhardy burning their hands on locked doors or trying to force bulletproof windows. Pointless efforts—the driver was dead from head trauma, and Motaki was curled in the fetal position on the smoldering headliner, baked to a turn.

CHAPTER THIRTY-THREE

Dugan lay in bed, arm around Anna as she dozed, her head on his chest. She stirred and lifted her head to smile at him sleepily, then put her head back down.

"Penny?" she said against his chest.

"Just thinking about the Russians and Iran," he said.

"Hmmm. Just what a girl wants to hear after fantastic sex."

"Sorry," Dugan said, to which Anna mumbled something inaudible, patted his chest, and rolled on her side.

"I'm just really surprised the Russians accepted our plan so readily," Dugan said a few minutes later.

"Hmmm…" Anna muttered. "…Braun's smirking face on video must have… done the trick…" Her voice trailed off into the steady breathing of sleep.

***

Dugan sat alone in the dark living room, a half-finished beer on the coffee table in a puddle of condensation. He looked up at a sound from the bedroom door.

"Tom?" Anna said.

He heard her move through the dark and shut his eyes against the glare as she turned on a lamp. He opened them again as she wrapped the thin silk robe around herself and sat down across from him.

"What's the matter, Tom?"

"How many people do you know that smirk on their deathbed? And if there was a video of Braun, why didn't I see it?"

"Tom… I…"

"The bastard's alive, isn't he." It wasn't a question.

"Tom… please… you don't under—"

"Don't what? Don't understand? Oh, I understand all right. It's all professional spook 'need to know' bullshit. Some sort of 'the end justifies the means' deal with the Devil. What could possibly motivate you and Jesse to cut any sort of deal with this murdering bastard?"

Anna was calm now, her voice ice. "Your bloody freedom, for one thing, and Alex's as well. Has it occurred to you that, despite everything that happened, we had not a scintilla of hard evidence against Braun? Alex had confessed and implicated you, and at the time we made the deal, we didn't even know if he would survive to recant. And even if he did, it was essentially his word against Braun's."

She continued before Dugan could interrupt.

"Just how do you think we got the name of the ship out of Braun?" Anna asked. "Did you think Jesse water boarded him in the recovery room? Despite your disdain for 'professional spooks,' on occasion we do have a better appreciation for the realities. We did what we had to do, and you and Alex are free men because of it."

"OK," Dugan said, somewhat mollified, "but why not tell me?"

"Because we concluded you were incapable of keeping the truth from Alex," she said. "Given what he and his family endured, we feel it better if he never knows Braun is free."

"Free? What do you mean free?" Dugan said. "I assumed you promised the bastard some sort of sentence reduction, but this is… this is…"

Anna sighed and reached for her phone. "I'm calling Ward over," she said. "I don't want to go over this with you more than once."

***

"Full immunity," Ward repeated two hours later. "All jurisdictions—UK, US, Turkey, Singapore, Panama, Indonesia, and Malaysia—and upon recovery, a private jet with a five thousand-mile range to take him anywhere he wants to go."

"Where is he now?" Dugan asked.

"In an apartment in Kensington," Anna said, "set up as a private hospital. The doctors specified a three-week convalescence. He'll be released day after tomorrow."

"So that's it then," Dugan said, "you just kiss him bye-bye at the airport, and you're done. Karl Braun no longer exists. You don't keep track of him?"

"He didn't even bother to put that in the agreement," Ward said, "because he knows we'll try to track him. But he's a slippery bastard, and somewhere there'll be another plane waiting, or maybe a whole series of planes. When he hits the ground the first time, chances are we've lost him. If there's a third cutout plane, or maybe two waiting at the same airport that go in different directions, we're toast. I think losing him is a near certainty."

"If he's officially dead anyway," Dugan asked, "why not just grease the bastard now?"

Ward looked at Anna, then back to Dugan. "Because it doesn't work that way, Tom. The heads of state of seven countries have signed off on this. If it somehow leaked that either the US or UK reneged on a deal we ourselves brokered, it could have severe adverse consequences on future diplomatic efforts, even if the deal in question is with a murdering thug."

Dugan sighed and picked up the written agreement from the coffee table.

"Tom," Ward said, "you're wasting your time with that. The State Department and Anna's folks have had a dozen lawyers going over that agreement with a fine-tooth comb. Braun's no fool. The agreement is very specific and airtight."

Dugan ignored Ward and kept reading. After a while, he looked up, a slow smile spreading across his face.

"Now let me get this straight," Dugan said to Ward. "You and Anna put him on the plane, and you're done, right?"

"Essentially. But Tom," Ward warned, "whatever you're thinking won't work. Our orders are to follow this agreement to the letter."

"I wouldn't have it any other way, pal," Dugan said.

HEATHROW AIRPORT
LONDON
28 JULY

"Off," Braun said, extending cuffed wrists to Lou and Harry.

"Not yet," Lou said as they rolled through security. Harry just glared.

"Idiotic," Braun said, "but have your petty victory."

Braun brightened as the limo rolled across the tarmac toward the plane, and he spied familiar figures. "Agent Ward. Agent Walsh. How nice of you to see me off," he gushed as he was dragged from the car.

"Cut the crap, Braun," Ward said.

"I suggest you lot cut the crap as well," Braun said, holding up cuffed wrists. "You can start by telling these baboons to uncuff me."

Anna nodded, and Lou uncuffed the German, none too gently.

"Much better," Braun said, rubbing his wrists. "But now, if there's nothing further, I'll just be on my way."

"Bon voyage," Ward said.

Braun laughed and bounded up the short steps into the plane. As soon as he entered the plane, two large black men grabbed him by the arms, forced him into a seat, and cuffed his wrists to the armrests.

"What the bloody hell—"

A much-smaller, well-tailored black man stood looking down at him and spoke.

"Karl Enrique Braun," he intoned. "You are under arrest for terrorist acts committed against the Liberian flag vessels M/T *China Star* and M/T *Asian Trader* on 4 July of this year. Under Liberian law, statements you make or have made can and will be used against you."

"What is this nonsense?" Braun said. "I have immunity, you idiot. Now remo—"

"Actually, you don't," said a voice behind him, and Braun twisted his head to see Dugan walking up the aisle, rolled papers in his right hand tapping the open palm of his left.

"Meet Mr. Ernest Dolo Macabee," Dugan said, nodding at the smaller black man, "Foreign minister of the Republic of Liberia."

"I don't give a damn who he is," Braun said. "I have full immunity. Now—"

Dugan held up the papers. "Turns out you aren't quite as bulletproof as you thought, Braun. There's no mention of Liberia in this agreement."

Braun sneered. "Your games don't fool me, Dugan. The intent of the agreement was global immunity. I don't believe for a moment your government will allow you to turn me over to these monkeys."

Macabee stiffened. Smooth move, Karl, thought Dugan as he smiled down at Braun.

"The governments involved *are* following the agreement, Braun. To the letter, in fact. What's happening isn't covered by the agreement."

"I HAVE FULL IMMUNITY!" Braun shouted.

"Alas, Mr. Braun, not in Liberia," Macabee said as if lecturing a dull student. "But it's not surprising we were overlooked. We have many ships under our flag and limited administrative resources. We invariably cede jurisdiction to the country where crimes occur or, if at sea, authorities in the next port. But we always retain the right to prosecute, if necessary. Justice must be served, Mr. Braun." He paused. "Even 'monkeys' know that."

"This is preposterous," Braun said. "This will never hold up, Dugan. I was promised freedom and a plane to take me anywhere I wanted to go."

"And you walked aboard this plane a free man," Dugan said, "whereupon you were arrested by different authorities. And as far as the plane goes," he continued, tapping the paper in his palm, "it says absolutely nothing about the ownership of the plane. It merely specifies range capability and that you will be transported to a destination of your choice."

Dugan turned to Macabee.

"Mr. Minister," he asked, "are you prepared to transport Mr. Braun from here to the destination of his choice before you return with him to Liberia?"

Macabee nodded. "Most assuredly, Mr. Dugan, though I regret he will be unable to deplane at his chosen destination."

Dugan made a show of studying the agreement, enjoying himself.

"Hmm… nothing in here about deplaning," he said.

Braun strained at the cuffs and screamed abuse. Macabee nodded to one of his men, who stifled the tirade with a piece of duct tape over Braun's mouth.

"I will discuss Mr. Braun's desired itinerary with him once we become airborne," said Macabee. "May I have a word with you on the tarmac, Mr. Dugan?"

Dugan nodded and followed the dapper African down the short steps. As agreed, Ward and the Brits were long gone, having fulfilled their part of the agreement and left. On the tarmac, Macabee turned to face Dugan.

"Well, justice delayed is justice denied, so I'll get Mr. Braun home," he said, extending his hand. "However, I did not want to leave before thanking you and your government for the generous gift."

Dugan gripped the man's hand. "My pleasure, Mr. Minister, though please be discreet regarding the plane. Agent Ward had to call in a few favors from friends in the Drug Enforcement Agency. The transfer wasn't completely according to Hoyle, but I'm sure you'll make much better use of it than the drug smugglers from whom it was confiscated."

Macabee smiled. "I understand," he said and bounded up the short steps into the plane.

Ten minutes later, Dugan watched the jet roar skyward, at ease for the first time since he'd met Ward and Gardner in Singapore two months and a lifetime ago.

EPILOGUE

"Great, Jesse," Gardner said, "please go on."

"That's it for Panama. In Iran, the situation is confused since Motaki's death. The unrest is being brutally suppressed, but the student-led opposition is winning. The regime is collapsing, and Ayatollah Rahmani has requested asylum in France."

Gardner scowled. "Why wasn't I told?"

"I just got it. I'm telling you now."

Gardner bit off a reply and smiled. "I understand, Jesse. Sorry to interrupt. Prognosis?"

What's with this asshole? Ward thought as he continued.

"Unknown," he said. "The likely beneficiary is the Council of Resistance. They pay lip service to democracy but have Marxist roots, even though most of the world knows that ship has sailed. They'll dominate any coalition. Not so bad, really. Sometimes"—he sighed —"a rational and predictable enemy is the best one can hope for."

Gardner filed that away.

"Great job, Jesse." He paused as if embarrassed. "I… I want to apologize for past behavior. I should have listened to you."

Ward gave a wary nod as Gardner extended his hand.

"Friends?" Gardner asked with a hopeful smile.

"Ah, sure," Ward said as he shook.

"Good man." Gardner walked Ward to the door with a hand on his shoulder.

Ward walked back to his own office, ill at ease and counting his fingers.

OFFICE OF THE DDO
(DEPUTY DIRECTOR FOR OPERATIONS)
CIA HEADQUARTERS
LANGLEY, VIRGINIA

"At times," Gardner said with a practiced sigh, "a rational and predictable enemy is the best one can hope for."

The deputy director looked puzzled.

"Yes, well, all in all a great briefing," he said, recovering.

"Just doing my job, Mr. Director."

"And quite well. But where's Ward?"

"Off today." Gardner lowered his voice. "Personal problems."

"I'm sorry to hear that," the DDO said. "Ward's a good man."

Gardner's silence spoke volumes.

"If you've something to say, son, say it."

"Sir, I think he's a burnout. The fitness report I just finished reflects that."

The DDO nodded. "Sad, but it happens. I don't second-guess supervisors."

"Yes, sir. Thank you, sir."

"And you've impressed me. How'd you like to work directly for me?"

"In what capacity, sir?"

"Something I've considered for years," the Old Man said. "We use tons of support, an effort decentralized across many groups. I want a sort of 'czar' to take charge. You've done operations. A staff position will enhance your résumé. How does assistant deputy director for administrative services sound?"

"It… it sounds fine, sir," Gardner stammered, "ah… when…"

"Right now. We'll get you moved over. Any loose ends?"

"No, sir." Gardner stopped. "Well, yes. I have to review Ward's fitness report with him."

"Leave that for his next supervisor."

"I better do it, sir. He'll be upset. He may even make groundless accusations."

"He's not the first burnout we've dealt with," sighed the DDO. "We'll handle it."

***

Ward fidgeted. He'd arrived at work to find Gardner's office empty and an e-mail that his performance review would be done by "his next supervisor," whatever that meant. Then this summons to the DDO's office.

"Jesse. Sorry for the wait," the DDO said, emerging from his office. "Come on in."

He pointed Ward toward a sofa, and as he sat, the Old Man retrieved a file from his desk before sitting opposite, a coffee table between them.

"Damned impressive." The DDO tapped Ward's personnel file. "A string of superior ratings and a Director's Citation. The only negative—a repeated refusal to accept advancement. Don't you like hanging around the office, Jesse?"

Ward squirmed. "I'm better in the field and—"

"And you hate office politics. Believe me, Jesse, I know the downside of advancement."

"Yes, sir, I suspect you do."

"More on that later. First, tell me how you became a fuckup."

"Sir?"

"Your latest fitness report." The DDO passed him a single sheet of paper.

Ward read with building anger. "This is… this is complete horseshit!"

"I take it you dispute the evaluation?"

"You're goddamned right I dispute—" Ward looked up to see the Old Man grinning.

"Good enough." The DDO snatched the report and crossed to his desk. A shredder whirred.

"This," the Old Man said, returning with a form, "says a disputed report was reviewed by senior management, that's me, and voided. This"—he laid a report in front of Ward—"is a fitness report from your new supervisor, also me, full of praise. Some of it might even be true. Sign."

"But, but… you're not… I'm way down the food chain."

"We'll get to that. Sign," ordered the Old Man, smiling as Ward complied.

"Now a question," the DDO said. "Think before answering. An American citizen named Borqei died recently. What do you know about it?"

"Just what the FBI told us, sir. We suspect a hit by foreign nationals of unknown origin. The trail disappears in Mexico City."

"Good answer," the Old Man said. "Now, the next issue. Recent events showed everyone, including the president, the potential of maritime threats. At his order, I'm forming a Maritime Threat Assessment Section reporting to me. You're gonna run it."

"Sir, I'm just a field spook. I don't—"

"Don't give me that crap. I'm a field spook too, but here I sit, long past retirement. Because the country needs me, just like it needs you." His face softened. "Jesse, it's a good deal. You get a chunk of the black budget, and I'll keep the politicians off your ass."

"I don't know what to say."

"'Yes, sir, thank you, sir,' would be appropriate."

They locked eyes. "Yes, sir, thank you, sir," Ward said.

"Fantastic." The Old Man thrust out his hand. "The paperwork's ready. Start forming a team. And get that Dugan guy. He knows the industry, and I like his instincts."

"I'm all over that."

"Good. You and Dee Dee ever been to the White House?"

Ward looked confused. "Uh… we took a tour when the kids were little.…"

The Old Man laughed. "Well, you and Dee Dee are dining there next week. Just a quiet private dinner where you'll receive a Presidential Commendation."

"I… I don't know what to say."

"For a smart fellow, Ward, you sure have a limited vocabulary."

"But what about Gardner?"

The Old Man's smile faded. "Yeah, we need to cover that, but what I'm about to say never leaves this room. Understood?" Ward nodded.

"You know Gardner's being groomed for office. Intelligence work enhances the résumé, and his family leaned on enough senators to get him forced on me. It had to be a "leadership position." Since you'd refused the top job in your group, I figured he could sit at that desk a while, and you'd keep him from stepping on his dick. I was prepared to step in if required, but Gardner's idiotic actions caught me flat-footed. Thankfully you salvaged things."

"So where's he going now?"

"I was gonna fire him regardless, but then I realized that wasn't enough. He might eventually end up somewhere he can do some real harm. I made him office-supply czar with a big title. Now he can't cause any disasters except maybe a stapler shortage."

"But won't he just move on in a year or so?"

"That's all I need. Like everyone else, he signed a privacy waiver. He's been under surveillance a month and already documented with underage prostitutes and buying cocaine. Soon, I'll have more than enough to leak to the press if he runs for so much as dog catcher."

"The surveillance is legal but leaking it isn't. Why tell me this, sir?"

"Because he'll be around long after I'm dead. I'll give you a copy of his file and rest easy knowing his balls are in the palm of your very capable hand. Can you live with that?"

"Yes, sir, I can."

"Good, then we're done." He started to rise but stopped. "By the way, Gardner tried to snow me with some bullshit about 'a rational and predictable enemy.' Sounded familiar."

Ward grinned. "It's from a speech you gave. I knew he'd use it sooner or later."

TEMPORARY OFFICES
PHOENIX SHIPPING LTD.
LAMBETH ROAD, LONDON
19 AUGUST

Like its legendary namesake, Phoenix Shipping rose from the ashes in temporary space with rented equipment, the hum of voices punctuated by ringing phones as monitors flashed atop a sea of cheap metal desks. Mrs. Coutts sat as gatekeeper to the closet-size cubicle of Mr. Thomas Dugan, acting managing director of Phoenix Shipping Ltd.

Dugan smiled out at the scene. Business was booming, and an able assist from MI5 hadn't hurt, providing quiet assurance in the right ears that Alex had performed exemplary service to the Crown and that Her Majesty's Government would take a dim view of allegations to the contrary. Claims on M/T *Asian Trader* were paid promptly and in full, and lines of credit were restored, and in most cases, increased.

Dugan left each night tired but happy, usually to meet Anna for dinner. They'd taken an apartment in Belgravia, and nothing had felt so right since that long-ago time when life was full of promise and he'd return from sea to find Ginny on the dock, laughing as she held up a sign reading HEY SAILOR. LOOKING FOR A GOOD TIME? Ginny would approve, he thought.

"Mr. Ward on line one, sir," Mrs. Coutts said.

Dugan lifted the phone. "Jesse. How's it going?"

"Good," Ward said. "Better than good. We've formed a dedicated maritime-threat section. They're letting me run it until I screw up."

"Fantastic, Jesse, and well deserved." Dugan paused. "What about that asshole Gardner?"

"Managing paper clips. He's no longer a factor."

"Well, that's good. At least you won't have to watch your back."

"And speaking of watching things, you know how badly we need—"

"Stop right there, pal. I like what I'm doing."

"Great," Ward persisted. "Stay there. It's perfect cover. We'll make it worth Alex's while financially, and you just keep your eyes and ears open. Piece of cake."

"Let's recap, shall we? The last time you said that, I was beaten by a crazy Panamanian, forced to jump out of a helicopter onto a moving ship, nearly washed overboard by gasoline, shot at, just escaped being blown up, and almost drowned. Oh yeah, I forgot the broken nose."

"Nothing like that's likely to happen again."

"Damn right, because I'm not playing."

"Just think about it, Tom. That's all I ask."

"Listen closely, Jesse. I—DO—NOT—WANT—TO—DO—THIS. Understood?"

"Just think about it. Talk to Anna. I'll call back. Sorry, but the DDO is calling. Bye."

Dugan stared at the receiver. Some friggin' nerve, he thought as he hung up.

Five time zones away, Ward smiled. He'll come around, he thought.

KAIROUZ RESIDENCE

Dugan and Anna held hands under the table. Dinner had been pleasant, and Gillian seemed a different person from the hollow-eyed wraith that had haunted Alex's bedside a month earlier. For that matter, she seemed a different person than she'd ever been. She had on a modest but stylish dress, obviously new, and most of the white had disappeared from her hair. Both she and Alex fairly glowed, trading sly smiles as Cassie seemed near bursting with some great secret. As they all finished coffee, Alex asked Mrs. Hogan and Daniel to join them and addressed the table, his voice raspy.

"We want you all to share a special moment. Recent events have been life changing, and they've led me to count my blessings"—he beamed at Cassie and Gillian—"and take some long-overdue action. I asked, and Gillian has done me the great honor of—"

"Mrs. Farnsworth's gonna be my new mom," Cassie blurted.

Alex sat bemused as Gillian struggled in vain to suppress a peal of laughter. "Well, yes, I suppose that's what I was taking rather too long to say," Alex said with a broad smile.

Dugan and Daniel rose and pumped Alex's hand, while Anna and Mrs. Hogan beamed approval.

"Out with it," Anna said, "the juicy details. When did this happen?"

Alex took Gillian's hand. "When I realized what I'd overlooked for many years."

"It caught me a bit off guard," Gillian said, actually blushing.

"But to quote a very wise woman," Dugan said, "'a lady is prepared for any eventuality.' And you, Gillian, are, and always have been, a great lady to the bone."

"Hear, hear." Alex squeezed Gillian's hand as Cassie held the other, and Gillian blinked back happy tears.

"Right, then," she said, "there's champagne chilling. Mrs. Hogan,"—she started to rise —"I'll help with the glasses."

She had to wipe away more tears as Cassie jumped up. "I'll do it, Mom."

***

After toasts, the ladies slipped away to discuss the wedding, and Alex led Dugan to the library. They sipped brandy in amicable silence until Alex spoke.

"Thomas, I'll be spending more time at home. I need you here. As managing director and an equal partner. In addition to salary, of course."

"Alex, that's extremely generous. I don't know what to say."

"'Yes' comes to mind."

"If I agree, how do you see things structured?"

"You handle operational matters; I look after finances. A perfect team, really."

Dugan stared into his glass. "Ward wants us to help the CIA. I said no, but I'm waffling."

Alex chuckled. "He is persistent. As is Anna. They've both pressed me, you know."

"How do you feel about it?"

"Positively, as long as it places neither you nor my family at risk."

"Agreed. Having the gratitude of the US and British governments is mighty helpful."

"So you're accepting my offer?"

Dugan smiled as he offered his hand. "I guess I am, partner."

CENTRAL PRISON
MONROVIA, REPUBLIC OF LIBERIA
8 SEPTEMBER

Concrete grated Braun's knees as he lapped at the puddle, grateful for the leaky roof; rain water was cleaner than the murky liquid his jailers dispensed. Mold thickened the walls over his rotten, sodden mattress, and he'd long ago sacrificed his shirt and underwear as rags to keep himself as clean as possible. His ragged pants hung loose, a legacy of the gruel ladled into his bowl with indifferent frequency. He devoured the sludge, saving some to attract cockroaches and other protein, and saving some of those to bait up geckos and rats. His thin face, framed by a beard and greasy hair, smiled back from the puddle. He was a survivor.

But he was concerned. He'd sent word to Macabee weeks ago, yet here he rotted. He was considering the likelihood of a double cross when a key rattled in the lock and Macabee entered, impeccably dressed and nose wrinkled, taking pains to avoid touching anything.

"Well, Mr. Braun, here I am."

"Where the hell have you been, Macabee? Why the delay?"

Macabee shrugged. "I felt time would make you more fully appreciative of the benefits of my assistance. Then there was the matter of a trial. The court docket is quite full."

"And when is my trial?"

Macabee smiled. "Last week. You pled guilty and were sentenced to hang."

"What—"

"Don't be tedious, Mr. Braun. A timely 'death' is perfect. Unless you want to stay?"

"No, no. I'm quite ready to leave."

Macabee nodded. "Let's hear your offer."

"It hasn't changed from what I offered on the plane, Macabee. Two million dollars."

"Method of payment?"

"I'll give you the number of my solicitor in London along with a code word. He, in turn, will give you account numbers and authorize the bank to verify availability of funds to you directly. I text you the authorization code to withdraw funds once I'm safely away."

Macabee laughed. "And I'm to trust you? That's as idiotic as your offer. Let's settle that first. Ten million US dollars."

"Preposterous," Braun said. Macabee turned to go.

"Wait! Ten million leaves me nothing. Make it five."

"Your ultimate solvency is both unknowable and irrelevant, Mr. Braun." Macabee smiled at a gnawed rat carcass in the corner. "Ten million—final offer."

Braun hid his elation. "Very well. Ten million."

"Good," Macabee said. "How is the money held?"

"Three accounts. Approximately two, three, and five million, respectively. Why?"

"You'll give me the account number and authorization code to withdraw the two million now as a deposit," Macabee said. "I'll confirm the existence of the rest with your solicitor, in the manner you indicated. I'll fly you under guard to wherever you want, but you won't be released from the plane until the remaining eight million is in my account. Agreed?"

"Agreed," Braun said, mulling plans to outwit the Liberian.

Macabee pulled out a notebook and pen. "Details, please."

***

Four hours later, Macabee sat at his desk, undecided and regretful he hadn't squeezed more from the German. He'd realized his mistake later as he mulled how easy it had been. He'd expected Braun to up the ante, especially after he'd tasted weeks of Central Prison hospitality, but still, it had been a bit too easy.

He sighed; perhaps he shouldn't be too greedy. He hesitated a moment more, then made his decision. He picked up the phone and dialed a London number.

CENTRAL PRISON
MONROVIA, REPUBLIC OF LIBERIA
10 SEPTEMBER

Braun trudged, wrists tied behind him and sandwiched between ragged guards with feet bare as his own, as the trio picked their way between puddles to the gallows. The ragged shirt provided by Macabee hid a wide belt around his torso. At the back of the belt, accessible through a rip in the shirt, was a strong eyelet. A thin wire braided into the rope above the noose would be hooked into the eyelet, transferring the force of the drop into the belt. The death certificate was signed, and the space below the trapdoor was shielded from prying eyes by plywood, concealing men waiting to help Braun down and into a coffin for his ride to freedom.

"Ah, Macabee," he said, topping the crude stairs, "good of you to see me off."

Macabee nodded as Braun was moved onto the trapdoor and hooded. Braun smiled under the hood as the noose was snugged and a metal tape unrolled to touch him at the heel and back of the head, measuring to set slack in the rope. Good showmanship.

Hands released him, and the trapdoor shifted as the others stepped off. Braun turned his hooded head toward Macabee. "The wire," he whispered.

"Alas, Mr. Braun. There will be no wire. I'm afraid you've been outbid."

"What? You can't do this, Macabee!"

"Actually, I can."

"Wait, Macabee! We can work this out. There's more money, much more. I lied."

"I know, Mr. Bruan," Macabee said, "and it's such a pity you waited until this late date to be forthcoming. And by the way, I've a message from Alex Kairouz. He asked me to tell you to enjoy your trip to Hell."

Macabee nodded, and the hangman pulled the lever.

M/T LUTHER HURD
GATUN LAKE ANCHORAGE, PANAMA
15 SEPTEMBER

Milam clung to the ladder and looked down into the tank, bright with work lights, the crackle of the welding arcs mixing with the clang of steel on steel—the din of progress. He grabbed the top rung and pushed his head through the manhole to find himself gazing at worn boots and an outstretched palm.

"Need a hand, old timer?" Captain Vince Blake asked, grinning down at Milam.

Milam smiled back and gripped Blake's hand to haul himself up onto main deck. He tugged sweat-drenched coveralls away from his skin as he moved to the rail in search of a breeze. "Christ. And the sun's barely up. Calderon was right about more productivity on the night shift. By noon it'll be tough to work down there."

Blake nodded, watching a line of passing ships. "Good to see the canal at full capacity," he said. "I can't wait to get in that line."

The ship had been refloated two days earlier, Blake and Milam dogging the salvage master's steps until he threatened to put them ashore. They'd maintained silence with difficulty and shared relieved grins when *Luther Hurd* was finally towed sternforemost to the lake for temporary repairs.

They had debated taking other assignments, but leaving *Luther Hurd* to others didn't seem right. Arnett had rejoined them, promoted to chief mate at Blake's behest. A new first engineer completed the group, a man Milam recruited. They'd ride on the tow north, inspecting and making repair lists.

Blake looked around and shook his head. Generator sets and welding rigs crowded the deck amid debris of ongoing repair work. Clean decks and bright paint had fallen victim to blowing sand and dirt from dam construction, and rains had washed the filth into hard-to-reach places or carried it to leach down the sides in dirty streaks. The port side and starboard stern were masses of rust, twin legacies of rocks and equipment that laid the steel bare and impact with the guide wall. The ship rode deep at the stern, exposing the mangled bulbous bow.

"God, she's a shit house."

"Yep," Milam agreed, "damn sand went everywhere: glands, seals, you name it."

Blake nodded. "How's the engine room?"

"Not as bad," Milam said. "I closed the dampers, so not much got below. Crankshaft deflections are in limits. We'll recheck when the engine is warm, but there's no bottom damage aft; at least none that carried to the engine. Prop and rudder are OK. Except for the tank holed by the anchor and the forepeak tank, the hull's tight. Divers are plugging those outside so we can make temporary repairs inside. When she's tight and we patch the holes between tanks, we can go. Two days maybe." His eyes narrowed. "If Little Dutch Boy gets his head out of his ass."

Blake suppressed a groan as he saw Pedro Calderon approach with Captain Frans Brinkerhoff, the salvage master's face flushed bright red. The Dutchman zeroed in on Milam.

"Vat is this nonsense about running the main engine, Milam?"

"I need to test it. I figure we leave on the main engine and make up tow outside."

"Oh, you do? I must remind you that it is not your decision to make."

Here we go, Blake thought as Milam reddened. By agreement, the Panamanians were responsible for returning the ship to service, including the return to the builder's yard in San Diego for repairs. They had in turn contracted a Dutch salvage company, relegating Blake and Milam to observers, a part neither liked but which Blake handled better than Milam.

"Actually, Captain Brinkerhoff," Blake said, "the chief is right. I'm sure you won't break tow at sea to let us test the engine. This will be our only chance."

"*Nee*. This is not my problem. We lock down with tugs and make up tow at Miraflores guide wall and tow straight to sea. This is most efficient, *ja*?"

"Look, asshole," Milam said, "no ship I'm chief on leaves port on a rope, so—"

"Ahhh… so this is about saving the pride of the chief engineer, *ja*? And who is to pay?"

"Pay for what?" Milam asked.

"Extra cost for harbor tugs to stand by, launch to return line handlers to shore, time lost, all costs not in our quoted price," Brinkerhoff said. "We follow my plan."

Milam glared as Calderon spoke. "Perhaps I can help, *Capitán* Brinkerhoff. The ACP will provide the needed services at no charge. Is that satisfactory?"

Brinkerhoff glared at Milam. "*Ja*," he said at last before stalking away in disgust.

"Thank you, *Señor*," Blake said as Milam nodded.

"It is nothing, *Capitán*," Calderon said. "I can at least ensure your departure is dignified."

M/T *Luther Hurd*
Gatun Lake Anchorage, Panama
18 September

Chief Mate Lynda Arnett stood at the main-deck rail, peering straight down as the pilot boat inched closer to the ship's side. The pilot stepped off the boat onto the rope ladder and began his climb toward her, showing her only the top of his head as he concentrated on the swaying ladder and the task at hand. As he neared the deck, Arnett stepped back to give him room to come aboard.

"Captain McCluskey," Arnett said as a smiling face appeared.

"You didn't think I'd let anyone else take you out, did you?" Roy McCluskey asked as he ignored Arnett's outstretched hand to fold her in a hug.

"I have to say, this is the first time I've ever hugged a second mate," McCluskey said, releasing her.

"Chief mate," Arnett corrected him.

His smile widened. "Fantastic. And well deserved."

Arnett tried not to glance at McCluskey's feet and failed.

"How's the… how are you?" she asked, her eyes back on his face.

"Right as rain." McCluskey stamped his prosthetic foot on the deck for emphasis. "They were able to save the knee, and that made a huge difference."

Arnett nodded, smiling back, and they stood for a moment in awkward silence.

"Lynda. If it wasn't for you—"

"Just doing my job, Captain," Arnett cut him off.

"Well, thank you just the same," McCluskey said.

Arnett nodded again, thankful he'd sensed her discomfort and cut his thanks short.

"Now," McCluskey said, "let's go see Captain Blake and start you on your way."

Bridge of the Americas
Balboa, Panama

No event save the opening of the canal itself had impacted Panama like the attack of July 4. It was named by consensus, but unlike 9/11, date alone was unsuitable, the people instinctively rejecting a name that relegated their tragedy to second place behind the birthday of their huge northern neighbor. Instead, it became simply "Pedro Miguel," a division in time. Things occurred "before Pedro Miguel" or "a week after Pedro Miguel," spoken with sadness and growing pride as the story unfolded.

Many stories, actually: the pilot who delayed the flames, quick-thinking tug captains who herded burning gasoline with their propeller wash, firefighters who abandoned traffic-snarled vehicles to run kilometers in the heat in a heroic but unsuccessful bid to save children at Miraflores; the list was long. But in a visual age, none was quite like the plunge of the *Luther Hurd.*

The video was viewed globally, but as the Bosphorus, then Iran and a dozen fresh stories dominated the news, it faded. But not in Panama, where it was shown repeatedly, and the *yanqui* ship with the strange name became, regardless of her flag, a Panamanian icon. Her repair progress was widely reported, unnoticed by the four Americans, lacking the time to watch the news and the Spanish to understand it if they had. But the people of Panama had no intention of letting *Luther Hurd* slip away quietly.

***

Manuel Reyes stood on the walkway, peering through the chain-link barrier, a hand on the shoulder of each of his boys. His sons held flags, Panamanian in one hand and American in the other. He'd been uneasy with the gringo flag, but the old plea of "But Papa, all the other kids…" had stolen his resolve. And, he thought, the *yanquis* helped him avenge Maria. He gave each shoulder a gentle squeeze. They were beginning to show signs of their old spirit.

"Look, Papa." Miguelito pointed. "There. Where the little boat is shooting water."

"Hah. A lot you know, Miguel," scoffed Paco, irritated his twin had spotted the ship first. "That is a fireboat. You should use the right name."

Reyes smiled. Much improved. "You are both right. Yes, Paco, that is a fireboat, and yes, Miguelito, I do believe the ship is *Luther Hurd*."

His words were drowned out as the people of Panama bid farewell to *Luther Hurd*.

M/T *Luther Hurd*
Passing Balboa Docks, Panama

Blake paced the bridge as McCluskey conned the ship. Arnett was at the console, and the ACP had provided a helmsman, leaving Blake no real duties and edgy. And, he admitted, gazing down at his filthy, rust-streaked ship, embarrassed. It was like walking around with your fly open, hoping no one noticed. He wished again they'd departed at night.

McCluskey smiled. "Don't worry, Captain Blake. I won't run into anything."

Probably wouldn't matter much, Blake thought as Balboa docks loomed to port. "What the hell's that?" he asked as berthed ships all began to sound their horns.

"Ships in port wishing *Luther Hurd* Godspeed," said McCluskey, puzzled at the reaction.

Blake gave a tight-lipped nod. So much for slipping away, he thought as they negotiated the waters of the port and turned south. "What the hell—"

"Dead slow ahead," McCluskey ordered.

"Dead slow ahead, aye," Arnett confirmed.

McCluskey grinned. "This may be a bit tricky, Captain, but I think we'll get through OK."

***

"Slowing down," said the first engineer. "Wonder what's up?"

Milam shrugged. "Who knows? We gave up sightseeing when we decided to push her rather than point her." The phone buzzed before the first could reply.

"Engine Room. Chief."

"Jim. Come up. You've got to see this."

"I've seen Balboa before, Cap. I need—"

"Just come, Chief! Now." Blake hung up.

"Shit," Milam said. "You got it, First? The Old Man has a bug up his ass."

The first engineer nodded, and Milam started the long climb, muttering about rope chokers with no regard for people who worked for a living.

As he exited the machinery space into the quarters, he heard a strange noise outside. Concerned, he raced up the central stairwell, two steps at a time, and burst onto the bridge to join Blake at the forward windows. The harbor was jammed with boats of all descriptions, stretching under the Bridge of the Americas to the sea. *Luther Hurd* moved slowly seaward through a narrow lane marked with temporary buoys and patrolled by police boats, tugs bow and stern to see her safely through, and a fireboat preceded her, throwing arcs of water skyward. The air rang with handheld air horns and whistles and sirens and bells, the less well equipped beating pots with large spoons. Flags were everywhere, most Panamanian, but also a liberal sprinkling of US flags among them. People were cheering and waving signs saying Thank You and *Muchas Gracias*.

"Christ," Milam said as they moved toward the Bridge of the Americas, where a banner hung reading *Muchas Gracias, Luther Hurd*, and in smaller letters below *De parte de los niños de Panamá*. The bridge walkway shimmered with flags in thousands of small hands.

"Who's that on the bridge?" Milam managed as Blake raised his binoculars.

"It's… it's kids," Blake said, "a lot of 'em."

As they moved under the span, McCluskey shot them a knowing smile, and a large net hidden by the banner released thousands of tropical flowers and handwritten well-wishes to cascade on the ship, covering *Luther Hurd* like a float in the *Carnival* parade. Milam lost it.

"Damned allergies," he growled, wiping his eyes with the back of his hand. "Christ, these fucking petunias are gonna clog the ventilation intakes. I gotta go reverse the fans." He fled to the sanctuary of his engine room as Blake and Arnett smiled at his retreating back.

***

Later under tow, Milam stood with Blake on the bridge wing as the coast receded.

"What do you figure, Jim," Blake asked, "three months?"

Milam shrugged. "Should take two, but it'll probably be four, depending on the priority they give us. And you know everybody has a warm and fuzzy feeling now, but as soon as I start insisting we tear into things and somebody has to pay, the honeymoon's over." He sighed theatrically. "Everybody wants to save a buck, but when it goes tits up at sea, I'm the guy stuck with it. I see nothing but arguments, long hours, and midnight inspections ahead."

Blake couldn't contain his laughter. "Who're you bullshitting? You love it."

Milam failed miserably in an attempt to look indignant. "Well anyway, we should start our second 'maiden voyage' in four months."

"Maybe this time I can get her to the load port," Blake said.

Milam chuckled and leaned back against the wind dodger as the battered bow of *Luther Hurd* plowed slowly through the swell behind the tug. Blake watched scattered flowers blow along her dirty deck and drift down her rust-streaked sides, but somehow, he didn't feel the slightest bit ashamed.

DEADLY COAST

In Memoriam
Rita McDermott Mayer
1942 - 2002

Sister, Aunt, Friend, and
Wordsmith Extraordinaire

PROLOGUE

PINGFANG COMPLEX TEST GROUND
UNIT 731
EPIDEMIC PREVENTION RESEARCH LAB
HYGIENE CORP
JAPANESE IMPERIAL ARMY
HARBIN, CHINA - 20 JUNE 1944

Shiro Ishii struggled to suppress his impatience as the last of the fifty *marutas* was led blindfolded into the test area and bound to one of the stout upright poles. He regretted the waste—a dozen subjects would have sufficed, but he wanted to impress. He lowered the binoculars and turned to his visitor, a man in the field gray uniform of a Waffen SS colonel, adorned with the crested serpent insignia of a medical doctor.

"That's the last of the marutas, Doctor," Ishii said. "It won't be long now."

The German grunted and continued to peer through his binoculars at the circle of poles and a pair of Japanese medical technicians fussing over a device in the center of the circle. He lowered the binoculars and turned to his host.

"I'm unfamiliar with the term. Does *maruta* mean 'test subject'?"

Ishii smiled. "In a manner of speaking. It means 'log.' As you can see, our complex is quite large, and we can hardly publicize the nature of our work, so the curious are told the facility is a lumber mill." Ishii's smile widened. "And what does a lumber mill process but logs? In fact, a number of the overly curious have themselves become logs."

The German smiled politely as Ishii turned his attention back to the distant circle just as the two technicians started toward him in a run. They crossed the five-hundred-meter separation and came to stiff attention in front of him, bowing deeply. He returned their bows with a shallow bow, and then barked at them in Japanese, sending them to a control panel. Ishii turned back to his guest.

"We're ready, Doctor," he said.

"You're sure we're safe here?" the German asked.

"Quite sure." Ishii pointed to telltales, streaming from a pole in the light wind. "We're well upwind. Now please watch closely. It will be over quickly."

The German nodded and raised his binoculars as Ishii gave orders to the technicians and then peered through his own field glasses. Ishii saw a small puff of smoke in the center of the distant circle as his technicians triggered the device, and began a running commentary for his visitor's benefit.

"Efficient distribution is dependent on the delivery device. For this test, we're simulating delivery by artillery shell, with each maruta twenty meters from the point of impact. The gas inhibits the central nervous system, producing cardiac and respiratory arrests. The effect is immediate and near one hundred percent lethal, even in very small doses."

Ishii paused his narration and watched through the binoculars as the test subjects stiffened and strained desperately at their restraints before collapsing like rag dolls, hanging from their posts by tethered hands. Within five minutes, all were dead. Next to him, the German lowered his binoculars and spoke.

"Very efficient. But what of residual evidence?"

"None," Ishii said. "Unlike earlier agents, the gas causes no burning or scarring. Victims appear to have died of natural causes, as you'll see during the autopsies. Of course, the enemy will know you've used gas, but proving it is a different matter. We've used the gas extensively here in China against both military and civilian targets for several months without problems." He smiled. "Of course, the world cares little about the Chinese."

The German appeared skeptical. "That may be true, but I hardly think we can use gas in the European theater with impunity. I remind you that, unlike Japan, Germany is a signatory to the Geneva Convention."

"And if Germany is defeated, what will your fellow signatories make of your efforts at Dachau, Auschwitz, and elsewhere?"

The German stiffened.

"I mean no disrespect, Doctor," Ishii said. "But there's a time for propaganda and a time for truth. We both know this war isn't winnable. The Allies have taken Rome and established a beachhead in Normandy, and your cities are being bombed into rubble. And here in the Pacific, we've been on the defensive for months. Last week, American bombers based in India destroyed the steelworks at Yawata. With American air power increasingly able to reach Japan, the situation is grave."

"Such defeatist talk is bordering on treason!"

"I didn't say we're defeated, merely that we can't win—a different matter entirely. Besides, what I'm proposing has approval of the highest authority in both your government and mine. Hardly treason."

"And what *are* you proposing?" the German asked.

"A fighting retreat to our respective homelands, using *every* weapon at our disposal to convince the Allies that invading our countries would result in unacceptable casualties. We can't win, but perhaps we can avoid losing. But we must act together. If either of our countries fall, the other must face the Allies alone. Japan leads the world in chemical and biological weapons development, and it's in our best interests to share those weapons with Germany."

The German nodded and Ishii turned and gave more orders before turning back to his guest.

"My men will wait for the gas to dissipate and move the marutas to the morgue for the autopsies. It'll take an hour or so. May I offer you lunch? We've a great deal of work this afternoon, and I wouldn't like to approach it with empty stomachs."

HEADQUARTERS
UNIT 731
EPIDEMIC PREVENTION RESEARCH LAB
HYGIENE CORP
JAPANESE IMPERIAL ARMY
HARBIN, CHINA - 23 JUNE 1944

Shiro Ishii sat at his desk and stared down at the plain, thin folder. Such a simple container for the last best hope of Imperial Japan. *Operation Minogame* was neatly hand printed on the cover, beside a TOP-SECRET EYES ONLY stamp. Everything in the folder was handwritten as well—details so sensitive that no clerical personnel were allowed to see them, regardless of security clearance.

Ishii looked up at a soft knock on his door, and slipped the file into a desk drawer before calling for the visitor to enter. Seconds later, Dr. Yoshi Imamura stood before Ishii's desk, bent at the waist in a deep bow.

"So, Imamura-san. Did our German guest get away safely?" Ishii asked.

"Hai!" Imamura straightened from his bow. "He left an hour ago, Ishii-san."

Ishii nodded. "And do you think he suspected?"

Imamura looked thoughtful. "I don't think so. Why would he? Your presentation was very logical and convincing."

Ishii smiled. "Thank you, Imamura-san. Is the shipment prepared?"

"As you ordered. Everything crated and ready. It'll be taken by one of our destroyers to our submarine base at Penang and transferred to a German U-boat for the trip to Germany."

"And have you given thought to who will accompany the shipment?"

"I have," Imamura said. "Honda and Sato are the best candidates. They've both worked with the agent extensively and know enough of the plan to deflect any of the Germans' questions."

Ishii nodded. "I agree, Imamura-san, with one addition. You'll join them."

Blood drained from Imamura's face. "Forgive me, Ishii-san, but is that the… best use of our resources? I've many other projects under development here and—"

Ishii cut his underling off. "None remotely as important as this, Imamura-san. You have time to brief a replacement on your other projects."

"But Ishii-san, I—"

Ishii's face clouded. "Imamura-san. You will go. It is the will of the emperor!"

"Hai!" Imamura cried, and bowed deeply.

Unterseeboot U-859
ARABIAN SEA, OFF OMAN
28 AUGUST 1944

Imamura lay sweating in the narrow bunk, cursing his inability to sleep and dreading the moment he'd have to surrender even the scant comfort of the bunk to Sato. Space was at a premium in the U-boat, and the three Japanese were allotted a single bunk they occupied in eight-hours shifts, spending the remainder of each interminable day trying to keep out of the crew's way—a difficult task in the cramped confines of the submarine.

The boat smelled of unwashed men, and the *gaijin* submariners' diet produced a body odor unpleasant to Japanese sensibilities in the best of circumstances—in the congested U-boat it was overpowering. Worse still was the ever-present smell of diesel exhaust as the boat ran submerged at snorkel depth. The Germans took it in stride, but Imamura had been plagued with headaches since the second day out of Penang, and bouts of nausea caused by the unfamiliar diet sent him to the cramped and complicated common toilet with increasing frequency.

His mood brightened as he heard the rumble of ventilation fans and smelled a faint hint of fresh salt air through the miasma of the sub. They had surfaced! He crawled from the bunk and joined Sato and Honda, faces lifted to the nearest ventilation register like hungry pups nursing.

Korvettenkapitän Johan Jebsen stood in the conning tower of *U-859*, binoculars pressed to his eyes as he cursed under his breath and scanned the moonlit horizon. He cursed the luck that had seen *U-859* make two combat patrols without a single kill, and wondered if that had motivated his superiors to strip his boat of all but six torpedoes to turn it into a carrier of mysterious cargo. He cursed Allied air cover that forced him to run at snorkel depth during daylight at six knots. But mostly he cursed the fact that his rather liberal interpretation of his current orders had come to naught.

He was tasked with getting his cargo and passengers to Germany, but nothing precluded kills en route if the opportunity presented itself. He'd swung farther and farther north in pursuit of just such an opportunity, with no results.

Jebsen lowered his binoculars and heaved a sigh as he looked over the calm surface of the sea. The full moon was bright enough to make the horizon visible and the slight lightening in the eastern sky signaled the coming day. He had perhaps an hour of darkness left and then he would submerge and head south, thoughts of a kill forgotten. He started at the voice of the lookout beside him.

"Herr Kapitän, I have a ship. Two points on the starboard bow!"

Jebsen jerked up his binoculars and peered in the direction indicated. Sure enough, visible on the western horizon was a ship.

"Excellent! A straggler from some convoy, no doubt. Good work, Müller!"

Jebsen lowered his glasses and glanced again at the eastern horizon. The ship was steaming at a right angle to his own course. He could never overtake her submerged, but it would soon be daylight. If the ship saw him too early and got off a distress call, he was well within range of shore-based aircraft. Still, he'd be approaching the target from out of the rising sun and could probably sink her before she even saw him. Beside him, Müller seemed to sense his indecision, and Jebsen read disappointment on the man's face. His crew needed a victory.

"Well, Müller," Jebsen said, "what say we go hunting?"

"Jawohl, Herr Kapitän!"

Jebsen returned Müller's grin and ordered flank speed.

It took well over an hour to close to torpedo range, but Jebsen's timing was perfect. The rising sun was just above the horizon and felt good on the back of his neck as he approached the ship, hidden in the glare. He studied it in his binoculars. An American Liberty ship, ugly but utilitarian. He could just make out the name SS *John Barry* on the bow.

Jebsen wasted no time in taking his shot. He fired two torpedoes from the forward tubes, his heart in his throat as the twin tracks sped away from *U-859*. The bridge watch on the Liberty ship must have seen them as well, because the ship started a desperate turn toward the sub to present a smaller target. But it was too little, too late, and the *John Barry* had hardly started the turn when both torpedoes slammed into her starboard side. The sound of the explosion carried through the water, and Jebsen didn't even have to report success before the cheers of his crew echoed up from the open hatch. Across the water, he heard the strident clanging of the ship's general alarm bell and the moan of her whistle sounding abandon ship.

Minutes later Jebsen stood off the sinking Liberty ship and watched as the crew launched lifeboats and tossed rafts overboard. The ship was well down by the bow and sinking. He was debating another torpedo to hasten the process when he heard the drone of an approaching plane.

"Dive! Dive! Dive!" he screamed into the voice tube, and the loud *ooh-gah, ooh-gah* of the dive klaxon filled his ears. He watched Müller disappear down the hatch as the sea washed over the foredeck, and took a last nervous look astern at the British plane lining up for a run. Jebsen followed Müller down, closing the hatch behind himself and spinning the locking wheel. As soon as they were submerged, he'd make a drastic course change and dive deep. He prayed it wasn't too late.

Imamura stumbled to the cramped toilet, oblivious to the submariners' cheers or anything else but his own cresting nausea. He got there barely in time, and steadied himself against the bulkhead as he leaned face-down over the stainless-steel bowl. It was a long and gut-twisting ordeal, punctuated by dry heaves, leaving him trembling and sweat-soaked just as the terrifying sound of the dive klaxon filled the sub.

The deck tilted at a crazy angle, slamming him against the bulkhead. Imamura recovered and wrestled the toilet door open a second before a powerful explosion rocked the sub. The lights failed, plunging him into a pitch-blackness filled with the terrified cries of dying men. He felt water on his feet, then his knees. Rising pressure sent ice picks of pain into his ears, and he groped his way down the corridor as water rose above his head. He swam underwater, moving blindly and banging his head and limbs on unseen obstacles. Then suddenly he was free.

Imamura spotted light above, and kicked for all he was worth. He surfaced in a patch of diesel oil, the noxious smell ambrosia now, mixed as it was with breathable air. The sea was littered with debris, and he pulled himself up on a sizable piece of wood he recognized as the wardroom table.

CHAPTER ONE

LONDON, UK
PRESENT DAY

Dugan awakened slowly as the erotic dream faded, leaving him with a throbbing erection. Anna lay naked in the crook of his arm, pressed against his side, and he could just make out her sleeping face in the moonlight leaking around the window blinds. He smiled and suppressed an impulse to stroke her cheek, fearful of waking her.

"You awake?" she mumbled into his chest.

"And so are you, I see."

Anna lifted her head. "I could hardly be anything else, now could I? You've been poking me with that bloody thing for half an hour. And what ungodly hour is it, might I ask?"

Dugan turned to peer at the glowing face of the alarm clock. "Four thirty."

"Bloody hell! Why did I have to fall in love with a morning person," Anna groused, as she rolled on top of Dugan and nibbled his ear. "But since we're both awake, I think one good poke deserves another. Don't you, Mr. Dugan?"

Dugan responded with kiss, just as his cell phone vibrated on the bedside table. He turned his head to stare at the phone.

Anna sighed. "Go ahead and answer it. No one is calling with trivial news at this hour. Even if you don't take it, you'll be distracted." She kissed him and smiled. "And I do want your full attention."

Dugan reached for the phone. "Dugan."

"Thomas. This is Alex. I need you to join me in the office as soon as possible."

"What is it? Are Cassie and Gillian—"

"No. No. They're fine. But *Phoenix Lynx* has been taken by the bloody pirates."

"On my way," Dugan said.

OFFICES OF PHOENIX SHIPPING LTD.
LONDON, UK

Dugan paced the windowed wall of Alex's spacious office, oblivious to the magnificent view of the Thames below in the dawn's light. The knot of his tie hung loose at his neck and the sleeves of his dress shirt were rolled to his elbows. He glanced at Alex, slumped morosely at his desk, and like Dugan, unshaven. Anna, sitting in a chair across from Alex, appeared unruffled. But Anna could look calm—and gorgeous—in a hurricane.

"Right, then," Anna said, glancing at a yellow legal pad in her lap. "Why don't we go back over what we know and put together a plan of action?"

Dugan saw Alex nod a weary affirmation, and he moved away from the windows to the chair beside Anna's.

"Notifications," Anna said. "Who do we need to call?"

"The International Maritime Bureau in Kuala Lumpur already knows," Alex said. "I'll ring the underwriters as soon as they open. Beyond that, we should begin notifying the crew's families. They should hear the news from us first and know we're doing all we can to get their loved ones back."

Anna nodded. "I'll get a contact list from HR as soon as someone comes in." She looked out the window at the lightening sky. "There are always some early birds down there, so I suspect we'll see someone within the hour. What about the ransom?"

"Fifteen million is pretty stiff," Dugan said. "Thank God for the hijacking-and-ransom policy. I just hope those guys don't drag out the negotiations too long. How does that work, Alex?"

"W… we don't have coverage any longer, Thomas," Alex said. "I'm afraid I dropped it two months ago."

The color drained from Dugan's face. "You *WHAT*?"

"I dropped it," Alex said. "Premiums had risen into the millions. We just can't afford it— no ship owner can in this market. It's not like a year ago when premiums were reasonable and freight rates high after the Panama closure. Since the global economic meltdown, we barely cover costs."

"So you just dropped it? Just like that? No discussion? No joint decision?"

Alex's face colored. "Yes, I suppose I did. But let's pretend for a moment that I had come to you two months ago and solicited your opinion. Would you have studied the issue and given me an opinion, or would I have received the standard Tom Dugan 'I'm the technical guy. You take care of all that financial stuff' response?"

Dugan glared, then sighed.

"You're right," he said. "I would've left it to you anyway, so I guess the point is moot. But where does that leave us on the ransom? How about the P&I club?"

Alex shook his head. "No help there. If there's a pollution incident arising from the hijacking, or crewmembers are killed or injured, protection and indemnity will cover liability, but they won't pay a penny toward ransom."

"So we're screwed."

"Not completely," Alex said. "Hull and machinery insurers might contribute to a ransom, as will the cargo insurers. Both will suffer smaller losses from a ransom than by declaring the ship and cargo as total losses. But that means protracted negotiations not only with the pirates but between themselves, as each seeks to minimize their contribution."

"God, I hate the thought of paying off these bastards, no matter who does it," Dugan said. "Are you sure there's no other option, Alex?"

"None that I can see," Alex said. "None of the Western naval forces will consider a rescue attempt if the crew is under pirate control—it's too risky for the hostages."

"What about your people, Anna?" Dugan asked. "Any help there?"

Anna Walsh, in addition to being Dugan's significant other and holding down a cover job as his secretary, was also a senior field operative with the British Security Service (MI5), currently tasked with maritime threat assessment.

She shook her head. "The official view of these hijackings is that they're a strictly criminal activity. As such, they aren't considered a threat to national security. In fact, you should be thankful the government isn't involved."

Dugan looked puzzled. "What do you mean?"

"What she means is, for Her Majesty's Government to get involved, terrorism must be at least suspected," Alex said. "And if terrorism is involved, the payment of ransom becomes illegal. As much as I dislike the thought of paying off these people, I wouldn't like the option precluded."

Dugan turned at the sound of activity coming through the open door.

"Sounds like people are starting to arrive," Anna said, rising. "I'll pop down to HR and get that contact list."

Alex nodded. "I'll get off emails to the insurers, and follow up by phone as soon as their offices open. Thomas, when Anna gets the contact list, could you begin notifying the families. I think it imperative that they hear the news from senior management first. We must reassure them we're doing all we can."

Dugan grimaced. "Those aren't calls I ever wanted to make, but yeah, OK."

By noon Dugan was finished—and emotionally drained. He'd started in the Philippines, where it was early evening, alerting the families of the unlicensed crew. From there he'd moved to various European countries where most of the officers lived.

By the time he'd made a few calls, word raced ahead of him along the informal and mysterious networks that connected a ship's crew and their families, regardless of nationality, and soon his calls were expected. Some reacted with stoicism, long accustomed to the possibility their loved one might one day fail to return. Others reacted more emotionally. Dugan listened to them all, for as long as they needed him to listen, then left them with a special number and the address of a dedicated website Anna was setting up to provide information.

He checked the time and did a mental calculation. Early morning in Virginia. Jesse would be at his desk. Dugan made another call.

"Maritime Threat Assessment, Ward speaking."

"Jesse. Tom Dugan."

"Tom! How the hell are you?"

"We got problems, Jesse. *Phoenix Lynx* has been hijacked by Somali pirates."

"Christ! I'm sorry. Is there anything I can do?"

"I don't know. *Is* there anything you can do? We don't seem to have many options at the moment," Dugan said.

"Well, admittedly I can't do much. There aren't any links between the pirates and terrorists—"

"I think I've heard that speech from Anna, but it's nice to know MI5 and the CIA are on the same page," Dugan said. "Though, frankly, I'm getting a little tired of you intelligence folks apologizing. When the shoe's on the other foot, it seems Alex and I bend way over to help you out."

Silence.

"What's eating you?" Ward asked, at last. "I just got to the party here. I don't think I deserved that."

Dugan sighed. "I'm sorry. I guess I'm wound a bit tight. It hasn't been a fun morning. But you're right. You didn't deserve that. What can you do?"

"I can share intel, if I stretch the point. Are there any US nationals involved?"

"Just me," Dugan said.

"I meant in danger," Ward said. "Our resources are spread thin as it is."

"Yeah, I get the picture, but at least keep me posted on whatever you have, satellite imagery or whatever, OK?"

"Will do," Ward replied. "What's the ship again?"

"*Phoenix Lynx.*"

"Being held where?"

"I'm hoping you can tell us," Dugan said. "The pirates knew enough to disable the AIS before they diverted the ship to Somalia."

"OK," said Ward. "I'll check the birds. She shouldn't be too tough to find; the various pirate clans tend to use the same anchorages. And I do have limited assets on the ground there. But Tom, she's not a US-flag ship, so I'm really off the reservation here. If I get any push back from up the food chain about expending resources—"

"I understand," Dugan said. "I appreciate whatever you can do."

"OK. I'll get back to you."

Dugan hung up and stared at the crew contact list. He ran his hands through his hair and said a silent prayer he'd never have to work his way down that list to deliver even more tragic news.

CHAPTER TWO

US-FLAG SHIP
M/T LUTHER HURD
AT ANCHOR
PORT SAID, EGYPT
SUEZ CANAL NORTHERN TERMINUS

Captain Lynda Arnett sat on the sofa in her office and glared at the brightly colored cartons of cigarettes stacked high on the coffee table. "This pisses me off," she said through clenched teeth.

"Can't say as I blame you," Chief Engineer Jim Milam replied from the chair across from her. "They don't call it the Marlboro Canal for nothing; *baksheesh* is the name of the game here." He nodded to the towering stack of cigarettes. "And I have a suggestion. Better put most of that stash out of sight in your credenza, and just leave a few cartons out at a time. There's going to be a steady stream of 'officials' knocking at your door, from the pilot to the rat inspector to the frigging dogcatcher. If they see all that, they'll get greedy."

Arnett sighed. "Good point," she said, rising to gather an armload of cartons and carry them to her desk. Milam followed her with the rest. Arnett squatted behind her desk and stacked the cartons inside the credenza as Milam handed them to her, one by one, until the space was full. Arnett closed the cabinet and rose to face him.

"That should do it," she said. "Any more advice, Obi-Wan? What about this Charlie Brown character? I've been ignoring him, but he called three times on the VHF while I was anchoring. I wish the damned agent communicated as well."

Milam shrugged. "Your call, Captain, but Vince Blake and other captains I've sailed with usually let him on. Thing is, we'll be swarmed by these guys selling trinkets or whatever, and it's tough to keep them off, short of injuring them, and then there'd be hell to pay. Vince always figured Charlie Brown at least seemed to manage the swarm, and establish a sort of half-assed controlled chaos. And besides," Milam added, "rumor is this guy has a lot of lower-level officials in his pocket. All it takes to lose our position in the next convoy is a little delay here or there. It's happened before."

"OK, so you're telling me a 'normal' Suez transit means the ship's going to be swarming with Charlie Brown and his gang of thieves, a bunch of line handlers, the useless Suez searchlight 'electricians,' and an unknown number of bogus officials. And I get to be the friggin' cruise director and pass out smokes. Is that about the size of it?"

Milam grinned. "Almost. You also get the blame if anything goes wrong."

"Christ," Arnett said. "Captain Blake picked a great time to get appendicitis."

"Look, Lynda, I've sailed with Vince Blake for ten years, and he thinks you're up to it, and so do I. We both told Hanley that on the sat-phone before the chopper took Vince off at Gibraltar." Milam grinned again. "Besides, you're the only one with a master's license."

"Yeah," Arnett said. "For a whole month. I need a lot more experience as chief mate before I'm ready for this. I wanted—"

"You wanted to be totally prepared so you could do a remarkable job and no one could say you were promoted fast because you're a woman. And now you're terrified you're going to screw up, and people will say that anyway."

Arnett glared at Milam, then her face softened. "Well, yeah."

Milam shrugged. "News flash. Some guys are going to say that regardless, so screw 'em. Lynda, we've been shipmates four years, and you pull your weight and then some. Better than most of the candy asses in the fleet that'll be complaining."

Arnett smiled. "Well, thanks for the vote of confidence, Chief, but frankly I'm surprised Hanley didn't relieve me here in Suez. I was looking forward to going back to chief mate."

"Ray Hanley's not stupid," Milam said. "He's the most hands-on, unmitigated, pain-in-the-ass control freak you ever want to meet. If the city's patching a pothole in the street outside his office in Houston, Ray is probably out supervising. He knows exactly who you are and figures there's no point in wasting airfare to bring out a relief when he's got a perfectly good captain in place." He smiled. "Also, I reckon he's crunched the numbers and figured that even with the remaining mates splitting extra watches and collecting overtime, he's still saving money by sailing a mate short once you figure vacation pay and benefits."

"I'm not sure whether to be flattered or pissed," Arnett said.

"Go with flattered," Milam advised. "If Hanley didn't think you were up to it, he'd relieve you in a heartbeat."

Arnett shrugged. "Well, flattered or pissed, there's nothing much I can do about it. Which brings me to this little turd the agent sent an hour ago." She picked up a piece of paper from her desk and handed it to Milam. His eyes widened as he read.

"Son of a bitch," Milam said. "The Egyptians aren't going to let the security team board?"

"That's what it says," Arnett said. "Seems arms and ammunition aboard a merchant vessel are a violation of 'law number 394 for the year 1954.' I guess the new government's decided to dust off the old law and enforce it. They turned our security team back at the airport."

"So where will they board?" Milam asked. "No matter how eager Military Sealift Command is to get this jet fuel to Diego Garcia, I doubt they'll want us sailing past the Horn of Africa without security. I'm not too keen on the idea myself."

Arnett shook her head. "Egypt was our best shot. But we'll have a US Navy escort from the southern end of the canal at least through the Gulf of Aden. Maybe MSC can work something out with the navy." She sighed. "One more thing over which I have zero control."

Arnett looked down from the bridge wing and drummed her fingers impatiently against the wind dodger, watching the chaotic scene on the main deck below. Stan Jones, the newly promoted chief mate, was scurrying about with a clipboard, trying valiantly to do a headcount as people left the ship to board multiple boats jockeying for position at the bottom of the accommodation ladder. The "official" personnel—petty officials, line handlers, and searchlight electricians—asserted privilege and bulled their way down the crowded accommodation ladder through hordes of Charlie Brown's vendors descending with bundles of unsold inventory and whatever they'd been able to steal while aboard. Here and there on the accommodation ladder, violent arguments ensued as a few of the vendors got far enough down the accommodation ladder to toss their bundles to comrades in the waiting boats and then turned to force their way against traffic, back up to the ship for a second load. Charlie Brown watched from his place near the gangway, smiling benignly and offering no assistance whatsoever.

Elsewhere on deck, Milam and one of his engineers were helping the deck gang discourage other late-arriving vendors from trying to board. Arnett watched as Milam and a seaman unhooked a homemade ladder from the ship's side and let it splash into the water, earning them curses and shaking fists from the Egyptians in the boat below. *Please, God! Get these people off my ship!* Arnett prayed, as she took it all in.

She turned and glowered as Akil Shehadi, the ship's agent, limped out of the wheelhouse toward her, clipboard in hand. The limp was of recent origin, a result of miscalculation. Assuming a female as young and attractive as Arnett had risen to her current rank by unprofessional means, Shehadi had decided to try his luck. His tender application of a hand to her ass had been rewarded by the significantly less tender application of her knee to his balls. From the man's gait, the impact of the lesson was still being felt.

Shehadi stopped a safe distance away and displayed his crooked teeth in an unctuous smile. "Almost done, Capitan Arnett. I require one more signature."

Arnett grunted and held out her hand, and Shehadi extended his arm to hand her the clipboard, keeping his distance. She suppressed a smile and the impulse to inquire as to the state of his testicular health, then signed the form and returned the clipboard.

"That it?" she asked.

"Yes, Capitan. But I was wondering. Do you think it would be possible for me to have a few more cartons of—"

Arnett froze him with a look.

"Perhaps not," he said. "Forgive me for asking, and may Allah grant you a safe journey."

Arnett nodded, and as Shehadi limped back into the wheelhouse, she turned back to the scene on the main deck, relieved the chaos was abating. The last of the Egyptians were going down the accommodation ladder, and as if by some silent signal, the late-coming vendors that circled the ship were moving off to other prey. Soon she saw Shehadi appear on deck, limping forward to accompany Charlie Brown down the accommodation ladder. She smiled as Charlie Brown stepped into the last boat and she saw the bosun begin to raise the ladder.

Thank you, God. She lifted her radio to order Stan Jones forward to stand by the anchor.

Ahmed Chahine, aka Charlie Brown, stood in the launch and watched as the stern of M/T *Luther Hurd* receded into the distance. Relief washed over him in waves. He was done now. His family was safe, and the men who had threatened them were gone. And he had been careful—no one could ever connect the men with him. He didn't know who they were—nor did he wish to. What you don't know, you can't be forced to tell, and that was best for everyone.

CHAPTER THREE

M/T *Phoenix Lynx*
At anchor
Harardheere, Somalia

Ali Ismail Ahmed, aka Gaal ("The Foreigner"), crouched in the bow of the boat as it circled *Phoenix Lynx* to the cheers of the Somalis lining the big ship's rail. The daily arrival of the *khat* boat was a much-anticipated event, a break in the pirates' otherwise boring existence. He looked back at the boat's cargo of the narcotic leaf, wrapped in damp cloths to preserve freshness and packed into plastic bags, and sent up a silent prayer to Allah for his good fortune. Catching a ride on the khat boat was a stroke of luck. He had quite a sales job before him, and it would be infinitely easier if the pirates were in a good mood.

He worried again about his potential reception. Despite his embrace of jihad, al-Shabaab, the local al-Qaeda affiliate, had been wary of his American roots. He hoped the pirates would be more welcoming.

His musings were interrupted by the bump of the boat against the ship's side, and the pirates lining the sloping accommodation ladder began to clamor for khat. Smiling broadly, Gaal passed bags of the narcotic leaf to the men at the bottom of the ladder, who passed them hand-over-hand up to the deck of the ship. When the last bag had been delivered, he nodded to the boatman and trailed the happy pirates up the ladder.

Gaal hung back a bit, fearing a challenge as he followed them aft to the deckhouse, but the khat-obsessed pirates didn't look back. Reassured, he closed the distance, and entered the deckhouse on their heels. The passageway was thronged with more pirates, but they parted willingly to allow passage of the khat bearers, Gaal among them now. Through an open doorway of what must be a mess room, he glimpsed hostages, hollow-eyed and fearful.

Knowing Zahra would have appropriated the best quarters for himself, Gaal separated from the group at the central stairwell and pushed through the door. He mentally rehearsed his pitch as he climbed the stairs.

Zahra Askar leaned back on the sofa in the captain's quarters—now his own—and transferred the wad of khat leaves from one cheek to the other with his tongue.

"Forgive me if I'm skeptical of your sudden change of heart, Gaal," he said in Somali. "But your activities aren't unknown to me. For months you've been proclaiming your allegiance to al-Shabaab and holy jihad, and now you ask to join us. Surely you know those fanatics consider our business, and any money flowing from it, *haram*. Now, why would an enthusiastic jihadist decide to join a forbidden business to earn tainted money? You can understand my confusion."

Gaal shrugged. "Al-Shabaab isn't what I thought. The same rigid philosophy that leads them to declare your operation haram makes me suspect because of my origin. I assumed my knowledge of the enemy would earn me a prominent place among them, but they use me as little more than an errand boy. I can't help being born in belly of the Great Satan, but because of that, I will never be a true brother in their eyes. I realize that now."

Zahra seemed to consider that, then shifted the wad of khat again and smiled. "Then perhaps we can offer duties more in tune with your abilities." He gestured to a chair and turned to a small man seated beside him. "Omar, offer our guest some khat."

The small man glared as Gaal took the offered chair, then tossed a plastic bag on the coffee table. Gaal nodded and extracted a stem of khat leaves.

"So you're American," said Zahra, as Gaal stripped the leaves, rolled them into a ball, and popped it into his cheek. "I suppose your English is very good."

Gaal nodded. "I speak without accent. Or more correctly, with an American accent," he said around the wad in his cheek. "I could interpret."

"I'm the interpreter," Omar said.

"Our only interpreter," Zahra said. "We could use another."

Omar's scowl deepened, and Zahra moved to defuse the situation. "In time, of course," he added, looking at Gaal. "For the moment, Omar here is handling all our needs quite well. And you could hardly expect to *start* as interpreter. You must work your way up—first holder, then attacker, perhaps first attacker if you have the courage. After that..." Zahra shrugged. "We'll see."

"I don't trust him," Omar said. "He's a spy from al-Shabaab."

"It's precisely because that's such an obvious possibility that it's unlikely," Zahra said. "The jihadists are fanatics, not stupid. If they wanted a spy, they'd corrupt someone already in our midst."

"I could be useful if you do take an American ship," Gaal suggested. The Somalis shook their heads in unison.

"Far too much trouble," Zahra said. "Now, when the Americans or the Western navies catch us at sea, they take our weapons and free us. Even if they catch us during an attack on some foreign ship, they're very careful to avoid killing us. They just send us to Kenyan prisons." He smiled and rubbed his thumb against his forefinger. "And with proper placement of a little cash, we're soon home."

"But if we take many Americans, that may change," he continued. "The Americans will come with guns to kill us. Then maybe we kill the hostages, and soon we'll have American drones looking for us and bombs falling on our heads. All because the Americans don't understand business." He shook his head. "It's much better to stick to capturing ships with Filipino and Indian crews. The insurance pays to get the ship and cargo back and no one causes trouble, even if we do kill a few crewmen. It is foolish to capture an American ship."

"What of the *Maersk Alabama*?" Gaal asked.

Zahra smiled. "I didn't say there weren't fools among us. I can't control the actions of others."

Gaal nodded, and Zahra turned to Omar. "Give him a chance to prove himself. Put him to work."

Omar glared before standing and motioning Gaal to do the same. "Come with me. The cook can use a helper. We'll start you gutting goats."

OFFICES OF PHOENIX SHIPPING LTD.
LONDON, UK

"This is useless," Dugan said. "Jesse gives us intel and then says we can't use it? What the hell good does it do us if we can't share it with our negotiators?"

Alex nodded and sighed. "I admit it's disappointing. The insurers aren't very forthcoming. One gets the impression they're haggling among themselves. I'd hoped if we could offer them insights into how the pirates were reacting to their counters, we might play a larger role. "

Anna appeared impatient. "I don't think either of you appreciate just how far Ward has his neck stuck out on this. He's re-tasked assets to help us on his own authority. If those assets are compromised, he could be in serious trouble. The least we can do is cover his back."

"We don't even know what his assets are," Dugan said. "How can we compromise them?"

"By seeming to know more than we should," Anna said. "If the insurance blokes doing the negotiating begin to seem clairvoyant, the pirates may well suspect a leak. And if they start looking, they may well find it."

"OK," Dugan said. "But the intel is still useless unless we can act on it. How do we do that without screwing Jesse?"

"We vet the information carefully, sharing only things that have an impact," Anna said. "And *only* if I can invent some plausible source that doesn't compromise Ward's assets."

"Sounds easier said than done," Alex said.

"Perhaps not," she said. "Phoenix is a British company. There is no official government involvement, but suppose I chat with the insurers and imply there is? That might buy us a bit more participation in the negotiating process. We can then selectively share intel and vaguely attribute our source to MI5 involvement and monitor and control how the information is used." She smiled. "And, of course, I'll also threaten them with charges under the Official Secrets Act if they deviate so much as an iota from our instructions regarding use of the information."

Dugan smiled. "God, you're a devious woman."

"And whose neck is stuck out now?" asked Alex.

M/T *LUTHER HURD*
GULF OF ADEN
SOUTH OF BAB-EL-MANDEB

Arnett took a last look at the chart and walked from the chart room to the wall of windows at the front of the bridge. Night was beginning to fall, and she set her coffee cup on the windowsill and raised binoculars to watch ships on the sea around *Luther Hurd* melt into pinpoints of red, green, and white lights—lights that revealed not only their positions, packed close to transit the narrow waters of Bab-el-Mandeb, but also their courses. She heaved a relieved sigh as those courses diverged, every captain taking advantage of the greater sea room of the Gulf of Aden to spread out.

"Come left to zero-eight-eight," she said to the helmsman.

"Come left to zero-eight-eight, aye," the helmsman parroted, and Arnett watched in the gathering gloom as the big ship's bow swung to port.

"Steady on zero-eight-eight, Captain," the helmsman said a moment later.

"OK, Green. Put her on the mike," Arnett said.

"Put her on the mike, aye," said Green, as he transferred steering control to the autopilot, or "Iron Mike," and stood watching the course heading for a moment to make sure the autopilot had engaged.

"Helm's on the mike at zero-eight-eight, Captain."

"Helm's on the mike at zero-eight-eight," Arnett confirmed. She took a sip of her coffee and shuddered. "Did you make this friggin' coffee, Green?"

Green's grin was a flash of white in his dark face. "No ma'am. That was Gomez."

Arnett shook her head. "Well, I don't want to hurt Gomez's feelings, but while he's on lookout, would you please pour it out and make a fresh pot. And if you see Gomez even look at the coffeepot again, please break both his thumbs."

Green's grin widened. "Yes, Captain," he said, and headed toward the coffeepot as Arnett turned back to the window. She looked up as Stan Jones walked in from the bridge wing.

"We're getting close," Jones said. "Where the hell's the navy?"

"We're two hours from the rendezvous, Stan," Arnett said. "I wouldn't start worrying just yet."

Despite her reassuring words, Arnett shared Jones's concern. Something seemed off somehow. A feeling vague and undefined, shared but unspoken. Whether it was the Egyptians' refusal to board the security team at Suez or running into dangerous waters with a new, untested skipper, she couldn't tell. But she felt it. The crew had been twitchy for the whole four-day Red Sea passage, Jones most of all.

"They should have met us at Suez," Jones said. "Especially after the security team was a no-show. Just watch, this is all going to turn into a big clusterfu—"

"*Luther Hurd, Luther Hurd,*" squawked the VHF. "This is USS *Carney,* do you copy? Over."

"Well, I guess your worries are over, Stan," Arnett said, moving to the radio.

"*Carney,* this is *Luther Hurd,*" she said into the mike. "We copy five by five. Nice to hear from you. We were afraid you didn't love us anymore. Over."

She heard a chuckle on the other end. "Negative that, *Luther Hurd.* We've been waiting with bated breath. Understand you did not receive houseguests at your last stop. Do you require boarders? Over."

Arnett considered the offer. Extra people had a way of disrupting the routine of a working ship. "I am considering your last transmission, *Carney.* What are your orders? Over."

"I'm to stay with you to the discharge port, keeping you in sight at all times. Your cargo is required soonest. Over."

"In that case, *Carney,* then negative boarders; repeat, negative boarders. You should be able to scramble assistance if needed. Is that affirmative? Over."

"That's a roger, *Luther Hurd.* Though you've broken my Marines' hearts. They heard your chow was outstanding. Over."

Arnett laughed. "Get us to Diego safe and sound, and I'll have Cookie put together a big feed. Over."

"Roger that, *Luther Hurd*. We have you on the scope and will maintain station one mile on your bow. USS *Carney*, out."

Mukhtar knelt with his three men, facing the stern of the ship and Mecca beyond, as they prayed the *Maghrib*, the sunset prayer, in the dim glow of the electric lantern. They couldn't see the setting sun, but Mukhtar had carefully inscribed prayer times on a scrap of paper and checked his watch faithfully. When they finished the prayer, he rolled up his prayer rug on the aluminum floor plates of the ballast tunnel walkway and watched his men do the same. He'd yet to make his own *hajj*, and the four-day voyage down the Red Sea in the belly of the great ship took him as close to the holy city of Mecca as he'd ever been. He felt a twinge of guilt that here, so close to the Holy of Holies, he was compelled to pray in such filth.

He'd done all he could, of course. Even though his men had complained, he'd forced them to walk far forward in the pipe tunnel, almost to the bow, to relieve themselves in the bilge. He'd realized his mistake on the second day. The ship was trimmed by the stern, and condensation on the ballast piping and tunnel bulkheads fed a tiny but constant flow of water into the tunnel bilge. Only millimeters deep as it trickled aft to the bilge wells, it was sufficient to carry stale urine and fecal matter a meter below the walkway where he perched with his men. By the third day, the tunnel reeked of human waste; so much so, Mukhtar worried the smell might carry to the main deck almost twenty meters above.

Nor was that the only problem. The cavern-like tunnel, running the length of the ship along the keel, was the perfect hiding place—hard to access, seldom visited by the crew, and far enough below the waterline that the flow of water against the hull kept it cool. But *cool* in the Red Sea was a relative concept, and soon the rank smell of sweat and unwashed bodies mixed with the effluvium wafting up from below.

To pray in such conditions was an abomination, and he'd compensated as best he could, diverting ever more of their limited water supply for ritual ablutions and ending each prayer session with an entreaty to Allah to forgive their transgressions and to bless their mission with success. It was in Allah's hands, but as he watched his men move listlessly in the dim light, he struggled to suppress his doubts.

Hiding in the American ship until its closest approach to the Somali coast had seemed an easy thing on paper, but who could foresee these conditions? Minutes had turned to hours as the men crouched in fetid blackness, saving the lantern batteries for prayer and mealtimes. At first they'd passed the time reciting and discussing Quranic scripture in the dark, but they were fighters, not scholars. Discussion turned to other things, and then stopped altogether.

The men became fixated on food and water; so much so, Mukhtar felt compelled to guard their limited stores of both. They were near mutiny, and he was increasingly uneasy leaving them alone, even for his nightly twenty-meter climb up the ladder to the main deck to take a GPS reading through the open hatch.

Mukhtar was pulled back to the present by a sudden change in the pitch of vibration in the steel hull, a change he'd come to understand signaled a major course adjustment. He nodded to himself as he felt the ship turn to port, and realized the significance. Last night's GPS reading had them just north of Bab-el-Mandeb, and he'd been waiting for a sign they'd moved through the narrow strait into the Gulf of Aden.

The men had sensed the change as well, and turned toward him, every face a question. Mukhtar ignored them and pulled the last water bottle from his pack. Less than a liter remained. They were not as close to home as he would have liked, but he could delay no more.

He straightened and handed the bottle to the man beside him.

"One swallow and pass it on," he said. "We save the rest to cleanse ourselves this evening before *Isha'a*." Mukhtar smiled at his men's expectant looks. "We strike tonight, when everyone except the bridge watch is asleep."

"Allahu Akbar," murmured his men in unison.

CHAPTER FOUR

Mukhtar squatted in the darkness on the starboard bridge wing, his left shoulder pressed against the wheelhouse bulkhead, and his senses heightened by a rush of adrenaline. He felt the rhythmic throb of the engine through the steel at his feet and heard the soft breathing of the man squatting behind him. The others were similarly deployed on the port side, waiting for his signal.

He rose until his eyes just cleared the bottom of the waist-high side window of the wheelhouse. The helmsman and the watch officer had their backs to him as they stood side by side, leaning on their elbows on the forward windowsill and gazing out at the ship's bow. They appeared to be chatting, and even without the night-vision goggles, he would've been able to make out their silhouettes in the soft glow of moonlight. Good, the ship was on automatic pilot. Should something go awry, he wouldn't have to worry about veering off course and alerting any escort.

The sudden thought of an escort chilled him. The plan called for the infidels to be subdued silently, but fire discipline was always a challenge with the mujahideen, and their weapons were not suppressed. The flash and sound of gunfire would carry a long way over water, and it wouldn't do to alert either the sleeping crew or an escort before he was prepared. Mukhtar sank back into a crouch and reconsidered his plan to rush the wheelhouse from each bridge wing.

After a time, he smiled, and motioned for his man to follow as he duck-walked forward, staying below the wheelhouse windows. He stopped a few feet aft of the open door into the wheelhouse and pulled a spare magazine from his pants pocket. He turned to see his underling nod in understanding and follow suit. Mukhtar held up three fingers for a silent countdown, and they lobbed the magazines in unison, away from the wheelhouse, which struck the steel deck with a sharp metallic clatter.

As expected, the watch officer came to investigate, intent on reaching the source of the sound farther out on the bridge wing. He moved through the open door with the helmsman on his heels, both playing small penlights on the deck in front of them. The pirates let them pass, then rose as one from the darkness to press the muzzles of their weapons against the backs of the seamen's heads.

"Move or make a sound, and you're dead," said Mukhtar.

Arnett hadn't had a decent night's sleep since she'd watched the chopper carry Vince Blake away at Gibraltar. Sleep came in patches, punctuated by weird dreams, the latest of which was unfolding behind her twitching eyelids. In it, she watched helplessly as Charlie Brown and thousands of his minions sailed off with *Luther Hurd*, leaving her adrift in the lifeboat in her underwear. She screamed curses, and then jerked awake in the dark—wakened by a sound that shouldn't be there.

She lay panting in the twisted sheets, trying to get her bearings and straining to hear what had wakened her, rewarded only with the distant throb of the engine and the familiar sounds of a ship at sea. She debated getting up, then decided against it. She wouldn't be a nervous pain-in-the-ass captain that didn't trust her people. The watch would call if she was needed, and she needed rest. She'd almost convinced herself that was going to happen when her phone buzzed.

"Captain," she answered.

"Captain," said the third mate, "I need you on the bridge."

"OK. Be right up," Arnett said, rolling out of bed.

Arnett pushed open the door from the central stairwell and made her way across the chart room, her path illuminated by the dim red lights of the chart table. She stepped through the curtains onto the darkened bridge, taking care to close them behind her, and then stopped a moment to let her eyes adjust.

"I'm here, Joe," she said. "Give me a minute to get my night vision and—" The smell hit her first—the sickening odor of an unwashed body and excrement. Before she could react, strong arms encircled her, pinning her own arms to her sides, as she was pulled close to that unwashed body. Then her training kicked in.

At five foot two, 120 pounds dripping wet, and determined to make her way in what was still very much a man's world, Lynda Arnett had carefully selected interests. Chief among them was martial arts. Rather than resist, Arnett tensed her legs and forced her back into her captor's chest. She sensed his surprise and a slight loosening of his grip, and still in the circle of his arms, she spun violently to the right, raising her right arm to deliver a savage elbow strike at the place where his head should be. There was a sharp pain as her elbow struck teeth, mitigated by the satisfying feel of the teeth giving way and arms releasing her as her attacker spewed unintelligible curses. She stepped back, still night-blind, and stumbled through the dark toward the general alarm.

Then the night exploded in stars, and she felt, rather than saw, the deck rising up to meet her face.

Mukhtar pocketed the leather-covered sap, and squatted over the motionless woman. He felt her pulse at the neck. Strong and steady—she'd have little more than a headache. Which was more than he could say for his second-in-command. He looked over to where the man stood, florescent in the night-vision glasses, holding his face.

"Are you injured, Diriyi?" he called, as he bound the whore's hands with a plastic restraint.

Mukhtar heard the sound of spitting and a soft click as something hard and small hit the deck. Diriyi's reply came as a wet, lisping rasp. "The bitch broke my teeth. I'll kill her!"

"Not yet," Mukhtar said, as he felt Arnett's pockets and extracted a key ring. "I'll stay here and guard the bridge. You take her master key and the other men and secure the rest of the crew. Enter their quarters and take them while they sleep. Leave each bound and gagged in their room for now. Start on the top deck and work your way down to neutralize the officers first. If you must kill anyone, use your knives. Now hurry!" He rose, and pressed the key ring into Diriyi's hand.

Arnett drifted back into consciousness, her head throbbing and a tightness enveloping the right side of her face as her flesh swelled from the savage blow she'd received. She couldn't see, and she fought down rising panic as she attempted to touch her aching face and couldn't. The panic worsened as she attempted to speak and couldn't open her mouth.

She forced herself calm and tried to assess her situation. She was sitting on the deck with her back against a bulkhead. Her hands were bound behind her and something sticky covered both her mouth and eyes—duct tape, she guessed. Light leaked around the edge of her blindfold, so she knew it was daytime, and from the sounds around her, she knew she was on the bridge. It sounded like her attackers had released Joe Silva to con the ship.

The VHF squawked. "*Luther Hurd, Luther Hurd.* This is USS *Carney.* How do you copy? Over."

"What do they want?" asked a foreign-accented voice.

"I don't know. Probably just a communications check," Silva said. Arnett heard the terror in his voice.

"Answer it and get rid of them," said the foreign voice. "And do not attempt to warn them, or first the whore dies, and then you."

"I'll try," said Silva, "but the captain's been talking to them. They may be expecting her."

Something hard pressed into Arnett's temple and she heard the foreign voice from just above her. "Do it," the man said. "And be convincing, or the whore dies."

"This is *Luther Hurd, Carney,*" she heard Silva say. "We copy five by five. Over."

Joe Silva had been in the States for most of his forty years—a US citizen for thirty—but there was still a ghost of his native Brazil in his speech, evidently enough to draw interest.

"*Luther Hurd,* this is *Carney.* Please identify the speaker. Over."

"*Carney,* I'm Joe Silva, third mate of *Luther Hurd.* Over," said Silva, his accent becoming more pronounced due to stress.

"*Luther Hurd,* stand by. Over."

The radio fell dead for over a minute, then squawked again.

"*Luther Hurd,* this is *Carney.* Is Captain Arnett available? Over."

Arnett could hear the panic in Silva's voice as he addressed their attacker.

"They want to talk to the captain! What do I do?"

"Make some excuse to delay," ordered the foreign voice. "Then break communications."

Arnett heard Silva sigh and then key the mike.

"*Carney,* this is *Luther Hurd.* I must call Captain Arnett to the bridge. She will contact you soonest. *Luther Hurd,* out."

"Understood, *Luther Hurd.* We will stand by. USS *Carney,* out."

Arnett felt strong hands in her armpits as she was hoisted to her feet and pushed forward. She stumbled a few steps and felt the chart-room curtain brush her face as she was pushed through it. Rough hands seized her arms again, and she sensed she was being held between two men, her attackers having apparently learned not to underestimate her. The body odor was mixed with a shit smell that was overpowering and nauseating, and she thought of her taped mouth, visions of strangling on her own vomit flashing through her mind.

She flinched as duct tape was ripped from her eyes and mouth, and blinked in the light as her eyes focused on the scene around her. The chart room was crowded. Two men held her against the chart table, and another stood across the room pointing an automatic weapon down at Joe Silva and Gomez, a young ordinary seaman on his first trip to sea. The terrified crewmen had been forced to their knees, and Gomez's hands were bound behind him.

Silva's hands were free, but he looked almost catatonic from fear. In the middle of the small space stood a fourth man, very much in charge. The men were all black, armed, and of medium height and indeterminate age. They were dressed very much like the vendors that swarmed aboard at Suez.

Mr. In Charge smiled as Arnett's eyes watered in the unaccustomed light, and a tear rolled down her cheek.

"Ah, the whore captain cries," he said in accented English. "Did we upset you?"

He said something in his own language, drawing laughter from the pair holding her and a grin from the man across the cabin holding her crewmen. A grin somewhat spoiled by missing front teeth.

Arnett smiled back at the man across the cabin. "Nice teeth, asshole," she said.

The man scowled and started for her, then stopped at the upraised hand of the man in charge.

Now she knew at least two of them spoke English.

Mr. In Charge moved in front of her.

"My name is Mukhtar, whore," he said. "But you will call me master. In a few moments, you will radio your navy friends and convince them everything is in order, or you will live to regret it. Any questions?"

"Yeah. Would you assholes like some deodorant? I've got some in my cabin."

Mukhtar's fist flew back, then he stopped.

"No," he said, "I must not damage your mouth. I want you to speak clearly on the radio. Diriyi," he called over his shoulder to the man with the missing teeth, "show the whore we mean business."

Without hesitation, the man raised his weapon to Gomez's head.

"No!" shouted Mukhtar. "Use your knife."

Toothless nodded and lowered his weapon to dangle from a shoulder strap, and whipped a knife from his side. He jerked Gomez's head back by his hair and sliced the young seaman's throat in one fluid motion, and bright arterial blood sprayed forward onto the deck. Toothless released him, and Gomez toppled forward, face-down as blood pumped from the wound and puddled in a spreading pool. Beside him, Joe Silva blanched, and dark stains of blood from the spray dotted his face in stark contrast to his skin. He trembled in wordless terror, trying to speak, but his mouth opened and closed soundlessly, like a fresh-caught fish in the bottom of a boat.

Shock coursed through Arnett, followed by rage. There was no training now, just undiluted hatred. She struggled to escape, but her captors were prepared and held her tightly. She aimed a kick at Mukhtar's groin, but he sidestepped.

"You bastard," she screamed. "I'm going to kill you!"

"I don't think so," he said, then turned to his underling. "Diriyi!"

Toothless moved toward Joe Silva with the knife.

"Wait!" screamed Arnett.

Mukhtar turned back toward Arnett and smiled. "Will you cooperate?"

"Let the crew go," Arnett said. "You have me and the ship. That should be enough for whatever you plan."

Mukhtar came close and grabbed her chin, putting his face inches from her own. "Listen to me, whore, because I will tell you once. What I 'plan' is of no concern to you, and you are in no position to negotiate. I can kill you all in five minutes, much sooner than any help can arrive, and I will do so if I must. My men and I are not afraid to die, and in fact, assume we will, so there is no threat you can use against me. Whether or not we complete our mission is the will of Allah, but you should hope for our success as well. It is the only way you and these other infidels will survive. Now, will you cooperate?"

Arnett glared at him. "Yes," she said at last.

Arnett lay face-down on the chart-room settee, bound hand and foot and once again blindfolded with duct tape. Mukhtar kept her there, always within sight, allowing her to use the bridge toilet and having food brought up sporadically. From the sounds around her, she knew he'd released at least a few crew members to run the ship, their good behavior guaranteed by threats against their shipmates.

It was hard to judge the passage of time, but she'd been hauled to her feet to participate in three more communications checks, so she figured they'd been running at least a day or so. She felt dull and lethargic, drugged by failure, racked by doubt, and denied any visual stimulation. She tried to keep herself alert, but monotony and fatigue overcame her at times, lulling her into fitful sleep. Sleep full of dreams of Gomez, a kid just out of high school and on his first big adventure. She remembered his eagerness to please, and the unmerciful but good-natured teasing he got from his shipmates, herself included.

And she remembered her big mouth had gotten him killed.

Tough-talking, take-no-shit-from-anyone Lynda Arnett. She'd always been proud of that image, and the respect that came with it. But someone else had paid the price, and she was determined no one else would die for her pride. So each time the *Carney*'s captain used the word *storm* in their conversations, she'd worked *good weather* into her response, signaling that all was well aboard *Luther Hurd*. And each time she'd been tempted to respond with *bad blow*—the prearranged signal to alert *Carney* she was under duress—she thought of young Gomez lying on the deck. She saw no way *Carney* could intercede without getting more of her crew killed, and she couldn't take that chance.

She roused at the sound of several people moving through the chart room, some of the steps hesitant, like those of blind men in unfamiliar surroundings, mixed with the more confident footfalls. The sound moved away onto the bridge, and despite her situation, she took comfort in the sound of a familiar voice coming from that direction.

"Get your goddamn hands off me," said Jim Milam.

She flinched at the sound of a blow, followed by a moan.

"Get the woman," she heard Mukhtar say, and moments later she felt the restraints on her ankles being cut. She was hauled to her feet and half dragged onto the bridge, where Mukhtar ripped the tape from her face and stood waiting for her eyes to adjust.

Chief Engineer Jim Milam stood on the bridge, his hands bound behind his back, with what looked like a small horse collar sprouting multicolored wires around his neck, held down by straps under his armpits. The cook, the bosun, and a seaman stood beside him, similarly bound and outfitted with the strange collars.

"Take them to the top of the wheelhouse," said Mukhtar to Diriyi, in English for Arnett's benefit. "Bind one to the rail at each corner." He smiled at Arnett. "That should keep them far enough apart to allow us to detonate them one by one."

"Just a minute, Mukhtar! You said—"

"Silence," screamed Mukhtar, as he backhanded her. Caught off guard, and with hands bound behind her, she stumbled backward and lost her balance, crashing to the deck in a heap.

Milam started toward Mukhtar, to be folded over by a rifle butt to the midsection.

"Take them up," said Mukhtar, jerking his head toward the door to the bridge wing, and Diriyi towed the still-gasping Milam toward the door. The other two terrorists herded the three bound seamen in their wake.

Mukhtar grabbed a handful of Arnett's short hair and hauled her to her feet.

She twisted her head and glared at him. "What're you going to do?"

He ignored her question and dragged her to the steering stand. Holding her with one hand, he fished handcuffs from his pocket and locked one cuff around the storm rail on the steering stand. He moved behind her, and she felt his gun at the base of her skull and heard the soft click of a switchblade opening.

"I am going to cut your hands free," Mukhtar said, pressing the gun harder to her skull. "I want you to handcuff your right hand to the steering stand. Move slowly. Try any of your tricks and your whole crew will die. Understand?"

Arnett nodded, and she felt the blade between her wrists, slicing through the plastic cable tie like butter. She wanted desperately to rub her raw wrists, but did as ordered and cuffed herself to the steering stand. She heard the slightest sigh of relief from behind her.

He was afraid of her. Despite her circumstances, the realization brought a small thrill of satisfaction and a ray of hope.

"Now," said Mukhtar, "place steering in manual and come right to a new course of one-eight-zero degrees."

Arnett did as ordered, without bothering to repeat the course back to him. A mile or more ahead, she could see the stern of the USS *Carney*, moving out of view to port as the bow of *Luther Hurd* swung due south.

"What are you doing?" Arnett asked.

"What I'm doing is changing our destination," Mukhtar said. "Very soon I'll be showing your navy friends they can do nothing about it."

The words were hardly out of his mouth when the VHF squawked. "*Luther Hurd, Luther Hurd*, this is USS *Carney*. Why have you changed course? Over."

"There they are now," he said. "The show is about to begin."

CHAPTER FIVE

Dugan gazed at Alex Kairouz across a conference table littered with sandwich wrappers, the debris of a working lunch.

"For Christ's sake," Dugan said. "It took the insurers ten days just to agree on a five-million counter on a fifteen-million ransom demand? While our ship and crew are rotting in some Somali shithole? What's the matter with those guys?"

"I'm afraid feeding them intel may actually be working against a speedy conclusion," Alex said. "They haven't said it in so many words, but I'm increasingly of the opinion the insurers see this as a golden opportunity to drive the ransom as low as possible, with a possible knock-on effect on future ransom demands."

"Then we need to explain to the insurers that our intel is a perishable commodity," Dugan said. "I'm sure there's a limit to Jesse's patience."

"And mine," Anna added. "Given the nature of my involvement, I'm not keen to see this drag out either. I'll drop some veiled threats to the insurers that Her Majesty's Government would like this concluded expeditiously."

Alex sighed. "Well, there's nothing more we can do now. The counter has been made. We just have to hope it isn't so low that it's angered the buggers and hardened their position. I'm anxious to hear from Ward on that point."

Dugan's cell phone vibrated on the table, and he glanced at the caller ID. "Speak of the devil," he said.

"Jesse," said Dugan. "We were just talking about you. Any word—"

"We? Are you with Alex and Anna?" Ward asked.

"Yeah, they're right here."

"Best put me on speaker," Ward said. "They'll want to hear this. And check your email."

Dugan activated the speaker function, placed his phone in the middle of the table, then pulled his laptop over and opened his email. "Go ahead, Jesse," he said. "You're on speaker and I'm opening my email. I see one message from you with an attachment. Looks like a video clip."

"That's it," Ward said. "Yesterday an American flag ship, M/T *Luther Hurd*, carrying a full cargo of jet fuel for Diego Garcia was hijacked off the Horn of Africa. There were—"

"As in the Panama *Luther Hurd*, the Hanley new build?" asked Dugan.

"The same," Ward said.

"But how could that happen?" Alex asked. "Surely, given the cargo and destination, there was a security presence."

They heard Ward's sigh through the speaker. "It's easier to show you than tell you," Ward said. "Play the video clip. But be warned, it's tough to watch."

Anna and Alex moved around the conference table beside Dugan, as he opened the video. They saw an aerial view of a ship in the distance, taken from an aircraft. The ship loomed larger as the camera closed on it, and then the camera circled the ship, making it obvious it was footage taken from a helicopter.

The ship was underway, but no one was visible on deck or on the bridge wings. However, there were four men on the flying bridge, standing by the handrails at each corner of the wheelhouse. The camera zoomed in to show the men bound to the handrails, each with a strange collar around his neck. As the camera panned over them, the men stared up at it, their terror obvious.

"Wh... what are those collars?" asked Alex.

A light began blinking on one of the collars, and the man wearing it screamed and tugged at the restraints binding him to the handrail, attracting the attention of the cameraman, who zoomed in closer still. There was a flash and the man's head disappeared, to reappear tumbling through the air. It landed on the main deck below, as the headless body collapsed to sit on the deck, torso held upright by wrists bound to the top handrail. The three other men looked dazed, the closest covered with his shipmate's blood, then all began to scream and tug at their bonds. The cameraman held focus on the ship, but the ship began to fade into the distance as the chopper beat a hasty retreat.

Dugan stared at the screen, blood drained from his face, the pencil he'd been twiddling snapped in half. Anna suppressed a strangled sob, and Alex sat wordless, moving his mouth as if trying to speak but not producing a sound. Dugan spoke first.

"The bastards," he said through clenched teeth.

Ward's voice came from the speaker. "That was filmed by a chopper from *Luther Hurd*'s escort, the USS *Carney*. The hijackers didn't even issue a warning until they'd killed the first guy to prove they meant business. Only then did they contact *Carney* on the VHF and order the immediate withdrawal of the chopper. The chopper withdrew, of course, and the hijackers informed *Carney* they would execute a crewman every thirty seconds if *Carney* violated a buffer zone of five nautical miles."

"If *Luther Hurd* had an escort, how the hell did the pirates get on in the first place? And wasn't there a security force onboard as well?" Dugan asked.

"There was supposed to be a private security team onboard," Ward said. "But since the revolution last year, the Egyptians haven't been very accommodating. Last week they began to enforce a 'no security team, no weapons' ban on merchant ships in Egyptian waters. My guess is that wasn't a coincidence, and it left the ship wide-open for the hijackers to stow away at Suez."

"What's the navy doing now?" Dugan asked.

"What can they do?" Ward said. "After the hijackers decapitated the crewman, the *Carney* pulled back and shadowed the *Luther Hurd* at the specified five-mile distance. We're dispatching more ships to the area, as are the UK and several NATO allies. Based on her current course, it looks like she's headed for Harardheere, where your own *Phoenix Lynx* is being held."

"Bloody hell," Anna said, now recovered. "Does it get any worse?"

"Unfortunately, it does," Ward said. "The hijackers must have had a camera of their own mounted to film the decapitation. It's starting to show up on several radical Islamic websites."

"Radical Islamic websites?" Dugan said. "Aren't we dealing with pirates?"

"I was coming to that," Ward said. "Al-Shabaab, the al-Qaeda affiliate, has taken credit. They've issued a statement via al-Jazeera, refusing any monetary ransom, and a list of terrorists they insist be freed. The list includes the names of over a hundred dangerous terrorists held in a dozen countries. The logistics alone of dealing with that many jurisdictions make it an impossible demand on its face, even if anyone was inclined to free terrorists. They claim they'll kill all the hostages and blow up the ship if their demands aren't met."

Dugan buried his face in his hands, then looked up. "OK. We understand, Jesse. Where do we stand?"

"I'm scrambling to get in front of this new situation, which leaves you without help, I'm afraid. I need to focus all my resources on al-Shabaab."

"Understood," Dugan said. "But could you try to get the pirates' reaction to the five-million-dollar counter before you pull out?"

There was a prolonged pause. "I don't think you understand, Tom. This is a game changer," Ward said.

"What do you mean?"

"I mean that Somali piracy just became unambiguously linked to terrorist activity, and the US, the UK, and many other countries have a clear policy of refusing to negotiate with terrorists. That includes allowing ransoms to be paid by US or UK citizens or companies."

"But they're different groups," Dugan said.

"Not to the general public," Ward said. "Public perception drives politics, and politicians make policy. Homeland Security is notifying US ship owners and insurers as we speak. Anna can check on her end, but I'll be very surprised if the Brits aren't doing something similar. It's always been a gray area, and rightly or wrongly, this pushed it over the line."

"Agent Ward," Alex asked, "are these public pronouncements or private notices to the owners and insurers? At any given time, the pirates hold over a dozen ships and several hundred crewmen, all the subject of negotiations. There's no telling what impact such a public pronouncement would have on the safety of the hostages, but I suspect the pirates will murder a few just to test the governments' resolve."

"That's been considered," Ward said. "For the moment, the notifications are verbal and no statements will be issued. Owners and insurers are free to continue talks, but no money can change hands. At least, that's what US owners are being told. But it's moot for us. The only US ship being held is the *Luther Hurd*, and Hanley's not talking to anyone, except calling me every thirty minutes to scream in my ear."

"So what you're saying is that we're screwed and there's not a damn thing we can do about it. Does that about cover it?" Dugan asked.

"Look, Tom. I'm sorry about—"

"We understand," Anna said. "But unless you've something else, we should ring off and check things from our end before someone lets the cat out of the bag."

"No. That's it," Ward said, and they said their goodbyes.

Anna looked at Alex. "I'll ring MI5 HQ if you'll contact the insurers."

Alex nodded, reaching for his phone, and Dugan stood to pace in front of the windows. He was not reassured by the bits of overheard conversation. Anna finished first, and Dugan sat down again, as they both waited for Alex to hang up. When he did, he didn't look pleased. He motioned for Anna to go first.

"Right," she said. "Long story short, HQ basically confirmed what Ward told us. Ransoms are prohibited and they're in the process of notifying owners and insurers. We're on the list to be notified, but they're starting with the major insurers first. No public announcement and no prohibition against talking to the pirates, but no money can change hands. What'd you find out, Alex?"

"Much the same. Our insurers intend to drag out negotiations as long as possible. From what they said, it seems all the major insurers are taking the same approach. I suppose no one wants to worsen an already horrible situation." Alex sighed. "In retrospect, I suppose our low-ball offer puts us ahead of the game. We can't have the buggers agreeing to a ransom we can't pay."

"How much time do you think we have before the pirates figure things out and it starts to get ugly?" Dugan asked.

"God alone knows," Alex said.

CHAPTER SIX

M/T PHOENIX LYNX
AT ANCHOR
HARARDHEERE, SOMALIA

"How many did we lose?" Zahra asked, leaning on the bridge-wing rail as he gazed at *Luther Hurd* in the distance.

"Four holders from here onboard," Omar replied, "including Gaal." He shifted the ball of khat to his other cheek and spit over the side, as if the American's name left a bad taste in his mouth. "Not that it's a great loss. He wasn't even a competent cook's helper. I can't imagine how he thought he could be an interpreter."

"And from our core group ashore?"

Omar hesitated. "That's more troubling. Five more holders—"

"Forget the holders! Any fool can be a holder," Zahra said. "Did we lose any attackers?"

Omar nodded. "Three."

Zahra stifled a curse and looked out over the anchorage dotted with captive vessels. He said nothing for a long moment, then shifted his gaze farther seaward, at the two American warships and those of half a dozen other countries, all drawn here by the presence of the *Luther Hurd*. He turned back to Omar.

"What're they doing, Omar? Al-Shabaab is full of fanatics, but they're not fools. Why, after months of declaring our business haram, have they decided to take it up themselves?"

"I don't know," Omar said. "But they've been recruiting for over a week now, and not the standard 'join the jihad and earn a place in Paradise,' either. They're promising holders twice the going rate and offering *four times* the going rate for attackers. In both cases, with half as cash in advance." He shook his head. "We can't compete with that. All the groups are losing men to them. Clan loyalty is keeping most groups together, but everyone has some men without strong clan ties, and they're flocking to the al-Shabaab operation."

"But that's just it," Zahra said. "There is no 'al-Shabaab operation.' They've captured one American ship, murdered crewmen, and drawn half the warships in the region to our doorstep. That isn't an 'operation.' It's insanity."

Omar hesitated. "There's more, I'm afraid."

Zahra sighed. "You're full of good news this morning. What is it?"

"Something strange is going on with negotiations. I was surprised when the initial counter on *Phoenix Lynx* was so low, but thought it a negotiating tactic. But I've been talking to interpreters for the other groups, and now I'm not so sure. They all tell me that their negotiations have slowed. In fact, one group was within days of finalizing a ransom amount and the ship owner and insurer suddenly raised objections to the terms of the deal. Terms agreed weeks before. It seems like a concerted effort to stall. What's it mean?"

Zahra glared out across the water at the *Luther Hurd*. "It means the fanatics have complicated our lives, and that negotiations will be more difficult." He sighed. "We must become more aggressive, both in pressing our ransom demands and acquiring more hostages to enhance our bargaining position. It will be best if we can coordinate our efforts and move quickly. I will contact the other leaders."

He shifted his gaze to the warships. "Perhaps, in a strange way, the fanatics have done us a favor. The more warships that collect here, the more freely we can operate out of the other ports and at sea. And Omar, find out more of the fanatics' plans. Pick out one of our most loyal men to defect to al-Shabaab." He turned and smiled. "Tell him he can take the fanatics' money, but not to forget where his loyalty lies."

M/T *LUTHER HURD*
AT ANCHOR
HARARDHEERE, SOMALIA

Mukhtar stood beside Diriyi on the bridge wing of the *Luther Hurd*, staring across the water at the *Phoenix Lynx*, three miles away.

"You were right, my brother," Diriyi said, as he gazed in the opposite direction, seaward toward the line of warships. "More arrive every day. But how can you be sure they won't attack?"

"On the contrary," Mukhtar said. "I'm quite sure they will, but not immediately. The killings make them wary, and as long as we don't force their hands with more executions, they'll talk." He smiled. "The Americans like to show the world how reasonable they are before they murder the faithful. They'll talk and talk, and meanwhile, their Navy SEALs will find a sister ship and familiarize themselves with every detail. Then they'll build a mockup and plan the attack meticulously, and count themselves very clever to have bought the time to do so. And *Inshallah*, by the time they attack it'll make no difference." He placed a hand on Diriyi's shoulder. "I'm counting on you to buy me at least two weeks—four would be better. But if you sense attack is imminent, kill as many of the hostages as you can, then save yourself. Go ashore on some pretext and leave our new recruits to face the Americans' wrath."

"As you order," Diriyi said. "I think my job is less difficult than yours. Are you sure our other recruits can be relied upon?"

Mukhtar shrugged. "They're motivated by dreams of wealth, which will buy their loyalty as long as needed. Besides, we've no choice. The faithful are few, and none of us have experience attacking ships. It made little difference with this one, because we got aboard and attacked by surprise in the middle of the night. But our next attack will be very different." He paused. "Which brings me to my next question. How's recruitment going?"

"We're almost ready. I've screened twenty experienced attackers, including two first-boarders, and begun to send them north to Eyl in twos and threes to avoid arousing the infidels' suspicions. Their satellites and drones are snooping everywhere."

"Good, good," Mukhtar said. "Holders?"

Diriyi snorted. "Holders we can have without number at the wages we're promising. Each day brings another boatload. I'm going to start turning them away."

"No. Bring them aboard and arm them to the teeth. The more armed men the Americans see aboard, the longer they'll delay and plan."

"All right," he said. "A few more then, but remember, every man aboard means more food and khat we must bring from shore. And with nothing to do, the men quarrel." Diriyi sighed. "I think I'd prefer to face death at your side than manage this pack of greedy and unruly children."

"And I'd prefer to have you there, my brother," Mukhtar said. "But none of the other faithful has enough English to deal with the Americans."

"Which reminds me. The boat this morning brought our runaway American back to us. I suppose the promise of cash was more alluring than faith."

"Gaal? Do you trust him?"

Diriyi shrugged. "He's a fool, like all these American jihadists. They all come impressed with their own sacrifice, and most are so squeamish they faint at the sight of a little blood. And then they expect us to make them leaders. " Diriyi spit over the side. "I didn't trust him before he deserted us, and I trust him even less now. I have him under guard, but it just occurred to me that his language skills might be useful."

Mukhtar stroked his chin. "You may be right, and even if you're wrong, he's expendable. But he's an unknown. We must test him somehow."

"But how?" Diriyi asked.

Mukhtar smiled. "I have an idea. Bring Gaal to the captain's office. And have someone bring up the woman."

Gaal's mind raced as, hands bound behind him, he was half dragged up the stairs toward an upper deck. At D-deck, he was tugged into the passageway and hustled toward the captain's office. He tensed involuntarily as Diriyi released his arm and pushed him through the open door.

Mukhtar stood in the middle of the room, and kneeling before him was a slight figure, head concealed by a pillowcase. The kneeling figure was dressed in the khakis of a ship's officer, and the diminutive frame and body shape left no doubt the captive was female.

"Ah, Gaal. You've come back," Mukhtar said in Somali. "So you find the promise of cash more alluring than that of Paradise."

"A believer may serve Allah in many ways, Mukhtar. I wish only to use the skills I've acquired in His service."

Beside him, Diriyi scoffed. "From the others who arrived with him, it seems his most recently acquired skill is gutting goats."

Mukhtar smiled at Gaal. "Not a skill in short supply, I'm afraid, but still, you may be of some use. Of course, given both your background and your recent betrayal, your loyalty is very much in doubt. As I'm sure you understand, we will require some proof of your renewed commitment."

Gaal nodded, but said nothing.

Mukhtar inclined his head toward the kneeling woman as he drew a Glock from his belt. "This whore is one of your former countrymen. I want you to kill her." He paused, as if he just remembered something. "Ah. But what am I thinking? We must watch her face while you do it." Mukhtar ripped the pillowcase off the woman's head.

The woman looked up, confused and blinking in the light. There was duct tape over her mouth. Mukhtar leaned down and spoke in English.

"You are about to die, whore. I would allow you some last words, but I don't care to hear anything you have to say."

Then he straightened and faced away from Gaal as he pointed the Glock down and racked the slide. He turned and held out the gun to Gaal, butt first.

Behind him, Gaal heard the click of a spring knife and felt cold steel against his wrists as Diriyi sliced through the plastic restraints.

"Kill her," Mukhtar ordered, thrusting the Glock at Gaal.

Gaal hesitated for an instant before taking the gun and pointing it between the woman's eyes, inches from her head. He said a silent prayer to Allah for her soul and pulled the trigger.

OFFICES OF PHOENIX SHIPPING LTD.
LONDON, UK

Dugan sat before his open laptop and steeled himself. Anna and Alex flanked him at the conference table on either side, just out of range of the laptop webcam.

"Thomas, you don't have to do this alone. I'll join you on the call," Alex said.

Dugan shook his head. "We agreed I should be the point of contact for the families, and based on the emails and voice mail, some of them already hate my guts. I may as well continue as the face of the company until my credibility is completely shot." He smiled wanly. "The way things are going, that won't be much longer. Then you can come in as backup."

"I think 'hate' is a bit harsh," Alex said. "I'm sure most of the families realize we're doing all we can."

"Are you?" Dugan asked. "Well, I'm not, and who can blame them? The friggin' pirates are calling them on their loved ones' cell phones, spreading the lie that we're stalling to save money, and all I can respond with are lies—yes, the negotiations are progressing… no, I can't discuss the negotiations… yes, we're hopeful of a breakthrough at any time. Christ! I'm beginning to hate myself."

"Still," Alex said, "are you sure a group video call is wise?"

"Hell no," Dugan said. "But it can't be any worse than individual phone calls day after day. It'll be intense, but at least it'll be over faster than having the same conversation twenty-plus times."

"And wise or not," Anna added, "we can hardly call it off now. We've had the time posted on the family website for three days, and I emailed the families the call-in number yesterday." She glanced at her watch, then at Dugan. "And speaking of that, you've got five minutes."

Dugan nodded and focused on the laptop. "Might as well open it up now," he said, moving the mouse. "So people can sign in and we can start on time."

He opened the conference call and watched as caller names popped up on the participant list. A few little squares of video flashed on the screen as some participants joined in video mode, but most preferred to listen and watch unseen. At the scheduled time, Dugan opened the call.

"Hello everyone, and thank you for joining the call. As I've told you previously, negotiations are progressing. The insurers' negotiating team is in daily contact with the pirates. I'm afraid I don't have anything substantial to report, but our best information is the crew is healthy and—"

As Dugan spoke, another square of video flashed onscreen, freezing him mid-sentence. A man sat restrained in a straight-back chair, a car tire draped over his neck. It was Luna, the bosun of the *Phoenix Lynx*. The tire glistened wetly, and as Dugan watched, hands appeared to upend a gasoline can on Luna's head, the liquid soaked him and his clothes. The hands withdrew as an accented voice narrated.

"We have been patient long enough," the voice said. "Phoenix Shipping is not bargaining in good faith. This is a small preview of what will happen if our demands are not met promptly."

A lighted match came sailing into the video, and Luna burst into flames, his tortured screams blaring from the speakers until they were cut off abruptly as Dugan ended the call.

Dugan was still trembling with rage fifteen minutes later. "How the hell did they get on our call?"

"I suppose we might have anticipated it," said Anna. "We know they've been calling the families to put pressure on us. I suppose somehow they found out about the private website and monitored it. When we posted the call time, they must have intimidated one of the families into producing the call-in number."

Alex nodded, his jaw clenched. "So we provided the audience for their barbaric exhibition. The question is, what do we do? If the families were distraught before, I can imagine their state now."

"There's nothing we can do about the families now," Dugan said. "I doubt any of them will believe a word we say anyway. We've got to do something to solve the problem, because this is going to get worse—much worse."

"I agree," Alex said. "And it's not just our ship. The insurance chaps tell me things are breaking down across the board. Apparently, some groups are copying al-Shabaab and adding a demand for the exchange of their own men captured at sea. That's *in addition* to monetary ransom. That and the fact that no money is flowing mean discussions are becoming more acrimonious."

"Exchanges? Christ! Why the hell is that an issue?" Dugan asked. "Most captured pirates end up in Kenyan prisons and back in Somalia before the ink's dry on the paperwork. It's a joke."

"Not entirely," Anna said. "Captured pirates are increasingly being bound over for trial in Yemen and especially neighboring Somaliland. And given centuries-old animosity between the clans in what are now Somali and Somaliland, Somali pirates aren't going to escape from a Somaliland prison quite so easily."

Dugan shrugged. "That doesn't seem to have made much of a difference so far, and this is going to end badly. I think we all know that. Sooner or later, the US Navy or Special Forces or someone is going to take back the *Luther Hurd*—public opinion in the US won't allow anything less. But there are hundreds of other captives, on two dozen ships scattered up and down the Somali coast, and when the *Luther Hurd* is free and the money dries up, you know what's going to happen."

Alex looked distressed. "Perhaps all the navies acting in concert—"

"Can what?" asked Dugan? "Mount a simultaneous rescue operation of two dozen ships? If that was going to happen, it would have happened months ago. Hell, Alex, no one was willing to take that risk when there were a few crews held captive and rescue was possible. No one's going to step up to the plate now that hundreds of lives are at stake. I doubt even the US would risk attacking the *Luther Hurd* if there was an option. These al-Shabaab assholes are clearly out to provoke a confrontation, and will murder as many crewmen as necessary to get one."

Alex sighed. "You're right, of course. As much as we all hated paying these murderers off, ransom was the only practical recourse to safeguard the crews. I shudder to think what will happen now that we can't give them what they want."

Dugan nodded. After a moment, he spoke.

"Suppose we do give them what they want?"

"What? How, Thomas? The government isn't going to allow ransom. What else do we have they want?"

Dugan smiled. "Oh, we don't have it yet. And they don't know they want it yet. But they will, they will." He glanced at his watch. "Let's take a little cab ride. I'll fill you in on the way."

EMBASSY OF THE REPUBLIC OF LIBERIA
FITZROY SQUARE, LONDON, UK

Given the nature of the visit, both Dugan and Alex had prevailed upon Anna to absent herself. As he looked around the richly appointed conference room, Dugan wondered if he should be here himself. A question made moot by the arrival of the Honorable Ernest Dolo Macabee, Foreign Minister of the Republic of Liberia, who bustled in and took a seat opposite them across the table.

"May I offer you some refreshment, gentlemen?" he asked. "Coffee? Tea? Something stronger?"

Dugan looked at Alex, who shook his head.

"No, we're fine, Mr. Minister, thank you," Alex said. "And thank you also for seeing us on such short notice."

Macabee made a dismissive gesture. "Not at all, Mr. Kairouz. I'm just glad you caught me in London." He smiled. "And I'm always happy to see you and Mr. Dugan. I always find our discussions agreeable."

To say nothing of profitable, thought Dugan.

"Now," Macabee said, "how can I be of service?"

Alex glanced at Dugan again, seemingly hesitant, and then began.

"We'd like to discuss the issue of piracy," he said. "Specifically in Somalia."

Macabee nodded as he leaned back in his chair and steepled his fingers. "A serious issue. Not only in Somalia but increasingly in West Africa as well. We, of course, decry these barbarous acts, and are fully supportive of international efforts to end the blight of piracy wherever it exists."

"What we'd like, Mr. Minister," Dugan said, "is some clarification of the Liberian position regarding the penalties for piracy and enforcement of anti-piracy laws. The Liberian statutes seem a bit…" Dugan smiled. "Shall we say, vague."

The Liberian returned his smile. "I think of them as flexible, Mr. Dugan. After all, no law can anticipate the circumstances of every incident." He shrugged. "Alas, the point is moot. My poor country lacks resources to enforce criminal laws on an international basis. But what, may I inquire, is your interest?"

Dugan looked at Alex, who extracted a small notepad from his breast pocket, scribbled a figure on it, and slid it across the table to Macabee. The Liberian picked up the pad and peered at it at arm's length, before fumbling in his shirt pocket for a pair of half-lens reading glasses with expensive tortoiseshell frames. He donned the glasses and stared down his nose at the note.

"Your interest is quite… substantial," he said at last.

"And available for deposit in the offshore bank of your choice," Alex said.

Macabee smiled. "Once again, Mr. Kairouz, how may I help you?"

"As Mr. Dugan indicated," Alex said, "we'd like to know your country's position on piracy."

Macabee's smile widened. "My dear Mr. Kairouz, what would you like it to be?"

CHAPTER SEVEN

Alex pecked at the keyboard, studying the spreadsheet as Dugan and Anna looked on.

"Are we going to have enough?" Dugan asked.

"It's tight," Alex said. "Between Macabee and the projected costs of the operation, we'll consume our entire cash reserve, to say nothing of loss of the ship. I've got to find some contingency funds somewhere." Alex sighed. "And then hope like bloody hell I can convince the insurers to make us whole later."

Dugan nodded, as Anna spoke.

"Not to change the subject," she said, "but what about Ward? Have you filled him in on this bloody insanity? If not, I'm going to have to, I'm afraid. Besides, he has the best intel, presuming he's inclined to share instead of having you two locked up as dangers to yourselves and others."

"I'll call him later," Dugan said, "after I've—"

"Now, Tom. Or I will," Anna said, holding up her cell phone.

Dugan glared at her, then sighed and punched Ward's number into the phone on the conference table.

"On the speaker, please," Anna said sweetly, and suppressed a smile as Dugan jabbed the speaker button.

"Are you nuts?" Ward asked, ten minutes later.

Dugan looked at Anna. "I get that a lot."

"Seriously," Ward said. "You can't go around making up your own laws, even if it is the high seas."

"They're not our laws," Dugan said. "They're laws of the sovereign Republic of Liberia, and *Phoenix Lynx* and well over half the hostage ships fly the Liberian flag. It's all legal."

"Laws you influenced and—"

"Give it a rest, Jesse," Dugan said. "The US and UK and every other nation tries to influence other countries' policies all the time. How else did corrupt shitholes like Yemen and Somaliland become so cooperative about taking captured pirates when no other countries want to get involved?"

"Those were *government-to-government* deals, and you know it. Not greasing some minister's palm."

Dugan scoffed. "Which means there were a few more layers and some fancy bookkeeping involved before the money got in some minister's pocket. The US probably paid about a hundred times what we did, so there'd be a bit left to spread around to make the common folk happy. I think you're just pissed because we're better at this than you bureaucrats."

"Dammit! You're jeopardizing an ongoing operation."

"Am I?" Dugan asked. "As I see it, our failure won't hurt you a bit, but if we're successful, it will damn sure help you. On the other hand, a rescue op on the *Luther Hurd* alone, followed by the continuation of the ban on ransoms, leaves over three hundred seamen in the hands of very pissed-off pirates. Isn't that about the size of it?"

Ward didn't answer, and the silence built.

"Look, Jesse," Dugan said, "I know you're doing what you have to do, and no one wants to see you get *Luther Hurd* back more than I do. But what I'm proposing won't hinder that at all. And as I see it, it's our only chance at getting everyone back. All I'm asking is that you provide us as much intel as possible."

Ward still didn't speak, and Dugan began to think he'd hung up.

"Anna?" Ward said, at last.

"Here," Anna said.

"What's your take on this?" Ward asked.

Anna sighed. "My take is that Tom and Alex are both certifiable, but that doesn't mean they're wrong. I can't see any other solution."

"All right," Ward said. "I guess when you get right down to it, everything they're proposing occurs well beyond the jurisdiction of either the US or UK anyway, so there's not a damn thing we can do about it. I'll tell you what I know, such as it is."

"Great," Dugan said. "We can start now. What can you tell us about their organizational structure?"

"Best we can tell," Ward said, "there are between fifteen hundred to two thousand active pirates, divided into gangs, roughly along clan lines. The gangs form alliances and work together as necessary, but that changes relatively frequently. For your plan to work, you'll have to spread your net pretty wide. I have a chart that shows the various clan relationships. I'll email it to you."

"Thanks," Dugan said.

Alex spoke for the first time. "Agent Ward? Did I understand you to say there may be as many as two thousand pirates at sea?"

"No, two thousand total," Ward said. "And I emphasize that's an *estimate*. Ninety percent of those guys are holders, with the rest attackers. They're sort of the rock stars of pirates, for want of a better term. They've had some military training. They take all the risks and get much larger cuts of the ransom. Also, each group has a first-boarder, the first one aboard the ship. He gets an even bigger cut of the ransom, and sometimes a bonus."

"Basically, the varsity," Dugan said.

"Yeah," Ward said. "Evidently they're arrogant pricks. They're excused from holding duty and spend their off time ashore, chewing khat and bragging. A lot of them have escaped from Kenyan prisons or been caught at sea and disarmed and released. They're pretty contemptuous of the Western navies, but seem terrified of the Russians."

"Understandable," Dugan said. "I doubt the Russians worry overly much about due process."

"They don't care about bad press, either," Ward said. "That's pretty much the sum of my intel on the pirates."

"You left out the most important point," Dugan said. "Time?"

"Honestly? Not a clue. But as long as al-Shabaab isn't murdering people, the navy's holding off to refine rescue plans. The more complacent and sloppy the pirates get, the better for us." Ward paused. "But understand this, Tom. If an opportunity presents itself, we'll take it. In two minutes or two months, and regardless of what's going on with *your* plan."

"I wouldn't expect anything else. Thanks for the help."

"You're welcome," Ward said. "Now you can return the favor. You know Ray Hanley, right?"

"I doubt there's anyone in the industry who doesn't. Why?"

"Because he's been crawling up my ass daily about the lack of progress of getting his people back, supplemented by calls from what seems like every elected official in the great state of Texas. I also have it on good authority that he's inquiring about Somali interpreters and airstrips in Kenya and Somalia." Ward sighed. "He's about to do something stupid and there's nothing I can do about it. He's a force of nature."

"And you're telling me this why?" Dugan asked.

"Because your harebrained plan is orders of magnitude better than whatever harebrained plan he's concocting," Ward said. "And yours has the added advantage of taking place a long way from my plan. Let's invite him to your party."

"He's not exactly a team player, Jesse. He doesn't want to lead the band, he wants to *be* the band. Besides, why join us? Our focus isn't *Luther Hurd*."

"No, but I can sell it to him as a necessary diversion, and if I don't do something, he'll screw things up for both of us," Ward said.

"I don't know," Dugan said, "Hanley can be—"

"Agent Ward, this is Alex Kairouz. Tell Mr. Hanley he is most welcome to join us." Alex shot Dugan a pointed look. "And tell him to bring his checkbook."

Ray Hanley, force of nature, arrived in London the very next morning on a nonstop redeye from Houston, all five foot seven and 180 pounds of him. He sat now at one end of the conference table, an unlit cigar jammed in the corner of his mouth, as he glared at the speaker phone in the middle of the table. Dugan sat at the opposite end of the table, and Alex and Anna flanked them on either side, all listening to the latest intel update from Ward.

"And there's been a huge increase in traffic out of Eyl as well as Garacad and Hobyo, all main pirate ports," said Ward's voice from the speaker. "It's beginning to look like some sort of major pirate offensive, and it's very unusual for them to be coordinated to this degree."

"What does that have to do with anything, Ward?" Hanley asked.

Ward's exasperated sigh was audible through the speaker. "I don't know, Hanley," he said. "It may have an impact, so I think we need to stay on top of it."

"Maybe this 'offensive' is what the *Luther Hurd* snatch is all about," Dugan suggested, ignoring Hanley. "To draw Western naval presence to a high-profile target and clear the field for more hijackings."

"Except that al-Shabaab and your regular pirates don't get along," Ward said. "Make no mistake, it's the terrorist angle that's drawing all the official attention. If *Luther Hurd* had been hijacked by garden-variety pirates, I'm sure the US Navy would be there alone." He paused. "No, al-Shabaab is doing this for their own reasons. The others may be taking advantage of it, but that's just a sideshow."

Hanley interjected himself back in the conversation. "Well, whatever's causing it, having the damn pirates out in force will help our operation."

"Ah… I don't think I want to hear about that," Ward said.

Anna smiled and reached across the table to the speaker phone. "Goodbye, Jesse. And thank you," she said, and disconnected.

Dugan looked down the table at Ray Hanley. "I think you need to tone down the attitude, Hanley. Ward is helping us, after all."

Hanley took the unlit cigar from his mouth and smiled. "He works for the government, and that makes him a bureaucrat in my book. And I have a standing policy of never cutting a bureaucrat any slack. They shovel BS on a daily basis, and you have to question everything that comes out of their mouths."

Anna stiffened.

"Present company excepted, of course," Hanley added. "Besides, Ward brought it on himself. He wasn't telling me a damn thing about what was happening on *Luther Hurd* until I forced his hand by putting out feelers for Somali interpreters and intel on airstrips and whatnot."

"That was a ruse?" Alex asked.

Hanley snorted. "Of course it was a ruse." He looked around the table. "Y'all think I'm a dumbass? I know I can't mount a rescue operation on my own. And those murdering al-Shabaab bastards don't want a ransom, and the government wouldn't let me pay it if they did, so the navy's the only option. I just wanted Ward to let me in on the plan, which he did." Hanley smiled. "He even told me about your little party."

Dugan looked puzzled. "If you got what you were after, why join us?"

"Plan B," Hanley said. "I didn't have one. I figure if the navy boys screw the pooch and there's anyone left alive on *Luther Hurd*, y'all's plan is my only shot at getting them home. Besides, we need to do something about these damned pirates."

There was a lull in the conversation, broken by Dugan.

"Right. Where were we when Ward called? Oh yeah," he said, looking at Alex. "Where do we stand with the Liberians?"

"They're set to expedite the flag change on Mr. Hanley's *Marie Floyd*, and to issue letters of marque for both *Marie Floyd* and our own *Pacific Endurance*." He smiled. "There was a bit of delay, since no one in the Liberian Ministry of Transport had ever *seen* letters of marque and reprisal. I had to get our solicitors to dig out the history books and cobble one together. However, they assure me everything is quite legal." He smiled again. "All according to recently enacted statutes."

Dugan nodded and turned to Hanley. "How about your end?"

"*Marie Floyd* is eastbound, in the Arabian Sea. I got word to her this morning to divert to Muscat, and I reckon she'll be there inside of two days." Hanley shrugged. "It's not too tough to change from US to Liberian flag. It's going the other way that would be a problem. Besides, between y'all greasing things on the Liberian side and my Washington contacts pushing on my side, there won't be any trouble. Of course, everyone sort of figures I've got a screw loose, paying to reflag a ship that was already on her way to scrap."

"We're happy to have her," Alex said. "Odds are much better with two ships."

"I've still got doubts if we can do it, even with two ships," said Hanley.

"We'll have to," Dugan said. "We can sacrifice two old, tired ships, but remember it's a long shot as to whether the insurers are going to make us whole. We have to survive this financially, come what may."

Hanley nodded as Dugan continued. "What about the riding crew? You sure these guys are up to it? Maybe I should get some of my—"

"Dammit, Dugan! Give it a rest," Hanley said. "I been using Woody and his boys for twenty years. They can do everything we need done, and they're bringing all the electronic gear with them. Besides, I left 'em my plane so they could fly straight into Muscat." He looked at his watch. "They're already on the way." He looked back up at Dugan. "You let me worry about my boys, you just worry about these friggin' Russians of yours."

"Look, Hanley—"

"Gentlemen," Anna said, "and I use the term loosely. Do you think you two could stop comparing penises long enough to allow us to finish our discussion?"

Dugan and Hanley looked indignant. Alex suppressed a smile and changed the subject. "Speaking of planes, Thomas, when are you leaving for Muscat?"

"Tomorrow morning," Dugan said. "I'll use the time before the ships arrive to start rounding up material. I don't want to stay in port any longer than necessary."

CHAPTER EIGHT

M/T *LUTHER HURD*
AT ANCHOR
HARARDHEERE, SOMALIA

Mukhtar and Diriyi stood on the main deck and gazed down at the boat bobbing at the foot of the accommodation ladder.

"Remember," Mukhtar said, "drag things out as long as possible. Take a hard line in negotiations, but do nothing to provoke the Americans into a premature strike. They'll expect us to kill more hostages, so do the unexpected. If absolutely necessary, release one or two of the lowly crewmen, but make sure that before they go they see the others with the collars around their necks. They'll report that to the Americans, and perhaps it'll reinforce their indecision. Then—"

"I know, my brother, I know," Diriyi said. "We've discussed this many times. Don't worry. I'll buy you your time, Inshallah."

Mukhtar smiled. "Forgive me, my friend. I know you will." He changed the subject. "I should be in Eyl in two days. The rest of the men are already there, and the boats are ready."

Diriyi nodded, and embraced Mukhtar. "May Allah protect you."

"And you as well, my brother," Mukhtar said, returning the embrace before moving down the sloping accommodation ladder to the boat.

Diriyi stood on deck watching the boat move toward shore. He gave one last look and smiled, as he turned to walk back toward the deckhouse. He'd do all that he'd promised and more, but first he had a score to settle and wagging tongues to still. He could hardly maintain control of this rabble when they whispered behind his back, calling him the Toothless One or He Who Was Beaten by a Woman. No, he must put things right, and quickly.

He entered the deckhouse and moved down the passageway to the crew lounge. Men sat squabbling over the dregs of the previous day's khat, a few wilted leaves of diminished potency, as they awaited the arrival of a fresh supply. He spotted the American at a table near the door, and nodded.

Arnett drifted in and out of consciousness. The darkness of the windowless storeroom was complete, and she'd lost all sense of time. The stench of stale urine was overpowering, and even now, hours or perhaps days later, her cheeks burned with shame. She remembered the muzzle of the Glock, inches from her eyes, and the abject terror. She remembered the click of the striker on the empty chamber, the terror yielding to confusion, and then the wonderful realization that she was alive. She remembered her soaked crotch and the shame of having wet herself, and the laughter of her captors. But most of all, she remembered the face of the bastard that pulled the trigger.

They'd dumped her in the storeroom shortly thereafter, still bound hand and foot. She'd been ignored since, without food or water, a blessing of sorts, since she had no access to a toilet. The hunger was bearable, but she was severely dehydrated, her tongue thick and swollen in her taped mouth. It was becoming increasingly difficult to tell dreams from reality, and images of Glock muzzles, Gomez, and the *Luther Hurd* sailing away flashed through her mind like an insane slide show.

She jumped involuntarily as the dogs on the watertight door disengaged with squeaks and thumps, and blinked in the sudden harsh glare of the overhead light.

Diriyi looked up as Gaal stepped into the room, the woman over his shoulder. He ordered Gaal to dump her on a table at the far end of the room. The men all looked up, interest on their faces, in anticipation of a break from their boring routine. Diriyi walked to the table and glared down at the woman. She lay on her back, her bound hands beneath her. She was totally helpless, but there was hatred in her eyes as she returned his glare. *We'll soon have that out of you,* Diriyi thought. He turned to his men, who had begun to gather around.

"This, if you can believe it, is what the Americans call a ship's captain," he said in Somali, and nodded at the laughter that followed. "This shameless whore, who doesn't even cover herself properly, would think to order men about. And what's most fantastic, these Americans follow those orders like small boys." He paused to let his words sink in, gratified at the sounds of disgust coming from scattered voices.

"But what's to be expected of infidels who keep unclean and dangerous animals like dogs as pets? And like a dog, even a woman can be treacherous to the unprepared." Diriyi smiled, displaying his missing teeth. "And I'll admit that I was unprepared when the bitch decided to bite." All of the men were laughing now, won over by Diriyi's admission.

"Like an infidel dog, this whore must learn her master, so I'm going to take her now in front of you. And when I'm finished, I'll take her to my cabin and have her many more times every day, until I grow tired of her. After that, you may have her. There are many of you and but one of her, so I suppose you'll have to use your imaginations to arrive at the most efficient combinations." He gave them a gap-toothed smile. "But I'm sure you'll think of something. Do try to make sure the bitch's heart is still beating when we sell her back to the Americans."

Diriyi finished his monologue to cheers, as the mob pressed close to watch. He ripped open the woman's shirt, popping buttons and shredding cloth to expose bare skin and a bra. He reached in his pocket for a switchblade, and the woman's eyes went wide as he slid the blade beneath the center of the bra. It yielded, exposing small but well-formed breasts. Diriyi was moving to slice the plastic tie on her ankles when a voice spoke behind him.

"But like the infidel dog, Diriyi, this woman's unclean," said Gaal in Somali. "She reeks of piss and sweat, and is unworthy of your dick. Better to wash the whore and take her slowly, rather than take her like this and pollute your manhood."

Diriyi glared at Gaal. "What do you think you're doing?" he asked in English.

Gaal smiled for the benefit of the mob, and answered in the same language.

"Stopping you from making a mistake," Gaal replied, his bantering tone in contrast to his words. "There are over forty men here, with only khat to pass the time. There are no women but her, and now you've promised her to them. Do you think you're going to be able to control them if you take her in front of them? Their blood's up, and she won't survive. And then what'll you do when the Americans demand proof that everyone's unharmed?" Gaal ended with a raucous laugh, as if he'd just told Diriyi a great joke.

The men grew quiet, their confusion palpable, and Diriyi smiled and stepped back, his nose wrinkled in mock disgust. "It seems our friend Gaal is right," he said in Somali. "The whore is filthy! Let's be thankful he didn't spend so much time among the Americans that he lost his good sense." Diriyi turned to Gaal. "Take the whore to my cabin and wash her. I'll be along shortly."

Gaal moved to the table, but the others made no move to return to their previous activities. Diriyi had worked them into a mob, and tension lingered, an ill-defined and unspoken threat. Then came the bellow of a hand-held air horn, announcing the arrival of the khat boat. The muttering morphed into shouts of joy as the men rushed out to bring the drug aboard.

Arnett lay on the table as the men rushed out. She was bare to the waist, and felt not shame but white-hot rage. She'd been biding her time, waiting to kick Toothless in the face the moment he cut her ankles free. Then she heard the voice. An American voice. Coming out of the other one, the one that tried to shoot her. A traitor! And he was discussing her like she was a piece of meat.

Traitor bent over the table to pick her up, and she jackknifed at the waist, sitting up and using her neck muscles to deliver a head-butt. The pain of teeth biting into her forehead was dulled by the pure joy of striking back, and she tried to swivel on her butt to sink her bound feet into his gut.

But Traitor was too fast and delivered a vicious openhanded slap, driving her once again onto her back, as he cursed her. Blood leaked into Arnett's eyes from her cut forehead, but not before she saw him step back, blood streaming from his mouth.

On the other side of her, Toothless erupted in laughter.

"She likes to take teeth, this one," Toothless said in English. "How do you like the bitch's sting, American? Did you too sacrifice teeth to the jihad?"

Traitor spit out blood and probed his upper teeth with a finger. "Just a split lip," he said, and spit more blood on the deck.

Arnett watched Toothless, still chuckling, move toward the door. "See if you can get her to my cabin and cleaned up without suffering any more injuries. I must go supervise the distribution of khat before these fools end up shooting one another."

Gaal trudged up the central stairwell with the woman over his shoulder, his arms clamped around her knees. She'd struggled at first, trying to raise herself off his shoulder. Her struggles had ceased when he'd rushed through the doorway into the stairwell, purposely clipping the back of her head on the metal door frame. All in all, she was being a pain in the ass.

Gaal exited the stairwell on D-deck and entered the captain's cabin, which Diriyi had claimed before Mukhtar even left the ship. He moved through the office into the bedroom to dump the woman on the bed. He collected the wastebasket from the corner and searched the bedroom and bathroom, scanning for anything that might be used as a weapon. Finding nothing, he moved back into the office and searched her desk and credenza, dumping a pair of scissors, a letter opener, and a heavy paperweight into the wastebasket. He moved to the door and set the wastebasket down in the passageway, and returned to the bedroom.

"I'm going to roll you onto your stomach and cut your hands free," he said to the woman. "If you so much as twitch, I'll shoot you. I've no doubt you'll get your legs free in short order. Clean yourself and tend to your wounds as best you can."

She glared up at him.

"If you don't like that arrangement, I'll leave you bound, cut your clothes off, and wash you myself. Now, will you cooperate?"

There was hatred in the woman's eyes, but she nodded.

"Good," Gaal said, as he rolled her onto her stomach. "I'll be back later with food. I saw a bottle of water in the bedside table. I'll bring more when I come back."

Gaal pulled out a knife and sliced the plastic tie binding the woman's wrists, and backed out the bedroom door, through the office, and into the passageway beyond. He closed the office door, and wrapped one end of a plastic tie around the doorknob before pulling the tie tight and securing the other end to the bulkhead storm rail. He moved down the passageway and repeated the process on the door from the captain's bedroom into the passageway. He moved back toward the central stairwell, collecting the wastebasket along the way, and descended to look for Diriyi.

Arnett's hunger and thirst had been niggling concerns during her near rape, blotted out by fear and rage. But the mere mention of food and water brought suppressed needs to the fore, and Arnett clawed her way across the bed to the bedside table. Lying on her stomach, she ripped the duct tape from her mouth and fished the water bottle from the drawer to drink in long, greedy gulps. Water leaked out the cracked corners of her mouth as she sucked the bottle dry.

It was soon gone, and she dropped the bottle and twisted on the bed to get her bound feet to the deck. Suddenly conscious of her nakedness, she pulled the shredded remains of her shirt together and stuffed shirttails into her waistband. She felt her rage rising again, and suppressed it. Food was the priority now, and who the hell knew if Traitor would be back with any, no matter what he said.

She pushed herself up and attempted to hop toward her office door, but dehydration and the rapid change in posture did her in. Head spinning, she crashed to the deck, to rise onto her hands and knees and move through the door to her desk like an inchworm, stretching forward and supporting her weight on her hands before dragging her knees up under her. Head still reeling, she hardly noticed when her shirttails pulled free and her tattered shirt fell open again.

She reached her objective and, still on the deck, pulled open a bottom desk drawer to reveal two boxes of protein bars. Ripping open wrapper after wrapper, she leaned back against the credenza and stuffed bars into her mouth, swallowing almost without chewing, as crumbs fell from her chin onto bare breasts. She finished and pulled herself to her knees, and rummaged in another drawer for a small pair of nail clippers to nibble at the thick plastic tie that bound her ankles. Soon she was free.

To do what?

Arnett dragged herself up into the desk chair, her mental fog lifted by the intake of calories. The respite from immediate personal danger allowed her to consider the bigger picture, and panic gripped her. She was responsible for the ship, but more importantly the crew, and she had no idea where they were being held or even how many were still alive. Gomez's frightened face rose in her mind's eye, and angrily she brushed tears from her cheeks with the back of her hand.

Since they'd separated her from the rest of the crew, she'd been reacting to her personal circumstances, but she had to reconnect and establish some sort of control. As much as she despised her captors, she knew she should try to defuse the situation.

She looked around at her cabin—now her cell—and rose to try the door from the office into the passageway. It was blocked closed from the outside, as she knew it would be. She moved to the bedroom and found that exit door blocked as well. Her eyes fell on her wardrobe closet, reminding her she was half naked. Despite her reluctance to comply with Traitor's orders, she knew she'd feel more confident and in control after a shower. Arnett walked to the bathroom, leaving a trail of sweaty, bloodstained clothes in her wake. One thought consumed her as she stepped into the shower—she'd see Traitor dead if it was the last thing she did.

Gaal's jaws moved in vigorous chewing motions, but he purposefully maneuvered the ball of khat leaves so few were crushed between his teeth to release their sap. It was a skill at which he'd become quite adept in the last months. He sat in an easy chair in the sitting area of the chief engineer's office, across a low coffee table from where Diriyi sat on a sofa.

"You're sure the whore can't get out?" asked Diriyi, his speech slurred a bit from the effects of his own wad of khat.

"Relax," Gaal said. "The doors are secured from outside, and the windows don't open. And even if they did, it's a twenty-meter drop to the main deck."

Diriyi nodded, then looked at his watch. He sat up straight, preparing to stand. "Come," he said. "She should be clean by now. I think it's time I kept my promise."

Gaal shrugged and made no move to rise. "If you think that wise."

Diriyi's eyes narrowed. "What do you mean?"

"I mean, the woman's face is already bruised, and now she has an ugly cut on her forehead from my teeth. She's had some training, and won't be easy to rape. I think it'll take more than you and I to hold her down, and we'll have to beat her into submission."

"What of it?" Diriyi asked.

"Think, Diriyi," Gaal said. "At some point the Americans will demand proof the crew's alive. They'll be insistent on seeing the woman, given their foolish tendency to place women in these positions and then agonize over what happens to them. Don't forget, I know how they think. Abuse of the woman will accelerate any rescue attempt." Gaal fixed Diriyi with a meaningful look. "And I think the idea's to delay that as long as possible, right?"

Diriyi tensed. "And what do you know of our plan, American?"

"I know your demands are impossible on their face and have no chance of being fulfilled," Gaal said. "I know Mukhtar has disappeared with all of the faithful and the cream of the crop of new recruits, leaving you and me here with this mob of rejects. I know you are promising these men an insane amount of money when the mission is over, and I suspect that's because you expect none to be alive to collect it." Gaal smiled. "Don't mistake me for one of these idiots, Diriyi."

Diriyi relaxed a bit and sank back on the sofa, studying Gaal.

"Perhaps I misjudged you, Gaal," he said at last. "What do you suggest?"

"Put the woman with the others. They'll all take comfort at being together, and each can confirm the safety of the others." Gaal paused, as if in thought. "When negotiations with the Americans get tense, let them talk to the woman if necessary. Perhaps at that point we can fit a few crew with collars and link the existing well-being of the crew with the immediate danger of their death, should we be attacked. That might buy a few days, or a week."

"You forget one thing," said Diriyi. "The men expect me to rape her then turn her over to them."

Gaal smiled. "But then you opened her legs in your cabin and found her diseased. The men will believe that, especially when I confirm it."

Diriyi returned his smile. "You're a clever fellow, Gaal. We'll do as you suggest." Then the smile faded, and his voice took on a hard edge. "But make no mistake. Before this is over I'll take her." He tongued the gap in his teeth. "And then I'll kill her."

CHAPTER NINE

M/T *Luther Hurd*
At anchor
Harardheere, Somalia

Gaal walked the length of the A-deck passageway, an assault rifle slung over his shoulder, stepping around a pirate squatting on the deck with thumbs flying as he sent a text message. Al-Shabaab had originally confiscated all phones, but with Mukhtar and the others safely away for over a week and the motley crew of bored pirates growing increasingly restless, Diriyi returned the phones to placate the men. Gaal smiled as he looked along the passageway and saw several other pirates engrossed with their phones. It was something he would never understand. Most of the country didn't even have running water or basic sanitation, yet every Somali seemed to have a cell phone and be addicted to using it.

The man he stepped around looked up and smiled, and Gaal returned the smile with a nod. He was accepted as second-in-command now; in fact, the pirates seemed to respect him more than they did Diriyi, a legacy perhaps of Diriyi's missing teeth and the manner of their extraction. But Gaal was careful not to encourage that, and had developed a wary rapport with Diriyi. The man didn't trust him, but Gaal had proven his worth in managing the unruly mob of pirates.

He glanced through the open door of the officers' mess room. The deck was littered with mattresses, on which several men were sprawled. The woman captain and several officers sat at a table, playing cards to pass the time before the next meal of goat meat and rice. The hijackers had concentrated the hostages for ease of surveillance, but at Gaal's suggestion they'd separated the officers. The unlicensed crew had similar communal arrangements in the crew mess room.

The days had a sameness, stitched together by routine. The hostages spent their days in languid monotony, punctuated by periods of terror and speculation when the pirates would fit crewmen with explosive collars and drag the captain out to speak on the phone. The pirates spent their days chewing khat, texting, and squabbling amongst themselves, watched over by Gaal.

Gaal watched the woman. Her cuts and bruises were healing, and she was looking increasingly attractive and obviously healthy. Soon it might be difficult to keep the men at bay, even with the story he'd spread that she was a petri dish of STDs. As if she felt his eyes, she looked up and glared. He smiled and moved down the passageway. She was a pain in the ass.

ARABIAN SEA
120 MILES FROM THE COAST OF OMAN

The Yemini fishing boat bobbed in the gentle swell as it chugged along at six knots, one of the scores of fishing boats ubiquitous to the area, a threat to no one. That was an image Mukhtar very much wanted to project, and he'd strolled the crowded wharf in Aden until he found just the right vessel.

The grateful captain hadn't asked questions when Mukhtar offered to charter his boat for several times the going rate, implying with a wink and a nod there may be a bit of smuggling involved. The poor man realized his mistake five miles outside the breakwater, when fast boats converged on his vessel and he was overrun by pirates. He'd little time to regret his action before Mukhtar shot him and his three-man crew and dumped their bodies over the side.

Mukhtar had no qualms about his actions. The fishing-boat captain was not one of the Faithful, or he wouldn't have accepted such an exorbitant sum nor been so eager to participate in illegal activity. And the crewmen were equally guilty, for what man would serve such a corrupt master if he weren't corrupt himself?

He raised the binoculars and studied the vessel in the distance. The tower of the drillship pointed to the heavens, like a great skeletal finger, and faint sounds of machinery and the ring of steel on steel carried across the water. Mukhtar forced himself to be patient.

DRILLSHIP *OCEAN GOLIATH*
ARABIAN SEA
120 MILES FROM THE COAST OF OMAN

The tool pusher stood on the centerline of the ship, staring down through the moon pool into the clear water, straining to catch a glimpse of the huge hydraulic grab. He cursed under his breath as the ascent of the drill pipe slowed, then stopped, and he heard the clang of steel on steel on the drill floor above. In his mind's eye, he envisioned the slips being placed and the tongs at work, unthreading a long stand of pipe to be moved aside so another could be lifted to bring the grab that much closer to the surface.

A roundtrip to the bottom—over eight thousand feet below—and back took hours. A pity the weight of the treasure and limited carrying capacity of the ROV forced them into this time-consuming process. But the remotely operated vehicle had proven its worth in other ways. Steering the little submersible to depths beyond the capacity of any human, the operator on the drillship had expertly placed explosive charges around the hull of the SS *John Barry*, ripping the old Liberty ship open and exposing her treasure for the first time in over sixty years.

The tool pusher fidgeted and shot a squirt of tobacco juice into the clear waters below. *Exposed* was still over eight thousand feet from *recovered*. He glanced at the immobile pipe. It was ingenious, really, the idea of turning a drillship into a giant version of the coin-operated claw arcade game. Of course, they expected their claw to pull up a hell of a lot more than a stuffed bunny.

He flinched at a sudden sound, then realized it was the massive thrusters kicking in, directed by the dynamic positioning system to keep the drillship precisely located over her target. He glanced once more at the unmoving pipe, checked his watch, and turned to head up to the drill floor to chew somebody's ass, just as there was a clank and a groan, and the pipe resumed its measured ascent.

When the massive hydraulic grab broke the surface an hour later, the moon pool was surrounded by crewmen and the excitement was palpable. Next to the tool pusher stood Sheik Mustafa and his American partners and the documentary film crew with their cameras at the ready. A hush fell over the crowd as the grab reached deck level and was maneuvered to its resting place. A hush broken by the tool pusher's gravelly voice.

"All right, all right! Get your thumbs out of your asses, and let's get her open."

At his command, crewmen jumped to hit the releases, and hydraulic cylinders groaned as they jacked open massive jaws to disgorge their contents. There was a rattle of metal on metal, not unlike a giant slot machine, as thousands of large silver coins hit the deck, mixed with mud and sand and bits of wooden packing crate. The rattle was replaced by cheers and screams of delight, and a grin was plastered on every face as the men thumped each other's backs in congratulation. But celebration soon yielded to practicality.

"There's more where that came from," the tool pusher yelled over the tumult. "Let's get her cleaned out and back in the water." He clapped his hands to get the attention of a few still celebrating. "Come on, come on, move it! Y'all can count your money later."

He smiled. He was already counting his.

M/T *PHOENIX LYNX*
AT ANCHOR
HARARDHEERE, SOMALIA

Zahra stood on the bridge wing of *Phoenix Lynx* and looked at the *Luther Hurd* in the distance, then turned his gaze seaward to the flotilla of naval vessels.

"So why's our friend Mukhtar so interested in this drilling vessel?" he asked, still looking seaward.

Beside him, Omar shrugged. "It's unclear. He's confiding in no one aboard the fishing boat. But I can't believe he intends to capture a drilling vessel so far from our waters."

Zahra nodded. "They're slow and conspicuous. Even the reduced naval forces would surround him long before he got to safe anchorage here. And if he meets Russians or Indians or South Koreans, he can't count on being handled with kid gloves. No, he wants something *on* the ship, and it's important enough to risk hijacking an American ship as a diversion." He shook his head. "I don't have a good feeling about this. We've had nothing but problems since the fanatics inserted themselves in our business."

"True," Omar said. "But at least the diversion is working in our favor as well. All the groups have men at sea or preparing to go, and this morning Wahid's group brought another captive to the anchorage at Garacad."

Zahra snorted. "Yes, I heard. An oceangoing tug with a four-man crew and no tow. Let's hope that the other groups bring home more worthy prizes. What of the negotiations?"

"Nothing," Omar said. "All the groups are reporting negotiations stalled."

Zahra sighed. "Very well. I suppose we can't delay without appearing weak. I'll call the other leaders and we'll start regular executions."

Omar hesitated, looking toward the naval vessels. "Are you sure, Zahra? Won't that invite attack?"

"That's why we'll start in the other ports with no naval presence. And the executions will be measured—shocking, but not wholesale slaughter. We'll release video on the Internet. An execution every few days should be enough, I think."

Omar nodded. "When should we start?"

Zahra pulled out his phone. "No time like the present."

USS Cᴀʀɴᴇʏ (DDG-64)
Dʀɪꜰᴛɪɴɢ
Hᴀʀᴀʀᴅʜᴇᴇʀᴇ, Sᴏᴍᴀʟɪᴀ

Commander Frank Lorenzo, USN, Captain of the USS Carney, stood on the bridge and looked down at the group of sailors walking up the deck, led by Culinary Specialist 3 Jerry Harkness. The cook carried a pail full of meat scraps and other garbage, and was trailed by a half dozen off-watch sailors, all carrying cameras. Harkness waited for the would-be photographers to line the rail, then transferred the bail of the bucket to his left hand and put his right beneath the bottom to heave the contents overboard.

Nothing happened for a moment, and then the water boiled with heavy gray bodies and large triangular fins, as the cheering photographers snapped away.

"*Carcarinus Zambenzensis*, more commonly known as the Zambezi River Shark," the man beside Lorenzo said. "The most dangerous and aggressive of the shark family. They'll eat anything or anyone, and frequently do."

Lorenzo turned. "I didn't know you were a shark specialist, Lieutenant."

The man smiled. "I try to know a little about all the creatures I share the water with," he said. "Seals and sharks are old enemies." The smile faded. "But seriously, this is one of the worst areas in the world for those beasts. You won't find people frolicking in the surf in Somalia."

"I bet that's right," said Lorenzo. "I sure as hell—"

"Excuse me, Captain," the officer of the watch said from the opposite side of the bridge. "There's movement on the *Luther Hurd*. Looks like they're swapping out the hostage on display."

Ten minutes later, Lorenzo lowered his binoculars and watched the lieutenant note the date and time in a three-ring binder, right beside a picture of Jim Milam.

"OK, that's Jergens, the chief steward, up there now, and Milam, the chief engineer they just took down, right?" asked Lorenzo, continuing without awaiting an answer. "That's all the crew accounted for?"

The young SEAL looked up. "Affirmative, sir," he said. "They're rotating all the hostages on top of the wheelhouse. That's for our benefit. They want us to see the hostages are unharmed, but that any threatening move on our part will result in immediate deaths."

"But when the hell are we going to *do* something about it?" Lorenzo asked. "Every time I talk to that captain, I feel more helpless. I'm a sailor, not a hostage negotiator. Someone from your team should be handling this."

"Negative, sir," the SEAL said. "You're doing fine. You've been here from the beginning and have a rapport. We *want* them to get comfortable, because comfortable equals sloppy. Our whole mission is intelligence gathering to support planning and training. They're building a mockup back in Virginia, and our guys are training on possible scenarios. My orders are to go early only if the hostages are in immediate danger and there's no option."

Lorenzo nodded, and turned to stare across the water at *Luther Hurd*.

M/T *LUTHER HURD*
AT ANCHOR
HARARDHEERE, SOMALIA

Milam sat next to Arnett in a corner of the officers' mess room, watching Traitor fit a collar on Chief Mate Stan Jones. Jones tried to smile as he was led out to take his turn as the display hostage, but managed only a sickly grimace.

"I hate all of them," Arnett said under her breath. "But I hate that friggin' Traitor the worst."

"I can't argue with that," Milam replied. "Every time I hear that American voice coming out of his pie hole, I want to kill him. I think his name's Gaal, by the way, or something like that. Anyway, that's what these other assholes call him."

"Well, they'll be calling the bastard dead if I have my way," Arnett said.

Milam nodded as he looked around the room.

The pirates had him secure the air conditioning days before to conserve fuel, and the room was stifling. The sour smell of body odor and sweat-soaked mattresses assailed his nostrils, and out in the passageway he could hear Somali voices raised in anger. Probably an argument over khat. Such arguments were increasingly frequent now, and all the pirates were on a hair trigger. They ogled Arnett with undisguised lust, and for the life of him, Milam couldn't figure how she'd avoided gang rape. He turned back to Arnett, speaking softly.

"These assholes are getting restless. You picking up anything from your little chats with *Carney*?"

"Toothless or Traitor do most of the talking and then put the phone on speaker to prove I'm alive and kicking. Last time, before they could get it off speaker, the *Carney*'s captain asked for assurances there would be no more executions. I can't remember his exact words, but I got the impression he wasn't talking about our two guys. It was, I don't know, like he was talking about something more recent."

"You sure?" Milam asked.

She shook her head. "No, I'm not sure," she said, her voice cracking. She struggled to compose herself. "Look, Jim. If anything happens to me…"

"Shut up, Lynda. Nothing's going to happen to you."

She grabbed his hand and squeezed, her eyes blazing. "Listen to me. I've been thinking about this, and how these assholes think. I don't know how this is going to end, but I'm pretty sure there won't be any negotiated deal. The US Navy's going to be coming in here as soon as they can figure out a way to do it without killing too many of us. Politically, they can't afford to do anything else. We both know that, and so do the pirates." She shook her head. "What I can't figure out is why they haven't moved the crew ashore or split us up, at least me. Let's face it, an American woman captain has to be a high-value hostage for them. Leaving us all here aboard the ship is keeping all their eggs in the same basket, so I figure that means they want all eyes on the basket."

Milam nodded. "Makes sense, but so what? Where you going with this?"

"What happens when they finish whatever else they have going on?"

"I don't know, I guess… oh shit!"

"That's right," Arnett said. "If the navy hasn't rescued us by then, they may decide to spread out their eggs. We have to stop ignoring the elephant in the room. I'm the prize egg, and I suspect I'll be the first moved."

"So what're you saying?"

"I'm saying, if and when that happens, don't do something stupid and get yourself killed. Understood?"

Milam's jaw clenched. "We can surround you—put you in the middle. We're no good to them dead. They won't risk killing—"

Arnett squeezed his hand again. "Yes. They. Will," she said. "No heroics. OK?"

Milam looked unconvinced.

"Jim?" Arnett said. Milam didn't respond. "That's an order, Chief," Arnett said.

"I'll consider it," Milam said at last, relieved she seemed to accept that.

"There's something else," Arnett said. "The crew looks up to you, and if anything happens to me, I want you in charge."

"How the hell am I going to do that?" Milam asked. "If something happens to you, Jones becomes captain, and if something happens to him, it's Joe Silva."

"Yeah, technically," Arnett said, "and Stan Jones may be acting chief mate, but he's got five years' experience to your thirty—and as far as poor Joe goes…" She looked across the room to where Joe Silva was coiled on a bare mattress in the fetal position. "All he ever wanted to be is third mate, and he's practically catatonic since they murdered Gomez."

Milam followed her gaze and nodded sadly. "Well, you're right about Silva, poor bastard." He turned to face her. "But Stan may view things differently." Milam's voice softened. "After all, Lynda, he may be green, but he's got a year more sea time than you."

"Jesus! Don't you think I've thought of that? But I still don't think—"

"I'm not saying I disagree," Milam said. "But what do you expect me to do? Stage a mutiny and appoint myself captain?"

"Of course not. But… I don't know… guide him… offer advice…"

Milam sighed. "Well, it won't come to that, but if it does, I'll do my best." Milam turned around and smiled ruefully. "It's not like there'll be too many command decisions made here in the mess room."

"Maybe not," Arnett said, "but if there are, I'll feel a lot better knowing you're making them. Job one is getting as many of the crew home alive as you can."

"Well, hopefully the cavalry will arrive soon."

"Maybe," Arnett replied, the doubt obvious in her voice, "but my gut tells me something's up, and I wish I knew what it was."

CHAPTER TEN

Mukhtar sat in the Zodiac in the inky darkness three hours before dawn, relieved the wait was over. It wouldn't serve his purposes to capture the high-profile sheik and his American partners, and the two days of waiting for them to leave the drillship had seemed a lifetime. Finally, the helicopter lifted off the vessel and headed ashore, and his man aboard confirmed the sheik's departure.

Both the hour of the attack and the initial assault craft had been chosen with care. The security detail would be less alert at this hour, and looking outward at the sea. His man onboard was good with a knife and could silence each of the unsuspecting sentries with ease. The small inflatable had a minimal radar return and would show poorly or not at all on the drillship radar, supposing it was even being monitored. He'd had his men stop the outboard some minutes before, and they now paddled through the darkness, awaiting the signal.

And there it was—three short blinks followed by a pause, then repeated. He called softly to the men and they bent to the paddles. In minutes they found the rope ladder down the side of the drillship, right where he'd ordered. Mukhtar rushed aboard with seven men, and within five minutes they captured the surprised crew on watch and took control of communications. With the threat of a warning eliminated, Mukhtar pointed a flashlight into the night and flashed another signal. He was rewarded by the sound of powerful outboards awakening in the distance, and smiled as the sound drew closer.

Within fifteen minutes the deck of the drillship was swarming with pirates. Within twenty the entire crew of the drillship had been subdued. He watched as the pirates, most of them new recruits drawn by the promise of money, cavorted around the huge piles of silver coins on deck. He would give it all to the fools, for he was after something of far greater value, and now he had the means to obtain it.

Mukhtar smiled at the man sitting in the chair in the control room. "Now, my friend," he said, as he held the muzzle of his assault rifle inches from the man's forehead, "we're going to take a little trip. Not too far, just a few kilometers. Will you help, or do I need to retire you and find someone more helpful?"

"No. I mean, yes… I'll help," the tool pusher said. "But we can't move in this condition. There's too much pipe racked in the derrick. The stability is—"

Mukhtar jammed the muzzle of his weapon into the man's mouth, breaking a tooth and stifling the protest. "Enough of your tricks, infidel! Move the vessel or die! Those are your options. Do you understand?"

The terrified tool pusher tried to nod, his head held almost immobile by Mukhtar's weapon.

"Good," Mukhtar said, and withdrew his rifle.

The man looked up, blood running from his mouth. "I… I have a family. D-don't kill me. Please."

Mukhtar nodded and smiled. "Cooperate, and you've nothing to fear."

M/T *MARIE FLOYD*
PORT SULTAN QABOOS, BERTH NO. 1
MUSCAT, SULTANATE OF OMAN

The three men stood on the main deck of the *Marie Floyd*, sweating in the noonday heat despite the shade of the bridge wing.

"I don't like it, Dugan," said the classification-society surveyor as he glared out at the deck, "not one little bit. This rust bucket was supposed to be headed to the Bangladesh breakers, and suddenly I get a call from Houston HQ telling me to get my ass down here from Dubai to expedite a *flag change*. Who changes the flag on a ship headed for the boneyard? And how the hell are you involved anyway? I thought you worked with Kairouz in London."

Dugan opened his mouth to speak, but Captain Vince Blake beat him to it.

"We're short superintendents," Blake said. "Mr. Dugan is a consultant."

The surveyor cocked an eyebrow. "So Hanley hires the *managing director* of a major competitor to babysit a flag change in the back of beyond?" The man turned and pointed across the open deck to where M/T *Pacific Endurance* floated at the next berth. "Where another of that major competitor's ships just happens to be berthed." He pointed down to the dock, where men unloaded steel plate, crates, and welding gear from a flatbed truck. "And I guess I'm not supposed to notice a newly arrived bunch of rednecks, looking suspiciously like a riding gang, loading material on both vessels. And I don't even want to know how that bunch of Russians fits into things or what's in those cases." He sighed. "Why me?"

"Look, it's just a flag change," Blake said. "The coast guard has no issue with it, so I don't see why it should be a problem for you."

"Why the hell *should* our USCG friends have heartburn?" the surveyor asked. "She's leaving US flag, and not their problem anymore. The only thing I got from my USCG counterpart was an email to the effect of 'be a pal and pull the Certificate of Inspection when you leave.' They're not even sending anyone to our little party. Which leaves me out on a limb all by myself, getting the bum's rush from HQ to do all the acceptance inspections on behalf of Liberia. But it's *my* signature that'll be on the new certificates and reports, and *my* ass on the line if whatever you screwballs are planning goes south and this bucket sinks."

Dugan stroked his chin. "Maybe we can keep everyone happy."

"That'd be a nice trick. How?" asked the surveyor.

"Your marching orders are to expedite the flag change, right?"

"Yeeeaaah."

"So do the flag change today with interim certificates. Defer all major inspections for a week and throw in as many 'outstanding recommendations to be cleared before leaving ports' as you want. Go back to Dubai on the afternoon flight, and come back next week before we sail to finish up the inspections and make sure everything is OK. That way you've expedited the flag change and covered your own ass at the same time." Dugan paused for emphasis. "Everybody's happy, and no very important people will be calling Houston to bitch about you."

The surveyor hesitated. "I guess that'll work, but I still don't like it!"

Blake took advantage of the opening. "Let's go up to my office. I'll pull the certificates for you," he said, leading the man into the deckhouse.

Ten minutes later Dugan stood at the rail, watching activity on the dock below. He turned at the sound of Blake's footsteps.

"He happy?" Dugan asked.

"Well, cooperative at least," Blake replied. "He's up to his neck in certificates and muttering to himself, but I think we'll officially be Liberian when he leaves. But what's this about sailing next week? I thought we were leaving tonight."

"He doesn't have to know that," Dugan said. "As long as we're officially Liberian, we're golden. All those outstanding recommendations he's going to saddle us with are meaningless since we don't intend to trade the ship, but they'll cover his ass and get him out of our hair."

Both men turned at the sound of a load being landed on the deck amidships by the ship's crane. Dugan noticed Blake wince at the sudden movement.

He fixed Blake with an appraising stare. "Pushing the envelope a bit on recovery time, aren't you?"

"Don't worry about me. It was laparoscopic surgery. I get a twinge now and then is all." His voice hardened. "And besides, *Luther Hurd* is my ship and those are my people. I may not be able to do anything for them, but I can do this."

"When we sail we can't turn back," Dugan said. "If there's any doubt—"

"I said I'm fine, Dugan. Drop it, OK?"

Dugan hesitated, then nodded and changed the subject. "Ever think you'd end up doing something like this?"

Blake grinned. "Can't say as I did. Maybe I should get an eye patch and a parrot to sit on my shoulder."

Dugan laughed. "Nah. He'd just crap down the back of your shirt."

His laughter was interrupted by angry voices, a distinctive Texas accent countered by another speaking—or rather, shouting—Russian-accented English.

"Crap," Dugan muttered, looking down at the dock. "Looks like there's a bit of friction between elements of our little band of swashbucklers." He started for the gangway, with Blake on his heels.

Dugan arrived on the dock to find two men toe to toe. The Texan was slender and of medium height. He was older, but appeared fit, and the well-muscled arm below the sleeve of his tee shirt was graced by a faded tattoo that read *USMC*. His Russian adversary was a head taller and decades younger, and neither was showing the slightest signs of backing down. A dozen men moved up in support of the Texan, as a similar number closed ranks behind the Russian, including a blond giant who towered above the others.

"Now hear this, Boris," said the Texan. "I don't give a damn who you are or what's in your little boxes." He punctuated his sentence by squirting tobacco juice on a stack of fiberglass cases. "I don't take orders from you. I got my own stuff to load, and when I finish, I'll load your crap if—and I do mean if—my boss tells me to. Got that?"

"My name is not Boris, little man. It is Andrei Borgdanov—*Major* Andrei Borgdanov. But you can call me *sir*. And if my equipment is not loaded on ship in—"

"All right, knock it off, both of you," said Dugan.

The Texan shot Dugan an irritated look, but brightened when he saw Blake.

"Cap'n," he said to Blake. "I was loading the gear like we agreed when this commie shows up and starts throwin' his weight—"

Borgdanov reddened. "I am Russian but not communist. Perhaps you should come into twenty-first century, *da*?"

"*Da* yourself, Ivan. You're all commies as far as I can tell."

"Cool it, Woody," Blake said.

The Texan nodded but seemed to think better of it, and sent another squirt of tobacco juice through the air to land inches from Borgdanov's foot. The big Russian got even redder and clenched massive fists. Dugan saw a smile flicker at the corners of Woody's mouth, as the smaller man clenched his own fists and set himself to take the Russian's charge.

"Enough!" Dugan yelled, as he stepped between them, facing Borgdanov as he pushed him back a step. "Captain Blake," Dugan said over his shoulder, "why don't you take Woody up the dock a ways and have a chat, while I discuss international cooperation with the major here."

No one moved at first, then Woody shot another squirt of tobacco juice onto the dock, well away from the Russian this time. He turned to the men behind him, as if seeing them for the first time. "What are y'all doing standing around!" he yelled. "Git back to work! This gear ain't gonna load itself."

Woody's men sprang back into action, as he watched a moment, then nodded to Blake. The two men walked off up the dock without looking back.

Borgdanov stared after them.

"OK, Andrei," Dugan said. "What's going on here?"

The major jerked his head in the direction of the retreating Texan. "This foreman is big pain in the ass," he said. "We wait here in sun two hours, and I order him *three* times"—the Russian held up three fingers for emphasis—"to load gear on ship so we can begin stowing properly. Two times, he ignores me, so last time I grab his arm to get attention." Borgdanov shrugged. "Then we have argument. I think maybe better you let me finish argument, then maybe he is no longer big pain is ass, *da*?"

"I think the *order* part is the problem," Dugan said.

"But *Dyed*," the Russian protested, "in Russia—"

Dugan reddened. "God damn it, Borgdanov, we're not in Russia! And I told you to stop calling me gramps!"

Despite the tension, the Russian grinned, as did the blond giant beside him.

"But Dugan," Borgdanov said, nodding toward his companion, Sergeant Ilya Denosovich, "as Ilya and I keep telling you, *dyed* is term of great respect."

"Yeah," Dugan said. "I can tell that by grin on the sergeant's face every time he hears it."

Both Russians laughed, the tension broken. Sensing the new dynamic, the other Russians moved away. Dugan lowered his voice.

"But understand you can't go ordering these guys around," Dugan said. "Woody and his boys have priority for the moment. Until they get the mods done, we can't proceed. Your work comes later." Dugan glanced at the other Russians. "For now, we need to cool things down a bit on all fronts. Why don't you leave a couple of guys to watch your gear and let the others wait in the crew mess? It's a lot cooler in the air conditioning."

Borgdanov considered that a moment. "*Da*," he said at last, before turning to the sergeant and spitting out a stream of Russian. The sergeant nodded and set about organizing the men, as Dugan and Borgdanov moved away a few steps and continued talking.

"But why do we even need these workers, *Dyed*?" Borgdanov asked. "Is easier to just make pirates disappear, *da*?"

"Don't call me… oh, to hell with it," Dugan said, knowing from experience he'd never win that contest. "We've been over this. We need the pirates alive."

The Russian shrugged. "OK, but seems a complicated plan. In Russia—"

Dugan sighed. "But we're not in Russia."

Borgdanov held up his hands, palms outward. "Yes, yes, I know. We are not in Russia. This you tell me many times," he smiled ruefully. "Not that I need you to tell me this. Anyway, since Istanbul, things have not been so wonderful for me in Russia."

Dugan paused, considering his next words. "You did everything you could in Istanbul, and saved thousands of lives. You should've been promoted."

"You do not get promoted when you lose eleven of thirteen men in operation, *Dyed*." Borgdanov looked away, and spoke almost as if speaking to himself. "Good men. *Spetsnaz*. The best," he said. He glanced over to where the blond sergeant was organizing the men, then turned back to Dugan.

"But my great regret is Ilya. I tried to have him transferred away from me, so he is not tarnished by my failure. But he is stubborn man, my Ilya. He refuses to go."

Borgdanov shook his head, as if to clear it of melancholy thoughts, and grinned.

"But now Ilya and I are, what is term? Ah yes, soldiers of fortune. And the pay from Mr. Alex Kairouz is very much like fortune to simple Russian soldier."

"You sure you're OK with this?" Dugan asked.

Borgdanov shrugged. "There is no future for me or Ilya in Russia, so I think this is not so bad. And the world is changing with many more opportunities for people with our training." He smiled again. "So we become, as you Americans say, private contractors. Just so long as we must do nothing against Russia."

"What about the others? What's their story?" Dugan asked.

"All different, yet all the same," Borgdanov said. "Things are not so good in Russia now. Putin is big asshole but powerful. Many people think there may be problems, and no soldier wants to shoot other Russians." He shrugged. "But any decision is dangerous, not only for soldier but family. Better to work outside Russia. This way, we don't have to choose side." He smiled again. "Is good opportunity, and for this we thank you, *Dyed*."

Dugan smiled back. "It's the least I could do since you saved my life."

"Yes," Borgdanov said. "Is like they say in India, karma."

"I didn't know you were a student of Indian philosophy."

"Even savages can have good ideas," Borgdanov said.

"I wouldn't call the Indians savages."

"Of course they are savages," Borgdanov said, then grinned. "They are not Russian! But don't worry, *Dyed*. You, we make honorary Russian."

CHAPTER ELEVEN

Dugan felt a slight vibration under his feet, as a fixed-tank washing machine blasted the underside of the deck. He watched crewmen move between the machines, checking remote indicators for nozzle angle and rotation, while he paced the main deck. And worried.

Bound for the scrapyard, *Marie Floyd*'s tanks were already clean and gas-free, allowing Blake to reduce her normal marine crew to the minimum necessary to sail. And Blake had taken over as captain of *Marie Floyd*, dropping the headcount even further to minimize noncombatants. Dugan's situation here on *Pacific Endurance* was a bit different. She'd been trading, and though empty, her tanks still had gasoline residue. She had to be clean before they could complete the mods, and to clean her, Dugan had to keep the whole crew. He paced the main deck and worried.

"You better mosey on down the deck a bit," said a voice behind him. "You're gonna wear a hole in this part. Reckon you're a worrier."

Dugan turned to see Joshua Woodley, aka Woody, grinning at him around the ever-present wad of tobacco in his cheek. Woody's coveralls were streaked with rust and mud and plastered to his body by sweat.

"Yeah, I guess I am at that," Dugan said.

Woody nodded. "Got no problems with worriers, long as they're doing something about what they're worrying about. I reckon you qualify."

"How's it coming?" Dugan asked.

"Well, we got the safe room rigged in the aft-peak tank and installed the controls. The biggest problem there was the mud, but we got 'er washed down all right," Woody said.

"Access?"

"We cut the engine-room bulkhead, but I got to thinkin' about it and just put in a plywood door instead of steel. All it has to do is stop the light. We painted it to match the bulkhead, and you can't hardly tell it's there even with the lights on. I don't reckon a pirate with a flashlight's likely to find it in the dark, even if he's brave enough to venture into a pitch-black engine room."

"What about—"

"Relax, Dugan. It's all in hand. Cameras, steering, sound-powered phones, jammers, everything. Just like you told me." Woody nodded at the men moving around the deck. "This here's the part that worries me. Edgar's already workin' on the tanks over on *Marie Floyd*, and we're still cleaning. When y'all gonna be finished?"

"Not a problem," Dugan said. "Tank mods don't have to be finished before we hunt. We'll work them along the way. When will everything else be finished?"

Woody looked at his watch again. "Long about noon I expect, give or take an hour." He paused. "Two days, start to finish. Not too shabby, if I do say so myself."

"Not too shabby at all," Dugan agreed, then added, "I'll tell the major."

The mention of the Russian earned him a scowl.

"What do you have against the Russians, Woody?"

Woody grunted. "Just don't like commies. My daddy died in Korea, and I fought the bastards in Vietnam. Kicked their asses, too."

Dugan hesitated. "I seem to recall we lost that one."

Woody cocked an eyebrow and turned his head to send a stream of tobacco juice over the rail. "Not the part I was in."

"You know they're not commies," Dugan said, changing his approach.

"Near enough. Just give it a rest, Dugan. Me and Ivan ain't never gonna be bass-fishin' buddies. Got it?"

"Loud and clear." Dugan turned to head for the deckhouse, as Woody fell in beside him. "I'll get Blake on the horn and see if he's ready to go hunting."

M/T MARIE FLOYD
ARABIAN SEA
125 MILES OFF OMAN

Blake peered down at the radar screen as the *Marie Floyd* steamed west at ten knots. She was ballasted deep and, for all appearances, a tempting target—a slow ship full of valuable cargo with her main deck near the waterline. He nodded at the blip showing *Pacific Endurance* running a parallel course on his port beam, well to the south. He and Dugan had agreed to run separately to avoid raising suspicions, but close enough to support each other if necessary. Otherwise, the radar screen was surprisingly clear except for a drillship he'd passed fifteen miles back, now showing on his starboard quarter. He wasn't too surprised, most ships were running farther to the north in the supposed safe lanes thinly patrolled by the warships of various nations. But for their plan to work, they had to steam into the heart of 'injun country,' as Dugan had called it.

As Blake started to move away from the radar, something caught his eye. A faint blip that, as he watched, changed from an intermittent to a steady target. Something small. He watched and waited, and positions at six-minute intervals showed the craft moving at twenty knots on a course taking it between his ship and *Pacific Endurance*. If it was a pirate, he'd turn toward whichever ship he saw first, and *Marie Floyd's* bridge was ten feet higher than that of *Pacific Endurance*.

As if reading Blake's mind, the blip changed course toward *Marie Floyd* and increased speed. Blake crossed to the phone on the bridge control console and dialed into the ship's public-address system. "Attention all hands. Pirates sighted on fast approach. All hands to their stations. All nonessential crew to safe room. Now! This is not a drill. Repeat. This is not a drill."

Blake hung up, moved to the VHF, and keyed the mike. "Big Brother, this is Little Sister. Do you copy? Over."

"We read you five by five, Little Sister" came Dugan's voice over the speaker. "And we have you on radar and understand your situation. Over."

"Roger that, bro," Blake said. "Going dark. Will call when we're done. Out."

"We'll be waiting, sis. Good Luck. Big Brother, out."

Blake was re-racking the mike when the console phone rang.

"Ready to switch steering to emergency local," said the chief engineer from the steering gear room.

"Take it, Chief," said Blake, and hung up. The phone rang again, this time from the engine room.

"Ready to switch engine to local control," said the first engineer.

"Take it, First," said Blake, and hung up again as the console alarms began to buzz discordantly, informing him that systems were in emergency override.

He silenced the alarms, and moved to a set of recently installed switches on the aft bulkhead, activating jammers to cancel all radio and cell-phone signals, making *Marie Floyd* a black hole communications-wise. He glanced around to ensure he'd missed nothing and then raced through the chart room to the central stairway, flying down the stairs two at a time. He stopped on A-deck to watch the dark-haired young Russian sergeant divide his men three and three between the officers' and crew mess rooms.

"Ready?" asked Blake.

The young Russian nodded. "*Da*," he said, and patted his gas mask before pointing through the door at the sound-powered phone on the bulkhead of the officers' mess. "We wait your order."

Blake nodded as the Russian stepped into the officers' mess and closed the door behind him. Blake opened the door to the machinery spaces and started down the stairs, the oppressive air wrapping him like hot, thick cotton, as the noise of the main engine and generators assaulted his ears. Bypassing the engine control room, he continued down to the generator platform level and aft to the rear bulkhead of the engine room. He swung open the almost-invisible plywood door and stepped into the jury-rigged safe room, closing the door behind him to block out at least a bit of the noise, if not the heat. The second mate sat in a folding chair tack-welded to the deck in front of a makeshift control panel facing the bulkhead. He was peering into one of two monitors mounted on the bulkhead in front of him, which displayed the sea ahead of the ship. In his hands was an oblong control box with a thick black cable running from it and up the bulkhead. He looked up as the captain entered.

"Everything OK?" Blake asked.

"Seems to be," the second mate said, glancing down at the control in his hand. "It takes a bit of getting used to. But it works fine as long as I remember that up is right rudder and down is left rudder."

Blake nodded, looking up to where the cable disappeared through the overhead into the steering gear room above. He smiled despite the tension. Trust an engineer to come up with the idea of wiring the spare crane control pigtail into the emergency steering servos. He looked over at the benches that lined the bulkhead, now occupied by his reduced crew and the Texans of the riding gang. He nodded at them and turned back to the second mate.

"Everybody accounted for?" Blake asked.

"Yes sir," the man responded. "Everyone is here except the Russians. The chief and the first engineer are at the engine-side controls."

Blake nodded and picked up the sound-powered phone mounted on the console, moved the selector switch, and turned the crank. Forty feet away, beside the big main engine, a light lit on a similar phone and the chief engineer answered.

"Engine side."

"All accounted for, Chief," said Blake. "Have the First kill the engine-room lights, then stand by to stop the engine. I'll call you when we're ready."

"Roger that," said the chief engineer, and he hung up and slipped the earmuff back over his ear. He nodded to the first engineer, who stood ready at the door to the plywood enclosure they'd built around the engine-side control station, and the first exited the little room and walked to a breaker box. They'd disabled the emergency-lighting circuits earlier, so as the First toggled breaker after breaker, the engine room was plunged into pitch darkness. The man looked around in the inky gloom, satisfied no pirate would brave the dark, and switched on his flashlight to make his way back to the little sanctuary.

When he opened the door to the little hut, the single 40-watt bulb was like a blazing sun. He stepped inside and closed the wooden door behind himself before releasing a rolled-up tarp, which fell over the door. Even if a pirate was brave enough to descend to their level, no light would leak out to reveal their position. The chief nodded his approval, and both engineers settled in to wait.

PIRATE LAUNCH
ARABIAN SEA
125 MILES OFF OMAN

Abdi grinned at his men as the Zodiac sped down the starboard side of the big ship fifty meters away. They'd been at the extreme end of their search pattern and ready to turn back when he'd spotted the tanker. He passed the ship's stern, then circled and cut speed to trail her, expecting evasive maneuvers. He read her name—M/T *Marie Floyd*—and below that, in strangely fresh-looking paint, her hailing port—Monrovia, Liberia. His smile broadened as the ship began the expected radical course changes to slew the stern from side to side and make boarding more difficult. But difficult was childishly easy for him, for he was Abdi, first among the first-boarders of the clan *Ali Saleeban*. He was already dreaming of his first-boarder bonus.

He signaled his best driver to take the tiller of the outboard, then moved through his men to the bow as the driver edged the inflatable closer to the ship, matching her maneuvers. Abdi pulled his sat-phone to alert the rest of the group far behind that he was about to begin an attack, and emitted an irritated grunt when he saw he had no signal. No matter, they'd know soon enough. He pocketed the phone and balanced himself in the bow of the boat, and motioned for the short ladder with hooks on the end.

His tiller man was good, and he didn't have to wait long. As the next course change started the ship's stern moving away from them, the launch shot forward against the ship side, and Abdi hooked the ladder over the bottom rail of the handrail and leaped onto it. He scampered up the ladder like a spider and jumped over the rail, unslinging his assault rifle, ready to ward off any counterattack. But there was none. He flashed a grin over the side and motioned his men up, and in seconds they joined him as the driver moved the Zodiac off a safe distance.

M/T *Marie Floyd*
SAFE ROOM

Blake stared at the monitor, swinging the stern from side to side as he watched the pirate launch close on the port quarter.

"Yes! There he is," Blake said. "First guy aboard. And here come the rest. I count five… six… seven aboard, one pulling the boat away."

Blake turned the selector on the sound-powered phone and cranked.

"*Da?*" said the young Russian.

"Seven pirates, repeat, seven papas aboard," Blake said. "One papa in boat."

"We are ready."

"Good. Get your masks on and stay on the phone," Blake said.

Blake watched the second monitor as the pirates moved out of sight. He switched to the camera in the A-deck passageway and waited. Within seconds the lead pirate burst through the door, gun at the ready, then called back to his men, who joined him in the passageway. The pirates moved toward the central stairwell, as beside Blake, the second mate counted. "… five… six… seven! They're all in, Cap!"

Blake threw a switch on the makeshift control panel and powerful magnets sucked home bolts in all the outside deckhouse doors and the doors to the stairwell on all the upper decks. He threw another switch and the lights went out in the deckhouse, plunging the pirates into darkness.

Blake picked up the phone. "Gas 'em," he said.

"*Da*," answered the Russian, as Blake toggled on the night-vision camera just in time to see pre-constructed slots open in the doors from the officers' and crew mess rooms to disgorge tear-gas grenades, one after another. Trapped in the passageway and unable to see, the pirates were screaming and slamming into each other in their panic, which increased as the grenades clattered unseen on the deck and choking gas billowed around them. In seconds they began to fall, coughing and gagging.

"Five papas down in the passageway, two in the stairwell. Round 'em up, Sergeant," Blake said into the phone.

The doors from the mess rooms opened and the black-clad Russians emerged, the helmet-mounted night-vision goggles flipped down over their gas masks, giving them the appearance of large black insects. Within seconds they bound the pirates' hands with plastic cuffs and covered their eyes with duct tape. Blake watched as the Russians dragged the pirates back into the relatively fresher air of the officers' mess room and shut the door. The light on Blake's phone flashed, and he picked it up.

"All secure," the Russian said, his voice muffled by the mask.

"Acknowledged," Blake said. "Tell your guys to secure their night-vision glasses, and I'll turn the lights back on and start ventilation to clear out the deckhouse. The papa in the boat can't be allowed to escape. I'll try to draw him closer, but if you can't take him alive, make sure he doesn't get away. Clear?"

"Clear."

"OK, stand by," said Blake, as he turned the selector switch on the phone.

"Engine side, Chief speaking."

"Stop her, Chief," Blake said.

"Stop, aye" came the reply.

Blake heard and felt the big engine rumbling to a stop as he ordered the rudder amidships. He switched cameras again to gaze at the pirate launch, keeping station a hundred yards away on his port side. He willed the pirate closer to the ship.

Five minutes later, Blake watched in the monitor as the Russians crept up the starboard side of the main deck toward the midships pipe manifold. He switched the other monitor to the camera on the port bridge wing, which gave him a clear view of the port side of the ship, and watched the pirate, apparently encouraged by the ship's loss of speed, maneuver the boat closer until he was too close to see the main deck above him.

The Russians worked their way across the deck from starboard to port and stopped well short of the rail. The young sergeant crept forward alone, keeping low, until he was close enough to peek over the rail with a hand-held periscope. He spotted the pirate and drew back, repositioning his men with a series of hand signals. When satisfied with their placement, he gave another signal, and six men charged the rail as one, spraying the Zodiac with automatic fire.

Three Russians concentrated on the idling outboard, and it coughed to a stop, riddled with holes and belching smoke. The remaining three men targeted the craft's starboard inflation tube and shredded it, as the terrified pirate crouched in what was left of his boat, clinging to the still-intact port side. Blake saw the man raise his head cautiously and then raise one hand over his head while he used his other to jettison weapons that lay awash in the boat. A line snaked out from the main deck and landed across the boat, and the pirate grabbed it and was hauled aboard and secured, none too gently. Blake heaved a sigh of relief and dialed the phone.

"Engine side, Chief speaking."

"We got 'em, Chief," Blake said. "I'm going back to the bridge and we'll switch back to normal running."

"Roger that. How many did we get?"

"Eight," Blake replied.

"It's a start," said the chief.

"That it is," said Blake. "That it is."

CHAPTER TWELVE

Mukhtar watched over the operator's shoulder as the man stared into the monitor and directed the little ROV over the seabed. It was cool in the air-conditioned control room, but sweat beaded the man's forehead and formed dark circles under the arms of his khaki shirt. Mukhtar rested his hand on the operator's shoulder and smiled as the man flinched.

"Move to the left," said Mukhtar, pointing on the monitor that displayed the camera feed from the ROV. "There."

Sure enough, as the ROV moved closer to the area he'd indicated, the objects came into focus: small gas cylinders half buried in silt.

"Good," Mukhtar said. "Gather them."

The operator nodded and engaged a joystick, and a robotic arm came into camera view, plucking cylinders from the silt to put them in the front basket on the ROV.

"Six," the operator said. "The basket's full. We'll have to bring her up."

"All right," said Mukhtar. "But get it back down as soon as possible. Gather as many of the cylinders as you can." The operator nodded, and Mukhtar left the control room, stopping on the way out to admonish his two men on duty to keep an eye on the infidels and summon him if anything looked suspicious.

He moved from the deckhouse to stand by the rail on the open deck, the outside temperature more to his liking. He gazed out to sea, assessing his situation. The prize was in reach, but it had been a long, hard path. One he'd hardly chosen.

Like others in the far-flung Somali diaspora, he'd left his afflicted land a student with high hopes of bettering himself. What he'd found in the UK, and later in Europe, was hatred and prejudice, both for the color of his skin and his religion. And though he'd never been there, by all accounts the US was even worse.

Oh, they spoke fine words of tolerance and equality, but eyes tracked him everywhere, even when he was in Western dress. Eyes that spoke eloquently, if silently. *What are you doing here? You're not one of us. Go back to where you belong.*

And so he had, but not before wandering Europe and working menial jobs, always the outsider. In time, he learned to become invisible. As a man, he was a foreign threat; as a fawning, obsequious servant, he was unremarkable and unthreatening.

He studied the ways of these people, so different from the clan system of his home. He met with others of the True Faith—some Somali, some not—in mosques and coffee shops, and they commiserated over their lives and the lack of respect for their faith and culture. He ended his European trek in Germany, becoming ever surer with each passing month that

Islam could never coexist with the infidels. How ironic it was to reach that understanding in the country that had done so much to eradicate the hated Jews. Contrary to popular wisdom, the enemy of his enemy was not always his friend.

There in Germany, Allah had first set Mukhtar's feet on the true path. He'd worked as an orderly in a hospice—another job no one wanted—wiping the asses of the dying and listening to the drug-induced revelations of the medicated. The old man had been blind, just another lump of wasted flesh with no visitors, stubbornly refusing to die. But his rambling rants against the Jews had been interesting, as had the discovery this human husk had once been a doctor in the Waffen SS.

The real revelation had been a deathbed tale of regret, a story of a submarine going down with a cargo of nerve gas—a gas so potent it would have changed the course of that long-ago war. Intrigued, Mukhtar's research revealed *U-859* had indeed sunk after torpedoing an American ship. He speculated as to the value of such nerve gas to the jihad, but ultimately lost interest. What good was a weapon on the ocean bottom, over twenty-five hundred meters deep?

By the time he returned to Somalia, Mukhtar was a dedicated jihadist. He joined al-Shabaab and rose through its ranks, and daydreamed no more of *U-859* and her cargo of nerve gas. Until, that is, he saw the press release from the flamboyant and extravagantly rich playboy Sheik Mustafa of Oman announcing purchase of the salvage rights on the SS *John Barry*, the very ship sunk by *U-859*.

Historical accounts said *U-859* had been sunk after torpedoing the *John Barry*, so after *Ocean Goliath* located the Liberty ship, finding *U-859* had been child's play. And as he'd hoped, the sub had cracked open like an egg when she hit the bottom and littered the sea floor with her cargo. They found gas cylinders almost immediately. He sighed. If only the rest of it had been as easy.

He'd expected some deterioration, given the time involved, but he'd hoped for better results. When he'd dressed one of his men in the chemical suit and had him test the gas on a hostage, the results were hardly promising. Of the first six cylinders salvaged, five had been duds. His man had opened the gas in the hostage's face, and the first three cylinders produced a puff of white powder with no discernible impact. The gas was still potent in the fourth cylinder and the hostage died, but testing of the last two cylinders on a new victim produced the same white powder and no results. He'd thrown the live hostage back with the others and contemplated his next move.

He'd no choice but to salvage as many of the cylinders as possible. Once they got the cylinders to a lab, he could harvest and concentrate the gas that was still effective. But it was all going to take time—more time than he'd allotted. He had the tool pusher making daily reports, and to those ashore, the salvage operation appeared to be proceeding normally. However, he could never tell when the sheik might visit.

He had to scoop up all the cylinders quickly and move the drillship back over the *John Barry*. They'd then take the gas cylinders, loot the silver, kill the crew, and leave. Investigators would find a ship looted for her treasure. No one would know of the gas—until they found out about it in a most unpleasant manner.

Mukhtar sighed. One thing at a time. First, he had to collect all the cylinders.

CIA HEADQUARTERS
MARITIME THREAT ASSESSMENT
LANGLEY, VA

"You're sure about this?" Ward asked for the third time.

"As sure as I can be," the analyst replied. "He's used the phone twice. The message was scrambled, but it's definitely this guy Mukhtar's phone."

Ward fell silent for a moment and studied the chart on the conference table as he stroked his chin. "And what's he doing on a drillship?"

"More to the point," the analyst said, indicating two positions marked on the chart, "why did the drillship move after he got onboard?"

"What've you got on her?" Ward asked.

The analyst shuffled some papers. "Let's see. The *Ocean Goliath*. Owned by Emerald Offshore Drilling, Houston, Texas. Currently on charter to a consortium controlled by Sheik Ali Hassan Mustafa of Oman."

"What's the story with the sheik? Is he a radical? Any chance our friend Mukhtar is aboard as an invited guest?" Ward asked.

"Don't think so," the analyst said. "Sheik Mustafa is the stereotypical rich-playboy type, educated in the UK, hobnobs with the glitterati, the whole nine yards. All the financial checks come up clean as far as funding suspect charities and similar activities." He shrugged. "He's a rich dickhead, but an unlikely terrorist."

"So what's the connection then?" Ward persisted. "Our friend Mukhtar is hijacking a drilling operation? That doesn't make sense."

"It's more of a treasure hunt." The analyst slid a press release across the table. Ward picked it up and saw a picture of the smiling sheik holding up a model of a World War II Liberty ship. The press release ran several pages.

"Give me the high points," Ward said.

"The SS *John Barry* was en route to Iran with military supplies for Russia with a scheduled port call in Saudi Arabia, where she was to offload three million silver *riyals* minted in Philadelphia for the Saudi government. She never made it. On 28 August 1944, she was torpedoed by *U-859*, which was in turn sunk by a British fighter shadowing the *John Barry*. The sheik and his partners are after the silver."

Ward looked skeptical. "So how much are three million riyals worth today?"

"It's not the riyals, it's the silver. It was worth about half a million bucks in 1944, but silver was eighteen cents an ounce. Now, it's over thirty bucks an ounce, so the coins are worth between ninety and a hundred million for the silver content. But that's not the whole story. There were persistent rumors that *John Barry* was carrying a secret cargo of another twenty-six million dollars of uncoined silver bullion, and that's at 1944 silver prices."

Ward let out a low whistle. "How much is that worth?"

"At today's silver prices? Several billion—with a *b*—dollars."

"So let me get this straight," said Ward. "You're telling me the location of this wreck has been known for over sixty years, and no one's gone after it?"

"Too deep," the analyst replied. "It's in over eighty-five hundred feet of water, and silver's heavy. No one ever figured out how to salvage it before now. And it's not a cheap operation—the average day rate on a drillship like *Ocean Goliath* is almost a half million bucks. It took someone with deep pockets and an appetite for risk to even consider it. Remember, the only *verified* treasure is the coins."

"But an al-Shabaab connection still doesn't make sense," Ward said. "Even if there is a fortune in silver and this Mukhtar guy loots it, he's still got to turn it into something he can use to fund his operation, and I don't think converting that much silver to cash can be done under the radar." Ward stroked his chin and looked back down at the chart. "You said the ship moved sometime after Mukhtar went aboard. What do you make of that?"

The analyst shrugged. "Could be any number of legitimate reasons. The wreck might be in two or more pieces, or maybe they missed it on the first try and are trying another position."

"How long were they in the first position?" Ward asked.

The analyst shuffled through various satellite photos until he found the one he wanted. "Ten days."

"Sounds like they were already where they wanted to be," Ward said. "So what else could draw our friend Mukhtar's interest?"

"The only wreck that's even close is the sub."

"The submarine," Ward said. "Get me everything you can on this *U-859*."

Two hours later, Ward sat fidgeting at his desk, trying to get some work done as he stole glances at his phone. He answered it on the first ring.

"Ward."

"*U-859*. Keel laid in Bremen, Germany, in 1942. She was delivered to the *Kriegsmarine* in 1943 and assigned to the *Monsun Gruppe*, or 'Monsoon Group,' to operate in the Far East alongside the Imperial Japanese Navy. She was a Type IXD2 U-boat, fitted with a snorkel to enable extensive underwater operation during the passage from Kiel, Germany, to her Far East base at Penang, Malaysia."

"Thanks for the history lesson," said Ward. "Did you get anything that might be of actual use?"

"Look, Ward. There's not a lot there, OK?"

But there was more; Ward could sense it in the analyst's voice. He was just waiting for Ward to be properly appreciative.

Ward sighed. "OK, Joe. I know you're about to hit me with an 'oh, by the way.' I can hear it in your voice. Don't make me drag it out of you."

He could picture the analyst smiling.

"Oh, by the way," the man said. "There was one survivor from the sub."

"So what?" Ward replied. "I'm supposed to fly to Germany and interview a ninety-year-old Kraut, presuming he's even alive?"

"Japanese, actually," said the analyst. "He's ninety-four and lives in Frederick, Maryland. Would you like his address?"

Jesse Ward drove down the quiet tree-lined street of well-maintained older homes set on large, immaculately landscaped lots—the American dream. The irritating mechanical voice of the GPS jarred him from his reverie.

"Arriving… at… one… twelve… Shady… Oak… Lane… on… right."

Ward pulled into the long drive and down toward a large detached garage set back some distance from the house. He stopped beside the house and got out, feigning an exaggerated stretch as he looked around. From his vantage point, he could see a manicured front lawn, complemented by an even larger area behind the house, dominated by a well-tended vegetable garden. He turned and started for the front door when he was hailed from the backyard.

"Agent Ward?"

He turned to see a small bespectacled man moving out of the vegetable garden, clad in a plaid work shirt with the sleeves rolled to the elbows. There was dirt on the knees of his well-worn jeans, and a straw hat was perched on his head, its broad brim hiding his face in shadow. He pulled off a pair of work gloves and dropped them to the ground at the edge of the garden as he continued toward Ward. He was bent with age and moved with arthritic slowness, leaning on a cane.

"Dr. Imamura?" asked Ward.

"Please, call me Yoshi," said the man, with the slightest trace of an accent. "I have not doctored anyone in some time." He smiled before gesturing to the garden. "Except, of course, my poor plants, who have no choice in the matter."

Ward followed the doctor's gaze. "It's a beautiful garden."

"My wife's passion." Imamura's smile turned wistful. "She got me interested in it after I retired. I lost her some years ago to cancer, but somehow, with my hands in the dirt I often feel she is still here, just out of sight in the next row. " He looked back at Ward. "But I don't think you came from Langley to listen to the maudlin ramblings of a very old man. Come. Let's sit on the patio and you can tell me what I can do for the CIA."

Imamura hobbled to a covered patio at the back of the house, with Ward in tow. They were met by a large black woman who looked to be in her sixties. She set a pitcher of lemonade and two glasses on a lawn table and fixed Ward with an inquisitive, none-too-friendly stare.

"Ahh… thank you, Mrs. Lomax," Imamura said. "Agent Ward, this is Mrs. Lomax. She does all the work around here and frees me to putter about in the garden. Mrs. Lomax, this is Agent Ward."

"Nice to meet you," Ward said. The woman nodded and turned to leave.

"I don't think she likes me," Ward said, as the back door closed.

Imamura chuckled. "Mrs. Lomax is quite reserved, but she is my rock. She's worked here for over twenty-five years, and her continued presence allows me my independence. My wife and I weren't blessed with children, so…" He shrugged. "I've enjoyed a full life, Agent Ward. I hope one day in the not-too-distant future Mrs. Lomax finds me in the garden, resting peacefully with a smile on my face."

Ward found himself warming to the little Japanese, despite what he suspected of the man's past. He nodded. "Sounds like a plan."

Imamura gestured Ward to a chair beside the lawn table as he took off his hat and placed it in another chair. He poured two glasses of lemonade, his hands shaking with the palsy of age, before taking a seat himself. "So tell me, Agent Ward. How may I help you?"

Ward scratched his head. "Well, to be honest, I'm not sure. Perhaps we can start with your own background and how you came to the US."

Imamura looked puzzled. "I hardly see how events of over sixty years ago can… oh, all right, I suppose it makes no difference. I was a doctor in Japan after the war, and I was offered the opportunity to come to the US in 1946. I was a young man, just married, and times in postwar Japan were extremely difficult. We were quite apprehensive because we did not know how *Japs* would be received in the US." He paused. "And it was hard at first. But we worked very hard at perfecting our English and fitting in. My new colleagues were very supportive, and my wife and I became citizens in 1955. We never returned to Japan."

"And by your 'new colleagues,' I assume you're referring to your co-workers at USAMRIID?" Ward asked, pronouncing it "U-sam-rid," the acronym for the US Army Medical Research Institute of Infectious Diseases.

"Yes," said Imamura, "though it was called the Biological Warfare Laboratories when I first joined it."

"One thing—no, make that several things puzzle me," Ward said. "War refugees were clamoring to enter the US at the time, but we were taking very few from Japan. Yet you were picked from the crowd, and as best I can tell from existing records—and there are damn few of those, by the way—you were fast-tracked straight to a good job in the US. Why is that?"

"Let us say that I had skills which were in demand."

"Such as?"

Imamura avoided eye contact, and lifted his glass to sip at the lemonade. The glass shook in his hand from a bit more than his normal palsy and ice cubes clinked in a steady rattle. "Agent Ward," Imamura said, "all details of my employment at USAMRIID and its predecessor are classified. You, of all people, should know that."

"You're right, Doctor. Forget I asked. My interest has nothing to do with USAMRIID, or your time here in the US."

"What interest is that?" Imamura asked over the rim of his glass.

"What were you doing on a German U-boat in the Arabian Sea in 1944?"

The sound of the glass shattering on the flagstone patio was like a gunshot. Lemonade splashed on both men's shoes and bits of glass and ice skittered across the patio, but neither man moved.

"Ho… how did you know that?"

"British war records," Ward replied. "Everything's being digitized now for historical purposes, and it's a lot easier than it used to be to make connections. Your name showed up as a POW with details of your capture and repatriation to Japan. It wasn't in the US records, and I doubt anyone would have thought to ask in 1946, or if they'd have even cared if they knew. But let's just say I've developed an interest. Now. What can you tell me?"

"It… it was long ago. Another world. I… I don't remember things well—"

"A sub sinks and you're the only survivor, and you don't even remember why you were there?" Ward fixed Imamura with a level gaze. "Somehow that seems unlikely."

Imamura had almost visibly shrunk as he slumped in his chair. He spoke not to Ward but to his own feet. "Please. Agent Ward. I… I am an old man—"

Ward cut him off. "Look, Doctor. Anything that happened is history. I'm not trying to root up bad memories, but I need—"

"I think you better go now!"

Ward looked up to see Mrs. Lomax standing in the back door. As he watched, she came out on the patio and started toward him.

"I just have to ask the doctor a few more questions."

"You're upsetting the doctor, Agent Ward. Please leave."

Ward ignored her. "Dr. Imamura, something's up with that sub, and I think lives may be at stake. I just need—"

"Now!" Mrs. Lomax said. "Or I'm calling the police."

Ward sighed and rose, dropping his card on the table before he turned to go. "Call me if you'd like to continue, Doctor."

"Go!" said Mrs. Lomax, pointing to his car.

Ward started for his car, trailed closely by the woman. She stood watching, arms folded, as he got in his car and pulled out of the drive.

Mrs. Lomax fussed about the patio, sweeping up the glass, the lemonade, and bits of melting ice, leaving wet streaks in the wake of her broom. She looked up, surprised, as Imamura leaned on his cane and struggled to his feet.

"Now don't you overdo it, Doctor," she said. "Just sit yourself back down. As soon as I get this cleaned up, I'll fix you some lunch. I got some of that soup you like simmerin' on the stove."

The doctor gave her a wan smile. "Thank you, Mrs. Lomax, but I'm not hungry. I think I'll finish my weeding."

"Now, you know the doctors said—"

Imamura waved a frail hand to cut her off. "I know, I know," he said. "But indulge me if you will. I have some thinking to do, and it's peaceful in the garden."

She opened her mouth to object further, then seemed to think better of it, and nodded. Imamura hobbled toward the garden, leaning on the cane. In a few minutes he was on his knees again, weeding around a row of tomato plants. The mindless work cast its usual spell, and he was soon moving more or less automatically, lost in his own thoughts. But much less-pleasant thoughts than usual.

Had it come to this after all these years? After working so hard to become thoroughly American? He'd been terrified at first that his role in the plan would be discovered. A plan so horrific that, even though never carried out, knowledge of his association would be sufficient to condemn him in the eyes of the world. Gradually he'd relaxed, increasingly sure that the past was buried and forgotten. And now this man Ward appeared from nowhere, asking questions. To what end? What did he want? *U-859* and its horrible cargo lay on the sea floor, over a mile deep, no threat to anyone. Imamura closed his eyes and his mind flashed back to a simple file folder, hand-lettered *Operation Minogame*.

What if it was true? What if, as impossible as it seemed, someone had found the secret and was going after the sub? Drops fell on Imamura's hands as he worked in the dirt. At first he thought it had begun to rain, despite the cloudless sky, but then he realized tears were rolling down his sunken cheeks. But the tears were not enough to relieve the stress of harboring a horrible secret for decades, and when the chest pain came, it was almost welcome—a sign that he could put down his burden at last and move on to whatever place in Heaven or Hell had been allotted him. He didn't cry out, but toppled over almost gently into the tomato plants, his last conscious thoughts of his wife and whether or not he would meet her.

CHAPTER THIRTEEN

Dugan stood on the main deck, braced against the slight motion of the ship as she drifted in a gentle swell, watching the M/T *Marie Floyd* drifting nearby. He turned his eyes from the ship to an inflatable roaring toward *Pacific Endurance*, a seaman at the outboard and carrying a single passenger. In minutes the roar died as the seaman cut power and expertly maneuvered the boat alongside the Jacob's ladder hanging down the side of *Pacific Endurance*. The passenger leaped onto the rope ladder and began to climb. Dugan met the man at the top.

"Welcome aboard, Vince. Glad you could make it," he said, extending his hand.

"Wouldn't have missed it for the world," Blake replied, shaking the offered hand. "Everything all ready?"

Dugan nodded as he led Blake across the deck. "Borgdanov's got them all lined up on the port side. He's going to flush out some translators first—all the gangs have English speakers to communicate with captive crews. After that, he'll go to work on confessions and clan connections."

"And what're we supposed to do?" Blake asked.

"Nothing," Dugan said. "It'll be more effective if they think it's a Russian operation. We just keep our mouths shut and try to look Russian."

"One thing I don't quite understand," Blake said. "Shouldn't we wait until we get more captives? Otherwise, we'll just have to do this all over again."

"Maybe not," said Dugan. "We've got thirty-four and you've got twenty-eight on *Marie Floyd*. If the Russians can convince these guys we mean business, we'll just toss any new captives we take in with them for a few days before we interrogate them. That may do the trick. I don't want to have to stop and go through this every few days unless we have to."

Blake nodded as the pair rounded the corner of the deckhouse and stopped to survey the scene on the port side of the main deck. The captive pirates were lined up with their backs against the deckhouse, their bare feet bound at the ankles with plastic ties and their wrists similarly restrained in front of them. All had duct tape across their mouths, and some were leaning back against the deckhouse to balance against the slight movement of the ship. Major Borgdanov and five of his black-clad Russians faced the prisoners, looking very much like the elite *spetsnaz* troops they formerly were. Each had a Russian tricolor flag patch on his shoulder. The major glanced over as the Americans arrived, and gave the briefest of nods before beginning to stalk up and down in front of the prisoners.

"I will need translator," the major yelled. "I am sure none of you savages is smart enough to speak *culturnyi* language like Russian. So! I think we must use English, *da*? So. If you speak English, raise hands. Now!"

His speech was met with a combination of uncomprehending stares and sullen glares, to which he responded with an exaggerated shrug.

"So. No translator? Is too bad. Without translator you are all useless to me." He spoke to Sergeant Ilya Denosovitch in Russian, who grinned and motioned to another Russian. The two men grabbed the first captive in line, carried him the few steps to the rail, and heaved him over, as effortlessly as if he were a feather. He fell out of sight and there was the sound of a splash. The sergeant unslung his automatic weapon and fired two three-round bursts down toward the water before turning back and saying something that caused the other Russians to convulse in laughter.

The major studied the remaining captives.

"Is too bad none of you speak English or Russian, so you cannot appreciate sergeant's little joke," said the major. "He said you savages are so skinny, you sink so fast he hardly has time to shoot you. But I am thinking about this. Maybe you are not useless after all. Maybe we have shooting competition and I give bottle of very good vodka to man who shoots most savages before they sink." He shrugged. "Not what I planned, but we should never pass up training opportunity, *da*?"

The major nodded toward the sergeant, who approached the next man in line. A dozen pairs of bound hands shot into the air.

The major held up his hand to stop the sergeant.

"What is this?" the major asked. "Could it be miracle? Some mysterious power that gives gift of tongues? Can I be so fortunate?" He walked to the first man with his hands raised and ripped the tape from his mouth. "Lower your hands and answer questions," he said, and the man nodded.

"What is your name?"

"Abukar."

"Abukar what?"

"Just Abukar."

"What is your clan?" the major asked.

"Ali Saleeban," the man replied.

"How long have you been a pirate?"

"I… I am not a pirate. I am a fisherman."

"Silence!" the major screamed, and the terrified Somali snapped his mouth shut.

The major re-taped the man's mouth with exaggerated gentleness, then patted his cheek as he stepped back and looked down the line at the other prisoners.

"Forgive me," said the Russian, "for not making myself clear. Is not quite enough to speak English, you must speak *truth* in English."

The major nodded to his men, who grabbed the would-be translator and tossed him over the side, followed by another burst of automatic fire.

The major moved to the next English speaker in line and untaped his mouth. "Maybe is more efficient if we start with hard question, *da*? How long have you been pirate?"

"Four years and three months," said the man without hesitation.

The Russian smiled and patted the man's cheek.

"Good! Very good! I think we have good translator, *da*?"

Joshua Woodley sat in the inflatable and cursed under his breath as the Somali plunged into the water ten feet away and soaked him with the splash. He looked up just in time to see the Russian sergeant step to the ship's rail and fire two short bursts down into the water, a good twenty feet from where the bound pirate struggled in the cargo net suspended loosely underwater between the inflatable and one of the ship's lifeboats. He had to admit, the commies were puttin' on a damn good show.

Woody gestured to Junior West, his companion in the inflatable, who reached out with a long boat hook and snagged the back of the struggling pirate's shirt to drag him to the boat. Together, they pulled the man onboard. The pirate flopped about in the bottom of the boat, his bare heels making a dull thump on the plywood floorboards, and Woody unholstered a Glock and dropped down beside him. He held the pistol to the man's head and put his finger to his own lips, the message clear. Wide-eyed, the pirate nodded enthusiastically and stopped making noise. Together, Woody and Junior dragged the pirate forward, out of the way.

They hardly had time to resume their positions before the second pirate splashed down. Junior pulled the man to the boat side, and wrinkled his nose in disgust.

"Woody," he whispered. "This one's done shit himself!"

"Jeees-us Christ," muttered Woody, as he unsheathed a Buck knife. "Here," he whispered, handing Junior the knife. "I'll hold the boat hook and you reach down and cut his pants off. Then we'll dunk him up and down until he's clean. Ain't nothin' in this deal about ridin' around in a boat fulla pirate shit."

He waited while Junior sawed through the pirate's belt. A man had to have standards, after all.

Dugan and Blake watched as one of the Russians put the video camera back in its case as the others taped the prisoners' eyes and cut their ankle restraints, so they could move back to the jury-rigged holding cells under their own power. Dugan looked down at the clipboard in his hand, and nodded.

"It's a damn good start," he said. "Of thirty-four prisoners, we've got good representation from ten of the twelve pirate clans, complete with video confessions. Hopefully, when we complete the same drill on your bunch, we'll pick up some members of the other two clans. If we can pick up at least that many more between here and Harardheere, we'll have made a real dent in their operation and be in a pretty good negotiating position."

"What about the 'dead' pirates?" Blake asked.

Dugan shrugged. "We'll keep them isolated from the rest. I doubt we'll have many more from *Marie Floyd* after Borgdanov finishes his little act."

"Yeah, well, I'm not real sure the Russians were acting," Blake said. "I suspect they'd do it for real in a heartbeat, and that's what made it convincing. And speaking of convincing, what about these confessions? I mean, we nailed them in the act, so there's no question of their guilt, but I doubt these confessions would hold up in court. It's pretty obvious they were coerced."

"Maybe not a US or UK court," he said, "but I don't think we'll have any problem in Liberia." He shrugged. "But it won't come to that. The confessions are just window-dressing for negotiations."

Blake nodded, then stared off in the distance with a troubled look on his face.

"What's up, Vince?" Dugan asked. "Things couldn't be going any better, and you look like someone just killed your puppy."

Blake looked back at Dugan with a wan smile. "Sorry. Just engaging in the time-honored tradition among captains of worrying about what's over the horizon. It's been easy so far. We've been at this less than a week and snapped up over sixty pirates. Sooner or later, the rest of them have to start worrying about all their buddies just disappearing. Then they may start getting cagey."

Dugan shrugged. "Maybe, but remember, these guys are pretty decentralized. I think realization is going to dawn gradually."

Blake looked doubtful. "I don't know, we may be pushing our luck. What happens if they stop sending out far-ranging scout-attack boats and keep operations closer to the mother ships? We might find ourselves up to our asses in more pirates than we can handle. If we lose the element of surprise, we're not in real good shape."

"Well, pal," Dugan said, "I guess we just have to hope that doesn't happen."

M/T PHOENIX LYNX
AT ANCHOR
HARARDHEERE, SOMALIA

"Silver? You're sure?" Zahra asked.

Omar nodded. "Great piles of it on deck, according to our man. At least a million of the old silver Saudi riyals. Worth much more than face value now."

"A fortune, no doubt," Zahra said. "But it still doesn't seem the sort of operation one would expect from the fanatics. And why hasn't Mukhtar looted the treasure and withdrawn? Surely he knows it's only a matter of time before he has company from the Omanis."

"I don't know, Zahra, but apparently he's promised the whole treasure will be divided among the men, and he's moved the ship to go after something else. Our man doesn't know what. Mukhtar allows no one but hard-core al-Shabaab followers in the control and operations areas. The speculation onboard is that he's going after an even richer treasure of gold or diamonds."

Zahra scoffed. "The speculation of fools. If there were such riches in the offing, the salvage operation would have brought those up first." He considered that a moment. "But still, Mukhtar is a fanatic, not a fool. If he's ignoring the treasure at hand to continue a search, then he's after something of immense value."

"What'll we do?" Omar asked.

"Nothing, for the moment. Have our man notify us the instant he discovers what Mukhtar's after. Then we'll decide."

"It will be done," Omar said, then hesitated.

"What is it, Omar?"

"These disappearances. Do you think they're somehow linked to Mukhtar?"

Zahra nodded. "It's crossed my mind. We've lost two boats and twelve men. The other bands are reporting similar strange disappearances, not so far from Mukhtar's drillship."

"A coincidence?"

"A bit too much of a coincidence," Zahra said. "I suspect he may have hunter boats of his own out to establish a perimeter."

"But surely, if he destroyed so many boats, a few of them would have gotten off a warning to their mother ships," Omar said.

Zahra shrugged. "Perhaps not. The turncoats that defected to al-Shabaab have no strong clan ties, and the lure of treasure is great. If they approached one of our boats, they'd be greeted as brothers. They could kill everyone in the boat before anyone got off a warning."

Omar nodded. "I suppose that explanation might fit."

"It's the only one that does," Zahra replied. "Warn our boats to be suspicious of any launches that approach them. I'll alert the other bands to the possibility."

Omar turned to go, but Zahra stopped him with an upraised hand.

"And Omar, I've been discussing the hostage executions with the other groups. It's clear they're having little impact. We've executed three so far, and still no owner has paid a ransom. We're going increase the rate of executions to one a day. Tomorrow's our turn to contribute a hostage. Pick one of the sick ones that might die anyway."

"It will be done," said Omar.

CHAPTER FOURTEEN

Jesse Ward closed the yellowed folder and pushed it away, almost as if he was afraid it might contaminate him. He looked across the conference table.

"Jesus Christ, Joe. *Logs*?"

The analyst nodded. "I'm not making it up. Apparently when they built their research facility in China in the 1930s, the Japanese claimed it was a lumber mill. I guess calling their human guinea pigs 'logs' was some sick bastard's idea of humor."

Ward looked shaken. "I'd heard of Unit 731 before, but I never checked out the specifics. These were some seriously bad people. What happened to them?"

"To most of them, nothing," said the analyst. "A lot of them, apparently including our friend Dr. Imamura, ended up working for us."

"That's disgusting!"

Joe shrugged. "Can't say I disagree. On the other hand, as nasty as these people were, they were the leading experts on chemical and biological warfare. The Cold War was upon us. We had the atomic bomb and the Soviets were looking for a counter. A lot of the 'logs' the Japs used were Soviet citizens kidnapped in cross-border raids from Manchuria, and the Soviets were demanding that all Unit 731 personnel be turned over to them for trial. Everyone was pretty sure they'd just fake executions and put these scientists to work on their own CBW program."

"So we just beat the Soviets to the punch and did the same thing, without fake executions," Ward finished. "Makes me proud to be an American."

"Well, at least for us they were working on defensive stuff, not weapons."

Ward scoffed. "Yeah, well. If you believe that, I've got a bridge to sell you."

"Look, Jesse. As long as other countries have—"

"I know, I know. You're right," Ward said. "I just have a problem with programs that make it hard to tell us from the bad guys."

The man nodded and changed the subject. "Any word on Imamura?"

"Still unconscious in the hospital. He may have had a stroke along with his heart attack. The guy's ninety-four with a do-not-resuscitate order. I suspect they're just checking him occasionally to see when to hang a toe tag." Ward sighed. "I doubt we'll get anything from him. Any luck connecting him to the sub?"

"None. What're we going to do?"

"What can we do?" Ward asked. "We have a hunch, no clue what was on the sub, and no idea if this guy Mukhtar is going after it. And our naval assets are all at least three days' steaming time away. I can't request repositioning on a hunch."

"So we…"

"So we wait and watch," Ward said. "And hope like hell nothing bad happens."

M/T Pacific Endurance
Arabian Sea

Dugan stood at the radar next to the captain in the early-morning light and watched the blip that was M/T *Marie Floyd*, well south of them. After much discussion, they'd decided to stay in the area for a few days, to continue to hunt at the edges of the pirates' normal range. They'd done well in this area, and as long as the pirate launches were ranging in front of the mother ships, they figured it safer to work the fringes. With luck, they could net enough captives to turn and head straight for the Somali coast and Hararardheere. Running at full speed, they had more than enough fire power to discourage pirates from boarding, a much less-hazardous operation than offering themselves as bait.

The strategy had borne fruit. In the day since the interrogation of the prisoners, *Marie Floyd* had taken two more launches and *Pacific Endurance* had taken another, twenty more captives between the three boats. But it seemed a hollow victory when this morning's call to Alex had brought news of the murder of another of *Phoenix Lynx*'s crew, and the pirates' pledge to murder another seaman daily until payment of ransoms resumed. He swallowed his anger and wrestled with the idea of heading to Somalia with the hostages they had now, knowing every day's delay would cost another life.

"You got something, Cap?" asked Dugan.

"Possibly," said the captain, pointing at the screen. "She's on a reciprocal course and should pass us to starboard."

Dugan followed his finger and saw a faint blip. "Pirate?"

"Too soon to tell," the captain said, staring at the screen. "I don't think so. Too big and too slow. A fishing boat, if I had to guess. I'll keep an eye on her."

Twenty minutes later, the captain watched as the target seemed to split, with the smaller target on a direct course toward *Pacific Endurance* and moving fast.

"Trouble!" he said. "Looks like a mother ship, and she just launched an attack boat. They'll be on us in twenty minutes."

The captain moved to the console to dial in to the public-address system and order all hands to action stations. Dugan watched as the crew went through the transfer of steering and engine controls, and the captain moved back to Dugan's side at the radar for one final look before evacuating the bridge.

"Any chance *Marie Floyd* can close with us and present them two targets?" Dugan asked.

The captain moved the radar cursor to check the distance to their sister vessel. "Negative," he said, shaking his head. "The mother ship's slower, but she's too close. She'll be on us an hour before *Marie Floyd* can get close, even in the best of circumstances."

"Well," said Dugan, "not much we can do about it. I guess we just have to make sure we take care of the launch before momma shows up, and then play it by ear."

Dugan pulled out his sat-phone. "I'll let *Marie Floyd* know what's going on before we activate the jammers."

CIA HEADQUARTERS
MARITIME THREAT ASSESSMENT
LANGLEY, VA

Ward leaned back in his chair and stretched before looking at his watch. He'd lost track of time and missed dinner. Again. There'd be hell to pay from Dee Dee when he got home, if she wasn't already in bed when he got there. He turned off his computer and was locking his file cabinets when the phone rang. He considered not answering until he checked the caller ID.

"Ward," he said into the phone.

"Agent Ward, this is Dorothy Lomax."

"Yes, Mrs. Lomax. Thanks for returning my call."

"To be clear, Agent Ward, I'm not returning your call. I think you're a despicable person who has nothing better to do than harass a kind old man, even to the point of death. I could quite happily go to my grave having never spoken to you again."

"Ah… OK," Ward said. "Then suppose you tell me why you *did* call."

"Because despite my pleas, Dr. Imamura insists he must speak to you."

"He's awake?"

"He regained consciousness two hours ago."

"I'll be right there," Ward said.

Dorothy Lomax met Ward at the door to the hospital room and shooed him out into the hall. She glared at him.

"You're not to upset him. Is that clear?" she asked in a low voice.

"How is he?" Ward asked, ignoring her question.

"He's dying, Agent Ward," she said sadly, a gleam of moisture in her eye. "The doctor doesn't expect him to last the night." The glare returned. "And why he wants to spend even a second of what little time he has left talking to the likes of you, I have no idea. But I do know I'll not have you upsetting him."

"I'll try not to upset him," Ward said, moving around her toward the door.

"Oh, you'll do much more than try, Agent Ward," she said, following him into the room. "I'll see to it personally."

Imamura was a shriveled husk of a man, swallowed by the hospital bed. An IV tube was taped to one arm, and a multicolored display above the bed flashed the news to all who could interpret it that this was a man not long for the world. He turned his head on the pillow as Ward entered.

"Thank you for coming, Agent Ward," he said, his voice weak.

Ward nodded, as Imamura looked at Mrs. Lomax.

"Mrs. Lomax, you've been here constantly. Why don't you go get a bite to eat while I chat with Agent Ward?"

"I think I should stay, Doctor."

Imamura smiled weakly. "I know you do, my dear. But what I must discuss with Agent Ward involves my work, and you don't have the necessary security clearance. So as much as I would like to spend all my remaining hours in your company, I must ask you to leave us."

Mrs. Lomax opened her mouth to speak, then shut it and nodded. She left the room, closing the door behind her. Imamura turned back to Ward.

"A small deceit, Agent Ward. Mrs. Lomax is the last living person I care about and I hope to spare her details of my sordid past. But before I begin, perhaps you would share with me the nature of your interest in a German submarine sunk more than sixty years ago."

Ward shrugged. "I was hoping, as the only survivor of that sinking, you could tell me what my interest *should* be, especially since some very bad people seem intent on salvaging the sub."

"That... that's impossible," Imamura said. "*U-859* sank in over a mile and a half of water. Too deep to salvage."

"Perhaps it *was* impossible," Ward said. "But what was impossible yesterday is merely difficult and expensive today. The question is, what's there to salvage worth the cost and risk?"

"Perhaps you'd better sit, Agent Ward," Imamura said, his voice quaking. "It's rather a long story."

Ward shifted uncomfortably in the chair, his mind numb from Imamura's recitation. He struggled to get his mind around the horrific tale he'd just heard. "But that makes no sense," he said. "Just how did you even think Japan could survive this Operation Mi... Migoname?"

"*Minogame*," Imamura corrected. "The Minogame is a creature from Japanese folklore—a giant thousand-year-old turtle representing both longevity and protection. By withdrawing into the protection of his shell, Minogame lived one thousand years. That's how we intended to survive."

Ward looked puzzled, and Imamura continued.

"The virus was to be introduced in the European theater, as far from Japan as possible. The Germans were to deploy it in front-line weapons against both Allied and Soviet troops, but the incubation period was relatively long, up to a week before victims became symptomatic."

Imamura stopped and closed his eyes. Ward was afraid he'd lost consciousness, but the little man opened his eyes, took a labored breath, and continued. "However, we knew from our own experiments most were contagious within twenty-four hours of exposure. That would allow time for wounded men to rotate to the rear to aid stations, and visiting VIPs—who, of course, were always accorded priority air travel—to visit the field hospitals and carry the virus back to London, Washington, and Moscow. The long incubation period ensured the virus would be well established before the epidemic was even identified as such."

"But this... this engineered hantavirus. You claim it had a mortality rate of over seventy percent?"

"Seventy percent in an indigenous Chinese population that enjoyed some resistance to the original virus," corrected Imamura. "We projected a higher mortality rate in other populations, but we had no test data."

Ward wrestled with his disgust. "So back to my question. How could you hope to survive?"

"We anticipated we'd have time," Imamura said. "It would take several weeks or perhaps a month for the epidemic to become obvious. The first response would be denial, and the knee-jerk reaction would be to suppress the news to avoid panic. That, of course, is the exact opposite of what is needed to contain an epidemic. When we saw signs the epidemic was taking hold, we already had plans in place to begin a massive withdrawal of troops to the Japanese home islands, leaving twenty percent of our manpower in place facing the Allies. Those troops left in place would have firm orders to die where they stood, opposing an Allied breakthrough. They did not have to win, only sell their lives dearly to buy time for the virus to do its work."

"But when the Allies figured out they were the victims of biological warfare, they'd strike back hard, with massive air raids if nothing else," Ward said.

Imamura nodded. "We assumed as much, but who would they strike? Remember, all indications would point to the Germans, whose cities were already being pounded. At the time we initiated Operation Minogame, the Americans had limited ability to reach the Japanese home islands with land-based bombers. We hoped that, in their fury, the Allies would spend more of their resources striking the easiest targets, as the epidemic sapped their ability to strike at all."

"Which brings me to another part of this story I find a bit hard to swallow," Ward said. "I can't believe the Germans would go along with this."

"The Germans were duped, and I was part of that deception. They were shown a nerve toxin of Japanese origin to be used strategically in artillery shells. We—that is, the Japanese—were supposedly to use the toxin at the same time, with the stated purpose of demonstrating a united front to the Allies to prove that the Axis powers were willing to go to any lengths to stop them. The theory was, presented with the prospect of massive and unacceptable losses, the Allies would become amenable to a negotiated peace that would leave both Germany and Japan unoccupied."

Imamura drew a long, ragged breath. Ward reached for a glass of water on the bedside table, and held it while Imamura sucked from the bent straw. He moved his mouth from the straw and water dribbled on his hospital gown.

"Thank you," he said, as Ward put the glass back on the table.

"I led a three-man team," Imamura said. "Our mission was to load the virus into the artillery shells, but approximately ten percent of the cylinders held nerve gas, should the Germans want to perform tests. Also, some of the artillery shells had to perform as advertised to ensure the Germans kept using them, at least for a time. Of course, a virus isn't a weapon one delivers with pinpoint accuracy. It was inevitable that the Germans would be infected as well."

"That means you…"

Imamura nodded. "I was sure to be infected, and if by some miracle I wasn't, I'm sure the enraged Germans would've killed me. I was to die for the emperor."

"Look, this is still nuts," Ward said. "How could Japan expect to survive?"

"Like Minogame, Agent Ward, inside a tight shell. The twenty percent of our forces still facing the Allies were to be only the first line of defense. There were to be three more concentric circles, with every ship or boat that floated and aircraft that flew prepared to hold the Allies at bay. They were to fight with what they had, with no more contact with Japan, and the home islands were to be isolated. As the epidemic took hold, it would, soon enough, spread from America to the troops facing Japan, attacking them from the rear, so to speak.

On the US mainland, there'd be fewer Americans to build weapons, and no one to man the ships to bring the weapons to the front. In six months America would be fighting for its life, struggling to maintain any sort of civilization, as seventy to eighty percent of the world population perished. Japan would be the least of their worries."

"And then what?" asked Ward. "Japan's not self-sufficient, then or now."

"The people were already inured to hardship because of the war, a bit more was bearable. Rationing would be even more strictly enforced, and as military resistance against us collapsed, we'd plans to devote all the resources of the war effort into survival. We'd subsistence-farm every square meter of land, including rooftop gardens in the cities, and send out fishing fleets with navy escorts to ensure they came in contact with no one. We'd hoard every bit of fuel left over from the war effort to supply the fishing fleet and their escorts. Survival would be hard, but Japan would survive as a cohesive nation, and as such, the most powerful force on earth. When we did eventually emerge, we'd have the power to take what we needed, for there would be no one left to oppose us."

Ward bit back his anger. He was both repulsed and fascinated by what he was hearing. "And how'd you plan to 'emerge'? Did you have a vaccine?"

Imamura shook his head. "There was no vaccine—not that we didn't try to develop one. The virus defeated our every attempt. But every virus mutates with each generation as it spreads through a population, and the more successful it is—and by that I mean, the more virulent and deadly it is—the faster it seems to mutate to something weaker and more benign. A case in point is the Bubonic plague, the Black Death of the Middle Ages. Though a bacteria rather than a virus, there are parallels. Bubonic plague still exists today, but it's much less a threat than the form that wiped out a significant percentage of the world's population." Imamura drew another ragged breath. "Japanese are patient people. We planned to send out survey teams periodically, in contact by radio, to check on the mutation of the virus. They, of course, would never return to Japan, but set up monitoring enclaves. We were prepared to wait five, or even twenty-five, years for the virus to mutate into a less virulent form. Of course, we hoped it wouldn't take so long."

"Yeah, I'd have hated for you to be inconvenienced," Ward said, unable to contain himself any longer.

"I understand your anger, Agent Ward. And whether you believe me or not, you can't hate me more than I've hated myself for many years."

Ward nodded, calmer now. "I'd be much angrier if I didn't doubt the whole story. Something like you're describing would have required cooperation and coordination with a lot of people, and I've never even heard a hint of anything like it. I'm supposed to believe that you're the only one who knew?"

"The secret was closely guarded. Dr. Ishii's concept was—"

Ward interrupted. "That's Dr. Shiro Ishii, the head of Unit 731?"

"Correct," Imamura said. "Ishii was a powerful man with the emperor's ear. Less than fifty people knew of Operation Minogame, and as soon as surrender was announced, they all died or disappeared under mysterious circumstances, days before MacArthur ever set foot on Japanese soil. I was interned in a British POW camp in Oman and presumed dead, so no one was looking for me in the chaos of postwar Japan. The British knew nothing of my background and seemed indifferent. To them, I was just another Jap. When I was repatriated in 1946, my wife was terrified and told me of the deaths of all my former colleagues. The very next morning, we bundled up our few belongings and went to the

American occupation authorities. I confessed I was a former member of Unit 731 and offered my services. By blind luck, I was interrogated by an OSS officer who recognized my potential usefulness. I didn't tell him of Operation Minogame, nor have I spoken to anyone about it until today, for the very reason you just confirmed. I knew no one would believe me. I'm telling you now because of what you've told me of this salvage operation." Imamura looked at Ward. *"You cannot let that happen!"*

Ward processed what he'd just learned. He didn't know quite what he'd expected, but certainly not the fantastic tale he'd just heard.

"Even assuming what you've told me is true, that was decades ago. You can't possibly imagine these weapons are still viable."

"Believe me, Agent Ward," Imamura said, "I've imagined little else for over sixty years. The containers were stainless steel of the finest grade, so corrosion will be minimal. Pressure will be extreme due to the depth—over thirty-five hundred pounds per square inch by my rough calculations—but the cylinders were thick-walled, with a small cross-sectional diameter. They may be crushed, but I doubt they ruptured."

"So what," Ward said. "Even if everything is intact, the nerve gas and virus would have degraded over time."

"Possibly, but it's very cold at that depth—a degree or two above freezing. I suspect there would be degradation of the nerve gas, though some of it's probably still lethal. But I'm most concerned about the virus. In our tests it was extremely hardy, and able to survive in all manner of environments. At extremely low temperatures, it almost seemed to hibernate, for want of a better word. I think, given the size of the shipment, some might survive. It takes only a tiny bit to begin replicating."

"Let me get this straight," Ward said. "You help engineer a deadly virus that can wipe out civilization as we know it, and thankfully, it gets sent to the bottom of the ocean. You then say nothing for over sixty years until you're on your deathbed. Don't you think it would have been a bit more useful to tell us about it a bit sooner—say, fifty-nine years ago—so we could have been working on a vaccine?"

"Did your investigation reveal my former position at USAMRIID?"

"Sure," Ward said. "Senior researcher in infectious diseases."

"And did it also," Imamura asked, "reveal my specialty?" He continued without waiting for an answer. "I was senior researcher for hantavirus and related viruses. I worked on nothing but finding a vaccine or cure for over forty years, but I was hampered by both inability and unwillingness to reproduce the actual strain we'd developed in Japan." He smiled wanly. "So condemn me as a monster if you will, Agent Ward, for I deserve that. But never doubt I labored mightily to put the genie back in the bottle. I regret that I failed."

The silence grew until Ward broke it. "If someone *is* trying to raise this virus, what do you recommend?"

"Do everything in your power to see that it doesn't surface," Imamura said, with a fierceness that belied his fragile condition. "If you fail, then redouble your efforts to destroy it. And most importantly, if it does come into your control, don't be swayed by those who will want to keep it to study for 'defensive purposes,' because that's the siren song. Unit 731 started with the noble aim of preventing disease, and ended cultivating those very diseases as weapons. Power corrupts, Agent Ward, as surely as the sun rises."

Imamura had risen onto one elbow as he spoke, gesturing at Ward with his hand for emphasis. The effort proved too much for him and he collapsed back on the bed with those last words, his breathing labored.

Ward stood. "Are you all right?"

A smile flickered at the corners of the old man's mouth. "As 'all right' as a dying man can be, I suppose."

"I… I meant…"

"I know what you meant, Agent Ward, and thank you. I'm fine, but if there's nothing else I can tell you…"

"No. I can't think of anything."

"Very well then," said Imamura. "Good luck in your operation."

"Thank you," Ward said, moving toward the door.

Mrs. Lomax was sitting in an uncomfortable-looking plastic chair in the hallway, clutching a well-worn Bible. She rose as soon as she saw Ward, and pushed past him before he could speak. He shrugged and headed for the elevator.

"Dr. Imamura?" Mrs. Lomax called.

Eyes flickered open and Imamura gave her a weak smile.

"Would you like me to read you some scripture, Doctor?"

"Why yes, Mrs. Lomax," Imamura said, "I'd like that very much."

CHAPTER FIFTEEN

CIA HEADQUARTERS
MARITIME THREAT ASSESSMENT
LANGLEY, VA

Ward hadn't bothered to go home—he was already in the doghouse with Dee Dee. He'd just texted her he was working over and gone back to the office. He was still there after midnight, peering through a magnifying glass at satellite photos of *Ocean Goliath*, searching for some clue of a problem aboard. As far as he could tell, it was business as usual aboard the drillship, with Mukhtar's presence the only indication something might be wrong. And even that was circumstantial, revealed by the presence of a sat-phone signal, hardly conclusive. He didn't even know for sure the drillship was going after the damned sub. But what if it was? Imamura's nightmarish scenario replayed itself in his mind's eye.

He laid the magnifying glass on his desk and leaned back in his chair, pondering his options. How could he mount an operation against a perfectly legal and high-profile salvage operation taking place in international waters, funded by a rich Omani with American connections? Based on what? A *suspicion* there was a terrorist aboard? A *suspicion* that they were trying to salvage devastating bioweapons from a long-lost submarine? A *suspicion* based on no hard evidence whatsoever, but on the dying words of a ninety-four-year-old man who may or may not be delusional? No one above him in the food chain would authorize an operation based on what he had. But then, no one else had heard Imamura's story, and Ward knew in his gut the man had been telling the truth.

But he couldn't proceed without more intel, and collecting it without alerting the terrorists was a problem. He couldn't very well contact the company in Houston, since he didn't know who might be involved in an effort to salvage a bioweapon, or even if such an operation was underway. And even if no one ashore was involved, they might inadvertently let something slip during later communications with the drillship. No, he had to figure some way to gather intel independently, and it was pretty damn tough to sneak up on someone in the middle of the ocean. Unless you look like something they expect to see.

He thought of Dugan's nondescript tankers. According to his last unofficial report from Anna, the two ships were a day's run from the *Ocean Goliath*. What if one of those tankers could pass close to *Ocean Goliath* in the night? Nothing to cause alarm, just a tanker in innocent passage. And what if that tanker pumped a bit of oil overboard in the darkness? Not a lot, just enough to cause a sheen. Enough of a sheen to attract attention from shore to investigate the source of the pollution. His resources in Oman were limited, but he'd deal with that later—for now, he just needed to talk Dugan into a little side trip.

He looked at his watch—coming up on midmorning in the Arabian Sea. He dialed Dugan's sat-phone and got a recording, hung up without leaving a message, and tried again five minutes later with the same result. After three tries, he left Dugan a message to call him no matter what the time, and hung up.

He sat for a moment, weighing the benefits of going home. He'd have to be back in the office in four hours anyway, and the hour and a half roundtrip to his house would have to come out of that time. He sighed and moved to his office sofa, and stretched out to wait for sleep that never came.

M/T *Pacific Endurance*
Arabian Sea

Dugan watched on the safe-room monitor as the first pirate scrambled aboard, trailed by five more. Following what Dugan now knew was standard pirate operating procedure, one man remained in the boat and moved it away from the ship to starboard, maintaining his distance from the wildly swinging stern of *Pacific Endurance*. Dugan nodded, and cranked the sound-powered phone.

"*Da*," answered Borgdanov in the officers' mess room.

"Six, repeat, six papas onboard," Dugan said. "Stand by and I'll notify you when they're inside and locked down."

"Standing by," Borgdanov replied.

Dugan watched as the pirates left the field of vision of the deck cameras and waited for them to appear on the passageway cameras inside the house. He didn't have to wait long before he saw the outside door open and the pirates move into the passageway.

"Papas are in the house," he said into the phone. "I count one, two, three, four—damn! Four papas inside, repeat, four papas inside. I'll wait a bit on the other two before I lock down."

"Standing by," Borgdanov said.

As Dugan watched the monitor, the four pirates moved toward the centerline of the ship and began to file into the central stairwell. Dugan spoke into the phone.

"All four papas in stairwell, I am locking down before we lose what we have. You'll have to adjust," he said.

"OK," Borgdanov replied, and Dugan threw the switch that sucked the magnetic bolts home on all the exterior deckhouse doors and all the stairwell doors above A-Deck, trapping the pirates. Then he turned off the lights in the windowless passageway and stairwell, plunging the pirates into darkness.

"Locked and dark," he said into the phone. "All four papas in the stairwell but out of camera range. I have no visual."

"Do not worry, *Dyed*," Borgdanov said. "We will get them."

I sure as hell hope so, thought Dugan, as he watched Borgdanov and his men in the feed from the night-vision cameras as they moved into the darkened passageway, the combination of night-vision goggles over gas masks making them look strangely alien. They moved to the central stairwell and Borgdanov directed his men with hand signals, his silent commands revealing nothing to the pirates in the darkness. At his signal, one Russian held open the fire door and two more rushed into the stairwell, returning in seconds, each dragging a scrawny pirate they had clubbed senseless in the darkness. Two more Russians rushed into the breach with tear-gas grenades and they also returned in seconds, empty-handed, as the Russian holding the door pulled it closed. Dugan saw flashes of light around the edges of the stairwell fire door and Borgdanov making a wait signal, holding his men for what seemed like an eternity before sending them back into the stairwell. They emerged with one man with bound hands and taped eyes and another who appeared unconscious. Borgdanov waved his men and their captives back toward the officers' mess room, blocked open the fire door to the stairwell, and moved after his men to enter the door to the officers' mess and close it behind him. Dugan nodded and started the ventilation fans just as the light of the sound-powered phone flashed.

"I am sorry, *Dyed*," Borgdanov's voice came from the phone, "but we lost one. I hoped to take the last two with the gas, but I think the one highest up the stairs panicked when he heard his comrade behind him in the dark. Before the gas got him, he shot down stairs and killed his comrade." Borgdanov paused. "Where are other two papas?"

Dugan was flipping through the other monitor feeds as he listened to Borgdanov. He located the missing pirates just as the Russian finished speaking.

"They're both on the bridge, looking confused," Dugan said. "You think they heard the gunfire in the stairwell?"

"Is impossible that they did not," Borgdanov said. "What about papa in boat?"

Dugan pulled up the starboard bridge-wing camera feed in the second monitor.

"He's maintaining position. I don't think he's on to us, and I think he's close enough to still be inside our jammer range," Dugan said. "But it's close."

"OK," said Borgdanov. "I think these two on bridge are scared and will stay together now. We must take them without alerting comrade in boat. If he warns mother ship, we have big problem I think. I will take one man up stairwell to bridge deck and wait. I send Ilya and three men to port side, out of sight of man in boat. They will make distraction and draw papas to port side. When you see them react and rush to port, you throw switch and unlock stairwell door. That will be my signal to rush out and take them from behind. I think they will surrender, but if not, we shoot first and our weapons are suppressed. If we are lucky, man in boat hears nothing. Then we make plan to take him."

"Why don't I just unlock the doors now? Maybe they'll come to you."

"No, *Dyed*. Stairwell smells of tear gas even with ventilation. They will not enter, I think. Also, magnetic locks make noise, and they will be already jumpy, as you say in English. Trust me, *Dyed*. These are not soldiers, only *piraty* and *prestupnikov*—pirates and criminals."

"OK, how do you want to time it?" Dugan asked.

"Is self-timing, *Dyed*. Ilya's diversion makes prestupnikov go to port side. You watch and unlock doors after they move to port. Door unlocking is my signal to spring trap. Simple plan is always best, *da*?"

"All right," Dugan said. "Make sure your guys have their night vision secured and I'll give you some light."

Korfa crouched on the port side, one deck below the bridge, tensing for his final charge. He took a deep breath and rushed up the steep stairs, his footsteps ringing on the metal treads, and covered the distance from the top of the ladder to the wheelhouse door in seconds, his weapon at the ready. To find—Ghedi charging in from the starboard side.

The two pirates stared at each other in confusion.

"Where's the crew?" Ghedi asked.

Korfa said nothing, but tried to absorb what he was seeing. The big ship was plowing ahead, its bow swinging radically as the tanker made rapid and frequent course changes, the standard evasive technique to prevent pirate boarding.

Except no one was at the wheel, or on the bridge at all.

"It's a ghost ship," Ghedi whispered.

Korfa snorted. "Don't be a superstitious fool."

Both men flinched at the sound of gunfire.

"That was no ghost," Korfa said, nodding to the stairwell door and raising his weapon. "Go check it! I'll cover you."

"Perhaps you should check it, and I'll cover you," Ghedi replied.

"All right," Korfa said. "Perhaps we should both just cover the door and see who emerges."

Ghedi nodded, and the pirates took positions on either side of the chart table, weapons pointed at the stairwell door.

Dugan watched the pirates on the monitor and cursed the lack of communication. With the jammers activated and Borgdanov away from a sound-powered phone, there was no way to warn him that the pirates lay in wait outside the door. He switched the other monitor from the pirate in the boat and started cycling through the port-side camera feeds, hoping to catch a glimpse of the other Russians who were preparing the diversion. There was a flash of black as one of the Russians moved into view on the port-side exterior stairway, and Dugan's mind raced as he tried to figure out what to do. If the pirates *didn't* take the bait and move to the port bridge wing, there was no way he was releasing the magnetic lock and sending Borgdanov into a trap. Then what? Perhaps "simple plan" was *not* always the best.

Sergeant Ilya Denosovitch stood on A-deck and debated whether to space his men out on the charge up the outside stairway or to group them together. Any way he spaced them, they would be sitting ducks for even a halfway-competent marksman firing down on them from the bridge wing. But that wasn't likely, given what he'd seen of the *piraty's* competence, coupled with the fact that the major would be attacking them from the rear as soon as they rushed to port. Presuming, of course, *Dyed* got the door unlocked promptly. The sergeant decided to rush the ladder as a group and nodded, sending his men clamoring up the ladder, each man pounding the rail with a free hand as he climbed, multiplying the sound of their approach.

Both pirates jerked at the din coming from the port side.

"What's that?" asked Ghedi.

"Go check," said Korfa, and after a slight hesitation, Ghedi moved to the port door and onto the bridge wing.

Korfa heard a burst of automatic fire to port, and Ghedi was back on the bridge. "Soldiers," he yelled. "Coming up the port stairway."

"How many?" Korfa demanded.

"At least a dozen," Ghedi gasped, moving toward the starboard door. "I didn't stay to count."

Korfa took a last look at the closed stairwell door, and turned to flee to starboard with Ghedi.

Dugan watched, racked with indecision, as one pirate moved to port and the other maintained his watch on the stairwell door. The pirate to port fired a burst down the outside stairway, and then rushed back across the bridge, shouting at the other pirate. The man at the stairwell door gave the door one last look, and then joined his companion, both headed for the outside starboard stairway. So much for the plan. Dugan released the lock on the stairwell door.

Borgdanov heard the magnetic bolt release and burst onto the bridge, his weapon at the ready. Instead of seeing the *piraty* to port as he expected, they were fleeing to starboard, and had almost reached the door to the starboard bridge wing. He fired a short burst ahead of them, in an attempt to contain but not kill them, spider-webbing the thick glass of the bridge window. The *piraty* didn't even slow down. They were through the door to the bridge wing and starting down the open stairway on the starboard side before he even reached the door to the bridge wing.

He turned as Denosovitch and his men rushed onto the bridge.

"Ilya," Borgdanov said. "Send your men down the central stairwell to keep the pirates from entering the deckhouse from below. I will keep pressure on them from above. It will be easier to hunt them on the open deck without so much cover. You set up here on the bridge wing. You know what to do."

"*Da*," Denosovitch said, and deployed his men as ordered.

Dugan watched the scene unfold on the bridge, and switched the second monitor to the pirate launch. The boat driver was staring toward the ship, aware something was wrong. The cat was out of the bag.

Erasto kept an eye on the ship and matched her movements expertly, as the vessel maintained her foolish evasive maneuvers. Didn't they know his brothers were already aboard? He jerked at the sound of gunfire from the bridge. He saw two Somalis emerge and rush down the outside stairway. He couldn't make out their features, but he recognized his cousin Korfa from his red shirt. The men were halfway down the ladder when a large soldier in a black uniform appeared above them, chasing them and loosing an occasional burst of gunfire as he came.

He maintained station, unsure what to do, and as he watched, the Somalis reached the main deck. He heard them scream his name just before they leaped over the starboard side, and he turned the Zodiac toward them, intent on rescue.

Dugan watched the pirates jump. *Idiots!*

"Stop the engine!" he said, and the captain cranked furiously on the sound-powered phone to alert the chief engineer beside the engine.

But it wasn't a finely tuned control system, and Dugan knew it was over before it started. *Pacific Endurance* was halfway through a hard turn to port when the pirates jumped, with her stern slewing to starboard. The pirates slipped under the stern and through the big propeller before the chief engineer even touched the engine control.

Erasto knew it was too late, even as his friends hit the water. Their heads surfaced less than a meter from the ship's hull, and then it was moving over them and toward Erasto, a giant steel wall rushing forward with the combined speed of the ship's swing added to the speed of his own boat. He shoved the outboard tiller hard to starboard, and the Zodiac veered to port, slamming the starboard side of the little craft hard against the advancing steel wall of the hull. For one terrible moment he thought the boat would turn over, but it was pushed along by the swinging hull, trapped by the force of the water, the bow of the little Zodiac pointing toward the stern of the ship.

The ship began to slow, loosening its hold on the Zodiac, and Erasto gave the outboard full throttle to shoot down the hull, under the ship's stern and away from her. Astern of the ship, water stained red with his comrades blood still roiled from the slowing propeller. He circled far to starboard of the tanker, intent on getting back to the mother ship. He'd be back, and he wouldn't be alone.

The steel deck was hot on the sergeant's chest and stomach as he lay prone on the rear of the bridge wing, even through the body armor and uniform. He wished he'd had something to lie on. Denosovitch put his eye to the scope of the Dragunov sniper rifle and zeroed in on the passing pirate launch. It'd be easier now that the ship had stopped turning and was drifting through the calm water. The shooting platform grew more stable by the second.

He zeroed in on the outboard motor, leading a bit to compensate, and placed two shots into it in quick succession. He was rewarded by an almost-instant cessation of the noise drifting across the water and a thick smoke billowing out of the outboard, as the Zodiac drifted to a stop. Now to collect Mr. Pirate. He sighed as he saw the man dig in his pocket.

The sat-phone wasn't quite to the pirate's ear when the man's head exploded.

The sergeant shrugged. Some *piraty* just had a death wish.

CHAPTER SIXTEEN

M/T PACIFIC ENDURANCE
ARABIAN SEA

"We can outrun them," Dugan said, as he peered into the radar.

"*Da*," Borgdanov said. "The mother ship we can outrun. But her attack boats? How many does she have? This we do not know. And remember, *Dyed*, we just took out attack boat from this mother ship while she is in radar range. *This* mother ship will know we either have comrades aboard or that we killed them. She will trail us, I think, sending out attack boats to harass us, and call others to join the hunt. And if we, how you say… ziggy… ziggy…"

"Zigzag," Dugan said.

"*Da*. Zigzag. If we zigzag to help hold off attack from chase boats, I think we cannot even outrun mother ship. To escape, we must first at least cripple them so we can break contact."

"And just how do we do that?" Dugan asked.

"They will be cautious, but also confused. If we outrun her, she will send attack boats. But if we drift…" Borgdanov shrugged. "I think maybe she is curious and will come close enough for us to damage mother ship and attack boats. Then we run."

"If that's a mother ship, they've got a lot of men aboard. You've got six men."

"Make that twelve," said a voice behind him. Dugan turned to find Woody and his five-man crew just coming onto the bridge.

"Goddammit, Woody," Dugan said. "What're you doing here? I told you all to stay in the safe room."

"Reckoned y'all could use a hand," said Woody. "And if you think I'm gonna be stuck down in some hidey hole waiting for a bunch of friggin' pirates to overrun the ship and capture my ass, you got another think coming, Dugan."

"Look, Woody," Dugan said, "you're not trained—"

"Screw you, Dugan. I was in the Corps." He nodded at the older man beside him. "And so was Dave here. He was in Hue while I was at Khe Sanh." Woody glared at Dugan. "And Junior here was at Fallujah. Maybe you heard of 'em all?" Woody kept his eyes on Dugan and spoke back over his shoulder. "How 'bout you other boys?"

"Fallujah. Both times."

"Nasiriyah."

"Najaf."

Woody smiled at Dugan. "Ole Ray Hanley likes us vets," he said. "And I expect we got enough training to take on a buncha raggedy-ass pirates."

"Maybe so," Dugan said. "But you'd have to use the captured guns, and there's not much ammo for them."

Woody's smile broadened. "Nice thing about those private jets, the security ain't quite so tight. You didn't think all those crates we brought aboard were tools, did you?" Woody extended his arm toward Junior West, who produced an M-4 carbine from behind his back and handed it to Woody.

Dugan opened his mouth to say something, then seemed to think better of it. He turned to Borgdanov. "What do you say, Major?"

The Russian stared at the Americans, then nodded, looking straight at Woody. "I think is good thing, so long as you understand there can be but one leader. You agree to follow my orders?"

Woody nodded back. "I reckon I can live with that. Provided you're open to a suggestion from an old sergeant now and again."

Dugan stood on the starboard bridge wing of the drifting *Pacific Endurance*, clad in one of the captain's extra uniform shirts with four-stripe epaulettes, with his hands raised in the universal sign of surrender, watching the approaching mother ship. Of course, *ship* was a bit of a misnomer. She looked to be a fishing boat, about eighty feet long, hard-used and rust-streaked. The name *Kyung Yang No. 173* on her battered bow confirmed her to be Korean—no doubt hijacked and pressed into service by the pirates. But the most prominent feature of the approaching vessel was not hardware but humans.

"Christ!" Dugan said under his breath. "She's crawling with friggin' pirates! There must be fifty of them."

"Weapons?" asked Borgdanov from where he crouched out of sight behind the wind dodger.

"Assault rifles. Some RPGs. I count six—no, seven RPGs. Nothing heavier."

"Boats?" asked the Russian.

"Three," Dugan said. "All rigid inflatables. Two towed along their starboard side and one on the aft deck. So far, so good. No one in the boats. Looks like they're going to check us out from the mother ship before they send anyone over."

"That is good," said Borgdanov. "How are they approaching?"

"They're coming alongside with their starboard side to ours and their bow pointed at our stern," Dugan said. "The boat on deck will be below you and to your left when you stand where I am now. You should have a clear shot at it, leaving the other two for your guys."

"What about the others?"

Dugan looked down the length of the main deck. "They're ready," he said.

Borgdanov's black-clad Russians were all hidden from sight in the pump room or behind machinery, but Woody's men were hidden in plain sight. Four were sprawled on the deck from the stern to the midship manifold, apparent victims of the pirate attack. Woody and Junior were draped across the rail, as if they'd been killed trying to repel boarders. Liberal use of blood from the pirate slain in the stairwell completed the illusion. Each of the 'victims' was within a few steps of the cover of a mooring winch or tank hatch, where their M-4 assault rifles waited. The theory was that with the ship dead in the water, littered with bodies, and the captain on the bridge making an obvious gesture of surrender, the pirates would be less suspicious. Dugan looked back toward the approaching vessel. That was the theory. He sure as hell hoped it would work.

"Remember, *Dyed*," said Borgdanov's voice below him, "the closer they come, the better. They must be within fifty meters for me to have the best chance to take out the boat with the RPG. My shot will also be signal for others to open fire."

"How could I forget?" Dugan said out of the side of his mouth. "That's about the tenth time you've told me."

Borgdanov said nothing, and Dugan watched the pirate approach at dead slow. The boat pulled even with him, a bit beyond Borgdanov's specified fifty meters, and Dugan saw the water roil at the stern of the boat as she reversed engine to stop her forward motion.

"We got a couple of little problems," said Dugan, trying to keep his mouth from moving.

"What problems?" asked the Russian.

"They're a bit farther away than fifty meters, but I figure we have to take what we can get. The bigger problem is, about twenty of the assholes have me in their sights and look like they'd really like to pull their triggers."

"Just drop straight to the deck very fast. You will be out of sight before they can react."

"I'm not worried about *me*, genius. What happens when you pop up in the same exact spot seconds later? They'll blow you away in a heartbeat. We should've thought this through a little more."

"Where are my men?" yelled a pirate across the gap.

Oops! Dugan hadn't figured on a speaking part.

"Como?" he yelled back. "No hablo Ingles."

Even over the distance, Dugan could read the confused body language of the head pirate as he conferred with the man next to him.

"Look," Dugan said out of the side of his mouth. "I'm going to drop, then try to draw their fire away. Don't pop up until you hear them shooting at me. Got it?"

Silence.

"God damn it, Borgdanov. Got it?"

"*Da*, but be careful, *Dyed*," the Russian said.

Dugan dropped straight down to the deck, out of sight of the pirates in their lower position. He heard indignant shouts, and a hail of automatic fire filled the area where he'd previously stood, the bullets smashing into the thick glass of the side bridge windows behind him. He crawled across the deck on elbows and knees, the hot steel burning his unprotected forearms as the anti-skid surface scraped his elbows. He stopped fifteen feet from the rear of the wheelhouse and got into a runner's starting stance, higher than he was before but still low enough to be out of the line of sight of the pirates in the lower vessel. He counted to three and then bolted upright, his upper body in full view of the pirates, covering the distance to the back of the wheelhouse in four long strides. He slipped out of sight around the corner of the wheelhouse as bullets slammed into the structure where he'd been, whining off into the distance. He leaned back against the wheelhouse bulkhead, his heart pounding, as he heard the explosion of the major's RPG. Then all hell broke loose.

Borgdanov was up as soon as Dugan disappeared from sight around the corner of the wheelhouse. He found his target exactly where Dugan had said it would be, and fired the RPG as he heard cries of alarm from the *piraty* that spotted him. Even without looking, he saw them in his mind's eye turning their weapons toward him, and he dropped out of sight just before a tsunami of automatic fire engulfed the bridge of *Pacific Endurance*, the din magnified as the hail of fire smashed the side windows of the bridge or ricocheted off steel bulkheads. He heard two more explosions, distinct even in the cacophony of noise, and crawled on his stomach to peek down over the edge of the deck. There was nothing but smoking debris where the two launches had previously floated alongside the pirate vessel, proof his men's RPGs had been successful as well.

There was bedlam on the pirate ship as the surprised *piraty* fell from covering fire laid down by his remaining men and the Americans. The *piraty* dived for cover and responded with wild, undisciplined fire at the ship itself, as if they thought they could sink the huge vessel with small-arms fire. Then he saw a man rise with an RPG, and turned and crawled for all he was worth away from his former firing position. He had no doubt where that RPG would be aimed.

Woody hung over the rail, playing possum with one eye open. As soon as Borgdanov's RPG took out the boat on the aft deck of the pirate vessel, he bolted from the rail.

"Cover," he yelled to Junior. "Pass it on!"

On the pirate ship all eyes were on *Pacific Endurance*'s bridge, and the Americans were under cover and armed in seconds, well before any of the pirates noticed. Woody yelled for his men to lay down covering fire as two more Russians leaped from their hiding places with RPGs to take out the boats tied to the mother ship.

He watched as the raggedy-ass pirates scrambled for cover, some dropping along the way. Their return fire, when it came, was furious but inaccurate. Their AKs weren't much in the accuracy department to begin with, and the dumbasses were keeping them on full automatic, pretty much making hitting anything a matter of luck. But even dumbasses can get lucky, Woody reminded himself, and glanced along the deck to make sure all his boys were staying under cover.

When he glanced back, he saw a pirate rising with an RPG hit by at least two rounds, but not before he fired his weapon. Woody flinched as the starboard bridge wing was enveloped in an explosion, and hoped no one was on the receiving end.

"Take out the RPGs!" Woody shouted, and the order was relayed from man to man.

The next pirate that tried to fire was hit before he could aim, but the rocket leaped across the distance between the two vessels and slammed into the hull of *Pacific Endurance* to explode in a fireball, well above the waterline. Another pirate died before he even raised the tube of the weapon, and taking note, the four remaining RPG men fired from cover without aiming, in the general direction of *Pacific Endurance*. Two rockets flew over the ship, missing her completely, as one obliterated the starboard lifeboat. But in keeping with Woody's observation that even dumbasses get lucky, the fourth slammed into the hull at the waterline, in way of the aft-peak tank.

The captain sat at the makeshift control console in the safe room jury-rigged in the aft-peak tank, feeling neither in control or safe as he'd watched the pirate vessel approach via the feed from the starboard-bridge-wing camera. His functions were to be ready to pass engine orders to the chief engineer at the local controls of the main engine and to steer the ship away from the pirate vessel when the time came.

Well, at least he could see what was going on. The pirate vessel moved alongside and stopped. He saw the pirates pointing and shooting and the boat on the deck of the pirate ship disappear in a fire ball just before a rocket leaped from the pirate vessel and seemed, for an instant, to be coming straight at him in the camera. The monitor flashed black at the same time he felt, rather than heard, a terrific explosion high above him. He cycled the feed through all the rest of the cameras and confirmed them operable. He was blind on the starboard side, which, of course, was where he needed to see.

There was another terrific concussion forward of him—how far forward he couldn't tell—and then something struck the ship's side below him to starboard. The hull rang with the impact, and it was like being inside a giant bell. The concussion lifted him from his chair and unseated the rest of the noncombatants from their benches, throwing them all to the deck in a jumble of tangled bodies and limbs. The temporary lights blinked out and the space filled with smoke and steam.

The captain struggled to his feet in the darkness, shaking his head in an attempt to clear the ringing in his ears. As his hearing returned, he heard the sound of rushing water in the tank below him.

"Anybody hurt?" he called into the darkness, as here and there a flashlight winked on. Scattered voices responded, confirming no serious injuries.

"I have to stay at the console," he said to the chief mate. "Count heads and get everyone into the engine room, then come back and go down to see how much water we're taking on."

The light blinked on the sound-powered phone.

"Everybody OK?" Dugan asked before the captain could speak.

"No one's hurt," the captain said, attempting to cycle through the camera feeds as he talked. "But we got no lights and they blew a hole in the hull at or below the waterline. I can hear water coming in. I don't know how bad. We'll check it."

"OK," Dugan said. "Stand by to get us out of here."

"That's going to be a pretty good trick," the captain replied, looking at the blank monitors. "That last impact shook up the monitors. I got no visual to steer by!"

CHAPTER SEVENTEEN

M/T PACIFIC ENDURANCE
ARABIAN SEA

Borgdanov crept to the edge of what was left of the starboard bridge wing and looked down with a worried frown. His men and the Americans had the *piraty* pinned down for now, but they were starting to recover from their surprise and to fire more economically and more accurately. He mentally willed his two men with the RPGs to hurry, and was rewarded by the sight of a rocket leaping from below him, stabbing toward the mother ship and exploding at her waterline, followed by another, which detonated three meters farther aft.

He raised his own RPG and took aim at the wheelhouse of the fishing vessel.

"No!" said a voice behind him. He snapped his head around to see Dugan crouched in the door to the wheelhouse.

"What is problem, *Dyed*?" Borgdanov said. "*Piraty* are in range of our jammers now, but if we move out of jammer range and leave them with communications, they will call other pirates. One RPG in wheelhouse will knock out radios."

"And kill some innocent fishermen in the bargain," Dugan said. "You know they make hostages of the crews of the vessels they hijack as mother ships."

Borgdanov shrugged. "This may be true, but we cannot leave them with communications."

"There are probably half a dozen sat-phones on that boat in addition to the radios," Dugan said. "Even if you take out the radios, we can't cut their communications, short of boarding and destroying their individual sat-phones. Do you think that's likely to happen without at least some of your guys taking a bullet?"

The Russian looked down at the fishing boat, where the pirates still outnumbered his combined force at least three to one.

"*Nyet*, but what will we do?"

"Do you think they've used up all their RPGs?"

"*Da*, otherwise I think they would still be using them."

Dugan crept up beside the Russian, keeping his head down as he approached the edge of the deck. "Then I think we should just sit tight, stay close with our heads down, and wait until they're ready for us to rescue them," he said.

Borgdanov looked skeptical. "That was not plan."

"Plans change," Dugan said, leaning over to peek at the fishing boat, already listing to starboard as water gushed into the holes in her hull. "Besides, we can't be sure of knocking out all communications without unacceptable risks, so dealing with this bunch here and now is the best option, even if it does cost us time. If we leave them behind and they *do* sic other pirates on us, losing time may be the least of our problems. Let's bag this bunch as quickly as possible and head for the coast."

Borgdanov followed his gaze. "Maybe you are right, *Dyed*."

Dugan gave a resigned nod. The delay from being right might cost another innocent seaman his life.

M/T *PACIFIC ENDURANCE*
ARABIAN SEA

"Well, they're stubborn, I'll give them that," Dugan said to Borgdanov. "I figured when we put *Marie Floyd* up close and personal on the opposite side of them, they'd get the message and give up."

Marie Floyd had arrived an hour or so after the gunfight with the pirates. Unable to communicate because of the jamming, Blake had come aboard *Pacific Endurance* via Zodiac to confer with Dugan and Borgdanov. They'd attempted to intimidate the pirates by having Blake move *Marie Floyd* to the other side of the crippled *Kyung Yang No. 173*, boxing her in and towering over her, but too far away for the pirates to attempt a boarding of either tanker.

The fishing boat was listing badly to starboard, her engine room flooded. But her condition had stabilized, and she appeared in no immediate danger of sinking. Far from surrendering, the pirates were using the captive crewmen of the *Kyung Yang No. 173* as human shields. The helpless South Koreans were tied to the handrails, four on each side of the fishing boat, with a pirate under cover in the house behind them, ready to fire from his protected position and kill the hostages at the first sign of attack from either tanker.

"These *piraty* think they are untouchable as long as they have hostages," said Borgdanov. "And everyone plays their game. Is for this reason they become so strong, *da*? Maybe better we just sink them with grenades and RPGs. Is bad to lose these eight fishermen, but how many more fishermen do we save if we kill so many pirates?"

"Christ! So we just bomb the hell out them, sink them, and leave? Is that your idea of a friggin' plan?" Dugan asked.

"This is big delay, and we have primary mission. But"—Borgdanov shrugged—"you are boss. If you say wait, we wait."

"Maybe I can negotiate—"

"*Dyed*, I'm sorry, but this is bad idea. Is obvious you are American."

"So what?" asked Dugan.

"So they know you are concerned about hostages and they will drag out negotiation forever, hoping their comrades will come looking for them. I think is better if I negotiate."

It was Dugan's turn to shrug. "Well, I can't deny you seem to be pretty good at dealing with these assholes. What do you have in mind?"

Borgdanov grinned. "Nothing complicated. Simple plan is always best, *da*?"

Borgdanov moved to the handrail at the edge of A-deck, the lowest deck on *Pacific Endurance* where he still enjoyed a height advantage over any place on the fishing vessel. He appeared to those below him like a man looking down on them from the edge of a cliff, a commanding figure despite the white flag in his hand.

"I want to talk," Borgdanov called down. "Summon your leader."

A thin Somali of medium height stepped out of the wheelhouse and looked up.

"I am the leader. What do you want?" shouted the man.

Borgdanov shrugged. "I want you to surrender. Lay down arms and you will be treated fairly and your wounded will get medical attention."

"I don't think so," the pirate replied in British-accented English, nodding to the South Koreans tied to the rail. "Perhaps you've noticed we have hostages. It will go badly for them if you attack us, but you can save them all if you're prepared to be reasonable and let us go."

Borgdanov snorted. "Well, you are big comedian, I think. How do you suppose that will happen?"

"Give us one of your ships and six crewmen to run it. Move everyone else to the other ship. We will give you two hostages as a show of good faith as soon as we see you moving your men to the second ship. After we've boarded the ship and confirmed the six crewmen you leave behind can run it and that no one else is hiding aboard, we'll release the remaining six hostages. Then we go our separate ways."

"And if I refuse?" Borgdanov asked.

"Then we will begin executing the hostages," the pirate said, making a show of looking at his watch. "You have one hour."

Borgdanov stroked his chin, as if considering the proposal, then responded. "Thank you for generous offer of one hour to consider, but is not necessary. Ilya!" he called back over his shoulder, never taking his eyes off the pirate.

Sergeant Ilya Denosovitch and three other Russians herded two dozen Somalis to the rail, including the three captured earlier in the day. All were naked, with duct tape over their eyes and mouths and hands bound before them with plastic ties.

Borgdanov suppressed a smile at the look of shock on the head pirate's face.

"You see," he said, "I think you have good idea to shoot hostages. Is very clear what you intend. Anybody can understand. So. I think I do the same, *da*? But I am more generous. You have eight, so I decided twenty-four—three to one. Is bargain, *da*? And by the way, these *piraty* are spares. I have plenty more. So please"—Borgdanov gestured to the pirate leader—"you go first. I insist."

The pirate stood motionless and speechless until Borgdanov continued. "OK. OK. I know is difficult to start sometime. I go first."

Borgdanov grabbed the pirate nearest him at the rail and threw him to the deck. The pirate fell out of sight of the fishing boat and the Russian unholstered a Makarov pistol and fired down at the deck three times. There was an angry cry from the pirates on the fishing boat and weapons rose, stopped halfway up by an urgent order from the pirate leader as he stared at the guns of the other Russians, all targeting him.

Borgdanov nodded to the Russian sergeant, who helped him lift the executed captive and hurl his body over the rail, into the sea. The body splashed down face-up and floated a moment before slipping below the clear water, staring up at the world he was leaving behind.

"Now please. Go ahead," called Borgdanov. "Execute hostage. We do not have all day, I am afraid. Ahh, but where are my manners? You were so nice to tell me your plan, so I should tell you mine before we continue, *da*? Is very simple. You kill those hostages and I kill all the rest of these fellows here, and then we get this silly kill-the-hostage game out of way, *da*? Then we finish blowing up your ship with RPGs and we pick up whoever can swim. Then we kill them. Not fast like bullet, but slow like hot steel rod in ass and things like that. Not everybody, of course. Maybe two or three we leave alive to tell others is not good thing to fuck with Russians." Borgdanov shook his head, feigning sadness. "But you, my friend, I am sorry to say, will not be one who lives. You are leader, so leader must become example. You I will sit on steel deck naked and stomp your balls flat with my heel, then I will tear off your head and piss in the hole." Borgdanov smiled. "Is quite easy to tear off head, especially skinny little fellow like you. Now—any questions?"

The pirate leader licked his lips. He tried to speak twice before anything came out of his mouth. "If… if we surrender, how do we know you won't do that anyway?"

Borgdanov inclined his head toward the Somali captives that lined the rail. "You do not. But if I executed captives, why are these fellows still alive? I will turn you over to proper authorities unless something forces me to do otherwise, like problem we have here."

"Do we have your word?"

"No," said Borgdanov. "But I will give you my word that if you don't surrender within sixty seconds and stop wasting my time, I will kill you."

The pirate leader swallowed hard, then laid his assault rifle on the deck and raised his hands.

Dugan stood with Woody out of sight of the pirates and watched the Russians push the Somalis to the rail. He flinched when Borgdanov unexpectedly threw a pirate to the deck beside the corpse of the man that had died earlier in the stairwell and then put three bullets in the dead man. The corpse was flying over the side before he figured it out. He was still scratching his head when the pirates surrendered minutes later.

"Sure didn't see that one coming," he said.

Beside him, Woody was equally impressed. "I'll be damned if I ain't getting to kinda like the commie bastard."

M/T *PACIFIC ENDURANCE*
ARABIAN SEA

"One hundred and sixteen," Dugan said, looking down at the list. "With at least a half dozen from every major pirate clan. We'll divide them up evenly, and as soon as Woody can get us patched up, I think we're ready to head for Somalia."

"How are the four wounded pirates doing?" Blake asked.

Borgdanov shrugged. "Not so bad. Ilya is cross-trained as combat medic and is very good. He says no problem. All wounds are in arms or legs. I think these *piraty* were shot by Woody's men. My men never miss kill shot."

Beside him, Woody bristled. "Screw you, Ivan. My boys—"

Borgdanov laughed. "Is joke, little man. I think you must… how do you say… lighten up, *da*?"

Woody looked somewhat mollified and was about to speak when Dugan changed the subject. "What about repairs, Woody? When can we get underway?"

Woody shot a stream of tobacco juice over the rail and into the sea, and looked up as if he were envisioning the repair process.

"Let's see," he said. "Nothing much we can do about the starboard lifeboat or the bridge wing. The RPG took out the starboard navigation light, but I got Junior riggin' up a temporary. Doubt it'll meet regulations, but at least she'll show a green light. One of the RPGs blowed a hole in number-five starboard ballast tank, but she's way above the waterline and hit between frames. That ain't much of a problem—most of the steel just peeled back, but it's still attached. We can close up the hole by heating and hammering it back in place, then we'll throw a doubler plate on the inside and weld it up. It'll be a beat-to-fit, paint-to-match homeward-bound job, but it'll do." Woody paused. "The biggest delay's gonna be the after peak tank. A hit right at the waterline took out a chunk of one of the frames. That ain't quite as easy to fix with what we got onboard. Lucky the water didn't quite make it up to the safe room."

"So where do we stand on that?" Dugan asked.

Woody shrugged. "The captain's ballasting to give us a port list so we can get the hole on the starboard side out of the water and have a better look at it. I'm thinking the quickest way is to just weld a light plate over the outside and box around the hole on the inside of the tank. We can put a bunch of scrap metal in the box for reinforcement and tack-weld it all together, then fill the whole damn thing with concrete." Woody looked over at Blake. "I called Edgar over on *Marie Floyd*. He told me there's a bunch of sacks of Speed Crete up in the foc'sle storeroom." Woody smiled. "I figured there would be. If Ray Hanley's gettin' ready to scrap a ship, I reckon a good supply of cement has been standard supply onboard a few years."

"No comment," Blake said, and Woody laughed.

"What about the monitors?" Dugan asked. "We're out of the pirate-hunting business for now, but that doesn't mean we won't run into some. If so, I'd still like to be able to steer from the safe room."

"The fiber optics is OK," Woody said. "The monitors themselves got a shaking—more than they could tolerate, I reckon. I got the boys stealing the TVs out of the officer and crew lounges. I think we can jury-rig somethin' up."

"Good," Dugan said. "Which brings me back to, how long?"

"I got Edgar and his boys coming over to give us a hand," Woody said. "I figure twelve, maybe fourteen hours." He looked past Dugan at an approaching figure who stopped several feet away, intent on catching Woody's eye but seemingly reluctant to intrude on the conversation. Woody shifted his stance so the man was no longer in his line of sight and lowered his voice.

"That is," he said, "if you can keep that damn Korean off my ass. Somehow he figured out I'm the go-to guy for repairs, and he's been followin' me all over the damn ship. I can't seem to shake him."

Dugan took a quick glance at the Korean, then turned back to Woody.

"What's he want?"

"Best I can tell, he wants me to patch up the *Ding Dong 173*, or whatever he calls that tub, so he can go back to fishing." Woody gave Dugan a hard look. "I take it you ain't told him he's now officially a passenger."

Dugan smiled. "Captain Kwok's understanding of English seems to deteriorate rapidly when the discussion turns to something he doesn't want to hear. Just keep politely ignoring him. I'm sure it will sink in sooner or later."

"For the last time, Jesse, no!" Dugan said into the sat-phone, so forcefully Ward figured he might have been able to hear him even without a phone. "I got guys working over the side in the dark with flashlights, trying to get out of here as soon as possible for Somalia. I'm sure as hell not going to burn a day going in the opposite direction and then a day coming back to do a drive-by oil spill in the middle of the night. You'll have to think of something else."

"I have no one else," Ward said.

"You've got navy ships, and helicopters, and jets, and all sorts of resources you could use for—"

"All the ships are too far away and way too obvious, as is a military chopper. I told you, I can't risk alerting the terrorists. If there *is* something going on and they think we're on to them, they could scramble with—" Ward caught himself. "Well, it would just be very bad, that's all. I need you to do this for me. Trust me, OK?"

"Two days' delay means two more dead hostages," Dugan said. "I'm sorry, pal, but I need more than 'trust me' if I'm going to carry that on my conscience."

"Tom," Ward said, "if I don't get some intel on this drillship, and soon, we both might have a lot more than *two* lives on our consciences."

"What are you talking about?"

Ward hesitated. The story was so fantastic he was having trouble convincing any of his own superiors it was anything but a fairy tale. He hoped he could be more convincing with Dugan. He took a deep breath and began.

Five minutes later Dugan had stopped pacing the main deck and stood motionless, the phone pressed to his ear.

"Jesus Christ!" he whispered into the phone. "That… that can't be true, Jesse. How could anyone… I mean… do you believe this?"

"I don't know what I believe, but I don't think Imamura was lying, if that's what you mean. We have to at least check it out."

"But why us?" Dugan asked. "We're a day away, and even if you don't have any navy ships close enough, a chopper from a navy ship or ashore would—"

"Make them suspicious as hell," Ward said. "I can't put a chopper over them until I'm ready to set it down on her helideck with an assault force, and I've got no grounds to board her at the moment. Not without further confirmation." Ward hesitated. "But it goes beyond that, Tom. The few people above me in the food chain I've talked to about this think I'm nuts, but they didn't sit there with Imamura. I need more proof before I'm likely to get much support for going after an American drillship chartered by a well-connected foreign ally, engaged in an outwardly legal activity in international waters. And the satellite imagery of the drillship pretty much shows business as usual. I need an excuse for getting closer— one that won't make al-Shabaab take the virus, assuming they have it, and run."

"For all you know, they already have," Dugan said.

"I don't think so. We've had the drillship under constant satellite surveillance. There have been no boats or chopper flights from the drillship since then. There's a fishing boat tied up alongside, which is a bit suspicious in itself, but not illegal. We think that's how Mukhtar got there, but it hasn't left the side of the drillship. Whatever was there is still there."

Dugan fell silent, considering what he'd just learned.

"Tom?"

"Oh! Sorry, Jesse," Dugan said. "I was just trying to come up with a plan. We have a few hours before we finish here. Let me think things over and get back to you."

"All right. But call me as soon as you can."

"Will do, pal," Dugan replied, and hung up to resume pacing the deck.

CHAPTER EIGHTEEN

Dugan picked his way across the canted upper deck of the engine room by the light of his headlamp, trailed by Woody and the Korean chief engineer. They moved cautiously over the tilted grating, watching their footing and holding on to piping and equipment to steady themselves. Dugan started down a stairway to the next level, the descent made difficult by the heavy starboard list tilting the already steep stairway at a crazy angle. He stepped off the stairway at the next level down and illuminated the ladder treads for Woody and the Korean to descend.

"Ain't as bad as I figured," Woody said to Dugan when all three were at the bottom. "The generator flat is above the water, and"—he examined the space below in the light of his headlamp—"only the lower level flooded above the deck plates, and just on the starboard side." He played his light over the partially submerged electric motors of two pumps and turned to the Korean. "*What those pumps?*" he shouted.

The little Korean frowned, then seemed to understand. "*They are bilge pumps,*" he yelled back. "*And I am Korean, not deaf.*"

Dugan suppressed a smile and interjected himself into the conversation. "What else is under, Chief?"

The Korean played his light over the water below, where the tops of electric motors showed in scattered places like small islands. "Both bilge pumps, ballast pump, sanitary pumps, cooling-water pump, refrigeration plant for fish hold"—he ticked them off on his fingers—"motors all gone."

"Well, we won't get any motors out here. How about work-arounds?" Dugan asked.

The chief nodded as he considered the possibilities. "General-service pump has bilge suction and crossover to ballast system. Can maybe make temporary hookup and use fire pump for cooling water, sanitary, and ballast. Reefer plant…" He shrugged.

"Yeah, I don't reckon y'all will be needing the reefer plant since the first RPG went into the fish hold," Woody said.

"What about the main engine?" Dugan asked. "Did the water rise high enough to get into the sump?"

The Korean shook his head. "I check before. Water not rise to shaft seal. I pull oil sample already. No water."

Dugan nodded. "Then it's just a matter of getting her patched up and pumped out. What do you think, Woody?"

Woody scratched his chin. "Well, best not to run them generators with this kind of list. We need to get her back up a bit straighter first. I saw two or three Wilden pumps in the foc'sle store on *Marie Floyd*, and y'all have some on your ship too. We can bring both ships right up alongside and drop air hoses down to run the pumps. We'll rig a couple of mattresses over the holes on the outside of the hull to slow down the water." He looked down at the water. "Ain't that much volume, so she should pump out pretty fast. We'll list her to port and get the holes out of the water and patch 'em best we can—doublers or cement boxes, or both. Won't be pretty, but she'll be tight."

"How long?" Dugan asked.

Woody sighed. "It's still the middle of the damn night and we ain't even finished with *Pacific Endurance*, so which one do you want first?"

"I want them both first," Dugan said.

"Yeah, that's what I figured," Woody said. He looked at the Korean. "Can your men tend the pumps and rig the piping crossovers?"

"Yes, yes," he said.

Woody turned back to Dugan. "OK, we'll see what we can do. Maybe noon."

M/T *MARIE FLOYD*
ARABIAN SEA

"You told me noon," Dugan said, looking at his watch.

"I told you *maybe* noon," Woody replied. "And now I'm tellin' you fifteen hundred for sure. And you're damned lucky to get that."

"All right, all right," Dugan said. "Sorry to lean on you, but we need to get moving as soon as possible."

"Get moving *where*, is the question." Blake stared across the mess-room table at Dugan. "Why the hell are you taking off for parts unknown in a Korean fishing boat?"

"I can't tell you," Dugan said. "It's something I have to do and this was the only way I could figure to do it without slowing our operation down. As soon as you show up off Harardheere, you can demand that they stop executing hostages or threaten to match the executions man for man, but they won't believe it until they see what you've got. It's going to take you four and a half days to get there as it is, and I don't want to add any time to that."

"I understand that part," Blake said. "What I don't understand is why you're going and how you intend to join back up with us."

"And the answers are, I can't tell you and I don't know," Dugan said. "And if I don't get to Harardheere, it doesn't matter. You know the plan. Start without me. Getting our captives there and setting up the deal is the important thing." Dugan looked at Woody. "And speaking of that, you know what you have left to do, right?"

"Well, I thought I did until you explained it to me ten times, but now I'm all fucked-up," Woody said.

Dugan turned red and Woody raised his hands in a calm-down gesture. "Yes, I got it down. The tank mods are already finished on *Marie Floyd*, so I can put everybody on finishing up *Pacific Endurance*. Don't worry."

Dugan nodded, mollified, and Woody continued. "But I'll tell you something else, for whatever it's worth. I don't know where the hell you're headed, but I'll be damned if I'd sail off with those Koreans without someone to watch my back. That chief's OK, but I think Captain Kwok just wants to get the hell out of Dodge, and if you think he's gonna cooperate when it's just you and him and his crew, you might want to rethink that. As soon as you have a difference of opinion, I reckon you're either gonna become a passenger or be dumped over the side."

Dugan nodded. "I was thinking the same thing myself."

Vince Blake stood on the port bridge wing of the *Marie Floyd* staring down at the *Kyung Yang No. 173* as she got underway. Dugan and the three Russians waved up at him from the afterdeck and Blake returned the wave, as the fishing boat slipped from between the two ships and headed east.

Blake waved across to the captain of *Pacific Endurance* and got a nod in reply, then started the agreed upon separation maneuver.

"Dead slow ahead," he called into the wheelhouse.

"Dead slow ahead, aye," parroted the third mate.

"Rudder amidships," he called.

"Rudder amidships, aye," the helmsman confirmed.

He stood watching on the bridge wing until he was well clear of the other ship, then set the new course and began to gradually increase speed, knowing *Pacific Endurance* would soon fall in a mile away on his port beam. There would be no intentional slow steaming now, not that it mattered much. Two tired old tankers near the end of their economic life weren't greyhounds of the sea, but he hoped they could maintain thirteen knots. Four and a half days at that speed—and five lives.

An hour later and at full sea speed, he let his mind wander to the *Luther Hurd*, and Lynda Arnett, and Jim Milam, and the rest of the crew. He wondered again if he was doing the right thing, and then suppressed those doubts. If he could do nothing for his own crew, at least he could help others. He glanced at the digital readout of the speed log and nodded. Thirteen-point-two knots. Not bad.

On a whim, he walked to the console, picked up the phone, and hit a preselect.

"Engine Room, Chief speaking," a voice answered.

"This is the old girl's last run, Chief," Blake said. "I'd like all she's got."

Blake listened patiently to a long tale about exhaust temperatures, overload protector settings, and a variety of other things about which he knew little as he awaited the words he knew were coming.

"… but I'll see what I can do," the chief said.

"Thanks, Chief. I appreciate it," Blake said, before cradling the phone.

Five minutes later, he smiled as he watched the RPM indicator creep up, and the speed log output move to thirteen-point-eight knots. If they could pick up a favorable current, they might beat his ETA. Four lives lost was better than five.

M/T LUTHER HURD
AT ANCHOR
HARARDHEERE, SOMALIA

Gaal adjusted the explosive collar around the chief engineer's neck, preparing him for his turn as display hostage. Milam glared at him, his hatred palpable. Gaal had insisted that he and Diriyi take over the tasks of changing the collars, citing his concern that the rest of the holders were so perpetually stoned on khat that they risked blowing themselves and the hostages up. Diriyi had acquiesced reluctantly, feeling the task was beneath him. Sensing that, Gaal had assumed most of the work himself, and the hostages grew to hate him even more.

Gaal pulled the last strap tight and nodded to a waiting pirate, who came over and jerked his head toward the door. The chief engineer started his trek up to the flying bridge, the exercise now routine. Gaal ignored the glares of the other hostages and fell in behind the chief and his guard, and followed them into the passageway and up the central stairs. He exited the stairwell at D-deck and walked a dozen steps down the passageway to the captain's office, and entered without knocking.

Diriyi was on the sofa, staring at his sat-phone on the coffee table in front of him. He looked up as Gaal entered. "I think something is wrong," he said. "Mukhtar should have called hours ago."

Gaal shrugged and dropped into the easy chair across from Diriyi. "It's probably nothing," he said. "Maybe he's having trouble with his phone."

"No. There are other phones, and he's eager to confirm the naval vessels are still in place watching us," Diriyi said. "Also, he knows I'm eager to know when he's done, so we may finish our business and leave. Things have been greatly complicated by Zahra and those other fools and their executions."

"Don't worry, Diriyi," Gaal said. "I know the Americans. They're single-minded and focused on us. They'll do nothing unless we provoke them by executing *our* hostages. They care nothing for the others."

Diriyi looked unconvinced. "Perhaps," he said. "But all the same, I wish Zahra and those other idiots had not complicated the situation. What can they be thinking?"

M/T PHOENIX LYNX
AT ANCHOR
HARARDHEERE, SOMALIA

"A mother ship?" Zahra asked. "You're sure? Maybe it's just late checking in."

"I don't think so," Omar said. "No one has heard from them in over two days. And she vanished in the same area as all the rest."

"How many now?"

"All the bands are reporting disappearances. Over a hundred now, I think," Omar said. "Do you think it's the work of Mukhtar and his fanatics?"

"Who else? The naval forces are eager to show the world how effective they are. If they'd done it, they'd trumpet the news." Zahra shook his head. "No. The only ones who might do this secretly are the fanatics. What's our man on the drillship say? If Mukhtar is targeting us, he should know."

"His report is long overdue," Omar said. "I fear he's been discovered. What should we do?"

Zahra said nothing for a moment. "How close is our remaining mother ship?"

Omar shrugged. "At her speed, perhaps three days from the drillship. Less, of course, for the launches she supports."

"And the other bands?" Zahra asked.

"More or less all at the same distance, but some have faster mother ships. Why? What're you thinking?"

"That there's little point in wandering around aimlessly to be picked off by Mukhtar at his leisure," Zahra said. "If we combine forces, perhaps we can end his interference once and for all."

Omar stroked his beard, then nodded. "It might work. We could rendezvous at sea and pick the two fastest mother ships to carry the men, then use them to support a larger force of attack boats. It'll take a little time to organize, but we could strike by surprise and overwhelm him."

Zahra smiled and reached for his phone. "I know it'll work. I'll confer with the leaders of the other bands. I think it's time we pay Mukhtar a little visit. And while we're at it, we can relieve him of his treasure."

CHAPTER NINETEEN

"You same pirate, Dugan," Captain Kwok said, glaring across the small wheelhouse of *Kyung Yang No. 173*. "Pirates take ship. You take ship." He shifted his gaze to include Borgdanov. "Somalis. You. Commie friends. All same. All pirate."

"I am not Communist. I am independent contractor," Borgdanov said, earning himself an even harder glare from the Korean.

"We *did* salvage your vessel, Captain Kwok," Dugan said.

That seemed to stoke the fires of the little Korean's anger even hotter.

"YOU SHOOT HOLES IN SHIP! NO HOLES! NO NEED SALVAGE!" he shouted, before spitting out a stream of Korean that Dugan was just as glad he didn't understand. Kwok returned to English. "First port, you see! I file charges. You big pirate!"

Dugan lost it. "File whatever you damn please. You looked plenty happy for our help when we untied you from that handrail, as I recall."

Kwok clamped his mouth shut and ignored Dugan to stare out at the sunlit sea. Sergeant Denosovitch came up the interior stairway and into the wheelhouse to relieve Borgdanov, and Dugan motioned for the major to follow and headed out of the wheelhouse to the aft deck of the fishing boat.

"Thank you for agreeing to come, Andrei," Dugan said. "I know it's not what you signed on for."

Borgdanov shrugged. "After you explained situation, I cannot let you go off alone." He grinned. "Ilya and I must keep you from trouble, *da*? And Corporal Anisimov, he likes the bonus. Besides, seems most difficult part is to get there."

"Yeah, Woody sure called that one right," Dugan said. "Captain Kwok's not a real happy camper."

Borgdanov nodded. "He is not so cooperative. But makes no difference, I think. We are four, and one of us can stay in wheelhouse to make sure boat stays on GPS track." He looked out at the sea. "And weather is fine. How long do you think?"

Dugan snorted. "Our tankers are speedboats next to this thing. I doubt she'll make more than eight knots, maybe less with all the jury-rigging in the engine room. It'll take us the better part of two days to get there."

"Good," Borgdanov said. "Maybe we use time to figure out what we do when we arrive. You have plan?"

Dugan shrugged. "Nothing firm. Plan A is to pretend to fish and get as close as we can without drawing attention. If we see anything suspicious, we pass it to Ward so he can convince people the threat is real. Assuming we *don't* see anything Ward can use, plan B is to pump a bit of oil over in the middle of the night so it drifts down around the drillship, and then we'll haul ass. Ward can use investigation of the oil spill as a pretext to get agents aboard for a closer look. Either way, when we're done, we head back toward the tankers. Ward promised me to start a navy ship in this direction, and get close enough to meet us with a chopper en route. With a bit of luck, we should get to Harardheere not long after the tankers arrive."

Borgdanov nodded. "Do you think this virus is real, *Dyed*? It seems like fantastic story."

"Not a clue, but Ward is certainly taking it seriously."

DRILLSHIP *OCEAN GOLIATH*
ARABIAN SEA

Mukhtar ignored his throbbing head as he watched the little ROV surface beside the ship. His men were working with the drillship crew now to supplement the work force and help hoist the craft back onboard. The men's movements were dull and lethargic, almost as if they were moving in slow motion. Half the regular ship's crew lay dead or dying in the crew lounge, and four of Mukhtar's men lay with them.

They all realized they were dying, but some undefinable will to live kept them moving, just as fear of Mukhtar drove them to their tasks. Just to be sure, he had two loyal men stationed on the fishing boat. No one was leaving until he'd brought up all the cylinders, a task made more difficult as men dropped of the disease hourly.

The revelation had come to him as the drillship crew began to sicken and die, starting with those who had survived the nerve-gas exposure. It was a miracle. In His great wisdom, Allah, blessed be His Name, had transformed the nerve gas into a deadly plague. *Yawm ad-Din*, the Day of Judgment, was at hand, and Allah had chosen Mukhtar as his instrument. The honor and responsibility were almost more than he could bear, but he would not fail!

His initial actions had been correct. He'd isolated the infected men in the crew's lounge, not realizing it was already too late, and spent the next four days scouring the sea floor to bring up every cylinder he could find. For what seemed the hundredth time, he debated leaving with what he had, and for the hundredth time he ignored the urge. He knew nothing about this new weapon, but sensed more was better than less, and he was determined to have it all.

He watched impatiently as the ROV was hoisted aboard, and his dwindling work force started to transfer cylinders from the ROV into a half-filled cargo basket on deck. Another full basket sat nearby. When he was sure he had all the cylinders, he would hoist the baskets aboard the fishing boat with the ship's crane. And then he would get God's great cleansing plague ashore somewhere, Inshallah.

Gaal's eyes flew open as he heard the key in the lock of his cabin door. He feigned sleep as his hand sought the grip of the Glock beneath his pillow. He heard his door open and his hand tightened on the Glock.

"Gaal," called Diriyi's voice. Gaal opened one eye and saw the Somali's form silhouetted against the light of the passageway. He looked at his watch.

"What do you want? It's one o'clock in the morning."

"Take the spare collars to the top of the wheelhouse, then join me in the officers' mess room."

"Why?"

"Never mind why," said Diriyi. "Just do as I say." He closed the door before Gaal could respond.

Gaal got up and dressed before going to the spare room, where he kept the extra explosive collars. He carried them to the top of the wheelhouse and laid them on the deck not far from where the bosun dozed in a lounge chair, fatigue having overcome his anxiety at being shackled to the handrail with two pounds of explosive wrapped around his neck.

The bosun started awake, wild-eyed in the light of the small penlight, as Gaal bent over him. The man jerked away and tried to stand, but Gaal pushed him back down in the chair.

"Relax," Gaal said. "I'm not going to harm you. Do you understand?"

The bosun nodded, distrust in his eyes, as Gaal held the light in his mouth and lifted the explosive collar to poke around beneath it. Terrified, the bosun tried to force his chin down to see what Gaal was doing, but Gaal pushed the collar up harder to keep the bosun looking straight up at the stars. Then Gaal pressed the collar back in place, straightened, and walked off, his progress marked by the faint glow of the penlight lighting his way.

He made his way down the central stairwell to A-deck, and found Diriyi waiting outside the officers' mess staring down in disgust at the man supposedly guarding the hostages. The pirate sat on the deck snoring, his back against the bulkhead, an AK draped across his outstretched legs.

Diriyi sneered. "This rabble now seems to look to you as a leader, Gaal. I'm happy to see you command such a disciplined group."

Gaal grimaced and kicked the sleeping man hard. The man jerked awake and scrambled to his feet in a flurry of elbows and knees.

"Sorry to disturb your nap," Gaal said, as the man stood blinking, his head swiveling between Gaal and Diriyi.

"Leave him," Diriyi said, and motioned for Gaal to come closer. When he did so, Diriyi lowered his voice. "Something is wrong," he said. "We will go in and bring out the woman and three other hostages one at a time. Bind their hands and tape their eyes here in the passageway, and then shackle them with the other one on top of the wheelhouse."

"There are only three extra collars," Gaal said.

"I know that," Diriyi said. "Have this fool"—he nodded at the guard—"take the woman to my cabin."

"But why?"

"I will explain later, in my cabin. For now, just do as I say."

Gaal hesitated, then nodded and followed Diriyi into the mess room.

Something was definitely wrong. Diriyi seemed agitated and nervous, and for the first time in days, he followed Gaal to the flying bridge and assisted in collaring the hostages. Diriyi handed Gaal each collar, and then held a penlight as Gaal fitted it. Gaal felt Diriyi's eyes on him as he worked. He finished and stepped back. The third mate, the chief mate, and the chief engineer now stood with the bosun, each fastened to a corner of the flying bridge.

"Good," Diriyi said, and moved toward the bosun.

"Where are you going?" Gaal asked.

"To check his collar," Diriyi said.

"I checked it when I brought the other collars up," Gaal said. "It's fine. Do you think I'm not competent to fit a simple collar?"

Diriyi hesitated. "Very well," he said. "Let's go down."

Gaal nodded and followed Diriyi down the stairs.

"What's going on?" Gaal asked minutes later in the captain's cabin.

"Mukhtar called and he sounded crazy," said Diriyi. "He was raving about Yawm ad-Din, the Day of Judgment, and saying something about a cleansing plague. None of it made sense, but it's clear the operation is coming to an end and now's the time to leave."

"I don't understand," Gaal said. "What about the woman? Why's she here?"

Diriyi smiled a gap-tooth smile. "I'm keeping my promise, but since I plan to take my time, I'm taking her ashore. After that…" He shrugged and pointed to where Arnett sat on the sofa, duct tape over her eyes and binding her wrists together behind her back. An oversized duffel lay on the sofa beside her.

"I need help getting her in the bag," Diriyi said.

Gaal smiled back, with a composure he didn't feel. "You'll need help taping her feet as well," he said. "Else you might be missing a few more teeth."

Diriyi frowned and extracted something from his pocket and moved to the sofa. He pressed the stun gun to Arnett's bare neck and held it there as she jerked and spasmed before toppling over.

Diriyi looked back and smiled again, as he slipped the stun gun into his pocket and reached down to pick up a roll of duct tape from the coffee table. He tossed it to Gaal. "That should hold her awhile. Tape the bitch's ankles."

Gaal did as instructed, uneasy as he watched Diriyi grab the big duffel and open the heavy zipper that ran its length. Diriyi spread the bag open on the deck, then came over and grabbed Arnett under the armpits and gestured for Gaal to take her feet. In seconds, they had her in the duffel and zipped up. A tight fit, but Diriyi didn't seem concerned with the woman's comfort.

"So what now?" Gaal asked.

"We take her ashore," Diriyi said, "and leave these fools to face the Americans when they come."

"They may be watching us with night-vision equipment."

"They'll see two men leave with a bag. Hardly enough to trigger action." He smiled. "And besides, I'm counting on their night vision, because they'll also notice the new hostages on display." He held up a remote actuator. "And when we're far enough away, they'll see those hostages lose their heads. I'm sure that will bring the attack."

Diriyi laughed. "It's a pity I didn't think of this earlier. We could've made collars for the whole crew." He sighed. "I guess we just have to do the best we can under the circumstances—Beard of the Prophet." Diriyi looked toward the cabin door. "What's that?"

Gaal turned to follow Diriyi's gaze, then felt the electrodes on his neck. *Dumb, dumb, dumb* was his last conscious thought before he fell to the deck. When his brain started functioning five minutes later, he was lying on his side with his wrists and ankles bound with duct tape. His mouth was untaped, but the last thing Gaal wanted to do at the moment was call for help from another pirate. He moved his bound wrists to the knife he wore on his belt, but the sheath was empty. He lifted his wrists to his mouth and began to gnaw at the tape.

CHAPTER TWENTY

M/T *Luther Hurd*
At anchor
Harardheere, Somalia

Jim Milam stood trying to assess the situation as the pirates' footsteps faded on the steel treads of the ladder. He heard the rattle of steel chain on the deck.

"This is Milam. Who's there?" he called into the dark.

"Me, Chief. Johnson."

"Boats," Milam said to the bosun. "Are we on the flying bridge? Can you see? How many others—"

"I'm here. Jones," called Stan Jones.

"M-me too. Silva," added Joe Silva.

"I can see," said the bosun. "We're on the flying bridge." The bosun looked around, his eyes accustomed to the moonlight. "I'm chained as usual, but it looks like y'all are pulled up short on the handrail. They left y'all's hands tied and no piss bucket or water bottles, so I'm thinkin' they ain't figuring on y'all being around too long." He paused. "That asshole Traitor was up here earlier, messing around with my collar. I don't know what that was about either."

"OK," Milam said. "Is everyone all right?"

"You mean other than being chained to a handrail with a friggin' bomb strapped to my neck?" Jones asked. "Yeah, other than that, I'm just peachy."

"What about you, Joe?" Milam asked.

"I… I'm OK, Chief," Silva replied. "But I wish they hadn't left us blind. It makes it all worse somehow."

"Yeah, I know," Milam said, as chains rattled on the deck to his right.

"I got some slack in my chain and my hands are free," the bosun said. "Move toward me, Chief, and I might be able to get that tape off your eyes."

Milam's hands were bound behind his back, his wrists chained to the handrail. He moved toward the sound of the bosun's voice until his short chain was taut.

He heard chain rattling on the deck as the bosun moved, then "Crap! That's as far as I can go. Can you bend toward me, Chief? Maybe I can reach your head with one hand."

Milam's shoulders were burning from being twisted in directions they weren't intended to flex, but he gritted his teeth and inched his head farther and lower, to be rewarded with a tentative touch to the crown of his head.

"Oof. Almost," the bosun said, strain in his voice. "Just a bit more and I might be able to hook my fingers under the tape."

Milam willed the pain away and surged forward. A half inch.

He heard a snort from the bosun's direction and felt the fingers slipping down the side of his face, and then—

"Got it!" the bosun said, and Milam clamped his eyes shut to a new pain as the ring of duct tape was torn from his head, taking a substantial wad of hair along with it.

Milam staggered back against the rail. "Christ, Boats! I think you friggin' scalped me!"

The bosun peered down at the hairy ring in his hand. "Sorry, Chief."

"That's OK, Boats. Thanks," Milam said.

"Can either of you reach us?" asked Stan Jones.

"Sorry, Stan," Milam said. "Both of you are too far away."

"Wonderful," Jones said.

"Well, if it's any consolation," Milam said, "things don't look any better with my eyes open."

The woman squirmed unexpectedly halfway down the sloping accommodation ladder, almost causing Diriyi to drop her over the side. It would serve the bitch right if her unseemly stubbornness resulted in her going to a watery grave. He managed to balance the moving bag on his shoulder the rest of the way down to the bottom landing, and then bent at the waist to drop the bag onto the floorboards of the Zodiac. It hit with a satisfying thump and stopped moving. Diriyi smiled his gap-tooth smile and jumped into the boat, untying the craft and cranking the outboard. He looked at the second inflatable tied to the accommodation ladder and considered sinking it, then discounted the idea. He was no doubt being watched from the infidel ship, and he didn't want to draw undue attention.

He turned the little boat toward shore, and increased speed. Not too fast, he must make sure Gaal had time to free himself and collect his weapons. He certainly didn't want the infidels to find Gaal all tied up and think him a victim. Diriyi laughed aloud, pleased with himself, as he slipped a phone battery from his pocket and tossed it over the side. It had puzzled him at first when his mole on the *Phoenix Lynx* had reported that Zahra seemed to know a great deal about Mukhtar's operation against the drilling vessel, but it soon became clear. Only he and Gaal had been privy to that information. Of course, there could be a mole on the drilling vessel itself, but Gaal was the more likely spy. He'd already proven his readiness to turn his coat at the first opportunity. And besides, Gaal was such a convenient scapegoat. The Americans were sure to take some of that rabble alive, and they would all claim Gaal as their leader. And if the Americans captured a leader, they'd be less inclined to look for him.

Gaal ripped at the last stubborn strand of tape with his teeth and it parted. He separated his wrists and tore the clinging remnants of the tape away, as he hawked and spit on the deck, trying to rid himself of the foul taste of the adhesive. His hands free, he made short work of the ankle binding, then leaped to his feet and rushed into the passageway. He stopped, surprised to see his knife and Glock on the passageway deck.

He collected his weapons and then rushed out of the deckhouse, onto the exterior staircase zigzagging up the starboard side, and looked overboard. There, at the edge of the circle of light around the bottom of the accommodation ladder, he saw a Zodiac moving away from the ship, and knew he was too late to save Arnett. He pounded up the stairs.

The guard inside the bridge heard his heavy tread and met him as he came up the stairway, onto the bridge wing.

"Quickly," Gaal said. "I think we'll be attacked. Go reinforce the guard on the hostages. I'll take care of things here."

The man nodded, and rushed down the stairs, as Gaal moved into the wheelhouse to a lighting panel. Without hesitation, he threw on the deck lights, and the main deck and the exterior of the deckhouse lit up like high noon, providing any force attacking from the dark a decided advantage. He dug in his pocket for his sat-phone—and found it dead. He mashed the power button repeatedly, then gave up and rushed back to the bridge wing and up the steel stairway to the flying bridge.

Milam clamped his eyes shut and then opened them cautiously, blinking in the harsh glare of the deck lights. He heard steps and turned to see Traitor top the open stairs from the bridge deck below.

"I'm Sergeant Al Ahmed, US Army Special Forces," Traitor said. "I'm going to get you out of here, but you have to do exactly as I say."

And I'm the friggin' Easter Bunny, thought Milam, as his mind raced, trying to figure out what Traitor was up to. He watched the pirate rush to a cringing Joe Silva and probe under the third mate's explosive collar. Stan Jones, blind like Joe Silva, was next, and the pirate was on him before he could react. Milam had no clue what the bastard was doing, but sensed the end was near and vowed not to die without at least getting in his licks.

He tensed as Traitor approached. One good one in the family jewels might bring the pirate down between him and Boats. If they could stomp the son of a bitch to death, maybe Boats could find the key on him. A lot of friggin' maybes, but it was the only plan he had.

Traitor was moving toward him now, holding something in his right hand. Milam turned toward him, and when Traitor was close enough, aimed a savage kick at the pirate's groin. But Traitor was fast, deflecting the kick with a forearm block that sent the wire cutters in his hand flying over the rail.

"You stupid son of a bitch!" Traitor said. "I'm trying to help you!"

"Yeah, right. Screw you," Milam said, and braced himself against the handrail, ready to kick again.

Traitor pulled a knife from his belt and started toward Milam.

"There is no time for this, you idiot," Traitor screamed, threatening Milam with the knife. He raised the knife high as he approached and Milam tracked it with his eyes. Milam was surprised by the side kick, and Traitor's heel slammed into his solar plexus like a jackhammer, driving the air from his lungs. Milam began to collapse, but Traitor was on him in an instant, driving his shoulder into Milam's chest to pin him upright against the rail. The knife flashed in Gaal's hand, slashing the straps that secured the collar under Milam's armpits. Then Traitor stepped back, and as Milam sagged to the deck, Traitor dropped the knife and grasped the collar with both hands in one fluid motion, ripping it over Milam's head. He continued in a whirling motion, like an Olympian throwing a discus, and released the collar.

Diriyi mashed the button and felt a rush of exhilaration as a fireball bloomed in the distance, followed by the delayed rumble of an explosion. The thrill faded as he realized there was one fireball, not four. Something was very wrong. First, the lights had come on, making the *Luther Hurd* an island of light on the dark surface of the surrounding sea. Then the movement on top of the wheelhouse. He cursed himself for not thinking to bring binoculars, then twisted the throttle on the outboard and roared toward shore.

USS CARNEY (DDG-64)
DRIFTING
HARARDHEERE, SOMALIA

"Jesus Christ!" Captain Frank Lorenzo said, as he peered through the binoculars toward *Luther Hurd.* "That was definitely Ahmed. Are they all down?"

"Can't tell," the SEAL beside him said. "But what the hell's he doing? He was supposed to give us at least thirty minutes' warning when he was ready for us."

"Well, that didn't happen, Lieutenant," Lorenzo said. "Are your SEALs ready to rock-and-roll?"

"The bird's warming up now," the SEAL said. "And I have two more waterborne teams ready to go when we give the word."

"That would be now, Lieutenant!" Lorenzo said, but he was already talking to the SEAL's back.

M/T LUTHER HURD
AT ANCHOR
HARARDHEERE, SOMALIA

Gaal, aka Sergeant Al Ahmed, struggled to his feet and took inventory. The collar had barely cleared the bridge wing when it detonated with an ear-shattering crash, driving him to the deck. The chief engineer was on his knees, his arms tethered to the top rail, twisted up painfully behind him. He'd recovered enough of his wind to moan as he put a foot on the deck and struggled to his feet. The two blindfolded men appeared to be terrified. They stood chained and alone in their darkness, begging someone to tell them what had happened. The bosun was least effected, having seen what was coming and thrown himself to the deck. As he struggled to his feet, Ahmed started toward him, when he felt as well as heard the pounding footsteps of men on the steel stairway below.

"Can you hear me?" asked Ahmed, letting out a relieved sigh when the bosun nodded. Ahmed handed the bosun a set of keys.

"Unshackle yourself and help the chief," Ahmed said. "Get him to lie down on the deck where he can't be seen from below and tell him to be very quiet. Then return to your position, but stand up so you can be seen by any pirates who look up from below. We have to fool them a bit longer. I'll be back as soon as I can. Understand?"

The bosun nodded and Ahmed turned to rush down the stairs to the bridge deck. He got to the starboard bridge wing as three pirates topped the stairs from below.

"Gaal! What's happening? What was the explosion?" the first man asked.

"One of the hostages lost his head," Gaal-Ahmed said. "There's no time to explain. The infidels will attack very soon, and we must be ready. Go below and get everyone to take defensive positions on the main deck, both sides, from bow to stern. They could approach from any direction, and we can't let them get aboard."

"But what of the hostages?" asked the man.

Ahmed looked up at the flying bridge, relieved to see the bosun standing there, the collar around his neck and chains draped around his wrists to give the impression he was restrained. "We still have three collared hostages to discourage the infidels. Move all the rest into the officers' mess before you disperse on the main deck, then block the doors from the outside. Leave one guard."

The pirates looked confused.

"*Move!*" Ahmed shouted, and the three took off down the stairway.

CHAPTER TWENTY-ONE

M/T *Luther Hurd*
At anchor
Harardheere, Somalia

Ahmed waited until the pirates were two decks below before he raced back up the stairs to the flying bridge.

"Release the others," he said to the bosun. "I'll help the chief."

Milam was steadying himself on the handrail as he climbed to his feet. Ahmed grabbed his other arm to assist him. Milam jerked away.

"Special Forces, huh. You took your own sweet time gettin' in the game," Milam snarled. "Don't you think you could have let us know?"

Ahmed shook his head. "I was already suspect because I'm American. Having you all hate me was the best cover. But things are about to get very interesting, so make up your mind if you believe me or not. If you won't let me save you, I'm sure as hell going to save myself."

Milam glared at Ahmed, then nodded, as the bosun and his newly freed shipmates gathered round.

"Where's the captain?" Milam asked.

"Diriyi, the one you call Toothless, zapped me with a stun gun and took her ashore," Ahmed said. "I couldn't stop him. When you're all safe, I'll go after her."

"What's your plan?"

"I expect a SEAL team from the *Carney* will be arriving soon," Ahmed said. "But the original plan won't work. I've decoyed the pirates away for the moment. I'll free the rest of the crew, and I want you to take them and escape in the free-fall lifeboat. The pirates are all watching out at sea, awaiting attack. They won't be looking up. If you board quietly, the launch will catch them by surprise. You should meet SEALs coming over water. Tell them there are no hostages left aboard."

"What about you?" Milam asked.

"I can take care of myself," Ahmed said.

"Why trust this son of a bitch?" Stan Jones demanded. "All we have is his word the captain's not onboard. I say we search for her before we take off in a lifeboat."

"Look, Stan," Milam said, "Lynda and I talked about this. I don't think—"

"Sorry, Chief," Jones said, taking a step toward him. "It's not your call. With Lynda gone, I'm the acting captain, and I—"

The sap came out of Ahmed's pocket and struck the back of Jones's head so fast it was almost a blur, toppling him. On Ahmed's right, he caught movement from the corner of his eye and ducked a retaliatory swing from the bosun, the big man's fist striking air where Ahmed's head had been. Ahmed danced away, his hand on his Glock as a warning.

"What the hell did you do that for?" Milam demanded.

"Because we don't have time for a debate," Ahmed said. "Decide if you're in or out. Right now. Or I go my own way."

Milam looked at the others, then nodded. "OK, we're in. What should we do?"

"Go to the lifeboat, as quietly as possible. Get it ready to drop, and wait. I'll take care of the guard and lead the rest of the crew to the boat."

"They won't trust you," Milam said. "I'll come with you." He turned. "Joe, can you and Boats get Stan to the boat while I go with Traito—the sergeant."

The two nodded, and Ahmed watched as they began to help a now-conscious Jones to his feet. Ahmed motioned for Milam to follow and moved to the stairs.

Ahmed stopped at his cabin on C-deck, then raced down to A-deck, Milam in tow. He left Milam in the central stairwell and walked down the passageway to the officers' mess. The single guard in the passageway glanced at the pillow wrapped around Ahmed's right hand, held there with his left.

"Did you injure yourself—"

The Glock spoke twice, its bark reduced to dull thuds by the pillow. The guard collapsed, his AK clattering to the deck. Ahmed picked up the assault rifle and called down the passageway to Milam.

With the whole crew together for the first time since capture, the atmosphere in the crowded officers' mess was tense. Milam was besieged with questions—faster than he could answer them, each louder than the last.

"Quiet!" he yelled, repeating the order several times before it took. "I don't have time to explain, but we're getting out of here. Right now I need everyone to just shut the hell up and listen to me. Got that?"

There were murmurs and nods of assent as he continued.

"First, I need a headcount," he said, looking around until he spotted Dave Jergens, the chief steward. "Dave?"

"I did a count when they put us together, Chief," he said. "Eighteen. Everyone's here, except the four of y'all they pulled out of here earlier and the bosun."

Milam nodded. "All of those are accounted for. Now listen, we're going to the lifeboat and everyone has to—"

"Why are you doing this? Where's Captain Arnett?" the steward asked.

Milam hesitated. "They took her ashore."

His announcement was met with shocked silence, and he continued before the crew had time to digest the news. "But there's nothing we can do about that. We got one chance to get out of here, and not much time to do it. We're going to move out of here and back to the lifeboat. No talking. No noise. We'll launch the boat and head toward the navy ships."

"How?" a seaman asked. "There's friggin' pirates all over the ship. Even if we get the boat in the water, it ain't exactly a speedboat. They'll blow the hell out of us before we get a hundred yards."

"We'll have a little help," Milam said, opening the door and motioning to Ahmed.

There was a low collective snarl. "That friggin' Traitor," said someone.

"Not exactly," Milam said. "Meet Sergeant Ahmed, US Army Special Forces."

At Ahmed's suggestion, the men left their shoes in the mess room, and followed Milam single file up the stairwell to D-deck. The elevated exterior catwalk to the top of the machinery casing was exposed, in full view of the pirates on the main deck below should they look up. Milam crept across in stocking feet, hoping like hell they wouldn't.

On the top of the machinery casing, he peeked over the starboard rail. Two pirates sat on a set of mooring bits, AKs across their knees, as they chewed khat and chatted, the alarm of a few minutes before seemingly forgotten. Milam turned and motioned to Ahmed, crouched out of sight across the catwalk, and the next man started across.

Milam had half the crew crouching out of sight on the machinery casing when a young seaman's sock snagged in the catwalk grating. The man finished the crossing in a stumbling run, his first unbalanced step on to the top of the machinery casing producing a dull but audible thump.

Milam took a quick peek over the rail. The pirates were looking up.

Ahmed crouched in the shadows of D-deck, listening to the pirates below.

"I tell you, I heard something."

"Bah! You're an old woman, jumping at shadows. Sit back down and have some khat."

"Maybe you're right. I can't see a thing with these bloody lights glaring in my eyes anyway," the first pirate said.

Ahmed crept to the edge of the deck and peeked over, seeing the pirate shading his eyes with his hand and peering upward. He watched as the man dropped his hand and returned to his seat on the mooring bit. The man looked around.

"I don't like these lights. We're exposed," the pirate said.

"Relax," the other pirate said. "The lights also show the hostages ready to lose their heads. The Americans won't attack. Otherwise, they'd have come long ago."

Ahmed moved back to his position, signaled Milam, and sent the next man across the catwalk. The rest followed at ten-second intervals, then Ahmed joined them. Getting into the free-fall lifeboat was a repeat of the catwalk exercise, requiring transit of another exposed walkway while pirates sat in plain sight on the stern two decks below. Milam stayed back this time, sending the men to the open rear door of the enclosed boat, where a recovered Stan Jones counted heads and ushered them into the boat. Milam sent the last man across and turned to Ahmed.

"The fools will be surprised," Ahmed whispered. "But they'll recover quickly. I'll cover your escape, then go after the woman. I must find her soon, or she's dead."

Ahmed saw Milam swallow and extend his hand.

Ahmed took the offered hand and felt Milam's hand tighten on his. "Get her back," Milam said, his voice cracking.

"With the help of Allah, I will," Ahmed replied. "But now you must go." He glanced toward the lifeboat, where Jones stood in the open door beckoning Milam to come. "Tell Mr. Jones I'm sorry I struck him, and also to keep the boat going straight away from the ship. You need to get out of the light cast by the ship quickly."

Milam nodded and gave Ahmed's hand a final squeeze.

Ahmed watched Milam move into the lifeboat and swing the stern door shut quietly. He waited, knowing it would take a moment before Milam settled himself into a rear-facing seat and strapped himself in for the sudden deceleration when the lifeboat hit the water.

He surveyed the pirates on the main deck below while he waited. There were four on the stern, and the pair he'd overheard farther forward on the starboard side. No doubt there were more on the port side out of his direct line of sight, but that didn't matter. They'd have to move into his field of fire to target the lifeboat and he'd have the advantage of surprise. He decided to let his first target be self-selecting. The pirate with the quickest reflexes would be the first to die. It seemed fair.

He'd no sooner made the decision than the lifeboat began to move, plunging over the side bow first. It struck the water at a sharp angle, submerged, then broke the surface some distance from the ship, the momentum of the dive carrying it away even before the engine cranked to hasten the progress. The pirate directly below Ahmed won the reaction-time lottery. His rifle was at his shoulder before Ahmed drilled him with a three-round burst in the back.

Ahmed shifted his aim to take out the second pirate of the pair, also before the man got off a shot, just as the second pair of pirates on the stern opened up on the lifeboat. But the boat was a moving target, and both pirates had their AKs on full automatic—noisy but inaccurate. Few of their bullets found a mark before their fusillade was cut short by two three-round bursts from Ahmed.

He ducked as a hail of fire ricocheted off the side of the machinery casing, well above his head, and realized he was taking fire from the two pirates on the starboard side. They were firing blind into the lights above them, and Ahmed fought his urge to flee and finished them with two aimed bursts.

He heard shouts coming from below him to starboard and spun, just as two more pirates rounded the machinery casing and rushed onto the stern. They froze, confused at the sight of their dead comrades, and Ahmed shot them down before they recovered. He looked out and saw the lifeboat, a dim patch of orange in the gloom now, and he turned to the deckhouse. Time to get the hell out of Dodge.

US Navy SH-60 Sea Hawk
Airborne near *Luther Hurd*
Harardheere, Somalia

The SEAL lieutenant watched from the chopper as the free-fall lifeboat dived off the stern of *Luther Hurd*, followed by the flash of gunfire. He cursed under his breath as he saw what little was left of his rescue plan evaporate, along with plans B and C. All the plans called for Ahmed to get the hostages centralized in one room and the explosive collars neutralized before calling in a request for rescue along with the hostage location. Now, at least some of the hostages had escaped in the lifeboat. Or was it all of them? If not, where were the rest? And where the hell was Ahmed and why hadn't he called? This was turning into a grade-A clusterfuck! He looked at the screen in front of him and the symbols of his two waterborne teams now closing on *Luther Hurd*. He keyed his mike and ordered one to hold its position and vectored the other toward the lifeboat. No way in hell was he going to charge in without at least some idea of what was going on.

Milam braced for impact as the boat dropped bow first into the sea. He felt the strange sensation as the boat plunged underwater before surfacing, followed by the rumble of the diesel as Stan Jones hit the electric start. He heard the rattle of gunfire and a sharp knock as something hit the fiberglass canopy.

He looked up to Jones in the elevated seat, with its glass ports to provide visibility for the coxswain. "You better get down lower, Stan," he said. "You're a sitting duck up there, and it doesn't much matter where we're going until we get away from the ship. Sit on the deck and reach up and hold the bottom of the wheel."

Jones didn't respond for a moment, then turned and gave Milam a strange look as he reached his left hand across his chest and felt behind his right shoulder. He pulled back a bloody hand. "Thanks for the advice, Chief, but I think you're a little friggin' late."

"Christ," Milam said, and began to unbuckle his harness, as beside him the bosun did the same. Both men were up and beside Jones seconds before he slumped in his harness.

"I'll hold him, Boats. You unfasten his harness," Milam said.

The bosun did as instructed, and between them, they maneuvered Jones to the seat just vacated by Milam.

"You steer, Boats," Milam said. "Just take a quick look to make sure we're still headed away from the damn ship and then stay down and hold on to the bottom of the wheel. We'll take care of Stan."

The bosun nodded and moved to the wheel, as Milam tried to get Jones's shirt off so he could see the wound. Frustrated, he tore it, just as the chief steward made his way up the aisle with the first-aid kit.

"Let me help, Chief," said the steward, as footfalls sounded at the rear of the boat, followed by rapping on the stern door.

"US Navy. Open up," said a voice on the other side of the door.

"Thank God," Milam said, leaving Jones in the steward's care and moving aft. "Boats, get on back in the coxswain's seat and let me by."

He moved aft and threw open the stern door.

"We've got an injured man—"

"Hands on your head and don't move!" said a black-clad figure, his face obscured by goggles, unlike the assault rifle pointed at Milam, which was quite visible.

Milam hesitated, confused.

"Hands on your head! Now!" the man shouted again. "And have someone open the forward door."

"Christ on a crutch," Milam said, putting his hands on his head. "Somebody open the bow door before this moron shoots me," he called over his shoulder.

He heard the bow door open, and after a moment a voice from the bow called to the SEAL holding him at gunpoint. "Clear. No bad guys inside."

The SEAL lowered his weapon. "Sorry," he said. "It could've been a trap. What's your situation?"

Milam's anger vanished. "We got an injured man. Gunshot wound. Everybody else is OK."

The SEAL nodded. "We'll leave our medic with you. *Carney*'s sending out another boat. Any hostages left aboard the ship?"

"No," said Milam. "But they took the captain ashore. And there's a US Army guy aboard, but he looks like a pirate."

"We know," the SEAL said, and keyed his mike.

M/T *LUTHER HURD*
AT ANCHOR
HARARDHEERE, SOMALIA

Ahmed raced down the stairwell, feeling strangely exhilarated. It was good to have a taste of his own identity, but now he had to be Gaal again, if only for a few moments. He reached main-deck level and ran out the starboard door of the deckhouse, and into a confused melee of pirates. He ran up the starboard side of the main deck toward the accommodation ladder, shouting as he ran to gain attention.

"Everyone listen!" he yelled, as he stopped on the main deck and pointed back toward the deckhouse. "The hostages overpowered me and escaped, and the Americans will attack any minute. Everyone back to the deckhouse. It's more defensible. We can hold them off long enough for boats to rescue us from shore."

Ahmed turned to the nearest pirate. "The infidels took my phone," he said. "Give me yours so I can call and arrange the boats!"

The pirate hesitated.

"Now! You idiot," Ahmed yelled, and the man pulled a phone from his pocket and handed it over. Ahmed pocketed it and turned back to the milling crowd.

"What are you waiting for?" he screamed, and fired a burst from his AK near the feet of the nearest group, sending bullets whining off the steel deck and into the darkness. "Go now, or by the Beard of the Prophet, I will shoot you down myself."

The startled pirates started running toward the deckhouse, and as soon as they were all in motion, Ahmed turned and ran for the accommodation ladder. As he started down the sloping aluminum stairway, his heart sank as he heard an outboard crank and saw a man in the remaining Zodiac untying the boat from the ladder. One of the pirates was a bit smarter than the rest.

"Stop!" Ahmed screamed, and brought up his AK, but the pirate twisted the throttle and the boat roared off. Ahmed's burst hit him in the back and he toppled out of the boat, which slowed abruptly and veered against the hull, thirty feet away from the bottom landing of the accommodation ladder.

Ahmed slung his AK on his back and flew down the ladder, hardly hesitating at the bottom before diving in. He reached the boat in half a dozen strong strokes, and pulled himself aboard as angry shouts reached him from the main deck above. Their attention drawn by his gunfire, even the dullest pirate understood Ahmed was abandoning them.

He twisted the throttle and veered away from the ship in a series of erratic turns to avoid the fire of two dozen assault rifles on full automatic.

"Christ! I think that's our guy they're shooting at," the SEAL lieutenant said.

"What should I do?" the pilot asked.

"Fire a burst over their heads," the SEAL said, picking up the mike.

"Roger that," the pilot said. The chopper swooped down, gun blazing, to hover just off the ship.

"This is the United States Navy," the speaker boomed. "Lay down your weapons and raise your hands."

Weapons clattered to the deck below and hands shot in the air.

"Well, that was tough," the pilot said. "Ah, what do we do now?"

"Damned if I know," the SEAL said. "I guess we hold them here until the guys in the boats arrive."

"What about our guy in the Zodiac?"

"They didn't hit him, and he can see what's going on. I figure if he needs help, he'll either circle back or call."

Ahmed looked back over his shoulder at the chopper hovering beside the ship. He considered going back for help, but dismissed the idea. If he had any chance of finding the woman at all, he must act now. If he returned, he knew he'd be forced into a planned, structured mission, and there wasn't time. He reached over in the darkness to feel the firmness of the starboard inflation tube. It had been hit, but the leak wasn't too bad. He'd be ashore long before it was a problem.

Halfway to shore, he was no longer as confident. The starboard tube had lost over half its buoyancy and the little craft was listing. The strange trim was causing the boat to track to starboard as well, so to compensate and maintain course, he had to steer continually farther to port. The maneuver cut his forward speed by half, and the scattered lights of the harbor didn't seem to be getting any closer. That's when he noticed the port tube was leaking as well.

Reflexively, Ahmed reached into the pocket of his sodden pants and pulled out the pirate's phone, hoping by some miracle it had survived the dunking. The screen was dark and resisted all efforts to revive it. He cursed and tossed the phone over the side and stared ahead at the lights, willing the boat forward.

A half mile from shore, he figured he could still make it, even as the tubes lost most of their buoyancy and let the transom sag to the point of drowning out the outboard. There was still air left in pockets and he could ride in the collapsed mess, propelling himself with the paddle.

Unfortunately, he neglected to think about the weight of the outboard until it was too late to jettison it, and the motor pulled the whole mass from beneath him, leaving him treading water. No worries. He was a strong swimmer.

A hundred yards away, a dark fin broke the water.

CHAPTER TWENTY-TWO

DRILLSHIP *O*CEAN *G*OLIATH
ARABIAN **S**EA

Mukhtar stood swaying at the control panel, clutching the storm rail to steady himself, as he stared at the bank of brightly lit displays and bewildering profusion of controls. He concentrated, trying to remember why he was standing here, and it came to him. He was the only one left, far too weak to transfer the cylinders or man the fishing boat alone, even if he'd had the strength to throw off the lines.

That's why he was here, staring down at the controls of the dynamic positioning system, watching it work its magic unattended. He didn't understand it, but knew it contained powerful computers. Computers that monitored a satellite, then automatically adjusted the vessel's thrusters to keep her rock steady over her chosen work area more precisely than any human hand.

And somewhere in his fever-racked brain, he knew the thrusters that held the ship steady also moved her. If only he'd paid more attention when he watched the drillship crew do it. He fingered the joystick and sent up a prayer for Allah to guide him. He must get the Great Cleansing Plague ashore!

*K*YUNG *Y*ANG *N*O. 173
ARABIAN **S**EA

"Piece of shit!" Dugan said, as the screen of the ancient radar went black for the fourth time in the last hour. He gave the cabinet a hard whack with the flat of his hand, and nodded when the screen jumped back to life.

"You break my new radar! Radar OK till you come! I say Phoenix replace."

Dugan sighed and cursed his own stupidity. Ever since he'd attempted to shut Captain Kwok up by offering to charter the fishing boat on behalf of Phoenix, the little Korean had been compiling a massive repair list, which, through some tortured logic, he had deduced was the charterer's responsibility.

"Look, Kwok," he said. "This friggin' radar was *new* about twenty years—"

He was interrupted by the trill of his sat-phone. He fished it out of a pocket.

"Dugan."

"Tom. This is Jesse."

"I'm glad you called. We're almost at the location you gave us and—"

"And the drillship's not there," Ward finished his sentence.

"That's right," Dugan said. "What's up?"

"I wish I knew," Ward said. "An earlier sat photo showed her off location, but I wanted to get a follow-up on another pass to confirm. She's moving. Looks to be ten or twelve miles north of you, moving northeast at two knots."

Dugan looked back at the blinking radar, and suppressed an urge to kick it.

"I see her now. I saw that target earlier but didn't realize it was her," Dugan said. "Ah… this kind of shoots our hang-around-and-pretend-to-fish plan in the head. What do you want me to do, Jesse?"

"I don't see we have a choice," Ward said. "Just pretend you're on the same course, overtake her, and get as good a look as possible."

"Roger that," Dugan said, as he caught Kwok's eye and pointed to the radar screen. Kwok leaned over from the wheel and looked, and Dugan mimed turning. Kwok nodded and made the course change.

"We're turning for her now," Dugan said.

"ETA?"

"If she's doing two knots, we should be able to overtake her in a couple of hours if the weather holds." Dugan eyed a building thunderhead on the horizon. "But I can't guarantee that. It looks like we have a storm building to the south."

"OK. Let me know," Ward said, and hung up.

"Son of a bitch," Dugan said, as the little fishing boat overtook the drillship and moved even with her port side. The larger vessel wallowed in the moderate swells, and the top of her towering derrick cut a regular arc through the air. She was typical of her class, with an engine room aft and deckhouse and navigation bridge forward, topped with a cantilevered helipad that jutted out over her bow. But the ship design wasn't the cause of Dugan's concern.

"Sea is not so bad. Why is ship rolling so much?" Borgdanov asked.

Dugan raised his glasses and studied the ship.

"Christ," he said. "There's a lot of pipe racked back in the derrick. She's got to be top-heavy as hell. With the swell, that's got her rolling pretty good."

"What do you mean?" Borgdanov asked.

Dugan pointed. "You see that dark vertical shape inside the derrick? That's drill pipe, and it's heavy. When they're putting pipe down, it's faster if they keep sections screwed together into what they call a stand. They keep a few stands stored vertically in the derrick. But that's when they're sitting in one place. They normally lay everything flat on deck when they're moving. And she's got way more racked back in the derrick than I've ever seen." Dugan glanced over his shoulder to the south. "When this storm hits, she may capsize."

He raised the glasses again, studying the drillship as they grew closer. He started at the bow and moved aft, lingering on the fishing boat tied to the port side. The smaller vessel was bobbing erratically as it was dragged along, straining at the thick hawsers that secured it, as the two vessels intermittently banged together with hollow booms. He spotted a pile of rags on the open aft deck of the drillship, and adjusted the binoculars until the pile jumped into focus—a dead man, between two large gray mounds. There were other, smaller mounds scattered on the deck, and as he examined them more closely, Dugan realized he was looking at piles of silver coins. Coins slid from the piles as the big ship rolled, covering the deck with a fortune in silver. A fatal temptation moving toward the Omani coast, the derrick top swinging through the sky like a gigantic metronome of death.

Dugan's hand trembled as he reached for his phone.

Ward answered on the first ring.

"We got a little problem here," Dugan said.

CIA HEADQUARTERS
MARITIME THREAT ASSESSMENT
LANGLEY, VA

Ward studied the latest satellite imagery. The front was more defined now, moving toward Dugan's position, but the more imminent threat was to the west. He was reaching for the phone when it rang.

"We got a little problem here," Dugan said. "From the looks of it, everyone is dead, and I'd say the virus is definitely onboard, along with a huge pile of silver." He paused. "But on the positive side, given the condition the ship's in, this storm will probably sink her within a few hours at most."

"You don't have that long," Ward said. "We've picked up what we think are two pirate mother ships west of you, on a course for the last position of the drillship. I don't know if they're al-Shabaab or garden-variety pirates, but they're headed your way. As soon as they pick up the drillship on radar, they'll figure out it's moving and launch their high-speed attack boats."

"It doesn't matter who they are," Dugan said. "If they're after the virus, all they have to do is grab a few bodies and haul ass, and if they're after the silver, I don't think they're going to let a few bodies slow them down. It's just too damn tempting. Intentional or otherwise, these guys are going to end up carrying the virus ashore. I can send you pictures via my phone. Is that enough evidence to get a strike to sink this thing before the pirates get here?"

"Maybe," Ward said. "But that's not the problem. Even if we sink her with a missile or air strike, we can't get anyone else there quickly enough to police the wreckage. There'll be debris and infected bodies floating around when the pirates arrive. If your visitors are al-Shabaab, they may harvest a few. And no matter who they are, chances are they'll pick up any floating bodies to take them ashore for a proper Muslim burial." Ward sighed. "Either way, we're screwed. If the virus gets off the ship, there's no way we'll ever be able to contain it. According to Imamura, the only way to kill the virus is to burn the bodies."

"At least you might have some time to start distributing a vaccine," Dugan said.

Ward said nothing.

"Jesse? Are you there?" Dugan asked.

"Yeah," Ward said. "I'm still here, but, ahh… there is no vaccine, Tom. Imamura worked on one for over fifty years and came up dry."

"Holy Mother of God!" Dugan said. "What's the mortality rate?"

"A minimum of seventy percent," Ward said. "Imamura speculated it would be much higher. If everyone on the drillship is dead, that would make it a hundred percent." Ward paused. "Tom, if this isn't contained…"

"Yeah, I can figure that part out, Jesse."

Ward said nothing, and the silence grew. Dugan broke it at last. "Look, Jesse, we're not equipped to deal with this. I wouldn't know where to start. Aren't there any other naval forces nearby?"

"Sure, a few. Chinese, Indian, Russian. Take your pick. They all have ships in the area as part of the anti-piracy effort. Do you really want any of those guys getting access to this bug? Hell, I don't even want our side to get it. Everyone will pay lip service to destroying it, but the temptation to keep 'just a little for research purposes' will be great."

Dugan cursed, then lapsed into silence again.

Ward waited a bit, then asked, "What are you going to do, Tom?"

"Not a clue," Dugan said. "But I guess I better figure something out. And by the way, Jesse, thanks for dropping me in the crapper again."

Ward heard a click.

KYUNG YANG NO. 173
ARABIAN SEA

"You don't have to go," Dugan said.

Borgdanov shrugged. "I am Russian, so I am fatalist. And if what Ward says is true, we will all die in few months anyway. If I must die, I prefer to die trying to prevent epidemic." He smiled at Sergeant Denosovitch, who was nodding in agreement. "And besides, without us, who will look after you, *Dyed*?"

"Well, thanks anyway," Dugan said.

The corporal said something in Russian and the others laughed, as Dugan looked on, a question on his face.

"Corporal Anisimov says Ilya and I must go with you to keep you alive to sign bonus check at end of mission. He has already picked out nice car," Borgdanov said.

Dugan smiled wanly and bent to apply more duct tape to the juncture between his survival suit and rubber boot. He, Borgdanov, and Denosovitch were dressed in bulky bright-orange cold-water survival suits they'd pilfered from the emergency-gear locker of the *Kyung Yang No. 173*. They were the typical Gumby suits with integral mittens and booties, designed to be donned over clothing. At least they *had* sported integral mittens and booties until Dugan had cut off the clumsy appendages at the ankle and wrist, enduring outraged screams from Captain Kwok as he did so.

"You cut survival suit!" Kwok screamed. "This no good. Suits very expensive. Phoenix pay, I tell you."

The look on Dugan's face and the knife in his hand had forestalled further protests, and the little Korean had hurried back to the wheelhouse to record this latest outrage on his growing list of expenses.

The initial roominess of the suits and Dugan's impromptu modifications meant that, stripped to their underwear, Dugan and the two much larger Russians could fit in the suits sized for the much smaller Korean crewmen. For all of that, the suits were tight, snug on

Dugan and approaching skintight on the Russians, and all three looked like gangly teenage boys after growth spurts, with wrists and ankles exposed.

The foul-weather-gear locker yielded three pairs of rubber boots they could squeeze their feet into and some long rubber gloves that would provide much better manual dexterity than the clumsy mittens Dugan cut off the suits. The trio had donned the boots and gloves and then slipped the sleeves and legs of the survival suits down over them before taping the resultant seams with duct tape. With the tight-fitting hoods of the survival suits in place and the full-faced tear-gas masks the Russians had in their gear, the trio would be about as microbe-proof as was possible, considering the circumstances.

And hot as hell. Suits designed to prevent hypothermia in arctic waters were not the most comfortable apparel in near-equatorial heat. Dugan could already feel the sweat puddling in his boots. He pressed the last piece of tape into place and straightened, finding Borgdanov holding a gas mask and eyeing it skeptically.

"Do you think masks will do any good, *Dyed*?" he asked. "They are for tear gas. I think not so good for biologicals."

"Ward says the main mode of transmission is contact, except when the stuff's embedded in a powder medium and intentionally delivered as an aerosol. If the masks will filter out the powder, we should be OK." Dugan grimaced. "And it's not like we have anything else."

Borgdanov nodded, and Dugan continued. "Christ," he said. "We better get this done before we die of heat stroke. Get the corporal here up in the wheelhouse to keep an eye on Kwok. When we're ready to leave, I want to make sure our ride's still around."

Borgdanov nodded and spoke to the corporal in Russian. The man moved toward the wheelhouse as Dugan and the two other Russians pulled on their hoods, donned their gas masks, and moved to the bow of the fishing boat. The pocketless survival suits complicated things a bit, so the trio had improvised. The big sergeant had an assault rifle slung across his body in one direction and a coil of rope in the other, almost like crossed bandoliers. Borgdanov and Dugan both carried small backpacks. The Russian's holding a radio, a Glock, flash-bang grenades, and spare ammunition for both the assault rifle and the Glock. They didn't anticipate resistance, but they could hardly go into the unknown unarmed. Dugan's backpack held tools and other things he'd pilfered from the fishing boat—anything he anticipated he might need for his half-formed plan.

They'd spotted the rope ladder earlier, trailing down the starboard side just forward of the after house. Dugan surmised it was how the pirates had come aboard initially. They hadn't bothered to pull it in. A lucky break, because boarding the rolling drillship would be tough, even if they weren't covered from head to toe in rubber.

Dugan watched the ladder now as Kwok inched the fishing boat toward it. As the drillship rolled toward them, the bottom of the ladder swung away from the hull, only to reverse course and slam back against the hull as the big ship rolled away. Far too soon, they were alongside the ladder, and as it swung toward the fishing vessel, Sergeant Denosovitch scampered over the rail and stepped on the bottom tread, grasping the vertical ropes of the ladder in each hand. As Dugan had advised him, he kept only his toes on the ladder rungs and his hands on the ropes, not the wooden rungs—advice that served him well when the ladder slammed back against the hull.

On the next out-swing, the sergeant climbed two rungs before he had to brace himself for the swing into the hull, and on the out-swing after that, he managed four. The higher he got, the closer the ladder stayed to the ship's side. Dugan watched from below as the Russian scaled the ladder with ease. *Frigging showoff.*

In no time the sergeant peered down at them from the deck of the drillship. He slipped the coil of rope from his shoulder and lowered the end to where Dugan and Borgdanov waited. Borgdanov grabbed the dangling rope and threaded it through the straps of the backpacks as Dugan held them up. Borgdanov tied a knot expertly and signaled the sergeant, who hoisted the backpacks aboard. As the backpacks ascended, Dugan crawled over the rail.

He stood facing outward, his feet on the gunwale, gripping the waist-high rail at his back with one hand, sweat pooling in his boots not just from the heat. The end of the rope came down again, this time with a loop tied in it, and Dugan grabbed it with one hand. In a brief moment of machismo, he considered refusing the safety line. A very brief moment. He dragged the loop over his head and under his arms. Moments later he felt the rope snug up across his chest, as above, the sergeant took a turn around the handrail and took slack out of the line.

Dugan watched the ladder swing back toward him and tensed to make the step, but at the last second his nerve failed. He clung to the rail of the fishing boat, just as Kwok overcorrected to pull a bit away from the drillship. As the vessels separated and the drillship rolled away, the rope bit into Dugan's chest to rip him from the rail, and he saw the black expanse of the hull rushing toward him.

50 YARDS FROM THE BEACH
HARARDHEERE, SOMALIA

Ahmed saw the fin again from the corner of his eye and murmured a silent prayer to Allah. From what he could see in the moonlight, it wasn't a huge shark, perhaps five or six feet, but it was plenty big enough to kill a defenseless swimmer. And he was, for all intents and purposes, defenseless. He'd jettisoned his AK when the boat sank, and though he still had the Glock stuck in his waistband, he knew the shark would strike from the dark depths before he ever saw it. Once he was crippled, he'd no doubt other sharks would join the feeding frenzy. As if confirming that grim thought, he spotted a second fin to his left as he turned his head to breathe. Ahmed banished such thoughts and focused on the distant shore. *There is no God but Allah, and Muhammad is the Messenger of Allah,* he repeated to hold dark thoughts at bay.

First contact was a brush against his leg, filling him with terror. A terror unabated as he stroked even harder for shore and felt the brush of a large body against his side. They were toying with him, like a cat with a mouse before the kill. He felt hard contact to his chest as he was lifted clear of the water, and clutched at the gray mass below him, shocked and bewildered. A blast of air and water erupted in his face.

Ahmed wiped his eyes with the back of a hand and blinked down at what he realized was a dolphin's blowhole inches below his face. The dolphin submerged, and Ahmed treaded water as elation replaced terror.

"*Allahu Akbar,*" he shouted into the night sky, then turned to stroke hard for the beach. Around him, dolphins rolled and leaped from the water, shedding droplets that gleamed silver in the moonlight.

Arnett felt the bag shift on the man's shoulder, followed by a short sensation of weightlessness—too short for her to prepare herself for the landing. She grunted as she landed flat on her back and air rushed from her lungs, and then struggled with the horrible feeling of being unable to take a breath. She heard the zipper an inch from her nose and smelled the khat on Toothless's breath as he leaned over to unzip the bag. Dim light leaked around the edges of the duct tape over her eyes, and the canvas shifted beneath her as Toothless upended the open bag and turned her out face-down on the floor. Rough concrete scraped Arnett's cheek and she smelled animal dung, just before rough hands rolled her onto her back.

"Where is your smart mouth now, whore?" Toothless asked.

Arnett sucked in air until she was able to respond.

"You… your brea… breath smells worse than the goat shit on this floor, asshole. Don't you own a toothbrush? Oh, that's right. You don't have many teeth left, do you?"

The savage kick landed in her side, and she was unable to suppress a moan at the unseen assault. Then she sensed Toothless leaning over her again, his closeness confirmed by his fetid breath and spittle spraying on her face as he spoke.

"That's right, whore. Moan," Toothless said. "Soon you'll have even more reason to moan as I fill your holes with my manhood."

Her head was jerked to the left by a vicious openhanded slap.

"Lie here and think about that," Toothless said. "I must gather supplies before the infidels decide to strike our safe house. And perhaps I'll have a cup of tea and a bite to eat. Whore-training is hard work, and I must keep my strength up."

She heard Toothless laughing as he moved away from her. The light leaking around her blindfold lessened—Toothless was apparently taking the light source with him. Moments later, she heard the complaining squeak of an un-oiled hinge followed by the rattle of a chain. Then an engine started and faded, and all was quiet.

Arnett rolled onto her stomach and inched her knees forward, elevating her butt and grinding her face into the foul-smelling concrete. She pushed her bound wrists toward her butt, trying to get her butt through the circle of her bound arms to get her hands in front of her. The first attempt wasn't close—nor was the twenty-first. She was sweating now, her panic rising at the thought of Toothless's return. She made herself relax and imagined her body was rubber, stretchable at her whim. She focused on her shoulders, willing muscles to relax, glorying in each fractional gain, until her wrists were below her butt and she was—stuck!

She was a tortured pretzel, her shoulders burning now, unable to continue or to return her hands to their previous position behind her back. Her right cheek was scraped raw on the rough concrete. Arnett threw her weight to the right and rolled up on her butt, her hands partially pinned beneath her. She took a deep breath, drew her knees to her chin, and pulled up on her arms with all her might to slide her bound wrists past her butt. Something tore in her left shoulder and she felt blinding pain, and then her wrists were under her knees. Arnett collapsed onto her right side, gasping at the pain in her shoulder, on the verge of passing out. She fought down nausea and forced herself to bring her knees to her chest once again, and worked her feet out of the circle of her bound arms.

Her shoulder throbbed and her left arm was useless. She tried raising her bound hands to loosen the tape around her eyes, but the required movement was too painful. She had to separate her hands first so she could immobilize the left one. She tried rolling onto her left side to support her left arm on the floor, as she lowered her head and gnawed at the tape binding her wrists. The adhesive tasted bitter in her mouth, and bits of tape stuck to her lips, but finally, the tape parted.

She moaned as she sat back up, holding her left arm tight against her side and picking at the tape circling her head with her good right hand. Her fingers found the end and picked it free. She unwound the tape quickly until she got to the last round stuck to her hair, then squeezed her eyes shut and gave one final jerk, hardly flinching as the tape tore at her hair.

Arnett blinked in the dim light. She was in some sort of dilapidated outbuilding, one that had housed livestock from the smell. It was poorly constructed and cracks in the plank walls let in moonlight that striped the rough floor. She reached down with her good hand to free her ankles. It was a matter of feel versus sight in the dim light, but her fingers found the tiny ridge that marked the end of the tape and picked it free. It unwound in one long strip.

Her first thought was escape, and she struggled to her feet and found the door in the dark. It yielded a half inch, then stopped with a metallic rattle, chained shut from the outside. She took a step back and the movement sent a stabbing pain down her left arm. She had to attend to that.

Arnett retraced her steps, kneeling and groping for the discarded tape with her good hand. She found it and fashioned a large loop with part of the tape, then tore the rest of the strip away by holding it in her teeth and tearing with her good hand. She slipped the loop over her head as a sling to support the weight of her useless left arm, then used the rest of the tape to circle her slight torso twice, immobilizing her now-supported arm against her body. Crude but effective.

Hurting and exhausted, Arnett leaned against the wall and tried to figure out what to do next.

A half-hour later, she clutched the handle she'd broken off an old rake found in the corner of the shed behind a stack of mud bricks. It had taken what seemed like forever to carry the bricks to the duffel bag, one at a time in her good hand. When the bag would hold no more, she'd managed to zip it. It was barely visible on the dim moonlight-striped floor.

She knew she had to kill Diriyi. Her guess was he'd brought her here on the spur of the moment and no one knew he'd done so; otherwise, there'd be a crowd, eager to participate in her rape. If his body was found, his death would be a mystery. If found alive, he'd raise the alarm.

Arnett pressed the end of the short rake handle against her useless left arm, testing the sharpness of the jagged point at the broken end. It wasn't much of a weapon, wielded by an exhausted and brutalized woman with a wrecked shoulder against an armed adversary. However, the odds seemed a bit better when you considered she was Lynda Arnett, five times Isshinyru Karate National Champion in the Black Belt Weapons Division. Her weapon of choice was the traditional Okinawan short sword, the *sai*.

Arnett closed her eyes and centered herself, visualizing Toothless in her mind's eye and mentally walking through her strike a half dozen times, each time changing Toothless's reaction and the necessary response on her part. When she'd covered the possibilities mentally, she practiced them physically in slow motion, testing every footfall, feeling the wooden rod in her hand. She'd reached the point of trying them full speed with her eyes closed when her heart leaped into her throat. A car engine!

Diriyi smiled to himself as he parked the SUV. The town was abuzz with the news of the American attack, and the few occupants of the al-Shabaab safe house had fled, fearing an

American retaliatory strike ashore. That the cowards had left in haste had been obvious, and they left plenty of food and provisions.

It was strange how these things worked out. Mukhtar's gamble on the drillship had gone wrong, and Diriyi's gut told him he would never see the man again. The fool had risked everything to get the nerve gas, and for what? Fame as the most effective fighter of the jihad? Notoriety as the favored of Allah who had slain the most infidels? Such delusions of grandeur were invariably costly. Now there'd be few of al-Shabaab left, and Diriyi was the most visible. He'd no intention of becoming the recipient of the Americans' wrath. He'd lay low awhile, then return to a life of piracy. After, of course, he'd enjoyed and killed the woman. Who knows, perhaps in a year or so he could claim a reward for leading the Americans to her grave. His smile widened.

Diriyi glanced in the back of the SUV before he got out. He'd enough provisions for several weeks. He'd have to cut some brush to camouflage the SUV, but that could wait. It hadn't yet begun to lighten in the east. Time for a little romp with the whore. He grew hard at the thought, and reached down to touch himself through his trousers.

He picked his way down the path to the goat shed in the light of the battery-powered lantern. The key turned in the padlock, and the chain rattled as he pulled it through the door handle. The dry hinge squealed its lament as he pushed the door inward. Time for some fun.

"Are you ready for some fun, whore?" he asked. He held the lantern high and moved into the shed, the complaining door swinging shut behind him.

Diriyi stopped, puzzled. The duffel bag, obviously full, was just visible at the edge of the circle of light cast by the lantern, but he couldn't see the woman. Then he understood and laughed.

"So you think you can hide from me in the bag, like an ostrich with its head in the sand? You are truly a stupid bitch. Giving me pleasure is going to be the only thing of value you will ever accomplish in your short life."

Diriyi held the lantern high and covered the short distance in a few long strides, aiming a savage kick at where he figured the woman's stomach would be.

Arnett stood with her back to the wall on the hinge side of the door as the door swung shut behind Toothless, revealing his back. She heard his derisive words, and nodded as he moved forward and drew his leg back to kick the bag. It was the response she'd hoped for, and she was moving even before the toe of his running shoe contacted the pile of bricks.

Toothless screamed as the toes of his right foot shattered, and he stumbled back, dropping the lantern, which flickered but didn't go out.

"Toothless!" yelled Arnett, and the pirate turned toward her, reaching for the Glock in his waistband. Too late.

"Kiii… aiii!" screamed Arnett, just as the jagged end of the rake handle contacted the man's Adam's apple and she threw her hip to put all her body weight and momentum into the blow. The wood ripped through voice box, jugular vein, and esophagus, and impacted the pirate's cervical vertebrae, forcing him backward even as he sank to the ground. Arnett drew her makeshift weapon back sharply, and arterial blood gushed from the gaping wound, spraying her before she could jump away.

Toothless lay on his back on top of the bag of bricks, blood pumping from the hole where his throat had been, moving his lips in wordless comprehension. His eyes fluttered shut and his lips stopped moving, and the air in the shed became even more foul as he lost sphincter control. Arnett stood motionless, staring down at him in the soft glow of the overturned lantern.

The trembling started in her good right hand and got increasingly violent. The bloodied stake slipped from her grasp, and the palsy spread to her legs, which buckled. She fell to her knees and retched, adding the stench of her own vomit to the miasma of death and goat dung. She felt an urgent need to flee and dragged herself toward the door on her three functioning limbs, the rough concrete punishing her hand and shredding her pants at the knees.

The door squeaked as she clawed it open and crawled into the moonlight, collapsing against the rough plank wall. She was suddenly very cold, even in the equatorial night, and she shivered uncontrollably. Shivers turned to sobs—whimpers at first, then growing to deep, wracking cries of anguish and freely flowing tears. Tears of sorrow for Gomez and the other dead crewman, tears of relief that she'd escaped Toothless, and finally tears of rage at the murderers that had done this to her and her crew. She hugged herself with her good arm and let her emotions out, crying until she was drained and exhausted.

Arnett jerked awake with the sun in her eyes, enraged at herself for falling asleep. She struggled to her feet. All her joints were stiff and her left arm and shoulder throbbed. She saw the SUV parked fifty yards away beside a dirt track, at the end of a narrow footpath through low brush and small boulders. There wasn't a house in sight.

She moved back into the shed, breathing through her mouth to avoid the stench, and knelt to pull the Glock from the dead pirate's waistband. A search of his pockets yielded another full magazine, a sat-phone, and car keys. She stuck the Glock in her waistband and pocketed the other things before she turned toward the shed door.

Arnett froze at a sound from outside, then bolted to the wall seconds before the door flew open and banged against her. The door swung closed to reveal Traitor, gun in hand, kneeling over Toothless with his back to Arnett. She raised the Glock in her right hand and drew a bead on the back of Traitor's head. Her hand trembled not at all as her finger tightened on the trigger.

CHAPTER TWENTY-THREE

M/T *Marie Floyd*
Arabian Sea
En route to Harardheere, Somalia

Captain Vince Blake paced the bridge, glancing at the speed log each time he passed. A building south wind on the beam steadily increased the swell, and the old tanker had a pronounced roll now—and a speed of 13.5 knots, despite the chief engineer's best efforts to coax more from the tired old engine.

Blake's pacing was interrupted by the buzz of the sat-phone.

"*Marie Floyd*, Captain speaking," he answered.

"Captain Blake, this is Ray Hanley. The navy boys took back the *Luther Hurd* last night—"

"How's the crew? Everyone all right?"

"Just the two guys we already knew about," Hanley said. "Jones, the acting captain, was injured, but not seriously."

"Don't you mean acting chief mate? Arnett's the capt…" Blake's voice trailed off. "You… you said there were no more deaths. Why is Stan Jones acting captain? What about Lynda?" Blake asked at last.

"Truth is, we don't know," Hanley said. "They took her ashore just before the attack. All we can do at this point is hold a good thought for her."

Blake didn't trust himself to respond. He composed himself, then changed the subject. "How about the other ships? Any more executions?"

"Two days, two dead seamen," Hanley said. "Just like the bastards threatened."

Blake glanced at the speed log and resisted an impulse to punch the control console.

"Maybe we should tell them we're coming with hostages of our own," Blake said. "And tell them to hold off executions until we get there."

"Except we don't know where all their boats are," Hanley said. "If they figure out where all their missing buddies are before you get under the protection of the USS *Carney* and the other navy ships off Somalia, you can bet they'll swarm you. Don't forget, this little operation of ours is totally off the books. We can pull up next to the navy boys and the pirates will *think* we're under their protection, but the truth is, none of the Western governments want to touch our little privateering operation with a ten-foot pole. They'll help us by ignoring us, but that's as far as it goes. Tough as it is, we have to stick with the plan."

Blake sighed. "I understand. We're almost ready."

"What do you mean, *almost*? You should be done."

"We are here," Blake replied. "Woody has the whole gang finishing up *Pacific Endurance*." Blake turned as he spoke and looked across at where *Pacific Endurance* was keeping station with him, a mile away.

"Hey, Junior. Get your ass up here," Woody called down into the tank.

Seconds later, Junior West's head and shoulders emerged from the open expansion trunk of number-one starboard cargo tank, a welding hood tilted back and a cap worn backward under the hood soaked with sweat.

"Whatcha need, Woody?" asked Junior. "You're holding up progress."

"Where are you?"

"Last seam. Maybe three feet," Junior said. "Course, that's just the first pass. I figure I ought to give 'em all at least one more."

"No need," said Woody. "Just seal all the seams with epoxy. It ain't like it's a permanent job."

Junior nodded. "Whatever you say. You think this is gonna work?"

"Don't see why not," Woody replied. "All any pirate opening the tank cover or the ullage hatch is gonna see is gasoline. They won't know they're looking at a six-foot-square box with a couple of tons at most and that the rest of the tank is full of seawater. The digital readout in the cargo control room will show the tanks all full."

Woody shrugged. "And even if they're suspicious enough to gauge the tanks by hand, those funnels and capped pipes we have rigged to line up under the ullage hatches will let the tape go all the way to the tank bottom and show gasoline all the way." Woody smiled. "I gotta admit, that Dugan's smart."

Junior nodded, and started back down into the tank.

"Junior," Woody said, and Junior stopped and looked over. "Don't forget to cut a couple of little holes in the tops of the walls of the false tanks so the inert gas can equalize. Put 'em way up at the top, right below the main deck where nobody can see 'em. I don't know how savvy these pirates are, but I don't want any of them getting suspicious 'cause there's no inert-gas blanket on the cargo."

Junior nodded again and disappeared into the tank.

DRILLSHIP *OCEAN GOLIATH*
ARABIAN SEA

The black hull rushed toward Dugan as he threw his weight to the side, attempting to spin on the rope. At the last moment, he twisted in flight and his back slapped against the hull, snapping his head against the steel with a dull thud, cushioned by the thick neoprene of the survival-suit hood. The impact drove the air from his lungs. He clung to the rope and saw stars and fought to retain consciousness.

He saw Borgdanov at the rail of the fishing boat, screaming up at the deck of the drillship and gesturing wildly. Then Dugan was moving again, almost in slow motion at first, then rushing toward Borgdanov as the drillship rolled and Kwok overcorrected again, sending the fishing boat charging at the drillship. Dugan dipped into the water to his knees, staring up helplessly at Borgdanov as the bow of the fishing boat towered above him on the crest of an approaching swell. He squeezed his eyes shut in anticipation of being crushed between the steel hulls.

Then the rope bit his chest even harder, and he was jerked upward as the drillship reached the end of her roll and started back in the opposite direction. Dugan opened his eyes to see Borgdanov flash by, as if Dugan was ascending past him on an express elevator. A strong hand grabbed his leg, and he heard a thunderous crash and the screech of steel on steel as the rope slackened its grip on his chest and he felt himself falling—not swinging now, but straight down.

Dugan landed on top of Borgdanov, driving him to the deck of the fishing boat some feet back from the mangled handrail. He heard muffled Russian curses below him, as Borgdanov rolled him off and got to his feet before reaching down to help Dugan. Dugan took the offered hand and pulled himself up.

Borgdanov put his facemask against Dugan's so he could be heard over the engine. "Are you injured, *Dyed*?"

"Ju-just my pride," Dugan said, as his breath returned. "Thanks."

The Russian gestured up toward the drillship. "Is thanks to Ilya. He pulled very hard when you were in water, and then released rope at just right moment so I can pull you in. We are very lucky, I think."

Dugan stepped back and nodded before waving up at the sergeant, who returned his wave. He took in the situation. Kwok was maintaining station next to the drillship, and Dugan could make out a steady stream of abuse in English and Korean coming through the open window of the wheelhouse, even with the noise and the mask. He had no doubt the little Korean was tallying repair expenses mentally, even as he maneuvered his boat. There was a sizable dent in the hull of the drillship, and the gunwale of *Kyung Yang No. 173* was set in a good eighteen inches, with the attached handrail mangled. Dugan had a fleeting thought about Woody's cement-box patches and put it out of his mind. First things first. He put his facemask against Borgdanov's.

"OK. Let's try this again. Do you think you should remind Ilya to make damn sure I'm on the ladder before he snubs up the safety line?"

Borgdanov smiled through the mask. "*Nyet*. I think he remembers now."

Dugan nodded and moved to the side of the boat. He jumped on the ladder without hesitation this time, and ten terrifying seconds later, he crawled over the handrail onto the deck of the drillship. Borgdanov was on the ladder and starting up as soon as Dugan cleared the rail, and the *Kyung Yang No. 173* moved away to trail the drillship.

As previously agreed, the Russians armed themselves and took the lead, communicating with long-familiar hand signals. The ship's movement was different than the fishing boat's, more extreme due to the weight of the pipe in the derrick but less erratic. Dugan cast a worried look at the storm clouds to the south. The seas were coming from the starboard quarter now, striking the vessel diagonally on the stern. If the wind and waves shifted to the beam, things could deteriorate quickly. He pushed the thought from his mind and fell in behind the Russians.

Besides the single body they'd already spotted on the open deck, they found several more in the deckhouse passageways. When they pushed open the crew lounge, Dugan almost lost it. Bodies were everywhere, leaking blood and fluids. It was all he could do to keep from vomiting in his mask. He closed the door, and they began a room-by-room search of the rest of the quarters, faster now, sure they would encounter no armed resistance.

They found two more bodies in upper-deck rooms and encountered the last one on the bridge, lying in a pool of his own blood and vomit on the deck next to the dynamic positioning console. Dugan studied the bank of flashing video monitors on the DP console and considered trying to bring the vessel's bow into the weather. One look at the controls dissuaded him. He didn't know the system, and this wasn't the time for on-the-job training. He could make things worse.

Instead, he gestured the two Russians close. Without the noise of the fishing boat engine, they could hear each other better now, but they still had to yell to communicate through the masks and hoods.

"I think that's all of them," Dugan yelled. "We need to get all the bodies into the crew lounge with the rest so we can burn them." He looked at Borgdanov. "If the sergeant can do that, I need to show you something."

The two Russians nodded, and the sergeant moved toward the body, but Dugan caught his arm. "Don't touch them directly," Dugan said, and pointed to the curtain between the chart room and the main area of the bridge. "Throw a curtain or shower curtain over the bodies and then roll them over onto it. Then you can drag them down the stairs or into the elevator without touching them any more than you have to. After you get the bodies taken care of, find the laundry and look for some bleach. Slosh it over any body fluids on the deck."

The sergeant looked confused. "Bletch?" he said.

"*Klornogo otbelivatelya*," the major said, and the sergeant nodded his understanding before moving to tear down the chart-room curtain.

Dugan motioned Borgdanov to follow, and led him out the bridge door and up the external stairway to the helideck perched high over the bow of the drillship. He found the nearest fire station, freed the fire monitor, and swiveled it to point overboard before opening the valve wide to send a stream of water arcing over the ship's side. He left it there, and with the Russian in tow, crossed the helideck to the fire station on the opposite side of the ship and repeated the operation.

"These monitors will spray water until I stop the fire pump and drain the line," Dugan said. "That may take a few minutes. While that's happening and Ilya is moving the bodies, I want you to look for the gas cylinders. According to Ward, they look something like scuba tanks. When you find them, put them with the bodies in the crew lounge. Get the sergeant to help you when he finishes with the bodies."

Borgdanov nodded, and Dugan continued. "But remember, while you're doing that, keep an eye up here on these monitors. If you see diesel shooting over the side, one of you needs to get up here quick and close the valves. Got it?"

"*Da*. As you explained on the boat, I understand."

Dugan nodded and headed for the stairs.

Sweat squished between Dugan's toes as he raced down the external stairs on the port side of the deckhouse. Only the fact that the boots were tight kept his feet from slipping around inside them. He hit the main deck and moved aft toward the machinery casing, his footing made even more treacherous by the loose layer of silver coins shifting across the open deck with each roll of the ship.

He slipped twice, the second time falling to his hands and knees as the ship took a hard roll to port. He froze at the metallic clang of drill pipe shifting in the towering derrick beside him, then breathed a sigh of relief as the vessel began to right herself. His relief was short-lived.

There was a thunderous boom, and he felt the steel deck vibrate through his gloves as the pirates' fishing vessel once again lost its fight with the mooring lines holding it captive and surged back against the side of the drillship. Dugan struggled to his feet on the tilting deck. *Christ!* How the hell did he get into this mess? He swallowed his fear and pressed aft to the machinery casing, hoping the layout wasn't too different from what he was used to.

He found the main fire pumps on a lower level, turned off the one that was running, and closed the discharge valve before dropping into the bilge to trace the system piping. He found the drain valve a few feet away. Water gushed over his legs and into the bilge when he opened it, cooling him a bit. He was tempted to linger, but he had no time. Truth be told, not even enough time to drain the system properly—there would be water trapped in branch lines unless he opened the valves on every single fire station—but that didn't matter. Opening the two monitors at the very top of the system would allow enough air into the system to drain the main line and allow it to vent when he refilled it. That would have to do. Reluctantly, Dugan climbed out of the cool bilge in pursuit of his next objective.

He spotted the centrifugal purifiers first, and found the diesel-oil transfer pump not far away. He traced the pump discharge piping until he found what he needed—a branch line about the same size as a fire hose—then traced the system farther, closing valves as he found them, isolating the branch line.

The hacksaw he'd taken from the Korean boat was old and dull. Undoubtedly, there were better tools aboard the drillship, but he had little time to find them and figured they might be under lock and key. His hands were sweating in the clumsy rubber gloves, and he almost lost his grip on the saw several times before it began to bite into the pipe. When he penetrated the top of the pipe, diesel gushed out, covering his hands and making the pipe and saw slick under his rubber gloves.

Dugan bore down hard on the saw and his right arm ached with the effort, as the dull blade sank through the pipe with glacial slowness. The pipe finally parted with a snap, and Dugan lurched forward as the hacksaw slipped from his grasp and clattered in the bilge below. *Good riddance!* He moved to the nearest fire station.

He cut the fitting off the end of the hose with a knife from his backpack and dragged the hose to the severed diesel line. The hose slipped over the end of the pipe easily. It was a bit bigger than the pipe, and it might leak, but he prayed it would hold long enough. Five minutes later, the hose was clamped securely to the pipe with a half dozen stainless-steel hose clamps scavenged from the fishing boat.

Water dribbled from the fire-system drain valve in a feeble stream, intermittently petering out then increasing with each roll of the ship. Close enough. Dugan shut the drain valve, lined up the other valves in his jury-rigged system, and started the diesel-oil transfer pump. The pump growled to life and the flat fire hose ballooned to a cylindrical shape as diesel gushed through it to fill the fire main. *So far, so good.* He rushed up a steep stairway to the engine control room.

The ballast control console was straightforward, and the mimic board allowed him to understand the system immediately. He started a single ballast pump, opened and closed several remotely operated valves, and then left the engine room to dash up the stairs and pick his way forward over the shifting silver carpet of the open deck. The ship took another bad roll, accompanied by the thunderous boom of the fishing boat against the side and a sound like a huge slot machine disgorging a jackpot, as coins spilled from the last intact pile to skitter across the deck.

He spotted the Russians on the starboard side, each with a cylinder on their shoulder, and worked his way across the pitching deck.

"Are the monitors—"

"Do not worry, *Dyed*," Borgdanov said. "Ilya closed monitor valves."

Dugan glanced at the sergeant and saw confirmation in the stain on his legs where diesel had splashed him.

"And I found cylinders," Borgdanov said. "Thirty-seven in two cargo baskets near crane. These are the last two."

Dugan nodded and fell in behind the Russians, just as the captive fishing boat banged against the hull again.

The Yemeni fishing boat Mukhtar had hijacked had seen better days when her previous—recently deceased—owner had acquired her a decade earlier. Maintenance since had been as needed, leaving her thinning hull a patchwork of steel of various thicknesses, held together by welds of indifferent quality. It was a miracle she had survived pounding against the stronger hull of the drillship as long as she had.

But even miracles have limits, and the repeated hammer blows took their toll. Steel bent and welds cracked, spreading through hull plating and frames as well. Water wept through the hull in a dozen places. Then the weeps became trickles; the trickles, streams; and the boat, heavy with water, moved more ponderously as it wallowed low in the water beside the drillship, straining on the lines that held it there.

CHAPTER TWENTY-FOUR

Ahmed squatted beside Diriyi's lifeless body. The ripped throat, blood pool, and stench left no doubt the man was dead. He wasn't surprised that he'd found Diriyi—Harardheere was spread out, but still easily covered on foot by a man fit enough to run at a steady pace. And Diriyi hadn't been popular. The few people that had seen his tricked-out SUV pass were only too happy to share that information with Ahmed. That same SUV on the side of the road led Ahmed to the shed.

He was surprised, however, to find Diriyi dead and the woman missing, and that complicated things. Known now as a man of shifting loyalties, his alter ego, Gaal, was undoubtedly unpopular with the various pirate gangs that called Harardheere home. He'd no doubt that the same people so eager to point out Diriyi would be equally happy to point him out to anyone interested. His best option was to rescue the woman and call for extraction. There were two problems with that, of course—he couldn't find the woman and he had no means to call anyone. Ahmed held the Glock in his right hand and began to search Diriyi's pockets with his left. Diriyi's cell phone would solve at least one of those problems.

The sound behind him was less than a whisper, but enough. He dived to the right as a bullet whistled past his ear. He landed on his shoulder and followed through in a tumbling roll, ending up with his Glock trained on—the woman!

"Don't shoot!" Ahmed said. "I'm on your side. Sergeant Al Ahmed, US Army Special Forces."

The woman's own gun was trained on Ahmed's forehead from less than five feet away, and it didn't waver. "Pleased to meet you," she said. "I'm Queen Elizabeth. Drop the gun! Now!"

Ahmed considered the situation. He couldn't shoot the woman, so holding a gun on her was rather pointless. He bent, keeping both hands in sight, and laid the gun on the concrete floor.

"I've been undercover the whole time," Ahmed said. "I helped the chief engineer and the others escape, and then I came after you."

"Really?" the woman said. "Seems like the last thing I recall was you coming up to the captain's quarters to help Toothless here stuff me in a duffel bag."

"He zapped me with the stun gun too," Ahmed said. "That's why I couldn't stop him from taking you."

"I guess I missed that part, though I do remember you holding a gun to my head and pulling the trigger."

"An empty gun," Ahmed said.

"That would carry a bit more weight with me if we hadn't both found out it was empty at the same time," the woman said.

Ahmed shrugged. "I suspected. The terrorists disarmed me when I came aboard. They were unlikely to hand me a loaded gun before I proved my loyalty. Then Mukhtar turned away from me when he racked the slide to fake chambering a round, and when he did hand me the gun, it felt light, like the magazine was empty. And besides, if they planned to test me, I didn't think they'd waste a high-value hostage like you. So I was pretty sure."

"Pretty sure?" she asked, her face reddening. "Did you say *PRETTY SURE*?"

Ahmed shrugged again. "It was a calculated risk."

Her hand twitched and the gun barked. Ahmed's hand flew to where his left earlobe had been.

"You stupid bitch!" he screamed. "You could've killed me!"

She stared at him with ice-cold eyes as he clutched his bleeding ear. "A calculated risk," she replied. "And if I wanted to kill you, there'd be a hole between your eyes. But as you've probably figured out, I don't believe your little fairy tale. That is, I'm ninety-nine percent sure it's a lie. That one percent is keeping you alive, so here's what we're going to do. If you're who you say you are, you must have a contact. Someone who can convince me you're legit. So you're going to call them now and let me talk to them. Got it?"

"My phone was trashed when I went in the water," Ahmed said. "I was about to take Diriyi's when you shot at me."

"I already took his phone." She grimaced in obvious pain as she worked her left arm out of a makeshift sling and free of tape wrappings to dig in her front pocket. She produced a phone and held it out with a shaky left hand, all the while keeping him covered with the Glock in her right.

"Call whoever you need to," she said, "but don't say a word. I don't want you warning anyone or giving away our position. You hand it back to me as soon as it starts ringing, and so help me God, if I hear as much as a peep out of you, you'll get a bullet in the head. Is that clear?"

"Very clear," Ahmed said, as he dialed.

A moment later he held the phone out, and the woman took it with her left hand and held it to her ear.

Arnett glared at Traitor and listened to the phone ring, her finger on the Glock's trigger. She was about to hang up when a man answered, his accent distinctly American.

"482-5555," he said.

"Who is this?" asked Arnett.

There was a long silence, then the voice asked, "Who're you calling?"

"I'm calling anyone who can verify there's a guy in Somalia pretending to be a pirate when he's actually a sergeant in the US Army Special Forces," Arnett said. "And you better talk fast, because I'm about to put a bullet in his head."

There was a long pause. "Captain Arnett?" asked the voice.

Arnett's heart jumped, but she caught herself. It could still be a trick. "That's me," she said. "Who's this?"

"Agent Jesse Ward, Central Intelligence Agency, ma'am. And I must ask you, are you having a storm there?"

Storm? What was he talking about? Then she remembered.

"No, Agent Ward. I believe *good weather* are the words you're waiting for."

"They are indeed, Captain," Ward replied. "I take it you've met Sergeant Ahmed. Please don't shoot him. He's one of my most valuable assets."

Arnett realized she was still pointing the Glock at Ahmed and lowered it as Ward continued. "Hold one, ma'am. There's someone I know wants to talk to you."

Arnett listened as she heard connection noises, then a phone ringing.

"*Marie Floyd*, Captain Blake speaking."

Relief washed over Arnett in waves, and for the first time in days, she believed she was going home.

DRILLSHIP *OCEAN GOLIATH*
ARABIAN SEA

Dugan stood on the open deck and braced himself against the roll of the ship as he nodded to Borgdanov.

"All of them," he said. "We need to get as much oxygen to the fire as possible."

Borgdanov nodded back and opened fire, rounds from his assault rifle stitching holes in the thick shatterproof glass of the crew-lounge windows. He worked his way down the row, stopping to pop in a fresh magazine, and Dugan followed behind him, beating the remnants of the shattered glass out with a fire extinguisher. When they'd finished, Dugan moved to the two fire hoses stretched out on deck, and bent to double-check the nozzles. He'd opened both to *fog* position, and wrapped the levers with wire from his backpack to prevent accidental closure. Satisfied, he nodded to Borgdanov, grabbed one of the hoses, and fed it through a glassless window, nozzle first, as the Russian did the same with the second hose farther down the row of windows.

"I don't know how much they're going to dance around when we pressurize them, and we don't want them popping out," Dugan said, "so feed in plenty."

Borgdanov nodded, as Dugan finished and duct-taped his own hose to the storm rail just below the ruined window. He used half a roll, wrapping the hose and rail repeatedly. Ugly but strong, at least strong enough to help prevent the hose from backing out of the broken window. He moved to Borgdanov's hose and repeated the procedure, then looked out at the building seas. The ship had a perceptible port list now, as Dugan's ballast adjustment began to manifest itself—perhaps a little too soon. He gave the ocean a last worried look, and hurried into the deckhouse with Borgdanov at his heels, fighting their way uphill as the ship took a roll.

They found the sergeant outside the crew lounge using the safety line to lash oxygen and acetylene cylinders to the passageway storm rail. Dugan looked into the open door of the crew lounge and nodded. Dead crewmen and pirates covered the deck, and trapped between the bodies were the gas cylinders. Scattered about the large room were cans of various shapes and sizes—paint thinner, alcohol, cooking oil, anything and everything flammable. Zigzagging across the room was a fire hose leading through the open door and arranged over the bodies. The nozzle at the end of the hose was wired shut and firmly secured to a table pedestal. Visible along the length of the hose were punctures Dugan had made with his knife. Not bad for a jury-rigged crematorium.

"I do not see why we need torch, *Dyed*," Borgdanov said. "I think alcohol and other things are enough."

Dugan shook his head. "All that stuff will burn fast. We need the diesel to keep feeding the fire, and diesel's not like gasoline—it's damned hard to get going. The torch is our insurance." Dugan glanced over at the sergeant. "Looks like Ilya's finished. Let's get it done."

Borgdanov nodded and spoke to the sergeant in Russian, as Dugan opened the valves on the oxygen and acetylene cylinders and plucked a friction striker from where it hung on a loop over one of the valves. The Russians moved up the passageway to the fire station that served the perforated fire hose.

Dugan stepped through the door and followed the oxygen and acetylene hoses down a narrow path through the bodies to the center of the room. The hoses terminated at a cutting torch taped to the leg of a coffee table inches away from a five-gallon can of cooking oil. Dugan squatted, opened the valves, and then struck a spark at the head of the torch. A flame flared to life against the silver side of the oil can. Dugan adjusted the valves on the torch to maximize the heat, dropped the striker, and raced from the room. He nodded down the passageway to Borgdanov, who opened the valve on the fire station a single turn, just enough to send diesel coursing through the hose to leak through the perforations over the pile of bodies. They fled the deckhouse.

"I think something is wrong, *Dyed*," said Borgdanov five minutes later, as Dugan and the two Russians balanced on the pitching deck some distance from the broken windows of the lounge.

"Give it a minute more," Dugan said. "When the cooking oil ignites, flames will spread to the rest of the more volatile stuff fast, then we'll see result—"

They all flinched at a loud explosion, and a ball of flame rolled out the farthest of the broken windows of the crew lounge. In seconds, flames were licking out of all the windows.

"There we go," Dugan said. "Time to add a little more fuel to the fire. Remember, open the valve wide."

Borgdanov nodded and rushed to the far fire station, while Dugan manned the nearer one. He twisted the valve open and diesel rushed into the flat hose, inflating it like a thick white snake, and Dugan watched the bulge at the leading edge travel down the hose and through the broken window into the lounge. In moments, there was a loud *whomp*, as diesel misted from the fog nozzle and ignited in a violent burst, followed by another as the spray from the second nozzle ignited. Flames boiled from the windows, topped by smoke that rose in a thick black cloud, caught and ripped away by the increasingly violent wind.

The fire was roaring now, and Dugan had to once again shout to make himself heard through the suits and masks. "That should do it. Let's get the hell off this thing."

Dugan started aft along the pitching main deck, starting down the port side, then changing course to traverse to starboard. There was a definite port list now, with the vessel rolling more to port than starboard, and the layer of silver coins had started to shift across the open deck, leaving surer footing to starboard. Even as Dugan rushed aft, he knew something was wrong. When he reached the stern, he moved across the ship and looked down the port side.

He cursed as the two Russians joined him.

"What is wrong?" Borgdanov asked.

"I wanted to give the fire plenty of time to burn," Dugan said. "So I set the ballast system up to slowly give her a port list. I figured that, being top-heavy, she'd capsize in an hour or so."

Dugan pointed to the Yemeni fishing boat, awash to its main deck and tight against the side of the larger vessel, hanging off half a dozen thick mooring hawsers. "I didn't figure on this. That friggin' boat's sinking, and she's heavy enough to increase the list, at least until those mooring lines part. Now it's a crapshoot."

The Russian looked confused. "What means 'crapshoot'?"

"It means we got to get the hell out of here. Now!" Dugan said, turning to look out at the increasingly violent sea. "Where the hell is Kwok?"

He swiveled his head, and a moment later, spotted the *Kyung Yang No. 173* in the distance, listing to starboard and headed away from the drillship. Dugan looked at Borgdanov and started to speak, but the Russian was already digging the radio from his backpack. His hands in the thick gloves were clumsy, but he pressed the radio to his hood near his ear and shouted through the facemask. After several attempts, he lowered the radio.

"Anisimov does not answer," Borgdanov said. "I think is big problem."

Dugan stared at the distant boat in disbelief. "Wonderful. The son of a bitch is abandoning us. Can it get any worse?"

The sergeant pointed into the distance, in the opposite direction from the *Kyung Yang No. 173*. Dugan saw a flash of white on the crest of a wave, and recognized it as a small craft headed their way, fast. As he watched, there were more flashes, until he'd counted eight, all undoubtedly loaded with pirates.

CHAPTER TWENTY-FIVE

Kwok looked out across the building seas at the drillship and cursed Dugan. He glanced back down at his radar and cursed again, as the flickering display went black, and he slapped the side of the cabinet with his open hand. The display blinked back to life and Kwok stared in disbelief, then rubbed his eyes and looked again.

Eight targets were closing on his position, not more than ten miles away, and closing fast. They were small and fast, their radar signatures indistinct. He had no doubt who they were. He turned to the impassive black-clad Russian, who watched from the rear of the small wheelhouse.

"Many pirates come!" Kwok said. "We must leave. Now!"

The Russian stepped forward and studied the display, then spoke into the radio mike clipped to his web gear. After several attempts, it was obvious he'd received no response. He looked at Kwok and shrugged.

"Major does not answer. I think maybe he is in noisy place and cannot hear radio in backpack," he said. "So. We must wait. He will call soon, I think."

Kwok looked across at the drillship. She was rolling more now, but also seemed to be developing a port list. He spotted faint traces of smoke rising from the deckhouse.

"We cannot wait! If we stay, pirates will catch us too." Kwok spoke to the helmsman in Korean, and the man began to turn the wheel.

"*Nyet!*" The Russian leveled his rifle. "We wait for others. Stay here."

Kwok raised his hands in surrender, and spoke over his shoulder to countermand the order. *Kyung Yang No. 173* returned to her previous course, creeping along in the lee of *Ocean Goliath* at two knots. She'd hardly settled back on course when the chief engineer rushed up the short stairway and into the wheelhouse.

"We're taking on water," he said to Kwok in Korean. "A lot of water!"

"What? How? Where?" Kwok asked.

The engineer shook his head. "I can't tell yet," he said. "But I think when you struck the drillship you disturbed one of the concrete patches. I'm pumping most of it out, but the pump can't keep up. We're already developing a starboard list."

"Can you repair it?" Kwok asked.

"Possibly," the engineer said. "If I can find it."

"Show me." Kwok started to follow the engineer down the stairs.

"Where you go?" the Russian demanded, stepping in front of Kwok.

"Hole in hull. Ship sinking," Kwok said. "I go look. You get out of way now."

The Russian stepped aside, confused, then fell in behind the Koreans.

Kwok turned over the situation in his mind, even as he raced downstairs after the engineer. He'd been with the Americans and the Russians when many pirates had been killed, and now he was—for all the pirates knew—voluntarily helping them. Eventually the pirates would find out about their dead colleagues and figure out who killed them. It wouldn't go well for him if he was their prisoner when that happened. Kwok reached that conclusion just as he stepped into the engine room, and the stench of diesel filled his nose and the engine assaulted his ears. He knew what he had to do.

Kwok followed the chief down the starboard side, and nodded as the man played the beam of his flashlight over the rising water in the bilge. Kwok turned to the Russian and motioned for him to stoop down, then spoke into the man's ear.

"Much water," Kwok shouted, to make himself understood over the engine. "We have leak. There." He pointed to a random place in the bilge. "You look. You see. You must bend down and look under that pipe."

Kwok motioned for the chief to shine his flashlight on the place where he pointed. Confused, the engineer did as ordered.

As the Russian bent to peer into the bilge, Kwok slipped a wheel wrench from a holder along the handrail and cracked him in the back of the head. The Russian collapsed, unconscious, and Kwok shouted in the chief's ear.

"Get two men to bind him and carry him to the wheelhouse, where I can keep my eye on him," Kwok said.

"Are you crazy?" the chief shouted back. "The other Russians will kill us!"

"And if we wait around for those fools, the pirates will kill us instead. We're getting out of here, so do as you're told. And I want full power from the engine when I ask for it. Now, take care of the Russian and find that leak. Understood?"

Kwok had just reached the wheelhouse when he saw a fireball rise from the deckhouse on the drillship. He ordered the helmsman to point the boat's bow southwest and increased speed to full power before he moved to the radar. The pirates would be on the drillship in less than ten minutes, but he figured their initial reaction would center on the silver, and he hoped to slip away in the confusion. Even if that miserable engineer couldn't get the leak fixed, floating around in a life raft awaiting rescue was a better alternative than being killed by pirates.

Kwok decided to improve his odds. He twisted the dial on the VHF to channel sixteen and keyed the mike.

"Mayday, mayday, mayday," he said, then repeated the name of his vessel and location. "Ship sinking. Many pirates come. Mayday, mayday, mayday."

He was on his fourth repetition when two crewmen dragged the Russian up the stairs and dumped him on the deck. The Russian moaned, and Kwok looked down at him, momentarily distracted. His head snapped back up as the VHF squawked.

"*Kyung Yang No. 173*," said an accented voice. "This is Russian naval vessel *Admiral Vinogradov*. We acknowledge your mayday and are coming to assist. Over."

Kwok looked back at the bound Russian, and blood drained from his face.

"We have assault rifle," Borgdanov said. "But most of ammunition I use to break windows. I have part of magazine left. Also the Glock with three magazines. But eight boats means twenty or thirty *piraty* at least. I think we have big problem, *Dyed*."

"Agreed," Dugan said. "But I'll be damned if I'm going to surrender just yet. Maybe we can—Jesus Christ!"

Dugan lost his footing and slammed into a mooring winch as the *Ocean Goliath* rolled to port on a particularly large wave. This time she lingered at the bottom of the roll, as if deciding between righting herself and lying on her side on the storm-tossed surface. Dugan held his breath at metallic clanging from the derrick as the drill pipe shifted, then let it out as the big vessel shuddered and rolled upright. But just upright, she was hardly rolling to starboard now. He regained his balance and moved back to where the Russians gripped a set of mooring bitts, bracing themselves against the roll.

"This baby's going over anytime," Dugan said. "The pirates might not recognize that right away, or realize everyone is dead. They'll come at us from the port side because it's lower and they can board easier. Then they'll either get distracted by all that silver or they'll head forward to the bridge and quarters to seize control of the ship. Either way, I don't think they'll head back aft, at least not initially. I figure we squat out of sight back here behind the machinery casing and see what develops." He looked up at the darkening sky. "There's bound to be a lot of confusion, and this storm will hit anytime. Maybe we use that to our advantage."

As if responding to Dugan's words, a raindrop hit his facemask, and in seconds, they were in a downpour. He looked forward at the smoke and flames billowing from the starboard-side lounge windows. Strangely enough, the wind was decreasing, and the smoke was rising in a black, greasy column. He turned away, reassured. No rainstorm, no matter how fierce, would quench the diesel-fed fire now, and when the ship went over, the lounge would be on the high side. She'd burn right up until she sank.

Dugan moved to the port side, and squatted out of sight behind the machinery casing. The Russians followed suit as the rain came down in sheets and collected on the pitching deck to form small waves on its way to the deck scuppers and overboard. The water accumulated on the exposed top deck of the machinery casing as well, faster than it could drain. Running to port because of the list, the water spilled over the edge of the upper deck like a minor waterfall, surging stronger with each roll of the ship.

"We can flush off under that water," Dugan shouted to Borgdanov over the noise of the downpour. "Then we can take these damned masks off. I doubt there's any airborne dust floating around in this mess. Remember to flush your gloves and boots well too—just in case—and don't touch your face. Tell Ilya."

Borgdanov nodded and turned to the sergeant, as Dugan crawled under the powerful stream. He turned his face up, staying there through several surges, as the water gushed over him from head to toe. Then he held his gloved hands under the flood, rubbing them vigorously to flush any residue off their slick surface. He looked to his right and saw the Russians similarly engaged, then stripped off his gas mask and closed his eyes before turning his bare face back into the stream. He crawled out of the direct stream and opened his eyes, blinking furiously and fighting an urge to wipe his eyes. He'd been in the suit less than two hours, but it seemed like two days, and the cool water on his face was comforting, even under the circumstances. His respite was cut short by the sound of approaching outboards, and Dugan shouted for the others to get down.

The pirates approached like a band of howling Comanches, their swift boats speeding up swells and crashing down the other side. The first boats drew close and cut their speed to match that of the wallowing drillship, and the more daring of the pirates balanced in their boats, timing the movement of the big ship. At the bottom of *Ocean Goliath*'s port roll, several leaped to catch the bottom handrail and hauled themselves aboard.

Dugan's guess the pirates would be distracted by the silver was correct, and the first aboard screamed through the rain to their brethren, alerting them to their great good fortune. Here and there, pirates in the boats fired celebratory shots into the air.

Waabberi balanced on the shifting layer of silver as the big ship rolled, his initial exuberance at discovering the treasure mitigated by sudden terror as the port rail dipped toward the water and metallic clanging filled the air from the derrick. Something was very wrong. There was no evidence of Mukhtar or anyone, and the ship was close to capsizing. They couldn't stay here long, but—he looked down at his feet—he wouldn't abandon this treasure. He turned to the men beside him.

"You," he said, "position four men halfway between here and the deckhouse. If Mukhtar and his fanatics are about, I don't want to be taken by surprise." The man nodded and rushed to do as ordered, and Waabberi turned to the second man.

"We don't have long," he said, "and we must save the silver. Have the men scoop it up and dump it in the boats."

The man looked out at the seas. "The silver's heavy. We can't load the boats so heavily in these seas."

"The mother ships will be here in an hour, maybe two," said Waabberi. "Load the boats and shelter in the lee of the drillship until they arrive. Her hull is breaking the waves a bit. Even if she rolls over, she'll float awhile. We'll be all right as long as no one is in the shadow of the derrick when she goes over."

The man looked doubtful, and Waabberi lost his patience.

"Don't question me!" he screamed. "Get moving! Now!"

The man glanced at Waabberi's hand moving toward the pistol in his waistband, and turned away.

"At once, Waabberi," he said over his shoulder, and began to shout orders.

Soon pirates swarmed aboard with empty backpacks, having hastily emptied ammunition bags and anything else that could hold coins. Those without containers spread their shirts on deck and piled coins to be gathered into bundles. The drivers stayed in the boats, circling on the stormy seas, waiting their turn to nose up to the ship to take on silver.

Dugan squatted at the corner of the machinery casing and peered through the pouring rain at the controlled chaos. He felt Borgdanov beside him.

"What do you think, *Dyed*?"

"They're pretty occupied. If we had a boat, we could slip away. But I'll be damned if I can figure out how to get one."

"Lifeboats?"

"They'll all be forward near the quarters. There are life rafts back here, but I don't think we can slip away from these guys in a raft. And besides. We'll never catch Kwok in a raft."

As they spoke, the first boat moved away from the side to make room for the next. It was a semirigid inflatable, visible through the driving rain as it wallowed up a swell and circled close in the relatively calmer waters beside the rolling drillship.

"That's it!" Dugan said, pointing to the boat. "He's loaded and staying in the lee of the hull. My bet is he'll wait for the others back here beside the stern. He'll be by himself until another boat is loaded. That's our shot."

Borgdanov nodded and motioned Dugan back out of sight behind the machinery-casing bulkhead. The Russians conversed in hush tones, the sergeant looking doubtful, then nodding in reluctant concurrence. Borgdanov turned to Dugan.

"Ilya will go first without weapon," he said. "He must take out pirate without attracting attention, or we have little chance. After Ilya captures boat, you and I jump and he picks us up. If we are lucky, we sneak away in rain without being seen."

"And if we aren't lucky?" Dugan asked.

Borgdanov shrugged. "You and I will have weapons. We empty them at pirates to keep their heads down and maybe make them a little cautious. Then we jump and hope for best." He looked at the sergeant, then turned back to Dugan. "This you should know, *Dyed*. Ilya and I do not surrender, no matter what. Russian military is not so kind to *piraty*, so I think they will not be so kind to us."

"You're out of uniform, how will they know?"

Borgdanov shrugged. "We both have unit tattoos. Sooner or later, they will figure it out. Then it will not go so well with us. But you are American. You, I think, they hold for ransom."

"Thanks for the thought," Dugan said. "But apart from the Fruit of the Loom label in my underwear, I suspect we're all going to look alike to these guys."

Borgdanov smiled and clapped Dugan on the shoulder. "Is true, and also I now remember I make you honorary Russian. So, *tovarishch*, do you want rifle or Glock?"

Dugan shrugged. "I doubt I'll hit anything anyway, but I have a better chance with the rifle."

The sergeant passed Dugan the assault rifle, as Borgdanov dug in his backpack for the Glock, the spare magazines, and a roll of duct tape he used to tape the magazines to his thigh. Dugan held the unfamiliar weapon and looked back and forth at the Russians, then down at himself and his bright orange suit, and wondered if this was how the redcoats felt.

He heard the muted mutter of the outboard now as the pirate boat crept along beside the ship at two knots. Borgdanov dug in his backpack again and pulled out a small mirror on a collapsible extension, and then discarded the backpack on the deck. He pulled the extension out full length, and then crouched low and crept near the port side, examining the water near the ship. He nodded and motioned the others to join him.

"Is good," Borgdanov said. "He is very close. And he looks forward, at the others, not up. I think we can make nice surprise for him, *da*?"

Dugan nodded, and Borgdanov spoke to the sergeant. On the next roll upright, both Russians stood and moved to the rail, and Dugan followed suit. The sergeant scampered over the rail and stood with his heels on the deck edge, holding the rail behind him.

Dugan looked down and saw the pirate in the boat below him, just as Borgdanov had described, oblivious to their presence. The ship rolled back to port, and the sergeant timed his drop perfectly at the lowest point of the roll, a mere ten feet above the pirate's head. He entered the water feet first beside the boat, close enough to grab the side as he flashed by the startled pirate. His head submerged, but he kept his hands on the edge of the boat, and heaved himself upward, propelled by both his tremendous arm strength and the additional buoyancy of the survival suit.

The Russian shot out of the water like an orange porpoise, and flopped far enough into the boat to wrap his massive right hand around the pirate's bicep. He fell back into the water, attempting to drag the pirate with him, but the terrified man clung to the tiller of the outboard, pulling it hard over and sending the boat into a tight circle, as he found his voice and began to scream. Desperate to silence the pirate, the sergeant gave a mighty heave and pulled the man into the water, then clung to the boat with his left hand as he held the now-thrashing pirate underwater with his right.

Dugan and Borgdanov watched as the tightly circling boat slipped astern, no longer matching the drillship's speed. Dugan looked forward, relieved no one seemed to have heard the pirate's cries.

"I must help Ilya," Borgdanov said. "Stay here, *Dyed*. We will be back with boat." Without waiting for Dugan's concurrence, he slipped over the rail and dropped into the sea.

Terrific. Dugan looked after the boat, alone on a sinking ship with three dozen bloodthirsty pirates. He was moving back to the shelter of the machinery casing when they spotted him. He saw one of the pirates shout, then point, and several moved down the deck toward him. His first instinct was to run, but there was nowhere to go, and if he jumped overboard, he'd draw attention to the Russians and the boat, and both he and the Russians would make nice orange targets for pirates shooting off the stern. No, the best option was to keep them forward awhile. If they didn't *see* him jump overboard, they might be cautious about charging aft. And every second they delayed, the drillship would move away, increasing the range.

Dugan raised the assault rifle and opened fire, sending pirates scrambling for cover. His fire was indiscriminate—he had no illusions about his own marksmanship—and he emptied the magazine in seconds before moving to the cover of the machinery casing. Out of sight, he moved aft, keeping the bulk of the machinery casing between him and any approaching pirates. At the stern rail, he dropped the now-useless rifle overboard and crawled over the rail to drop feet first into the water.

"Is it one of Mukhtar's fanatics?" Waabberi asked.

"I don't think so. He was a big white man in orange coveralls with a hood."

Waabberi scratched his chin. "One of the crew then. But where did he get the weapon? Crews aren't normally armed."

His underling shrugged. "Perhaps he took it from one of the fanatics."

"It doesn't matter," Waabberi said, looking up at the derrick as the ship started another roll to port. "Put one man on guard in case he returns, and get everyone else back to the silver. We don't have time to waste on—"

He ducked at the crack of a gunshot, then realized it wasn't a shot at all, but the forward mooring line on the doomed Yemeni fishing boat parting at last. Deprived of this last crucial bit of support, the boat's bow dipped below a swell, and the forward motion of the drillship drove it deeper still, increasing the load on the remaining forward lines that, stretched to the limit of their elasticity, snapped in quick succession. Attached to the drillship now by only her stern lines, the bow of the boat swung away from the hull, and for one critical moment, the sinking boat acted as a rudder.

The big ship veered to port, at the very bottom of her port roll, and never recovered. The rest of the drill pipe in the derrick broke free to join the loose single string that had been producing the doleful clanging, and the ship pitched on her side, spilling pirates and silver into the storm-tossed sea. Despite Waabberi's warning, two of the boats were caught in the shadow of the derrick and disappeared, while the rest sped away from the ship in panic, then returned to circle the sinking ship, like flies disturbed from a dead carcass.

Dugan plunged through the water, turned end over end in the powerful prop wash from the drillship's thrusters. He felt a moment of disorientation and panic, but then he was free of the turbulence and the buoyancy of the survival suit carried him to the surface. He panicked again when his head broke the water, and he looked around in the driving rain. His visual range in the water was considerably less than it had been from the higher vantage point on the ship, and it was reduced even further as he bobbed up and down in the waves. How would he find the Russians? Even the huge ship was becoming a blur as it moved through the rain away from him and intermittently disappeared as he got caught in wave troughs.

A massive groan reached him, like the death rattle of some great beast, and he rode up on the crest of a wave in time to see the dim outline of *Ocean Goliath* rolling over. Then things went quiet, the only sound the hiss of the rain on the water.

And Dugan felt very, very alone.

CHAPTER TWENTY-SIX

KYUNG YANG NO. 173
ARABIAN SEA

Kwok looked aft and eyed the edge of the rainsquall, now stretched across the near horizon like a gray-white curtain, obscuring his view of the threat he was trying so desperately to escape. The storm front had passed with remarkable speed, and *Kyung Yang No. 173* had run out of it, into clear skies and troubled but calming seas. She struggled over a big wave as Kwok turned to watch the helmsman fight the wheel, compensating for the increasing starboard list.

Kwok dropped his gaze to the Russian bound on the deck, blood dried on the side of his head, glaring up at Kwok with hate in his eyes. Kwok ignored him and looked back out to sea, as he mentally parsed the possible outcomes of his current situation. His reverie was disturbed by hurried footsteps on the stairs, and moments later the chief engineer burst into the wheelhouse, soaking wet and dripping water on the deck.

"I found the leak!" the chief said in Korean, "but we must—"

"Is it fixed?" Kwok asked.

The engineer shook his head and tried to speak, but Kwok cut him off.

"Why not? Can you do it?"

The chief nodded. "Yes, but I must—"

Kwok exploded. "Then don't stand here talking to me! Repair it at once! Why'd you even come here?"

"That's what I'm trying to tell you," the chief said. "It's the most forward of the concrete patches the Americans placed. They left some materials onboard, so I think I can make the repair, but the force of the water against the hull is making the leak worse. I must slow it down a lot before I can hope to patch it. We must reduce speed until I can get it patched and the concrete sets."

Kwok looked back, as if trying to peer through the curtain of rain.

"Out of the question," he said. "The pirates could overtake us and capture us before the Russians arrive. We must get as far away from them as possible."

"And if the boat sinks?" the chief asked.

"Then we take to the raft," Kwok said. "The Russians should be here anytime to rescue us."

"And how do you intend to explain abandoning their countrymen, or the fact that we're floating around in a raft with a bound Russian?"

Kwok shrugged. "Dugan and the other two fools won't survive the pirates, so no one will know we abandoned anyone, and as far as our friend here goes"—he looked down at the

Russian—"I don't think he'll be joining us in the raft. I suspect he'll drown if the ship sinks, or perhaps fall over the side before then."

The chief glared at Kwok. "*We* didn't abandon anyone, Captain. You're the one who ran away."

"And saved your neck in the process, you ungrateful fool," Kwok said.

"I doubt it was *my* neck you were concerned with," the chief said. "And it remains to be seen whether you saved any of us. Besides, running away is one thing; murder to cover it up is quite another."

"I'll deal with the Russian as I see fit," Kwok said. "Now stop your insubordination and get below and fix the leak. Without stopping the engine. Is that clear?"

"But I can't—"

"I said, is that *CLEAR*?" Kwok screamed.

The chief fixed Kwok with a silent glare. "I'll try," he said at last, and turned to the stairs.

ARABIAN SEA
ASTERN OF CAPSIZED *OCEAN GOLIATH*

Dugan bobbed in the water and fought rising panic. Staying afloat was no problem in the suit, but that was about the only positive. He imagined a slow death, floating around without food or water—unless, of course, a shark happened along. He compartmentalized his fear and tried to concentrate on the task at hand.

Visibility was awful. The raindrops whipped the sea into a fine mist a few inches above the water—inconsequential if you were in a boat, but blinding if the only thing above water was your head. Each time a wave lifted him, Dugan fought to lift his head higher and swiveled it frantically, hoping to catch sight of the Russians. He slipped back into each trough disappointed.

Then he heard it—the muted mutter of an idling outboard. On the next crest, he looked toward the sound and glimpsed a flash of orange before he tumbled back between the waves.

"Help! I'm here," he cried on the next crest.

"I hear you, *Dyed*," came the reply. "Keep shouting!"

Moments later, the boat almost ran over him as it crested a wave and crashed down toward him. It sheared away at the last minute, and then it was beside him, and Borgdanov pulled him in. Dugan lay with his back against a mound of coins.

"It's good to see you guys," he said, looking around. "Wherever the hell we are. I think I drifted quite a ways after the ship went over."

Borgdanov pointed through the rain. "Ship is there. Maybe five hundred meters away. We were closer just before she turned over, but still, we could barely see ship. But we heard gunfire and saw flash of orange and think maybe you jump in water. We have been searching."

Dugan nodded. "Thanks," he said, as he looked around.

The boat was heavy, plowing through the confused seas rather than riding over them, and the sergeant was fighting the tiller of the outboard to keep her from broaching sideways to the swell. Dugan turned to Borgdanov.

"What's our situation?"

"I lost Glock when I jumped" Borgdanov said. "But some *piraty* left weapons in boat when they go to take silver. We have two AKs and one RPG." He shrugged. "Fuel, not so much, but I think we have enough to catch Kwok. Anyway, we must try, *da*? You remember which way he goes?"

"Looked like southwest," said Dugan, looking around in the rain. "Wherever the hell that is."

Borgdanov smiled and said something to the sergeant, who patted a wooden case at his feet.

"*Piraty* left us nice compass," Borgdanov said. "So we go southwest. But *Dyed*, I think you should drive. Ilya and I keep watch with guns."

Dugan nodded, and moved to change places with the sergeant.

"I suggest one of you keep watch and the other start dumping the silver," Dugan said, as he pointed the boat southwest. "Loaded like this in these seas, we'll be lucky not to sink. Much less overtake anything."

The Russians stared at the pile, reluctant to jettison the treasure.

"Don't forget," Dugan said, "some of the dead men on the ship may have handled this stuff. I doubt viruses prefer to live on silver, and it's had a hell of a lot of water flushed over it, but make sure to keep your gloves on."

The idea the silver might be contaminated ended the Russians' reluctance, and Borgdanov jettisoned silver while the sergeant kept watch. As the boat lightened, Dugan increased speed, and the boat labored through the seas to the growl of the outboard.

ARABIAN SEA
BESIDE CAPSIZED *OCEAN GOLIATH*

"I warned the fools to stay out of the shadow of the derrick," Waabberi said to no one in particular, as he studied his band of bedraggled survivors. Miraculously, all of his men had survived the capsizing, except the drivers of the boats caught under the derrick. The survivors filled the five remaining boats to capacity, and floated together in a group in the lee of the overturned drillship, clustered around Waabberi's boat.

"Beard of the Prophet," Waabberi said. "If we were so unfortunate as to lose three boats, why did one of them have to be loaded with silver?"

"But Waabberi," a pirate said, "only two boats perished under the derrick. The silver boat was farther aft. The strange men took it."

"Strange men? What are you talking about, you fool? What strange men?"

"Big white men, dressed in orange," the pirate said. "I looked up and saw—"

"And you're telling me this now!" Waabberi screamed. "Why didn't you tell me at the time?"

"I tried," the man said. "But I was farthest away from the ship and I couldn't get your attention. Then the gunfire from the ship drowned out my shouts, and the ship capsized. Then I was rescuing our brothers—"

"Enough," Waabberi said. "Which way did they go?"

"I… I don't know. I lost of them in the rain."

Waabberi nodded and sat thinking to the combined soft muttering of the outboards, as the boats maintained station against wind and waves in the lee of the stricken drillship. Who were these strange men? Crewmen, no doubt; but where could they go? They didn't have enough fuel to go far. They must be close by, even now.

"Stop the motors!" he shouted, and the five outboards sputtered to silence. "Now," Waabberi said, "everyone listen. They can't be far."

Several men pointed at once, then Waabberi heard it himself—the distant sound of a straining outboard. He turned to his driver. "What direction is that?"

The man looked at his compass. "Southwest," he said.

Waabberi nodded and took quick inventory of his little flotilla, grateful now that some of his men had ignored orders and left their weapons in the boats when they boarded the ship to load silver.

"Quickly," he said, motioning over the fastest boat of the five and jumping aboard. "Three men here with me in the chase boat. The rest of you spread yourselves evenly among the other boats and follow. Unarmed men, get in the boat with the silver." Waabberi looked at the driver of the boat loaded with silver. "You'll be slow, so bring up the rear. Don't take risks in these seas. We've little enough to show for our efforts, and I don't want to lose any more silver. Is that clear?"

The man nodded as all the outboards roared to life, and Waabberi squatted in his own boat and pointed southwest.

ARABIAN SEA
5 MILES SOUTHWEST OF *OCEAN GOLIATH*

Dugan raised his free hand to shade his eyes from the bright sun reflecting off the water. They'd run out of the rainsquall a mile back, and it had been like switching on a light in a darkened room. The wind had calmed as well, and the sea was settling but still choppy, marked here and there with whitecaps. He shot a worried glance over his shoulder at the gray-white curtain of rain and took a chance on increasing speed.

The sun was a mixed blessing. No longer deluged by cooling rain, Dugan once again broiled in the survival suit, and saw sweat running down the Russians' faces as well. He was contemplating stripping off the suit when a shout rang out in front of him.

"*Dyed*! There!" Borgdanov cried, just as the boat crested a wave. Dugan squinted into the distance in the direction of the Russian's pointing finger.

He smiled as he made out the unmistakable profile of the *Kyung Yang No. 173*. His smile faded.

"She's listing badly," Dugan said.

"No matter," Borgdanov replied. "I think is better to be on listing fishing boat than in middle of ocean on Zodiac with little fuel and no food and water, *da*?"

"I can't argue with that," Dugan said.

"How long before we catch her?" Borgdanov asked.

"Hard to say. She's not making full speed, but neither are we. I'd guess maybe half an hour—less if the seas cooperate."

Borgdanov nodded. "Is good—"

The sergeant yelled something to Borgdanov and pointed aft, and Dugan swiveled his head to see a pirate boat emerging from the rainsquall. As he watched, three more boats appeared out of the curtain of rain in quick succession. He looked forward to find the Russians checking their weapons.

"Can we beat *piraty* to fishing boat, *Dyed*?" Borgdanov asked.

"Doubtful," Dugan said. "Not that it'll make much difference."

"Will make big difference," Borgdanov said. "Is better platform to defend, and we add Anisimov's gun to our firepower."

"I'll do my best." Dugan increased speed, capsizing now the lesser risk.

Ten minutes later, it was obvious Dugan's initial doubts were justified. For every yard they had gained on the fishing boat, the lead pirate seemed to gain a yard and a half on them, and the rest of the pirate boats weren't far behind. Dugan noticed a fifth boat now, breaking the rain curtain and moving more slowly than the others. The pirates in the lead boat began a sporadic, if wildly inaccurate, fire in Dugan's direction. He took no comfort in the poor marksmanship; when they got closer, it wouldn't matter.

"I don't think we're going to make it to Kwok's boat," Dugan said. "And at this speed, we're burning a lot of—"

The outboard began to sputter and cough, then stopped.

"—fuel," Dugan finished, as his boat lost power and coasted down a wave.

Dugan tried unsuccessfully to restart the outboard, then threw a worried glance back at the pirates. He moved to the collapsible fuel bladder and opened the fill cap. There was a slight hiss as air rushed into the collapsed container, and Dugan released it from its securing straps, lifting and tilting it so that every last bit of fuel could drain through the attached hose to the outboard. He motioned the sergeant to take his place.

"Hold this up," Dugan said. "Not much there, but we'll go as far as we can."

He returned to the outboard. It started on the second attempt.

Kyung Yang No. 173
Arabian Sea

The chief engineer kneeled in the bilge, shoulder deep in oily water as he groped beneath the water's surface, searching by feel for the crack in the concrete patch. There! He'd found it again, and felt the rush of water on his fingertips. It was about 150 millimeters long from the feel of it. The thin wooden wedges he'd made should plug it enough for the bilge pump to catch up, then he could work on a more durable repair—if he could get one of the damn things tapped into the crack to stay this time. Broken remnants of half a dozen wedges floated on the water sloshing around him, testimony to his failure so far.

He closed his eyes and held his breath in anticipation as the boat rolled to starboard, and the water rose over his head. He grabbed a grating support with his left hand to steady himself, but kept his right hand firmly pressed to the crack—he wasn't going to lose contact with it again.

The boat rolled back almost upright, and as his head broke water, the chief braced his knees against the tank top and threw up his left hand. The crewman assisting him on the deck plates above leaned down to press a wooden wedge into it.

"Last one, Chief," the man yelled over the engine noise.

The chief nodded. He couldn't afford to lose this one, there was no time to make more. He lowered the wedge beneath the water and worked the thin edge into the crack by feel, using both hands. Once started, he then held it there against the incoming rush of water with his left hand as he reached up his right toward the deck plates. He was coated head to toe from the oil floating in the bilge, and he felt a rag in his open palm as his assistant above tried to wipe the oil away to improve his grip. Then came the firm slap in his palm, and he gripped the hammer handle.

He drew in another deep breath and closed his eyes as the boat rolled and the bilge water enveloped him again, and he groped underwater with the hammer until he felt the top of the thin wedge. He tapped tentatively and felt the wedge ease through the fingers of his left hand, deeper into the crack. He tapped again, just enough to seat the plug but not break the thin wood, as he had on his previous attempts. It only had to hold long enough to get the bilge pumped; he mustn't overdo it again.

He made a final light tap, his left fingers on the wood telling him the wedge was no longer moving into the crack, then he let go of it, just as the boat rolled back upright and his oily head broke the water.

"Got it!" he shouted to his helper, and started to climb out of the bilge. No sooner were the words out of his mouth than the wedge popped to the surface, borne away into a maze of piping on the wave of water rolling through the bilge. He considered trying to find it, but knew it was futile. He grimaced and started for the wheelhouse. He had to convince Kwok to stop the boat.

As he exited the engine room onto the open deck, he looked aft and saw the parade following his own boat. There was no mistaking the orange-clad figures in the lead boat. He rushed up to the wheelhouse, finding Kwok staring aft.

"Dugan and the Russians are—"

"I can see them, you fool," Kwok said. "And they're leading the damned pirates right to us! But what're you doing here? Is the leak fixed?"

"No. Our speed's making the leak worse. I can't repair it unless we stop."

Kwok looked aft again. "In ten minutes it'll be over, I think. We must maintain our speed until then. After that, it'll be safe to stop."

"Wha... what do you mean?"

Kwok pointed and the engineer squinted. The rainsquall had moved farther north, revealing the capsized drillship. Hovering over it was a black dot.

"That'll be a Russian helicopter," Kwok said. "If we can maintain our distance, I think they'll take care of our pirate friends. But if the pirates get here first, I'm sure we'll become human shields again."

"But Dugan and—"

"Screw Dugan!" Kwok shouted. "He's the one that put us in danger to start with. Now he's leading the pirates right back to us, so I think it only fair he helps us for a change. When the pirates catch him, they'll slow down to deal with him and the Russians. If he and those crazy Russians resist, all the better—it'll slow the pirates even more. And if the Russian chopper arrives while they are all mixed together and kills them all"—Kwok shrugged—"so be it. It's none of our affair."

The chief looked down at the bound Russian.

"That chopper is undoubtedly attached to a Russian ship, probably on the way here now. How do you intend to explain him?" The chief nodded at the Russian.

Kwok shrugged again. "If by some miracle Dugan and his crazy Russians survive, we'll just release the corporal here, claim it was a misunderstanding, and apologize. They'll be angry, but I doubt much will happen. But if Dugan and his companions perish, no one knows the corporal's here. I doubt the helicopter has fuel to stay for a prolonged period, so we'll have some time after they leave before the Russian ship arrives. We'll just wrap our friend here in chains and slip him over the side, as if he never existed."

Kwok smiled at the chief, pleased with his own cleverness. "When the Russians arrive, we are simply a poor fishing boat that was attacked by pirates. If you can get the leak repaired, we will continue to port. If not, we ask the Russians for help. Either way, we can forget we ever met Dugan and his crazy Russians."

"Yo... you're insane! I won't be involved with murder!" the chief said.

Kwok narrowed his eyes. "I suggest you rethink that position," he said. "Or you'll go over the side with your new Russian friend. Now get below where you belong and keep us afloat. I'll tell you when you can stop the engine."

RUSSIAN KA-29TB HELICOPTER
1 NORTHEAST OF *OCEAN GOLIATH*
ARABIAN SEA

The pilot stayed in the clear air behind the rapidly moving front, wary of any developments that might endanger his craft. He dropped low to the water and moved toward the plume of black, greasy smoke. The drillship was lying port side down, her hull awash, and as the pilot reached the ship and hovered over her, she lost her fight with gravity and slipped below the waves. The pilot circled and keyed his mike.

"Momma Bear, this is Baby Bear. How do you copy? Over."

One hundred nautical miles to the east, the comm center on the Russian naval vessel *Admiral Vinogradov* answered. "Baby Bear, this is Momma Bear. We read you five by five. What is your situation? Over."

"We had to divert to avoid weather," the pilot said. "We're presently over the site of a large drillship that burned and sank. No apparent survivors. Request you come to this position to extend search. Do you copy? Over."

"Baby Bear, we copy and confirm we're en route to your present position. What of your original mission? Over."

"There is activity to my southwest. En route to investigate. Over," the pilot said.

"Acknowledged, Baby Bear. Keep us informed. Momma Bear, out."

ARABIAN SEA
300 YARDS ASTERN OF
KYUNG YANG NO. 173

Dugan flinched as a bullet whizzed by his ear.

"Not to be critical," Dugan yelled to Borgdanov over the roar of the outboard, "but maybe you should start shooting back at these assholes."

"*Nyet*," said Borgdanov. "Is waste of ammunition. Do not worry, *Dyed*. We open fire when they get closer."

The outboard coughed to a halt just as he finished speaking.

"Well, that'll be anytime now," Dugan said. "We just ran out of fuel. Tell me when to start worrying."

ARABIAN SEA
700 YARDS ASTERN OF
KYUNG YANG NO. 173

Waabberi raised the binoculars and fiddled with the focus until the distant dot revealed itself as a Russian chopper. He shifted his gaze to the following boats, and watched them break pursuit and turn to run for the protection of the rainsquall as each identified the threat. Being caught on the open sea by a Russian chopper was a pirate's worst nightmare. It was survivable with hostages as shields, but when they caught a boat manned solely by pirates, the Russians were merciless.

He looked after the fleeing boats. The fools would never make the protection of the squall line. The chopper was too fast.

But how had the Russians found them? He turned back to study the orange men's boat. Someone must have called for help, but who? It couldn't be the fishing boat—they'd been chasing it only a few minutes, far too short a time for anyone to respond to a distress call. But the orange men came from the drillship, and they must have a radio. And if the Russians were coming to rescue the orange men, the way to avoid immediate and violent death at the muzzles of Russian guns was to get as close to the orange men as possible, whoever they might be.

He turned back to his quarry, just as the orange men's boat died.

"Faster," he said to his driver.

"But Waabberi," the driver said, "we should follow the others—"

"Silence, fool!" Waabberi said. "Our only hope is hostages, and the hostages are there. Keep at least one of them alive," he yelled above the outboard.

KYUNG YANG NO. 173
ARABIAN SEA

The chief engineer stared down at the water sloshing in the bilge. They were listing over ten degrees, and each roll of the boat brought water up to the deck plates on the starboard side of the engine room, dangerously close to shorting out the electric motor of the general-service pump, his last remaining way to pump bilges. This was lunacy and Kwok was an idiot. He touched his pocketknife through the cloth of his sodden coveralls, and made a decision.

He climbed from the engine room to the wheelhouse, taking the steps two at a time. His knife was open in his hand as he burst through the wheelhouse door.

Kwok turned, his scowl turning to concern as he saw the knife. "Yo… you dare attack me?" he shouted, as he moved to where the Russian's assault rifle lay on deck against the wheelhouse bulkhead.

The chief ignored Kwok and stooped to slice the tape at the Russian's wrists and ankles. The Russian sprang up, covering the distance to Kwok in two long strides.

He looked at Kwok with contempt. "To shoot, Kwok," he said as he disarmed the Korean, "you must first move safety selector."

"I… I meant no harm," Kwok said. "I left the drillship to save us all. You too. Bu… but I was wrong. It was a misunderstanding. I am very sorry."

The Russian smiled at Kwok, then shrugged. Kwok visibly relaxed seconds before a great ham of a fist smashed him in the face.

"Apology accepted," the Russian said, looking down to where Kwok lay on the deck, his face already purpling. He aimed a savage kick into the little Korean's midsection, and then turned back to the chief.

"You," he said. "Tie this bastard up, then tell me what is happening."

"We are sinking, and your countrymen are coming," the chief said, as he fished a roll of duct tape from his pocket and tossed it to the Russian. "And tie him up yourself. I have to stop us from sinking."

The chief turned on his heel and rushed to the engine room.

Unarmed, Dugan crouched as low as he could in the boat, then realized how stupid it was to expect an inflatable boat to provide any protection from a bullet. He scooted over to put as much of the outboard as possible between himself and the pirates. Borgdanov and the sergeant knelt on either side of him, calmly firing an occasional three-round burst back at the pirates. Dugan looked up at Borgdanov.

"For Christ's sake," Dugan said. "There's only one left. Use the RPG!"

"*Nyet*," Borgdanov replied without looking down. "He is still too far for RPG. We must be sure of kill shot. Anyway, chopper is coming soon, and the *piraty* are terrible shots. At this distance, it would be accident if they hit anything."

Just as the Russian finished speaking, bullets stitched the starboard tube of the inflatable, followed by the hiss of escaping air. Borgdanov looked down and shrugged. "Even *piraty* get lucky sometime," he said. "But maybe you are right. We are not moving and they are coming fast." He glanced over. "Ilya, the RPG."

Anisimov balanced himself on the canted open deck of the listing fishing boat, holding his assault rifle and looking for an opportunity to add his fire to that of his comrades. But it wasn't to be. Without her forward motion to maintain rudder control, the *Kyung Yang No. 173* was wallowing in the remaining swell, making her a very unstable firing platform. Given the range to the pirate boat and the fact that he would be firing past his comrades, he stood as much chance of hitting them as he did the pirates. He lowered his weapon and glanced up at the approaching chopper.

He did a double take. The chopper had stopped its approach and was hovering. What's wrong? Surely they can see the situation. They should be closing on the *piraty* with their mini-gun to provide cover for the major and—

Then it hit him, and he rushed for the wheelhouse and the radio.

Dugan peeked around the outboard and watched the pirate boat go airborne as it topped a swell fifty yards behind them, moving at full throttle now. He glanced at the sergeant on his knees beside him, the RPG to his shoulder, and willed him to pull the trigger. There was a muffled thump, and he watched the round fly from the weapon and plunge into the sea, thirty feet from their own boat.

"*Mat' ublyudkek*," the sergeant muttered, as he tossed the now-useless weapon over the side and reached for his assault rifle.

"What the hell?" Dugan said.

"RPG is dud," Borgdanov said from Dugan's opposite side, continuing to stare aft as he fired at the pirates. "Where is chopper, *Dyed*? We could use help now."

Dugan rolled on his back and searched the sky. He spotted the chopper just as it went into a hover, and watched, waiting for it to charge forward and take out the pirates. *What's he waiting for?*

"Ahh… Andrei. This guy's not acting too friendly. If you have any secret hey-I'm-a-Russian-too signals, now would be the time to trot them out."

The co-pilot peered through the sight. The heat-seeker would do the work, but the range was relatively short and he had to ensure he got the weapon close enough to acquire the target. He was intent on his task, undistracted by the sudden chatter on the radio. Only slowly did it penetrate.

"Russian chopper! Abort! Abort!" a frantic voice screamed in Russian. "You are targeting friendlies!"

But he'd already launched.

CHAPTER TWENTY-SEVEN

Dugan sensed something was wrong and was rising even before the flame bloomed from the chopper.

"Get *DOWN, Dyed*," screamed Borgdanov, as Dugan rose between the two Russians firing at the advancing pirate boat.

Dugan, with no time to explain, placed a hand on the shoulder of each Russian and shoved with all his strength. The surprised Russians cursed as they tumbled into the water, and Dugan threw himself backward over the outboard. He was still in midair when the missile struck. The concussion drove the air from his lungs, and he plunged beneath the surface of the water just as a fireball rolled over it.

Disoriented, he surfaced seconds later, more from the buoyancy of the survival suit than from his own efforts. He felt a strong hand on his arm, and turned his head to find the sergeant towing him toward the charred remains of their deflating Zodiac. Soon, he was clinging to the side of the damaged craft with the two Russians, looking at a debris field where the pirate boat had been.

"Wh… what happened?" Dugan asked. "I was sure he was aiming for us."

"Maybe he was, *Dyed*," Borgdanov said. "But *piraty* boat was very near with engine at full power. Our own motor was cooling. So. I think heat-seeker made targeting correction." He looked at the smoldering remains of the Zodiac. "Even so, was very close. Being underwater and in suits saved us, I think."

Dugan looked up, searching the sky.

"Let's hope the chopper doesn't come back to finish the job," he said.

Oblivious to the VHF squawking demands that he identify himself, Anisimov watched in horror through the wheelhouse window as the fireball erupted on the sea behind him. Then as the fire dissipated, he saw an orange head bob to the surface, then two more, and all three moved to the charred remains of the first Zodiac. Relief flooded over him, and he heard the radio for the first time.

"—demand you identify yourself at once. Over."

Anisimov started to key the mike, then stopped. He looked down at his black utilities, devoid of rank markings but clearly Russian Special Forces. Instinctively, he touched the Russian tricolor flag patch on his shoulder. The Russian government didn't particularly like it when their elite soldiers resigned to become private contractors, and Anisimov and the others had done so under assumed names. And he was quite sure that Russian officials would like it even less if they knew that private contractors were impersonating active-duty Russian personnel. When Major Borgdanov accepted the assignment, the clear understanding was that there would be no possible contact with regular Russian forces. This could be tricky.

Anisimov stared at the mike. What did the major always say? Ah yes, when your back was to the wall, attack! Surprise assault is always the best defense. He walked to the wheelhouse window, where his uniform was visible to the hovering chopper and keyed the mike.

"Russian helicopter over my position! Identify yourself at once! Over," he said.

"This is flight Bravo Three from Russian naval vessel *Admiral Vinogradov*. I say again. Identify *yourself*," came the reply.

Anisimov ignored the request. "What is your name and rank?" he demanded.

"*Identify yourself at once*. Over," the chopper pilot said.

"Very well," Anisimov said. "This is Colonel Alexei Vetrov, Federal Security Service, Special Operations Group Alpha. Now. What is *your* name and rank? Over."

There was a long pause before the pilot responded, his voice tentative.

"Th... this is Captain Lieutenant Ivan Demidov," the pilot said. "Wh... what are you doing here, Colonel, if I might ask?"

"*Nyet*! You may *not* ask," Anisimov replied. "We are on classified mission, involving something you may have seen on way here. Beyond that, I cannot discuss on open radio. Is this clear, Captain Lieutenant Demidov?"

"*Da*, Colonel," Demidov said. "Do... do you require assistance? Would you like us to pick up the three men in the water?"

Anisimov hesitated and looked back at the charred Zodiac, and then around the fishing boat. Major Borgdanov and company seemed to be all right. The fishing boat was in bad shape, but if it sank, the Russians were nearby and he could always put out a distress call before taking to the raft. Better to get the chopper away for now.

"*Nyet*, Captain Lieutenant. Not at this time," Anisimov said. "What is your mission?"

"To rescue Korean fishing boat and arrest *piraty*," the pilot replied.

"Consider the first part of your mission successful," Anisimov said. "But I believe most of the *piraty* are escaping as we speak."

"We'll catch them, Colonel," said the pilot. "Though I suspect they'll all be killed resisting arrest."

Anisimov paused. He had no idea what had transpired on the drillship, nor if any of the pirates had been exposed to the virus. If they had, the results could be catastrophic. If they hadn't—well, they were still murdering pirates, weren't they?

"That outcome would be... helpful to our mission, Captain Lieutenant," Anisimov said. "In fact, it would be most helpful if these *piraty* disappeared without a trace. Is my meaning clear?"

"What *piraty*, Colonel?" the pilot asked. "Now, if there is nothing more, we'll undertake routine patrol to north and return to ship."

Thirty minutes later, Dugan and the two Russians sat in the charred, half-deflated Zodiac alongside the listing *Kyung Yang No. 173*. The seas had abated to a slight swell, and the two stricken vessels drifted side by side, tethered by a single thin line. Anisimov stood on the canting deck of the fishing boat and tossed Sergeant Denosovitch a plastic jug, as Dugan and Borgdanov opened cans and sloshed clear liquid around the crippled inflatable.

"That ought to do it," Dugan said. "We'll leave the rest of the stuff in the cans. It'll go up quick enough when it all starts burning."

He surveyed their handiwork. The air was thick with the pungent smell of paint thinner, mineral spirits, and whatever other flammables Anisimov had scrounged from the paint locker. They'd splashed it all over the boat until it puddled on the floorboards, and then stacked open cans of the liquid that remained in the middle of the boat.

"You got the bleach, Sergeant?" Dugan asked.

"*Da*," the sergeant said, and held up a large plastic jug in each hand.

"Let's get to it then," Dugan said, reaching for one of the jugs.

The three took turns helping each other douse the outsides of their survival suits with bleach. When all the suits were thoroughly wetted, Dugan nodded, and the men stripped the suits off and tossed them over the cans in the middle of the boat. Their underwear joined the pile, and they leaped, naked, to the deck of the fishing boat.

Anisimov had things prepared—buckets with a solution of strong soap and water, brushes, and sponges. One man stood still while the other two scrubbed him and flushed him with seawater. When they were done with that, each stepped under the powerful flow of the temporary shower Anisimov had rigged by securing a fire-hose nozzle to the handrail of the upper deck.

"That should do it," Dugan said, as he stepped from beneath the torrent and signaled Anisimov to turn off the water. He walked to the rail and untied the line holding the crippled Zodiac. Anisimov appeared with a flare gun, the other two Russians close behind. Dugan waited until the Zodiac was twenty feet away.

"Do it, Corporal," Dugan said. Anisimov nodded and fired, and the Zodiac burst into flames.

ISOLATION UNIT
SICKBAY
USS *BUNKER HILL* (CG-52)
ARABIAN SEA

"Christ, I'll be glad to get out of here," Dugan said to Borgdanov across the tiny room they shared with the other two Russians.

Borgdanov shrugged. "Is not so bad," he said. "Is only three more days, and is much better than the two days we spend on fishing boat, *da*? For sure food here is better." He shuddered. "I am not so fond of kimchi."

Dugan nodded. He was glad to be off the fishing boat, however impatient he was with the current situation. With his help, the Korean chief engineer managed to get the leak stopped.

A call to Ward had done the rest. They set a westerly course for Aden to get them out of the Russians' immediate operating area, while Ward arranged an extraction. Two days later, a Sea Hawk helicopter had lowered biohazard suits for Dugan and the Russians, not to protect them but to isolate them from contact with others.

They'd been winched aboard the chopper one by one, with Dugan the last to leave. Before going, he'd read the newly cooperative Kwok the riot act, reminding him of the realities. He would be shadowed by satellites and aircraft all the way to Aden, and if he changed course or attempted in any way to contact another vessel, he would be sunk without warning by a cruise missile. Ward's superiors had been much less reticent about authorizing decisive action after they'd learned what they were dealing with.

Given the speed of the fishing boat, the incubation period for the virus would elapse before the vessel reached Aden, and there she would be met by a medical team to assess the crew's health before releasing them.

"What about charter and repairs, Dugan?" Kwok had asked. "You promised."

Dugan had handed Kwok a card. "Mail your bill for the charter and *reasonable* expenses here, and it will get paid, Kwok," Dugan said, glancing at the chief engineer. "As long as it's accompanied by a signed statement from the chief here that you didn't retaliate against him and the other crewmen that helped us."

"This is blackmail!" Kwok said.

"Your call, Kwok. Money or revenge," Dugan countered, leaving the little Korean sputtering on deck as the chopper hoisted him skyward.

"Do not worry so, *Dyed*," Borgdanov said, pulling Dugan back to reality. "We will be finished incubation period soon, and by that time we arrive in Harardheere. Blake says executions have stopped since *piraty* now know about our hostages, and I think it is not bad thing to give them time to think. Like you say in English, give them time to boil, *da*?"

Dugan smiled, despite his mood. "I think you mean, give them time to stew," he said.

Borgdanov shrugged. "Boil. Stew. Whatever. How you cook *piraty*'s ass is not so important, I think—as long as you cook it."

CHAPTER TWENTY-EIGHT

M/T Phoenix Lynx
At anchor
Harardheere, Somalia

"QUIET!" Zahra shouted for the third time, slapping his open hand on the conference table.

Eleven faces snapped toward him, surprised and quieted by the explosive sound. Surprised looks turned to scowls as the men glared down the long table.

"And just who're you to give orders, Zahra," one said. "We're all equals here."

"Even among equals someone must maintain order," Zahra said.

The man sneered. "So you've appointed yourself. Is that it?" There were grumbles of agreement.

"I appointed myself to nothing," Zahra said evenly. "When these ships full of our brothers arrived, their captors contacted me. These people made it clear they'll only deal with a single point of contact. I didn't seek them. As soon as the situation became clear to me, I called you all here to Harardheere."

Zahra kept his face impassive and watched reactions as he spoke. In truth, he was elated the new arrivals contacted him first. As the possibilities had occurred to him over the last week, he'd become giddy with anticipation. If only he could pull it off. He sighed inwardly. But first he had to leash this pack of hyenas.

"And now that we're here, Zahra," asked another man, "just what would you have us do? We've come the length of the Somali coast to gather, and now you propose giving up all of our captives and half the ships. That's ridiculous. If they give us two ships and a hundred or so captives, we should give them back the same."

"I've been dealing with them for over a week," Zahra said. "This American Blake is a tough negotiator, and this fellow Dugan who arrived yesterday is worse. He threatens to take all the men to Liberia. He even joked that for ten thousand dollars he could ensure they all get the death penalty."

"Savages," muttered a man down the table.

"He's bluffing," the first man scoffed. "Western governments will never permit that. Many European governments won't even turn our captured brothers over to *any* country with the death penalty."

"But we aren't dealing with Europeans," Zahra said. "At least not in name. They showed me papers documenting themselves to be Liberians, but in truth I don't know who they are. There are both Americans and Russians among them, but I suspect the Russians are mercenaries. It doesn't matter. As long as Liberia is willing to provide them cover, I doubt any of the Western powers will make a fuss. In fact, I'm quite sure they're secretly happy they don't have to deal with the problem themselves. Make no mistake, my brothers, these Liberians are serious people. They allowed me to speak with a few of the prisoners, who told me the Russians murdered quite freely and laughed in the process."

"But their offer is outrageous! We can get more ransom—"

"Can we?" Zahra asked, cutting the man off. "Thanks to the al-Shabaab fanatics and their lunacy with the American ship, there's now a UN moratorium on the payment of ransoms. One which hasn't been broken despite the fact that we've executed over twenty hostages. That means even if owners and insurers are willing to deal with us, as these Liberians seem to be, it's now impossible for them to process the necessary transactions through their banks. I doubt we see another cent in ransom money, at least until things cool down, and that may take months, or even longer." Zahra stopped and stared down the table. "That makes the offer of two ships full of gasoline very attractive. The asset is already here; no government can stop its delivery. Together, they carry over one hundred and fifty million dollars' worth of petrol, even if we sell it below market price."

A man down the table looked doubtful. "So you say. But we're warriors, not merchants. We already have other tankers, and we've always ransomed them in the past. What's so special about these?"

Idiot! Zahra struggled to hide his contempt.

"Those are crude tankers," he said. "Their cargo is useless to anyone lacking the means to refine the crude. These are product tankers, full of premium gasoline. It's as good as cash."

"The ships and captives are here, within easy reach," said one of the others. "We greatly outnumber these Liberians. Why negotiate at all? Why not just take the hostages *and* the ships?"

Zahra could no longer hide his exasperation. "With what? A collection of khat-chewing holders? These Liberians have over a hundred of our best attackers, and the Russian assault after the drillship sinking wiped out over forty more. Must I remind you that only one mother ship survived that attack with a few men left alive? We hardly have enough experienced men left to conduct normal operations against single unarmed ships, and only then if we combine forces. We have nowhere near the necessary firepower to successfully attack targets defended by armed Russians!"

"I still say they're bluffing," came a reply from down the table, and the group once again dissolved in chaos, each man shouting his opinion to be heard above the melee. Zahra shook his head in disgust.

"Have you confirmed the cargos, Zahra?"

The voice was hardly above normal speaking level, yet it was heard through the commotion. The others fell silent and turned to the speaker. Gutaale was at least a decade older than the others, and universally respected—and feared.

"Have you confirmed the cargos, Zahra?" he repeated.

"Yes, Gutaale," Zahra said. "Several of my men have lived in Europe and worked as seamen on tankers, and the Liberians allowed us to inspect the ships. My men confirm that they are both full of gasoline."

"And whoever these Liberians are, doesn't it seem strange they have such a fortune in gasoline to trade? Something doesn't seem right to me," Gutaale said.

Zahra suppressed a smile. If he could win Gutaale over, the others would fall in line, and the man was asking the very questions he'd asked himself.

"Nor to me, Gutaale. At least at first. But things became clear during negotiations. Blake wouldn't answer that question, but this Dugan isn't quite so clever. He let a few things slip and Omar, my interpreter, was able to pick up on them. Between us, we pieced things together," Zahra said. "The tankers are both old, near the end of their lives. The cargoes belong to major oil companies, and the oil majors self-insure their cargo. I think these Liberians just diverted the tankers here to use the cargo as trade goods. They will, of course, claim that they were hijacked by pirates and that they were only able to negotiate the release of the crews. The ship insurers will be happy to get off by paying scrap value for the two old tankers, and the oil companies will be stuck with the bill for the gasoline." Zahra paused, his admiration obvious. "It's quite clever."

"And quite obvious," Gutaale said. "There'll be repercussions."

"Ah, but that's the beauty of it," Zahra said. "Repercussions from whom?"

He ticked off points on his fingers.

"All our captives will be released, so the great humanitarian issue is solved. With the captives out of the equation, pressure will be off the various governments. Maintaining the anti-pirate force is expensive, and I suspect they'll all jump at the chance to reduce their naval presence. Will the insurers complain? I don't think so. No hostages reduces the pressure on everyone. They'll let things calm down a bit, and in a few months start very low-key talks about payments to release the remaining ships.

"This is not a bad deal," Zahra continued. "Everyone is a winner except the oil companies, and how much sympathy can they expect? In three months' time, everyone will go back to ignoring poor, benighted, lawless Somalia. Then we do what we want."

Gutaale stared at Zahra. Zahra held his breath, then heaved an inward sigh as the corners of the older man's mouth twitched upward in a smile.

"You have it all figured out, Zahra," Gutaale said. "Exactly what is it that 'we' want to do?"

Zahra smiled back. "Organize, innovate, train, upgrade our equipment, and a dozen other things!" His voice grew excited as he warmed to the subject. "Just think of it Gutaale," he said. "This is the first time we will have such a sum all together. We have a chance to combine forces and use it wisely. Night-vision equipment. Remote-controlled drones to extend our search areas. Better, bigger, faster boats with better radar and evasion capabilities. Training to teach us to use it all. Intelligence assets in the world's shipping centers. The list is long," Zahra said, "and all possible with this influx of money."

"We've made good money in the past," Gutaale said.

"Yes. A million here, five million there," Zahra said. "All divided and spent foolishly. How many times have you seen the fools we employ crowd the khat market, waving fistfuls of hundred-dollar bills? We can do better. We must."

"What do you propose?" Gutaale asked.

"To make the deal," Zahra said. "I say we give them all the captive seamen, and negotiate for the remaining ships. We may get something for the ships from the insurers in a few months when things calm down a bit. In the meantime, we do nothing but acquire new equipment, train, and put our intelligence assets in place. The men we get back from the Liberians will be the core of our force, and they'll know how they were captured and how to develop countermeasures. When we launch again in six or eight months, we'll use our intelligence nets to select our targets carefully. Rather than scooping up every poxy fishing boat or rusty Greek freighter carrying cement, we'll focus on high-value targets—loaded tankers and container ships, or perhaps passenger vessels." Zahra paused, as if thinking.

"Yes," he said, "particularly passenger vessels. We can use the fanatics' trick and get people onboard ahead of time. If we make the very first capture of our new venture a passenger vessel, we'll have tremendous leverage. Think of having over a thousand European hostages!"

"Which it seems to me," Gutaale said, "would eventually bring back the warships and put us in a situation very similar to where we are now."

"Agreed," Zahra said. "But the key word is *eventually*. It'll take a year or more before we get to that point, and by that time, we'll have bought our way into what passes for a government here." He smiled and looked around the table. "We can all be ministers of something or other, and work diligently to free the hostages from the horrible pirates—in exchange, of course, for a sizable aid package from the Western powers."

Gutaale leaned back in his chair and nodded. "All right, Zahra," he said. "You've convinced me." He looked around the table. "Does anyone disagree?"

No one spoke.

"Very well, Zahra," Gutaale said. "Make your deal with these Liberians."

M/T *MARIE FLOYD*
AT ANCHOR
HARARDHEERE, SOMALIA

Dugan walked across the main deck to where Blake stood staring out at the M/T *Luther Hurd*, anchored in the shadow of USS *Carney*.

"How are your people, Vince?" he asked.

"Looks like they're both going to be OK," Blake said. "The navy's evacuating them to Bahrain for further evaluation, then they'll fly them home. Looks like Stan may heal faster than Lynda, but the doc on the *Carney* said she might be able to avoid surgery and get by with physical therapy."

Dugan nodded. "How about you? What're your plans?"

"I'll take the *Luther Hurd* on to Diego Garcia," Blake said. "Hanley leaned on some politicians who leaned on the navy, and they're flying some replacement crew out via Bahrain also. We'll tag along a few hours behind *Carney* until we get in chopper range." Blake looked a question at Dugan. "But I don't think you came up here to discuss my travel plans. What's up?"

Dugan grinned. "I just got off the phone with our new buddy Omar. Hook, line, and friggin' sinker! They bought the whole story."

"Terrific! You were smart to let them keep some of the ships. They think they got the best end of the deal. The crews are the issue."

Farther down the deck, Woody emerged from a ballast tank manhole and began to pull a cutting-torch hose from the tank and coil it on deck. He was finished by the time Dugan and Blake reached him.

"What's up?" Woody asked.

"You tell me," Dugan said. "How are the ballast-tank bulkheads coming?"

"Finished," Woody said.

"And the engine room?"

"Let's just cut to the chase, Dugan," Woody said. "I said 'finished.' That means every damn watertight bulkhead on this ship is like Swiss cheese."

"OK. How about the jammers and the li—"

"Jesus H. Christ on a crutch, Dugan! You sure you ain't related to Hanley? You could be twins separated at birth."

Dugan opened his mouth to protest, but Woody cut him off. "Every single thing on your list is finished. Here on *Marie Floyd*, and over on *Pacific Endurance* too."

Blake laughed, reducing Dugan's indignation to a sheepish grin.

"OK, OK," Dugan said. "Pack up and get your boys over to the *Carney*."

"If it's all the same to you," Woody said, "me and the boys will ride on *Luther Hurd* with Andrei and his guys till Bahrain."

"*Andrei*? You mean Borgdanov? The same guy you said you'd never be bass-fishing buddies with?"

"He ain't half bad," Woody said grudgingly. "For a foreigner, I mean."

Dugan laughed, then stroked his chin. "Not a bad idea. We'll have the Russians with us here on *Marie Floyd* right up to the last minute, but if Zahra gets any cute ideas, having you and your boys with your M-4s close by will be good backup."

M/T *MARIE FLOYD*
AT ANCHOR
HARARDHEERE, SOMALIA

Dugan stood with Blake near the accommodation ladder. Borgdanov and his black-clad Russians surrounded them facing outward, a threatening counterbalance to the fifty-strong contingent of the twelve clan leaders farther down the deck. The pirate presence was growing, as pirates released from their holding cells joined their leaders on deck.

But quantity didn't trump quality. Only the pirates who boarded with the clan leaders were armed, and even if they outnumbered the Russians more than four to one, the result of any firefight was far from certain. The Russians' superior weapons, body armor, and fire discipline made them formidable adversaries, and no pirate was eager to deal with them, despite the numerical imbalance.

By agreement, Dugan and Blake stayed aboard—hostages until the exchange was complete. It had begun early in the morning, starting with the release of *Phoenix Lynx* and her surviving crew, followed by release of the captive ships in the out ports. The freed vessels carried not only their own crews but those of ships Dugan allowed the pirates to keep. Each vessel released was met by a warship from the Western powers, and the identity of each hostage confirmed against a master list. When all the hostages were verified safe, *Carney* relayed the news to Dugan and escorted *Phoenix Lynx* a safe distance away. They waited now, out of sight just over the horizon.

Blake glanced nervously over the side, to where *Luther Hurd* rode at anchor, a half mile away. "I feel a bit naked without *Carney* in sight."

Dugan shook his head. "I had to lean on Ward to get them to leave in the first place. If we can't see them, they can't see us. Plausible deniability. Besides, *Carney*'s skipper already has his neck stretched out a bit by talking the SEALs into forgetting those boats."

Blake nodded and glanced down over the rail at two big high-speed Zodiacs tethered to the small landing at the bottom of the accommodation ladder. They rode there among half a dozen empty pirate launches of assorted shapes and sizes, clustered around the little landing like nursing piglets.

Dugan turned. "Well, we always knew this would be the tricky part," he said to Borgdanov. "Recommendations?"

"They will not attack until after we go down, I think," Borgdanov said. "I stay on top with six men while Ilya takes six more down ladder and prepares boats, *da? Dyed*, you and Captain Blake go with Ilya. When all is ready in the boats, Ilya signals me and we come down very fast, while Ilya and his men keep weapons pointed up at edge of the main deck. If any *piraty* leans over the main deck to shoot, Ilya's men kill him. Then we escape. Simple plan, *da?*"

"*Sounds* simple," Dugan said, hoping it would be.

"Good," Borgdanov said, and barked orders. The sergeant nodded and motioned Dugan and Blake to the ladder, then followed with his six men. Dugan moved down the sloping aluminum steps and into the first Zodiac, and Blake moved into the second. They fired up the outboards, as the Russians divided themselves between the two boats and trained their assault rifles up at the rail. The sergeant gave a sharp whistle and the remaining Russians rushed down, Borgdanov in the rear. By prearrangement, the second group also divided, filling both boats to capacity. The last Russian to board each boat cast off the lines, and Dugan and Blake backed the boats out of the cluster. Dugan looked up at the sergeant's shout.

Half a dozen pirates reached the rail, forced back by Russian fire. All the Russians targeted the rail, except Borgdanov and the sergeant, who were pulling the pins on grenades and tossing them into the pirate boats.

"*GO! GO! GO! Dyed!*" screamed Borgdanov, as he and the sergeant finished and raised their weapons to target the rail.

"*HANG ON!*" Dugan screamed, as he spun the boat around and hit full throttle, and Blake followed suit. Heavily loaded, the boats bucked in the water and bogged down as the propellers cavitated, but almost simultaneously Dugan and Blake realized their mistake and backed off the throttles a bit. In seconds, the boats were up and planing across the water, as Dugan felt the concussion of the grenade blasts on his back and heard the earsplitting explosions.

The pirates aboard *Marie Floyd* rushed back to the rail, pouring wild, undisciplined fire after the boats, joined by freed pirates on the deck of the nearby *Pacific Endurance*. But the boats were already difficult targets—too difficult for the marksmanship of the pirates.

Borgdanov pointed to the *Marie Floyd*, where three pirate launches clustered unharmed at the bottom of her accommodation ladder. Dugan shrugged.

"We'll just have to let those go," Dugan yelled over the noise of the outboard. "They're all stirred up now. If we go back to toss grenades in those boats, someone might get killed."

Borgdanov smiled. "We do not have to return," he yelled back. "Just because *piraty* are terrible shots, does not mean we are. Stop. I think we are safe here."

Dugan cut power to an idle, and the boat drifted to a stop. Blake did the same and the boats drifted together, the powerful outboards muttering.

"Just as well," Dugan said. "I wasn't going to go much farther anyway. I'm not totally sure of the range of the remotes."

Borgdanov nodded, then shouted orders to his men. The Russians opened fire on the distant boats, a steady *rat-tat-tat* of aimed three-round bursts from a dozen weapons. In minutes, the three pirate boats were riddled with holes and sinking. Dugan opened his mouth to congratulate Borgdanov on his men's marksmanship, but was distracted by an unexpected vibration from his pocket.

M/T *MARIE FLOYD*
AT ANCHOR
HARARDHEERE, SOMALIA

Omar stayed to one side and tried to make himself small as Zahra paced the deck and screamed curses after the fleeing Liberians.

"Those steaming piles of goat dung have the effrontery to betray me?" Zahra screamed. "To shoot my men and destroy my boats? They've reneged on the agreement, and we'll bring boats from ashore and hunt down this *Luther Hurd*! She can't outrun us! We'll blow them up and sink them all, and if the navy ships come back, we'll claim it has nothing to do with us! Tankers blow up all the time."

Omar didn't think it wise to point out that their men had been shooting at the Russians first.

"Omar!" Zahra screamed, and Omar scurried over.

"Call this Dugan on the cell phone you gave him for the negotiations. I want to let him know he's about to die so he can enjoy the anticipation," Zahra said.

"But Zahra—"

"*DO IT!*" Zahra screamed, and Omar pulled out his phone and hit a preset.

After a moment, Omar took the phone from his ear and spoke. "I have him, Zahra," he said.

"Good," Zahra said. "Tell him that he'll soon be dead."

Omar nodded and spoke into the phone, then looked back at Zahra.

"And now ask him if he knows what I'll soon be doing," Zahra commanded, preparing to launch into a long description of the slow torture he intended to inflict on Dugan and all his men.

Omar translated Zahra's words, and listened to the phone a moment. His face took on a strange expression, then morphed into a fearful look as Zahra continued.

"Tell him I'll—"

"I… I can't tell him anything, Zahra. He hung up."

"*WHAT*? He just hung up? What did he say?"

"Well, after I asked him if he knew what you'd be doing, he said… he said…"

"Out with it, you fool! What did he say!"

Omar was trembling now. "He… he said, 'I suggest the backstroke,' and then he hung up," Omar said.

ZODIACS
HARARDHEERE, SOMALIA

"—suggest the backstroke," Dugan said, then tossed the phone over the side. "Let's do it," he shouted across to Blake in the next boat.

Blake fished a small electronic device from his pocket and flipped up the guard over the single button. He thumbed the button and multiple explosions bloomed along the hulls of both *Marie Floyd* and *Pacific Endurance*, well below their waterlines. They caused small but obvious boils of white water, sending spray into the air as dull thumps echoed across the sea.

Dugan nodded and pulled a remote from his own pocket. He stared at the device a long moment, then looked back at the ships.

"These are very bad people, *Dyed*," Borgdanov said. "I think you should not worry about their fate. Whatever chance they have is better than chance they give people they burn to death and shoot in head, *da*?"

Dugan nodded and hit the button, sending a single signal to turn on half a dozen battery-powered jammers hidden on each ship. It was a one-time thing. As soon as the jammers came online, they blocked the signal that had activated them. Along with everything else.

M/T MARIE FLOYD
AT ANCHOR
HARARDHEERE, SOMALIA

The deck vibrated under Zahra's feet from a series of muffled explosions, and he looked across the water to see the water roiled by a similar series of explosions along the hull of the *Pacific Endurance.*

"They've sabotaged us," Zahra said, his mind racing. "Very well. Forget the Liberians for now, Omar. Organize the seamen among our men. We'll ground the ships in shallow water to save the cargo. Get them started, then call all available boats from ashore, just in case."

Zahra actually had good cause for optimism. Contrary to popular perception, tankers typically have a great deal of reserve buoyancy and can survive significant damage, given calm water and fair weather.

But this wasn't a casualty. This was destruction orchestrated by a man who spent his life keeping tankers floating, and who sure as hell knew how to sink one. So as much as Woody had griped as he crawled through tank after tank watching Dugan mark places to cut with a can of spray paint, he'd followed instructions to the letter. As had the Russians when Dugan showed them where to place the shaped charges for maximum effect.

The ships were going down, and they were going down fast.

Omar rushed from the deckhouse to where Zahra stood, watching the main deck a foot above the water.

"Zahra," he said. "The engine room is flooded. We can't move the ship!"

Zahra nodded, never taking his eyes off the water. "Have you managed to reach anyone ashore?"

"No," Omar said. "No phones. No radio. No nothing. We're being jammed."

Zahra looked up. Pirates boiled out of the deckhouse, alerted to the fact the engine room was flooded and that sinking was imminent.

"We must escape," he said, quiet urgency in his voice. "There aren't enough lifeboats. It'll be every man for himself when this mob realizes that. Go get them started launching the boats, then pick four of our most loyal men and sneak away to meet me on the stern. I saw a small life raft near there. We'll launch it and escape while the rest of these fools kill themselves over a place in the boats. Go now!"

"At once, Zahra," Omar said, and scurried away.

Zahra moved calmly, reassuring men as he met them. Telling them that tankers took a long time to sink, and that boats were on the way from shore, and that they were readying the lifeboats as a last resort.

He lied his way aft, then slipped from sight into the alleyway between the deckhouse and the machinery casing. He waited there impatiently until Omar arrived with four men in tow.

"Here," Zahra called, and motioned them aft to where the life-raft canister rested in its cradle near the ship's rail. "Quickly now," Zahra said. "Two men on each end. Lift the canister and toss it into the sea on my count of three. Omar, hold the rope, and don't let go!"

The men positioned themselves as instructed and prepared to heave.

"One. Two. Three. Heave!" Zahra shouted.

The men heaved on command, and an almost-weightless fiberglass canister shot ten feet in the air and plunged the short distance to the sea, splitting in two halves and revealing—nothing.

"It... it's empty," Omar said, holding a rope attached to nothing.

Zahra looked farther up the deck, where two other pirates intent on survival had attempted to launch another life-raft canister. It too was empty.

"They've sabotaged all the rafts," Zahra said. "That leaves only the lifeboats. Listen to me, all of you. We'll go to the nearest lifeboat. As soon as it's launched, shoot down anyone who gets in our way and get aboard. Is that clear?"

The men nodded, and Zahra led them up the port side to the lifeboat station. But they soon found they had no cause to use their weapons.

"It's welded!" Zahra heard a man cry as he neared the lifeboat. "The lifeboat davit is welded together! We can't launch the boat!"

Zahra looked around. The main deck was awash now and the tank vents were starting to go under, water boiling around them as the last pockets of air were forced from the tanks. He raced up the exterior stairway to the bridge wing, his underlings close behind. They gained the bridge wing and flew across it to the stairway up to the flying bridge above the wheelhouse, the highest spot on the ship.

And there they stopped.

Soon they were joined by others, and the small space was an island of humanity, its population staring down at the sea rushing to claim them, each knowing there was no escape.

ZODIACS
HARARDHEERE, SOMALIA

Dugan watched the main deck of the *Marie Floyd* dip below the water, with that of the *Pacific Endurance* not far behind. He did his best to ignore the masses of humanity collecting above the bridge on both vessels.

"Seen enough?" he yelled over to Blake.

Blake nodded, and headed toward the *Luther Hurd*, undoubtedly thinking of dead shipmates. Dugan gritted his teeth and fell in behind.

Halfway back to the *Luther Hurd* he saw them, two large black triangles cutting the water. He turned as the sharks swam past, and looked out over the water at a dozen fins converging on the sinking ships.

Dugan closed his eyes and thought of Bosun Luna, flaming tire around his neck, his agonizing death recorded to brutalize his family. He thought of other families in the Philippines, India, Europe, and the US—and victims yet to be. And his heart grew hard. *What goes around, comes around.*

"Bon appétit, boys," he whispered, and turned toward *Luther Hurd* without looking back.

Author's Notes
The Facts behind the Fiction

A novelist never lets the facts get in the way of a good story, but I firmly believe the strategic use of facts make a tale more compelling. Given that truth is often stranger than fiction, I thought a review of the facts behind *Deadly Coast* might be of interest.

UNIT 731
EPIDEMIC PREVENTION RESEARCH LAB
HYGIENE CORP
JAPANESE IMPERIAL ARMY

I've visited Japan many times, and found the Japanese to be gracious and friendly. So much so, it's often difficult to believe the events of the Second World War and the period leading up to it. Horrifying human experimentation carried out by Unit 731 was rumored for some time, and in the last fifteen years, well documented. The Dr. Ishii Shiro mentioned in the book was a real person. Under his leadership, Unit 731 committed atrocities that are almost beyond belief.

None of the perpetrators of these atrocities were brought to justice. At the war's end, members of Unit 731 were the world's foremost experts on chemical and biological warfare (largely as a result of their inhuman experimentation). Much documentation was destroyed before it was captured by occupying forces, and the world in 1945 was still a dangerous place. In that context, Ishii Shiro and his colleagues, a group unknown to the world at large, traded expertise for immunity. The rank and file of Unit 731 were sworn to secrecy and melted back into the general population, while higher-ranking members became advisors to classified US chemical- and biological-warfare programs. The official position was that Unit 731 never existed.

The Japanese government never changed that stance, but a decade or more ago, something extraordinary happened. Former members of the rank and file of Unit 731 began to tell their individual stories. Local governments, assisted by volunteers, many of whom were academics, set up exhibitions in sixty-one locations across Japan. In the course of eighteen months, the truth was told. Many of those testimonies are chronicled in a book by Hal Gold, titled *Unit 731 Testimony*. It isn't reading for the faint of heart.

While Mr. Gold's book provided the historical background, I did take license. None of the dialogue or actions attributed Ishii Shiro in *Deadly Coast* are factual, and the relationship with his Nazi counterparts is also my invention, as is Dr. Imamura. There was never an Operation Minogame, but there was an operation conceived by Dr. Ishii for a last-ditch biological attack against the US mainland.

Operation PX was finalized on March 26, 1945. It was to be a suicide attack against the US West Coast by the *I-400*, the largest Japanese submarine and one of only three vessels of its class. *I-400* carried three seaplanes in watertight hangars, and the sub's range was to be extended by converting ballast tanks to fuel tanks. She was to launch a seaplane attack against West Coast population centers with plague, cholera, and perhaps hantavirus. The crew was then to run the vessel aground and carry other pathogens ashore.

Ishii's plan was scrapped just prior to launch by General Umezu Yoshijiro, Chief of the General Staff. Umezu reportedly stated, "If bacteriological warfare is conducted, it will grow from the dimension of war between Japan and America to an endless battle of humanity against bacteria. Japan will earn the derision of the world." Umezu remained steadfast against the plan through the last five months of the war, even as the US bombed Tokyo to rubble. He faced violent opposition for his reticence.

General Umezu was given the inglorious duty of representing the Japanese Imperial Army at the surrender aboard the USS *Missouri*, and later was tried as a war criminal. He received a life sentence and died in Sugamo Prison in 1949. Dr. Ishii never served a day in prison, and died of throat cancer in 1959. Go figure. One can only hope Ishii's demise was a painful one.

THE LIBERTY SHIP
SS *JOHN BARRY*

Every good pirate tale needs a treasure ship, and I was pleased to find a real one in the neighborhood. Owned by the US War Shipping Administration and operated by Lykes Brothers Steamship Company of New Orleans, Louisiana, the SS *John Barry* sailed from Norfolk, Virginia, on July 24, 1944. She was bound for Iran with war materiel, with an intermediate stop in Saudi Arabia to deliver three million newly minted silver *riyal* coins. She never made it.

On the night of August 28, 1944, the *John Barry* was torpedoed by the German submarine *U-859*, and sank in over 8,500 feet of water, 127 nautical miles off the coast of Oman. Two seamen died in the attack, and the rest took to lifeboats. These survivors' tales placed the *John Barry* solidly in the ranks of history's lost treasure ships.

According to the captain's statement, there was an additional secret cargo of $26 million (at 1944 silver prices) in silver bullion aboard the *John Barry*. The captain's statement was backed by anecdotal evidence from other crewmen, and cryptic, if inconclusive, references scattered throughout official records. The existence of the additional silver was never established. Clearly out of reach over a mile and a half deep, the *John Barry* and her cargo became another legend in the pantheon of lost treasures.

And so it remained until 1992, when an unlikely alliance of American treasure hunters and an Omani sheik employed a British salvage expert and a French drilling vessel in an ambitious attempt to wrest treasure from the depths. Using an unmanned remotely operated vehicle to place explosives, the operators of the drillship *Flex LD* blew open the *John Barry*'s hull and used a mechanical grab of their own invention to scoop up the exposed silver coins. The salvors managed to raise 1.8 million of the confirmed cargo of 3 million silver riyals.

Unfortunately, the silver bullion (if it exists) couldn't be identified in the jumbled wreckage, and the rest of the silver coins were too mixed in the wreckage to allow easy extraction. The salvors terminated operations with a stated intention of making another attempt. To date, the remaining riches of the *John Barry* remain unrecovered.

I took obvious liberties with the story, but the methods employed by my fictional drillship, *Ocean Goliath*, closely parallel those used by the very real drillship *Flex LD*. Most importantly, the *U-859* was not sunk immediately after her attack on the *John Barry* as indicated in the story, but sailed on to make some very interesting history of her own.

U-859

Contrary to the portrayal in the novel, the real *U-859* was outward-bound from Germany to the German-Japanese submarine base in Malaysia when she encountered and sank the *John Barry*. *U-859* was a type IXD2 boat, the latest class of submarine in the *Kriegsmarine*, and on her maiden voyage. Class IXD2 boats were large, with a range of 30,000 miles, and charged with the increasingly perilous task of maintaining a sea link between the Third Reich and the Empire of Japan. By 1944, the subs provided the only remaining method for sharing technology and scarce resources. *U-859*, like many eastbound subs, carried a cargo of mercury, in perpetual short supply in Japan and vital in the manufacture of munitions. Other boats carried not only mercury but also parts and drawings for the Messerschmitt ME163, an early jet fighter. Drawings the Japanese used to develop the Mitsubishi J8M1. Five of these advanced planes were captured when the Japanese surrendered in 1945. Records show that radar technology, optical instruments, and parts for V-2 rockets, along with German technicians, all made the long undersea voyage in the bellies of German U-boats. Reading of the technology transfer from Germany to Japan, I wondered what Germany might have received in return, and the idea of Unit 731 transferring biological-warfare expertise was born.

Before encountering the *John Barry*, the real *U-859* had already sunk two Allied ships and survived an air attack from a British Catalina off South Africa. She managed to shoot down the British plane, but was depth-charged and damaged in the fight. By the time she found and sank the *John Barry*, the limping U-boat was the subject of a search by British forces, which the loss of the *Barry* intensified. Undeterred, three days later Korvettenkapitän Jan Jebsen, the skipper of *U-859*, attacked and sank the M/V *Troilus* of the Blue Funnel Line. *U-859* sailed on, evading all British attempts to locate her.

But all was not well aboard *U-859*. Her snorkel was damaged in the earlier depth-charging and was only partially effective. Forced to remain submerged almost constantly by British patrols, the atmosphere inside the boat was increasingly toxic. It was with great relief that Jebsen surfaced on the night of 16 September and received radio orders to proceed to base at Penang, Malaysia.

A week later, on the morning of 23 September, *U-859* was approximately twenty nautical miles northwest of the base at Penang. Confident he'd finally shaken pursuit, Jebsen was cruising on the surface and allowing his weary men the luxury of coming topside in shifts to suck in lungfuls of fresh sea air. He was a bit more than an hour from the safety of the port. At Swettenham Pier in Penang, garlands of flowers were prepared for *U-859*'s crew and a Japanese naval band was tuning up. A crowd of Japanese and German naval personnel stood ready to welcome *U-859*, giving the base a carnival air.

Much closer to *U-859*, HMS *Trenchant* slipped beneath the azure waters of the Malacca Straits as her captain, Commander Arthur Hezlet, RN, studied the approaching U-boat in his periscope—the Royal Navy had found *U-859* at last. Or more accurately, the U-boat found the Royal Navy, since the British had intercepted the Germans' signals to base and broken the code. Commander Hezlet had been in position for thirty-six hours, awaiting *U-859*'s arrival.

HMS *Trenchant* fired a spread of three torpedoes from her stern tubes, with the middle torpedo striking the German sub just astern of the conning tower. *U-859* broke in half and sank immediately. Of the sixty-seven men aboard, nineteen survivors were in the water, including seven who made an astonishing escape from inside the sinking boat. Among the seven was the only officer to survive, twenty-two-year-old Oberleutnant Horst Klatt, the sub's first engineer. Much like my fictional Japanese, Dr. Imamura, Oberleutnant Klatt was in the toilet at the time. I based my description of Imamura's escape on Klatt's firsthand account of his own harrowing and miraculous experience.

Though perilously close to Japanese forces, Commander Hezlet ordered HMS *Trenchant* to surface and rescue survivors. Minutes into that exercise, Japanese ships appeared on the horizon and a Japanese fighter appeared overhead. Hezlett managed to pick up eight survivors, including Oberleutnant Klatt, before the attack forced him to submerge and evade. The remaining eleven Germans were rescued by the Japanese.

The story doesn't quite end there, for *U-859* did indeed contain a biological hazard and she was salvaged years later. After researchers turned up the fact that the submarine sank with some thirty-one tons of toxic mercury aboard, there were wide-spread concerns the flasks would eventually leak, poisoning the seafood chain. After diplomatic discussions between West Germany and Malaysia, the West German government launched a salvage operation in the winter of 1973.

There were ethical as well as environmental concerns. Containing the bodies of almost fifty German submariners, the wreck had long since been designated a burial site by the German War Graves Commission. As *U-859*'s only surviving officer and the individual most familiar with the sub, Horst Klatt, then fifty-one years old, was asked to lead the expedition. And lead it he did, eventually recovering some thirty of the estimated thirty-one tons of mercury.

THE PIRATES

The world has a romanticized view of piracy; but with apologies to Johnny Depp and Captain Hook, there's nothing romantic about it. As I write these words on September 2, 2012, Somali pirate gangs hold eleven ships and 178 hostages of various nationalities. Yesterday, pirates in Haradheere murdered a crewman from the *M/V Orna* in cold blood and wounded another, announcing in a phone call to the press "More killings will follow if the owners continue to lie to us—we have lost patience with them." To most folks, those numbers and events mean little, but they represent a threat all too real to those who make their living on the world's oceans and their friends and families.

The total number of hostages at any given time is a moving target, with hostages being ransomed as new hostages are captured. The International Maritime Bureau reports that last year (2011), a total of 1,206 seamen were held hostage at some point during the year, including some held for more than two years. Hostages are forced to live in deplorable conditions and subjected to constant physical and psychological abuse. Based on interviews with freed hostages, over half report being beaten and approximately ten percent suffered severe abuse, including being tied up in the sun for hours, being locked in freezers, or having fingernails pulled out with pliers. Thirty-five hostages died in 2011, nineteen of whom died while used as human shields.

Deadly Coast is fiction, and none of the characters or their actions is real. As much as I might like to play God and wrap up the Somali pirate problem so neatly, I'm afraid the solution offered exists only between the covers of this book. But though the story is fiction, I did attempt to sketch the scenes in Somalia with some authenticity. I was greatly assisted in that effort by the book *The Pirates of Somalia* by Jay Bahadur. Mr. Bahadur is a Canadian journalist who spent time in Somalia interacting with the pirates. The result is a compelling narrative that is obligatory reading for anyone interested in learning about Somali pirates. I will add that Mr. Bahadur went to great lengths to present a balanced view and his book is wonderfully objective. As a novelist rather than a journalist, I labored under no such obligation, and my pirates are considerably nastier than Mr. Bahadur's. I leave it to the reader to decide which portrayal they find more compelling.

So there you have it—the threads unraveled from the fabric of history and woven around current events to produce *Deadly Coast*. I hope you enjoyed reading the story as much as I enjoyed writing it.

Fair Winds and Following Seas,
R.E. (Bob) McDermott

Postscript on the Somali pirate situation - October 2014 - It's been two years since I penned *Deadly Coast*, and I'm pleased to say that during that period the Somali pirate situation has changed for the better. Aggressive use of private marine security (i.e. armed guards) by shipowners coupled with more aggressive anti-piracy operations by the world's navies have reduced Somali pirate attacks to a seven year low. As portrayed in *Deadly Coast*, the pirates view the whole sordid thing as a 'business,' and when you increase the cost of doing that business, the smart money goes elsewhere. That's the good news. The bad news is that piracy is increasing off the West Coast of Africa, where both the motivations and methods of operation differ greatly. So piracy continues as it has for hundreds of years, with the sporadic efforts at eradication resembling nothing so much as a giant global game of Whack-a Mole.

DEADLY CROSSING

To Our Sons
Chris and Andy

Each passing day makes me prouder
to be your dad

PROLOGUE

PRAGUE
CZECH REPUBLIC

Karina shifted in her sleep and groaned, dragged by pain to the edge of consciousness. Her eyes flew open to stare into the darkness, and her heart began to pound like that of a captured bird. Had they heard her? If they knew she was conscious, they'd come back. Then it would all start again. She squeezed her eyes shut and willed herself to sleep. Just another hour, or even another minute. Anything to escape, if just for a moment.

But sleep would not come, and she lay still, listening for approaching footsteps. She heard none, and her pulse slowed, then spiked again as she turned on the bare mattress and pain shot through her naked body. Despair washed over her, and her shoulders began to shake in silent sobs, but there were no tears, for there were none left.

She thought again of killing herself, but that was impossible, even if she had the means. They had warned her what would happen to her sisters if she defied them.

Then there were footsteps in the hall, accompanied by laughter. She curled into the fetal position and trembled, dreading the squeak of the opening door.

CHAPTER ONE

"Whatever is wrong with you?" asked Anna Walsh in the back seat of the taxi. "You've been behaving strangely for days, and now you're sweating. Are you ill? Perhaps we should skip dinner."

Tom Dugan smiled to cover his unease. "I'm fine. I'm just preoccupied with work—and it is a bit stuffy in here. Besides it's your favorite restaurant, and we've had the reservation for a week."

He gave her hand a gentle, and what he hoped was reassuring, squeeze. Anna nodded but appeared unconvinced. He leaned over and kissed her, curtailing further discussion. One kiss led to another until she pushed him away, laughing.

"Yes, well, we best stop this and give you a chance to cool down a bit before you have to be seen in public. Otherwise, we'll have to turn the cab around and go home straightaway."

Dugan glanced down and moved back to his own side of the backseat with some reluctance. He gazed out the rain-speckled window, at the lights of London refracted through the drops clinging to the glass, and was soon lost in uneasy thoughts.

The source of his unease rested in his jacket pocket, a small black velvet ring box. He'd wrestled with 'popping the question' for weeks, but as the moment approached, he was beset by doubts. There was the age difference, of course, and the demands of her career and his, and a dozen reasons why their relationship shouldn't work. The fact that it had worked for the last three years was a source of continual amazement to him.

But what if she said no? She'd never even hinted at marriage, and if he crossed that line without invitation, the dynamic between them might be subtly but forever changed. Perhaps he was being greedy, wishing for more happiness when he already had more than any man deserved.

His reflections were interrupted by the trill of his cell phone, and as he fished it from his pocket, he reminded himself to turn it off before they got to the restaurant.

"Dugan," he said into the phone.

"*Dyed*, I am sorry to disturb you, but we need your help," said a familiar voice.

"Andrei?"

"*Da*, it is me, and I need to talk to you urgently," Andrei Borgdanov replied.

Dugan glanced over at Anna, who arched her eyebrows in a question. "Okay, I'll call you back in a couple of hours. I'm a bit tied up at the moment."

His reply was met with a momentary silence before the Russian responded. "Very well, *Dyed*, but please hurry."

Dugan sighed and suppressed his irritation at being addressed as *dyed*, Russian slang for 'gramps.' Borgdanov had given him the nickname at their first meeting, when they were far from being friends. Their relationship had changed, but the nickname was apparently here to stay.

"Okay," Dugan said. "But where are you? I thought you were still in the Indian Ocean."

"We are here."

"Here? As in London? Where?"

"In lobby of your building," Borgdanov said. "I tried to go to your apartment, but man at desk stopped us. He called your apartment to see if is all right, but he got no answer."

"Shit," Dugan said. "Pass the phone to the doorman. Wait a minute. You said 'we.' Who's with you?"

"Ilya."

"Okay. I'm going to have security let you in to the apartment. Make yourselves at home and wait for us. Now pass the phone to the guy at the desk."

"Security," said a voice.

"Walter, this is Tom Dugan. Do you recognize my voice?"

"Yes, Mr. Dugan."

"Great. Could you please escort these two gentlemen up to our apartment and let them in with your passkey?"

"Yes, sir."

"Thanks, Walter. We'll be home in a bit." Dugan hung up and slipped the phone back into his pocket.

"So Borgdanov is at our apartment," Anna said, "and there's someone with him?"

"Ilya Denosovitch, though damned if I can figure out what they're doing here. It's not like them to just show up out of the blue, so it must be something pretty serious."

"And something we'd both spend dinner worrying over, so we best go find out." She leaned forward and told the driver to take them home.

"That's probably the right call." Dugan felt the ring box in his pocket, and relief washed over him, along with a bit of guilt at his own reaction.

DUGAN AND ANNA'S APARTMENT
LONDON, UK

"But how do you even know she's in London?" asked Anna.

"We don't for sure," Borgdanov replied, "but we have information she is probably in the UK, and I think London is logical place if she is in hands of bad people."

"That's another thing," Dugan said. "Why do you think there's foul play? I mean, she's nineteen and out on her own for the first time. Maybe she's just caught up in the adventure of living life and has been too busy to write or phone home. It wouldn't be the first time."

"*Nyet!*" Ilya Denosovitch said. "My niece is good girl and very devoted to family. And even if she would be so cruel as not to contact my sister and brother-in-law, she is very close to her younger sisters and little brother." He shook his head. "If she doesn't contact family, can only mean she cannot do so, and that she is in trouble."

"Okay. Let's go over it again," Anna said. "You say she left home two months ago?"

"*Da*," Denosovitch said. "Besides being beautiful girl, Karina is very smart. She speaks very good English and also French and German. She also loves children and is very good with them. She applied for job with agency in Volgograd. This agency places Russian girls as…" Denosovitch looked to Borgdanov for help. "How you say *nyanya*?"

"Nanny," said Borgdanov.

"*Da*, nanny," Denosovitch said, continuing. "This was two months ago, and little Karina flew to Prague, where there is training school. She told my sister there is one month training course, and then she gets assignment in Western Europe or the UK, or maybe even USA. My sister got a phone call from her when she arrived in Prague, and Karina was very happy and excited. Since then, nothing."

"And your sister wasn't able to contact Karina?" Dugan asked.

Denosovitch shook his head. "After one week with no word, they tried calling number in Prague, but it is disconnected. Then my brother-in-law goes to the office of the agency in Volgograd, but office is closed, like no company ever exists. Police in Russia are no help, so my brother-in-law goes to Prague, but he has no address. He tries police there, but they have no record of the company. He tries many days but is difficult for him because he does not speak Czech. He goes everywhere, showing Karina's picture, but no one knows anything. Finally, he goes home to Volgograd. Then my sister contacts me, but I am with the major"—he nods at Borgdanov—"providing security on ship transiting near Somalia. It was ten days before we could leave ship in Aden; then we come straight here."

He looked down, composing himself. He was a blond giant, six foot five in his bare feet, and tipping the scales at two hundred and eighty pounds, none of it fat. Yet when he looked up, he was the picture of helplessness. His hands were trembling, and his eyes were wet with barely concealed grief.

He turned to Dugan. "Can you help us, *Dyed*?"

Dugan reached over and laid a hand on the big man's shoulder. "We'll do everything we can, Ilya."

The room grew quiet for a long moment before Anna broke the silence. "You said you had information Karina was in the UK. What kind of information?"

"Under the circumstances, I think it is clear that Karina was taken by the *mafiya*," Borgdanov said. "It seems only logical answer. I know a few ex-*Spetsnaz* that work for mob. I do not like what they do, and we are not friends but we are not enemies. I put out discreet inquiries, and one fellow told me that normally when the *mafiya* steals girls and takes them to Prague, final destination is usually the UK or USA. They have many clubs here, and they force the girls to…"

Borgdanov glanced over at Ilya, who was sitting with his jaw clenched and hands curled into fists.

"…to work in clubs. I think you understand."

Dugan and Anna nodded, and Borgdanov continued. "Maybe she is in US, but I figure we start here first."

Borgdanov looked at Anna. "We were hoping that maybe you could use your contacts to help us, and if we have no luck here, that maybe *Dyed*, could help us in US. We have nowhere else to turn."

Anna nodded. "Officially, of course, MI5 can do nothing regarding a personal matter that has no impact on national security. Unofficially, you'll have all the help I can give you, and if we do have to make inquiries in the States, I suspect Jesse Ward will make some very 'unofficial' inquiries as well."

"I think you can count on that," Dugan agreed.

"Thank you," said Borgdanov, relief in his voice.

Denosovitch merely nodded, not trusting himself to speak.

"But I think there's another person you haven't considered who may have some helpful contacts," Anna said, glancing at her watch. "Tom, would you please ring Alex and ask if we might all pay him a visit?"

KAIROUZ RESIDENCE
LONDON, UK

"And just how long has this been going on?" Alex Kairouz demanded, his face flushed.

His wife, Gillian, hesitated. "Almost a year, though Cassie only confided in me a month ago."

"A month ago!" Alex's face grew redder still. "You've known a month and you're just getting around to telling me?"

"And with good reason, obviously. I knew you'd overreact."

Alex glared. "I'm not overreacting. You know Cassie is vulnerable, and she's far too young to be romantically involved, even if she were... she were..."

Gillian's eyes narrowed to slits. "Even if she were what, Alex? Normal?"

Alex wilted under her gaze and slumped in his chair.

"I didn't mean it like that, and you know it. I just don't want her hurt, that's all."

Gillian shook her head. "I know you THINK that dear, but the problem is you really did mean it that way. You're so intent on protecting Cassie you can't see her as anyone except a flawed and fragile child. But she just turned eighteen, Alex, and the cognitive rehabilitation therapy has worked wonders over the last three years. She's come further than we ever dared hope. She tested low normal on the last battery of tests. That's low NORMAL, Alex. We can't keep her wrapped up in some sort of cocoon, and if we try, we'll only ruin her chances for a happy life." Her voice hardened. "And she WILL have a happy life, Alex, even if I have to fight you to achieve it. I promised that to Kathleen on her deathbed, and I keep my promises."

Alex softened at the memory of his dead wife. "I know you do, dear. And God knows no one's worked harder to give Cassie her chance in life. It's just so unsettling. Who is this boy? Where did she meet him, and how have they been seeing one another? She's hardly had the opportunity. She's always attended all-girl schools, and we've never allowed her to date."

"Apparently they've pursued their relationship through emails and texting."

"My God! She met him online? What if he's a predator!"

"I didn't say she met him online. I said they pursued their relationship online. She actually met him face to face last year. So did we."

"What? Where? Who is he?" Alex demanded.

"Do you remember when we all flew to the shipyard in Korea for the christening and delivery party for the *M/V Lynx*?"

"Yes, what of it?"

"Do you also remember the handsome young cadet that escorted Cassie and I on a private tour of the ship while you and Tom conferred with the captain?"

"Vaguely," Alex replied, awareness dawning.

"Well, evidently young Nigel Havelock was quite smitten with Cassie, and the feeling was reciprocated. He apparently slipped her his contact information, and they've been communicating ever since." Gillian paused. "Cassie told me proudly that 'her Nigel' is now third officer on the *Lynx*."

Alex exploded anew. "The bloody cheeky little bastard! Chatting up the boss's daughter in hopes of currying favor, is he? We'll just see about that. I'll sack the little bugger!"

"Alex Kairouz, you will do nothing of the sort. And quit being a pompous ass! Why do you think it's all about YOU and your company? Are you blind to the fact that our little girl is not so little any longer? She's a warm and beautiful young woman, and you best learn to accept that."

Alex sputtered, at a loss for words, and Gillian continued.

"And besides, you've often remarked on how Kathleen had an uncanny ability to read people and that Cassie inherited that gift. If this boy's feelings weren't genuine, don't you think Cassie would have seen through him by this time?"

"I suppose," Alex said, the concession grudging, "but if it's to continue, I insist we engage our security consultants to run a background check on him."

"Don't be ridiculous!"

Alex colored. "I'm NOT being ridiculous! And I would think you would be the first..." He stopped mid-sentence and looked quizzically at Gillian, a smile tugging at the corners of his mouth.

"You've already done it, haven't you?"

It was Gillian's turn to flush red. "It seemed prudent," she responded primly.

"And?"

"And he's just what he seems to be," Gillian said. "A nice English boy from a solidly middle-class family. No skeletons in the closet as far as the security people could determine. He got full marks through school and glowing recommendations from your own captains while he was a cadet. He seems a fine young man."

"Perhaps," Alex said, somewhat mollified, "but I think we should—" He was interrupted by the ring of the phone on the table beside him. He glanced down at the caller ID.

"Thomas," he said, reaching for the phone, "whatever can he want at this time of night."

"Yes, Thomas," he said into the receiver. "What? Borgdanov? Here? Yes, yes, of course you can come over. We'll see you in a few minutes." He hung up.

"What's that all about?" Gillian asked.

Alex shrugged. "I haven't a clue, but Thomas and Anna are coming over with Major Borgdanov and Sergeant Denosovitch. Thomas said it was urgent."

CHAPTER TWO

An hour later, Gillian sat in the comfortable and well-appointed living room of the Kairouz home, across from Dugan, Anna, and the Russians. Beside her on the sofa, Alex addressed their guests.

"Of course, we'll do anything we can to help," Alex said, "but I honestly don't see much we can contribute. I'll contact our security consultants and put them at your disposal." He looked at Anna. "But surely Anna's MI5 colleagues and her contacts at New Scotland Yard will be of more use."

The Russians nodded their thanks, but Anna cut Borgdanov off before he could respond.

"Actually, Alex," she said, "I was hoping Gillian might be able to help us."

"But whatever can I do, Anna?" asked Gillian. "As Alex says, surely your sources are far superior to any contacts I might have."

"Yes and no," Anna replied. "First thing tomorrow I'll start working those contacts, but if, as Andrei suspects, the Russian mob is involved, they've likely covered their tracks pretty well. I'll start with the UK Border Agency to check on work visas and immigration records, but if the girl IS here, she may be under a fictitious name."

Gillian looked unsure. "Well, of course I'll do anything I can to help. But again, what can I possibly do?"

Anna hesitated, obviously searching for words. "I'm interested in any contacts you might have from… from the time before you were a nanny. Do you keep in contact with any of them?"

Beside Gillian, Alex stiffened and took her hand. He glanced at the Russians and then across at Dugan and Anna.

"It's all right, Alex," Dugan said. "You can trust Alexei and Ilya."

"Well, it would seem Anna's given us no choice," Alex said. "And I fail to see how any of this—"

Gillian cut him off. "It's all right, Alex. I don't mind helping in a good cause."

"It's NOT all right! They've no right to ask you—"

Gillian reached over with her free hand and gently put her fingers to his lips. "I know you want to protect me, and I love you for it, but this really is my decision."

Alex slumped back on the sofa and glared at Dugan and Anna as Gillian continued. "What do you want to know, Anna?"

"Tomorrow I'm going down to the Clubs and Vice Unit of the Met to see what I can find out about Russian mob operations here in London. However, most of their officers are undercover, and they aren't likely to want to jeopardize ongoing investigations by sharing intel for a very 'unofficial' inquiry. That problem is compounded by the fact that I don't have a strong relationship with anyone in that unit. I'm really clutching at straws a bit, but I thought if you still have any contacts in that world, it could help a great deal. You might be able to provide some insights that even the Vice Unit fellows don't have."

Gillian gave a hesitant nod. "I may know someone who can help, but it might take a day or so. I'll get on it straightaway in the morning."

"Thank you, Gillian," said Anna.

The room grew silent, permeated by Alex's brooding disapproval, until Anna rose from her chair.

"Right then," she said, "we'd best be off. Thank you both for your help."

Dugan and the Russians echoed Anna's thanks, but Alex only looked at them and scowled before Gillian walked them to the door. She returned to find him standing at the sideboard, pouring himself a rather large measure of brandy.

Gillian sighed inwardly and joined him at the sideboard. "I'll have a small one, please, dear."

Alex nodded and reached for another snifter.

"Are you going to continue to sulk, or shall we discuss this like adults?"

Alex faced her and exploded. "They've no right to ask this of you. Your past is just that—past. Daisy Tatum is long dead and buried, and you're Gillian now. My wife and Cassie's mum. Delving into the past benefits no one, and this Russian mafia is dangerous. Who knows what they might—"

Gillian cut him off by wrapping her arms around him and pressing her cheek to his chest, hugging him tight until his anger dissipated. She turned her face up to his.

"You know I love you both beyond measure, and you've given me a wonderful life. I count my blessings each and every day. But you of all people should understand that I can't refuse this request. This poor girl may be suffering as I did, and I couldn't sleep at night knowing I might have helped her and didn't." She paused. "And neither could you, dear."

He took a ragged breath. "I suppose you're right, but I can hardly abide thinking of what you went through, and I'd spend the last breath in my body to shield you from having anything to do with that sordid world again. Were it in my power, I'd erase those horrible memories."

She touched his cheek. "I know you would, and I love you for it. But you can't, really, and I wouldn't let you if you could. Daisy will always be part of me, a hidden part perhaps, but always a source of strength. As the saying goes, what doesn't kill us makes us stronger."

Alex returned her hug before speaking.

"So are you going to see her?"

"You needn't say HER as if it were an epithet, dear. You know she's always been a staunch friend."

"That she has," Alex agreed, "and I owe her a debt I can never repay for rescuing you and giving you a new identity. I just can't agree with her lifestyle."

Gillian chuckled, the tension broken.

"Gloria has larceny in her DNA, Alex. The fact that she spurned your multiple attempts to set her up in legitimate businesses shouldn't be held against her."

"I was rather thinking of the time she DIDN'T spurn my offer and ended up fleecing one of the fellows at my club out of ten thousand pounds."

"It serves you right. She told me it was the only way she could think of to keep you from your incessant attempts to force her to go straight. And you made good the loss, so everything ended well," Gillian said, barely containing her laughter. "Besides, you said yourself that Clive Falworth was, to use your words, a wanker of the first order."

Alex sighed. "I suppose there's no way I'm going to win this argument?"

"Not a chance." Gillian kissed him tenderly before pulling her head back and staring up into his face.

"However, perhaps I can make it up to you. Cassie's spending the night over at her friend Ingrid's house. Does that suggest anything?"

CLUB *PYATNITSA*
LONDON, UK

Arsov sat at the end of the bar and surveyed the dim interior of Club *Pyatnitsa*, the flagship of his new London territory. It was quite a step up from his old territory in Prague, a dozen clubs and half a dozen high-end brothels in flats scattered throughout the city, owned through various front companies set up by the *Bratstvo*'s highly skilled London solicitors. Competent legal representation had been a problem initially, but the Brotherhood always sought out the best representation in each specialty. Those firms without sufficient moral flexibility to appreciate the extremely generous fees involved soon reconsidered after home visits from the more 'persuasive' members of the Brotherhood. Surveillance photos of solicitors' families as they went about their daily lives, coupled with detailed descriptions of possible fatal accidents (along with graphic photos of previous 'accidents'), never failed to do the trick. After all, the world was a dangerous place, and who could fault the attorneys for wanting to make sure their families were protected?

The solicitor arranging the real estate and business transactions had been particularly skillful. Arsov controlled his territory from a well-appointed office here at the rear of Club *Pyatnitsa*, or Club Friday, but nothing connected him to the other locations. He was a powerful spider, sitting in the middle of a web visible only to the *Bratstvo*.

His move from the *Federal'naya sluzhba bezopasnosti Rossiyskoy Federatsii*, or FSB, had been a natural one. As head of an FSB task force charged with controlling organized crime, it hadn't taken him long to realize the hopelessness of the task. Corruption was endemic in the government, and the *Bratstvo*'s tentacles reached deeply into the very agencies charged with controlling it, and had since Tsarist times. Ever the pragmatist, Arsov had soon decided that if he couldn't beat them, he'd join them, and quickly moved from taking the odd bribe to becoming a willing recruit.

He smiled at his new surroundings. The Brotherhood had given him more power and money than he could have ever acquired as a servant of the state (even a corrupt one), and the techniques he'd introduced in Prague had raised both the efficiency and profits of their trafficking operations tenfold. His reward had been London, and in the six weeks he'd been here, things were coming along nicely.

"That's Katya, there," said the man beside him, nodding to a girl clad only in a thong prancing onto a spotlit stage. The girl began a wildly erotic dance as rock music blared in the background.

Arsov watched a moment. "She looks too young."

"I'm following your new guidelines. She's completely legal. She turned eighteen last week, and I've got the documentation. I've sent all the younger girls out of sight to the brothels, just like you ordered." He hesitated. "But if you ask me, it will cost us business."

Arsov shook his head. "You have to understand the psychology of the clients, Nazarov. Men come here for a fantasy. Middle-aged men, with receding hairlines and expanding waistlines, who manage to convince themselves that a young woman who looks like a starlet cannot live until she has given them a blow job in a curtained booth. They want to feel strong, virile, desirable. But if they see a girl here that looks like their own teenage daughter, some percentage might feel guilty, maybe even call the police."

"It was never a problem before. We have lookouts on the street to alert us to the first sign of cops. We get the young ones out of here before the cops even get to the door."

"And how many men do you tie up standing around watching for the police? Two? Four? Now multiply that by a dozen clubs," Arsov said. "It is a huge waste of manpower."

Nazarov grunted noncommittally, and Arsov continued.

"It is all about knowing your customers, Nazarov. There is a different dynamic for the men who patronize the brothels; there is no illusion of romance. And a man who arrives at a brothel with a specific request to fuck children is unlikely to suddenly be stricken by a crisis of conscience." Arsov smiled. "Besides, customers with those particular tastes will pay a lot more. Why should we let them satisfy their urges here in the back rooms at the same price a normal john pays?"

"All right, I'll give you that, but I still don't like the other changes. London isn't Prague, and what we were doing before worked just fine."

Arsov suppressed a sigh. "Fine as opposed to what? As far as I could tell, you never tried anything different. You hooked all the girls on drugs and then managed them by close confinement, withholding the drugs, and beating them from time to time for no apparent reason. You may think a glassy-eyed, bruised and drugged-out whore is sexy, but I suspect it doesn't help sustain our clients' fantasies particularly well, to say nothing of the cost of the drugs. We turn a much better profit by distributing those drugs instead of using them to control the girls."

"That's another thing since you brought up control. I don't like this new plan at all. I think you're giving them too much freedom."

"On the contrary, we're making them control themselves, AFTER they've earned some freedom," Arsov said.

Nazarov looked unconvinced, and Arsov wondered if he'd have to replace the man. Some resistance was to be expected and tolerated, given that Nazarov had obviously been expecting to be promoted to head the London operation. However, Arsov had his limits.

His main concern was his new underling's refusal to grasp the obvious—his resistance to the new control plan being a case in point. The concept Arsov had perfected in Prague was brilliant in its application of psychology and elegant in its simplicity. Breaking a girl's spirit and perfecting her acting skills was only the first step—she still couldn't be trusted out of direct supervision. And even then, there was always the possibility she might convince some sympathetic customer to contact the police.

Arsov's solution was preemptive action. Though she didn't know it, among each new girl's first paying customers were *Bratstvo* men in disguise, alert to any attempt the girl might make at outside contact. If the girl passed that passive test, a *Bratstvo* 'john' would then actively attempt to gain her trust and offer to make outside contact for her. If the girl accepted, the fake john would reveal himself to be one of Arsov's men and the girl would be punished by repeated water-boarding and other torture that left no physical marks. Testing in a controlled club/brothel situation was repeated until the girl was deemed trustworthy enough to advance to the next level.

At the next level, a girl was allowed some limited freedom to run errands or perhaps go to lunch at a nearby fast-food restaurant. However, and again, all was not what it seemed. The girl was under continual close surveillance. If she attempted to escape or to contact anyone, she was immediately captured and summarily punished.

Girls who passed this challenge were tested even more stringently and given an errand that took them right by a uniformed policeman on patrol, one of Arsov's men in disguise. The imposter would stop the girl on a pretext and engage her in conversation, giving her ample opportunity to ask for help. If she did, he would appear sympathetic, then put her in his car and deliver her back to captivity. The fake 'policeman' would be given a large cash payment in front of the girl, cementing the idea that the police were in Arsov's pocket, and the girl would receive even harsher punishment, ostensibly for incurring the cost of the policeman's bribe.

'Graduates' of Arsov's program went from being unsure who to trust to being absolutely sure they could trust no one, even the police. That, along with frequent reminders of what might befall their loved ones back in Russia and of their videotaped porn sessions and interviews in which they waxed enthusiastic about their new life in the sex trade, served to destroy all resistance. The girls were free to come and go as they pleased, because there was no longer hope of rescue.

But it didn't stop there. After Arsov had broken the girls to his will, he proceeded to reshape them. Top producers got special privileges, good food, and lavish gifts. Less enthusiastic girls were ignored, and if they failed to earn the minimum set by Arsov, they were punished. Repeated failure to meet quota meant a girl would be 'sent away,' which was rumored to mean she'd be sold to a brothel in some Third World shit hole that would make even her current lot seem wonderful by comparison.

Arsov was the first to admit the process was time consuming, but he prided himself on taking the long view. After a girl was trained by his methods, she had a much longer working life than those controlled with drugs, and made much more money. Additionally, he needed almost no muscle to control the girls, and he could devote that manpower to growing other areas of the business. He could always use more manpower in the drug trafficking, and loan-sharking to the small but growing Russian expat community was an expanding business as well.

"What about the new girl, Karina?" Nazarov asked, breaking into his thoughts.

Arsov smiled. Beria had done a good job with that one, considering. She was by far the most challenging project he'd seen to date. Perhaps if things went well, he'd have Beria transferred here to London; he was a much more competent Number Two than this idiot Nazarov.

"I'm enjoying little Karina, but I think she needs a bit more seasoning. I'll keep her in my flat another week or so before she starts earning her keep."

Gillian Kairouz released the button as she heard the muffled sound of the bell chiming through the closed door. It wasn't a harsh buzz or rapid 'ding-dong' but a slow, stately chime, totally in keeping with the upscale building in which she found herself. She heard footsteps inside, and then the door opened to reveal an attractive woman of somewhat matronly aspect and indeterminate age, her faced wreathed in a broad and welcoming smile.

"Gillian, love," the woman said, stepping into the hall to fold Gillian in a tight embrace, "it's been far too long."

The woman released Gillian and stepped back, holding her at arm's length. "And let me look at you! Father Time has been kind to you, I see. You're as lovely as ever."

Gillian laughed. "And you're still the charmer, Gloria, and looking well yourself."

"A girl does what she can," the woman said, guiding Gillian through the door. "But come along. Let's have a spot of tea and catch up."

Gillian surveyed the apartment as Gloria closed the door.

"Belgravia no less. You seem to be doing well for yourself."

Gloria laughed again. "Appearances are everything, love. To be successful, one must first LOOK successful."

"I'm not even going to ask exactly what you're successful AT," Gillian said, moving through the well-appointed living room to a love seat Gloria indicated with a wave of her hand.

"Oh, this and that. Just this and that," Gloria said with a sly smile as she took a seat across from Gillian and busied herself pouring two cups of tea from the silver tea service that sat on the coffee table between them.

"And how's Cassie?" Gloria asked.

"Wonderful, thank you for asking. She's more lovely every day, and she scored absolutely brilliantly on her last battery of tests. She tested at the low end of the normal range."

"Well, bugger the tea!" Gloria stood and moved to an antique sideboard. "That calls for a toast!" She returned with an ornate cut-glass decanter and two brandy snifters on a tray.

"I really—"

"Just a small one," Gloria replied, brushing aside Gillian's objection and pouring a healthy measure into each snifter. "It's not every day I hear such good news, and we mustn't tempt fate by seeming unappreciative."

"Very well." Gillian took the proffered snifter.

"To Cassie." Gloria raised her glass.

Gillian joined the toast and set her glass on the coffee table after taking a small sip. Across from her, Gloria settled back in her chair, snifter still in hand.

"And is Cassie excited?" Gloria asked.

"Very. It's a heady time for her. She's even started something of a relationship with a young man."

"Well, good for her."

"Yes, I think it's healthy, but Alex is, of course, less excited."

Gloria snorted. "And how is His Nibs?"

"He's fine. And he sends his best, by the way."

"Yes, I'm sure."

"Really, Gloria. Alex is a good man."

Gloria nodded. "I never doubted it for a moment, but you have to admit he's a bit rigid."

"He is," Gillian replied, "and that's unlikely to change. He is who he is and so are you, and I've the rare privilege of loving you both. But I didn't come here to discuss Alex. Were you able to find out anything?"

Gloria's face clouded, and she leaned forward and put her glass on the coffee table before settling back in her chair.

"Aye, enough to concern me. Are you sure this is something you want to get involved with?"

"It's not a matter of wanting, Gloria. Sergeant Denosovitch has nowhere else to turn, and I couldn't live with myself if I didn't help him do everything possible to rescue his niece. Not after what I... not after—"

"I know, I know, love. But these Russians are orders of magnitude nastier than our homegrown British bastards. I just want to make sure you understand what you're getting into. To be honest, I'm a bit nervous to even be nosing around."

Gillian was taken aback; she'd seldom seen Gloria more tentative. "Go on."

"Well, the Russian mob is like an octopus with a lot of tentacles. The preeminent group at the moment seems to be called the Brotherhood, or *Bratstvo*. They're into everything, from legit businesses to every criminal enterprise imaginable. They have strong ties to the Russian government, and many of them are former members of Russian police or intelligence organizations, making them practically untouchable in Russia—I've heard they pretty much do what they want there."

Gillian nodded as Gloria continued.

"Outside Russia, they operate through legal fronts where possible. They always engage the best lawyers, and if they can, they buy police or government officials—their businesses throw off a lot of cash."

"What about here?"

"Drugs, girls, loan-sharking—the usual." Gloria shrugged. "As far as bribes go, it's hard to say. Your guess is as good as mine, but given the money they have to throw about, I'll wager at least a few coppers are on the take."

"What makes them any more dangerous than any other criminals?"

Gloria shuddered. "Utter ruthlessness. They began to arrive in the UK in significant numbers eight or ten years ago, but the Armenian mob got here ahead of them and had established a foothold. Within a year of the Russians' arrival, all the leaders of the Armenian mob were either dead, along with their families, or working for the *Bratstvo*. If you cross the *Bratstvo*, they'll murder you and anyone close to you or, for that matter, anyone they even suspect is close to you, and they'll probably torture all their victims first. Coercing people by targeting innocent family members is their stock and trade, and everyone is vulnerable. Italian mobsters are gentlemen by comparison."

"If they have the girl here in London, any idea where they might be holding her?"

Gloria shook her head. "None of my contacts would be brave enough to poke their noses that deeply into *Bratstvo* business, and I wouldn't even consider asking them to." She stared hard at Gillian. "And you shouldn't pursue this either. These blokes are VERY dangerous."

"I'm only going to be passing the information along, so you needn't worry."

"You haven't been listening, Gillian. If you're involved in any way, you'll be in danger."

"Perhaps, but I have to pass this along nonetheless. It's all general anyway. I take it you were unable to find anything more specific?"

Gloria opened her mouth to speak, then seemed to think better of it and shook her head.

"Gloria? What aren't you telling me?"

"You don't want to pursue this. Nothing good will come of it."

"Gloria, if you don't tell me, I'll be forced to make inquiries elsewhere, and that might prove even more dangerous."

Gloria sighed. "You're not going to drop this, are you?"

"Not a chance."

"All right. I don't have much more, but I did find that the impression on the street is that most of the *Bratstvo*'s operations seem to be controlled from a single nightclub in Soho called Club *Pyatnitsa*. That apparently means Club Friday."

Gillian took a notepad from her purse and began to write. "Do you know the address?"

"It's in Berwick Street," Gloria said, "but don't even think of going there!"

CHAPTER THREE

Alex was still at work when Gillian reached home, but an anxious Cassie greeted her in the hallway, and Gillian's plans to phone Dugan and Anna were momentarily deferred.

"Did you tell him?" Cassie asked. "What did he say?"

Gillian considered her reply.

"Your father wasn't exactly thrilled about your relationship, but I suspect he'll come around eventually. I think we best give him time to come to terms with it."

"He's not going to do anything mean to Nigel, is he?" Cassie asked, then continued without waiting for an answer. "I knew I shouldn't have said anything. Papa will ruin everything!"

Gillian wrapped her arms around her stepdaughter and pulled her close. "Calm down, sweetheart. Your father isn't an ogre; he's just concerned about you, that's all. He'd do anything to keep you from being hurt."

"But Nigel would never hurt me, Mum. He's kind and wonderful! He doesn't care at all about… about a lot of things. Actually, he's a lot like Papa."

Gillian smiled. "Perhaps you should keep that observation to yourself for the moment. I'm not sure how your father would take it." She held Cassie at arm's length. "And where is young Nigel now, and what do you hear from him?"

"He was in Europe, and we've been emailing when he could get a connection. But his ship gets into Southampton late tonight, and I hope we'll be able to video chat via Skype. It's ever so much better when we can see each other," Cassie said.

"I'm sure. Hmm… Southampton. Perhaps it's time we renewed our acquaintance with young Mr. Havelock. I think we should invite him to dinner while his ship's in port."

Cassie looked terrified. "No! I mean, I don't know. He… he doesn't know I told you, so I don't know if he would want to come to dinner."

Gillian nodded. "I suspect facing your girlfriend's parents is intimidating enough. When the girl's father is also your employer, it would be more daunting still. That said, he's got to do it sooner or later, so there's no time like the present. I think I can give Mr. Havelock an assurance that I can keep your father on good behavior."

"Okay," Cassie said, doubt in her voice. "I just hope Nigel's not mad. I… I didn't tell him I was going to tell you about us."

Gillian hugged Cassie again. "I'm sure it will be fine, dear. Now off you go. Are you having dinner with us tonight?"

"If it's all right, Ingrid and I were meeting some friends for pizza."

"That's fine, but finish your schoolwork before you go, and let Mrs. Hogan know you won't be here for dinner."

"Thanks, Mum." Cassie returned Gillian's hug and flashed her a bright smile before rushing off to the kitchen.

Gillian watched her stepdaughter's retreating back, momentarily overwhelmed. She'd cared for Cassie almost since birth but had only become 'Mum' in the few years since she'd been married to Alex. At times when Cassie called her that, Gillian was almost overcome with emotion. She hoped for his own sake that Nigel Havelock was as wonderful as Cassie believed, because if he hurt the girl, Alex Kairouz would be the least of his worries.

Gillian composed herself and moved to the phone.

Gillian arranged the meeting with a single phone call to the offices of Phoenix Shipping Ltd., where Alex Kairouz and Tom Dugan were equal partners and respectively the chairman of the board and the managing director. Dugan arranged to ride home from work with Alex and then called Anna at the MI5 offices in the nearby Thames House. She agreed to swing by their apartment and pick up the two Russians for a meeting at the Kairouzes'. They were assembled around the dining room table within an hour of Gillian's call.

"That generally tracks what I learned from the Clubs and Vice Unit boys at the Met," Anna said, after Gillian had related what she'd learned from Gloria. "They mentioned this Club *Pyatnitsa*, though they didn't identify it as the nerve center. Either they don't know that or they were purposely a bit obtuse. They weren't particularly keen about me poking my nose into their playpen."

"Well, if they don't want us mucking about, did they present an alternative?" Alex asked. "Perhaps an offer to investigate themselves?"

Anna shook her head. "No, and I've no leverage. Clubs and Vice are a very specialized unit within the Metropolitan Police, and they normally have very little contact with MI5. No one owes me any favors there."

"Okay, I guess I need to go to this Club *Pyatnitsa* and see what I can find out," Dugan said.

"*Nyet, Dyed*," Borgdanov said. "I think it is better if Ilya and I go. As Gillian says, these are very dangerous people. I appreciate help with information, but Ilya and I should do this thing."

"Actually, Tom's right," Anna said. "No offense, but you two would stick out like sore thumbs. And it's unlikely that you'll just go in and spot Karina. A more likely scenario would be having to ask around discreetly."

"But most girls are Russian, and we speak Russian," Borgdanov reasoned.

"Which might do more harm than good," Anna said. "You told me yourself that some former *Spetsnaz* accept employment with the Russian mob, right? You lot may as well have 'military' tattooed on your foreheads. Don't you think it likely that if you show up and start asking questions, the girls will think you either work for their employer or a rival? Either way, they'll be reluctant to talk or at best will tell you what they think you want to hear."

Both the Russians nodded. "*Da*, I had not thought of this," Borgdanov admitted.

"Perhaps I should go," Alex said.

Dugan shook his head. "I think I'm a more convincing john, Alex. You're too obviously a local, and if you just show up out of the blue, the mob boys might get suspicious as to why they haven't seen you before. With my accent, I can come off as a horny middle-aged American, in town for business and looking for a good time."

"Accurate on several counts," Anna said with a smirk, "though I'll refrain from specifying just which ones."

Dugan shot her a dirty look while Alex and Gillian laughed and the Russians looked confused. As the laughter died, Ilya Denosovitch shook his head.

"I do not like it. Is my family, so I should take risks. These are very bad people, *Dyed*."

"I'm not keen on putting Tom in harm's way either," Anna said, "but we can work around that. We'll fit him with a wire so we can hear everything he says and you two"—she nodded towards the Russians—"can wait with me just outside the club. If he runs into trouble, you can go to his aid."

"*Da*," Borgdanov said as Ilya nodded. "This, I think, will work."

"When?" Dugan asked.

"I have to organize the wire and a van," Anna said, looking at her watch. "Obviously this will be an evening operation, and it's too late to get things going tonight. I'd say tomorrow evening."

BERWICK STREET, SOHO
LONDON, UK

Dugan looked out the window of the cab as it turned south onto Berwick Street. Soho had changed in the last decades, transforming from a seamy area of sex shops and adult entertainment to a district of theaters and an eclectic mix of upscale shops, restaurants, and offices. But here and there remnants of the sordid past remained, sex shops and adult entertainment venues scattered in the mix, now almost 'upscale' by association. It was no wonder the Russians had chosen this more prosperous location for Club *Pyatnitsa*, where the clientele was undoubtedly more prosperous. It was almost respectable.

Anna and the Russians were already in place in a van parked on a side street near the club, and Dugan was arriving by cab, a typical foreigner on the prowl in the big city. He saw the club just ahead, and the cabbie pulled to the curb.

"Here we are, guv," the cabbie said, looking at the meter. "That'll be sixteen quid."

Dugan passed the driver a twenty and waved away the change.

"Thanks, mate," the driver said as Dugan closed the door.

Dugan looked around and pulled his cell phone from his pocket. He held it to his ear as if he were talking to someone and then said, "I'm here. How do you copy?"

"I hear you fine, Tom," said Anna's voice in his ear. "But are you making a spectacle of yourself by standing on the street and talking to your invisible friend?"

"Sheesh, give me a little credit, will you. I'm talking into my cell phone."

He heard Anna's laugh in his ear. "Okay, Tarzan. Now that we've got our com check, you best lose the earbud before you go in. You remember the safe word?"

"No," Dugan said, "I've forgotten it completely in the thirty minutes since we last spoke. Of course I remember the safe word. It's *Stoli*."

"Good. Just don't forget and order vodka by mistake, or our two Russian friends will come crashing in to rescue you."

"I'll try to fend off senility long enough to remember that. I'm taking out the earbud now, so I don't have to listen to any more of this abuse." He cut off Anna's laughter as he discreetly plucked the small earbud from his right ear and pocketed it.

Dugan crossed the sidewalk towards the club, and as he approached, the doors opened and a large well-dressed man emerged, his arms around two attractive girls, one on each side. Pounding rock music blared from the door before it closed, and the man gave Dugan a drunken smile. "A wonderful place," he said in a thick German accent. "I've invited these two lovely ladies to dinner."

"Ah…well, good luck with that," Dugan replied.

"Ah, but that's the beauty of it," said the man, his smile broadening. "No luck required. Come, my lovelies, dinner awaits."

Dugan watched the trio lurch to the curb as the drunken German hailed a cab.

"Don't get your blood pressure medication mixed up with your Viagra, asshole," Dugan muttered under his breath.

He pushed through the door to be engulfed by music. Just inside, a man at a podium gave Dugan an appraising look. "Good evening, sir," he said, with the slightest trace of a Russian accent. "The cover charge is forty pounds, which includes two drinks. However I'm sure a prosperous-looking gent like yourself will want a stage-side table—only ten pounds extra."

Dugan nodded. "I always go top shelf," he said, pulling out a money clip prepared for his little excursion, holding a thick wad of fifty-pound notes. He peeled one off and passed it to the man.

The man nodded and pocketed the note. "I could tell you were a man of distinction." He motioned for Dugan to follow him.

The music was even louder in the club proper. A long, wide, horseshoe-shaped stage dominated the room, with brass poles at regular intervals, each occupied by a gyrating girl. All the dancers were nearly nude except for lingerie designed to highlight rather than conceal. The stage also served as the bar, and the barmaids behind it were equally scantily clad and attractive, smiling at the customers nonstop in hopes of receiving some of the notes that weren't being stuffed into the dancers' lingerie—or elsewhere.

Tiny tables crowded one side of the stage/bar, each with two chairs. The less affluent were seated at larger tables some distance back from the stage. Girls not onstage circulated through the crowded room, drinking and talking to customers. Occasionally a girl would take a customer by the hand and lead him to one of the booths that lined the back wall and then close the black velvet curtains behind them.

"Here you are, sir," the Russian shouted into Dugan's ear, motioning him to a small table. Dugan nodded and sat down just below an amazingly flexible girl as the man deposited two drink tickets on the small table and left.

He was staring up at the smiling girl and reevaluating his seating choice in light of his plan to remain low profile, when another girl sat down in the empty seat at his table. She looked to be somewhere between eighteen and twenty, with long dark hair pulled back in a ponytail that reached the middle of her back, and she was wearing the briefest of black bikinis. He felt a hand on his thigh as she leaned over, her smiling face only inches from his, her ample breasts barely contained by her halter.

"Hello, handsome," she cooed in accented English as she picked up the drink tickets. "Buy me a drink?"

"Ah. Sure," Dugan replied, and the girl held up the tickets and beckoned to another scantily clad girl nearby who was carrying a tray of assorted drinks.

Dugan's new companion took something in a champagne flute off the tray, and Dugan took a glass of what turned out to be lukewarm and watery beer.

The girl sipped the drink and then bent close again, her hand now on his inner thigh. "So tell me, handsome, what is your name? I am Tanya."

"I'm Tom."

The girl's smile widened. "Ah. You are American, I think. What brings you here, Tom?"

"Business." Dugan returned her smile. "And now pleasure."

"I know much about pleasure," Tanya said as she leaned closer still, slipping her hand between Dugan's legs to begin rubbing his crotch—with the inevitable result. "Would you like me to suck you?"

So much for small talk, thought Dugan, as he glanced around self-consciously to find no one was paying the slightest attention.

"Ah… here?"

The girl laughed. "Of course not. You must upgrade to a champagne booth." She nodded toward the curtained booths along the back wall. "Only fifty pounds for a bottle of fine champagne and a private drinking place." She smiled. "My tip we can discuss in booth."

"I'd like a little more privacy. I saw a guy leaving with a couple of girls when I came in. How about coming back to my hotel?"

She shook her head. "*Nyet.* I am training. I cannot leave. But if you want more privacy, there are rooms in back but more expensive. One hundred pounds for thirty minutes. Room you must pay for before we go back."

Dugan nodded and reached into his pocket. He peeled two fifties off his roll and passed them to Tanya. She motioned him to keep his seat and moved to the front of the club, no doubt to give the money to the man at the podium, and returned a moment later with a key in hand. She led Dugan through a curtained doorway in the back wall and down a dimly lighted hallway with doors on either side. They stopped at the last door on the right, just short of an alarmed exit door, which Dugan presumed opened onto an alley.

"This hallway could use some more light," Dugan said, for the benefit of Anna in the van. "Does that door go outside into the alley? Maybe we could just slip out and go to my hotel."

"*Nyet.* I told you I cannot go out. And besides"—she smiled up at him—"you have already paid for room."

With that, she unlocked the door and led Dugan into an average-size and none-too-clean bedroom, with a door leading off it into an attached bath. She laid the key on a battered dresser and turned to Dugan, putting her arms around his neck and smiling up at him as she pressed her body against him.

"And now, Tom the American, we discuss what Tanya can do for you, *da*?"

Dugan gently disengaged the girl's arms before he stepped back and reached into his pocket. He pulled out his roll and peeled off a dozen bills and held them out.

He was surprised at the reaction. Tanya's eyes widened, and she looked apprehensive. Her body language telegraphed fear, and she took a half step back, her eyes on the money in his outstretched hand.

"Is a lot. Wh…what do you want me to do?"

"Nothing kinky. I just want some information."

The girl's face hardened.

"So you are police. I have nothing to tell you. Get out!"

"Take it easy. I'm not the police."

"Whoever you are, I don't want to talk to you. You must leave!"

"Okay, I'll leave." Dugan laid the money on the dresser and reached into his coat pocket. "But first just look at a picture and tell me if you recognize this girl."

Tanya turned her head, but Dugan moved the picture directly in front of her face so she had no choice but to look at it.

Blood drained from her face, but she shook her head.

"I have never seen her. I do not know her. Now get out!"

"You're getting awfully upset about a girl you don't know. C'mon, tell me what you know and the money's yours, and another five hundred along with it."

The girl looked about furtively, then lowered her voice and hissed at Dugan. "You are going to get us both killed, you fool! Take your money and go!"

***

In an office several doors away, Nazarov sat up straight at his desk, staring at the monitor. It was standard procedure to watch and listen when one of the girls took a john to the rooms. It was always much better to let the girls negotiate prices, because the johns were usually more generous if they thought the girl was getting the money. However, it was only good management to listen to the bargain and make sure the little bitches turned over all the money afterward. And besides, watching the sex was often amusing—he saved the funniest videos to watch again.

"Yuri," he said to a large man sitting on a nearby sofa perusing a girlie magazine, "Tanya is having some sort of problem with a john in room six. Bring him to me."

"*Da*," said the man as he stood up. He was at least six foot five and thick chested. Muscles bulged from the heavily veined arms protruding from the sleeves of his polo shirt, and he had all the telltales of steroid abuse. A tattoo on his neck peeked from beneath his shirt, barely concealed.

"Can I slap him around?"

Nazarov shrugged. "Just bring him here. Don't hurt him too bad unless he fights you, then do whatever is necessary."

Yuri nodded and started for the door.

"But don't kill him," Nazarov added. "He's up to something, and I need to know what."

There were heavy footfalls in the hall, and a surprised Dugan stepped back just as the door burst open to reveal a hulking Russian filling the doorway. Tanya fled to a far corner of the room and dropped to the floor, her arms wrapped above her head in a defensive position. Obviously she'd seen the man before. Dugan was rattled by the unexpected arrival, but tried to bluff it out.

"I paid for this room. Get the hell out!"

The Russian ignored Dugan and stepped into the room. "You must come with me." His English was heavily accented.

"I'm not going anywhere, pal," Dugan said as he took a step back, "unless it's back to the bar to get a shot of *Stoli*." He spoke the last sentence down at his chest, emphasizing *Stoli*.

"You come now." The Russian moved toward Dugan.

Dugan had circled around the bed now, to the opposite side, and the big Russian was at its foot, blocking the path to the door. Dugan wasn't a small guy himself, but there was no way he could stand toe to toe and trade punches with this guy. Where the hell were Borgdanov and Ilya?

"I sure could use some fucking *Stoli*!" he said again, almost shouting the last word.

The big Russian regarded him quizzically. "What is this talk of *Stoli*? Are you idiot? Now come before I hurt you." He punctuated the sentence by circling the bed, moving much faster than Dugan had thought possible.

Dugan leaped up on the bed, intent on crossing to the open door, but he felt the Russian's arms closing on his legs. Frantic, he turned in the man's grasp and hammered his right hand down hard on the top of the thug's bony skull, using the side of his fist to keep from breaking his knuckles. The Russian released Dugan and fell across the bed, and Dugan bolted.

But the Russian had other plans and managed to get a hand up, snagging a foot and pulling Dugan off balance. He fell off the bed and landed hard, flat on his back on the floor, the air rushing from his lungs. Then the Russian was towering above him with clenched fists—and an evil smile.

***

Anna sat in the driver's seat of the van and listened to Dugan's exchange through the speakers, privately amused at his imagined discomfort. The Russians were impassive and pointedly avoided Anna's gaze when the girl offered to perform oral sex on Dugan.

"He's letting us know he's on the move," she said, when Dugan mentioned the hallway lighting. "Sounds like he's near the rear exit. I'm going to pull around the corner to the entrance to the back alley, just in case."

The Russians nodded as she pulled the van away from the curve. Over the speakers, they heard Dugan cut to the chase and offer the girl money.

"A bit ham-handed," Ann muttered as she moved into light traffic. "He should have worked into that a bit more gradually."

She was pulling into a new parking place when through the speakers came the loud bang of the opening door, followed by Dugan's strange exchange with a male Russian.

"*Stoli*?…Bloody hell! He's in trouble," she said, tires squealing as she jack-rabbited from the curb and rocketed the fifty feet to the alley entrance. She slammed on the brakes and then threw the van in reverse and cut the wheel, rushing backwards down the narrow alley to come to a screeching stop near the rear entrance to the club. All three bolted from the van. Ilya reached the door first and tugged at the handle.

"Locked!" he said.

"Stand back." Anna drew her Glock from a belt holster and fired several rounds into the metal door by the lock.

Ilya jumped forward again and grabbed the handle with both hands. After a moment's resistance, the door opened with a metallic shriek followed immediately by the raucous clanging of an alarm.

Anna started in, but Borgdanov put a hand on her arm. "We will get *Dyed*. Better you have van ready to go immediately, so we waste no time."

She started to argue, thought better of it, and nodded. "Take this." She handed Borgdanov the Glock before rushing back to the driver's seat.

Borgdanov and Ilya rushed inside and found the open bedroom door only a few steps down the dimly lit hallway. Through the door they saw a big man crouched over Dugan, his fist drawn back as he prepared to land a blow.

"Stop!" Borgdanov yelled in Russian, and the big man's head snapped around just in time to receive a vicious front kick from Ilya that drove him over Dugan to land in a heap. Ilya was on the man in seconds, hammering his face with two more vicious haymakers.

"Enough, Ilya!" Borgdanov shouted in Russian. "He is finished. Help me get *Dyed* up."

Ilya turned back to see Borgdanov stuff the Glock in his belt and reach down to help Dugan. Dugan brushed off Borgdanov's hand and rose unsteadily on his own.

"I'm okay. I just got the wind knocked out of me."

"We must go!" Borgdanov said.

"Wait," Dugan said, looking at Tanya cowering in the corner. "She recognized the picture of Karina. She knows something. We have to question her."

Borgdanov stepped to the door and glanced down the long hallway. "There is no time, *Dyed*. I think we have company very soon."

Dugan looked from Borgdanov to the girl and back again, then motioned Ilya towards Tanya.

"Take her, and let's get out of here!" Dugan said, and Ilya rushed to the corner to scoop the girl up and flee the building on Dugan's and Borgdanov's heels.

They were nearly to the van before Tanya realized what was happening. She twisted in Ilya's arms and screamed curses in Russian as she struggled to escape. He clamped a hand across her mouth to silence her and got bitten for his efforts. At the van, Dugan waved the two Russians and their struggling captive through the cargo door and slid it shut behind them, then jumped into the front passenger seat.

"Go," Dugan said to Anna, as she looked back to see Borgdanov and Ilya struggling to restrain a half-naked girl who was fighting like a wildcat.

"Bloody hell!" Anna said.

"Go," Dugan repeated and was rewarded by the squeal of tires as Anna slammed the accelerator pedal to the floor.

Anna paced the expensive oriental carpet and muttered under her breath, pausing occasionally to glare at Dugan and the two Russians seated on the sofa. Alex watched her from a chair across from the subdued trio.

"Bloody unbelievable," she said out loud at last, directing her ire at Dugan. "You've really topped yourself this time, Tom. How could you?"

"It seemed like a good idea at the time. Besides, we rescued her."

"Let's just recap, shall we. It's a 'rescue' when the person wants to come with you. When you take them against their will, it's called kidnapping. Do you see the difference?"

"She'll thank us when she understands," Dugan said.

"And how's that working out so far?"

"Anna, I know you're upset," Alex said, "and there's no doubt Thomas's action was impulsive, but what's done is done. And if anyone can reach the girl, it's Gillian."

"And what's the plan if Gillian can't 'reach' her? Do we drag her down to the basement and water-board her until she tells us what we want to know?"

"Please, Anna. Do not be angry at *Dyed*," Ilya said. "Is my fault. You are trying to help me, so problem is my responsibility, and I took the girl, not *Dyed*."

"After he told you to," Anna persisted.

"You're right," Dugan said. "I didn't think it through, but as Alex says, what's done is done. Let's just hope Gillian can get through to her. For sure she's not likely to trust any of us otherwise."

***

Gillian sat at the kitchen table across from Tanya. The girl still wore the scanty black bikini, but it was covered by an old bathrobe Gillian had scrounged from Cassie's closet. Tanya was trembling but no longer crying—her eye makeup ran in dark streaks down her cheeks. She stared down in silence at her hands folded on the table in front of her. She hadn't said a word since Gillian had shooed the others from the room and sat down with the girl, thirty minutes earlier.

"Would you like something to eat, dear, or a nice cup of tea?" Gillian asked.

Tanya shook her head, eyes downcast.

Gillian let the silence drag on a few minutes more and then reached across the table and took the girl's hand, holding it tight when she tried to pull it away.

"I know what you're going through," Gillian said softly.

Tanya's head flew up, and there was fire in her eyes. "You know nothing. You are fine lady in big house, probably with many servants. You go where you want and do what you want. You think world is safe and beautiful place and bad things only happen on TV. You think you can fix everything with 'nice cup of tea,' *da*? Well, you know nothing of MY life, fine English lady, so please, do not tell me you know ANYTHING."

She tried to pull her hand away again, but Gillian held on, gently but firmly. Finally Tanya gave up and resumed staring down at the table. Gillian said nothing for a long while and then began to speak, her voice low and gentle, completely at odds with the raw story behind the words.

451

"My mother was a drug addict and street prostitute, and my father was her pimp. She delivered me in a charity hospital after my 'dad' attempted to induce a late-term abortion by means of a savage beating." Gillian paused. "But I survived, so I guess you could say I was tough from the start."

Tanya raised her head, shocked.

"I never knew my mother," Gillian continued, "as she died a short time later from a drug overdose. I suppose I was born addicted, but no one would waste drugs on an infant, so fortunately I have no memories of that first withdrawal. I was passed around among the other girls of my father's stable, but my memories of that time are fairly dim." Gillian shuddered and seemed to steel herself before she continued.

"I do remember my eighth birthday, when my father told me we were going to have a party with a new friend. He stripped me naked and tied me to a dirty mattress, then proceeded to sell my virginity to a fat old man with rotten teeth and stinking breath." She paused, as if bracing herself to continue. "He bragged to me later that he made five hundred pounds off the transaction, and he bought me a bag of Jelly Babies as a reward. I've hated the vile things to this day.

"It got worse after that, as impossible as that may seem. There were many pedophiles, and dear old Dad made good money. When I got too old, he put me on the street. By that time I'd begun using drugs like the rest of the girls, just to escape the horrid reality of our lives. When the drugs and the life had ravaged me to the point I wasn't producing much income as a whore, he turned me to selling drugs on the street. In time, I was arrested. He visited me in jail just once to warn me to keep my mouth shut, then left without bothering to bail me out. I was sentenced to five years."

"You went to prison?"

Gillian nodded. "The best thing that could have happened to me. I got free of the drugs, healthy for the first time in my life, and a bit of education. I was terrified when I was released after serving my sentence, but I got a job as a waitress, and everything was looking up. Then he showed up again."

"Your father? What did you do?"

Gillian lowered her head for a moment to compose herself. When she faced Tanya again, the gentleness was gone, and there was steel in her eyes.

"I buried a kitchen knife in the bastard's black heart."

"Bu-but did you not go back to prison?"

Gillian smiled at her and spoke, her voice gentle again. "That's a rather long story for another time perhaps. But first I must know, do you believe me?"

Tanya reflected a moment and then nodded slowly. "*Da.*"

"Good. Then you should know that most of the people who helped me find this new and wonderful life are sitting in the next room. I trust them with my life, and you can as well. And if you will trust us all, we may be able to give you your own life back."

Gillian could almost feel Tanya's emotional turmoil as fear and disbelief contorted the girl's features, chased by a flicker of something else—hope. And she watched as hope emerged victorious and Tanya's chin began to quiver. Fresh tears wet the makeup stains on her face, and Gillian rose from her chair and rounded the table to pull Tanya upright and into her tight embrace. The girl's body shuddered with silent racking sobs as she clung to Gillian, and the older woman held her close and whispered reassurance that her nightmare might soon be over.

CHAPTER FOUR

Tanya sat on the sofa beside Gillian, the robe wrapped tightly around her. The others surrounded them in the seating area of the comfortable living room. The girl was calmer now, but still clung to Gillian's hand. She'd hardly let go of the older woman since they'd come into the room, and every few moments she glanced over as if assuring herself that Gillian was still there. It had been quietly decided that Anna would do the questioning, given Tanya's recent experience with men.

"What can you tell us about Karina?" Anna asked gently. "Does she work at the club?"

Tanya shook her head. "I… I cannot speak. If they find out, they will hurt my family in Russia." She shuddered. "These are very bad men with powerful friends."

"Only if they know," Anna said, "and right now they think you were taken against your will. The room was obviously under surveillance, and the video will show you fighting Ilya. There will be no point in them harming your family."

The girl reflected a moment and slowly nodded.

"So please," Anna said, "tell us about Karina."

Tanya hesitated, then looked at Gillian, who gave a reassuring nod.

"I… I will try to help, but I do not know much."

"Good," Anna said. "Now, how do you know Karina? Does she work at the club?"

Tanya shook her head. "Not yet, but soon, I think. I met her at the boss's apartment."

"How long ago?" Anna asked.

"Three days," Tanya replied.

"Who is this man? What is his name? Where is apartment?" Ilya demanded.

Tanya flinched, earning Ilya a glare from Anna.

Gillian put a protective arm around Tanya's shoulders. "Gently, Sergeant, gently," she said to the big Russian.

Ilya nodded. "Forgive me, little Tanya. I did not mean to frighten you, but we are so close, and I must find my Karina."

Tanya relaxed and nodded. "He calls himself Sergei, but I don't know if that is true name. I know only that the others call him Boss. And I do not know where apartment is." She lowered her head. "I am in training. Not trusted to go outside yet. When they move us, we are in closed van or blindfolded, so we have no idea where we are. Until they put me in the club, I did not even know I was in London. This I learn from customers in club."

"Is the apartment where they hold all the girls?" Anna asked.

Tanya shook her head. "*Nyet*, not all. When we arrive, we go in place like warehouse. Is big room, but they put us each in small… small… I do not know English word. In Russian is *kletka*."

The others looked at Borgdanov. His face was a study in suppressed anger. "Cage," he translated between clenched teeth.

"*Da*, cage. But small, like for dog. They tell us we are all bitches, and we live naked in cages until we are properly trained."

No one spoke. "Bastards," muttered Alex after a long moment, but words failed the others, for no words could convey their building rage.

Anna recovered first. "So how did you end up in the apartment with Karina?"

"Each time there are new girls, Boss comes to look. They line girls up naked, and Boss picks one he likes to have for a while. He chose me, so they blindfold me and take me to his apartment. There I meet Veronika, who was Boss's choice from last group. Veronika told me she was there for ten days and told me before her there was Zoya. Zoya taught Veronika all the special sex things Boss likes, then she went back to club because Boss was bored with her. Veronika's job was to teach me all the things Boss likes then she goes back to club." Tanya hung her head and continued, her voice barely above a whisper. "Was my job to teach what Boss likes to Karina. But Karina was very… very…" She looked at Borgdanov. "I don't know English…*upornaya*."

"Stubborn," Borgdanov said.

"*Da*, stubborn. We must have sex together with boss, but Karina would not do some of the things Boss likes. Then she spit on him and called him pig." She lowered her head and shuddered. "It was very bad."

Gillian pulled the girl close and stroked her hair.

"Did he punish her?" Anna asked.

Tanya shook her head. "Not her. Me. And not the Boss. He does not get hands dirty. He just smiled and said, 'Why, Karina, you are being very unpleasant,' and then he leaves room. Three men come in and take us to kitchen. Then they… they…" She squeezed her eyes shut and shook her head again, pressing herself into Gillian.

"I think this is quite enough," Gillian said. "Let her rest."

"NO!" Tanya said, straightening in Gillian's embrace and looking the older woman in the eye. "You were strong. I will be strong. Like you,… and like Karina."

Tanya let go of Gillian and took a sip of tea from a cup on the coffee table in front of her. But she was still trembling, and the cup rattled on the saucer when she set it down.

"They do nothing to leave marks, because customers do not like to see bruises. But they shocked me with *elektricheskiy* wires here"—she motioned to her breasts—"and… and… between my legs. Then they held me down and put towel on my face and poured water on it until I cannot breathe and pass out. Then they wake me up and do again, many times."

"But why torture you to punish Karina?" Dugan asked.

"I think because they know she is very *upornaya*…stubborn, and will endure much herself. But they know also her heart is good, and to be the cause of pain to others is maybe worse for her than to take the pain herself. So while they do all these things to me, they make her watch and tell her to watch well, because this will soon happen to her sisters." Tanya paused and hung her head. "And the next day, Karina does everything the boss wants."

Ilya Denosovitch bolted upright and moved to the far side of the room, turning his face from the others. They watched his back in stunned silence as he clenched and unclenched his fists, struggling to control himself. When he turned, a single tear ran down his cheek, but his face was otherwise composed. His voice was full of quiet menace.

"When I catch these fuckers, they will beg for death."

Borgdanov rose and walked over to Denosovitch. He put his hands on his friend's shoulders and looked him in the eye. "*Da, tovarishch.* But you must not be greedy. There are enough of them for both of us, I think."

"Unfortunately, I think there are many more than enough," Anna said, "and they're now alerted to the fact that someone is watching them. We have to consider their probable reaction."

"Seems to me we still have the advantage," Dugan said. "They know some strange men abducted one of their girls, but they won't really know why. And even if they have me on the video asking about Karina, I never used her name, so there won't be any connec…"

Dugan trailed off mid-sentence to reach into his coat pocket. He blanched.

"What is it, Tom?" Anna asked.

"Karina's picture. I had it in my hand when the goon burst in the door. I thought I'd slipped it back into my pocket, but I must have dropped it."

ARSOV'S APARTMENT
LONDON, UK

Sergei Arsov stared at the picture, then tossed it on the coffee table in front of him.

"It's Karina. No doubt there. Now why do you suppose an American and two Russian military types are interested in our little Karina? And why would anyone be stupid enough to steal one of our girls?"

Across from him, Nazarov shrugged. "I don't know, Boss. Maybe someone is trying to move in on us. We are not the only organization."

Arsov shook his head. "I don't think any of our competitors would use an American, especially not an amateur like this fellow. The Russians are a different story. From the way the one held the gun and the way the other took care of Yuri, I think they are ex-*Spetsnaz* for sure." His face clouded. "Of course, if you hadn't let them waltz out of our club with the girl, we could question them directly."

"I… I had no choice. It happened very fast, and Yuri was the only one in the office with me. I called the boys from the front, but by the time they got back it was too late."

"And I don't suppose it ever occurred to you to defend our property? You were armed, were you not?" Arsov asked.

"Yes, but there were three of them and…"

"One of whom was lying on the floor, and the other two with apparently one gun between them. Hardly a formidable force, Nazarov."

Nazarov opened his mouth to protest further, but Arsov cut him off.

"Enough. Excuses get us nowhere. We must decide what to do about this."

"What if Tanya talks?" Nazarov asked.

Arsov shrugged. "To who will she talk? The men who took her are obviously not police, and even if they take her to the police, what can she say? The sex trade is not illegal in the UK. She is over eighteen, and we have a video tape of her describing how she loves being a whore and all the money she makes, and she hardly looks unwilling in the porn we shot. Her training is not complete, but I believe she understands what will happen to her family if she betrays us, but even if she does, it is her word against ours, and we have very good lawyers."

Nazarov nodded.

"No," Arsov said, "I'm not worried about the police. I want to find out about these stupid assholes who took our property. Go back to the club and check the security tapes again to try to figure out as much as you can about this American. Be sure to check the tapes for the street in front of the club, and see if you can determine how he arrived. If it was by car, perhaps we can get a license plate number and backtrack that."

Nazarov nodded but didn't move.

"Don't just sit there. Get moving."

"We have another problem," Nazarov said.

Arsov sighed—nothing but problems with this bastard. He silently vowed to bring Beria to London at the first opportunity.

"What is it now, Nazarov?"

"Our man in the US contacted me. His mole in ICE informed him that the US authorities know about the drug shipment on the *Igor Varaksin*. They plan to raid the vessel when she docks in Savannah."

Arsov glared. "Which means you may have a mole here as well."

"Not necessarily. The leak could have come from St. Petersburg. I cannot be held responsible for areas beyond my control."

Arsov just stared at his subordinate. Nazarov finally broke the uncomfortable silence.

"Wh… what do you want me to do?"

"What can we do? We have no choice but to jettison the container, and I assure you our superiors in St. Petersburg will not be pleased."

Nazarov rose. "I will notify the captain," he said and moved toward the door. Halfway there he turned back to Arsov.

"What about the security video?" He pointed to the open laptop on the coffee table.

"Leave that with me," Arsov said. "I'll share it with little Karina and see if she knows any of these men so eager to find her."

***

Arsov motioned Karina to the couch and patted the seat beside him.

"What is it?" Karina asked as she sat down beside him. There was a laptop open on the coffee table in front of them.

"I have a little video I'd like to watch, my dear." He reached over and clicked the mouse.

A poor-quality video appeared, showing Tanya in a room with an American. The American was trying to get her to look at something, but Tanya was resisting. Suddenly things began to move very fast, and Yuri burst into the room, and then two other large men and—Uncle Ilya! Karina gasped, and her hand flew to her mouth as she watched the remaining seconds before the screen blanked.

"Obviously you recognize one of our countrymen. Please tell me who he is and why these three men are looking for you."

"No, I was just startled and afraid they would hurt poor Tanya. Why do you suppose they took her? Did you get her back?"

Arsov smiled. This was a smart one, trying to deflect his question with a discussion of Tanya. He almost regretted what he had to do. Almost. He shrugged.

"I know you will never tell me voluntarily, and I admire you for it. But your obstinacy does become tedious at times."

At the snap of Arsov's fingers, two large men appeared in the doorway.

"Water-board her until she talks. Do it in the guest bathroom and try not to make too much of a mess this time."

CONTAINER SHIP IGOR VARAKSIN
EN ROUTE TO SAVANNAH, GEORGIA

The captain stood on the starboard bridge wing, peering out over the wind dodger at the sea ahead. The blue skies and moderate swells were hardly the weather associated with losing a container at sea, and he worried how he'd explain the loss when the authorities boarded in Savannah—a story of a 'rogue wave' perhaps?

The other officers would be no problem, of course. Like him, they were in on the plan. But he'd have to spread a great deal of money around to buy the unlicensed crew's silence and rehearse them thoroughly. Even then, he doubted he'd fool the authorities, but neither would there be proof to the contrary. He allowed himself a grim smile—innocent until proven guilty—a wonderful concept for those in his current profession.

None of the officers were smugglers by choice, and all had resisted initially, but when the third officer and his entire family were brutally murdered in St. Petersburg, the message was clear—cooperate or else. The captain sighed. They were all just unfortunate enough to be in the wrong place at the wrong time. The wrong place was a ship trading regularly into Savannah, Georgia, and the wrong time was when the Bratstvo was in need of 'mules' to bring their drugs into the lucrative US market. Savannah had been a natural choice—a smaller port with less enforcement presence than the much busier ports of the Northeast, and none of the extensive US Navy presence of Norfolk or Charleston. For even though the Cold War was long ended, Russian merchant vessels near US Navy facilities still received more than their fair share of scrutiny.

It had begun five long years ago, and accommodating the odd 'special cargo' was now routine, their consciences salved somewhat by large cash bonuses delivered personally to their homes by very dangerous-looking men—the very act of payment a tacit reminder of both the carrot and the stick. At least things had been routine, until this morning. The voice on the sat phone was emphatic, the container must be jettisoned, and the captain had set the long-planned but never executed operation in motion.

As usual, the 'special cargo' was in a twenty-foot container in the outermost top tier on the starboard side, near the flare of the bow—a spot chosen with care, where the containers were secured with twist locks and not tie rods. He watched as the first officer directed sailors releasing the twist locks and the chief engineer directed the placement of tough but thin rubber air bladders into the narrow space between the 'special cargo' container and the box below it. All the bladders were positioned on the inboard side of the container, so that when inflated, they would tip the container outboard, toward the side of the vessel.

The men finished their tasks and began to scramble out of harm's way, just as the radio on the captain's belt squawked.

"First officer to bridge."

"*Da.* This is bridge. Go ahead," the captain said.

"We are finished, and all men are clear."

"Good! *Spasibo*, Mr. Ivanov. Chief, do you copy?" the captain asked into the radio.

"*Da*, Captain. I am here," the chief engineer replied.

"Very well," the captain said. "Begin inflating."

He was answered by the hiss of air rushing through hoses, followed shortly thereafter by the distant sound of an air compressor cycling on. He watched in silence as the inside edge of the 'special cargo' container rose slowly into the air and the container tipped outward toward the starboard side. After a long ten minutes, progress stopped with the container at an odd angle. The captain keyed the mike on his radio.

"Chief, do you copy? What is the problem?"

"The bags will only lift seven hundred and fifty millimeters, Captain. I think we have hit the limit, and it is not enough to tip the container over. I can shore the container up with wood and reposition the bladders, but it will take some time."

The captain thought a moment and looked out at the sea around the ship.

"Let me try something first," the captain said into the radio as he moved into the wheelhouse. "It may take a moment. Make sure everyone stays well clear of the container."

"Understood," the chief replied.

"Put steering on hand," the captain ordered the helmsman, then glanced once again at the sea. A southerly wind was generating a moderate swell, striking the ship almost broad on the port beam, inducing a slight but gentle roll.

"Steering is on hand, Captain," the helmsman said.

"Very well. Five degrees right rudder," the captain said, and the helmsman confirmed the order and turned the wheel.

The captain moved to the wide windows at the front of the bridge and watched the sea with a practiced eye as the ship's bow swung northwest, and the swell began to strike the ship from astern and at an angle.

"Steady as she goes."

The helmsman repeated the captain's order and steadied the ship on her new course.

The captain nodded to himself at the anticipated effect as the ship began an increasingly violent corkscrew motion in the quartering seas, dipping further to starboard with each successive roll. On the fifth or sixth roll, the 'special container' reached the tipping point and rolled off the stack into the sea with a spectacular splash. He heard a cheer from the men assembled forward and allowed himself a small smile.

"Well done, Captain," said the chief over the radio.

"Come left to new course of two four zero," the captain said, waiting for the helmsman to confirm the order before moving back out on the starboard bridge wing to gaze over the side. In the ship's wake, the container was already sinking as it filled with water through holes pre-drilled near the bottom of the container for that very purpose. He lifted his own radio.

"And well done to you, gentlemen. Now, Chief, please take a sledgehammer to some spare twist locks so we have some evidence of the 'violent rogue wave' we encountered to present the authorities in Savannah."

The chief engineer acknowledged the order and the captain sighed. Now to craft some fairy tale for the logbook.

CHAPTER FIVE

"Sergei Arsov," Anna said, turning her laptop on the coffee table so the others could see the picture. "A lot of Russian nationals named 'Sergei' have entered the UK in the last year, but when we bumped the list against those with long stay or resident visas and with Tanya's description, the list got a lot shorter. This is our man; Tanya positively IDed him based on the photo."

"What else do you have on him?" Dugan asked.

Anna shook her head. "Not much. He entered the country with Indefinite Leave to Remain status, arranged very quickly, I might add. It looks like he has competent legal counsel or friends in high places. He listed his occupation as 'management consultant—self-employed.' He had to list a UK place of residence as part of the application, but that's a dead end. It's his solicitor's office. However, we'll find him now; it's just a matter of time."

"But time is what we do not have," Ilya said, rising to pace. "Already we have lost a day, and this Arsov now knows someone looks for Karina, so she is in more danger, I think. We must find this apartment and go there at once to save her."

"That might make things worse," Anna said. "The man's not stupid. I think we can assume he's already moved her somewhere. We know he's connected to Club *Pyatnitsa*, so we'll stake out the club until he shows up and then keep him under surveillance on the hope he leads us to Karina."

"I agree with Ilya," Borgdanov said. "I am not such big supporter of 'hope,' and we do not have time for this surveillance. If we catch this bastard, we will question him at once and make him tell us where he is keeping Karina. And HE can 'hope' we kill him quickly."

Anna stiffened. "Gentlemen, I'm prepared to do everything in my power to help you rescue Karina and turn this man over to the proper authorities. I understand and share your rage, and I've ignored your previous comments about killing this man, but I can't be a party to a murder, however justified."

Borgdanov glared. "And what will your authorities do to this bastard? You have already said that he has very smart lawyers, *da*? I think your authorities do nothing, just like in Russia."

Ilya muttered something in Russian, obviously in support of Borgdanov; then the room grew quiet, the tension palpable. Dugan moved to defuse it.

"Calm down, Andrei. Anna's sticking her neck way out here, and if this turns into a vigilante action, she could be in serious trouble."

Borgdanov glanced at Ilya, then turned back to Anna. "We had not thought of that, and we appreciate what you are doing. I promise we will not kill this bastard in the UK; beyond that I promise nothing."

Anna returned Borgdanov's gaze for a long moment before speaking. "We'll discuss that when the time comes. For the moment, let's concentrate on finding the elusive Mr. Arsov, shall we? Do I at least have your agreement that you won't rush in and beat him to a bloody pulp the moment we find him?"

Borgdanov looked at Ilya, who nodded.

"*Da*," Borgdanov said. "To this we will agree."

"It's settled then," Dugan turned to Gillian. "By the way, where is Tanya? I'm surprised she let you out of her sight."

Gillian smiled. "She's up in Cassie's room. Those two bonded immediately, and they're about the same size. Cassie is finding her something to wear."

In the chair beside Gillian, Alex stirred. "Do you think that's wise, my dear?"

"Well, I thought it preferable to having the poor girl run around half naked."

Alex scowled. "You know that's not what I meant. I just don't think Cassie should… should… associate too closely with this girl. One never knows… I mean…"

"Yes, I know exactly what you mean, Alex Kairouz!" Gillian's eyes flashed. "And you should bloody well be ashamed of yourself! Tanya is a victim, and I'll not have her treated like a leper because of what she was forced to do to survive and protect her family."

"I'm not suggesting she be treated like a leper, only that Cassie is innocent—still practically a child, for God's sake! I don't think she should be exposed to all this."

Gillian softened and leaned forward to lay her hand on Alex's cheek and look into his eyes. "The world is a dangerous place, Alex, and no one knows that better than I. I also knew from the beginning that Cassie could never protect herself from dangers she didn't understand, so I've taught her about 'all this,' as you call it, since puberty. She knows and understands what Tanya has endured, and wants to help her. I'm tremendously proud of our daughter, and you should be as well."

"Well, you could have told me."

Gillian smiled sweetly. "Yes, dear, but you would have objected, and I would have done it anyway, and we would likely have had a terrible and continuous argument. Isn't this much better?"

***

Tanya stood with Cassie in the walk-in closet and marveled at the racks of clothes.

"So many beautiful clothes. Is like Christmas. I do not know what to choose."

"You can have anything you like," Cassie said. "Mum said you can stay in the guest bedroom. Pick out what you want, and we'll move it in there. Except for underwear. I have some new stuff I haven't worn though so I'll give you that." Cassie made a face. "Wearing someone else's underwear is gross."

Tanya laughed. "I like you, Cassie. You make me laugh, and I have not laughed in very long time."

Cassie hugged her. "I like you too, and I'm glad you're staying with us. Mum says you can stay as long as you like."

They picked out a few outfits, and Tanya carried them to Cassie's bed. As she laid them down, Tanya noticed several pictures of a beautiful woman on Cassie's dresser. She had honey-blond hair and a peaches-and-cream complexion—she was the spitting image of Cassie.

"Who is this?"

"That's my birth mum. Her name was Kathleen, and she died when I was just a baby. But Mum Gillian told me all about her, and she gave me those pictures so I would never forget her. I think she loved my birth mum a lot."

"So Gillian is not your real mother?"

Cassie shook her head. "She was my nanny. My mum and dad hired her when I was a baby after I got real sick with a high fever. Then my mum got cancer and died, and Gillian stayed and took care of me and Dad. Then they fell in love and got married."

"Is like fairy tale." Tanya spied another picture at the back of the dresser.

"And so who is this handsome fellow that has you smiling so wide?" she asked, lifting a small photo of a beaming Cassie and a young man in uniform, obviously taken on a ship.

Cassie blushed. "That's Nigel. That was taken on his ship in Korea."

"So, your boyfriend is sailor man. Very nice!"

"He's not really my boyfriend," Cassie said, eyes downcast. "We only met in person one time. Mostly we text and email and video chat." She perked up. "But his ship got in to Southampton yesterday, and Mum is going to invite him to dinner."

"Trust me." Tanya looked at the picture. "I can tell by the way he is looking at you that he is your boyfriend."

"I really hope so. Do you have a boyfriend?"

Tanya looked away, tears welling up in her eyes.

"Oh, I'm sorry. That was really dumb! Please don't cry. I didn't mean to make you sad. I meant… you know… before. Oh, that's wrong too!"

Tanya turned back to face Cassie and wiped her eyes with the back of her hand. Then she put both her hands on Cassie's arms to calm her.

"Is okay, Cassie. Is just difficult to think of these things sometimes. And yes, I had boyfriend in St. Petersburg. His name is Ivan. He is very quiet but very nice. And very, very smart. He is computer programmer. We were going to marry."

"That's great!" Cassie got excited. "Maybe we can call him and let him know you're okay. Do you have his number?"

Tanya shook her head. "I think is dangerous for him if I call him now. And besides, I am not so sure that… after what has happened…" Tanya paused, once more on the verge of tears. "Maybe he doesn't feel the same way about me anymore."

Cassie looked perplexed. "What? Why?" she asked, then realization dawned. "You mean because of what you were forced to do? But that wasn't YOUR fault."

Tanya hung her head, her voice barely audible. "Perhaps his head will tell him this, but his heart may say something different. I am no longer the same person. Even I feel shamed and dirty. How can he feel any different?"

Cassie's temper flared. "That's terrible! If he stops loving you because of what someone else forced you to do, he's just a… just a…" Cassie groped for words. "Just a no-good wanker!"

Tanya looked up, shocked by Cassie's reaction, and her new friend's righteous indignation was so complete it struck Tanya as amusing. The corners of her mouth turned up in a smile, and though tears still ran down her cheeks, she burst out laughing and folded Cassie in a tight hug.

"I think you and I will become great friends," Tanya said, through the laughter and the tears.

CLUB *PYATNITSA*
LONDON, UK

"You're sure it's him?" Arsov asked.

Nazarov smiled. "Not just him. Them." He pulled a stack of photos out of his jacket pocket and tossed them on the desk.

"I found the cab," Nazarov said, "and the cabbie remembered the fare. He picked the guy up at a fancy house over near Kensington Square. I had Anatoli stake the place out, and he took those last night."

Arsov looked through the pictures. He recognized the American and both of the Russians. One photo showed the American exiting a large house in the company of a striking redhead. "Hmm. Kensington Square. That says money. Just who is this American?"

Nazavov's smile widened. "The Internet is a wonderful thing. His name is Thomas Dugan, and he is managing director of Phoenix Shipping Limited. The house belongs to an Alexander Kairouz, who is chairman of the board of the same company."

Arsov glanced back at the photo. "And the redhead?"

"Her name is Anna Walsh. She's this Dugan's live-in girlfriend. Other than that, I can find nothing on her, but we're still looking."

"And you saw no sign of Tanya?"

"Not so far. I slipped the doorman at this Dugan's flat a bribe, and according to him, he's seen no one resembling Tanya, so I think she must be at the Kairouz house. Anyway, we're covering Kairouz, Dugan, and the Russians around the clock. The Russians seem to be staying at Dugan's flat. Someone will lead us to Tanya sooner or later."

"You better make sure it's sooner," Arsov said. "We damn near had to kill Karina to get her to identify the *Spetsnaz* and admit the big blond fellow was her uncle, and I don't like unnecessary wear and tear on the merchandise. It's not good for business. We need to put an end to this."

"I don't understand why you just don't make a call to St. Petersburg. If they put pressure on the girl's family, this bastard Denosovitch and his old boss Borgdanov will get the message and back off. That's always worked before."

"Because, Nazarov, I am not eager to give our superiors in St. Petersburg the impression that we cannot handle one troublesome whore and her loving uncle. Must I remind you that our competence is already in question because of the loss of the drug shipment to Savannah?"

Nazarov bristled. "I told you, that was not our fault."

"And as I explained to you, it doesn't fucking matter. The leak was either here, in the US, or in St. Petersburg. We're responsible for the UK and the US, and do you really think our superiors in St. Petersburg will easily accept that the problem is on THEIR end? Perhaps I should send you to St. Petersburg so you can explain your theory to them in person, *da*?"

"I… I had not thought of that."

"Yes, well thinking does not seem to be a skill you've completely mastered." Arsov glanced at his watch. "It's almost noon. I want you to concentrate on finding Tanya, and then we'll take care of our *Spetsnaz* friends. They are the real threat. This American clown is just someone who is trying to help them. He will fade away without the Russians in the picture. I want you to locate Tanya by six o'clock. Use as many men as necessary, but get it done. Is that clear?"

Nazarov nodded and rose from his chair.

"Oh, and one other thing. Move Karina back to the holding warehouse, just to be on the safe side. I'm bored with the little bitch anyway. She's more trouble than she's worth."

NEAR KAIROUZ RESIDENCE
LONDON, UK

Nazarov slumped in the driver's seat of the car and took a sip of the cold, bitter coffee. He grimaced and set it back in the cup holder before glancing at his watch. He hated this surveillance and ordinarily would have delegated the task, but given Arsov's current mood, he couldn't afford a screw up. He'd decided to watch the Kairouz place himself. He had a man watching the back entrance as well, where the driveway led from a large garage on to a side street. So far, all they'd observed was Kairouz leaving for work, with his driver, and the arrival of a fat woman he assumed was a servant of some sort.

He had Yuri positioned outside Dugan's flat and Anatoli watching the Phoenix shipping offices, each with one man to help, but neither of the other two teams had reported anything of note. Bored, he dialed his cell phone.

"Yuri," he said when his man answered, "any activity there?"

"*Nyet*," Yuri replied. "The American and red-haired woman left earlier, and there was some activity as other people in building left for work. No sign of the *Spetsnaz*. I think they are still inside. Since then only minor foot traffic in and out of building, and one telephone repair truck goes into underground garage." Yuri paused. "We have been here long time. I am very sleepy and sick of pissing in bottle. When do we get relief?"

"You will get relieved when I say!" Nazarov snapped. "And I am pissing in bottle too, so quit whining. Call me if you see anything suspicious, and you better stay alert if you know what's good for you. Understand!"

Nazarov listened to the sullen "*da*," then hung up and called Anatoli.

"Anything new?"

"*Nyet*," Anatoli said. "Kairouz arrived, and his driver dropped him in front of building and then went into underground garage. The American and the woman arrived by taxi. She went into building with him and has not come out, so I think she must work here also. Everything else seems normal. Many people coming to work; no one leaving except some deliveries coming and going and one repair truck."

Nazarov sat up in his seat. "What kind of repair truck?"

"I'm not sure. Was a white van with design on the side. British Telecom, I think. Why?"

"Did it stay on the street? Can you still see it?"

"*Nyet*. It went into underground car park and left a few minutes later. Why? You think is problem?"

"I'm not sure," Nazarov said, "but stay alert, and call me if you notice anything at all."

Anatoli acknowledged the instruction, and Nazarov hung up and called Yuri back.

"Yuri, what did the telephone repair truck look like?"

"It was a white van," Yuri replied.

"Is it still there?"

"*Nyet*. It stayed only a few minutes and then left."

"Shit!" Nazarov hung up.

He tried to compose his thoughts. Something was up for sure. Having a telephone repair truck visit two of the locations they were staking out was just too much of a coincidence. Should he notify Arsov, or should he try to find out more first? He sat struggling with the decision when his phone chirped. The caller ID displayed the number of his man at the back entrance to the Kairouz house.

"What?"

"I spotted Tanya through the kitchen window," the man said.

"You're sure?"

"Absolutely. I had the binoculars on the window, watching the fat woman. Another woman came into the kitchen, Kairouz's wife I think from the way she was dressed. They were talking, but when they moved, I could see across the room, and I saw Tanya. I am sure."

"Did she look like she was a prisoner?"

"Not unless prisoners laugh and smile a lot."

"Okay, keep a close watch. I'll get back to you." Nazarov disconnected and dialed Arsov.

CHAPTER SIX

Anna watched from the back of the vehicle as Harry Albright, uniformed as a repairman, drove the British Telecom van slowly down Berwick Street and pulled to the curb near a utility manhole. He got out and quickly arranged a bright yellow plastic barricade in front of the manhole, stabbed a curved metal hook into a small opening in the heavy steel cover to drag it to one side, and placed a large 'Men at Work' sign in front of the barricade. He surveyed his work briefly and climbed into the back of the van.

"All set," he said to Anna Walsh.

"Thanks, Harry," Anna said. "And thanks again for doing this. I'd stand out as a repair person, and that lot in the club have all seen Tom and the others. We really appreciate the help." Beside her, Dugan and the Russians nodded in agreement.

"Glad to do it, Anna. But my chum in transport can only juggle things so long. The van is supposed to be in the shop for servicing."

Anna shrugged. "We can only use it for a while anyway. A BT van is a bit conspicuous for long-term surveillance. Hopefully we'll spot Arsov quickly and put a tail on him. Is Lou ready?"

"Parked around the corner in the chase car," Harry said, "ready to pick up the trail if Arsov starts moving."

"Brilliant." Anna's smile faded as she studied Harry's face.

"What is it, Harry? You look troubled."

"Nothing really, but are you sure you aren't attracting some attention of your own?"

"Why?"

"It's probably not related," Harry said, "but I did see a couple of blokes sitting in a parked car before I turned into the parking garage for your apartment."

"Did they seem overly interested in the building, or you?"

Harry shook his head. "Neither that I could tell, which is why I didn't mention it earlier. Nor did they look particularly observant, but I only got a quick look at them as I passed. It's more of a feeling, really. Quite frankly, I feel a bit foolish mentioning it now."

Anna was silent. Harry Albright was an experienced agent, and his 'feelings' were ignored at one's peril.

"What are you thinking, Anna?" Dugan asked from the seat beside her.

"I'm thinking if the bastards have identified us, we might have unknowingly led them to Alex's house, and Gillian is alone there with Tanya and Cassie."

"You think they've found us?" Dugan asked.

"No, I'm probably being paranoid. I guess I'm just overprotective of Tanya after all we know she went through. And I promised her we would keep her safe."

"Ilya or I will go there," Borgdanov said. "We do not need everyone to watch for this Arsov."

Anna shook her head. "You're both too conspicuous. If either of you leave the van here, someone from the club might spot you. Harry would be the logical choice, but we need him here to stay outside and fend off any police or anyone else that might show up. Tom's also a risk, because he's been seen, but at least he's a bit smaller and thus less conspicuous than you two, presuming we can disguise him somehow."

"I've got some spare BT repairman uniforms," Harry said. "They're part of the standard kit for the surveillance rig. One of them should fit our Yank friend here, and if he pulls the cap low on his face and walks directly away from the van and the club, he can be around the corner and out of sight in less than a minute. There's a taxi stand about four blocks away."

"Let's do it," Dugan said, and Anna nodded to Harry, who began pulling uniforms from a small cabinet mounted on the floor of the van and checking the labels for sizes.

"I'll ring Gillian," Anna said, reaching for her phone. "I don't want to alarm her, but she should know what's going on, and I'll tell her Tom is coming."

Five minutes later, Dugan was uniformed as a British Telecom repairman, pushing past the Russians to the rear door of the van when Harry stopped him.

"Are you armed, Yank?"

Dugan shook his head. "You folks aren't big on concealed carry permits."

"Permits be damned. These blokes are nasty bastards." He reached into another compartment and extracted a Glock and a spare loaded magazine. "The magazine in the gun is full," he said, handing both the Glock and the spare magazine to Dugan, "but there's not a round in the chamber."

Dugan nodded and slipped the spare magazine into his pants pocket and the Glock into his waistband. He adjusted his shirt to cover it and moved to the back of the van.

"Wish me luck," he said, hand on the door release.

"Let's wish you don't need it," Anna countered.

Dugan flashed her a hesitant smile, then crawled out of the van.

CLUB *PYATNITSA*
LONDON, UK

Arsov pulled his vibrating cell phone from his pocket and looked at the caller ID.

"Yes, Nazarov."

"We've spotted Tanya. She's in the Kairouz house."

"Is she being held?"

"No, she appears to be there willingly."

Arsov thought for a moment. "Too bad. That means we'll have to take her by force. Who else is there?"

"A woman I think is Kairouz's wife and a servant. A cook, I think. She seems to spend all her time in the kitchen."

"And no one else?"

"Not that we can see," Nazarov said. "Kairouz and his driver left this morning, and we followed him to his office."

"And the others?"

"The American and the Walsh women went to the office, and the two *Spetsnaz* stayed at the apartment. We did not see any of them leave either place," Nazarov hesitated. "But…"

"But what, Nazarov? Please do not tell me you couldn't even perform a simple surveillance."

"A… a British Telecom repair van, possibly the same one, entered and exited the underground garage of both buildings. I don't know for sure, but it seems too much of a coincidence…"

"So what is the problem? You have plenty of men. Surely you dispatched someone to follow this van."

"W-we did not realize it visited both places until it was out of sight. I do not know where the van went or if anyone was in it."

Arsov suppressed a sigh of exasperation and collected his thoughts. Now why would the American and the Russians conceal themselves in a repair van, assuming, of course, that this idiot Nazarov's suspicions were correct?

"Hold a moment," Arsov said into the phone as he moved from his office and into the club. The club wasn't open yet, and he motioned to a large man restocking the bar. "Victor, go out front and have a smoke. Look up and down the street casually, and see if you see a white British Telecom van anywhere, but don't be obvious."

The man nodded and moved from behind the bar and toward the door as Arsov reconnected with Nazarov.

"If they are moving around in a van," Arsov said, "perhaps they have decided to watch us. I sent Victor to check. However, it doesn't really matter where they are at the moment. In fact, whether they have obligingly gone to work as usual or collected in a van to try to watch us makes no difference. They are not around Tanya. Pull all the boys off the other surveillance and bring them to the Kairouz house. How long will it take them to get to you?"

"Not long. Both places are nearby. Ten minutes perhaps."

"Good. Leave two men watching the street outside the Kairouz place, and the rest of you go in and take Tanya. Understood?"

"*Da*," Nazarov said. "I will call the boys at once. Where do—"

"Hold a moment." Arsov looked up as Victor returned.

Victor nodded. "*Da*. There is this van as you said. It is far down the street out of the view of the security cameras, but I could see it. From the position of the van, I think they can see both the front entrance and the opening to the alley leading to the back door."

Arsov nodded, motioned Victor back to the bar, and spoke into the phone.

"The van is here, and since it stopped both places, we know both the *Spetsnaz* and their pet American are probably inside. Take the girl to the holding warehouse. I will join you shortly, and we can figure out what to do about our troublesome new friends." Arsov paused. "And Nazarov, listen carefully. We prosper here because we provide a needed service and we keep a low profile, so do not do anything stupid. Don't harm the cook or the Kairouz woman, but leave them tied up. The last thing we need is this escalating because of dead or injured British citizens, especially rich ones."

"*Da*," Nazarov replied, doubt in this voice, "but, Boss, surely when we take Tanya they will know it was us and report that to the police."

"Maybe not. We will have Tanya back under our control and will be able to remind her what will happen to her family. If they call the authorities at that point, the girl will say anything we want. They will know that, and they must also know, or at least suspect, that we have video from the club showing them kidnapping her. They will be the kidnappers, not us."

"But suppose a neighbor sees us or finds the women tied up before they free themselves?"

"Have the men wear ski masks, and no one is to speak Russian. In fact, have no one speak but yourself and then only two or three words at a time so your accent is not so obvious. And after you grab Tanya and tie up the women, ransack the house a bit and steal any valuables. That way, if it does get reported, it will look like a simple home invasion. The Kairouz woman and the others cannot say anything different without implicating themselves in Tanya's kidnapping."

"*Da*. But what about the American and the *Spetsnaz*?"

"One thing at a time, Nazarov. One thing at a time." Arsov disconnected.

He sat for a moment and considered his next move. It was very obliging of these fools to collect themselves in one spot where he could watch them, but what exactly did they expect to gain from watching the club? Surely they understood he knew they were after Karina and that he would never bring her near the club. Then it hit him—if little Tanya was now friendly with her kidnappers, she undoubtedly told them about him, and they probably expected him to lead them to Karina. His face clouded—he'd take care of Tanya later, but for the moment perhaps he should give his new fan club something to see. After all, he didn't want them to get too discouraged. If they kept watching him, he'd know exactly where to find them when the time came to deal with them.

Arsov sat for a moment and considered the possibilities. Tanya didn't know the location of his apartment, so these amateurs could only really know about the club. And since they had only just arrived, they couldn't know for sure he was inside. If he wanted to keep their interest focused on the club, he'd have to show himself. Should he take a stroll outside? Too obvious, especially after he'd just sent Victor out. Even amateurs wouldn't be that gullible. He dialed the number of a cab company and requested a pickup in ten minutes.

***

Arsov cracked the back door of the club and peered down the narrow alley through the slit. He couldn't see the surveillance van from the door, which meant that while the observers in the van could see the entrance to the alley, they couldn't see the club door itself. He smiled and opened the door wide to stroll across the alley to another door. He opened the door and stepped into the busy kitchen of an Italian restaurant preparing for the lunch rush. He was immediately confronted by a burly man in a once-white apron smeared with tomato sauce.

"You cannot come in this door—"

"Food Standards Agency. Surprise inspection." Arsov held up his open wallet as if it were credentials.

The surprised cook stepped back, and Arsov pushed past him, straight through the kitchen and into the dining room. He nodded at the servers setting up tables and continued out the front door without pausing. Five minutes and a block later, he climbed into a cab at the prearranged pickup point and gave the driver the address of the club.

"What?" said the angry cabbie. "My dispatcher said you was going to Heathrow. This bloody address is two streets away. You can walk it."

"Yes, but if you take me there, I'll pay the full fare to Heathrow with a nice tip besides."

The cabbie shrugged, mollified. "Your money, mate."

BERWICK STREET, SOHO
NEAR CLUB *PYATNITSA*
LONDON, UK

Harry Albright sat in the driver's seat of the van, pretending to study a clipboard as he conversed with Anna, unseen in the back of the van.

"You think they made us, Harry?"

"Hard to say. That was the world's fastest smoke break. The bloke only took a few puffs before he tossed the butt, and he did seem a bit too interested in what was up and down the street. Then again, they are a criminal enterprise, so I suppose it's only normal that they be cautious. It might just be routine. One thing's for sure though, whether they've twigged to us now or not, we can't be mucking about in this van too much longer without raising suspicions."

Anna sighed. "Agreed. However, I was hoping we'd at least spot Arsov before we had to come up with another means of surveillance. My inventory of favors subject to call is fairly limi—"

"Hello! What's this? You have that on your screen back there, Anna?" Harry asked.

"Affirmative." Anna watched on the monitor as a cab pulled up in front of Club *Pyatnitsa*. A tall man emerged from the cab, dressed impeccably in a suit that said Saville Row and wearing a snap-brim fedora set at a rakish angle. He stretched and checked the street in both directions, then strolled to the front door and entered the club."

"Well, well," Anna said. "Here's our guest of honor now. Now we just have to stay in touch."

"It shouldn't be too difficult, as long as he doesn't suspect we're onto him."

CHAPTER SEVEN

The smell of fresh-baked cookies filled the spacious kitchen, and Gillian watched as Tanya took two from the pile and then hesitated before placing a third on her plate. Mrs. Hogan beamed as she set a glass of cold milk beside Tanya's plate.

"Now that's what I like to see," the cook said. "A girl with a healthy appetite. A girl needs a few curves. None of this string bean stuff. It ain't healthy."

Tanya laughed around a mouthful of cookie and took a swallow of milk to wash it down. "If I keep eating your cooking, Mrs. Hogan, I think I have more than 'few' curves, *da*? Soon I look like beach ball."

"And a beautiful beach ball you'll be, dearie," Mrs. Hogan gave Tanya's back an affectionate pat.

Gillian smiled, amazed at the change in Tanya that even a short time in a safe environment had caused. The scars were deep, but Gillian knew they would heal, given time, and she wanted to keep the girl's life as stress free as possible.

Beside her on the counter, Gillian's cell phone chirped, and she recognized Anna's number on the caller ID.

"Yes, Anna," she said, and then listened a moment, tensing slightly.

"No, we're fine and enjoying some of Mrs. Hogan's delicious cookies. Thomas? He is? Well, we'll be sure to save him some cookies. Yes, dear, and thank you for calling." As Gillian disconnected, Mrs. Hogan gave her an inquisitive look.

"Mr. Dugan is coming over in a bit. Can you keep some of these cookies warm for him?"

"Aye," Mrs. Hogan said and began taking warm cookies from the plate and wrapping them in a tea towel.

Gillian strolled nonchalantly to the kitchen windows and gazed out into the backyard. "It's certainly a lovely day out." She locked the deadbolt on the back door as she passed.

"Why does Mr. Dugan come here?" Tanya asked, obviously still somewhat ill at ease in Dugan's presence.

"Oh, he's just coming to collect some papers Alex forgot on his desk this morning."

"And speaking of cookies gettin' cold," Mrs. Hogan said, "where is Cassie? She'll want some of these while they're nice and warm."

Tanya laughed. "I do not think she wants to be disturbed. She is in room, having video chat with Nigel. She is very nervous, I think, about asking him to dinner. I thought maybe better to give her some privacy. Do you think Nigel will come?"

Gillian paused, thoughts of Anna's call momentarily forgotten. With all that was going on, she'd contemplated postponing the dinner with Nigel, but his ship was only in port another two days, and Cassie had warmed to the idea of the dinner. At this point she couldn't postpone it without disappointing Cassie.

"He better, if he knows what's good for him," Mrs. Hogan said before Gillian could reply. "I need to get a look at him and decide whether or not he's suitable for our Cassie."

Gillian wondered, not for the first time, if young Nigel understood what he was in for.

OUTSIDE KAIROUZ RESIDENCE
LONDON, UK

Nazarov saw the Kairouz woman moving toward the kitchen window and ducked down behind the hedge. After a long moment he chanced another peek over the hedge and saw her back as she resumed her place near the center island. He nodded to himself. They were all in one place, and this should go quickly. He looked over at his men crouched beside him behind the hedge. He'd kept Yuri, Anatoli, and Dimitri with him and concealed the other two among the lush landscaping at the front and back of the stately home. He planned to be in and out in five minutes and doubted he'd need lookouts, but it was better safe than sorry.

"Remember," he whispered, "do not speak unless absolutely necessary, and then only in English and use few words. Yuri and I will grab the girl, and I want Anatoli and Dimitri to take care of the women. I don't think they will give us any trouble, but you are not to harm them. Keep your guns visible for intimidation, but do not draw them unless needed to enforce the point. I don't want one going off by mistake. We just tie them up, take the girl and leave. Understand?"

His men nodded.

"All right. Pull down your masks, and let's get this done."

His men did as instructed and followed him toward the kitchen door. He quietly tried the knob and, finding it locked, stepped back and nodded at Yuri. The massive Russian backed up half a dozen steps on the flagstone walk and launched his three hundred pounds pounds of muscle toward the door, striking it with his shoulder. It yielded with the sound of splintering wood, and Yuri crashed through with the others close behind.

Yuri and Nazarov wrestled Tanya off the stool, but to Nazarov's surprise, she was not the frightened girl of a few days before, and she fought like a tiger. As he struggled to hold the writhing girl, he glanced over to see Anatoli and Dimitri closing on the two women. The pair stood back to back and were obviously combative rather than intimidated. His men approached tentatively, mindful of orders not to harm the women. Anatoli shot Nazarov a questioning look.

"Take them! Now!" Nazarov barked, and his men rushed in. To unexpected results.

"Keep your bloody hands off me, you bastard!" shouted the older woman as she pulled a kitchen knife from the capacious pocket of her apron and slashed Anatoli's outstretched hand.

Anatoli cursed as he retreated, staring at the blood gushing through a cut in his glove.

His curses were soon joined by those of Dimitri, as his partner was on the receiving end of a savage kick to the groin from the Kairouz woman. Dimitri doubled over, and the woman shot past him toward the hallway.

"Cassie! Lock your door, and call the police!" the woman screamed as she ran toward the door.

"Shit," Nazarov said, as he struggled with the squirming Tanya. "Beat her down," he yelled at Yuri, and the big Russian nodded and delivered a massive blow to the side of the girl's head. She went limp, and Nazarov dumped her on the floor and took off after the Kairouz woman.

"Cassie! Lock your door," the woman screamed again, as he burst into a long hallway and spotted her at the far end, racing for an ornate staircase. Her toe caught on the edge of a carpet runner that stretched the length of the hall, and she sprawled on the hardwood stairs. As Nazarov rushed to her, she raised her head, intent on calling out again, and he silenced her with a vicious open-handed slap, Arsov's cautions forgotten in the crush of events.

He dragged the woman to her feet, savagely twisting her arm behind her and clamping his other hand over her mouth before pushing her toward the kitchen, controlling her with pressure on her arm. Christ, he couldn't believe things had gone completely to hell so quickly.

In the kitchen, he was greeted with the ludicrous sight of Tanya unconscious on the floor and his three underlings surrounding the fat cook. The woman was in a corner, holding them all at bay with her knife.

"Yuri, get over here and help me," Nazarov said, and Yuri left the cook to the others and rushed to Nazarov's side.

"Tape her mouth," Nazarov said, nodding at the woman squirming in his grasp. He twisted the woman's arm back further, and she gasped against his palm clamped over her mouth.

"I'm going to take my hand away while my friend tapes your mouth," Nazarov whispered in her ear. "And if you scream again, I'll break your bloody arm and then kill everyone in the house. Do you understand?"

The woman bobbed her head, and Nazarov checked to see that Yuri had a piece of duct tape ready before he moved his hand from the woman's mouth.

"Cassie! Call the police! Lock your doo—"

Nazarov gave the woman's arm a savage twist, but only Yuri mashing the tape across her mouth silenced her. It was an imperfect job with the woman's mouth open, and Yuri grabbed the roll and quickly wound a length of tape around her head several times, covering the bottom half of her face, as the woman fought.

"Tape her hands and feet, and cover her eyes! Quickly," Nazarov said. He restrained the woman, and Yuri rushed to comply, but no sooner than they had the Kairouz woman subdued, the fat cook took up the cry.

"Cassie! Call the police!" the cook shouted.

"God damn it! Shut that bitch up! Now!" Nazarov yelled at Anatoli and Dimitri as he pushed the bound Kairouz woman to the floor. "Go help those idiots," he said to Yuri before starting for the hallway.

"Where are you going?" Yuri asked.

"Obviously to find this Cassie. And I hope like hell she didn't hear any of this fiasco and call the police."

KAIROUZ RESIDENCE
LONDON, UK

Cassie laughed and shook her head at something Nigel said, and then winced as the headphones pinched her ear. As she reached up to adjust them, she saw a look of concern on Nigel's face as he stared up from the screen of her laptop.

"If the headphones are uncomfortable, why don't you take them off and just use the speakers?" he asked.

"Because," said Cassie, "there is NO privacy in this house. Everyone seems to think I'm two years old, and every time I close my door, I can just imagine them with their ears pressed against it."

Nigel laughed. "Surely it can't be that bad?"

"Well, I suppose not really, but sometimes it seems like it. I know they all love me, but it's really tiring to be treated like a child. It seems even worse after I told them about us, but maybe that's my imagination. Anyway, maybe it will be better after you come to dinner."

Nigel's face clouded. "About that, I really don't know—"

"Oh, Nigel, you ARE coming, aren't you? I couldn't bear it if you don't come after I've told everyone."

"Well, about that—"

"That's it isn't it? You're angry that I told about us without discussing it with you. I am SO sorry. Please don't be mad. I was just so happy, and it slipped out, and Mum pounced on it and wheedled the rest out of me—"

"Cassie, Cassie, calm down," Nigel said. "I'm not angry that you told. We had to tell them sooner or later. Perhaps it would have been better if we discussed it, but I understand how it happened, and I'm not the least bit angry. Okay?"

"O-okay. But then why don't you want to come to dinner?"

"I WANT to come, but I have the watch. I know you think I'm the commodore of the fleet, but I'm a very, very junior officer who must do as he is told."

"But can't you talk to the captain or something? I know, I'll have Papa call him and tell him to let you—"

"Absolutely not," Nigel said. "None of my shipmates must know about us."

Cassie's face fell, and tears welled up in her eyes.

"Cassie, what is it?"

"Is it… is it because I'm… I'm… you know…Are you ashamed of me?"

"Cassie, oh God, no! Ashamed of you? Never EVER think that. I'd shout your name to the rooftops if I could. You're beautiful and caring, and I feel incredibly fortunate that you care for me."

Cassie blushed at Nigel's praise. "And just who are these women you're comparing me to, Mr. Havelock?"

Nigel smiled, relieved at her mock indignation. "No one you have to worry about, and that's a promise."

"Well, I still don't understand why you want to keep our relationship a secret from everyone. I could understand it when Mum and Papa didn't know, but what's the point now?"

"The point is, that you're the daughter of the chairman of the board of my employer, and some cheeky bastard is bound to make a snide remark about you or our relationship. At that point, I'd be compelled to punch him in the nose, and I don't think that would be very good for my career."

"It's bound to come out sooner or later. You'll just have to learn to control yourself."

"I'm not quite rational in regard to you, but I'll try to work on it." Nigel touched the computer screen, partially obscuring his face.

Cassie touched her own screen in return, as if they could share a tactile connection digitally. When she removed her hand, Nigel's face came back into view and took on a look of concern.

"Cassie, the door behind you is opening."

Cassie turned as she spoke. "Probably just Mum—"

A man in a black ski mask burst into the room, and Cassie leaped from her chair, the cord from her headphones to the laptop almost dragging the laptop off the desk before tearing the headphones from her ears. The intruder closed the short distance between them, trapping Cassie against the desk before she could move away.

"Who are you?" Cassie demanded as the intruder threw her over his shoulder, then started through the door toward the stairs.

She struggled at first, then let herself go limp, dead weight over the man's shoulder. She felt him relax, and as they started down the stairs, she struck, driving her right knee into his chest and hammering the side of his head with her elbow as she threw all her weight to one side, overbalancing him.

The man cursed in a foreign language as they collapsed on the stairs in a jumbled heap, and Cassie felt his grip lessen. She squirmed from his grasp and almost got away, crawling back up the stairs, but a strong hand closed on her ankle.

"Not so fast, you little bitch," he said and pulled her back down.

She twisted in his grasp and flipped over on her back to kick at him with her free leg, but he was too strong and too fast and was soon on top of her, grabbing at her flailing arms. Cassie clawed at his face, and her fingers closed on his ski mask and ripped it from his head. The man stopped, as if shocked, and then his face flushed red.

He drew back his arm, and Cassie felt his fist explode against her face.

***

The cook was still bellowing when Nazarov returned to the kitchen, his mask back in place and the girl over his shoulder. The cook's cry died on her lips at the sight of the girl.

"Cassie!" she said, her eyes on the girl as Nazarov lowered the girl to the floor and began to tape her hands and feet.

Yuri took advantage of the cook's momentary distraction to grab her right wrist, and with the threat of the knife neutralized, Anatoli and Dimitri closed in. They subdued her quickly, physically but not verbally, for she continued to scream abuse until they got tape over her mouth. Seconds later, she was trussed up on the floor beside the Kairouz woman.

"What now?" Yuri asked.

"Put those two in the pantry, out of sight," Nazarov said, nodding toward the Kairouz woman and the cook. "And tape Tanya up and carry her to the van."

He looked around at the blood on the floor.

"And get some tape on Anatoli's hand so he's not bleeding all over the place and then clean up this blood. Use some bleach; there must be some around here somewhere."

"What about her?" Yuri nodded at the blond girl they'd called Cassie.

Nazarov thought for a moment. Arsov had been clear; no one was to see their faces. He shook his head. "She saw my face. We'll take her with us."

CHAPTER EIGHT

Arsov sat and drummed his fingers against his desk. He'd expected to hear from Nazarov by now, but he didn't want to call him if he was still in the middle of the operation. The simpleton would probably find snatching Tanya challenging enough without a distraction. He comforted himself with the thought that even Nazarov couldn't screw up such a simple mission.

His thoughts turned to his friends outside. They would expect him to move at some point, and if he just slipped away and left them sitting there, they would figure things out sooner or later. Besides, even these amateurs couldn't be so inept as to think they could tail him in a BT van without being spotted. They must have a chase car somewhere nearby, and it would be good to smoke that out as well. Arsov punched the intercom and summoned Victor from the bar. Twenty seconds later, the bartender stuck his head into the door to find Arsov undressing.

"Yes, Boss," Victor said, obviously confused.

"Get in here and change clothes with me," Arsov said.

***

"We have movement," Harry said from the driver's seat.

"I have him." In the back of the van, Anna watched on her monitor as a cab pulled up in front of the club. Moments later Arsov walked out the front door and climbed into the cab.

"He's moving," Anna said. "Call Lou and give him the plate number. The cab should pass him in the next block."

"On it," Harry said.

***

Arsov climbed into a cab several blocks away. His exit through the kitchen of the Italian restaurant had gone more smoothly this time, after he apologized for his earlier deception and explained to the cook that it was all really a matter of the heart. His jealous wife had hired a private investigator to watch him, making it difficult for him to slip away from his club to meet his mistress, and so he needed a way to enter and exit the club unobserved. The cook had smiled and nodded at the story, his understanding and future help assured by the gift of a hundred pounds to compensate for his 'inconvenience.'

It was working out well. Victor had orders to have the cab drive about aimlessly for an hour or so and then to go to Arsov's apartment and stay there. The chase car would no doubt sit on the apartment, and the van would likely remain at the club. He'd hesitated at leading the pursuers back to his own apartment and briefly considered having Victor lead the pursuit to his own place, but quickly dismissed that idea. Victor likely lived in some shit hole, and he wanted the deception to be realistic. Besides, there was little of value in his own apartment he couldn't abandon if necessary, so the risk was minimal. And while his bumbling pursuers were chasing ghosts, he'd go deal with Tanya, find out who these people were and what she'd told them, and then return to take care of them as necessary. After all, he knew just where to find them.

OUTSIDE THE KAIROUZ RESIDENCE
LONDON, UK

Dugan ordered the cab to the curb and shoved money over the seat, exiting the cab without waiting for change. The taxi stand had been empty when he got there, and he'd had difficulty flagging down a cab. Evidently his British Telecom repairman's uniform didn't mark him as a prospective customer. A dozen cabs passed him before he caught one discharging a passenger and jumped into the back before the cab pulled away.

He'd had the cab stop at the entrance to the long drive leading to the back of the house, knowing that Gillian was likely in the kitchen with Mrs. Hogan. He rushed up the curving drive and stopped short at the sight of a black panel truck pulled up near the kitchen door. As he watched, the door opened and a large man in a ski mask walked out with a bundle over his shoulder. Then he saw the blond hair. Cassie!

Dugan slipped the Glock from his waistband just as another masked man emerged, speaking and pointing toward the panel truck. Dugan racked the slide on the Glock to chamber a round, and the men's heads jerked toward the sound in unison. They found Dugan in a shooter's crouch, the Glock steady on the center mass of the man giving the orders.

"Hold it right there, assholes," Dugan said. "Put the girl on the ground gently, and then both of you move away slowly and lay face down. Now!"

Dugan felt a tremendous jolt on the back of his skull, and his world went black.

***

Nazarov looked at Ivan, standing over the unconscious American, holding a bloody landscaping stone he'd obviously picked up from the flower bed.

His man shrugged. "I didn't know what else to do. You said no shooting."

"*Da*. You did the right thing," Nazarov said.

"Should I kill him?" His man gestured with the rock.

"No, my orders were clear. We weren't to kill anyone. Leave him. Let's just get the girls in the truck and get the hell out of here."

Arsov sat at a battered desk in the office warehouse, seething as he stared across at Nazarov seated on a threadbare sofa. He suppressed an urge to scream. When he spoke, his voice was calm, almost conversational.

"You continually exceed my expectations, Nazarov. For instance, I knew you weren't the brightest fellow around, but I never expected that you were quite this stupid and so completely incompetent."

"It wasn't as easy as you think—"

"Yes, I'm eager to hear how six large men had difficulty subduing two middle-aged women? Go ahead, please. I'm all ears."

Nazarov glared. "We got Tanya back, didn't we?"

Arsov erupted. "You fucking idiot! Yes, you got Tanya back AND some girl who's likely Kairouz's daughter. And in the process, you assaulted two other British citizens. What part of 'low profile' don't you understand? A large part of our success here hinges on the fact that no one cares about these foreign girls. Even these people realize that, or they would have gone to the authorities by now. But things are a bit different now, aren't they? You've kidnapped a rich Brit, and I seriously doubt they'll hesitate to go to the police. This girl's face will probably be all over the media by this time tomorrow. How could you be so stupid?"

"I had to grab her. She saw my face."

"Which, from what you told me, would never have happened if you'd left her happily up in her room with her headphones clamped on her head. She'd have wandered down some time later and found the other two tied up, and that would have been the end of it. They couldn't report anything about Tanya, so at worst it would have been a home invasion by persons unknown."

Arsov sank back in his chair and glared at Nazarov, who wisely said nothing. After a long moment Arsov spoke.

"Well, I'll have to figure out something. We can't turn the girl loose, and she is a looker. Maybe we can get her out of the country and use her elsewhere. In the meantime, we have to take care of these damned *Spetsnaz* and the American. They seem to be the driving force, and with them out of the way, I suspect the authorities will give up in time, no matter how connected this Kairouz might be. We'll spread money around to hasten that result if need be."

Nazarov smirked.

"I don't think the American will be much of a problem for a while. I had Ivan brain him with a rock."

"What do you mean?"

"I was trying to tell you before. He showed up at the Kairouz place when we were loading the girls. I had Ivan on lookout, and he got behind him and smashed him with a rock."

"Where is he now?"

"W-we left him. He hadn't seen our faces, and you didn't say anything about snatching him. But we didn't kill anyone, just like you said."

Arsov buried his face in his hands and struggled to control himself.

CHAPTER NINE

Offices of Phoenix Shipping Ltd.
London, UK

Alex pressed the intercom button. "Yes, Mrs. Coutts."

"I'm sorry to disturb you, sir, but there's a Nigel Havelock on line one who insists he must speak to you. I wouldn't have bothered you, but he seems quite upset and says it's about Cassie."

"Very well. Thank you, Mrs. Coutts." Alex reached for his desk phone.

"This is Alex Kairouz. What can I do for yo—"

"Mr. Kairouz, thank God. Cassie's been attacked. We were—"

"Attacked? What the hell are you talking about, Havelock? If this is your idea of some sort of sick joke—"

"It's no joke, sir! We were video-chatting a few minutes ago, and a man in a black ski mask burst into her room and dragged her from her chair. The laptop was pulled out of position, and I couldn't see anything after that, but it sounded like he dragged her out the door."

Alex sat stunned.

"Mr. Kairouz, are you there?"

"Yes, yes, Havelock. The police—"

"I called them straightaway, sir. You were my second call."

"Good, good," Alex said absently. "Thank you. Now I must go."

"Of course, sir. If you could only—"

Alex hung up and started for the door. "Mrs. Coutts," he shouted, "have Daniel bring the car around straightaway."

M/V *Phoenix Lynx*
Port of Southampton, UK

Nigel Havelock heard the line go dead and resisted an urge to throw his cell phone over the side of the ship. Instead he put it in his pocket and tried to assess his options. He had none really; there was no way in hell he was going to sit here idly while Cassie was in danger. The train would get him to London faster than a car, and he didn't have the cash for an eighty mile cab ride in any event. He ran back into the deck house to have a word with the second officer, and then to his cabin to change. Five minutes later he rushed down the gangway and out to the street to flag down a cab for Southampton Central Station.

KAIROUZ RESIDENCE
LONDON, UK

Halfway down Alex's street, they encountered an ambulance speeding in the opposite direction, lights flashing. Alex swiveled in the back seat of the Bentley, momentarily torn between following the ambulance and continuing home. But no, he had no way of knowing if the ambulance was connected to events at his house, and he needed to find out what was going on. As they approached his house, there were several police cars parked on the street, colored lights flashing. Daniel pulled into the drive and was immediately confronted with yellow crime scene tape stretched across the drive between two trees. He brought the car to a stop, and Alex scrambled from the back.

"Hold it right there, sir," said a uniformed constable as Alex ducked under the tape. "No one's allowed beyond the tape."

"This is my house." Alex attempted to push past the policeman.

The policeman put a firm hand on Alex's chest. "Right, sir. That would make you Mr. Kairouz, then?"

"Of course I'm Kairouz. Now get out of my damned way. I want to see my family."

"Very good, sir," the policeman said, his hand still in place. "I'll just escort you to the house. Detective Sergeant Grimes will fill you in."

He removed his hand, and Alex shot toward the house, forcing the policeman to run beside him to keep up. As Alex rounded the turn of the drive, he saw Gillian outside the kitchen door, talking to a man in civilian clothes who was writing in a small notebook.

"Gillian!" Alex rushed to her and wrapped her in a hug.

"Alex, thank God you're here. They've taken Cassie and Tanya as well."

Alex released her and stepped back, his hand still on her arm. "Taken Cassie? Who?"

"That's what we're trying to determine, sir," the man in civilian clothes said. "I'm Detective Sergeant Grimes of the Metropolitan Police, and if you'll just step inside with Constable Hawkins here"—he nodded at the uniformed policeman—"I'll finish taking Mrs. Kairouz's statement, and we'll try to get this sorted."

"I'll do nothing of the sort." Alex put a protective arm around Gillian's shoulders. "I'm staying right here with my wife."

Gillian nodded, and Grimes started to protest but then seemed to think better of it. He looked at Constable Hawkins and jerked his head toward the drive, and Hawkins nodded and headed back down to the perimeter tape.

"Now, Mrs. Kairouz," Grimes began, "you say you'd never—"

Gillian faced the policeman and brushed back her hair, and Alex saw an ugly bruise below her ear along her jawline.

"My God, Gillian. You're injured."

"It's nothing," Gillian said. "The bastards slapped me and Mrs. Hogan around a bit, but nothing serious. Tom's injury was much more serious. He got a nasty crack on the head."

"Thomas? Here?" Then he remembered the ambulance. "Is he… is he… all right?"

"Mr. Dugan was apparently clubbed from behind with a rock," Grimes said. "He was groggy but conscious when we arrived, staggering around the back garden. The paramedics don't think it's too serious. However, they transported him to hospital for x-rays and scans. He may have a concussion."

Alex nodded, and Grimes waited a moment to see if he would continue; when he didn't, Grimes turned back to Gillian.

"Now, Mrs. Kairouz, this Russian girl…" He glanced at his notebook. "Tanya. You say she was taken along with your daughter. What was her relationship? Also, I'll need her address so we can notify her family."

Gillian hesitated for the slightest moment. "Tanya was Cassie's friend and our houseguest. To the best of my knowledge she has no family in this country."

Grimes nodded. "Fair enough, but I'll at least need her surname. Can you give me that?"

Gillian looked shaken. "Ah… no. I'm afraid I can't. She'd just been here for a day or so, you see. She told us, of course, but it was some unpronounceable Russian name that I didn't retain."

"Perfectly understandable," Grimes said. "Just how did Tanya and your daughter become friends?"

"Ah… well, they… ah—"

"What has all this got to do with anything?" Alex demanded. "This is a waste of time. We need to get on with finding them."

Grimes slowly closed his notebook and slipped it into his coat pocket, then cocked his head slightly as he stared at Alex.

"With all due respect, Mr. Kairouz, things aren't quite adding up here. Normally in a situation involving a family of obvious wealth, I'd treat this as a kidnap for ransom. However, we have this mysterious Russian girl no one seems to know much about, and the cook let something slip about 'bloody Russian bastards.' He paused. "And then there's this American Dugan found staggering around your back garden with an unregistered handgun. Fortunately he retained the presence of mind to drop it when ordered to, but that could have developed into a very bad situation."

Alex looked down and said nothing.

"If you expect our help, Mr. Kairouz, we have to know what's going on."

Alex looked at Gillian.

"Best call Anna," she said, and Alex nodded, pulling out his cell phone.

"I have to make a call, Detective Sergeant Grimes," Alex said. "Then I suggest we all go sit down in the house and wait. There's someone you need to meet."

ST. IGNATIUS HOSPITAL
LONDON, UK

Dugan saw Cassie's inert body slung over a man's shoulder, moving through a fog. He tried to run toward them, but his legs wouldn't move.

"Cassie!" he cried, then jerked awake. He was in an unfamiliar bed in a dimly lighted room, and he saw a silhouette at a nearby window, framed against the night sky and lights of London.

"Easy," Anna said as she moved from the window to his bedside and took his hand.

"Where the hell am I?"

"St. Ignatius Hospital. You took a nasty blow to the back of your head, but you're going to be all right."

"Is Cassie okay? I saw—"

"Cassie and Tanya were both abducted. Obviously Arsov's work. We're—"

"Abducted? Shit. I have to get out of here." Dugan began to sit up.

"Easy, tiger," Anna said, hands on his chest pressing him back down on the bed. "You took quite a pounding. They've done all the scans, and you appear to be all right, but they've been waiting for you to wake up to do some follow-up. I'll pop out to the nurse's station and let them know. Do NOT get out of that bed while I'm gone. Is that clear?"

"Yes, ma'am," Dugan said, and Anna left the room and returned in less than a minute.

"How long have I been here? Was anyone else hurt?" Dugan asked when she returned.

"You've been here most of the day, and Gillian and Mrs. Hogan were knocked about a bit, but not seriously injured. Mrs. Hogan evidently got a piece of one of the kidnappers with a kitchen knife."

"Good for her." Dugan started to push himself up in the bed.

"Hold on." Anna reached for the bed control. There was a whirring sound as Dugan's head elevated.

"Better?"

"Much," Dugan said. "Now what's the situation?"

Anna sighed. "Evolving, I guess would be the best way to describe it. A Detective Sergeant Grimes was the officer at the scene, and he wasn't particularly happy with our freelance activities or with your possession of an unlicensed handgun. However, between my association with MI5 and Alex's contacts in government, there won't be any repercussions on either score. The Clubs and Vice Unit of the Metropolitan Police are now officially involved, though recent events haven't exactly enhanced my relationship with them either, I'm afraid. Gillian is in a state of depression and hardly talks. I've never seen her like this. She obviously blames herself for Cassie's abduction. Alex is at the other extreme. He alternates between black silence and rage, and he's calling in every favor anyone in government ever owed him. He must have contacted at least half a dozen MPs and senior government officials. He's succeeding in raising awareness, but is simultaneously stirring up quite a bit of resentment among the Metropolitan Police. In short, and to use one of your colorful American expressions, it's a complete cluster fuck."

"What about Borgdanov and Ilya?"

"I had Borgdanov with Lou watching Arsov's apartment, and Ilya stayed with Harry on the club. The one piece of positive news is that the police have taken over those stakeouts, so we're not spread as thin. That said, there's been absolutely no movement by Arsov, so I'm beginning to think he may have given us the slip. I sent Harry and Lou home to get some rest, and the Russians are doing the same in our apartment. We have a meeting with the Clubs and Vice Unit tomorrow to plan and coordinate a city-wide raid on suspected Russian mob operations."

"That's it?"

"For the moment. We've also got pictures of Cassie up all over the media and will soon have pictures of Tanya. We didn't have any of her, but Ilya remembered that Tanya said they had taken her passport. He suggested that if they had her here working 'legally,' that she had to have some sort of entry paperwork, and we found some. We figure they must have used one of their 'trained' girls who looks like Tanya to pose as her for entry purposes, using Tanya's real passport. We found an entry permit with a passport photo, and we've posted her picture on the media beside Cassie's. Ilya had another photo of Karina, and we're giving that to the media as well; by the late evening news, their pictures should be everywhere."

Dugan looked doubtful. "That might have unintended consequences."

"We thought of that, but Arsov already knows we're looking for all three girls, so we didn't think we had anything to lose. Going public doesn't change that, it just makes it more difficult for him to hide or transport them."

"That's the best option, I guess." Dugan glanced toward the door. "Why do I have to see the doctor, anyway? I feel fine."

"I suppose they want to make sure you know who you are and where you are and that you're not loopy." She smiled and squeezed his hand. "At least not any loopier than normal."

"Very funny," he said and returned her squeeze. "I'm overwhelmed by your sympathy."

"Well, the shaved patch and stitches might garner you sympathy in some quarters, I suppose."

Dugan reflexively put his free hand to the back of his head and probed at the bump. "I vaguely recall a little of that. I think they used staples, without any anesthesia I might add. You Brits don't seem to be much on painkillers."

"Stiff upper lip, Yank. It builds character."

"Yeah, well, my character's just fine, thanks. Now where the hell is that doctor? I want to get home, crowded though it is."

"Oh yes," she said. "There is something I forgot to mention. It will be a bit more crowded than you realize, I'm afraid. We've added a houseguest."

"What? Who?"

"Cassie's boyfriend, Nigel, showed up at Alex's house while the police were questioning everyone. Evidently he saw Cassie's abduction while they were video-chatting and phoned the police straightaway. He also called Alex."

"Smart boy. But why is he at our place?"

"Because it was patently obvious to anyone with eyes that he has no intention of leaving with Cassie still in danger. And it was equally obvious to me that the poor boy is extremely uncomfortable in Alex's presence, so I invited him to our place and put him on the couch. The major didn't fit on it very well anyway, and Ilya can't fit on it at all. He barely fits on the bed in the spare room. I moved the major into the spare room and bought an inflatable mattress for Ilya and put it in the living room. I think everyone will be more comfortable, but we won't have much privacy for a while."

"Sounds real friggin' cozy," Dugan said. "I can hardly wait to sit around in our jammies and tell ghost stories by candlelight."

CHAPTER TEN

HOLDING WAREHOUSE
516 COPELAND ROAD
SOUTHWARK, LONDON, UK

Arsov glared at the collage of photos on the screen of the small TV in the shabby office and thumbed the remote to raise the volume.

"...believed to be victims of a kidnapping ring engaged in human trafficking. The suspected kidnappers are thought to be Russian or Eastern European, but that has yet to be confirmed. Anyone seeing these girls is requested to call the number on your screen. The Metropolitan Police have emphasized that the kidnappers are armed and dangerous, and no one should attempt to intervene. Again, if you see anything or have any information, you should call the number on—"

"Shit!" Arsov screamed and hurled the remote across the room at Nazarov sitting on the couch. His underling ducked, and the remote slammed against the cinder-block wall and popped open, raining batteries down on Nazarov as the TV screen blinked off.

"I hope you're happy, you idiot! Our very low profile and profitable business is now going to get a lot of attention. This is on every fucking station!"

"So what?" Nazarov said. "They couldn't prove anything before, and they can't prove anything now. We have the girls, and there are no witnesses. We keep the girls who aren't fully trained out of sight and threaten their families for good measure. The trained girls will support us as usual." He shrugged. "Nothing has changed."

"Can you really be this fucking obtuse? Of course things have changed. How much juice and influence do you think it takes to get these pictures all over the media this quickly? And the lead story on every single channel? The shit is about to hit the fan, Nazarov, and we're going to be splattered."

"But they know nothing—"

"They know about the connection to Club *Pyatnitsa*, or at least the American and the *Spetsnaz* do, so we can assume the police know now as well. And besides, do you think our little pleasure operations are a secret? Our methods make it impossible for them to get a conviction, and we don't get our girls from the local population, so they've learned that prosecuting us has a low political priority. We are out of sight and out of mind, at worst the public perception is that we are facilitators of a 'victimless crime.' In one afternoon you've managed to make us kidnappers and the subject of a media campaign. The authorities have no choice now. Even if they know it will be difficult to get convictions, they have to be seen as trying, and that will have a major impact on our operations."

Arsov could see from the expression on Nazarov's face that it was finally sinking in.

"Wh-what should we do?"

"Partially what you already suggested," Arsov said. "They already know about Club *Pyatnitsa*, so there's no point in shutting that down. However, make sure to leave no girls there except the most trustworthy. The same for the other clubs. They won't necessarily know of our ownership, but in this shit storm you've stirred up, they will likely be hitting any adult business with suspected Russian involvement. Bring any girls you have the slightest doubt about back here to the warehouse. And shut down all of the brothels for the time being. Close the ones with the kids first. Bring everyone here. Stop all drug operations as well—"

"The street distributors won't like that. The junkies will be howling, and the distributors may try to find other sources."

"The junkies can howl for a month or so. They'll come back when we're ready," Arsov said. "Brand loyalty is not exactly something junkies care about. And if the distributors desert us temporarily, it won't be a problem. If they won't come back when we're ready, we'll just kill a few and their families as well. Understood?"

"But where am I going to put all the whores? We don't have enough cages here to hold them all."

"There are plenty of empty containers in the warehouse. Lock them in those. Now get moving."

Nazarov nodded and rose. He stopped halfway to the door. "What about Tanya and the other two, should I put them with the rest of the whores?"

Arsov considered that for a moment. "No. They're troublemakers and would likely infect the others. We won't be able to use them in the UK any time soon. Export them."

"How? Their pictures are all over the place, and all the normal routes will be closely watched."

Arsov thought a moment. "Do we have any of the 'special cargo' boxes we can modify?"

"The only time we tried shipping whores by container, they were dead on arrival."

Arsov shrugged. "Then disposing of the bodies will be someone else's problem. Put Yuri and Anatoli on modifying a container while you attend to the other business."

Nazarov nodded and left the room, and Arsov sat staring down at his cell phone on the desk. He sighed and picked it up to dial St. Petersburg.

SPECIALIST CRIMES DIRECTORATE 9 (SCD9)
HUMAN EXPLOITATION/ORGANIZED CRIME
VICTORIA BLOCK, NEW SCOTLAND YARD
BOADWAY
LONDON, UK

"We're not the Clubs and Vice Unit any longer, Agent Walsh, and we haven't been for some time, though I expect you lot in the exalted halls of Thames House don't keep up with such mundane matters. However, I'd appreciate it if you'd use the correct unit designation."

Anna returned the man's gaze across the conference table and bit back a sharp retort. The meeting had started badly when the police inspector insisted on excluding Alex, Dugan, and the Russians. In fact, he made clear that the involvement of Anna and her MI5 colleagues was only tolerated on orders from above, a tolerance that did not extend to civilians. Alex had been near apoplectic at his exile to a waiting room along with Dugan and the others, and Anna was struggling to salvage the meeting. She gave the inspector her most winning smile.

"Apologies, Detective Inspector McKinnon," Anna said. "It's been 'Clubs and Vice' for so long I suppose it's just a habit to refer to it that way. However, I'll make a point to use the proper unit designation and make sure everyone else does as well."

Flanking her on either side, Lou and Harry nodded their assent, and McKinnon's glare softened—barely.

"That would be appreciated, Agent Walsh. As you're no doubt aware, the old Clubs and Vice Unit had a long history, not all of it positive. Most of us are now new to the unit, and we've done our best in the last eighteen months to distance SCD9 from that legacy." McKinnon sighed. "We've made some headway, but we're still very much a work in progress."

Anna nodded. The Clubs and Vice Unit had always been the backwater of the London Metropolitan Police and long considered a career-ending assignment. From its establishment in the 1930s, it had a checkered past, reaching its low ebb in the 1970s when chronic allegations of corruption were proven true and over twenty detectives were sacked. Since then, there had been periodic and to date unsuccessful attempts to upgrade the unit. The recent name change and infusion of new personnel was only the latest of those attempts.

"Understood," Anna said, "and I assure you will have MI5's support in that effort."

McKinnon cocked an eye. "Which brings me to my first question. How does any of this concern the Intelligence Service? This is clearly a police matter, and I can see no rhyme or reason for MI5 involvement. What am I missing?"

Anna hesitated. "Alexander Kairouz, Thomas Dugan, and their company have provided exemplary service to the Crown on prior occasions. Because of that, and Mr. Kairouz's political connections, they enjoy the favor of Her Majesty's government, so it's only natural that in a situation like this Mr. Kairouz would seek the government's help." She paused. "And as a word to the wise, Inspector, I'm not sure it's a good idea to exclude Mr. Kairouz from these discussions."

"Yes, well, I think there's rather more to it than that, Agent Walsh—I sense a personal connection, but I'll leave that for the moment. As far as this operation goes, I will deal with YOU with complete transparency, and what you tell Mr. Kairouz and his entourage or how you choose to involve them is entirely your concern. However, I also expect them to stay completely out of our way; is that clear enough?"

"Completely," Anna said. "Where do we begin?"

McKinnon opened a thick file folder in front of him and passed Anna a stapled packet of papers.

"Lacking detailed intelligence and with time an issue, with brute force," McKinnon said. "That's a list of every known or suspected Russian-operated illicit business in London and its environs. We're gearing up to raid all these locations simultaneously. No matter where the girls are, we should find them, and perhaps a lot of other things as well."

Anna paged through the list. "There must be over fifty locations here. How are you going to pull this off? It will require massive manpower."

"Fifty-seven, to be exact, and I suppose I have your Mr. Kairouz to thank for the manpower. People who would never give me the time of day are now calling to offer me resources, and magistrates who previously made us jump through hoops are now signing off search warrants with a minimum of hassle." He smiled for the first time. "Actually, it feels a bit like Christmas."

"Brilliant!" Anna said.

"When do you start?" Lou asked.

"In forty-eight hours, or maybe a bit longer," McKinnon replied.

"So long?" Anna asked.

"We have to make sure we get as many as we can, and that takes coordination. When we start the operation, word will spread quickly to any locations we miss. Understand that if we don't turn up the girls on this sweep, they'll likely get much more difficult to find."

"Maybe we should hold off a bit and try to pinpoint the girls first," Harry said.

McKinnon looked at Anna. "Do you think we have time for that, Agent Walsh?"

Anna looked down at the list and back up at McKinnon before slowly shaking her head. "No, unfortunately I don't. I think your massive quick sweep is our best shot, but God help us if we're wrong."

CHAPTER ELEVEN

Holding Warehouse
516 Copeland Road
Southwark, London, UK

Arsov stepped into the empty container with Nazarov close behind. Nazarov let out a relieved sigh as Arsov looked around and nodded. A rack along one wall of the container held a long row of one-gallon bottles of water, and a few cases of 'Meals, Ready-to-Eat' were lashed in a corner. Three bare mattresses lay on the deck in the far end of the container.

"Looks like you have enough water," Arsov said, "but are you sure there are enough MREs? We don't want them looking like survivors of the Gulag. It will make them less marketable until we can put some weight back on them."

"But we don't want them fat either," Nazarov replied. "Americans seem to like them skinny. Anyway, they have enough for one meal per day—it is enough, I think. But I don't know about these." He pointed to a row of empty twenty-liter plastic paint buckets with tight-fitting lids lashed to the opposite wall. "I think a chemical toilet would have been easier."

Arsov shook his head. "It would fill up too fast and slosh around when the ship rolls, splashing all over the place and stinking. If they do their business in the buckets, they can seal them tight and prevent that. Just make sure they have enough buckets."

Nazarov shrugged. "Who the fuck cares? So the whores arrive stinking—we give them a wash."

"I don't care about them, you idiot! I don't want to draw any attention to the container. It's not airtight, and don't you think a container reeking of shit and piss might draw more than a casual inspection from a boarding inspector?"

"I hadn't thought of that."

"Why doesn't that surprise me?"

Arsov ignored Nazarov's glare and continued. "Make sure they have a flashlight and some spare batteries. They'll need light to open the food and go to the toilet, but make them understand they are to use it sparingly—and put the fear of God in them about remaining quiet."

"*Da*," Nazarov said. "I will handle it."

"When will they leave?"

"A drug shipment was scheduled to leave Felixstowe tonight for Jacksonville, Florida, but I'm substituting this container. There should be no problem. Containers originating in the UK receive less scrutiny these days; that's why we've begun the drug transshipments through here."

"The crew is reliable?"

"*Da*. Mostly Ukrainians and Croatians," Nazarov said. "As usual, we first had to make a few examples to ensure their complete cooperation, but they've handled three 'special cargoes' for us so far. They know what to do, I don't foresee any problems."

"You'd best make sure there aren't any. St. Petersburg is far from pleased, so we can't afford any more screwups."

HOLDING WAREHOUSE
516 COPELAND ROAD
SOUTHWARK, LONDON, UK

Arsov looked around the seedy office and grimaced—it was a far cry from his well-appointed office at the club, and he was already sick of this dump. He cursed Nazarov's ineptitude and stood up from the squeaking office chair to stretch his aching back, a by-product of his night on the threadbare dilapidated sofa. He thought of the nights he had yet to spend here and regretted his own lack of forethought in establishing a more comfortable hideaway. Still, the warehouse was their most secure location, known only to a handful of his underlings, and he could manage here until the worst blew over. He'd send Nazarov to run things at Club *Pyatnitsa* and to take whatever heat might be generated there. It would serve him right, and a night in jail might teach the stupid bastard a lesson, presuming their solicitors couldn't free him within a few hours of any arrest.

He thought back over the day's events—he was as prepared as possible. All of the questionable whores and the children had been brought to the warehouse and locked in the cages or containers, and Yuri and Anatoli were here to watch and feed and water them. Drug operations had been temporarily suspended, and as Nazarov predicted, the distributors had started to moan, but that was a minor problem. And most importantly, the container with the troublemaking whores had left earlier this afternoon and should be at sea and out of reach by tonight. He was ready.

The big question was, ready for what? Security surrounding the anticipated police operation was tight—much tighter than usual. His informant could only tell him the planned operation was 'big' and that it would happen 'soon.' With preparations complete, the timing of the attack no longer concerned him as much as the scope. He'd downplayed the situation to his superiors in St. Petersburg, hoping he'd be able to contain things and ride out the storm. He could probably survive if the pending operation shut them down for a week or ten days—he'd skimmed enough cash to make up the shortfall—but beyond that there would be a serious cash-flow problem. Then he'd be faced not only with admitting his 'error,' but also explaining why it had taken so long for profits to dry up. A visit from an 'auditor' from St. Petersburg wasn't an event he'd likely survive.

All because that buffoon Nazarov couldn't obey a simple order. And that being the case, it was only right that Nazarov take the fall should things go badly. Arsov sat back down, ignoring the tortured squeal from the office chair as he swiveled back to the battered desk and opened his laptop.

Anna stood in front of the bathroom mirror, fresh from the shower and wrapped in a towel. She was reaching for her toothbrush when Dugan stepped in from the bedroom, clad only in a pair of boxers. He stepped close behind her and wrapped her in his arms as he smiled at their reflections in the mirror.

"Alone at last," he said as he pressed his body against hers. "All our houseguests are bedded down for the night."

Anna returned his smile and pressed back against him. "And why do I have the feeling that you have further plans for the evening, Mr. Dugan? I see the crack on the noggin had no impact on your libido."

"What can I say? I could never resist a woman in a towel."

"Yes, well, if you don't let me finish brushing my teeth, we'll see how you feel about a woman in a towel with the breath of a camel." She reached behind her with her free hand and placed it on his cheek. "Off with you now. I'll be in bed straightaway."

Dugan leaned down and kissed her neck. "See that you are." He caressed her bottom before moving away.

Five minutes later, Anna slipped naked between the sheets, to find Dugan lying on his back with his arms behind his head, staring up at the ceiling with a scowl on his face. She moved to his side, and she saw him smile in the dim half-light leaking from the partially closed bathroom door.

"All right, Dugan, what were you lying here thinking about? I could tell by the scowl it wasn't sex."

"Nothing that won't keep." He pulled her close and nuzzled her neck.

She pushed herself back from him and looked him in the eye. "Sorry, not good enough. I want your undivided attention. Now what's troubling you?"

Dugan sighed. "Nothing we can do anything about. I was talking to Borgdanov while you were in the shower. He and Ilya are very concerned with the impact all of this may have in Russia."

"You mean repercussions against their families?"

Dugan nodded. "Borgdanov's parents are dead, and he has no close relatives, but Ilya's concerned about his sister's family. He called them as soon as we figured out this asshole Arsov knew we were looking for Karina, and they went into hiding. But they can't hide forever, at least not in Russia."

"Have they had any indication anyone is looking for them?"

"That's the strange part. These Russian mob types don't normally screw around, but some of Borgdanov's old *Spetsnaz* buddies are keeping an eye on the house, and they've seen no indications anyone is after Karina's family. It's almost like what's happening here isn't being reported back to Russia. That doesn't add up."

"What do Borgdanov and Ilya think?"

Dugan shrugged. "They're clueless but don't think it will last indefinitely. They're working on some sort of plan for dealing with things in Russia, but they won't elaborate, at least not yet."

Anna looked concerned. "They're not going to go 'cowboy' on us, are they? Now that the Met is officially involved, I won't be able to protect them if they try to take things into their own hands."

"They understand the situation. I don't think they plan anything here in the UK."

"Well, that's good to know, if somewhat tentative. Let's just hope we get the girls back on the sweep tomorrow night."

Dugan nodded in the dim light. "Amen to that." He looked into Anna's eyes. "Are we done now?"

She pressed her body against him and ran a hand down his bare belly. "Not by half, Mr. Dugan. Not by half."

CHAPTER TWELVE

Dugan sat in the back seat and fidgeted as he looked out at the night lights of Soho, concentrating on the neon marquee above Club *Pyatnitsa*. Beside him he heard the low squawk of Anna's tactical radio, the volume lowered. He looked at his watch.

"How much longer?" he asked, not for the first time.

"From the sounds of the radio traffic, not long," Anna said from the front passenger seat. "But remember Detective Inspector McKinnon is coordinating a citywide strike, so he's got to ensure all the pieces are in place before he gives the go-ahead."

"I know, I know," Dugan said, "but it seems like we've been here all night."

"Two hours, actually," Harry said from behind the wheel. "Hardly any time at all as these things go, so don't get your knickers in a twist, Yank." Harry smiled at Anna. "He's an impatient sod, isn't he? I wonder if Lou is having to put up with this from the Russkis and the kid?"

"I suspect our Russian friends' military background has made them a bit more accustomed to lengthy waits," Anna said, "but I expect young Nigel is fit to be tied. He's been beside himself ever since the kidnapping." She looked over the seat back. "By the way, Tom, that was nice of you to square things for Nigel with the captain."

Dugan shrugged. "It was pretty obvious he wasn't going back to the ship, no matter what anyone said, and I didn't want the ship to sail shorthanded. He's just lucky personnel was able to find a replacement for a pier-head jump. Anyway, I figured I better do something, because Nigel's obviously not Alex's favorite person."

"I don't quite understand that," Anna said.

"I suspect it's a 'dad' thing," Dugan replied. "Remember Alex had just learned about Nigel and wasn't too happy about it to begin with, and then in the space of forty-eight hours, Cassie was taken and Nigel was the one who delivered the bad news. I'm sure Alex realizes it's unfair to associate that with Nigel, but on a gut level it's probably something he can't control. I think it's best just to keep them apart."

"Which reminds me, Yank," Harry said, "just how did you keep Kairouz away from our little party tonight?"

"With great difficulty, but ultimately with the truth. I pointed out that Gillian's at her wit's end, and he shouldn't leave her to wait for word alone. He was obviously torn but had to concede the point."

"Yeah, well, he's probably just as well off at home," Harry said. "It's not like any of us are anything more than spectators at McKinnon's show. We just have a bit better seats."

Anna and Dugan nodded agreement. Detective Inspector McKinnon had made it abundantly clear they were to take no part in the raids. Dugan and the other 'civilians' were allowed to observe only if accompanied by an MI5 agent. He did provide them radios to follow the progress and agreed that when the girls were located they would be informed and could go straight to them. He also allowed them to choose their vantage points, and they'd elected to split up into two cars and position themselves outside Club *Pyatnitsa* and Arsov's apartment building.

The radio squawked again, and Harry looked at Anna. "That sounds like it might be it. Turn up the volume."

Anna did so just in time to hear, "—ecute. Repeat. Execute."

Down the street, they watched as three uniformed constables exited an unmarked car and raced up the alley to seal the rear door of the club just as two patrol cars careened around the corner from a side street and skidded to a halt in front of the club. Six policemen boiled out of the cars and made a bee line for the front entrance of the club and pushed their way inside, followed shortly by the two policemen driving the cars, who stationed themselves at the front door to ensure no one entered or left.

"If all goes well, this is happening all over London," Harry said. "Now it's just a matter of sorting through the catch. That might take a while."

SPECIALIST CRIMES DIRECTORATE 9 (SCD9)
HUMAN EXPLOITATION/ORGANIZED CRIME
VICTORIA BLOCK, NEW SCOTLAND YARD
BOADWAY
LONDON, UK

The gray light of dawn leaked between the slats of the blinds into the Spartan conference room, competing with the harsh glow of the fluorescent fixtures. One tube in a fixture in the far corner blinked on and off sporadically and emitted a barely audible but annoying buzz, a fitting complement to the sullen mood that permeated the room.

"Bloody fuck all," McKinnon said. "Not only did we fail to find any of the girls, we uncovered nothing else of substance. One of the biggest operations in the history of the Metropolitan Police and we turn up nothing except a handful of immigration violations and a few minor offenses. I was sure if we hit them hard from every quarter, we'd turn up something to nail them with, at least." He slumped in his chair and shook his head. "I'm not likely to ever be able to marshal this much support again."

Across from him, Anna nodded sympathetically while Dugan and the Russians said nothing. It had been agreed that since they were there under sufferance, Anna would do all the talking. For that same reason, they'd excluded a quite agitated Nigel, but Lou and Harry were keeping him company elsewhere so the exclusion wouldn't seem so obvious.

"What do you think happened, Inspector?" Anna asked.

"It's clear as the nose on my face, isn't it? Though thank you for not pointing out the obvious. Someone tipped the bastards off, didn't they?"

"Perhaps it was the media campaign over the missing girls," Anna said. "I'm sure they may have been expecting something."

"Something, yes," McKinnon said, "but they were far too well prepared. We hit them simultaneously at eleven in the evening, and two hours later when we started hauling people in for questioning, there were already lawyers here waiting for them. And we found almost nothing—a bit of marijuana, some Russians that had overstayed their visas and the like, but no hard drugs, no guns, no girls that will admit to being anything but thrilled with their employers, and this bugger Arsov's a bloody ghost. Not only has no one seen him, no one even admits to knowing him."

"What are you going to do?" Anna asked.

McKinnon ran both his hands through his thinning hair and then clasped them behind his neck while he stared down at the table as if considering his reply. Finally he lifted his head.

"Whatever I can, which admittedly isn't much. We'll detain everyone guilty of any offense as long as legally possible. We caught a number of the girls engaged in sex in the back rooms, and for those clubs we can charge the managers with 'keeping a brothel.' We probably can't make those charges stick in the long run, because the johns will have to admit to paying for sex, and that's unlikely to happen. We may get the visas revoked for the girls that are supposed to be students or nannies, which only means they'll move them elsewhere." He shrugged. "I can tie a knot in their knickers for a few days or perhaps a week, but after that it will be back to business as usual."

"You said there was no sign of Arsov," Anna said, "even at his flat or Club *Pyatnitsa*?"

"There were clothes at his flat and toiletries, that sort of thing. Nothing at all in the way of papers or anything to indicate he'd lived there. The place was leased by a shell company that's another dead end. These buggers are smart."

"Then who was running the club?" Dugan asked, earning him a look from Anna.

"A bloke named Nazarov," McKinnon said. "He's been in the country a couple of years and is generally known by some of our undercovers as the man in charge. This Arsov is a relatively unknown quantity. If he is pulling the strings, he is doing so through Nazarov."

"Then we must question this Nazarov, *da*?" Borgdanov said. "If you have him, we must make him talk."

McKinnon stiffened. "We don't do things that way here, Mr. Borgda—"

"It is Major Borgdanov, Inspector," Borgdanov said.

"Very well, 'Major' Borgdanov. We can't very well just beat the information out of him, now can we?"

"Of course not," Borgdanov said. "I know many other ways that do not leave marks. We could—"

"Your point is well taken, Inspector," Anna said, cutting Borgdanov off. "I think perhaps you and I should continue this discussion in your office." She shot a pointed look at Dugan and the Russians. "Alone."

McKinnon nodded and rose without a word. He walked to the door and held it open for Anna and then followed her out into the corridor.

As the door closed, Dugan looked at Borgdanov. "Not too subtle, Andrei."

Borgdanov shrugged. "I do not know what means 'subtle,' *Dyed*. But I do know you will make no progress with *Bratstvo* bastards with nice questions and lawyers. I think we tried Anna's way and did not work. I think now we try our way."

Beside him, Ilya nodded.

"Aren't you forgetting your promise to Anna?"

"*Nyet*," Borgdanov said. "I promised I would not kill Arsov in UK, and Nazarov is not Arsov. And besides, we do not plan to kill Nazarov."

"And if we do, we take him outside UK," Ilya said. "We would never break promise to Anna."

CHAPTER THIRTEEN

CONTAINER SHIP *KAPITAN GODINA*
EN ROUTE TO JACKSONVILLE, FLORIDA

Cassie sat on the floor with her back against the steel side of the container, bracing herself against the constant roll of the ship and clutching a large plastic bucket as she fought down the gorge rising in her throat once again. She lost the battle and hung her head over the bucket as her stomach spasmed, but there was little left to eject, and she endured yet another round of painful, mostly dry heaves. The episode passed, and she slumped back against the wall and closed her eyes, hoping that when she opened them, she would find it had all been a bad dream. But that didn't happen.

The others slumped beside her, each girl clutching her own bucket, the odors rising from the open pails combining to produce an oppressive miasma in the dead air of the container. Cassie judged it was near midday, because the temperature in the container had risen steadily since the first bit of light began leaking through the holes high up on the container walls. It wasn't much light, barely enough for her to make out the other girls only a few feet away from her. Tanya was the worst off—the seasickness had hit her almost immediately, and she'd vomited on the container floor before she could make it to one of the buckets. The blond girl, Karina, seemed least effected, and as Cassie looked at her, Karina nodded and produced a wan smile.

"I think we will survive, *da*?"

"I…I guess so," Cassie said, "but where are they taking us?"

Karina shrugged. "It makes no difference. Everyplace is the same. Only the accents of the bastards they sell us to changes."

Cassie's lower lip started to tremble, and Karina reached across Tanya and gave Cassie's leg a reassuring pat. "But for now we cannot think of that. We must try to figure out how long we will be in this box." Karina passed her bucket over Tanya's legs. "Here. Hold my bucket so it does not turn over. I want to check something."

Cassie took the bucket and held it on the floor beside her own with her free hand, and watched Karina pull herself up and turn on the flashlight she had jammed in the pocket of her jeans.

"Wh-what are you going to do?" Cassie asked.

"I go to count the food they give us. Nazarov said to eat only one box each every day. It means if I count meals, I know how long they think to keep us here. If we know this, we can count water and see how much we have for each day. Maybe if there is little extra, we can wash a bit, *da*?"

Cassie nodded, encouraged, and followed the light as Karina's figure faded into the gloom toward the far end of the container. She saw the light moving around the boxes lashed in the corner and then saw it illuminate Karina's hand as she tore open one of the cartons. Then the light played over the water jugs in a rack along one wall and bobbed back through the darkness toward her.

"Is enough food for maybe ten days," Karina said as she resumed her place on the floor. "Assuming they would only put in whole cases, I think maybe our trip is seven or eight days. There is plenty of water—fifteen jugs." Karina held the flashlight out to Cassie. "Here, Cassie, hold light for me."

"Just a minute," Cassie said and transferred one of the cumbersome buckets to between her knees so she could hold it with her legs against the ship's motion. "Okay," she said and took the light.

"Hold it on my hands," Karina said, and Cassie watched as the Russian girl opened a package marked MEAL - READY TO EAT.

"How can you eat?" Cassie asked, surprise in her voice.

The mention of food propelled Tanya away from the wall and over her bucket in an episode of dry heaves. Karina reached out with her free hand and patted Tanya's back until her friend finished retching and slumped back against the wall.

"I am searching for crackers or biscuits," Karina said. "Something light to start. And we must drink water, or we will become dehydrated."

Tanya groaned. "What does it matter? It is hopeless."

Cassie saw Karina shake her head as she continued to rummage through the contents of the MRE. "There is always hope, no matter how dim. And we must keep ourselves strong to take advantage of any opportun—Aha!"

"Did you find biscuits?" Cassie asked.

"No, but I have the solution to something else that has been concerning me." Karina held up a packet of toilet paper.

HOLDING WAREHOUSE
516 COPELAND ROAD
SOUTHWARK, LONDON, UK

Arsov held the phone to his ear and listened to the attorney with a growing sense of relief.

"… and six girls have immigration violations—two Russians and four Ukrainians. They're subject to deportation, but I can file appeals—"

He cut the lawyer off. "On the contrary. Use all your contacts to expedite their deportations; then get me their names and flight information. I'll take it from there. Understood?"

The lawyer confirmed his understanding, and Arsov scribbled a note on the pad in front of him. The girls would be met by *Bratstvo* soldiers when they arrived in their homelands and shuttled right back into the system, after any refresher training needed. It was the quickest way to get them back to income-producing status. They could no longer sell the girls in the UK, but the world was a big place, and the *Bratstvo* served many markets.

"What of the club managers?"

"As I told you previously, Mr. Nazarov and three others are being charged with 'operating a brothel,' but the charges are unlikely to hold up unless the clients are willing to testify they exchanged money for sex. However, the authorities are holding the managers pending a bail hearing, stipulating that as foreign nationals they represent a flight risk. I'm pressing for a hearing this afternoon, so we should have them out by this evening at the latest."

Arsov was silent a moment. "Don't press so hard. Tomorrow afternoon will be fine."

"Yes… but don't you want me to get them out as soon as—"

"Do we have a bad connection, or are you just slow?"

"Ah… no… no, I understand," the lawyer said. "Tomorrow, then?"

"Or the next day. Whatever is convenient. Is there anything more?"

"No, not unless you—"

"Goodbye." Arsov hung up.

He sat back in the squeaking chair and put his feet on the battered desk. All in all, things were going much better than he had hoped. The raid would impact revenue, of course, but not as badly as he feared. It would slow, but not stop for a week or two, and then he could start ramping things up again. Better still, with Nazarov out of the way for a couple of days, he could continue his plan. He had already set up the Cayman Islands bank account in Nazarov's name, and he just had to plant a bit more evidence before he alerted St. Petersburg as to the full extent of the problem and his suspicions about Nazarov. Perhaps he would pick the least competent of the other club managers presently in custody as well. After all, Nazarov would undoubtedly have had an accomplice. He smiled. The bosses in St. Petersburg would be pleased that he'd come to London and uncovered these irregularities so quickly. Perhaps he would be in line for yet another promotion?

CHAPTER FOURTEEN

"Absolutely not!" Anna said. "I made this clear from the beginning. We have to be careful, and now that the Met is involved, we have even less room to maneuver. You can't just snatch Nazarov as he leaves New Scotland Yard and beat a confession out of him."

Borgdanov shrugged. "Actually, Anna, I think you mean the POLICE cannot do this. I think we can do what we want as long as we do not get caught. After all, is what the *mafiya* does, *da*? So we must, as you say in English, fight the fire with the fire. Is this not logical?"

"Andrei is right, Anna," Dugan said. "The police gave it their best shot and got nowhere. If we don't take matters into our own hands, what's Plan B?"

Anna opened her mouth to respond, but Alex cut her off.

"I concur with Thomas and Major Borgdanov." Beside Alex on the sofa, both Gillian and Ilya nodded.

Anna looked around the room. "I wasn't aware we were voting, but if you're all quite done, I'd like to make something clear. I love Cassie as much as anyone here, and I'm not about to abandon the effort to get her and the other girls back. What I said was that we had to be CAREFUL or the police will shut us down in a heartbeat." She looked at Borgdanov. "That means you can't just snatch Nazarov as he exits the police station. He'll undoubtedly be met by other mobsters, and that might result in a confrontation that draws attention. You must have a plan—where to grab him quickly and quietly, where to take him for interrogation, etc."

"You are right," Borgdanov said. "I am sorry, Anna. We must discuss these things."

"Yeah, but maybe Anna shouldn't be involved from here," Dugan said. "She's already pushed the envelope, and if things go south, it may be better if she has some plausible deniability."

Anna shook her head. "No, I'm in, but I'll keep my distance from the interrogation. If you turn up anything of use, I'll need to feed it back to the police and attribute it to a 'confidential source.' Given his desire to wipe out the Russian mob, I don't think McKinnon will ask too many questions. But I'm only speaking for myself—Lou and Harry can't be involved. They're both near retirement, and this could be costly for them if it goes badly."

"As far as a place for the interrogation," Alex offered, "we have some surplus warehouse space that's up for sale. It's empty and relatively isolated. I'll call the real estate agent tomorrow and tell him we're thinking about keeping it and not to show it to anyone for a few days."

"Good idea," Dugan said, "but you'd better let me do that, Alex. You probably need to keep your distance too. The police already know my face and my relationship with Andrei and Ilya, and if this goes badly, one of us needs to stay out of jail to keep the company going."

"Now see here, Thomas—"

Gillian reached over and took Alex's hand. "Tom is right, dear. I know you want to do more to save Cassie, but if something goes awry you have to be available to carry on the effort. We can't let our emotions overrule our intellect."

Alex gave a reluctant nod, and Gillian patted his hand.

"So," Ilya said, his impatience evident, "we will have place to question this bastard, but when do we take him?"

"He has a bail hearing tomorrow afternoon, and there's little doubt he'll be released," Anna said. "We'll shadow him from that point and figure out the best time and place to grab him. I don't think it will take very long."

"What about McKinnon?" Dugan asked. "Won't he have a tail on Nazarov and the others?"

"Maybe," Anna said, "but after the failure of the raid, he'll be back to limited resources, so he'll be a bit thin on the ground. We'll just have to cross that bridge when we come to it."

CLUB *PYATNITSA*
LONDON, UK

Nazarov sat behind Arsov's desk in the office, looking over the receipts from the previous evening. They were down, of course, given the raid, but even the threat of arrest couldn't dampen the allure of what they provided for long, and business was rebounding. With the 'trainees' out of action for a while, he'd have to work the remaining whores that much harder. He'd have Ivan gather them together before business picked up this evening and inform them they had to get more aggressive. Maybe he'd start opening earlier in the day and see if he could draw in a matinee crowd. He'd feed the whores uppers if he had to, Arsov's prohibition on drugging the bitches be damned.

Arsov! He knew that asshole would leave him to take the fall, but he hadn't expected to spend two nights as a guest of the government. He suspected that was Arsov's doing. To be sure, the UK jails were a paradise compared to some of the Russian jails he'd been in as a boy, before he smartened up and joined the *Bratstvo*, but that didn't mean he enjoyed spending time there. Just another thing he'd chalk up on the ledger. Arsov wasn't the only one who had a few friends in St. Petersburg.

Nazarov stretched and yawned; he hadn't slept well in jail. Everything seemed in order here, so he decided to go home and get some sleep. He let Ivan know he was leaving, then walked down the corridor to the rear exit. He cracked the door to verify it was all clear before he rushed across the alley to the back door of the Italian restaurant. He had to give Arsov credit for establishing this discreet access. The Italian chef no longer needed a cover story, and Nazarov didn't even slow down as he stuffed a fifty-pound note in the big man's hand and kept walking. Seconds later he was headed for the cab stand two blocks away.

BERWICK STREET, SOHO
NEAR CLUB *PYATNITSA*
LONDON, UK

"This could get a bit tricky," Dugan said, watching the two plain clothes cops in the car parked fifty feet away. "What if they follow us if we leave?"

"They won't," Anna said from the driver's seat. "And if they do, so much the better. We'll lead them away from Borgdanov and Ilya."

"You're sure this is gonna work?"

"It's the only thing that makes sense. We know Arsov successfully gave us the slip before, and we were watching both the front entrance and the opening to the alley. He never came out of either place. Therefore, he must have gone through one of the businesses facing onto the next street. If Nazarov leaves, he'll likely do the same, and our Russian friends can pick him up while we stay here and keep the constables company."

"Yeah, well, maybe the cops are doing the same thing?"

"I don't think so," Anna said, smiling sweetly, "because I never shared my conclusions with Detective Inspector McKinnon. Also, we're watching one location, but McKinnon's likely still trying to cover several, and he's back to being short on manpower."

"Let's hope you're right."

HOPKINS STREET CAR PARK
LONDON, UK

Ilya Denosovitch sat behind the wheel of the rental car, with binoculars pressed to his eyes, peering over the waist high side wall of the open-air car park into the street below. He'd been fortunate to find a vantage point on the third level of the facility that allowed him to look directly into the alley behind Club *Pyatnitsa*, two blocks away. He smiled as he saw the back door of the club open a crack and then fully, as Nazarov exited and scurried across the narrow alley and into another door. He picked up his radio and keyed the mike.

"Chase One, this is Eagle Eye. Do you copy, over?"

One block away on Wardour Street, Borgdanov responded from the driver's seat of his own rental car. "Eagle Eye, this is Chase One. I copy, over."

"Chase One, suspect should exit somewhere in your vicinity at any time. Be prepared. Over," Ilya said.

"Eagle Eye. I have him. Repeat. I have him. Over," Borgdanov said.

"Affirmative, Chase One. I am leaving my position to join you. Keep me advised as to your location, and I will catch up."

"Affirmative, Eagle Eye. Babysitter, this is Chase One. Did you copy last transmissions? Over."

Anna's voice came over the radio. "Chase One, this is Babysitter. We copied all transmissions. We will stay in place and watch our friends. Good hunting, and please advise when you are well out of area. We will disengage here and join hunt if possible."

"Affirmative, Babysitter. This is Chase One out."

Thirty minutes later, Anna's radio squawked. "Babysitter, this is Chase One. Do you copy? Over."

"This is Babysitter. Go ahead, Chase One. Over."

"We are well away from you. Target exited taxi and entered apartment building on Chesham Place. I think is his place. Over."

"We copy, Chase One. We are in transit to your location. Babysitter out." Anna started the car.

"Fancy. The Belgrave Square area," Anna said as she pulled away from the curb.

"Won't the cops think it strange if we leave?" Dugan asked.

"Not likely. They've only seen the two of us, and they know we can't stay here round the clock. They'll probably just attribute it to lack of resources and figure we'll rely on them. After all, they know half the team is amateur." Anna smiled. "Be sure to wave at them as we pass, so we can cement that impression."

CHAPTER FIFTEEN

Dugan stood in the beam of the car's headlights and unlocked the padlock before leaning his weight into the edge of the large sliding door. After a moment's resistance, the big door started to move, slowly at first and then faster as it built up momentum, the disused metal wheels on the track above squealing a lament. When it was halfway open, Dugan released the door and stepped back, and inertia carried it another few feet before it rumbled to a stop. He waved the car through the gap and took a quick, furtive look up and down the street before he stepped inside and tugged the door closed after him.

The car's headlights cut a bright tunnel through the pitch-black interior of the warehouse, illuminating a section of the back wall. Dugan pulled a flashlight from his pocket.

"Stay there a minute," he called out toward the car as he made his way to a breaker box near the door. "I'm going to get us some light."

Seconds later the interior of the warehouse was bathed in light, and Dugan watched as Borgdanov and Ilya climbed out of the vehicle and looked around. Dugan followed the Russians' gaze. It was a cavernous space, mostly empty, and the sound of the closing car doors was returned from the bare walls in a metallic echo. Here and there coils of old mooring lines and empty oil drums were stacked in disarray, the detritus of a successful shipping operation left behind when the expanding operations had necessitated a larger warehouse. They'd have to get this place cleaned up a bit before they sold it, Dugan thought, momentarily distracted. He looked back at Borgdanov as the Russian approached, shaking his head.

"I think we need quieter place, *Dyed*. In here the sound will be, how you say, amplified, and we do not want to attract attention."

Dugan pointed to a door in a cubic structure built into the far corner of the warehouse.

"That's the office. It's insulated and soundproofed, and there's probably some old furniture left. That should do."

Borgdanov nodded. "Ilya," he called to Denosovitch, who was dragging a bound and gagged Nazarov out of the trunk. "Take him to the door in the far corner."

Ilya nodded and tossed Nazarov over his shoulder, none too gently. He started for the door.

"Did you have any trouble?" Dugan asked.

"*Nyet*. The only real problem is keeping Ilya from killing him."

"You promised—"

"I know, *Dyed*. We promised Anna, and we keep promise. We kill no one in the UK." His face hardened. "But I assure you, very soon our friend Nazarov may wish he is dead. I think also, it may be better if you leave, *da*? We call you when we finish."

Dugan shook his head. "There are private security patrols on several of the nearby warehouses. If they see or hear anything, they may phone it in to the police. I have identification and work for Phoenix, so if they come, I can assure them everything is okay. Besides, maybe I can help out. I'm sure Nazarov is terrified of you guys, but maybe I can be the alternative. You know—bad cop, good cop."

Borgdanov shook his head. "I am afraid 'bad cop, good cop' does not work so well with Russian *mafiya*. For them we must use 'bad cop, worse cop,' *da*?"

PHOENIX SHIPPING WAREHOUSE B
EAST LONDON, UK

Dugan watched as Ilya tipped the chair and dumped Nazarov on his back on the tile floor, still bound to the chair hand and foot. Nazarov screamed what Dugan assumed was abuse in Russian until Ilya placed a thick towel over his face and slowly began to saturate the towel with water from a plastic jug. Nazarov grew silent as he held his breath for what seemed like forever, and then the silence was replaced by the sound of Nazarov's strangled attempts at breathing.

Ilya glanced at his watch, timing the man's struggles, and then hoisted the chair back upright to allow the sodden towel to fall away. Nazarov bent at the waist and alternated between wet, racking coughs and gasps. Dugan shook his head and moved toward the door into the warehouse, motioning for Borgdanov to join him. Once they were outside the office and in the warehouse proper, he turned to Borgdanov.

"This isn't working," Dugan said. "I don't know what the hell he's saying, but you've water-boarded him five times now, and it looks to me like he just gets more defiant each time."

Borgdanov shrugged. "We had to try easy way first, *Dyed*, but I did not really expect this to work. Also, he is *Bratstvo*, and these scum think they are very tough guys. Now he is congratulating himself that he has endured our punishment and is big tough guy. So. When we start more aggressive methods, he will have big surprise. Is how you say 'psychological.' *Da*?" Borgdanov patted Dugan's shoulder. "Do not worry so. We know what we are doing."

"I sure as hell hope so," Dugan muttered as he followed Borgdanov back into the office.

They found a silent Nazarov glaring defiantly at an impassive Ilya, and Dugan held back as Borgdanov approached, smiling before addressing Nazarov in Russian.

***

"So, Nazarov," Borgdanov said cheerfully, "did you enjoy your last little swim?"

Nazarov spit and screwed his head around to look at Borgdanov. "Is that the best you have, *Spetsnaz*? I am *Bratstvo*. You will never break me."

Borgdanov shrugged. "Well, we will in time, but I would prefer for you to cooperate with no more little unpleasant things, *da*? We are not savages. So, I ask you again, please tell me where you are keeping the girls and also where Arsov is hiding."

Nazarov sneered. "Fuck you, soldier boy. You want girls? Then come to club, I fix you up with many girls." Nazarov looked up at Ilya and grinned. "But too bad you missed one of the best ones. Her name is Karina, and she loved to suck my cock. Also she was crazy about taking it up the ass. We have some nice videos of her satisfying five big guys at once. Maybe I can get you two a copy. You can use it to jerk off."

Nazarov threw his head back and laughed, and Borgdanov watched Ilya, half-expecting him to kill the man immediately, but the big Russian remained outwardly calm; the only indication of his rage a red flush creeping up the back of his neck and into his-close cropped blond hair. Borgdanov shook his head and addressed Dugan in English.

"I see we must change methods, *Dyed*. Can I count on you to assure Anna we did at least try to do things nicely?"

Dugan nodded, and Borgdanov pulled a syringe from his pocket, uncapped it, and ejected a bit of fluid before sinking the needle into Nazarov's neck. The man jerked a few seconds and then slumped in the chair against his bonds.

"Come," Borgdanov said to Dugan as he recapped the syringe and tossed it in the corner. "Please help me carry in the rest of the supplies while Ilya prepares our friend."

Ten minutes and several trips to the car later, Borgdanov and Dugan stood watching Ilya cut Nazarov's clothes off. Borgdanov followed Dugan's gaze as the American looked at the floor and studied the collection they'd carried in.

"Christ, Andrei!" Dugan said. "Where the hell did you get all this stuff?"

Borgdanov smiled. "Harry and Lou are a little less concerned about methods than Anna. I gave them my shopping list. They got me the tranquilizer too."

***

Nazarov floated on the edge of consciousness, fighting unsuccessfully to open his eyes. Something was tickling his nose, and he tried to scratch it, but his limbs wouldn't respond. Then the acrid smell of ammonia filled his nostrils, burning the inside of his nose as he gasped for a breath. His eyes flew open in time to see a retreating pair of hands holding the crushed remains of an ammonia popper, and he gazed up the arms attached to those hands into the smiling face of Borgdanov.

"Very good, Nazarov. You've decided to rejoin us. Apologies for waking you so abruptly, but we are a bit pressed for time. I'm sure you understand."

"Fuck you." Nazarov studied his surroundings.

He was stark naked, seated semi-reclined on the floor, the cracked tile cool against his bare ass. He was leaned back against some sort of support, his arms stretched out to his sides and duct-taped at the wrist to a board stretched across his back to keep them that way. He tried to sit up but couldn't. The board was obviously securely fastened to something. His legs were also stretched wide and-duct taped at the ankles to another board. B-t most worrying were his balls. His genitals rested slightly elevated on a flat triangular piece of concrete that had been shoved between his legs. He felt the rough point against his anus and tried to shift his weight away from it, but he was totally immobile. He fought down his terror and grinned up at Borgdanov.

"You think you can scare me, soldier boy? You can't do this shit in the UK. This is all a bluff."

Borgdanov shrugged. "I think perhaps you should consider this warehouse to be a little piece of Mother Russia for the moment. That may help you focus your thoughts, *da*?"

"I will tell you nothing."

"On the contrary. You have already confessed to doing very bad things to my friend Ilya's favorite niece, so he very much wants to kill you. Fortunately for you"—Borgdanov shrugged—"or perhaps unfortunately—you have information we need. But I will not bother to ask you again, because I know you will only resist. Instead we will have to do things the hard way." Borgdanov stepped aside, and Nazarov lifted his head to see the one called Ilya standing nearby. At the big blond's feet lay an assortment of pliers, various sharp instruments and other tools, and a propane torch. Ilya smiled down at him.

"Fuck you too," Nazarov said again, but there was fear in his voice.

"I admire your courage," Borgdanov said. "And Ilya and I agree it may take some time for you to agree to cooperate. So we've decided to save all these little toys for later and to use them only if necessary. Instead we have decided to go to the most extreme measures immediately so you will understand we are very serious." Borgdanov shrugged. "Then, if you are still not convinced, we can always resort to the tedious cutting and burning."

Nazarov swallowed, his mouth dry. He tried to speak but didn't trust his voice.

"After some consideration," Borgdanov said, "we decided the worst thing we could do to a big stud like you was to remove your genitals. We considered various methods—you know, like dull knife or maybe burning them off with the propane torch. But my Ilya is a man of action. He said to me, 'We should not pull the wings off the fly like some cruel child. *Nyet*. We are not barbarians. We should be humane and crush the fly quickly.'"

Nazarov cut his eyes back to Ilya as the big blond reached down and rose with a long handled sledgehammer. It was a massive thing, with a flat face on one side of the head tapering to a rounded point on the opposite end. Nazarov watched with horror as Ilya stepped around the table, raised the hammer over his head, and charged forward, with the obvious intent of flattening Nazarov's genitals. The huge hammer descended in an arc, and Nazarov closed his eyes and screamed as he felt the hammer impact.

"Ilya, dammit, I told you to be careful. You missed completely."

Nazarov opened his eyes and moaned, his balls aching from the impact of the hammer on the concrete only millimeters away.

"It is not my fault," Ilya said. "I told you we needed to center his balls on the stone. Now look what you made me do. Put his balls back in the center, and I'll try again."

"I'm not going to touch his balls," Borgdanov said. "Use the pliers and... oh shit, Ilya. You cracked the stone. Now we'll have to get another one."

"All right, I'll talk," Nazarov whimpered.

"We don't need another stone," Ilya said, ignoring Nazarov. "This one is perfectly fine. It's only a small crack."

"I'LL TALK!"

Borgdanov looked down at Nazarov and then back at Ilya. "He wants to talk."

Ilya shook his head. "I don't care. He hurt Karina, and you promised me I could smash his balls. Besides, he talks with his tongue not his balls, and we have plenty of ways left to make him talk." Ilya stepped back and raised the hammer again.

"No... no, it wasn't me! I never touched Karina. Arsov wouldn't let me. He kept her for himself."

Ilya hesitated, the hammer raised.

"And where is Karina now?" Borgdanov asked.

"In a container on a ship bound for the US. All the girls are... that is the three troublemakers. They left port three days ago."

"And what is the name of this ship, and what is its exact destination?"

Nazarov looked from Borgdanov to the hammer raised above Ilya's head. "If I tell you, will you promise not to smash my balls?"

Borgdanov shook his head. "No. But I do promise you that if you don't tell me in five seconds, your balls will be looking very different."

Nazarov said nothing, and Borgdanov shrugged and nodded to Ilya, who grinned and repositioned the hammer for another swing.

"Wait! It's the *Kapitan Godina* bound for Jacksonville, Florida. That's all I know. I swear."

"I think you are far too modest my friend," Borgdanov said. "I think you also know where our friend Arsov is hiding, *da*?"

"I... I cannot. He... he will kill me if I tell."

"Then I think you are in a very bad situation, Nazarov, because we will kill you if you don't tell. After, of course... well, you know..."

"You must give me something."

Borgdanov sighed. "All right, all right. If you give us Arsov and then behave yourself, we will not smash your balls and we will not kill you. Okay?"

Nazarov looked at Ilya, who was still standing with the hammer in his hand. "What about him?"

Borgdanov looked over at his subordinate. "Ilya?"

Ilya scowled and lowered the hammer. "*Da*. But I am going to smash this Arsov's balls for sure."

"We'll see," Borgdanov said, turning back to Nazarov. "Now where is Arsov?"

"In our secret warehouse on Copeland Road in Southwark. Number 516."

"And who is there with him?"

"Just two men to take care of the unreliable whor— the girls."

"And no one else?"

"Just the kids," Nazarov said, then flinched as he saw Borgdanov's jaw tighten and Ilya tighten his grip on the hammer. "I have nothing to do with the children," he blurted. "That was all Arsov's doing. The perverts pay a fortune."

"What else is in this warehouse?"

"Just the drugs. It is our distribution center. Heroin, cocaine, Ecstasy, that sort of thing."

"All right." Borgdanov wrinkled his nose and turned to Ilya. "I think our tough guy shit himself. Cut the bastard loose and take him to the toilet to clean himself up. If he makes one wrong move, kill him."

∗∗∗

"Brutal but effective," Dugan said to Borgdanov as they waited for Ilya to return with Nazarov. "If Anna feeds this warehouse location to McKinnon, the cops can free the captives and scoop up Arsov and a couple of his men at the same time."

Borgdanov hesitated. "We want this Arsov, *Dyed*. I think the police do nothing."

"They can do plenty if they catch him with captives and drugs."

Borgdanov's skepticism was apparent. "I think with smart lawyers is never a sure thing. This Arsov is very clever."

"And if he turns up dead, the police are going to be looking for us, and that's not a distraction we need while we're still trying to get the girls back. Thanks to you, we know where they are, and we should be concentrating on freeing them and leave Arsov to the police. Besides, if we take out Arsov and his thugs by ourselves, what are we going to do with his captives? They'll need more help and support than we'll be able to provide. And just taking out Arsov won't solve the larger problem, because some other London-based thug will just step into his role. But if the police scoop up Arsov with a bunch of drugs and witnesses, they have at least a fighting chance of wiping out the whole *Bratstvo* operation, at least here in the UK. If, as you fear, he manages to escape or beat the charges, you can hunt him down later."

Borgdanov gave a reluctant nod. "*Da*, everything you say makes sense. I will think about it. Ilya will not be happy, but I know he will agree that nothing should interfere with our ability to rescue Karina and the others."

Dugan let out a relieved sigh. "Good. Now, what are you going to do with Nazarov."

"Perhaps you should not concern yourself with this, *Dyed*. In fact, is maybe better you wait for us outside in the warehouse, *da*?"

"Just a damn minute, Andrei! You promised Anna you wouldn't kill—"

Borgdanov held up his hands. "Calm yourself. We will not kill this scum, though you know he deserves it. But we cannot let him go or turn him over to the police either. If the police know we got information by force, I think your stupid law maybe will prevent them from raiding this warehouse, *da*? So we cannot give him to police, and we cannot let him go. We do not have enough people to keep him prisoner, and even if we did keep him prisoner, sooner or later we must either give him to police or release him, and either way he will eventually go free, I think." Borgdanov's face hardened. "And to this, I cannot agree. He deserves some punishment. He was here long time before Arsov, so I do not believe that he has nothing to do with selling children and these other things. You do not rise to a position in the *Bratstvo* without killing many people along the way."

"I can't argue with that, but what's left?"

"As I said, we have a plan. Now if you just go into the warehou—"

Borgdanov looked up as the toilet door opened, and a naked Nazarov re-entered the large office, trailed by Ilya still carrying the sledgehammer.

"I'll stay," Dugan said.

Borgdanov shrugged. "As you wish." He turned to face Nazarov.

"Nazarov! Take three steps forward and stand at attention!"

Obviously puzzled, Nazarov took three slouching steps toward Borgdanov and stood up marginally straighter, shooting a nervous glance over his shoulder at Ilya.

"Eyes on me," Borgdanov yelled, and when Nazarov hastened to comply, Borgdanov nodded to Ilya.

Without hesitation, Ilya stepped to one side and drew the hammer back to take a side arm swing as if he was chopping a tree. He landed a crushing blow to Nazarov's back, expertly centering the rounded point of the hammer on the man's spine just below the shoulder blades. And like a tree, Nazarov went down, collapsed in a heap on the floor.

For a long moment the quiet was broken only by Nazarov's strangled sobs.

"Jesus Christ!" Dugan moved back a step.

"I-I can't feel my legs," Nazarov sobbed as Borgdanov knelt beside him, speaking English now.

"And you will never feel them again, you worthless piece of shit. And in the future, while you're sitting in a wheel chair, wallowing in your own filth in some shit hole of a government nursing home, I want you to think about all the people you hurt and the lives you destroyed, *da*? Now we are going to dump you naked in the street beside the nearest charity hospital. I suggest that you tell the authorities that you have amnesia and that you never regain your memory. Because there will be a big raid on the warehouse, and we're going to make sure that the *Bratstvo* know that you were the informant. So you see, my friend, they will be looking for you, and you will not be able to run and hide. So it is best you remain anonymous, *da*? Then you can live out the rest of your miserable life begging God for forgiveness. I suspect He is more charitable than Ilya and I."

"You promised!"

"I promised not to kill you, and you are still alive. I promised not to crush your balls, and they are still there. The fact that you will never feel them again is not my problem. Oh, I keep my promises, Nazarov, and I will make you another one. If you ever open your fucking mouth, I will have Ilya visit you again and apply his hammer a bit further up your spine and remove the use of your arms. Understood?"

"You bastard!"

"I assume that means yes." Borgdanov turned to Ilya. "Put some tape over this asshole's mouth and help me get him to the car."

Dugan watched as Ilya complied, and the ex-*Spetsnaz* men each hooked a hand into an armpit and began dragging Nazarov toward the door. He wasn't sure what he'd expected, but it certainly wasn't what had just transpired. He trailed the Russians, trying to figure out how much of this to share with Anna.

CHAPTER SIXTEEN

Dugan watched Alex pace the room, wringing his hands. "How long before we can mount a rescue, Thomas?"

Dugan shook his head. "The *Kapitan Godina* is in the middle of the Atlantic. They're already out of reach from this side, and according to their AIS signal, it looks like three days minimum before they're in chopper range of the US coast. I've called Jesse Ward, and we're working on a plan, but we have to be discreet. Like Anna, Jesse's helping us off the books. By the time he got official approval for an op like this, presuming that's even possible, it would be too late."

"Yes, of course." Alex continued to pace. "But assure Ward we'll fund whatever resources are needed—"

"Alex! You're wearing a hole in the rug," Gillian said. "Come sit down and finish listening to what Tom has to say. This is all stressful enough without you dashing back and forth like a bear in a shooting gallery."

Alex bristled, then seemed to compose himself. He sat down beside Gillian on the sofa and she took his hand. "I'm sorry to be cross, dear. But we're all overwrought, and we can't let our emotions rule us, especially at this point." She turned to Dugan. "Finding the girls' location was brilliant, Tom. We can't thank you enough."

"You can thank the Russians."

"And speaking of our Russian friends, where are they?" Anna asked, then narrowed her eyes. "And just exactly how did they get this out of Nazarov?"

"I dropped them off at our apartment," Dugan said, ignoring the second part of the question. "Nigel has been there unsupervised, and I didn't want to leave him alone too long in case he might decide to do something stupid like storming into one of the clubs by himself."

"Answer the question, Tom."

"Borgdanov and Ilya can be quite convincing."

Anna sat quietly for a moment. "Is Nazarov still alive?"

"He's definitely alive and enjoying the finest care the National Health Service can provide," Dugan said, then added, "Under an assumed name. He's disappeared, and it's better for all concerned if he doesn't reappear, so you should really let it rest. You've often pointed out to me that MI5 is intelligence, not law enforcement, so it seems to me if you get the intelligence, how it was collected should make no difference as long as you personally didn't violate any laws."

"Still, how do you suggest that I present this to McKinnon, who DOES have legal restrictions on how information can be obtained?"

"Say you obtained it from a confidential informant whose identity you can't disclose for reasons of national security. Trot out the Official Secrets Act. You folks seem to use that as much as the US uses the Patriot Act."

Anna nodded. "I suppose that might work. McKinnon wants the bastards so badly I'm sure he won't look a gift horse in the mouth. If we act fast, we might be able to roll them up before you leave."

"That fast?" Dugan said. "I'm sure our Russian friends would be relieved to see Arsov behind bars before we head to the US to prepare our little arrival party for the *Kapitan Godina*."

"When do you plan to leave?" Alex asked.

"We can leave anytime within the next thirty-six hours and still make it," Dugan said. "So I figure we'll take off as soon as Arsov's behind bars."

"Hear, hear," Alex said. "I'll call and have the Gulfstream serviced. Gillian?"

"I'll have our bags packed within the hour. We'll be ready."

Dugan looked back and forth between the pair. "Just a minute, you two. You're not—"

"We most certainly ARE," Gillian said. "Surely you didn't think we were going to sit here by the phone when Cassie's in danger? We're going, and that's final, Tom."

SPECIALIST CRIMES DIRECTORATE 9 (SCD9)
HUMAN EXPLOITATION/ORGANIZED CRIME
VICTORIA BLOCK, NEW SCOTLAND YARD
BROADWAY
LONDON, UK

"I'm not even going to ask where you got this information, Agent Walsh," Detective Inspector McKinnon said. "I'm only going to ask if you're confident of its accuracy?"

"I am," Anna said.

McKinnon grinned. "Well, then it's bloody perfect. A single location with only three Russians and a large number of captives and illegal drugs—we may be able to sweep up enough evidence and testimony to smash their entire UK operation."

Anna hesitated. "About… before…"

McKinnon held up a hand. "You don't have to remind me, Agent Walsh. It was obvious we had a leak on the last operation. They have someone on the inside, and I don't know who." He sighed. "Given the amount of money they have to throw around, it's not surprising. And the last operation was so large that keeping it quiet was all but impossible. You can't run an operation of that size without involving a lot of people." He smiled again. "But that's what's so perfect about this setup you've given me. They have all their eggs in one basket, and I can mount this op with a half-dozen men. And I'm not taking any chances on a leak. I'm not even using my own men. A mate of mine in CO19 owes me a favor and got me authorization to use five of his SFOs. Trust me; I'm keeping security very, very tight on this one. I'm not even logging the paperwork until immediately before the strike."

Anna raised her eyebrows at the mention of CO19, the London Metropolitan Police Firearms Unit, made up of highly trained Specialist Firearms Officers or SFOs, the elite of the London Police.

"CO19 lads. Impressive. It would seem you still have some support from on high."

McKinnon shook his head. "I fear I'm rapidly running out of favors to call in, Agent Walsh, so I hope this works. At any rate, we can't afford to pass up this opportunity. I intend to hit them hard and fast."

"Fast means when?"

"How's tonight sound?" McKinnon asked, then added, "Would you like to ride along? After all, we wouldn't be there without you."

"Absolutely," Anna replied. "And about that, I was wondering if—"

McKinnon's face clouded. "No way. Your civilian colleagues will have to sit this one out. And you're to keep this absolutely confidential. I'm not taking a chance on a leak from ANY source. Is that clear."

"Perfectly."

DUGAN AND ANNA'S APARTMENT
LONDON, UK

"What do you mean we cannot be there?" Borgdanov demanded. "If not for Ilya and me, this policeman McKinnon would still be standing around with thumb up ass!"

"*DA!*" Ilya said, nodding his head in angry agreement.

"And you both know quite well that McKinnon can't officially KNOW that you two got the information or how you got it," Anna said. "And unless you want to taint the case completely, the best thing you can do is stay as far away as possible. McKinnon's right about that. He's not trying to slight you; he's trying to make sure some slick slimy solicitor doesn't get these bastards off on some technicality."

"Ms. Walsh is right," Nigel said. "We shouldn't waste time with this warehouse anyway. Leave it to the police."

Nigel flushed as all eyes turned to him, the Russians obviously angry at his interruption.

"I-I mean, it's a distraction, isn't it?" he stammered. "We should be concentrating on Cassie and the others, not wasting time trying to do the police's work."

Dugan laid a hand on Nigel's arm. "We're doing both, Nigel. I've already made some calls to get the ball rolling on the US side, but we can't overtake the ship quickly by any surface craft, and just flying over her in a plane won't do any good. We have to get to her by chopper, and she won't be in chopper range of the US coast for at least a couple of days. If I thought it would do Cassie any good, we'd be in the air right now. But since it won't, it makes sense to try to make sure this Arsov character is behind bars first."

"And besides," Borgdanov said to Nigel, "do you think Ilya and I would do anything to jeopardize rescue of Karina and the others?" Borgdanov's eyes narrowed, and he looked at Dugan. "I think maybe is better if you send little boy back to his ship. We have too much at stake and too few resources to waste time as babysitters, *da*?"

Nigel clenched his fists and started to stand, but Dugan grabbed his forearm and restrained him.

"Sit!" Dugan said to Nigel, then turned to Borgdanov. "Nigel's got a stake in this too, Andrei, so he has a right to be here. And you," he said, turning back to Nigel, "try to remember that you're here on sufferance, and that you have the least experience of anyone in this room. Behave accordingly."

Nigel stiffened and glared at Dugan a moment, then relaxed a bit and nodded.

"Good," Dugan said. "Now where were we?"

"I believe Major Borgdanov was berating me for incompetence, based on my demonstrated inability to have foreign national civilians included in an ongoing Metropolitan Police operation." Anna smiled sweetly.

Borgdanov flushed. "I do not know what means 'berating,' and I did not say you are incompetent. But I do not think it is right that we cannot at least observe the operation. Maybe we can help, *da*?"

Anna shook her head. "I'm sorry, Andrei, but that's not happening. McKinnon was firm on that and I'm already on shaky ground there. We have to play by his rules on this one."

Borgdanov said nothing for a long moment, and then nodded. "Okay, but we still have tactical radios from first raid, *da*? So if we are nearby listening in, I think this McKinnon will not know, and we will be there if needed. We do not want to sit here in apartment wondering what is going on."

"McKinnon's a bit sharper than that, I'm afraid," Anna said. "The Met has specially assigned frequencies for their tactical radios, and they rotate them between operations as a routine security precaution."

"But he will give you these new frequencies, *da*?"

"I asked, of course, but he refused."

Borgdanov looked confused. "But why?"

Anna said nothing, but Dugan read the look on her face.

"Son of a bitch!" Dugan said, and Borgdanov turned to face him.

"What do you mean, *Dyed*?"

"Think about it, Andrei. There was a leak on the last operation from an unknown source. You're Russian. Arsov and company are Russian. There are plenty of ex-*Spetsnaz* working for the Russian mob. McKinnon's not taking any chances."

Beside Borgdanov, Ilya exploded. "*yob tvoyu mat', ublyudok*!" he cursed. "So this policeman thinks we are *Bratstvo* scum!"

Borgdanov only nodded thoughtfully and rested his hand on Ilya's forearm. "Calm yourself, my friend. Is only logical for McKinnon to think this. In his position, we would think the same, *da*? I should have thought of this myself." He looked at Anna. "The question is, what do we do now?"

Anna looked at the Russians' faces and knew she was fighting a losing battle. Dugan had managed to convince them to let the police handle Arsov, but they obviously had limited confidence in the Met's ability to capture Arsov, and were equally skeptical the legal system could contain him if captured. Their forbearance was tenuous at best, and if they were shut out of the operation, she had little doubt they'd launch their own preemptive strike. She sighed and moved to the 'Plan B' she'd already put together in anticipation of their objections.

"The Met's tactical frequencies are limited by bandwidth, so they don't have that many options," Anna said. "They defeat most commercially available scanners or other equipment to which the criminal element might have access, but they're nothing our technical boys at MI5 can't easily defeat. I can get a scanner to monitor the tactical bandwidths. You won't be able to transmit, but that's all the better, because I definitely DO NOT want McKinnon to know you're listening. Is that clear?"

Borgdanov smiled, and Ilya nodded in agreement. "*Da*," Borgdanov said. "Thank you, Anna."

"Don't thank me yet. There's a condition."

"What is condition?"

"Under absolutely no circumstances are you to come within a mile of the warehouse. McKinnon cannot see you. And just to make sure you don't get 'confused,' I'll get you a map and draw a circle around the forbidden area. Agreed?"

Borgdanov stroked his chin. "Okay. *Da*. I agree."

Anna nodded and stood, obviously relieved at his agreement.

"I'm going back down to New Scotland Yard to go over some details with McKinnon. I'll have Harry or Lou bring you back the scanner." She paused for emphasis. "And a map."

"Good," Borgdanov said. "Ilya and I will stay here with *Dyed*. We must discuss how to approach the *Kapitan Godina*."

Dugan rose and followed Anna to the door. She pecked his cheek before leaving, and Dugan locked the door behind her. As he walked back into the living room, Borgdanov caught his eye and jerked his head toward the master bedroom. Dugan nodded and moved into the bedroom. Seconds later Borgdanov entered the room and closed the door.

Dugan sighed. "What is it now, Andrei?"

"I am concerned about the rescue operation. First I hear Alex is coming to US with us, and I cannot say no because, after all, is his jet. Now also I learn not only Gillian is coming but the little boy is coming. This will not work. I think we need only me, Ilya and you." Borgdanov flashed a fleeting smile. "After all, you I have pushed out of chopper before. You are not so useful in gunfight, but you know all things about ship if we should need expert, *da*?"

"I understand, but Alex and Gillian don't plan on coming on the rescue. They just want to be in the US so when we rescue the girls, they're close to provide what comfort or support they can."

"Okay, but what about this kid Nigel? He is nice kid, and I think he loves Cassie, but if we have to watch him, it will distract us from mission. Is not good idea."

"I agree, but perhaps you've noticed he's stubborn as hell. If we exclude him, he's not going to just go away, and I'm concerned he might do something stupid. I figure it's best to keep him with us for now, where we can keep an eye on him. We'll leave him ashore in the US."

"Okay. Is good. I should have known you would be thinking of this," Borgdanov replied, moving back toward the door to the living room.

"Andrei, one more thing. Thank you for agreeing to Anna's conditions. This is a difficult situation for her."

Borgdanov nodded. "I understand, and we will stay outside of her circle. And who knows? This Arsov is a crafty fox I think, and maybe the fox will run out of the circle, and they will need someone to chase him, *da*."

Christ, I hope not, thought Dugan.

CHAPTER SEVENTEEN

CONTAINER SHIP *KAPITAN GODINA*
EN ROUTE TO JACKSONVILLE, FLORIDA

Cassie sat on the mattress, breathing through her mouth, her back resting against the corrugated steel wall of the container. Like her two companions, she was stripped to her bra and panties, and the bare steel was hot on her back. Tanya's head rested in her lap, and Cassie tried to shift her weight without disturbing the other girl—a low moan signaled the failure of that effort. In an hour or so, the steel would be too hot to lean against, and she'd be faced with the unpleasant choice of sitting upright and bracing herself against the continual slow roll of the ship or lying on the fetid smelly mattress. The first choice was exhausting, the second vomit-inducing. Tanya moaned again, and Cassie mopped the girl's head with a precious piece of clean cloth torn from her skirt and soaked in water from their dwindling reserve.

"I think she's hotter, Karina. The fever is getting worse."

Beside her, Karina stirred and reached out to pat Cassie's arm. "Tanya will be fine. She is tough. All four of her grandparents survived the Battle of Stalingrad. Survival is in her genes, *da*?"

But her optimism seemed forced, and Cassie sensed the fear behind the words.

Cassie shook her head. "It's all just so horrible…" Her voice trailed off as she looked around in the dim light of the container.

It had been tolerable enough at first, when their seasickness had finally abated, but then the seas got really bad, and even stretching out on the mattresses gave no relief from the constant movement. Rest seemed impossible, and even when fatigue overcame them and they fell into exhausted sleep, they soon found themselves thrown off onto the hard floor of the container. Cassie remembered Nigel's tale of sleeping in rough seas by shoving his life jacket under the outer edge of his bunk to form a V-shaped trough along his cabin bulkhead, and they emulated the trick, shoving all three mattresses against the long wall of the container and then elevating the outside edges of the mattresses with the boxes of MREs. They'd slept secure for one night at least, resting in the notch they created, with gravity holding them in place and their backs against the steel wall.

Then the rolling got worse—far worse—and the second night one of the toilet buckets came loose from its lashing and slammed against the far wall of the container, losing its lid to dump its vile contents on the container floor. The girls' fumbling efforts to re-lash the bucket by flashlight had ended in failure when a huge roll caused Tanya to slip in the mess and go down hard, smashing the flashlight and cutting her hand on the broken lens. The girls had groped their way back to their mattresses, to huddle in the pitching dark, listening as one by one, other buckets and water bottles broke free to careen through the container.

Gradually the seas abated, and when dawn began to leak through the small holes near the top of the container, daylight found them clinging to their little mattress islands, awash in a half inch of unspeakable filth that sloshed back and forth with the roll of the ship. Over half their thin-walled plastic water jugs had burst and added their contents to the stew of vomit and body wastes disgorged from the toilet buckets, and the intact bottles rolled around in the filth, as the mattresses and the cardboard of the MRE boxes wicked up the sewage.

Karina had taken charge, wading through the sloshing filth to pull undamaged bottles of water onto her mattress. Then she'd retrieved the three empty and unused toilet buckets that hadn't broken free and brought them to the mattresses. She'd ordered everyone out of their clothes and sealed the relatively clean garments in one of the buckets, retaining her own dress, which she immediately began tearing into rags. Then she used one of the rags to wipe an intact water bottle as clean as possible before she opened it. While Cassie and Tanya held the other unopened jugs out off the mattresses, Karina sacrificed water from her open jug to frugally, but thoroughly, flush the exterior of the other bottles.

When she'd flushed the bottles, she had the other girls dry them with rags and resecure them in the wall rack, while she dug the MREs from the wet cardboard boxes and pushed all the sodden packing material to one side. Finally, she'd flushed the exterior of all the food packages, dried them, and packed and sealed them in the remaining two clean buckets. At last all three girls braved the ankle-deep mess one last time to stack the three mattresses on top of each other and crawl on top of the stack, discarding their sodden shoes and sacrificing another bit of precious water to rinse their feet.

They'd survived since crammed on their tiny mattress island, hoping against hope the rough seas would not return and destroy what they'd managed to salvage. The remaining food and water was lashed to the near wall within easy reach, along with a single toilet bucket. The bottom mattress had wicked up much of the effluvia from the floor of the container, leaving a slick sheen through which ever-smaller waves rippled with the roll of the ship. The second mattress was sodden as well, as it wicked up fluid from the bottom mattress and the remaining liquid from the top mattress drained into it. Only their small sanctuary was dry, but the mattresses seemed to concentrate the smell.

The discomfort of the hot steel on Cassie's back returned her to the present, and she shifted again. Tanya moaned in her sleep, moving her right hand as she did so. She cried out and came half awake. Cassie held her tight.

"Shhh… Tanya. It's okay. I have you. Go back to sleep. Rest is good for you," Cassie whispered, and Tanya whimpered and closed her eyes again.

When Tanya's breathing indicated she'd fallen back into a troubled sleep, Cassie studied Tanya's right hand in the dim light. It was swollen to almost twice its normal size, the skin stretched tight and shiny. The edges of the cut from the flashlight lens were red and angry, and the discoloration had begun to creep up her arm.

"It's getting worse, Karina," Cassie whispered.

"*Da*," Karina agreed. "No doubt some shit got into the cut. There is nothing we can do now but try to keep her comfortable and hope the ship arrives somewhere soon. I think is good thing she sleeps."

"Wh-what if we don't get there before… before… you know…"

"We will, Cassie," Karina said through clenched teeth. "We will all survive. It is the way we will beat these bastards, *da*?"

HOLDING WAREHOUSE
516 COPELAND ROAD
SOUTHWARK, LONDON, UK

"…and you haven't seen him at all?" Arsov asked into the phone.

"*Nyet*," said the voice, "not since we were released. We dropped him at Club *Pyatnitsa*. He said he was going to check a few things there and then go home to sleep."

"Okay. If you hear from him, tell him to call me."

"*Da*," the man responded and hung up.

Arsov laid the phone down and drummed his fingers on the battered desk. Where the hell was Nazarov? He hadn't showed up back at the club, and no one had heard from him for a full day. What was the idiot up to now? He wasn't in police custody—his informant had been sure about that—but he was nowhere to be found. Had Karina's uncle and that other ex-*Spetsnaz* asshole grabbed him? It seemed unlikely, but that was really the only explanation.

What were the possible implications? He wasn't worried that Nazarov would talk—no one was more aware of what the *Bratstvo* did to informers than other members of the *Bratstvo*. No, Nazarov would keep quiet even if it killed him. Arsov smiled—and it probably had. And what could be more perfect? He was on track to resume operations in a week or ten days, and Nazarov was no longer here to defend himself. His narrative was complete. He had come here from Prague and discovered irregularities. Nazarov was not only skimming money into an offshore account, but was also playing both ends against the middle as a paid police informant. The treacherous bastard had set up a massive police raid, and when he, Arsov, had discovered the offshore account and foiled the raid, Nazarov had disappeared.

Arsov hummed a little tune and considered his next move. He still needed to set up one of his other underlings as Nazarov's accomplice, but that could wait. In fact, hinting to St. Petersburg that he was still struggling valiantly to root out all the problems would make him seem even more indispensable.

He picked up his phone and speed-dialed St. Petersburg.

SPECIALIST CRIMES DIRECTORATE 9 (SCD9)
HUMAN EXPLOITATION/ORGANIZED CRIME
VICTORIA BLOCK, NEW SCOTLAND YARD
BOADWAY
LONDON, UK

Detective Constable Cecil Peterson sat at his desk, mouse in hand. He liked his desk position in the bullpen, with his back to the far wall and with the others able to see only the back of his monitor. He could pass his time playing computer solitaire without anyone sneaking up on him, and he had a good view of the whole squad room as well. He liked the late night shift too, without so many prying eyes. Not that he'd had any choice in the matter. No one else wanted it, and it had been 'offered' to him on a take-it-or-leave-it basis when they 'reinvented' his unit. They'd acted like he should bow down and kiss their bloody arses for the right to stay on a few more years until his full pension kicked in, rather than being sacked or pensioned off early at reduced pay like the rest of his mates.

Twenty-five years in Vice and that's what he got as a thank you. Twenty-five years of having Barbara's snooty family say things like, "Oh yes, Cecil's with the Met, but he's not a proper copper, is he? He's in Vice, you know, mucking about arresting whores and breaking up poker games. I don't see why he doesn't request a transfer to a real unit, but he seems to like it."

If only they knew. It wasn't like that at first—new men joined the unit intent on making a difference. But then they learned they couldn't, because no one really wanted things to change, did they? If they cracked down on prostitution, there were the inevitable campaigns ranting about the focus on 'victimless crime' while 'real' crimes went unsolved. And when they eased off, there were the equally strident news stories of the Vice cops 'allowing' pimps and other low-life scum to victimize innocent girls.' Damned if you did, damned if you didn't.

But you didn't know that at first, did you? And by the time you wised up a few years in, you were irrevocably tainted. Other departments shied away from accepting transfers from Vice, so you stuck it out and grew more cynical year after year. So what if a few of the lads took a few quid here or did a favor there? It's not like any of it made a difference. Everyone just wanted to eke it out to full pension, and crawl out of the cesspool. And then along comes Detective Inspector Colin bloody McKinnon, with his high and mighty attitude and new names, sacking good lads left and right. Peterson sneered. Specialist Crimes Directorate 9—Unit SCD9. It sounded like something in a damned James Bond movie.

He straightened at his desk as the object of his ire walked out of his office and into the squad room, trailed by the redheaded bitch from MI5. What the hell were they doing here at this hour? They both had on tactical vests and were armed, and as he watched, they hurried across the nearly deserted squad room and into the corridor. Through the open door, Peterson heard the chime as the lift arrived.

Peterson's mind raced. The MI5 bitch had been part of the big operation against the Russians, so it didn't take a genius to figure out something was up. He closed his game of solitaire and accessed the department server to check new warrants. And there it was—a search warrant for 516 Copeland Road, Southwark, filed less than thirty minutes earlier. McKinnon, you sneaky bastard.

This was bad. The money from Arsov was good, but penalties for failure didn't bear thinking about. If the Russkies went down to a raid and he hadn't at least tried to warn them, he doubted he'd survive the week. And they wouldn't stop with him—Barbara and the kids would be at risk too. But what the hell was McKinnon's game? He obviously wasn't planning on raiding Arsov with just himself and the woman, and he hadn't used any SCD9 assets. And giving Arsov sketchy information was almost as likely to incur his wrath as giving him none. He needed to find out more, and fast.

He stood up and stretched. "Christ, I'm knackered," he said to his nearest colleague a few desks away. "I'm going out for a smoke. Cover my phone for me while I'm gone, would you, mate? I'll be back straightaway."

The man shrugged. "Sure. Take your time. I doubt anything exciting is likely to happen anytime soon."

Peterson smiled and tried to appear nonchalant as he walked toward the door. *If you only knew mate*, he thought.

Once in the corridor, he raced straight to the stairwell and flew down the two flights to the ground floor. He cracked open the stairwell door and confirmed the corridor was empty before exiting and walking toward the car park at the back of the building. He slowed as he neared the glass door and exited quietly, ducking down behind the nearest patrol car to scan the car park. He spotted them in the far corner.

Bloody Hell! He spotted McKinnon's car parked behind a 'Trojan,' one of the ARVs, or Armed Response Vehicles, of Unit CO19. McKinnon and the Walsh woman were standing near his car, and McKinnon was obviously introducing the woman to a group of black-clad Specialist Firearms Officers. They were all well-equipped and all wearing tactical vests. Peterson spotted assault rifles, and at least one had night-vision glasses hanging from his web gear—likely they all did. This was bad!

Peterson slipped back through the door and raced down the corridor to the toilet. He did a quick check of the stalls to ensure he was alone and then pulled the burner phone from his pocket.

CHAPTER EIGHTEEN

Peckham Road and Talfourd Road
London, UK

"I think you can get a little closer, *Dyed*," Borgdanov said from the front passenger seat.

Behind the wheel, Dugan pointed to the GPS display mounted on the console. "We're already well inside the agreed one-mile radius. And besides, this is as good a spot as any. We're inconspicuous here, and the last thing we want is to be spotted and screw up the op."

They were parked on Talfourd Road, facing north toward the intersection of Peckham Road, just one car of many parked along the curb.

"Of course we are inconspicuous," Borgdanov grumbled. "We are so far away Arsov would need spy satellite to find us. It will not hurt to get a little closer. If nothing happens, Anna will never know, and if there is problem and we help, we will be forgiven, *da*?"

"*Da*," Ilya agreed from the seat behind Dugan.

Dugan twisted in his seat to look at Ilya and Nigel sitting beside him. Nigel remained silent, but his expression spoke volumes. It was clear he agreed with the two Russians.

"That's a big *nyet*," Dugan said. "Besides, exactly where else would you like me to go? In the unlikely event this operation fails, the bad guys could run in any direction, and we can't be everywhere. I think we can count on them having other safe houses, and they'll likely stay in the city center where they don't stand out as much, and Peckham Road is the fastest way back to the city. If that happens, we'll hear it on the scanner and be in a position to maybe cut them off."

"Okay, okay," Borgdanov said. "So we stay on this road, but maybe just a bit closer?"

"Absolutely not. Anna's got her neck stuck out on this as it is, and we promised her that McKinnon wouldn't even know we were nearby, so here we stay unless something goes amiss."

Borgdanov glared at him a long moment just as McKinnon's voice erupted from the scanner.

"Unit Two, this is Unit One. Do you copy? Over."

"Unit One, this is Unit Two. We copy," came the reply.

"Two, what is your status? Over," McKinnon asked.

"We are in position near the loading dock. All the large roller doors are closed. There is one man-door, a heavy metal industrial job. Suggest we use breaching charges on the masonry surround. Over."

"Affirmative, Two," McKinnon said. "Are there security cameras or vehicles? Over."

"Negative on cameras. There are two cars in the yard near the far end of the loading dock. We have eyes on the inside of the warehouse. Ramsey snaked fiber optics under one of the roller doors. There is movement in an area on the south wall. We can see the head and shoulders of two men over the back of a sofa. Some sort of makeshift living area. Third target is not visible, but there is what looks like a door to an office area on your side." He paused. "And there are cages and containers on the north end of the warehouse. The cages are full of… people."

The scanner fell silent, and Dugan looked at the Russians, his jaw clenched.

"Bastards," Nigel muttered, but the Russians sat in stoic silence, their expressions saying everything that needed saying.

"I copy, Two," McKinnon said. "Are the hostages in the line of fire? Over?"

"Negative, One. If you take the target in the office area and we enter simultaneously from both doors, we'll catch the other two in a cross fire. Over."

"Okay, Two. Disable the vehicles and set the breaching charges on the door. How long before you're ready? Over."

"Estimate five minutes. Should I keep Ramsey on the fiber optics?"

There was another pause, as if McKinnon was considering the question, then he responded. "Negative, Two. We're shorthanded as it is. I need all three of you to crash the door, and I want Ramsey to insert himself between the hostages and the targets. Advise when you have the charges set and are ready to breach. Over."

"Affirmative. Unit Two out."

Borgdanov nodded. "Okay, *Dyed*, we stay. I think we soon find out if McKinnon captures the fox, *da*?"

HOLDING WAREHOUSE
516 COPELAND ROAD
SOUTHWARK, LONDON, UK

Arsov answered his phone.

"It's me," a voice said. "You're about to be raided."

"What? When? By who?"

"McKinnon and that MI5 bitch," Peterson said. "NOW!"

"MI5? What the hell are you talking about? What's MI5 got to do with any of this?"

"That redhead bitch, Anna Walsh. I was wondering how she seemed so thick with McKinnon, and I sniffed around a bit and found out she's with British Intelligence," Peterson said.

"And you're just telling me now?"

"I-I just found out earlier today, and the big raid was already a bust, so I didn't think it was urgent. But when I saw her sniffing around tonight, I put it together and figured—"

"Or maybe you figured I might pay a little more for that information and were saving it for later, eh? Let me assure you, you'll be paid, but maybe not as you intended."

"No… really…I had no clue. I mean, I found out about the woman, but I just found out about the next raid by accident. That bastard McKinnon didn't even log the warrant until a half hour ago. I called you as soon as I found out. I swear."

Arsov's mind raced. There would be time enough to deal with Peterson later—assuming there was a later. Now he needed information.

"How many and when?" he demanded.

"Seven, including McKinnon and the bitch, at least as far as I could tell. But they're not from our unit. At least five are CO19 lads, full tactical gear, night-vision kit, the works. And if they're not outside your location now, they soon will be."

"All right. We'll talk later." Arsov hung up.

He took a deep breath and struggled to calm himself. He thought of the captives and the drugs in the warehouse—so much for staying under the radar. No lawyer could get him out of this, no matter how good he was. And MI5? What the hell could that mean? He pulled his laptop over and clicked on the feed from the security cameras concealed around the perimeter of the building. Other warehouses made sure the cameras were visible to discourage robberies, but the *Bratstvo*'s security needs were a bit different. They didn't need to discourage thieves; everyone in the underworld knew you didn't touch certain warehouses and you didn't talk about them—ever. He pulled up the feeds from the front of the building first and saw nothing within the range of the cameras, but the loading dock was a different story. Two black-clad figures worked around the back door, and when he zoomed in, he saw they were setting breaching charges. He zoomed out and panned the camera to see another man puncturing the tires on Yuri's Mercedes. He assumed his own car would be next.

Not much time, but he did have the element of surprise. He moved to a metal storage cabinet and pulled a canvas duffel bag from a lower shelf and quickly stuffed it with items from the cabinet. He slung the bag over his shoulder and raced out into the warehouse.

His underlings were in the makeshift living quarters along the south wall of the warehouse. There were two old sofas on either side of a card table where they ate their meals. A large refrigerator, a microwave on a stand, and a big-screen TV completed the furnishings. The two men spent their time eating, playing video games, or enjoying the pleasures of the whores they released from the cages when they felt the need. Yuri sat on a sofa with his pants around his ankles as he forced a naked teenage girl's face into his crotch. Anatoli was sitting at the other end of the sofa, laughing and making critical comments on the girl's performance.

Arsov heaved the duffel bag on to the card table and unzipped it as he gave orders with quiet urgency. "Pull your fucking pants up, and put her back in her cage," he said to Yuri. "We're about to be raided."

"What?" Anatoli asked as Yuri pushed the girl away roughly and stood to fumble with his pants. Arsov glared at him again, and he quickly zipped his pants and dragged the girl upright by her hair to push her in the direction of the cages across the cavernous warehouse.

"They'll be coming in the front and back doors any minute," Arsov said to Anatoli, as he laid out weapons in a line on the table, three compact Kedr submachine guns with extra box magazines, with a flashlight next to each. He flinched slightly as a cage door slammed, and looked up to see Yuri returning. He motioned him to hurry, and when Yuri got close, Arsov continued his instructions in a rush.

"They'll probably be three or four through each door, and we'll be waiting. Yuri, I want you to cover the door from the office area. Anatoli, take the back door, but be careful. They'll blow the door with explosives, so stay behind cover until they detonate. They'll be wearing vests, so take their legs out from under them first. I'll kill the interior lights, so each of you take a flashlight. You may need—"

Yuri looked confused. "But wha—"

"Shut the fuck up! I don't have time to explain."

Both men bobbed their heads and began to arm themselves, and Arsov continued as he donned the single pair of night-vision goggles and flipped them up out of his line of vision. "They'll probably use flash bangs from both doors, so be ready to shut your eyes and cover your ears."

"But how did they find us?" Anatoli asked, risking Arsov's wrath.

"That bastard Nazarov must have talked. But there aren't many of them, so we should be able to take them down. Now get in position."

Yuri nodded and rushed to cover the front entrance, but Anatoli hesitated.

"What are you going to do?"

"I'll stay mobile and arrange a little surprise and then support either you or Yuri, depending on circumstances. We have to kill all these bastards quickly and then take one of the cars and get the hell out. We're done in the UK for now, but if we can make it to a safe house, we can hole up a while and then get out of the country. Now quit asking questions and get to your god damned station."

Anatoli nodded and rushed to cover the rear door.

COPELAND ROAD
NEAR HOLDING WAREHOUSE
SOUTHWARK, LONDON, UK

"Unit One, do you copy? Over," the radio squawked.

McKinnon looked at Anna and spoke into his shoulder-mounted mike. "Two, this is One. I copy. Are you ready? Over."

"Affirmative, One. Over," came the reply.

"Good, Two. Prepare to breach on my order. Over," McKinnon said.

"This is Two standing by for your order. Be advised the bit of light leaking under the big roller doors just went out. It looks like they may be bedding down for the night. Over."

McKinnon frowned. "Do you think they've moved? Over."

"Possibly," Two replied, "but they'll either be on the sofas or somewhere in the office area. We didn't see anywhere else to sleep. Either way, the plan should work. Over."

"Affirmative. Stand by."

McKinnon turned and nodded at Anna as he opened the car door. "Well, wish us luck, Agent Walsh."

"I do indeed." Anna opened her own door.

"Just a minute. Where do you think you're going?"

"With you, obviously. You did invite me to ride along."

"Correct," McKinnon said. "As in 'ride,' which implies you're to stay in the car. Need I remind you that this isn't exactly a matter for MI5 and that I invited you to OBSERVE as a courtesy."

"Not likely," Anna said sweetly. "And besides, there are only six of you. That's not exactly an overwhelming force now, is it?"

"Six of us and complete surprise. This should be a fast and easy take down."

"In which case there's no harm in me OBSERVING from a closer vantage point than the car, is there? The word does mean 'to see,' you know, and I won't be able to see bloody fuck all from the car, now will I?"

McKinnon shook his head. "All right, damn it! But stay well behind us. If this doesn't go as planned, I'll have a hard enough time explaining your presence, and all the more so if you get shot in the bargain."

Anna smiled. "Your solicitude is touching, Inspector."

McKinnon muttered something under his breath and got out of the car, striding toward his two constables on the sidewalk without looking back. Both constables had their assault rifles slung, and one was carrying a crowbar and the other a short but obviously heavy breaching ram. McKinnon nodded as he reached them, and they all started for the front door of the warehouse in a crouching run, with Anna close behind.

The front of the warehouse appeared to be office space, with a vacant reception area opening on to the street. Large floor-to-ceiling windows dominated the front of the reception area, and the entrance was a glass door set in a heavy aluminum frame. McKinnon nodded to the constable with the crowbar, and the man inserted the flat end of the bar into the crack between the door and the frame just above the lock and leaned into the bar. The metal frame of the door resisted and then began to distort, as the heavy glass gave a soft pop and cracks spider-webbed across the door. The constable pushed harder, and the door came open.

McKinnon rushed inside, his two constables and Anna on his heels, as he whispered into his shoulder mike.

"Two, this is One. We're in the reception area. Blow your door and prepare to deploy flash bangs."

The words had hardly left his mouth when they heard a rumbling roar from the back of the building, followed immediately by the screams of terrified women, muffled slightly by the thin interior walls of the office area.

"Go! Go! Go!" McKinnon said, and the man with the ram ran forward and slammed the heavy weight against the door leading to the interior office area. The flimsy door frame shattered in an explosion of splinters as the door flew open and slammed against the wall. McKinnon and the two constables entered the short dark hallway, flipping down their night-vision glasses as they entered. Anna, with no NV equipment, trailed cautiously, her Glock in a two-handed grip, as the three policemen leapfrogged each other down the hallway, clearing the two empty offices. They stopped at another flimsy wooden door. The screams from the warehouse interior were deafening now.

"Flash bangs! Now!" McKinnon said into his mike as he nodded to his own men. Anna holstered her weapon as one man smashed the door open with a well-placed foot near the doorknob, and the second lobbed a flash-bang grenade into the black interior. All three policemen slung their weapons, and Anna followed their cue as they turned away with their eyes closed tight and palms pressed over their ears. Even then, Anna saw the lights from the twin explosions flash through her closed eyelids, and the concussions felt almost like physical blows.

She staggered a bit and opened her eyes as she groped for her Glock. After an instantaneous lull, the screaming started again, even louder.

"Go!" McKinnon said, and his constables rushed through the open door and deployed to either side. McKinnon followed and cleared the door just as the interior of the warehouse was bathed in bright light and the roar of automatic weapons fire drowned out the screams of the terrified women. Anna watched, paralyzed, as the three police men jerked from the impact of multiple rounds and collapsed.

She spotted the shooter through the open door, some distance into the warehouse, crouching near an oil drum. She raised her Glock and opened fire, trying to relieve the pressure on the three wounded cops lying in the open. A round hit the drum with a metallic clang, and the shooter turned his attention to her. She dived to the floor as concentrated automatic fire shredded the thin walls of the office area around her.

CHAPTER NINETEEN

Arsov waited among the caged whores on the north wall of the warehouse, his flashlight illuminating an electrical panel. He had his eyes averted from the door in the east wall, almost fifty meters away. His wait was finally rewarded by an explosion that sent masonry rubble sailing across the darkened warehouse, to pepper the floor like falling hail. He smiled as all around him the whores began to screech in terror. He hadn't thought of that—what a wonderful little addition to the confusion he wished to generate.

Anticipating what was to come, he held his small flashlight between his teeth, cupped his palms over his ears and faced the wall, presenting his back to the interior of the warehouse, his eyes tightly shut. Moments later, he felt the twin concussions of the flash bangs and held his position a second longer to make sure there wouldn't be a third. When he took his hands from his ears, the terrified wails of the whores were even louder. Even better! The cops should be coming in just about… now! He turned his flashlight on the electrical panel and threw the main breaker.

The interior of the warehouse was flooded with light, and the black-clad policemen stood in the open, stunned as their NV glasses made it seem as if the sun itself had gone supernova in their faces. Arsov nodded in satisfaction as Yuri stitched the three policemen charging in from the office area across their lower bodies, and they went down together. Someone returned fire from the office area—the MI5 bitch, no doubt—and he again nodded approval as Anatoli began shredding the office area on full auto, attempting to silence his unseen adversary.

Arsov turned to the rear door and shook his head. Anatoli had obviously not listened as well as Yuri. Two of the policemen were down, but the third had taken most of Anatoli's fire in the vest, though he was limping badly as he staggered towards the hole in the wall where the door had been. Arsov unfolded the stock of his Kedr, raised it to his shoulder, and took careful aim. He pulled the trigger and watched as the limping cop's head exploded, washing the masonry wall with a swath of blood and brains.

Anatoli redeemed himself in the next moments by killing the other two downed cops, and then Arsov turned back to check on Yuri's progress. Just in time. Yuri still hadn't silenced the woman and seemed oblivious to the fact that one of the wounded cops on the floor had his hand to his shoulder mike, attempting a distress call. Arsov cursed under his breath, the last thing he needed was more cops riding to the rescue before he got far enough away. He pressed the gun to his shoulder and aimed at the struggling cop.

***

Blinding light flashed in McKinnon's eyes, stunning him. *Ambush*, he thought, just as three hammer blows hit him mid-thigh, knocking his legs from under him. He hit the floor face first, the concrete driving the useless NV glasses into his face, and he felt them gouge into his forehead. He lay there a second, blinking beneath the now useless goggles, as something wet flooded his eyes and the air above his head filled with the cacophony of terrified screams and full automatic rifle fire.

He moved in slow motion and, with great effort, flipped up his damaged NV goggles, but he still could see nothing. He turned his head and willed his hand to key his shoulder mike. It came up gradually, almost as if it wasn't attached to his arm.

"All units near... near... 516 Cope... land... Road. Offi... officers down... ambush... auto..."

***

Blood sprayed from the back of the cop's head onto the shattered wall of the office area, and his ruined face rolled to one side, away from the shoulder mike. Almost done. Arsov jerked as a bullet ricocheted off the wall beside him into the caged whores, eliciting an even louder round of screams. One of the two wounded cops had his night-vision glasses flipped up and had recovered sufficiently to return fire, and the second was attempting to do so as well.

He couldn't have that, now could he. Arsov reached over and threw the breaker again, plunging the warehouse into darkness just before he flipped down his own NV glasses.

"Hold your fire," he bellowed in Russian, loud enough to be heard above the screams, just as Yuri stopped to change magazines. It wouldn't do if one of these idiots shot him by mistake.

He ran across the warehouse, watching as the two wounded policemen struggled with their NV glasses. But they were blind fish in a barrel, and Arsov killed them both before they got off another shot. He turned without breaking stride and ran back through the dark, flipping his NV glasses up just before he turned the lights back on. He glanced down at his watch—less than two minutes since the cops had blown the rear door—but he still had to hurry.

"Anatoli! Come to this side and help us finish off the woman. Hurry!"

Seconds later, the Russians were lined up in front of the office area, with fresh magazines in place. Arsov glanced over at the cages where the whores cowered, quiet now, as if afraid to attract attention.

"I think I hit her earlier, before you finished off the cops," Yuri said, as Arsov looked back. "I heard her yell. She's on the right side of the door."

Arsov nodded. "Keep your fire low. She will be on the floor."

All three men sprayed the base of the wall to the right of the door with automatic fire.

***

Anna flattened herself against the floor and gazed at her useless Glock. She'd expended both her first magazine and her spare and was out of ammunition. The walls were rapidly being blown away to nothing, and light shined through the ragged holes, suffusing the previously dark space with a dull glow that threatened to steal her invisibility. She hadn't caught a bullet, but the furious fire had turned the office walls into shrapnel, and blood puddled around her, leaking from a half-dozen wounds where ragged splinters had driven into the flesh of her unprotected limbs. She fumbled with her phone and had just pressed Dugan's preset when another burst of fire shredded the cheap carpet in front of her and ricocheted off the concrete floor beneath, sending her smashed phone flying out of her hand along with the tip of her right index finger.

"Shit!" Anna said before she could stop herself, and then she scrambled to her left and under an old metal desk just as a fresh burst ripped through the place she'd occupied seconds before. She was unarmed and helpless, and apparently the sole survivor. She was pondering surrender when hope surged as different guns joined the battle to the left of what remained of the door. There were others still fighting back! Then the lights went out again. Someone yelled in Russian, and hope died as she heard unanswered automatic fire from where she knew the cops had fallen. They were being executed. There would be no surrender to these bastards.

Moments later, the lights came back on, and there was more shouting in Russian before the fire directed at her increased in intensity, all of it ricocheting off the floor now at a shallow angle, walking toward her. She rolled over quickly and turned her back to the gunmen, ducking her head and drawing her legs up to her chest, presenting as little unprotected flesh to the unseen gunman as possible, and gasping as multiple rounds bounced off the floor and slammed into her protected back, hammering the breath from her. Then she felt a jolt and a searing pain in her left hip below the vest, and something warm and wet flowing down her legs. She thought she'd wet herself until she smelled the coppery odor of fresh blood and knew she was badly hurt.

Suddenly she just felt tired. Very tired. How very nice it would be to take a bit of a nap. If only they would stop making all that noise. She closed her eyes and was at the edge of consciousness before something slammed into the desk above her with a tremendous crash. *Bloody noise makers*, she thought again and then slipped away.

***

Arsov watched as the shattered remains of the office wall folded over and the suspended ceiling crashed down into the ruined office area in a great cloud of drywall dust.

"Hold your fire," he yelled and moved toward the rubble.

"Should we dig her out and make sure she's dead, Boss?" Yuri asked.

Arsov watched a growing puddle of blood leak out from under the wreckage, mixing with white drywall dust to form a pink sludge.

He shook his head. "No time. Look at the blood. She's either dead or soon will be. Besides, if she's still alive when help arrives, they'll waste a bit of time trying to save her."

"So we go?"

Arsov nodded. "Go gather up your stuff, and let's get out of here."

He watched as Anatoli and Yuri pushed past him, and when they were a few feet away, he shot them both in the back. Just on the off chance he did get captured, he needed someone to blame all the dead policemen on now, didn't he? He was congratulating himself on his cleverness when he looked up and saw the whores staring at him through the wire of the cages.

"Fuck!" He was so accustomed to thinking of them as furniture he'd totally forgotten about them as potential witnesses. He glanced at his watch again—five minutes since it had all started, though it seemed like an hour. He had no way of knowing if the cop got a call off before he killed him, but he had to assume he did. So first things first—he needed transportation.

He first searched the cop that tried to call and got lucky, pulling a set of car keys with an electronic key fob from the man's pants pocket. He wiped the blood off on a dry section of the cop's pants and looked over at the collapsed rubble of the office area. The collapsing walls had exposed a section of the glassed front of the reception area. He moved to the glass and pressed his face against it as he thumbed the button on the key fob and smiled as lights blinked in the distance up Copeland Road. Now to tidy up and leave.

He put a fresh magazine in his Kder and started toward the cages.

PECKHAM ROAD AND TALFOURD ROAD
LONDON, UK

Dugan sat with the others in tense anticipation as they listened to McKinnon's orders to breach the warehouse door and deploy the flash bangs. Then came the order to rush the warehouse, followed by—nothing.

He looked at Borgdanov. "Shouldn't we be hearing someth—"

Dugan's phone buzzed, and he fished it from his pocket and checked the caller ID before answering. "Yes, Anna?"

"Anna, are you there?" he asked into the phone as Borgdanov glanced over, a puzzled look on his face.

Dugan disconnected and stared at the phone.

"What is it, *Dyed*?"

"A call from Anna's phone," Dugan replied, still staring at the phone. "But I hardly think she'd call me in the middle of an operation, especially since we're not supposed to know it's going down. Maybe she just pocket dialed me by mistake." He looked up at Borgdanov. "Do you think I should try to call her back?"

Borgdanov shrugged. "I do not know, *Dyed*. Perhaps it is as you say, a mista—"

The scanner squawked, "All units near… near… 516 Cope… land… Road. Offi… officers down… ambush… auto…"

Dugan's blood ran cold.

"Go, *Dyed*!" Borgdanov yelled.

But Dugan was already starting the car. Tires squealed as they rocketed from the curb and careened around the corner onto Peckham Road.

CHAPTER TWENTY

Inside Holding Warehouse
516 Copeland Road
Southwark, London, UK

Arsov glanced at his watch again as he hurried back from the cages, his mind working overtime as he strode across the warehouse. If anyone was coming, he needed to buy some time, just in case, and the best diversions were always the unexpected.

He saw the answer from across the warehouse, provided courtesy of MI5. One of the drums Anatoli had ducked behind was punctured by the woman's fire, a single round just below the liquid level. A pungent smell assailed Arsov's nostrils, and he saw clear liquid leaking down the side of the drum and puddling around it. A rivulet crept across the concrete floor toward a floor drain ten meters away. He drew close to read the labels on the drum and a dozen others around it. Nitroethane—raw material to feed multiple methamphetamine labs the *Bratstvo* was establishing across the UK. He nodded to himself and hurried over to Yuri's body and searched the dead man's pockets.

Moments later Arsov moved across the warehouse, unwrapping one of Yuri's vile little cigars as he walked. He sniffed the air to make sure he no longer smelled the fruity odor of the nitroethane. He didn't want an open flame near the chemical—not yet. Satisfied, he lit the cigar with a book of matches from Club *Pyatnitsa* and drew on the disgusting thing until the end glowed red. He then placed the butt of the burning cigarillo next to the matches in the open book and closed the cover, pinning the butt of the little cigar in the match book before he moved back to where the stream of chemical inched its way toward the floor drain. He set the matchbook down on edge in the stream's path, two meters away, the matchbook forming a tiny stand to hold the burning end of the little cigar up in the air—an improvised, but effective fuse.

He took a last look around. Unlike the cages he'd been able to fire through, he'd no time to open each container and deal with the occupants, but the whores inside the containers hadn't seen anything, and the fire should take care of them. And if help arrived while they were still alive, their rescue would provide yet another time-consuming diversion. Then he remembered the caged whores screaming during his ambush and had a flash of inspiration. He rushed back and picked up Yuri's Sedr and opened fire, the bullets ricocheting noisily off the heavy metal containers. He ceased fire as screams rose from the terrified women and children trapped inside the boxes—he obviously had their attention. He moved closer, shouting, "Run! The whole place is about to explode! Forget the whores! Leave them, and let's get out of here!"

Arsov nodded, as the screams from the containers rose to a satisfying din—that should be enough to occupy any first responders. With any luck, everyone would die together.

He jogged toward the section of exposed reception area glass at the front of the warehouse, blasting it apart with Yuri's Sedr as he approached. The last bit of glass fell from the window just as he reached it, and he tossed the now empty automatic to the side and stepped lightly through the ruined window, fishing the cop's keys from his pocket as he did so. He pressed the key fob, and car lights blinked down the street. He set off toward it at a jog.

CLAYTON AND CONSORT ROADS
LONDON, UK

Dugan gripped the wheel tightly as he whipped around the roundabout and raced due south on Consort Road. He searched above him for the point where the London Overground tracks passed over the road, the landmark for a hard right on to Copeland Road.

"Hurry, *Dyed*," urged Borgdanov, but Dugan already had the accelerator floorboarded.

Then the tracks were overhead, and Dugan barely slowed as he braced for the right turn. He blew through the traffic signal on screaming tires in a barely controlled skid, only to encounter the headlights of another car coming in the opposite direction.

"Watch out, *Dyed*!" Borgdanov screamed, but Dugan was already cutting the wheel, avoiding a head-on collision by inches. He clipped the back of the other car and sent both cars spinning away from each other to lurch to a halt against the curbs at opposite corners of the intersection.

"Is everyone all right?" Dugan asked.

"Arsov!" Ilya yelled from the back seat, and Dugan looked across to see Arsov behind the wheel of the other car. The mobster obviously recognized them as well, and the tires of his car squealed as he fled north up Consort Road.

"After him, *Dyed*," Borgdanov shouted, but Dugan hesitated only an instant before he roared down Copeland Road toward the warehouse.

"What are you doing?" Borgdanov demanded.

"If Arsov's hauling ass and McKinnon called for help, things went to hell at the warehouse." Dugan handed Borgdanov his cell phone. "I doubt the cops will listen to us, so get Lou or Harry on the phone and tell them which way Arsov is headed so they can alert the cops. And tell them to get all the help they can over here. I have a feeling we're going to need it."

Borgdanov swallowed his frustration and nodded as he took the phone. Dugan accelerated toward the warehouse—and Anna.

A minute later, the car skidded to a halt, bucking as the front wheel rode up on the curb. Light leaked through a smashed floor-to-ceiling window at one end of the warehouse reception area, dimly illuminating the wreckage of the remainder of the office area visible through the intact panes. The car was still rocking on its suspension as Dugan threw open his door and tumbled out to race toward the shattered window.

"*Dyed*, wait!" Borgdanov cried. "It could be a trap."

Dugan ignored him and ran toward the warehouse, with Nigel close behind. The Russians had no choice but to follow.

As he approached, Dugan heard muffled screams, but nothing prepared him for the scene inside the warehouse. Bodies lay scattered, and the pools of blood glistening in the harsh lights left little hope anyone was still alive. Heart in his throat, he scanned the bodies, momentarily relieved that he didn't see Anna, then fearful at her absence. He scanned the walls, and fear turned to rage when he saw more inert and bloody forms on the floor inside the cages.

He stood trembling as Borgdanov walked through the blood and stooped at each inert policeman's body to check for a pulse. Then he saw Ilya rush to the steel containers, obviously drawn by the screams. Ilya ran down the line, disengaging the locking dogs on each set of container doors and throwing them open. The screams died, and women and children rushed out of each container, to stop and gaze at their rescuers, confusion and fear in their eyes.

"Is Anna there?" Dugan called.

Ilya surveyed the small crowd of milling hostages. "*Nyet,*" he called back. Dugan heard a gasp behind him.

He turned to see Nigel pointing at a flame racing across the floor towards a collection of drums stacked near the wall of the warehouse. The small flame reached the drums and ignited a larger puddle around them, engulfing all the drums.

"What the hell is that?" Nigel asked.

"Nothing good," Dugan said and screamed at the Russians, but they were already herding the hostages toward the hole in the back wall of the warehouse where the door had been.

"Go help them. I've got to find Anna," Dugan said to Nigel, then turned without waiting for a reply. He rushed toward the wreckage of the offices, the only place that might conceal her.

"Anna!" he called, wading into the debris. "If you can hear me, make a noise."

He stopped and listened, straining to hear over the growing roar of the fire behind him and feeling the heat on the back of his neck. Whatever was in the drums was burning hotly, and it was only a matter of time before the barrels ruptured and engulfed the whole building in flames. He pushed that from his mind and moved through the rubble calling Anna's name. Please God, let him find her in time.

Then he was deep into the wreckage, his movement raising thick, swirling clouds of drywall dust to mix with the acrid smoke of the chemical fire, stinging his nose and eyes and obscuring his vision. A section of shredded wall loomed out of the haze, blocking his path, and as he wrestled it aside, his foot slipped on something slick. He went down hard and cursed as his left knee slammed painfully into the concrete floor, and when he dropped his hand to steady himself, he felt something wet and slimy. He lifted his hand and squinted through stinging eyes.

Blood!

"Anna!" he screamed at the top of his lungs and was rewarded by a low moan from beneath a huge debris pile.

"I'm here! Hang on, Anna! I'll get you out of there."

It was becoming difficult to breathe in the increasingly toxic atmosphere, and Dugan succumbed to a bout of violent coughing. He struggled to his feet. Saving Anna was all that was important now.

What looked like half the suspended ceiling had collapsed upon the debris pile in front of him, the metal supports and acoustical tile twisted into a solid mass. The loose end of the obstruction rested on top of the pile of wreckage, and the other end was still connected overhead some distance away. Dugan squatted and put his shoulder under the free edge of the mass and lifted with a desperate, adrenaline-fueled strength. The load stubbornly resisted, and he redoubled his efforts until the whole mass began to creep upward, inch by inch. Dugan's straining hamstrings and butt muscles were on fire, but then he was upright, and he locked his knees, transferring part of the load to his skeletal structure. But what now? He heard a cough, and then someone shouted behind him.

"Mr. Dugan! Where are you? We have to get out. The whole place is going up!"

"Here, Nigel," Dugan yelled back over his shoulder, and Nigel scrambled through the rubble toward him, the sounds of his passage barely discernible over the increasing roar of the conflagration.

"Mr. Dugan. We hav—"

"Negative," Dugan shouted. "I found Anna. We've got to get her out!"

"Yes… yes, sir," Nigel said, moving to help Dugan shoulder the load.

"No," Dugan said. "I've got this. She's under the desk. Get that piece of wall out of the way and then slide the desk over so we can get at her."

Nigel set to work, his slight figure straining as the heavy wall section rose slowly and then crashed back onto the desk as his strength failed.

"It's too much for one man," Dugan yelled. "Go get the others!"

Nigel peered through the thick smoke and shook his head.

"It's too late. The fire's blocking the way. I came back just as they got the last of the hostages out the back, and I barely made it. I'm sure they're coming around the outside, but it's a long way, and there may be fences to deal with."

Dugan coughed and struggled for a breath.

"O-okay, then find something we can use to prop this ceiling up, then we can—"

"I understand," Nigel said, scanning the wreckage. He disappeared into the smoke and returned in seconds with a broken piece of wood slightly longer than Dugan was tall.

"This will have to do," Nigel said, tipping the wood at an angle and placing one end under the end of the collapsed ceiling near Dugan's shoulder and the other end on the floor. "If you can lift the ceiling a few more inches, I'll push the bottom of this board in along the floor until it's taking the weight."

"Let's do it," Dugan gasped, twisting to get the heel of his hands beneath the ceiling panel—and failing.

"What's the matter?"

"I-I've got to get out from under the load to reposition myself," Dugan said, "and as soon as I let go, this panel's coming down unless your little stick can hold the weight, so make damn sure the bottom of that thing doesn't slide out. Got it?"

"Just a minute," Nigel said, and Dugan felt the ceiling panel vibrate as Nigel kicked at the bottom of the board, trying to force it more vertical under the load. "Okay. I'm going to drop down and brace the bottom. Lower the load onto the board whenever you're ready."

Dugan nodded. "We'll go on three. One, two, THREE."

He twisted quickly and repositioned the heels of both palms under the edge of the ceiling panel. He'd barely gotten into position as the load began to increase.

"God damn it, Nigel! Hold it, I'm not ready! I can't hold it with my arms alone."

"The floor's… slick… with… blood. It's… sliding," Nigel gasped between grunts. "I can't… hold it… much longer. Get… clear!"

Dugan cursed and stepped back, releasing the load to sink on to the pile of debris, as the increased weight on the board pushed Nigel back a foot or so before the board came loose and clattered to the floor. Dugan stripped off his shirt and dropped to all fours to mop the blood off the floor.

"Take off your shirt and help me," Dugan yelled, and Nigel rushed to comply. In seconds they had cleared a small area of the floor of the sludge of blood and drywall dust.

Dugan squatted under the edge of the ceiling panel and extended his arms straight above his head, his palms resting on the load. Catching on immediately, Nigel worked the board back under the edge of the ceiling panel at an angle, pressing the bottom of the board to the newly cleaned floor to hold it in place.

"Okay," Dugan shouted above the fire. "At every count of three, I'll push up as hard as I can, and you push the bottom of the board in and let me know when you've stopped. You'll have to keep the bottom of the board in place while I'll rest for a second or so, and then we'll repeat. Start whenever you're ready. Got it?"

"Go," Nigel said, and Dugan began to take a deep breath and stopped as the smoke burned his throat. He coughed and steadied himself for the effort.

"One. Two. THREEEE…" Dugan clenched his teeth and pushed up with all his might.

"Stopped!" Nigel shouted.

Dugan relaxed a split second and squatted back down a bit to take advantage of the space his last push had gained him and began the count again. "One. Two. THREEE…" he called and fired upward on burning legs, gaining a bit of momentum before he shouldered the weight.

"Stopped," Nigel yelled. "That was a good one. A few more and we'll be done."

If I have 'a few more' in me, thought Dugan, as he dropped back down.

"Let's go for broke, junior. Just keep pushing and call out progress. Got it?"

"Ready when you are," Nigel replied.

"One. Two. THREEE…" Dugan fired upward, straining for all he was worth.

"Stopped," Nigel shouted, "just a bit more."

Dugan fought the urge to suck in a lungful of the smoke-filled air and tried to ignore his burning muscles. He closed his eyes and thought of Anna's face and strained harder still, oblivious to the pain.

"That's it! That's it! The board's vertical and taking the weight."

Dugan stumbled out from beneath the load, barely able to keep his feet, then gasped for breath and sucked in smoke instead. A coughing fit drove him to his knees, and as he struggled back to his feet, he squinted through the smoke toward the approaching inferno. The flames had reached the outer edges of the destroyed office area, and the heat was intense.

He stumbled toward the debris pile, and Nigel leaped to his side to help him wrestle the heavy section of destroyed wall off the desk. Seconds later they pulled the desk aside to reveal Anna's inert form lying in a pool of blood. Dugan's heart was in his throat as he dropped to her side and felt her carotid artery. Her pulse was weak but discernible, and Dugan gathered her in his arms and attempted to stand, but his exhausted legs betrayed him.

Nigel dropped down on Anna's opposite side, and between them, they lifted her and stumbled through the wreckage, breathing near impossible and their vision obscured as dense smoke burned their eyes. Bits of debris burst into flame, and they coughed as they staggered on, barely able to breathe.

"Wh-where's the window?" croaked Nigel. "Ca-can't see…"

"Just mo-move away from… fire. Hi-hit front wall and fo-follow it left t-to window," Dugan replied, with more certainty than he felt. Nigel stifled a cough, and they stumbled on, blind men in a maze.

"*Dyed*! Are you there?" came a voice.

"Here," Dugan croaked, and relief washed over him as two hulking figures appeared through the smoke. Ilya plucked Anna from their grasp and disappeared back the way he came. Borgdanov inserted himself between Dugan and Nigel and pulled them along in Ilya's wake.

"This way. Hold your breath," Borgdanov gasped through the thickening smoke as he dragged them through the wreckage.

Dugan slipped on a loose board and went down, rising with difficulty as Borgdanov tugged him to his feet. His lungs screamed for oxygen, but he dare not take a breath. Smoke burned his eyes, and he could see nothing, so he squeezed his eyes shut and stumbled on, relying on the big Russian to lead them to safety. Then he felt cool air on his face and sucked in a lungful of air tinged with the acrid stench of smoke. He blinked away the tears and rushed toward the blurry vision of the window, a rectangular outline in the glow of the streetlights.

"We are at the window," he heard Borgdanov say. "Watch your step—"

Dugan's toe caught on the low windowsill, and he pitched forward, landing hard on the sidewalk among the shards of broken window glass.

***

He came to sometime later, lying on a gurney as the flashing lights atop various emergency vehicles washed over him. He blinked and tried to sit up, but hands gently restrained him.

"Easy, sir," said a voice he didn't recognize. "You've had a nasty spill and inhaled quite a lot of smoke."

Dugan tried to speak, but there was something on his face. He tugged the oxygen mask free before the paramedic could stop him, and tried to sit up again.

"Anna," he said. "You need to be helping her! I'm—"

"Easy, *Dyed*," said Borgdanov's voice from the other side of him. "Ilya put Anna directly in first ambulance. She is already at hospital, I think. This ambulance will take you and Nigel to hospital."

The paramedic tried to put the oxygen mask back on, but Dugan pushed him away.

"How… how is she?" Dugan asked Borgdanov.

Borgdanov paused before answering. "Honestly, I do not know, *Dyed*. But she is alive, and she is strong woman, *da*?"

CHAPTER TWENTY-ONE

Dugan stole another glance at the clock on the wall and willed the time to pass, infuriated at the asinine hospital rules that allowed him only ten minutes at Anna's side every hour. He rose from the uncomfortable chair and began to pace just as Borgdanov and Ilya entered the tiny waiting room.

"How is she?" Borgdanov asked.

"She lost a lot of blood, but we got her here in time," Dugan said. "They repaired the damaged vein, and there was some muscle damage, but the doctor said she'll make a full recovery. The doc also said she was very lucky. The bullet barely missed the femoral artery. An inch lower and she'd have bled out for sure." Dugan paused and closed his eyes a moment, overcome by the thought of how close he'd come to losing her. Borgdanov rested a reassuring hand on his shoulder, and Dugan shook off the morbid thought and continued. "Anyway, she's still heavily sedated. I haven't had a chance to talk to her."

Both the Russians gave relieved nods. "Is good," Borgdanov said. "I told you she is strong woman, *da*? But what about you, *Dyed*? We went by your room first, but you were not there. Nurse did not seem so happy that you left against doctor's advice."

Dugan shrugged. "They were surprised to see me again after just releasing me from the crack on the head, so I think they're just being overly cautious. But I've got a pretty thick skull, and I don't have time to lie around in the hospital. As soon as I'm absolutely sure Anna's going to be okay, we have to get across to the US and get Cassie and the others back."

The Russians looked skeptical but said nothing, and Dugan changed the subject.

"How many did you save from the containers?"

Borgdanov's face darkened. "Twenty-three," he said through clenched teeth. "Eighteen women and five children. Three boys and two girls."

No one spoke for a long moment. Finally Dugan broke the silence.

"How many…" he hesitated, "… didn't make it?"

"All six policemen died, along with two of the *mafiya* bastards," Borgdanov replied. "And they found the charred remains of eleven women—girls, really—in the cages. Obviously Arsov's plan was for everyone to die."

"Son of a bitch!"

Borgdanov shook his head. "No, *Dyed*, son of a bitch is too kind for this scum. I think there is no word for him, but there is one I would like very much to apply to him. Ilya and I will not rest until he is *dokhlyy*—dead."

Ilya nodded, and Borgdanov lapsed into pensive silence for a moment before continuing.

"But we are few, and our priority is to rescue Karina, Cassie, and Tanya, but we cannot allow the trail of Arsov to grow cold either. We must be smart and careful."

"How are we going to do both? Lou and Harry told me the police lost Arsov. I figure he's out of the country by now."

"I am working on plan," Borgdanov said, "but for now we must—"

"Mr. Dugan?" said a nurse from the door of the waiting room.

Dugan turned to her. "Yes? Is Anna okay?"

The nurse smiled. "More than okay, Mr. Dugan. She's fully awake and asking for you." She glanced at the clock. "And I think under the circumstances we can relax the rules a bit."

INTENSIVE CARE UNIT
ST. IGNATIUS HOSPITAL
LONDON, UK

Anna looked up and gave Dugan a wan smile as he slipped through the curtains surrounding the bed.

"This place is rather like being in a fishbowl," she said, "but I did prevail upon the nurse to draw the curtains."

Dugan moved to the left side of her bed. An IV tube sprouted from Anna's right forearm, and on one finger of her right hand she wore a pulse monitor. Dugan took her left hand in both of his own and squeezed it gently.

"I'm told you're my savior."

"Well, I found you first, but if not for Nigel's help and then Borgdanov and Ilya getting us out, it would've been over for all of us."

Anna smiled. "Modest as always, I see." Her smile faded. "Ho...how are McKinnon and his men? No one will tell me anything."

Dugan was silent a long moment. "I'm sorry, Anna."

"All of them?"

Dugan nodded, then squeezed her hand.

"Bloody hell!" She turned her head away as a tear coursed down her cheek.

She struggled to compose herself and turned back to Dugan.

"The hostages?"

"The Russians managed to save over half of them." Dugan tried to soften the blow, but Anna wasn't deceived by semantics.

"Which means almost half of them are dead. How many, Tom?"

"Don't think about that now. Just worry about getting well."

"How many?"

"Eleven," Dugan replied softly and felt her flinch as if he'd struck her.

"What a complete fiasco."

Dugan felt the deaths all over again, Anna's pain combining with his own. He trembled when he thought how fragile life was and how close he'd come to losing her. He felt the ring box in his pocket and hesitated, but now was not the time. Not like this.

Suddenly the curtain parted, and the nurse appeared.

"I'm sorry, Mr. Dugan, but time's up," she said, not unkindly. "She needs her rest."

Dugan bent down and kissed Anna's lips, then pulled his face back a few inches.

"Rest now, and don't think of anything but getting better."

"I'll concentrate on recovering, right enough, but don't think I won't be thinking of Arsov." Her voice hardened. "Revenge is a powerful motivator."

Dugan nodded, and Anna continued. "What are you going to do?"

"We have to go after Cassie and the others. Now that you're out of immediate danger, we'll leave tonight."

Anna put her free hand behind his neck and pulled his face down to her. She kissed him tenderly, oblivious to the nurse clearing her throat at the curtain. She released him, and Dugan lifted his head to stare into her eyes.

"Do be careful, Tom," she said softly.

KAIROUZ RESIDENCE
LONDON, UK

Dugan shook his head. "I don't like it, Andrei," he said again. "You shouldn't go back to Russia alone. Come with us on the rescue, and we'll deal with Arsov after we've freed the girls."

"I don't like it either, *Dyed*, but we have no choice. I am sure Arsov is back with his superiors now, or soon will be, and the *Bratstvo* will know who we are. They will not take this lying down, and you can be sure they will retaliate. We must now, as you say, fight the war on two fronts, *da*?"

"Which is exactly why you going back to Russia alone makes no sense. If you insist on going, at least take Ilya to watch your back."

Borgdanov shook his head. "You do not know what resistance you will meet on ship, and while Agent Ward can maybe get you transport and logistical support, this is still an 'unofficial' matter as far as the US is concerned, and I don't think he can provide manpower. That leaves only you and young Nigel here to go on ship. Maybe you need help, and maybe not, but I do not think people on ship will just nicely deliver the girls to you. And if you must 'persuade' them…" he paused and nodded at Ilya, "I think Ilya is handy fellow to have around. And besides, I cannot ask Ilya to abandon the rescue of Karina and the others. Is primary mission, *da*?"

Beside Borgdanov, Ilya nodded his agreement.

"Still, I don't see what you can accomplish in Russia alone, other than get yourself killed."

"I think Mr. Dugan is right," Nigel added. "I can't see what you can accomplish alone in Russia either, but you would be an obvious asset on the rescue mission."

Dugan saw Borgdanov stiffen a bit at Nigel's implied criticism, and then visibly relax. Nigel's role in Anna's rescue had done much to raise the others' opinion of his usefulness, and he was now accepted as a member—though very much a junior one—of the team.

"Thank you for your high regard for my usefulness, Nigel," Borgdanov said, "but you and *Dyed* should not worry so about me. I am not so easy to kill, and Russia is my home. If all goes as planned, the *Bratstvo* bastards will not even know I'm there until I want them to know."

"But still, what can you do alone?" Nigel pressed.

"That is just the point. I do not plan on being alone. There are plenty of Russians who are sickened by what the *mafiya* and the corrupt politicians who protect them are doing to our country. Good people, many ex-*Spetsnaz* among them, who would like to do something about it."

"I don't doubt that," Dugan said, "but even if you recruit a few, I don't see you making much of an impact. This is a huge problem."

"But I am not trying to solve the whole problem, *Dyed*. The *mafiya* is too entrenched, and nothing will happen to them unless and until the government moves against them, and this will not happen. I also understand that even if I succeed in hurting this branch—this *Bratstvo*, another group of scum will arise to begin trading girls, drugs, and all the rest. My goal is not to solve the problem, because that is impossible, rather I only seek to make them leave us in peace."

"That's still a pretty tall order," Dugan said.

"True, but I know they will attempt to retaliate, and our choice is to sit here and wait for them to do so at the time and place of their own choosing, or to surprise them by striking first. You must understand that everything these bastards do is by calculation, and their brutality is by design, to intimidate their rivals. But we are not their rivals. They will only attack us now because we have annoyed them and they think we are weak, so punishing us will be easy. However, if we succeed in hitting them first, they will understand that retaliation against us will not be so easy. If they also realize we are not potential rivals attempting to take over their territories, the profit motive will be missing, and they will not be so eager to continue the attack. They are both bullies and businessmen. When faced with resistance, bullies turn away, and businessmen will not invest time and resources if there is no profit at the end of the operation."

"So essentially, your plan is to sucker punch them and hope it makes them go away," Dugan said.

Borgdanov nodded. "If 'sucker punch' means what I think it does, then *da*—that is my plan."

"And what if they don't stop coming?"

Borgdanov shrugged. "For sure, they will stop temporarily, to figure out what is happening. Then if they come after us again, I think they will concentrate on those of us who have hurt them. You who have helped us here in UK will be a minor concern, quickly forgotten." Borgdanov nodded both at Dugan and also Alex and Gillian, who had been sitting quietly, watching the exchange. "We will, as they say, draw their fire."

"Now see here, Andrei," Alex said, "we can't let you do that. Surely the authorities—"

Borgdanov held up his hand. "Alex, my friend, your authorities must play by certain rules, while the *Bratstvo* bastards have none. And how can they protect you, really? One lone assassin can come into the country, kill you all, and escape. Do you want to spend the rest of your life living in fear for Gillian and Cassie?" Borgdanov shook his head. "No. We brought these people to your door, and we will lead them away." He turned and looked at Ilya. "*Da?*"

"*Da,*" Ilya agreed.

"Lead them away where?" Dugan asked. "Aren't you forgetting something? What about Ilya and Karina's family, and the people you recruit to help you and all of their families? Surely nowhere in Russia, or even Europe will be safe for them."

Borgdanov nodded. "Is for this, I will need a bit more help."

CHAPTER TWENTY-TWO

MARITIME THREAT ASSESSMENT SECTION
CENTRAL INTELLIGENCE HEADQUARTERS
LANGLEY, VIRGINIA, USA

Jesse Ward slouched at his desk. A blue sports coat hung over the back of his chair, and the knot of his loosened tie hung at half mast, three inches below the open collar of his rumpled white shirt. His sleeves were rolled up, exposing corded muscles beneath the dark skin of his forearms, but here too he could see the beginnings of age-related decline. He sighed. It was inevitable he supposed, but things had only gotten worse since he took the job as section chief and no longer got into the field much. He'd have to start finding time to go to the gym or he'd turn into a complete marshmallow.

He abandoned thoughts of encroaching decrepitude and turned his attention back to the computer screen. These little 'unofficial favors' for Dugan and the Brits were always a challenge, and he studied the monitor again, trying to gauge just how far he could push the envelope without getting his ass in a crack. Or another crack, that is—dealing with Dugan always seemed to involve sticking his neck out.

His desk phone rang, and he looked over at the caller ID. Speak of the Devil.

"I hope you haven't called to ask me for another favor. I'm still working on the first one."

"And hello to you too," Dugan replied. "Are we in a bad mood, Jesse?"

"Well, I don't know about we, but I've been better. Do you have any idea how difficult it is to marshal government resources to interdict a foreign vessel in international waters when US security interests aren't at stake and I have absolutely no official justification for doing so?"

"I'm sure it's quite a challenge. How are you doing?"

"I'm still trying to figure out how to spin it," Ward said. "I thought about saying I had intel it was a big drug shipment, but then I'm sure everyone will want to let the ship actually dock. Then I thought about saying I'd received a tip the ship had a WMD aboard so that interdiction at sea was the safest option, but if I go that route, we'll attract a LOT of attention we probably don't want." He paused. "Are you sure we need to intercept them at sea?"

"Absolutely, Jesse. We don't know what condition the girls are in, and I want to get to them as soon as possible. We'd have tried to reach them from here in the UK if they hadn't already been out of chopper range. Even if a chopper only saves us a day, we need to do it."

Ward sighed. "Okay. I hear you. I'll make something work. Is there anything else?"

"Well, since you asked—"

"Shit. When will I learn to keep my mouth shut?"

"I need you to get some people into the US."

"What people?"

"Borgdanov and Denosovitch and some people they're recruiting in Russia."

"How many?"

"Maybe a dozen. Maybe fifteen."

"Just like that, huh?" Ward said. "I snap my fingers and produce fifteen visas?"

"Actually, I think they'll need green cards."

"Oh, really? Is that all, Mr. Dugan? I'll get right on it. Will there be anything else? We try to be a full service agency."

"Uh… yeah, well, they'll also have their families with them, and they'll all probably need new identities."

"Christ on a crutch, Tom! Let me get this straight. You're asking me to commit to getting permanent residence status for a large—but currently unknown—number of foreign nationals, none of whom have anything whatsoever to do with US national security. You then expect me to get them in some witness protection program—"

"I never said anything about a witness protection program. They'll take care of their own protection. I just need to get them in with new ID to help cover their tracks."

"You're really pushing the limits here, buddy. Maybe you better start at the beginning. If I'm gonna sell this to anyone, I need at least some way to connect this to a national security concern, however tenuously."

Dugan sighed and recounted Borgdanov's idea. Five minutes later, he finished and waited in silence for Ward to respond.

"Why do they want to come here? Why not stay close to home somewhere in Eastern Europe where they could blend in a bit better?"

"Because they'll be too many of them to hide in plain sight," Dugan said. "And any Russian mobsters searching for them in Europe will blend in well too. If they go to a rural area of the US, they may be conspicuous but they should be able to concoct at least a somewhat plausible cover story, and anyone searching for them will be equally conspicuous. Also, in the rural US they'll be able to arm themselves without constantly worrying about violating gun laws."

"And who's going to pay for all this?"

"Alex and I are kicking in, and I called Ray Hanley down in Houston. He still owes Borgdanov and Denosovitch for helping to get his crew back from the Somali pirates. He grumbled a bit but agreed to kick in. It won't cost the US taxpayers a cent."

Ward sighed. "All right. I still have access to some of the black op resources, so I may be able to swing the green cards and new IDs—but it can't be a 'favor'—not something this big. I report to people too, and I have to have some justification for this, and you better be sure the Russians understand what will be expected in return."

"Let's hear it."

"I will do anything Ward requires of me unless it involves acting against Russia," Borgdanov said. "Russia is our *Rodina*, our homeland, regardless of the bastards who are in power at the moment. I will never betray her."

Beside him, Ilya nodded agreement.

Dugan said nothing for a long moment.

"I think that's Ward's concern," Dugan said at last. "He was insistent I made that point clear to you. If he gets you the new identities and green cards, his expectation is complete loyalty in return. He has the ability to fast-track you all to citizenship, but he expects you all to commit to the US completely and unconditionally. He'll use you and whoever you recruit when needed as private contractors in future CIA operations and will pay you all well. He'll also try to make sure you're never forced to operate against Russia, but we have to face the facts. In situations where Russia and the US are at odds, there may be times when native Russian speakers are an asset, and I think you can count on being called upon to act against Russian interests. That's just a fact of life. If you can't do that, you should decline this deal and we'll have to work out something else."

"There IS nothing else, *Dyed*. We have no other connections, and we are not safe in Russia, even now."

"But I do not want to be a traitor to the *Rodina*," Ilya said, morosely. "Things are not so good there now, but it is my home."

"I understand," Dugan said, "but you have to decide, and also make sure that anyone you recruit understands the commitment. And I know it's a hard decision, but ask yourselves if you see any possible scenario in which the situation in Russia improves."

The Russians said nothing, and Dugan rose from the sofa.

"I'm going to the hospital to check on Anna before we take off. You guys think it over. I hate to rush you, but we need to leave for the US in a couple of hours, and if Ilya is coming with us and you're heading back to Russia, you need to make a decision before we leave so Ward can set things in motion."

Borgdanov merely nodded and continued to stare down at the coffee table. Dugan briefly laid a hand on the man's shoulder, then moved toward the apartment door. "I'll be back in an hour."

***

Borgdanov looked up when Dugan entered the apartment an hour later. The two Russians sat on opposite sides of the coffee table, a shot glass in front of each, and a much depleted bottle of vodka on the table between them.

"We did not think you would mind, *Dyed*," Borgdanov said. "We helped ourselves to your vodka."

"No problem." Dugan sat down on the sofa beside Borgdanov. "Did… did you make a decision?"

"We did." Borgdanov pushed his empty shot glass in front of Dugan and poured it full before refilling Ilya's glass. "But first, a toast."

Ilya picked up his glass and raised it in the air, and Borgdanov motioned for Dugan to take his glass as he raised the bottle.

"To Mother Russia, the *Rodina*," Borgdanov said, and Ilya raised the glass to his lips and threw back the shot as Borgdanov took a healthy pull from the bottle. Dugan's heart sank, but he courteously followed suit. The vodka burned his throat.

Not a good sign, thought Dugan, as he set the glass back down on the table and waited for the bad news. Borgdanov poured both glasses full again.

"A final toast." He looked at Dugan. "You know *Dyed*, once Ilya and I made you an honorary Russian, but now it seems we are to be countrymen for real." He raised the bottle, and Ilya raised his glass.

"To the USA, our new *Rodina*, and to a safer and better life for our families!"

ST. PETERSBURG
RUSSIAN FEDERATION

Arsov sat reviewing his story, struggling to hide his unease as he sat in the well-appointed outer office, a task made considerably more difficult by the presence of the two muscle-bound thugs flanking the ornate double door to the inner office beyond. The pair radiated malevolence, their ill-fitting suits stretched tight across steroid-enhanced musculatures, and they studied him with undisguised interest, sensing he might soon be the subject of interesting diversions. Arsov pretended to ignore them as he paged through a magazine he'd picked up from the end table beside his chair.

His reception so far had been chilly to say the least. London was a significant and growing market for the *Bratstvo* and, more importantly, was considered a training ground for seasoning the whores for the planned expansion of the US market. The near total collapse of the UK operation was not playing well here in St. Petersburg. His immediate superiors had been openly skeptical of his version of events, but with the death of his underlings and Nazarov's convenient disappearance, there was no one to dispute his story. And like all good fabrications, Arsov's tale contained elements of the truth. The police could only have learned of the warehouse from Nazarov, that much seemed apparent and added credibility to Arsov's claims. Ironically, Nazarov's obvious perfidy was the principal obstacle between Arsov and immediate execution and that, along with Arsov's voluntary return to Russia, had earned him a reprieve and led to his case being kicked up the chain of command. Far up the chain of command.

Arsov stiffened as one of the thugs guarding the door put his hand to his earbud, obviously listening to someone.

"*Da*," the thug said and then reached behind him and opened one side of the double door before pointing at Arsov.

"You," the guard said, "inside."

Arsov ignored the man's rudeness and casually tossed the magazine on the coffee table. He stood and moved toward the door with feigned confidence. Unimpressed, the guards smirked as he moved between them into the office beyond. It was much darker in the inner office and as Arsov stopped to let his eyes adjust, he heard the soft click of the closing door behind him and felt a momentary surge of fear.

"Do you intend to stand there all day like a statue, Arsov?" asked a disembodied voice from the far end of the palatial office, and Arsov moved toward a circle of light.

The man sat behind an ornately carved oak desk, lighted by a single desk lamp. The light was pointed down at the desk, and he sat in the shadows, a dim silhouette on the edge of the light. He was known only as *Glavnyy*—the Chief—and few people outside of his small circle of trusted associates had ever seen his face—and those who had never lived long enough to be a concern. Even in circumstances such as these, he was known to alter his voice and appearance in subtle ways, more to preclude the necessary elimination of the interviewee than out of any concern for his own safety. Arsov kept his eyes on the desk, encouraged. If the Chief intended to kill him, he had no doubt the meeting would have been face to face.

The Chief's right hand reached for a glass of tea on the desk and moved it into the shadows. Arsov heard a noisy slurp, and suddenly his own throat felt very dry. He watched as the hand moved back into the light and set the empty glass on the desk, and stood silently, waiting for the Chief to open the discussion. Seconds turned to minutes, and the minutes seemed like hours. Arsov felt sweat running down his cheeks.

The Chief slapped the desk with his open hand, upsetting the empty glass and producing a loud bang that caused Arsov to flinch.

"Tell me what happened in London, and don't give me that ridiculous fairy tale," the Chief said.

"I-I caught Nazarov skimming and—"

"Bullshit! Why is this the first we've heard of it?"

"I wasn't sure. I wanted to get evidence before I reported him. Bu-but he must have found out I was on to him and became a police informant."

"So let me see. Nazarov is stealing from us and then decided to become an informer. So that means we make no more money, so he has nothing to skim. Does that make sense to you, Arsov? Surely you can come up with something better than that?"

"But I explained! He must have figured out I was on to him and knew the money would dry up. Then he set us all up with the cops. I think his plan was that none of us would survive, and that he paid the cops to make sure that happened. I think the plan was to burn the building so the bodies would be unidentifiable; then he would disappear with his money. And it would have worked if I hadn't escaped. Besides, I have proof. The offshore accounts—"

"Yes, yes, the offshore accounts. And how convenient that you discovered those and so thoughtfully provided them to us. But I am a little confused, Arsov. First, you tell me you did not inform us because you were waiting to get proof, and in the very next breath you tell me you HAVE proof. I am sure you can see my problem, *da*?"

Arsov took a deep breath and struggled to calm himself.

"I discovered the accounts only shortly before Nazarov set us up and disappeared. So I DID get the proof, but I didn't have time to let you know before Nazarov sprang his trap. I came here as soon as possible after I escaped."

Arsov saw the head of the silhouette nod and relaxed a bit. Perhaps he could sell his story after all.

"That sounds… possible," the Chief said, "but there are still many little 'loose ends,' as the Americans say. For example, Nazarov has been in London for over four years, mostly as number two in that operation, but these offshore accounts you've discovered were opened only two months ago, and the balances are really quite small. If our Nazarov is an embezzler as you say, he must be quite incompetent or very patient."

"It makes perfect sense if you think about it," Arsov countered, warming to the discussion. "Nazarov was put in charge of the London operation for two months when Tsarko rotated back here to St. Petersburg and I had not yet arrived from Prague to replace him. I think Nazarov seized that opportunity to set up his skimming operations, assuming he could steal enough to escape before I discovered the problem. I just caught him sooner than he anticipated, that's all."

Again the silhouette nodded, and Arsov relaxed a bit, his hopes growing, only to be dashed.

"That is one explanation," the Chief said. "Nazarov is not a particularly clever fellow. But then again, I think he understands his own limitations. So, you will perhaps understand why I find it difficult to believe that he had the *yaytsa*—the balls—to steal from the Brotherhood."

The Chief paused, and even though Arsov could not see his face clearly, he felt the man's eyes boring into him.

"But you, Arsov. You are quite clever. Perhaps even as clever as you THINK you are. I can easily envision a scenario in which you convinced yourself that appropriating a little of the *Bratstvo*'s money as your own was a good idea. And it hasn't escaped me that these offshore accounts were opened AFTER your arrival in London. Perhaps YOU were the one skimming the money and our now absent friend Nazarov caught you? An interesting theory, is it not?"

"Never! I assure you, sir, that I—"

"Calm yourself, Arsov. Your assurances, however passionate, are meaningless, so don't bore me. Be content to know that with Nazarov missing, I will accept your story for the time being, but know also that your loyalty is now suspect. Because of your previous outstanding performance, you will be given a very rare second chance, but do not disappoint me again. Is that clear?"

"Perfectly, sir! I will do everything in my—"

"Save your assurances, Arsov. The only acceptable assurances are your actions. You will perform or you will die a slow and painful death. It is that simple, and no flowery speech will change it. Now. Tell me how you managed to attract such intense scrutiny from the police."

"I… I'm sorry if it seems like I'm repeating myself, but it was Nazarov."

The Chief sighed. "The absent are always guilty, it seems. So how did the conveniently absent Mr. Nazarov bring the police down upon us in such force?"

"We had a girl from Volgograd named Karina Bakhvalova. We seasoned her in Prague, but she was a real spitfire and needed additional work in London. Two ex-*Spetsnaz* showed up looking for her—one of them was her uncle—and evidently, and unbeknown to us, they had influential friends in London. They kidnapped Tanya—"

"I thought you said the girl's name was Karina?"

"I did. Tanya is a different girl they were questioning in the club. When Nazarov sent in a man to break it up, the *Spetsnaz* overpowered our guy and kidnapped Tanya. When I sent Nazarov and some men to get Tanya back, he also kidnapped another girl at the house where Tanya was staying. It turns out she was the daughter of a very influential and well-connected Brit, and the shit hit the fan."

"Am I to understand that after years of low-profile operations, you and Nazarov thrust us into the limelight with one incredibly stupid move?"

"Not me. Nazarov."

"And just who did Nazarov work for?"

Arsov said nothing, and the silence grew to the point that he feared the Chief might have a change of heart about giving him a second chance.

"We'll be toxic in the UK for months, if not years," the Chief muttered before addressing Arsov again. "Very well. What happened to this Tanya, or Karina, or whatever her name is, and this British girl? I trust you at least took care of them in a way that will not lead the police back to our door?"

Arsov's mind raced. He hadn't spared a thought for the troublemaking little bitches since he'd shoved them in the container. However, now was not the best time to appear uncertain and indecisive in front of the Chief.

"Absolutely. Dead and buried where they won't be found."

The silhouette nodded. "Well, at least you didn't screw that up."

Arsov hesitated a long moment and then ventured the question he'd been holding back.

"Where will I go next?"

"We'll put you back in your old position in Prague. You seemed to do well there, at least. But before you go, we have a few loose ends to clear up. Give me what you have on the whore that started all this trouble and the *Spetsnaz* idiots."

"The girl was Karina Bakhvalova from Volgograd. One of the *Spetsnaz* was her uncle, Ilya Denosovitch. He was formerly a sergeant, I believe, but I'm not sure what unit. The other was his commanding officer, a man named Borgdanov, first name unknown. However, I'm sure he won't be difficult to find."

"And the Brits?"

"Actually one was an American, Thomas Dugan. He's a business partner with a Brit named Alex Kairouz. It was Kairouz's daughter that Nazarov kidnapped."

"Anyone else involved?"

Arsov hesitated and briefly considered telling the Chief about the dead MI5 bitch, but was pretty sure that would be the straw that broke the camel's back. He was apparently getting out of this interview alive, and he didn't want to do anything to change that. Besides, he was the only one who knew she'd been MI5, and if that fact turned up later, he could just pretend he hadn't known.

"No. That's it. Are you going to retaliate?"

"Of course we're going to retaliate. We can't have people thinking they can fuck with the *Bratstvo*, now can we? But we have to consider how to go about it. We need to send a clear message, without making the situation worse. We'll have a difficult time getting reestablished in the UK as it is."

"I'd like to participate in the strike," Arsov said, the first honest statement he'd made since he walked in the door.

"Oh, you've done quite enough, Arsov. Now get out of here and get your ass on a plane to Prague. And remember. We're watching you."

Arsov nodded and turned for the door, hurrying before the Chief changed his mind. The guard thugs turned and scowled as he opened the door, then moved to block his exit.

"Let him go," said the Chief's voice in the gloom behind him, and the two men parted, their disappointment obvious. Arsov gave them a smirk. Who was laughing now?

His brief elation died in the elevator as his thoughts turned to the troublesome bitches en route to the US. Had Nazarov informed the receivers in the US of the girls' names? He doubted it. The receivers probably had no clue who the girls were, just another shipment of whores as far as they were concerned. The unorthodox method of delivery might generate some local curiosity, but other than that, his secret was probably safe. Or was it? None of the girls were stupid, and if they somehow escaped, it might come to the Chief's attention that Arsov had been less than forthcoming. And both the Russian girls could identify him to the authorities if it came to that. No, he had to make sure the shipment never arrived.

✳✳✳

Vladimir Glazkov, Chief of the St. Petersburg and Leningrad Oblast Directorate of the Federal Security Service of the Russian Federation, AKA "the Chief," watched Arsov's retreating back as the fool fled. Meeting with the idiot was perhaps unwise, but he really needed a better sense of the London debacle, and some things could not be communicated via underlings or even video. Sometimes you needed to be in the same room with a man, to sense his tension, to smell his fear. And besides, he had been juggling his dual identities as St. Petersburg's chief policeman and head criminal for so long, the deception was second nature to him.

One thing was clear—nothing was quite as this fool Arsov related it. While there was no doubt that Nazarov had somehow been compromised, the circumstances of that treachery were very much in question, and Arsov had likely played a role. He would have to be killed in time, but he was good at training the whores, and the Brotherhood might as well get as much use out of him as possible for the time being. It wasn't good business to squander resources, and Glazkov was nothing if not an astute businessman.

Which brought him back to this UK disaster. That there had to be retaliation was clear, but the scope and targets were problematic. These *Spetsnaz* bastards and their families would die, of course, but beyond that, things became more difficult. The *Bratstvo* operated with impunity throughout Russia and many of the former Soviet satellites, on the back of generous 'gifts' to politically connected 'friends.' But in those countries where bribery was not an accepted way of doing business, the model (which he had developed) always involved flying well below the radar. The sex trade was staffed by foreign talent acquired outside of the country being served, and drugs were sold primarily to the bottom tier of society, in both cases the 'victims' being persons held in low regard by the general population. It boggled the imagination that Arsov and Nazarov had managed to violate the most basic tenet of their operation.

And not just by targeting some common Brit—oh no—they had to kidnap the daughter of this Kairouz, who was obviously not only wealthy, but politically connected as well. The sheer idiocy of it made his head hurt.

Well, at least the girl was no longer a problem, and if Arsov was to be believed—a somewhat doubtful assumption—there was nothing left to lead the authorities back to the *Bratstvo*, except, of course, unprovable suspicion. But therein lay the rub. If everyone suspected that this Kairouz and his American partner had brought ruination down on the *Bratstvo*, their apparent weakness would encourage rivals to muscle in on the UK business. Viewed from that angle, retaliation against this Kairouz and Dugan seemed mandatory. However, if they DID retaliate, would that not raise their profile with the authorities even more and make reestablishment of their UK operations that much more difficult? He cursed Arsov once again for putting the Brotherhood in this difficult position.

Then again, things were going to be hot in the UK for some time anyway, so if they intended to eliminate the Kairouz family and this Dugan, there was no time like the present. The sooner things heated up, the more quickly they would cool down. He picked up the phone and pressed a preset. Halfway across the city, a voice answered.

"Arkady," Glazkov said, "get me everything you can find on an Alex Kairouz and Thomas Dugan in London. They're partners in a shipping company, I believe. I want everything on them and their families. Is that clear?"

"Yes, Boss. Since it's outside Russia it may take a bit longer, but I should have you a full report by tonight. Anything else?"

"Yes. Do a similar search for Ilya Denosovitch, who was previously a sergeant in some sort of *Spetsnaz* unit. He's from Volgograd, I think. And also check for a Borgdanov, first name and hometown unknown. However, he is also ex-*Spetsnaz*, and I believe he was Denosovitch's commanding officer, so you should find him in the records for the same unit. He was likely a field grade officer, a major or a lieutenant colonel."

"Much easier. I should have those within the hour."

∗∗∗

Arkady Baikov, Chief Data Analyst for the Federal Security Service for St. Petersburg and Leningrad Oblast, looked down at the name on his scratch pad. Borgdanov. He didn't have to look up the name. He knew it. Andrei Nikolaevich Borgdanov, Major Andrei Nikolaevich Borgdanov.

"Whatever you're doing, Dyusha," he said softly, "you're making a big mistake."

Arkady sighed and turned to his computer.

CHAPTER TWENTY-THREE

Container Ship *Kapitan Godina*
En route to Jacksonville, Florida

Tanya's hand was dark bluish black, the discoloration visible well up the inside of her right arm, almost to the elbow, and the festering wound leaked thick foul-smelling pus into the makeshift bandage they'd tied around her hand. The girl burned with fever and lapsed in and out of consciousness, rousing only enough to swallow small sips of water Cassie gently trickled into her mouth from one of the few remaining bottles of clean water. She slept now with her head in Cassie's lap, a troubled sleep punctuated by whimpers between labored breaths, and Cassie gently stroked her forehead with a wet rag, attempting to soothe her fevered brow.

"She's getting worse, I think," Cassie whispered.

In the dim light leaking through the holes near the top of the container, she saw Karina nod agreement.

"*Da*," Karina said. "The infection has spread, and there is nothing more we can do. Without treatment soon she will not survive."

"But she CAN'T die. Not like this. Not from a little cut!"

Karina shook her head sadly and laid a hand on Cassie's arm. "I don't want her to die either, Cassie, but you must be prepared. If we do not reach port today, I think she will not last the night, and even if we do, I think she will lose at least her hand and maybe part of her arm."

"But we're not even close. Look at the food, we have four or five days left," Cassie said.

"I honestly don't know, Cassie. We weren't eating much when we were seasick, and Tanya has hardly been able to eat at all. The days have run together, and I've lost track. I don't even know how long we've been in this damn box."

"We'll get there soon. We HAVE to. And then they'll treat Tanya. I mean if they intended to kill us, they wouldn't have bothered to put us on a ship, would they?"

Karina nodded, more to placate Cassie than because she believed it.

Airborne
En route to Jacksonville, Florida

Dugan fidgeted in the leather seat of the Gulfstream and considered having a drink from the bar, then decided against it. His stomach already boiled from too much coffee, and he was wired on a potent combination of adrenaline, caffeine, and anxiety. Alcohol would hardly improve things.

He worried for the hundredth time if he'd done the right thing leaving Anna in the hospital, even though she'd insisted he do so. Then he suppressed a pang of guilt at his insistence that Alex and Gillian stay behind to watch over Anna, arguing that they could do nothing ashore in the US. It was a totally logical argument, and they reluctantly agreed, even though they clearly wanted to come on the flight.

Dugan looked over at Nigel and Ilya, both apparently lost in their own thoughts. Leave-taking had been an emotional affair all the way around, with the two Russians embracing before Ilya climbed aboard the plane ahead of Dugan.

"Do you think Andrei will have any trouble in Russia? I'll bet these mafia bastards have eyes and ears everywhere."

Ilya looked up and shook his head. "*Nyet*. Part of the time the major and I were on counter terrorism assignments, we worked undercover. He has many contacts where he can get new identity papers, and with your generous support, he has all the money he needs. Is no problem, I think."

"Still, with automated video surveillance at all the international airports, I think it's dangerous. He can't change his appearance that much."

Ilya laughed. "More than you think, *Dyed*. But the major will not use any primary entry point. Since the end of Cold War and breakup of Soviet Union, our border is not so secure anymore. There are hundreds of possible overland entry points, and after he gets inside, traveling on domestic transportation with false papers is not big problem, especially if he keeps changing identities."

"I'm still worried. He's completely on his own."

Ilya shook his head again. "No, *Dyed*. We have many *tovarishchi*—comrades—there. Some will help him, some will not because of concern for families or similar things, but none will betray him, I think, especially not to *mafiya* scum."

"Do you know his plan?"

"He has no clear plan—yet," Ilya said. "First he must do reconnaissance. Then he can form plan and figure out resources he needs to proceed. He will contact us when he is ready, not before. Then we strike, *da*?"

"We?"

"Of course, I will be there. This rescue operation will be over in a day or two at most, one way or another. Then I go to Russia as soon as the major needs me."

Dugan scowled at the Russian fatalism inherent in the 'one way or another' but ignored it. He was much more irritated by what Ilya had just revealed.

"Christ! If that's the case, why the hell didn't he wait until we finished up here like I suggested? Then we could have all gone together?"

"Because we would have to separate anyway. The major and I can move about Russia independently with false papers, but together we would be very obvious, *da*? So—if we must separate anyway, is better the major goes ahead and gets things started." Ilya paused. "And besides, *Dyed*, you are not coming to Russia."

"What the hell do you mean I'm not coming? I want this asshole Arsov as much as you do."

"Forgive me, *Dyed*, but you are not Russian. The major and I can sneak across border and move freely in disguise, especially if we separate, but you, I think, will stick out like sore finger."

"I think you mean sore thumb."

Ilya shrugged. "Whatever. You are not going. The major was clear on this."

"I guess he forgot to tell me that part."

Ilya shrugged again, but said nothing.

We'll see about that, thought Dugan, but he didn't press the point with Ilya.

***

An hour later, Dugan dialed the satellite phone.

"Maritime Threat Assessment," Ward answered.

"Jesse, where do we stand?"

"You've got clearance to land at Cecil Field, which is a joint civil-military airport on the west side of Jacksonville. It's also the home base for the Coast Guard's HITRON, so that worked out well."

"Hit what?"

Ward chuckled. "HITRON. It's an acronym for Helicopter Interdiction Tactical Squadron. They're the Coasties that support ops against drug trafficking and that sort of thing. I have some contacts there because they also support the USCG Maritime Security Response Team. I ran a few drills with them right after we set up the Maritime Threat Assessment group here at Langley."

"Any problems arranging it?"

"Yes and no."

"That's not very illuminating, Jesse."

"No, it wasn't difficult to get you a chopper. These guys jump at any excuse to get some air time, especially if it can be back charged to some other agency's budget. And by the way, you're welcome. I was able to sneak this little joy ride on to what remains of my rapidly dwindling black budget."

"And that's much appreciated," Dugan said, "but what about the 'yes' part?"

"Yes, it was tough to figure out a plausible cover story, but I managed. This is being billed as an AOR—and before you ask, that's 'Area of Responsibility'—familiarization flight. In other words, an excuse to go up and fly around somewhere they might reasonably be expected to conduct operations someday. You guys are members of a 'multinational task force' going along as observers."

"How's that work?"

"There's an ongoing cooperation between our guys and the Royal Bahamian Defense Force called Operations Bahamas, Turks and Caicos or OPBAT. Since the Turks and Caicos Islands are still a British Overseas Territory, it's not too much of a stretch to think the Brits might send some observers to the operation from time to time."

"So we're all supposed to be Brits?"

"No, you're billed as a company man, working for me—which is partially true since you do that on occasion. The others are British intelligence. Lou and Harry are going to backstop us and confirm that if necessary," Ward said.

"That might work for Nigel, but what about Ilya. He's carrying a Russian Federation passport."

"Don't worry about it. I called in another favor. An immigration officer will board the plane on landing and take care of everything. After that, just tell Ilya to keep his mouth shut and nod a lot around the Coasties."

"Okay. I follow. And the Coasties know we're going after the *Kapitan Godina*?"

"Uhh… no."

"What do you mean, no? How the hell are we supposed to get to the ship if these guys don't know the target."

"I mean my imagination is tapped out, and I've stretched this about as far as I can. You have the AIS number for the ship, so after you get airborne, you'll have to use your boyish charm to convince the pilot to take you there. I can get you in the room, Tom, but you have to close the deal yourself. I'm sure you're up to it. By the way, are you armed?"

"Harry got us an assault rifle, which I gave to Ilya so I don't shoot myself in the foot. He also got us a couple of Glocks, but I'm not too worried about that. This is a merchant ship, and I doubt they're armed, or heavily armed anyway. I'm more concerned with what I'm going to tell the Coasties. What do they think they're supposed to be doing, anyway?"

"Right now they think they're just going to fly around offshore and pretend to be intercepting drug-traffickers for the edification of a group of their British cousins. If I push any harder, this whole thing could fall apart in a hurry."

Dugan was quiet a moment before responding.

"I understand. Thanks, Jesse," he said at last.

"Look Tom, these are good guys. I suspect that after you're in the air and all the bureaucrats are out of the way, you won't have any problem. Use your own judgment, but I suspect if you level with them, they'll find a way to help you."

"Your lips to God's ears, pal. And however it turns out, I appreciate the help."

"No problem. What's your ETA?"

Dugan looked at his watch, suddenly worried. "About 2100, I think. Listen, since the Coasties think this is a bullshit show-and-tell operation, do you think they'll be ready to deploy tonight? They may want to wait until daylight since they don't know it's urgent.'

"Damn, I didn't think of that. Do you want me to try and push from here?"

Dugan thought a moment. "No, you can't really push without setting off alarms, and like you said, it might all unravel. It's 1900 now, so we'll be on the ground in a couple of hours, and I'll see what I can do face to face."

"Okay. Call me if you need me to run interference."

"Will do," Dugan said and hung up.

He unfastened his seat belt and headed for the cockpit to tell the pilot to change his flight plan to Cecil Field.

CHAPTER TWENTY-FOUR

Arsov sat at his old desk and looked around. In a way, it was good to be back in Prague, especially considering the alternatives. True, Beria hadn't been particularly pleased at his return and only grudgingly vacated the office. However, Arsov had been able to placate his underling with the assurances that it was only a temporary situation.

But he had to take care of loose ends to keep it that way. He picked up his phone and dialed the sat phone on the *Kapitan Godina*, listening as the buzzes and clicks ended in the strange ring tone.

"*Kapitan Godina*, captain speaking," said a voice in English.

"Good evening, Captain," Arsov replied in Russian. "I trust you're taking very good care of our shipment?"

After a long pause, the man replied in Ukrainian-accented Russian. "Yes, sir, all is in order. We should dock in Jacksonville late tomorrow evening or early the following morning depending on the availability of a pilot."

"There has been a change of plans. I believe you will encounter a storm and lose the container overboard. Most regrettable."

"Bu-but we cannot! We are too close to port, and the weather is fine. And there are many ships in this area, converging on the US coast. No one will believe we encountered heavy weather. If you wanted to dump the shipment, you should have informed me when we were in mid-ocean with less traffic."

"I'm telling you now, and I won't tell you again."

"But what will I tell the insurers and the customs inspectors?"

"I'm sure you'll think of something, and while you're considering that, I suggest you think of your lovely wife and beautiful daughters for inspiration. Your wife is a bit old to be of any use, so regrettably, we'll have to dispose of her. Your daughters, however, are promising, and I'm sure we could find places for them in our operation."

"No. No. I'll take care of it. Don't worry."

"Oh, I never doubted it for a moment, Captain," Arsov said. "And if you have any trouble with the other officers, please remind them we have all of their loved ones under our protection."

"I… I will. It will be done. Don't worry."

"Thank you. Call me when it's done. And, Captain, do have a pleasant evening."

Arsov hung up and leaned back in his chair with his fingers laced behind his head, satisfied he was getting things back on track. As soon as the captain reported the death of the troublesome whores, there was absolutely nothing more that could connect him to the unfortunate events in London. He could forget about Karina and her little friends and go about rebuilding his reputation in the organization here in Prague. He regretted his missteps, but one always learned more from mistakes than successes. Next time, he'd be a bit more careful.

KAPITAN GODINA
AT SEA EAST OF JACKSONVILLE, FLORIDA

"Have you ever done it before," the captain asked the chief engineer.

"No, but it should not be too difficult, I think. The container is well positioned, and we have the air bladders they gave us aboard." He glanced out the porthole of the captain's office. "But I don't think we should do it at night."

"We must. Every hour we get closer to shore. And if we dump it at night, no one can see."

The chief shook his head. "On the contrary, everyone can see. We can't work in the dark, especially doing something we've never done before. You'll have to put on the deck lights, which will look strange and attract the attention of any passing ship. I think it's actually better to do it in the day time. The activity on deck won't attract any interest, and we can flip the container overboard when there are no ships nearby. You're sure the container has holes top and bottom, to flood and sink quickly?"

The captain nodded. "They told me that is standard for their 'special shipment' containers."

"So if we time it right, it will be over the side and gone before anyone sees. Right?"

"Very well, there is something to what you say. But we have to slow down. The closer we get to port, the more traffic, and I don't want anyone to see us dumping the container. Its disappearance will be hard enough to explain as it is."

The chief stood. "Okay. I'll go down to the engine room and prepare to reduce speed. Give the order whenever you're ready. I'll also have the first engineer gather all the tools and equipment. We'll be ready to start on the container at first light. It shouldn't take long."

The captain nodded and the chief started out the door, but turned back in the doorway.

"What do you think is in the damn thing, anyway?" the chief asked.

The captain shrugged. "Drugs or guns, I suppose. I don't know, and I don't really want to know. I just want my family safe."

CECIL FIELD
JACKSONVILLE, FLORIDA

Ward was as good as his word. An immigration officer boarded the plane as soon as they rolled to a stop beside a nondescript building. He took their passports and stamped them without saying a word, then returned them and shook hands all around.

"Gentlemen," he said, "welcome to the United States."

Then he left, hurrying down the short stairs without looking back.

"Very efficient," Ilya said, and Dugan nodded and looked at his watch.

"Well, boys, let's go see if we have a welcoming committee." Dugan started for the hatch. His feet had barely hit the tarmac when he heard his name being called, and looked up to see a man walking toward him. The newcomer was of medium height with sandy hair, and he wore the uniform of the US Coast Guard with lieutenant's bars on his shoulders.

"Mr. Dugan?" the man said again as he approached.

Dugan nodded, and the man smiled and extended his hand. "Joe Mason. I'm going to be your taxi driver tomorrow."

"Nice to meet you, Lieutenant Mason. But please, call me Tom."

"Only if you call me Joe."

Dugan grinned. "That's a deal, Joe. And these guys are Nigel Havelock and Ilya Denosovitch."

Mason shook Nigel's hand, and as he shook Ilya's, he regarded the big Russian with interest.

"*Dobro pozhalovat' v Ameriku*," Mason said.

Ilya struggled to hide his surprise. "*Spasibo*," he replied.

Mason studied Denosovitch a bit more closely.

"*Spetsnaz*?"

Ilya's discomfort was obvious. "*Da*," he said after a moment's hesitation.

Mason grinned. "I can always spot a snake eater, no matter what the nationality."

Well, there goes that plan, thought Dugan. Mason laughed at the group's obvious unease.

"My brother's a SEAL and two of my cousins are Army Special Forces, so I've been around a lot of special ops guys. They just carry themselves a little differently from most people. And my family is Russian. Our name was Kamenshchik, which translated—obviously—to Mason. I'm second generation, but my parents spoke Russian at home to my grandparents, so I sorta picked it up. Don't get to practice much, though."

"Sounds pretty good to me," Dugan said.

Ilya nodded. "*Da*, his pronunciation is perfect, *Dyed*."

Mason grinned. "*Dyed*? You don't look quite old enough to be this guy's grandpa, and you don't look Russian at all. What's with the *Dyed*?"

"It's a long story." Dugan glared at Ilya, who was struggling to suppress a grin.

Mason looked back and forth between the two. "Sounds interesting."

"Maybe later," Dugan said. "What's the plan?"

"Well, I apologize, but we don't have suitable quarters here at HITRON. Cecil Field isn't strictly speaking a full Coast Guard facility—we share it with the Florida Air National Guard support folks and some commercial operators. However, I booked you rooms in a Hampton Inn about six miles down I-10. I can take you there now, or if you're hungry, we can stop somewhere and get some chow first. I've got the boys coming in to preflight the chopper at oh five hundred, so we'll be ready anytime you folks are. Just let me know when you'd like a pickup in the morning."

"Ah… could we get started a little sooner?"

Mason looked puzzled. "Sooner? You mean, like… tonight?"

"Yeah, if that's possible."

"Well, sure, it's possible. We're equipped with night vision for twenty-four-hour ops, but I guess I'm a bit confused as to the point. My briefing said this was a routine familiarization and training flight for drug interdiction."

"That's right," Dugan said quickly.

Mason gave Dugan a strange look. "Mr. Dugan, do you mind if I ask you all for some identification. I was told to expect three intelligence agents, an American and two Brits, but Mr. Denosovitch doesn't look very British to me. I'd really like to know what's going on here."

Dugan noticed the use of the title and felt the situation slipping away. He knew he'd blown it somehow but decided to try to bluff it out. He smiled at Mason.

"If I told you, I'd have to kill you."

Mason said nothing and waited. The silence grew.

"Okay. I see you're uneasy," Dugan said. "Why don't you tell me what's bothering you?"

"What's bothering me is that for guys that are coming as observers on a drug interdiction exercise, you seem to know jack shit about the procedure. Our role is normally to scout for and intercept the drug-traffickers' small 'go fast' boats and force them to stop and remain in place while we vector surface vessels to their position. We're all about intimidation. If they refuse to stop, we either put a shot across their bow with our machine gun or try to take out their engines with a fifty-caliber sniper rifle. The point is, intimidation works best when your target can SEE you, so while we're capable of night operations, that isn't a standard training op. Besides which, night ops involve the crew using night-vision equipment and as 'observers,' you wouldn't have much to observe except the backs of our heads. All of which leads me to believe something isn't quite right here. This has all been a very low-key 'do me a favor' op, but I'm getting a real bad vibe. So, absent a direct order from my chain of command, I'm not risking my bird or my crew unless and until I know what the hell is going on. How about I take you to the hotel, and tomorrow at oh eight hundred we'll meet with my superiors and we can sort this all out?"

Dugan sighed. "Okay. I guess we need to start over. It's a long story, so why don't we go somewhere we can all sit down, and I'll tell you the deal over a cup of coffee. After that, we'll do it any way you want."

***

An hour later, they sat crowded into a corner booth in a near-deserted Denny's, well away from the few other customers, speaking in low tones. The waitress started toward them, coffee carafe in hand, but Dugan waved her away. She shrugged and turned toward the counter as Mason glanced over his shoulder to make sure she was out of earshot before continuing.

"So these girls are being held captive on the ship," Mason said. "I get that. But why not wait until the ship docks in a day or so and hit them then. I mean, they've been on the ship a week as it is, and a shore-based op would be way easier."

Dugan shook his head. "We have no idea what shape the girls are in, and we don't know that they'll even be on board when the ship docks. And there's all sorts of scrutiny when the ship reaches port. It's not like guns or drugs, people make noise, so for all we know, they intend to take them off at sea just before they make port. That's why I want to hit them as soon as they get into chopper range and before they can connect with anyone."

Mason still looked skeptical. "Well, maybe, but I still don't buy it. I mean, I'm sympathetic, but this looks very much like something for law enforcement, and for the life of me I can't understand why the CIA and British intelligence—assuming you guys actually are who you claim to be, which I doubt—has any skin in the game here. I don't see any national security issues involved at all, so what AREN'T you telling me, Dugan?"

Dugan wasn't sure whether the transition from 'Tom' to 'Mr. Dugan' and back to simply 'Dugan' marked progress in his relationship with Mason, but at least the Coastie was still listening. He decided he had nothing to lose by coming clean, and Mason wasn't anyone likely to be conned.

He sighed. "I work for the CIA part time, and I also have connections with British intelligence. However, these gentlemen are not affiliated with either organization. It's a very personal matter for us all, I'm afraid."

"I'm listening."

"One of the kidnapped girls, Cassie Kairouz, is my goddaughter. Another is Ilya's niece."

"What about Havelock here?" Mason inclined his head toward Nigel.

"Nigel is Cassie's…" Dugan hesitated; 'boyfriend' seemed diminishing somehow, but he didn't know what else to call him. "Nigel cares a great deal about Cassie," he said simply.

Mason shook his head. "Okay. That makes more sense. But this is WAY outside the lines. I really think we need to discuss this with the unit commander—"

"There's no TIME, Joe. Do you really think that discussion would end before the ship got to the pilot station? I mean, you're cleared for the flight, right? PLEASE, let's just make the flight as planned and adapt to circumstances as we find them. If we miss this chance, they might either be dead or out of our reach!"

Mason shook his head again, but didn't respond, and Dugan felt the opportunity slipping away. Then Ilya began to speak to Mason in Russian, his voice barely above a whisper.

***

Ilya watched with growing concern as Dugan's attempts to convince the Coast Guard pilot seemed to be failing. He couldn't follow all the nuances of the conversation, but there was no mistaking the pilot's body language, and the head shakes were growing more emphatic as the conversation progressed. When both men lapsed into what seemed a final silence, he could contain himself no longer.

"I am sorry, Joe Mason," Ilya said in Russian, "but I do not have the English words to say to you what I must. But I beg you to listen to *Dyed* and take us in your helicopter without delay. I suppose all families everywhere have a great bond, but I KNOW I feel these things, and if your family is Russian, I suspect you do as well. I think your parents and grandparents and brothers and sisters and cousins and nephews and nieces meet several times each year to eat and drink and laugh and dance and fight and argue. I think you have family members you love without limit and others that piss you off every time you think of them. But I think that when one is in trouble, no matter which one, you will help with your last ruble or ounce of strength if necessary, because this is family, *da*?"

Mason nodded, and Ilya continued.

"I was a teenager when little Karina was born, and I bounced her on my knee and took her to the park and the zoo and all the places children like. When I became a soldier, I knew it was not such a good life for family, and so I have never married, but my sister's children are like my own. And these scum, these *mafiya* bastards have taken my little Karina and done unspeakable things to her." The big Russian's look hardened. "And for this, they will pay, of that I assure you. But first, we must save Karina and the others. So before you say no or take the easy road of referring the matter to your superiors, I ask you to think of your OWN family and what you would do if one of them was in the clutches of these monsters. So the decision is yours Joe Mason, and I have nothing to give you but my gratitude, but I swear to you that if you do this thing, you will be my *tovarishch*—my comrade—for life."

***

Dugan watched the exchange, clueless as to the meaning of the words, though he sensed it was an appeal. Ilya leaned forward as he spoke, his intensity obvious, and when he finished, he leaned back in the booth as if the speech exhausted him. Dugan watched Mason. The silence grew.

"Okay," Mason said at last.

"Okay, what?" asked Dugan.

"Okay, I'll take you maniacs up, though I'm about ninety-nine percent sure I'm going to end up with my ass in a crack."

"*Spasibo,*" Ilya said.

"*Vsegda pozhaluysta,*" Mason replied. You're welcome.

"Great," Dugan said. "Let's get going."

"Not so fast. I'm STILL not taking you up tonight. There are way too many variables to attempt a landing or insertion on a hostile ship in the dark without recon. They could have wires strung up to foul us, or if we go in with NV, they could switch on all their lights at the last minute and blind us, and there are about a dozen other reasons a night approach is a bad idea. And apart from Ilya here, I'm guessing none of you have any experience fast-roping out of a chopper, so I may have to land, or at least hover, on top of the containers."

Ilya was nodding. "Joe is right, *Dyed*. I am eager to get to ship too, but these things he says are true."

"Besides," Mason added, "we need to figure out where the hell the ship is first. Do you have her Automatic Identification System number?"

"I do," Dugan said. "It's on my laptop in my bag in the car."

"I'll go get it," Nigel said, obviously eager to make a contribution.

Mason nodded and fished his car keys out of his pocket as Nigel stood up. Mason handed the keys to Nigel, and he hurried for the door.

"Any chance the bad guys have disabled their AIS?" Mason asked.

"I doubt it," Dugan replied. "She'll still show up on the Vessel Tracking System as an 'unknown' when she gets close enough to shore, and disabling the AIS would just be calling attention to herself."

Mason nodded, and they lapsed into silence until Nigel returned moments later and passed the laptop across the table to Dugan.

"This place got Wi-Fi?" asked Dugan as he booted the computer.

Mason shrugged. "Probably. Just about every place has nowadays."

The computer whirred to life and went through the boot routine, and Dugan heaved a little sigh of relief as he saw the icon at the bottom of the screen indicating a wireless connection was available. He connected to the internet and logged on to the subscription tracking service, where he'd already entered the *Kapitan Godina*'s AIS number.

"Right there," he said and centered the cursor over the icon for the *Kapitan Godina* before sliding the open laptop over in front of Mason.

Mason shook his head. "She's about a hundred miles beyond our maximum range anyway, so we have to wait until she gets closer." He studied the screen a moment. "Are these course and speed numbers accurate."

Dugan shrugged. "Mostly, I think. I believe they're projections calculated from the ship's previous positions over time, so I suspect they're always a bit behind. I'm not sure how often they refresh. What's her course and speed," he asked, leaning over to have a look himself.

"She's headed due west, right toward us. And this shows a speed of eighteen knots."

Mason looked at his watch. "It's almost eleven now. At her current speed, she'll be at the extreme edge of our range about daylight. If we leave at six or so, that should be about right."

"Why not earlier?" Dugan said. "Let's hit her at first light."

"Because I'm assuming that you'd like us to have enough fuel to stay over her long enough to do some good. Unless you just want to get close and wave at her in the distance before we turn back. One way trips in multimillion dollar helicopters are not exactly career-enhancing events."

"Can we, I don't know, get another chopper with longer range... or something," Dugan offered, knowing it sounded somewhat lame as soon as he said it.

Mason shook his head. "Not at this point and not with me. We fly the MH-65C at HITRON, and that's what you've got. Understand, Dugan, we normally operate as one element of a team and in concert with one of the flight-deck-equipped cutters. In fact, USCGC *Legare* was supposed to be our launch platform and home base for this little 'training exercise,' but then no one knew you had a specific target in mind."

"Can't she head in the direction of our target?" Dugan asked.

"Sure, but not on MY say so, and not without a good reason. I suppose I can say that our British guests have requested a change to the planned area of operations. Her skipper will be pissed, but he'll probably comply. After all, this is all supposed to be a dog and pony show for you 'Brits' anyway."

Dugan nodded. "Good idea. Put it on us. Tell 'em we're pushy assholes that threatened to create all sorts of waves, and you were just trying to satisfy us."

Mason grinned. "Well, you are sort of a pushy asshole now that you mention it. And I hope you and Ilya here can perfect your British accents before you have to talk to anyone above me. Otherwise you'll have to let Havelock do all the talking."

"Don't worry. We appreciate what you're doing, and we'll back you 100%."

"Okay," Mason said. "I'll get on the horn to *Legare* with the change of plan, but understand it probably won't do any good anyway. I think she's a bit too far south to do us much good on this accelerated timetable."

Dugan sat in the chopper and struggled to conceal his impatience as he looked out over the tarmac, watching in the predawn light as helicopters and fixed-wing aircraft took shape around him. He glanced over at Ilya seated in the web seat across from him, the borrowed assault rifle across his lap and the coveralls Mason had provided stretched tight across the big Russian's massive chest and bulging biceps. The Coasties inventory of flight coveralls for visitors seemed to be very much based on a 'one size fits all policy,' and sitting beside Ilya, Nigel was swallowed in his, the slight Brit looking for all the world like a kid in his father's clothing—except for the grip of the Glock protruding from his pocket. Only Dugan's coveralls fit reasonably well, as he was apparently what the US Coast Guard considered average.

The other three Coasties in the crew displayed no overt curiosity about the strangely armed multinational trio of 'observers,' leading Dugan to surmise that Mason had briefed them on the somewhat extralegal nature of their mission. If they had any qualms, they hid them well, and each had shaken hands and seemed friendly enough when Mason made the introductions. After settling their visitors as far out of the way as possible, they'd methodically worked their way through the preflight checklists.

When the checks seemed complete and nothing happened, Dugan risked breaking the silence.

"Uh… what are we waiting for?" he asked into his mike.

Ahead of him, he saw Mason swivel a bit in his seat and tilt his head back toward him.

"AIS shows the target still at 225 miles out, a bit beyond the edge of our range."

"Yeah, but she's closing on us," Dugan said, "and it'll take us time to get to her, so by that time she'll be within range, right?"

"Negative. Looks like she's slowed down considerably. She may have increased speed again, but we can't tell exactly how much until the next time the satellite data refreshes. If we leave now, we might not be able to stay over her very long—or maybe at all. I figure we sit tight another half hour to be on the safe side."

Dugan thought about that a minute. "Why the hell would she slow down that far from shore? You think maybe she's meeting another vessel? Christ, if that happens we could lose the girls completely."

"I hadn't thought of that," Mason said. "I guess we better get into the air." And with that he called the control tower and requested immediate clearance.

Ten minutes later, Dugan looked down through the open door as Jacksonville flashed by below them.

CHAPTER TWENTY-FIVE

KAPITAN GODINA
DUE EAST OF JACKSONVILLE, FLORIDA

The chief engineer grunted as he helped the first engineer drag the heavy rubber bladder up the deck. The damn things were cumbersome, even uninflated, and he didn't look forward to wrestling two of them into the small gap between the 'special container' and the one below it. As the two engineers approached, they saw the chief mate in the early morning light, directing sailors releasing the twist locks at each corner of the container. Soon only the weight of the container itself held it in place.

The sky was clear and the sea calm, with only a slight following wind that matched the speed of the ship, with the result that there seemed to be no wind at all over the deck. The chief engineer wondered again how in hell the Old Man was going to convince anyone they'd encountered heavy weather, and was glad it wasn't his problem.

As they neared the container, the chief engineer wrinkled his nose in disgust.

"Christ! What's that smell? It's like a mixture of rotten meat and shit."

The chief mate shrugged. "I don't know, but I think it's coming from this container. Some of the guys mentioned it a few days ago, but with the wind, it was only an occasional whiff, and we couldn't tell for sure where it was coming from."

"What do you think it is?" the chief engineer asked, his unease obvious.

"None of your business or mine," the chief mate growled. "Now let's get this fucking thing over the side, and we won't have to worry about it."

He turned from the engineers and barked orders to the sailors, who grabbed some loose staging planks and set about rigging a scaffold on each end of the short container stack.

***

"She's gone, Cassie," Karina said as she reached down into Cassie's lap and closed Tanya's sightless eyes. "We did all we could, but she's gone."

Cassie said nothing, but in the dim morning light leaking through the holes in the container, Karina saw her shake her head in wordless denial as she reached down and hugged Tanya's lifeless body.

"Sh…she can't be dead. It was only a tiny cut."

"But it got infected," Karina said as she eased Tanya's head off Cassie's lap and pulled Cassie to her in a comforting embrace. "We did all we could, but she's gone," Karina said again, and this time she felt Cassie nod against her chest, and she stroked the girl's hair and pulled her closer.

They both jumped as something struck the outside of the container with a metallic clang, and then they heard more thumps and muted voices. They had heard an occasional voice before, but always at a distance—and though they couldn't quite make out what was being said, these voices seemed to be right outside the container.

"Wh-what should we do?" Cassie asked.

"I'm not sure. Nothing for the moment, I think," Karina said. "Let's see what happens."

***

The two engineers connected the air hose to the second bladder and climbed down from the scaffold at the aft end of the container. The chief engineer surveyed their work and nodded to the chief mate.

"Both bladders are positioned and the air hoses are connected. Tell the Old Man we're ready," the chief engineer said. The chief mate, nodded and relayed the news to the bridge via his walkie-talkie.

"Go," came the captain's voice over the radio, and the chief engineer nodded to the first engineer to open the air valve.

Air hissed through the hoses, and the group watched as the bladders swelled, slowly at first, then faster. The container shuddered, and the inboard edge began to rise, lifted by the bladders and tilting the steel box toward the side of the ship—and the ocean beyond.

Then they heard muted thumps and the sound of movement inside the container, and the sailors looked at each other as the edge of the box continued to rise.

"What the hell is that?" the chief engineer asked.

"Nothing. Just something shifting in the box. Keep going," said the chief mate, just as an unmistakable human cry sounded above the air hissing through the hose.

"Help us! Please!"

The first engineer closed the air valve without asking permission.

"There's someone in there!" he said, and the chief mate raised the walkie-talkie.

"Captain," he said, "I think you should join us on deck."

***

The captain stood looking up at the tilted container, then shifted his gaze to the men grouped around him. He did his best to ignore the stench, and thankfully, the muted cries from within the container had stopped, its occupant or occupants apparently mollified by the fact the container was no longer moving. But those were minor concerns at the moment, as he studied the uneasy faces of his officers.

"What should we do?" the chief mate asked.

"What the hell do you mean, 'what should we do?' There's someone in there. A woman by the sound of it, maybe more than one. We must let them out," the first engineer said.

"How many voices did you hear?" the captain asked.

No one spoke at first. "Only one that I could tell," the chief engineer said at last.

The Captain nodded, as if considering that, and the silence grew.

"What does it matter if there is one or ten or a hundred?" the first engineer said. "We must help them, no matter how many there are."

"To what end?" the captain asked. "All of us have families. Even you, Ivan," he said, looking at the first engineer. "You are young and do not have a wife and kids, but what of your parents and grandparents? What if we save whoever is in the container? What do you think will become of us and our families? Do you have any doubt that we would pay dearly? It is a case of a life, or maybe a few lives, against many, and the many lives in question are those of our loved ones."

"We can go to the authorities when we dock in Jacksonville."

"And tell them what, exactly? Here are some people we rescued from a container? We think the Russian mob put them there, and oh, by the way, we know that because we are smugglers for the Russian *mafiya*, but never mind because we are all really good fellows. And, because we are all really good fellows, perhaps you could protect our families, who are thousands of miles away in Russia and Ukraine. Oh, I almost forgot to tell you, please do not notify the Russian authorities because they have ties to the *mafiya* and will most assuredly inform the mob and then look the other way while the bastards murder our families." The captain paused. "Is that what you would like us to do, Ivan?"

The first engineer shook his head. "If it were your wife or daughter in that fucking box, you would feel differently."

"Sadly, Ivan," the captain said, "if we don't finish this terrible business, it likely will be my wife and daughter in a box like that, perhaps with the rest of our loved ones with them, while we all rot in unmarked graves."

The captain turned to the chief engineer. "Finish the job. How long before you get it over the side."

The chief engineer swallowed. "I can get it a bit higher, but I don't think I can tip it with one inflation. We'll have to shore it up and reposition the bladders for another lift. Maybe another thirty minutes."

The captain nodded. "Get busy. The more quickly this is finished, the better for everyone."

"Okay," the chief engineer said, and as the captain walked back toward the deck house, he turned to the first engineer.

"Turn the air back on, Ivan," the chief engineer said.

"Fuck you. Do it yourself," the first engineer said, and stomped off after the captain.

USCG MH-65C HELICOPTER
75 MILES DUE WEST OF KAPITAN GODINA

"We've got a problem," said Mason's voice in Dugan's headphones. "I just got an update from the VTS guys ashore. We'll be over the target in less than thirty minutes, but she's still at the very edge of our range."

"Why is that a problem? We can reach her, right?"

"Yeah, just in time to maybe circle her twice and head for the barn."

Dugan was quiet a moment. "Okay, what's your plan?"

"What's MY plan? Christ, Dugan, I'm the taxi driver here! I don't HAVE a plan. I agreed to HELP, but none of this is by the book."

"How about the cutter, is she close enough for you to hang around a bit and still make it back to her?"

"Negative. When we reach the target we'll be about equidistant from both Cecil Field and the *Legare*, and both will be on the hairy edge of our range. She's closing on us, and another hour might make a difference, but we don't have an hour."

"But you CAN get us aboard?"

"Probably, one way or another," Mason said. "But that's what I'm trying to tell you. We normally stop the bad guys, then circle and wait for the fast-pursuit boat. But I can't do that, and I can't just set down on a potentially hostile vessel. That violates so many rules I couldn't even list them all. I assumed I was going to drop you aboard and hover to support you and intimidate the bad guys, but if I drop you at this range, I'll have to haul ass. And I'm sure as hell not leaving any of my guys in that situation. You'll be totally on your own for at least three hours."

Dugan glanced over at Ilya and Nigel, both of whom had been listening on their headphones. Both nodded.

"Let's do it," Dugan said.

USCG MH-65C Helicopter
In sight of *Kapitan Godina*

"Got her," Mason said, and Dugan craned his neck to peer forward through the windshield at a ship in the far distance.

"I'm going to circle wide and high and slow, so as not to alarm them. We'll look them over from a distance as we pass, and then I'll fall in behind them and overtake her fast from dead astern. I'll flare and drop straight down in front of the bridge onto the top of the container stack. Everyone copy?"

Through the headset, Dugan listened as each crewman confirmed their understanding and Mason continued.

"Landry," he said to the gunner, "I want you in the open door facing the bridge windows with the M240. Don't fire, but try to look threatening as hell. Sinclair," he said to the fourth crewman, "I want you at the other open door, ready to help our guests disembark. I'll have the skids within a foot of the containers, so they won't have to fast rope. Just get 'em out the door so we can get out of here. Got it?"

Again the crew acknowledged the orders.

"Dugan," Mason said, "Landry and his machine gun will probably be all the intimidation you need, but we can't hang around long. You guys have to bail out, go around the chopper and haul ass for the bridge. From what I see from here there's some sort of platform running across the front of the bridge you can climb up on from the top of the container stack. As soon as you reach the bridge, you're on your own. Got it?"

"Affirmative. Anything else?"

"Yeah," Mason said. "Make sure you keep your heads down and circle around in front of the bird so I can be sure none of you run into the tail rotor."

"Thanks for the tip."

"Think nothing of it," Mason said. "It's hard to take off with a fucked-up tail rotor. You guys go ahead and move over by the door. This is going to happen fast."

Dugan and his companions complied, crouching near the door as the chopper veered starboard as it approached the ship, passing down the vessel's port side at a distance.

"There looks like there's some activity over on the starboard side near the bow," Dugan said, "but I can't make out what it is."

"We'll probably get a better look from astern," Mason said. "I'll drift out a bit to starboard and give you a look through the side door before I start to close."

Dugan said nothing as the chopper completed its run and circled to steady up on the same heading as the *Kapitan Godina*. He waited impatiently, unable to see anything from his position until Mason changed the orientation of the chopper to give Dugan a view through the side door.

"What the hell are they doing?" Dugan asked aloud, as he saw a container on the short stack near the starboard bow tilted at a crazy angle. Then as he watched, the container began to move almost in slow motion as it tipped over the side and tumbled into the water with a great splash.

"Mason! They must be onto us, and they're dumping the girls. Forget the ship and get us over that container. Now!" Dugan screamed.

Seconds later the chopper hovered over the floating container, the downdraft from the rotor sending ripples across the water in all directions as Dugan and the others peered down at it through the open door.

"How long will it float?" Mason asked in Dugan's ear.

"How the hell should I know? A while at least, assuming the door seals are tight. But I'm not worried about that as much as what shape the girls are in. That wasn't any gentle drop, more like a car crash. If they're alive in there, they're probably injured. How long before that cutter can get here?"

"Five or six hours at least. I'll get on the horn and…"

"I think it's sinking!" Nigel said, and Dugan saw he was right. The container was sitting deeper in the water than it was when they arrived moments before.

"Shit! The bastards must have drilled—"

Nigel was out the open door and falling feet first toward the water twenty feet below, and before Dugan could stop him, Ilya stripped off his own headset and was out the door after Nigel.

Dugan watched helplessly as his friends swam toward the container, knowing there was no way they could open it in its present condition.

"Do you have any duct tape?" he asked into the mike.

"What the hell are…" Mason began and then stopped himself. "Actually we may have something better. Landry, you got any of that 100-mile-an-hour tape around?"

"Never leave home without it," replied the gunner, as he dug around in a bag at his feet and emerged with a roll of what looked like black duct tape. "This is the best shit I ever used. It'll stick to anything, wet, dry, oily—"

Dugan snatched the tape and slipped his hand through the roll, pushing it tight on his left wrist like a bracelet. Without another word, he ripped off his headset and jumped out of the chopper feet first.

CHAPTER TWENTY-SIX

Dugan splashed into the water beside the container and surfaced to find Nigel and Ilya clinging to the front of the steel box. His first sensation wasn't visual but olfactory—a putrid stench that seemed to engulf him. A fine mist of water whipped up by the chopper's rotor wash obscured his vision, and he wiped his eyes to clear them. Nigel was hammering the door of the container with his closed fist, and Dugan could just make out his shouted words over the roar of the chopper.

"Cassie! We're here! Hang on, we're going to get you out."

Dugan swam the few strokes to the container, and Ilya turned as he swam up. The look on the Russian's face belied the promise of Nigel's shout. The twenty-foot container was floating at a crazy angle, cocked with one long edge submerged perhaps two or three feet deep and the opposite bottom edge just under the surface of the water—Ilya pointed to the bottom of the doors.

"The bottom of both halves of the door are below water, *Dyed*," Ilya screamed to be heard over the chopper. "If we open them, water will pour in and fill box in seconds. We will have no chance to get them out."

Dugan nodded. "We have to stop the water going in now, and then figure out how to deal with the doors."

Without waiting for an acknowledgment, Dugan swam around to the high side of the container. The bottom edge was just below the water line, and he started at the near corner and found what he was looking for immediately—water was pouring through a two-inch hole drilled in the side wall just above the bottom of the container. Ilya and Nigel splashed up on either side of him.

"What are you doing?" Ilya shouted.

"Looking for the holes," Dugan shouted back. "If we can find them and plug them, we can keep the box afloat long enough to figure out how to get the girls out. You and Nigel go along this edge and see how many more there are while I try to plug this one. Whatever we find along this edge will probably be duplicated along the deeper side, but if we can plug these first we'll have an idea of what we're dealing with. Hurry!"

As the pair nodded and started to pull themselves down the length of the container, Dugan steadied himself on the container with his left hand, positioning the roll of tape around his left forearm directly in front of him. He picked at the edge of the tape with the fingers of his right hand, fumbling as he tried to tease the edge of the tape up, and hoping this stuff would stick as well to other things as it did to itself. He finally got it started and pulled off a foot-long strip before reaching down and taking the edge of the tape in his teeth so he could tear it with his free hand. As he finished, his companions were back beside him, Nigel in the lead.

"Two more holes," Nigel shouted, "one about halfway down and the other at the far corner."

Dugan nodded and turned back to his hole. He had no illusions he'd get a complete seal, but he hoped he could slap enough of the heavy tape across the hole to slow down the water and buy a little time. IF Landry's magic 'stick to anything tape' worked as advertised. It didn't. Apparently he'd never tried it under salt water.

"It's not working," Nigel said, panic in his voice. "Ball it up and try to make a plug."

"Worth a shot," Dugan agreed, wadding the tape. It still stuck to itself, at least. He studied the tiny ball and shook his head.

"Nice theory, but it will take a helluva lot more tape than we have to make six plugs," Dugan said. Then it hit him.

"Quick. Take off your socks and give me one," Dugan shouted.

"But what—"

"Just lose your shoes and give me a fucking sock! No time to explain!"

Nigel ducked his head under the water, and Dugan started to pull a strip of tape off the roll. Nigel surfaced a moment later, socks in hand.

"Okay," Dugan shouted. "Roll one of them into a ball, tight as you can get it, then hand it over."

Nigel nodded, holding the sodden sock up to let the water drain from it as he rolled it tight.

"That's good," Dugan said. "Now hold it tight while I wrap it."

Seconds later Dugan had a black ball, perhaps three inches in diameter, pliable but not overly so.

"Cross your fingers, junior." Dugan took the ball from Nigel and began to compress it and twist it into the hole. It worked.

"Brilliant," Nigel said, as he began to roll his second sock.

"*Dyed*, I think water is coming in lower holes faster, *da*? If you and Nigel make plugs, I will dive down and plug bottom holes first."

"Good point." Dugan pulled the first plug from the hole and passed it to Ilya. "Start with this one. We'll have another one ready by the time you get back."

USCG MH-65C HELICOPTER

"How much time?" Mason asked.

"None," his co-pilot replied. "We should have started back five minutes ago. Even now it'll be close, and the winds are shifting. Any sort of head wind at all, and we're getting our feet wet."

The 'and losing a twenty-million-dollar helicopter' went unspoken.

"Well, I can't just fucking leave them bobbing around a sinking container in the mid-ocean."

"Drop them the raft and locater beacon," the co-pilot suggested. "In this weather, *Legare* can be here in twelve hours at flank speed. For that matter, we can probably make it to her, refuel, and be back in three."

"And what if they get the girls out of the container? They're bound to need medical attention, and Sinclair has EMT training. Three hours could make a big difference."

"So could going in to the drink because we don't have enough fuel," the co-pilot said.

"Shit!" Mason said and shook his head. "Okay. Landry, you and Sinclair deploy the raft."

"What about the ship?" the co-pilot asked.

"What about her?" Mason replied. "She'll either continue for Jacksonville or she won't, but even at top speed, she's not getting away from us, not this close to home. We can have *Legare* send a boarding team or vector another chopper in on her anytime we want."

ATLANTIC OCEAN
EAST OF JACKSONVILLE, FLORIDA

Ilya pulled himself into the inflatable raft and then helped Nigel and Dugan in after him, as the thump of the chopper's blades faded to the west. Dugan spared a quick glance at the receding speck in the western sky and turned back to the container. He could hardly fault Mason, and right now he had other priorities. He grabbed a paddle and shot a quick glance at the reference marks he'd scratched on the side of the container with his pocket knife. They were still right at the waterline.

"She's tight, for now at least," Dugan said as he propelled the raft around to the door end of the container. "Now let's see what we can do about those doors."

"Is still no good, *Dyed*," Ilya said. "If we break door seal, the container will sink like stone."

"Maybe not. From the force of the water flowing into the holes, I don't think the water inside had equalized with the outside water level yet. That means the water level inside the box is below the outside waterline. If we can tilt it down on the far end, even a little, the water inside should run to that end, causing it to sink and lifting the door end a bit. Maybe."

"But how?" Ilya asked, but Nigel was already nodding and studying the end of the container.

"We'll have to climb up this end," Nigel said, "using the door locking bars as hand and footholds. But if we put more weight on this end, it might have the opposite effect."

"Which is why you'll go first," Dugan said, "since you're the lightest. Work your way down to the far end and then shout out. I'll go next, and when I get down there, our combined weight should more than compensate for Ilya."

Nigel nodded again and reached up for a hand hold, but Dugan put a hand on his arm.

"I don't have a clue how much weight it will take to shift this thing or how quickly it will happen, so get your ass to the far end as fast as you can. Got it?"

Nigel nodded and swallowed hard before grabbing one of the locking bars to steady himself and then standing up in the raft. He reached as high as he could for another handhold and then placed his foot on one of the tilted locking bars and launched himself up. The free-floating container rocked slightly under his weight as he struggled upward, and his foot began to slip down the bar. Ilya shot his hand out, grasping the bar just below Nigel's foot, forming a step with his wrist and forearm. Steadied, Nigel got a fresh grip and pulled himself up onto the top of the rocking container and disappeared.

"I'm here," he shouted a moment later from the far end of the container.

Dugan tied the raft off to one of the locking bars and looked up. He was thirty years older—and considerably less nimble—than the young Brit.

"*Dyed*, I have idea," Ilya said, rising to his knees and facing the end of the container. He reached up and grabbed a locking bar as far up as he could, then turned his head and spoke over his shoulder. "Use me like ladder, *da*? First my shoulder, then my wrist on bar. Will get you high enough very quickly, I think. And part of your weight will be on me in raft."

"Good idea, but try to keep all your weight on your knees. The way that thing rocked with Nigel's weight, it's tender as hell."

"*Da*. Now go."

Dugan put his hand on the side of the container to steady himself and stood in one swift motion, putting a foot on Ilya's shoulder and reaching as high as he could for a handhold. He heard the big Russian grunt as he pulled himself up and put his other foot on Ilya's wrist. In seconds, he was on the upraised top edge of the container, as if he were straddling the top ridge of a roof. He placed his hands and knees on either side of the raised corner and quickly worked his way down to Nigel. The container rocked even more violently from the shifting weight of his transit.

"I'm here, Ilya. Go," Dugan shouted.

Ilya was over the end of the container in a flash, moving toward them standing up in a strange crablike run, his bare feet splayed on either side of the upraised corner of the container. Dugan marveled at his ability to maintain his balance as Ilya settled down beside him.

The container rocked a bit more, then slowly subsided. For a long moment, nothing happened.

"Is not working," Ilya said.

"Give it a second." Dugan hid his fear the Russian was right. Then, almost imperceptibly, the high side of the container began to fall as the container turned on its axis, and just as gradually, their end of the container began to sink lower. Then it happened in a rush, the movement increasingly rapid as the water inside the box rushed to the lower end, driving it even lower, and the opposite end of the box began to elevate. In moments the box had reached a new equilibrium, and Dugan looked down the side of the box, toward the door end.

"Is it up, Mr. Dugan? Is it out of the water?" Nigel asked.

"It's close, but I can't tell for sure. Nigel, you're the lightest. Ilya and I will stay here to keep our weight in the equation. You swim around to the door end and have a look."

Nigel dove overboard before Dugan even finished his sentence. The container rocked violently from his sudden departure, causing his companions to clutch at the steel beneath them to maintain their balance. Nigel stroked furiously for the door end of the container and Dugan heard him splashing as he dragged himself up into the raft.

"What do you see, Nigel?"

"We did it! We bloody well did it," Nigel screamed. "It's only by an inch or so when the container isn't rocking, but the bottoms of the doors are above the water."

Dugan's mind raced. An inch wasn't much. If either he or Ilya left this end of the container, the door end might very well drop back below the waterline, and even a quarter inch would be deadly.

"Okay, Nigel. Ilya and I have to stay back here, so this is all on you. Do you think you can get both of the doors open so we can see what the situation is? We'll play it by ear from there."

"I'm on it," Nigel shouted, and Dugan whispered a prayer beneath his breath. *Please Lord, let them be alive.*

ATLANTIC OCEAN
EAST OF JACKSONVILLE, FLORIDA

Nigel untied the raft from the container so he could maneuver around the doors. He rotated the dogs on the four locking bars, disengaging them one by one, breaking the seal around the doors. The stench intensified, and he suppressed consideration of what that might portend.

The steel doors were heavy, tilted as they were, with gravity holding them closed. Nigel struggled to get a purchase, floating in the raft, but dare not climb on the container lest he tip the opening below the water level. Finally, through force of will and adrenaline-fueled strength, he succeeded in lifting the left door open ninety degrees. From that point gravity took over, pulling the door from his grasp as it fell open on its hinges with a crash, once again rocking the container violently.

***

Dugan and Ilya perched precariously on the far end of the container, and the stench wafted over them when Nigel broke the seal on the container door. Ilya turned to Dugan, his eyes wet.

"I know this smell, *Dyed*. Before I was not so sure, and I wanted to be wrong. But I have smelled it many times. Too often. It is death. We are too late, I think."

Dugan nodded, a lump in his throat, but as he reached over to lay a comforting hand on Ilya's shoulder, the box rocked violently. He tried to steady himself against the unexpected movement, but he lost his balance and went over backward. Ilya moved quickly, clutching at Dugan's leg as he went over, but the Russian was off balance himself, and both men tumbled into the water.

***

Nigel watched in horror as the now open end of the container sank toward the raft and water poured over the door sill into the dark maw of the container. Inside in the roiling water, he saw a flash of white flesh and glimpsed an arm, and acted instinctively, diving through the open door without thought or hesitation, a scant second before the box slid beneath the surface. He swam blindly through the filthy water inside the container, groping down the hard steel walls, and through a clutter of what felt like buckets or pails rising around him. And then flesh, a wrist. Let it be Cassie!

He was disoriented now, clueless as to up or down, his lungs near bursting. He followed the wall, ever faster as his lungs screamed for air, kicking and pulling himself along the corrugated steel with one hand, the other clamped tight around the wrist. He reached for another handhold and pulled with all his might, propelling himself upward in a rush—and smashed head first into unyielding steel—the still-closed right half of the container double door.

Stunned, he instinctively released the wrist to use both hands to claw his way around the unexpected obstacle. Then he was out of the container and sunlight filtering down from the surface far above showed the container plunging downward, already far below him. Cassie! He dove and was kicking for the container when he felt rather than saw a presence beside him, and then felt a jolt to the side of his head and… blackness.

∗∗∗

Nigel blinked, then opened his eyes. His head ached, and orange filled his vision. The raft. He was on the raft. He tried to lift his head and was unable to suppress a moan as he felt a stabbing pain on the side of his face.

"Easy," said Dugan's voice. "You took a pretty good hit."

Nigel stayed down but rolled toward Dugan's voice to find both his companions staring at him with concern in their eyes.

"Wh…what happened?"

"I am sorry, Nigel," Ilya said, "but I had to knock you unconscious. Even for strong swimmer is not possible to bring struggling man to surface from many meters below, and I knew you would fight me."

"Cassie!" Nigel said, sitting up this time, despite the pain.

"Gone," Dugan said. "I'm sure they were gone long before we opened the container. I suspect that's why the bastards dumped them. They were getting rid of the evidence."

"But I saw… I had someone," Nigel said.

"Alive?" Dugan asked gently.

"I… I don't know. I couldn't see. But they were very cold."

Nigel lay there, tears running down his cheeks, and nothing broke the silence for a long while. Finally Ilya spoke quietly to Dugan.

"*Dyed*, when we get ashore, we should have Nigel checked by doctor. I think the water in the container was very contaminated, and for sure he took some in."

Nigel overheard and responded. "What does it bloody matter?"

CHAPTER TWENTY-SEVEN

KAPITAN GODINA
DUE EAST OF JACKSONVILLE, FLORIDA

The captain peered far astern through the binoculars, tensing as he watched the orange helicopter leave the jettisoned container and fly straight toward his ship. It overtook the ship rapidly, passing just above bridge level on the starboard side, the door gunner tracking the ship with his machine gun, his clearly visible face a mix of anger and eagerness. The captain heaved a relieved sigh when the chopper continued westward without firing.

"They're leaving," the chief mate said, his relief obvious.

"They will be back. Or someone will, in any event," the captain said, turning to the chief mate. "Mr. Luchenko, you have the bridge. Notify me at once if we are approached by any aircraft or ships."

"Yes, Captain."

"Chief," the captain said to the chief engineer who had also been on the bridge watching the chopper, "let's go down to my office and get this over with, shall we."

The chief engineer nodded and followed the captain into the central stairwell and down to his office on the deck below. The captain motioned the chief to his sofa as he moved to his desk and picked up the sat phone. He dialed a number from memory.

"Is it done?" asked a voice on the other end.

"*Da.* The container is over the side and was sinking as we sailed away."

"Any problems?"

"*Nyet,*" the captain said.

"Good," said the voice and hung up without another word.

The captain hung up the phone and pursed his lips to blow out a relieved sigh.

"What will he do if he finds out you were lying?" the chief asked.

The captain shrugged. "If I told him the truth, he would likely harm my family because I failed, even though I tried. So what can he do, kill my family twice? This way at least, we have a little time. Anyway, we did what he said. If it comes to that, we merely say that the helicopter was unseen in the distance and apparently saw us dump the container, and that we were not aware of that until later, when they boarded us to investigate. After all, I did warn him we were too close to the coast to jettison the container."

"So you think the authorities will come?"

"Most assuredly, either at sea or when we reach Jacksonville. And we will be arrested, or at least I will, if everything goes well."

"You WANT to be arrested? Why?"

"Because I am much more afraid of these *mafiya* bastards than anything the US authorities can do to me, and being arrested will demonstrate to the *mafiya* that I followed instructions to the letter. And what can the Americans charge me with, exactly? They saw a container go over the side, and it sank, so they have no physical evidence. And it was in international waters, and we are a foreign flag ship, so I actually don't think we have broken any US laws. They can SUSPECT that there is some sort of insurance fraud going on, but unless the company files a claim, there is no fraud. They can suspect we are smugglers, but what are they going to use for evidence?"

"I hadn't thought of that," the chief admitted.

"Furthermore, I am sure that the *mafiya* has clever and expensive American lawyers, and they will want to make sure this goes away. So I doubt I will be spending much time in jail."

"Aren't you forgetting something?" the chief asked. "What about our other problem?"

"I'm forgetting nothing," the captain said. "We did what we had to do, and may God help us if we were wrong."

ATLANTIC OCEAN
EAST OF JACKSONVILLE, FLORIDA

Dugan sat in the raft with Ilya, his eyes half-closed against the mist of salt water being whipped up by the chopper's propeller wash as he watched Nigel being winched aboard the chopper. Moments later the empty harness came back down, and Dugan grabbed it and offered it to Ilya, who shook his head and indicated Dugan should go first. Dugan shrugged and slipped into the harness, then looked up and motioned for the chopper crew to take him up.

Five minutes later, he was strapped into a web seat beside a dejected Nigel, and he watched the two chopper crewman haul Ilya through the door. Ilya took a seat across from Dugan and put on the headset before he even strapped himself in.

"Where is ship?" Ilya demanded.

"About fifty or sixty miles due west," Dugan heard Mason reply in his headphones. "We passed her on the way here. She's evidently continuing to Jacksonville as if nothing happened."

"Good," Ilya said. "Take me to ship."

Dugan felt Nigel stir in the seat beside him, and a glance at his face showed his approval of the Russian's demand.

There was nothing but silence from the headsets.

"I said take me to ship. Now," Ilya said. "These bastards killed Karina and the others, and they must pay."

"I'm sorry, Ilya, but that's not happening. We've already dispatched another chopper with a boarding party. They should be getting aboard any time. They'll take it from here."

The Glock came out of Ilya's pocket and he half-turned to level it at Mason over his shoulder. Dugan saw the other crewmen tense, unsure what to do at the unexpected development.

"I am sorry, Joe Mason. But you must take me to ship. I do not want to kill you, but I will wound you, then co-pilot can take us to ship."

"So. Is this the way you treat a '*tovarishch* for life'?"

"No… I mean…" Ilya's momentary indecision faded, and his voice hardened. "I must avenge Karina. You are Russian. You understand this."

"I understand I agreed to risk my career and my life and these men's lives to SAVE the lives of your Karina and the others, not for your revenge. And you know that's true. If you are a man of honor, you will respect that agreement. And besides, the boarding party will reach the ship long before we do. What do you plan to do, leap aboard and single-handedly fight your way through a heavily armed and well-trained team in order to kill their prisoners? You know that as soon as you leave the chopper, we'll warn them you're coming. We must—unless, of course, you plan to kill us all first. Is that your plan, *tovarishch*?"

Dugan sat silently and watched the emotions play across Ilya's face—anger warred with resolve, and then uncertainty, and finally, anguish and defeat. The big Russian seemed almost to deflate, and he flung the Glock out of the open door of the chopper and buried his face in his hands.

"*Yob tvoyu mat', lokhi*," he said, between clenched teeth. "As God is my witness, someday I will kill them all."

"STOP!" said Mason into the headphones as Landry and Sinclair moved to restrain Ilya. "Leave him alone," Mason said more quietly. "Just leave him alone. He'll be okay."

Dugan looked at Ilya and Nigel slumped in their seats. Would any of them ever really be okay again? His thoughts turned to Cassie, and he tried to swallow the lump in his throat—and wondered what he would say to Alex and Gillian.

CHAPTER TWENTY-EIGHT

Anna sat on the side of the bed, fully clothed, and glared at Dugan.

"I'm perfectly capable of walking," she said. "I DO NOT need a wheelchair."

"Hey, don't get mad at me. I'm just telling you what they told me. Hospital rules. All released patients get a wheelchair ride to the exit. No wheelchair, no release."

"Well, in that case they should be a bit more efficient. I've been ready to go for an hour."

As if on cue, an orderly rolled a wheelchair into the room. "Who's ready to go home?" he asked with a bright smile, and Dugan saw Anna bite back a sharp response.

"That would be me," she said, and despite her previous attestation of fitness, she grimaced a bit as she stood, holding the bed for balance as she turned to allow the orderly to wheel the chair up behind her. Dugan jumped up from his own seat and steadied her arm as she sat down in the chair. She still had a bit of healing to do.

The orderly looked at Dugan. "Your car?"

"I have a taxi standing by at the front entrance," Dugan said, and the man nodded and rolled the chair out into the corridor with Dugan at his side. A few minutes later, after an elevator ride, the orderly rolled Anna across the expansive main lobby and out to the waiting cab.

Dugan helped Anna settle into the back seat of the taxi, and then ran around and climbed into the other side. He leaned forward and gave the driver the address of their apartment and then sat back as the car began to move. Anna reached over and took his hand.

"How are they?" she asked.

Dugan looked over and shrugged. "They were a bit numb at first, like us all, I think. But it's started to sink in over the last few days. I don't know who's more devastated, Alex or Gillian. The house is like a tomb. Mrs. Hogan is looking after them, but she can't get either of them to eat. Alex has taken to sitting alone in his study, staring at the empty fireplace. She tells me he's hitting the brandy pretty hard, very much like when Kathleen died, except that this time, Gillian is equally distraught and dealing with demons of her own."

"And how about you?"

Dugan shrugged again. "I… I guess I'm all right. I just can't help but feel if I'd done things differently—if we'd somehow gotten there even an hour earlier—"

"Tom, you can't blame yourself. You did everything in your power to save them. You all did. I'm sure Alex and Gillian know that."

"Maybe, but when they look at me—when they look at any of us—I can't help but feel they blame us on some level, whether it's conscious or not."

"You know that's ridiculous. Alex and Gillian know how much you loved Cassie, and Ilya lost his own niece."

Dugan nodded. "On an intellectual level, I know you're right, but there's just something about it that makes it hard to be around them now. It's like we're not sharing our grief, but somehow when we're all together it's compounded. I can't explain it, but the others feel it too."

"And how ARE Nigel and Ilya?"

"Nigel's nearly a basket case. I know he's having nightmares because he cries out in his sleep. Ilya's like a ticking time bomb. He doesn't talk much, and when he does speak, it's in monosyllables. You can almost feel the hatred and rage, no small part of it directed at me."

"YOU? Whatever for?"

"He really wanted the guys on the ship that dumped the container—we all did—but the Coast Guard pilot wouldn't land us on the ship. And the pilot apparently sent word up the line about the volatility of the situation, because before we even landed back at Cecil Field, I got a call from Ward. He told me that if we even tried to get near the ship and crew that the deal he'd cut for Borgdanov's 'recruits' was off. I can see his point. I'm sure selling the idea was difficult enough without one of the potential new permanent residents shooting up a ship full of foreign nationals in the Port of Jacksonville before the program even gets off the ground."

"How did Ilya take that?"

"Badly, but what could he do? Borgdanov's incommunicado at the moment, recruiting people on the strength of Ward's assurances. Ilya would never do anything to compromise Andrei, no matter how enraged he gets. But he's chomping at the bit for word from Borgdanov summoning him to go to Russia. I pity the bastards when he gets there."

"How did you leave things with Ward?"

"Not good. We hung around a day trying to find out what was happening with the crew of the Kapitan Godina—nothing much as it turns out. I mean, I was willing to let the authorities handle it, but I thought SOMETHING would happen to them. Ward told me the captain lawyered up, and with a very pricey shyster at that, and that it's likely nothing will stick at all."

"I can see why Ilya is upset. How did he take THAT?"

Dugan shook his head. "He was upset enough; I didn't dare share that with him. Christ, if he finds out the truth, there's no telling what he might do. Anyway, Ward and I had words, not nice ones. Let's just say he's not on my Christmas card list anymore, at least for the moment."

"You and Jesse Ward have been friends for a long time."

"And we still are, I suppose. And we'll continue to work together on the deal he promised Borgdanov. But for the moment, or the next few days anyway, I don't want to get into it again with him. He's actually called a few times, but what is there to say? I let it go to voice mail."

"Did you listen to the messages?"

"Nope, and I don't intend to for a while."

Anna nodded. "You're upset, I get that. But perhaps the memorial service will give everyone a bit of closure. Have Alex and Gillian decided on a time?"

"No. It's like if they plan a memorial service they're giving up on Cassie. I know Mrs. Hogan has been gently pushing them in that direction, but without result. She's set up a visit with Father O'Malley first thing tomorrow morning and asked me to come. I don't look forward to it."

"Would you like me to come?"

Dugan shook his head. "No. The doctor released you on the condition that you take it slow. I think the deal was no more than an hour or so on the crutches at a time for the first week. I intend to hold you to that." He put his face close to hers and looked into her eyes. "I've lost enough people in my life, Anna, and I intend to take good care of you, whether you want me to or not."

ST. PETERSBURG
RUSSIAN FEDERATION

Vladimir Glazkov held the phone to his ear, shaking his head in silent exasperation. He sighed. There was no professionalism anymore it seemed, only a dwindling pool of spoiled and whining practitioners of a dying art. Sometimes he missed the old days.

"... and you know multiple hits are difficult. As soon as I hit one of the targets, I'll no doubt spook the others. They may go into hiding and delay completion of the job, and you were emphatic that you wanted this finished quickly."

"Obviously you hit them all at the same time and place," Glazkov said. "A bomb or car crash when they're all in the same car perhaps."

"What about collateral damage? Are additional casualties acceptable?"

Glazkov sighed again. "Well, obviously we don't want to slaughter a dozen innocent school children or random tourists in a public place. That would elevate it to the level of terrorism and make matters even worse in regard to raising our profile with the authorities. However, so long as casualties are confined to these Kairouz people, their American friend, and close associates, I think that would be acceptable. My experience is that the general public doesn't react too strongly to the killing of wealthy people; I think there's even a certain subliminal sense of satisfaction. In a few months, it will all be pushed from the headlines by another sensational news event of some kind, and we can go quietly about rebuilding our UK operations."

"Getting them all in the same place at the same time may prove difficult. I can't guarantee a time frame. But I have them all under surveillance now, and I'll probably be able to move soon."

"Are you monitoring their communications?" Glazkov asked.

"Not so far. I haven't been able—"

"So let me understand, Fedosov. Your plan is to follow them around until they just happen to get together in one place and then kill them?"

"No, of course not, but we only just began discussing hitting them at the same time—"

Glazkov erupted. "We only just began discussing it because it was such an obvious requirement that only a simpleton such as yourself would have failed to grasp it. Now monitor their communications, find out when they'll be together, and TAKE THEM OUT! Is that sufficiently clear, or must I email you a diagram?"

"No, Boss. I'll get on it at once."

"You'd better. And keep me informed."

He slammed the receiver into the cradle, rested his elbows on the desk, and put his face in his hands. He definitely missed the old days.

CHAPTER TWENTY-NINE

Kairouz Residence
London, UK

The back garden was awash in the light of a full moon, augmented by nearby streetlights, and Fedosov cursed the time table that forced him to take risks he would normally avoid. But then any risk, no matter how high, was preferable to the certain danger if he disappointed the Chief. He shuddered at the possibility and tried to concentrate on the task at hand.

He was well concealed in the shrubbery and had been since he'd arrived at two in the morning to find lights still burning throughout the stately home. An hour later, the lights began to wink out, indicating the residents were retiring—all except one—which was still burning now almost an hour later. He glanced toward the east—it would be getting light soon—and other than the single light, he'd no other indications that anyone was still awake in the house. Common sense told him to abort, but the memory of the last conversation with the Chief was a strong motivator. He crept close to the window of the room still showing a light, keeping his head well below the sill.

Fedosov rose slowly, not wanting sudden movement to draw the gaze of anyone inside, and as his eyes rose above the windowsill, he looked through the open blinds. The light was coming from a shaded desk lamp on an ornately carved wooden desk. No one sat at the desk, but slumped in an overstuffed leather chair in the corner he saw Kairouz, obviously unconscious. He wore a dressing gown, sagging open at the waist to reveal a hairy chest. His bare feet were on a footstool, slippers lying below them on the floor at odd angles, as if they'd fallen off. His head had fallen to one side, and his mouth was slack in sleep, a tendril of drool leaking out of one corner and down his unshaven chin. Beside him on a side table was an empty brandy snifter and a decanter with perhaps a half inch of amber liquid left in the bottom. Out like a light, no problem there. That left only the woman, and based on the timing of the lights being extinguished, she'd been asleep for over an hour.

He glided around the house to the back door into the kitchen, keeping in the shadows. He picked the lock without difficulty, entered the kitchen, and moved quickly to the security panel. The technician from the security company had been reluctant at first and, to his credit, unpersuaded by any amount of money offered. However, in the end, the graphic videos of what might happen to his family had convinced him, along with the promise that the information would only be used to relieve an obviously wealthy man of some of his possessions. By the time the technician figured out differently, he would already be implicated in the crime.

Fedosov covered the small speaker on the panel with his right hand to muffle the chirps, and tapped in the security code with his left, nodding as the lights on the panel flashed to 'unarmed.' He crept to the basement doorway off the kitchen and descended, lighting his way with a small headlamp rather than risking turning on a light. The utility closet was in a far corner of the basement, and in minutes he'd wired a voice-activated transmitting device into the phone circuit, rearranging the wiring to conceal it. There were still the Kairouzes' mobile phones, of course, but since they seemed to be staying close to home, he reckoned they might be using their landline for the majority of calls. He quickly checked his work. Satisfied, he crept back up the stairs.

It was a moment's work to conceal tiny listening devices throughout the ground floor in locations likely to yield interesting conversations. He considered planting some in the upstairs bedrooms, but he had no idea how soundly the woman was sleeping. No point in pressing his luck. Stopping in the doorway to the study, he spotted Kairouz's mobile phone lying in plain sight on the desk just beyond the sleeping man. As he stood trying to decide whether to go for the phone, Kairouz moaned in his sleep and began to wave his arms as if he were struggling with some unseen assailant. His arm flew out to the side, and Fedosov jumped out of sight to the side of the door a scant second before he heard the sound of the brandy snifter smashing on the hardwood floor. He stood deathly still, his heart pounding.

"Alex? Are you all right?" came the woman's voice from up the stairs, followed by the sounds of someone rising and then footsteps across the floor above. "Alex?" the woman said again.

Fedosov willed himself calm and faded quietly down the hall and around the corner into the living room as the woman's footsteps sounded on the stairs. He fingered the silenced pistol in his pocket and considered killing them both now. But no. The Chief wanted them all killed together and quickly. If he snuffed these two now, an alerted Dugan would be an exponentially more difficult target. He waited.

He heard shuffling and muttered curses from the direction of the study, and then a moment later the woman's voice from the direction of the study door.

"For God's sake, Alex, put your slippers on. There's glass all over the floor and—oh, sit back down, you've cut your foot."

"Fuck offf," came the slurred reply. "… i's my bloody foot, isn't it?"

Fedosov heard noises as if someone was stumbling into furniture, followed by more muttered curses and then a bitter mocking laugh.

"And it IS a bloody foot, isn't it?"

"Alex, SIT DOWN and let me look at it."

"Oh? Givin' bloody orders are we, dear? You're good at that, aren't you? Always has to be YOUR way, doesn't it? You and Thomas bloody Dugan and those fuckin' Russkis. I told you to leave it alone. I told you they were dangerous. But no, everyone knows better than old Alex, don't they? She drowned in a box like a fucking rat! And where was I? Tending the bloody home fires while our little girl died. And what did Thomas and those fucking Russkis do? Bloody fuck all!"

"Alex, you don't mean that," the woman said. "You know Tom did everything—"

"THE HELL HE DID," screamed Kairouz, and Fedosov heard the crash of what he assumed was the brandy decanter smashing against a wall. "THE HELL HE DID! IF HE'D DONE ALL HE COULD, CASSIE WOULD BE ALIVE!"

The outburst was followed by an unintelligible cry of anguish and then dissolved into the sounds of wracking sobs mixed with cooing sounds, as if the woman was comforting an infant.

"Come along, dear," the woman's voice said. "Let's sit you down here on the sofa and have a look at that foot." There was a pause. "It doesn't look too bad, and the bleeding's mostly stopped. Let's get you up to bed. I have some plasters in our bathroom."

Fedosov heard them making their way up the stairs, the man's steps halting and stumbling, and he imagined Kairouz leaning on the woman. The sounds moved to the bedroom above, and he waited a moment, considering the risks. He had to reset the security system when he left, and with the woman fully awake, she might hear the chirps. Then the decision was made for him. He heard the woman coming down the stairs.

She seemed to stop at the bottom, and he heard muffled sobs. Slowly he peeked around the door, and in the light leaking into the hallway from the open door of the study, he saw the woman sitting on the bottom step, her face buried in her hands and her shoulders shaking.

He began to panic. It was close to sunrise, and the stupid bitch was between him and his planned exit point, and she had a clear view of the front door as well. If she sat there and bawled until daylight, he may have to take her out anyway, regardless of what the Chief preferred. She began to wipe her eyes with the back of her hand, and Fedosov ducked back into the living room.

Panic rose again as he heard her coming down the hall in his direction, and he put his hand on his gun. Then she stopped, and he heard her lift the receiver of the hall telephone.

"Tom," the woman said, "I'm sorry to wake you at this hour—"

"Oh, you weren't? Well, I guess none of us are sleeping too well these days," she said, then responded to another unheard question.

"Me? Oh, I'm fine, or as well as can be expected, I suppose, given the circumstances. It's Alex I'm concerned about. I'm going to cancel the meeting with Father O'Malley this morning, and I didn't want you to come over for nothing."

"I appreciate that Tom, but I really think it's better if you don't come over just now. Alex is in no state to see anyone, much less discuss the memorial service. I'm just going to tell Father O'Malley to schedule it for the day after tomorrow—well, I guess that's actually tomorrow now, given that it's almost morning—just after midday. We can all meet here at the house after the service. Just family and close friends."

The woman was silent, as if she was considering the answer to a difficult question.

"Of course you're welcome, Tom. But I can't pretend this isn't difficult for Alex. In truth I think he blames us all, myself included. They say that time heals all wounds, but…well, it's possible that some wounds are just too deep. Time will tell, I suppose."

"Thank you, Tom. I will. Best to Anna." She hung up.

Fedosov tensed, anxious about the woman's next move, then heaved an inward sigh of relief when he heard her footsteps on the stairs. He waited a moment and then slipped down the basement stairs and moved to one of the two small basement windows set high in the exterior wall and examined it critically. It would be tight, but he could make it. He pulled an all-purpose tool from his pocket and quickly wired around the security system sensor, so that the system would always show 'closed' regardless of the position of the window. He then unlocked it and made sure it would open easily before pulling it closed and gliding back up the stairs to exit through the kitchen, muffling the alarm and resetting the security system on his way out.

He tried to appear casual as he strolled through the predawn light to where his car was parked several blocks away. It had been a productive evening despite a rocky start. He had the place and time of the hit nailed down and had arranged access to the site. All he needed now was a little time and a lot of plastic explosive. And from the sound of things, he'd be putting them all out of their misery. It was practically an act of mercy.

DUGAN AND ANNA'S APARTMENT
LONDON, UK

Dugan disconnected from Gillian and sat down in the wrought-iron chair on the small balcony of the apartment. He'd being lying awake when she called, watching Anna sleep, and going over the events of the last few days in his mind. The phone vibrated on the night table before it rang, and he had snatched it up before it disturbed Anna, and retreated to the balcony.

He looked through the closed glass door into the living room and saw Nigel sprawled on the couch. With Ilya in the spare bedroom, there was literally no place in the small apartment other than the bathroom where Dugan wouldn't disturb someone. He considered going back to bed, but knew he'd only toss and turn and probably disturb Anna, and she needed her rest. He decided to stay out and watch the sunrise, so he set the phone on the table beside him, leaned back in the chair and put his feet up on the rail of the balcony.

He jumped as the phone vibrated on the table beside him and picked it up, thinking Gillian had forgotten something and was calling back, but he didn't recognize the number on the caller ID.

"Dugan."

"I was beginning to think you were dead," Ward said. "Don't you check your voice mail?"

Dugan felt a flash of guilt, followed immediately by irritation.

"Yeah, well, I've been kind of busy. Where are you calling from, anyway? I didn't recognize the number."

"I was counting on that. I'm calling on the plane's satellite phone. I'm over the Atlantic, and we should be landing in London in an hour. I need you to meet me."

"For Christ's sake. It's five o'clock in the morning—"

"So if you leave soon, you can beat the traffic."

"This isn't the best time, Jesse. Care to tell me what this is all about?"

"I can't, not over the phone. Just meet me there, okay? You won't be sorry."

"Yeah, well, I've heard that before." Dugan sighed. "All right. I'll meet you. The private terminal at Heathrow, I presume?"

"Negative. Meet us at London RAF Northolt. Do you know it?"

"I know of it, but I've never been there. I can get there all right."

"Great! I'll wait for you on board. There are some things we need to discuss before we disembark. I'll arrange clearance for you straight to the plane. The stairs will be down, just come aboard when you get there."

Dugan rolled to a stop at the gate and lowered his window as the uniformed guard approached.

"My name is Tom Dugan." He offered his passport. "I'm supposed to meet Mr. Jesse Ward, who's arriving by private jet."

The guard took Dugan's passport and scrutinized it closely before looking back at him with the same intensity. He then turned to a companion in the small guard shack and nodded, and the man walked out of the shack and got into a golf cart parked just inside the open gate.

"Yes, Mr. Dugan," the guard said. "Mr. Ward touched down a few minutes ago. If you would be kind enough to follow my colleague, he'll escort you to the plane."

"Thanks." Dugan accepted his passport back from the guard and put the car in gear.

He followed the golf cart down a perimeter road and around the end of what appeared to be a terminal building. Arrayed along the back side of the building were a number of executive jets of various sizes, but they bypassed them all and went to the last parking place some distance from the others, to a large Gulfstream sitting alone. The guard motioned for him to stop and then circled the golf cart around beside the car.

"Park your car there near the fence, if you will, sir. You'll see some spaces marked as you get nearer. Then board the aircraft. I understand they're expecting you."

"Thank you," Dugan said, and the guard touched his finger to his cap and sped away.

Dugan parked the car and walked across the tarmac, puzzled at the unusual manner of Ward's arrival. On those rare occasions when he traveled on the CIA's private jet rather than the more customary trips by commercial carrier, Ward normally landed at the private terminal at Heathrow. Thoroughly confused, Dugan mounted the short flight of steps up into the plane.

He turned to his right as he entered the small but luxurious cabin of the executive jet, and saw Ward facing him at the far end, sitting across a coffee table from two dark-haired men, both with their backs to the door of the plane. Ward smiled as he saw Dugan and began to stand.

"Okay, Jesse," Dugan said. "Care to tell me what all the cloak and dagger shit is—"

"UNCLE THOMAS!"

Dugan froze, confused, as both dark heads turned in unison, and one man leaped from his seat and moved toward him, wearing Cassie's smiling face topped with a short mop of black hair.

"UNCLE THOMAS!" the figure cried again, and there was no mistaking the voice. It was Cassie, however impossible that seemed, and she flew into his arms. He hugged her tight, unable to speak as tears flowed down his cheeks and his shoulders shook.

"Oh, Uncle Thomas, I'm so glad to see you!" Cassie was crying herself now as she returned his hug, and they both lapsed into silence, clinging together and unable to speak. Time seemed to stand still, and they stood there motionless, as a thousand questions crowded Dugan's mind and he was unable to articulate any of them. He just stood in joyful acceptance of the miracle, indifferent for the time being as to how it came about.

Dugan looked over Cassie's head to see Jesse Ward standing a few feet away, beaming.

"Can I assume," Ward asked, "that you're no longer pissed off at me?"

Dugan blinked back tears and returned Ward's smile, still unable to speak. He nodded.

"Good," Ward said, "and I don't want to rush your reunion, but we have a lot to talk about. But first, I don't think you've met Karina."

Dugan looked at the other person he'd assumed was a man, to see a beautiful young woman perhaps an inch taller than Cassie. There was no mistaking the family resemblance.

"Yo-you're Ilya's niece."

Karina nodded. "*Da*, but I am not so sure he will recognize me with new hairstyle."

Dugan returned her smile. "Trust me. He won't care if you're bald. I can't wait to see his face when I tell him—"

"About that," Ward said, "you can't tell him, at least not yet. But that's going to take some explaining, so take a seat."

Dugan raised his eyebrows but allowed Cassie to lead him to a seat by the coffee table. He settled in the seat as Ward sat down across from him.

"So when did you find them?" Dugan asked.

"Yesterday. I was goin—"

"YESTERDAY! Why the hell didn't you call…"

Dugan shut his mouth and stared down at the coffee table.

"That's right," Ward said, "not exactly the kind of information I'd leave in a voice mail, is it? So why the hell didn't YOU return my calls?"

Dugan nodded. "You're right. I'm sorry. I'll shut up and let you bring me up to speed."

"Can I get you something to drink first? This may take a while."

"Well, the sun's hardly up, but I think I could use a drink. Bourbon if you got it. Neat."

***

Half an hour later, Dugan drained his glass, then looked at the two girls and shook his head. "Well, the hair makes a huge difference, but these two still don't look like Filipino seamen to me. I'm amazed they were able to sneak past the authorities and get ashore."

"The crew hid us when the authorities were searching the ship," Cassie said. "We only pretended to be seamen to get out the port gate, and it was at night."

"*Da*," Karina added, "and we did not try to pass the guards at the gangway, because they were checking very carefully. We went by rope ladder down the side of ship away from dock and swam further down the wharf. Then, out of sight of ship's gangway guards, we met with a group of the Filipino seamen who went down the gangway in normal manner. They wore extra dry clothes under their own clothes and also had identification cards for two of their shipmates who remained on board. We all walked out the port gate together, holding up identification cards. Port guards don't pay so much attention to seaman leaving; they seem more interested in people coming into the terminal. When we got away from the port, we gave them the identification cards back, and they gave us some money the ship's officers had collected for us."

"I didn't know what else to do," Cassie said, "so I called Agent Ward."

Dugan nodded. "Well, I think you both did great." He turned to Ward. "But what are we supposed to do now, Jesse? Are they supposed to disappear forever and live under assumed names? That doesn't sound too workable."

"Truthfully, I don't know," Ward said. "But I do know that we need to keep them under wraps for the next few weeks at least until we can figure out what to do. I mean you may be able to protect THEM here in the UK, but there are all sorts of vulnerable targets you can't protect, like Karina's family, and now the families of the guys on the Kapitan Godina. Hitting the soft targets is the way these Russian mobsters work."

Dugan nodded. "Well, hopefully Borgdanov will have some ideas along those lines. Just because we've gotten the girls back, I don't think he's going to cancel his plans. If anything, I expect he may see them as even more of a necessity to keep these bastards at bay. That's probably the solution to everything anyway, just making the Russian mob guys understand that their least damaging option is just to leave us all the hell alone."

"Have you heard from him?"

Dugan shook his head. "No, and that's a bit troubling. Ilya's chomping at the bit to get to Russia and getting nervous, but he promised Borgdanov he'd wait for word. Borgdanov's playing it by ear, and he didn't want Ilya to show up until he'd established a firm cover."

"Well, I hope he knows what he's doing. This could backfire big time."

"We'll cross that bridge when we come to it. Right now, I'd like to take these young ladies for a little visit and make some people I know very happy."

"Ahh, at the risk of pissing you off again, I don't think you should do that just yet. That's the main reason I contacted you alone."

"I understand. We'll continue to play along. We'll go ahead with the memorial service and—"

"That's my point. The Kairouzes have many friends as well as business colleagues and associates, and I'm presuming the service is going to be well attended?"

Dugan shrugged. "I'm sure it will be. What of it?"

"And just how do you think Alex and Gillian will behave if they see Cassie before the service? They'll be a lot of eyes on them, perhaps even from our Russian friends. They have to be convincing as grieving parents."

"I'm sure they can handle it."

"Really? Like you? Whether you know it or not, you've had a shit-eating grin plastered all over your face from the moment you realized Cassie was alive. Relief and elation are hard to disguise, especially to trained observers."

"Then we'll cancel the service."

"You're not thinking straight. How would that look? You'd likely draw even more attention to the situation." He shook his head. "No, best have the service with the Kairouzes and Ilya genuinely distraught in plain sight. Then we can secretly reunite them with the girls."

"I'm not putting those people through another twenty-four hours of hell just as window dressing," Dugan said through clenched teeth. "Alex and Gillian are already—"

"Mr. Dugan," Karina said, "I am sorry to interrupt, but I think Agent Ward is right. I do not want to see Uncle Ilya suffer more, and I think Cassie also feels pain for the additional suffering of her poor parents, but it is MY family that may be in danger if we are somehow discovered, so I would beg you to listen to Agent Ward. Also, I am not sure what means 'shit-eating grin' or why anyone would smile while eating that, but he is right that you have been very happy since you saw Cassie. I think it will be even more difficult for her parents to hide their joy."

Dugan looked at Karina and then turned to Cassie, who nodded.

"I don't want Mum and Papa to suffer anymore either, Uncle Thomas, bu-but they're right, I think," Cassie said.

Dugan sighed. "Shit! All right. So how do we do this?"

"Good," Ward said. "What I figure is that I'll bring the girls to Alex's house during the memorial service. If you can get the Kairouzes and Ilya there, with maybe Anna and Mrs. Hogan, we can tell them all at once right after the service. Will that work?"

"I'm not sure. When Mrs. Hogan was first talking about the service yesterday, I believe the plan was for people to come back to the house afterwards. I think people have already begun dropping off food."

"Can you kill that? Maybe have the minister announce that the family's too distraught to receive visitors?"

"I can try, and that's not far from the truth. But things are a bit strained at the moment, and I'm not sure I can just go in rearrange whatever they've already set up."

"The quicker we can get everyone together without an audience, the quicker we can end their anguish."

"I'll try."

"Do you think there's any safe way to get word to Nigel on his ship?" Cassie asked, obviously hesitant. "I don't want to put anyone in danger, but I'm sure he's worried. We were video-chatting when I was taken and—"

"Nigel hasn't left our sides since you were taken, Cassie. In fact, he alerted the police and left his ship right away to search for you."

"He did?" Cassie beamed.

Dugan nodded. "Yes, he's quite a resourceful and determined young man. I'll make sure he's there along with everyone else. He certainly deserves to be included."

"All right then, it's settled," Ward said. "I have a place here to stash the young ladies. I'll take them there, and you try to get the after-service gathering canceled. We'll play it by ear from there. And Tom"—Ward laid a hand on Dugan's shoulder,—"when the others see the girls alive, they'll forget all about being mad at you."

"Yeah, until they realize I could have told them about it twenty-four hours earlier. Then they'll get really pissed."

Ward grinned. "Well, concentrate on that. It'll help you keep a grief-stricken look on your face for the next day or so."

"You know, Jesse, sometimes you're an asshole."

"You know, Tom, sometimes I have to be. It comes with the territory."

Borgdanov sat at a corner table in the Starbucks, still crowded at late morning, sipping a double espresso. He would have preferred a local place, but anything Western was popular in Russia, and crowds were his friend. Even so, it didn't pay to get too comfortable, and he studied the patrons around him over a folded newspaper as he reflected on his progress. Crowds might be his friend, but situational awareness was his best friend.

He wasn't overly concerned with being spotted. Russia was the last place the *Bratstvo* would expect him to be, and his disguise was complete. His week-old beard was dyed jet black, a bit in contrast to his now salt-and-pepper hair—just another aging man vainly trying to hold time at bay. The oral prostheses in his cheeks made them look puffy and bloated, and a bit of padding under his loose and somewhat shapeless clothing spoke of a man attempting to disguise a thickening waistline rather than conceal a rock-hard body. A pair of horn-rim glasses completed the disguise, and he looked threatening to no one or nothing, except perhaps the half-eaten pastry that sat on a plate on the table in front of him.

In his pocket was a passport and wallet full of credit cards, a driver's license, and other documentation identifying him as Vasily Gagarin, a Ukrainian of ethnic Russian descent who was in town to purchase textiles. His ethnicity accounted for his flawless Russian, and now that Ukraine was a separate country, the foreign passport made things a bit more difficult for local law enforcement to verify his identity should he be stopped for any reason. Most police wouldn't bother to follow up if there was too much work involved.

Despite his ability to move freely, things had been more difficult than he'd imagined. Corporal Anisimov had been a willing recruit, even before Borgdanov had described his need, but the others had been less enthusiastic. While some warmed to the idea of a fresh start with new names in America, they balked at doing so as fugitives from the *Bratstvo*, especially since Borgdanov could not yet clearly define the mission. So far, he had Anisimov and two other former comrades, but he was nearing the end of the short list of people he felt safe contacting, and rapidly coming to the conclusion that he would have to organize the men he had and summon Ilya. Then they would do the most damage they could with the manpower available.

He raised his cup and took a sip of the now lukewarm coffee, the bitter dregs a suitable companion to his growing disappointment.

CHAPTER THIRTY

OFFICES OF PHOENIX SHIPPING LTD.
LONDON, UK

Dugan sat at his desk, reviewing vessel position reports and making a few notes to email to his subordinates. After returning to the flat to check on Anna, he'd decided to come into the office for a few hours, if only to escape the funereal gloom that permeated the apartment. With nothing to occupy their time or thoughts, both Nigel and Ilya merely sat listlessly staring at the television, present but disengaged, no doubt reliving the events of the past few days.

The atmosphere in the office was only marginally better, but there was some mindless comfort to be found in familiar tasks, and before he knew it, Mrs. Coutts walked in and set a bottle of water and a sandwich from the corner deli on his desk. Dugan looked up, surprised.

"Is it lunch time already?"

She nodded. "I just assumed you'd want your usual."

"I'm really not hungry, Mrs. Coutts. But thank you."

"That's what I thought you'd say, which is why I didn't ask. Did you have breakfast?"

Dugan thought back to the bourbon he'd had on Ward's plane.

"Ah… sort of."

"Which means no. So you can either promise to eat that sandwich, or I'm going to sit here and stare at you until you do." As if to back up her words, she sat down in the chair across from Dugan's desk and fixed him with a disapproving stare.

Dugan smiled. "All right, you win. But why is it I'm often unsure exactly which of us is the managing director around here?"

"I'm sure I don't know what you're talking about, sir. And talk is cheap. I haven't yet seen any action to back up your promise."

Dugan sighed and reached down for the sandwich. He took a big bite.

"Sah-dis-vied?" he asked, around a mouthful of food.

"Yes." she stood up, "But don't talk with your mouth full. And don't think you can get away with throwing half of it in the rubbish bin, because I intend to check."

Dugan watched her retreating back and shook his head. For all, or perhaps because of, Alicia Coutts's peremptory ways, she was hands down the best secretary he'd ever had, and seldom wrong. A fact he was rediscovering once again, as he realized he really was famished and wolfed down the rest of the sandwich. He washed it down with the water, feeling a great deal better than when he'd arrived at the office. The feeling quickly evaporated when he turned to the next task at hand.

He'd given it a lot of thought and decided the best approach was through Father O'Malley. He looked the priest's number up and dialed.

"Saint Mary's. Father O'Malley speaking."

"Father, Tom Dugan. How are you?"

"I'm fine, Tom, though it's me that should be asking you that. How're you holding up, lad?"

"As well as can be expected, I guess, Father."

"Things will heal in God's own time and not our own, though it's a bitter pill to swallow. Now how can I help you?"

"It's about the memorial service tomorrow, or more specifically, the gathering after. I just… I just don't think either Alex or Gillian are up for it."

"Aye, you might be right. I have spoken to Gillian, and though she seems understandably distraught, I'm more concerned about Alex. Mrs. Hogan has made a couple of attempts to get us together, but they've come to naught. I understand Alex isn't handling it well."

"That's an understatement, I think. My understanding is that he's neither dressed nor bathed nor shaved since he heard the news, and mainly crawled inside a brandy bottle."

"Your understanding? So you've not seen him, then?"

Dugan hesitated. "He… he hasn't wanted to see me, Father. I think he blames me for what happened to Cassie, and to be honest, he's probably right."

"It's a black day that causes us to harden our hearts against those that love us and mean us no harm. I'm sure it's just his grief talking, Tom. When he can see clearly again, he'll be sorry for his actions now, I've no doubt."

"I hope you're right, Father, but Alex is pretty much a basket case right now. I'm sure he can probably sit through a short service, but I don't know if he'll be able to handle a houseful of people attempting to comfort and console him. He just doesn't seem ready to interact with anyone right now—like you said, it will require God's own time, and we're not even close yet."

There was silence on the line, as if the priest was mulling over what he'd just heard.

"All right, Tom. I'll discuss it with Gillian and suggest canceling the post-service gathering. If she agrees, I'll make an announcement at the end of the service to the effect that the family is too distraught at the moment to receive visitors, and ask all gathered to keep you all in their thoughts and prayers. I'll suggest to Gillian that perhaps we can have a celebration of Cassie's life in a few weeks, when the wounds aren't quite so fresh. Of course, you know it will be up to her?"

"Of course. Thank you, Father."

"And Tom, though this is Gillian's decision, if she decides to cancel the post-service gathering be aware it might upset Mrs. Hogan. I just thought you should know that."

"Ahh Okay. But why?"

"Well, I can't be sure, of course, but Mrs. Hogan's a bit traditional. I'm not trying to borrow trouble, mind you, but I thought I'd mention it."

"Okay, thanks."

"You're welcome. And while I have you on the phone, why don't you come round in a few days? It sounds like you might need a sympathetic ear yourself."

"Ahh… thanks for the offer, Father. I'll keep it in mind."

O'Malley sensed the hesitation.

"Sure and that sympathetic ear is nondenominational, lad," O'Malley said, a smile in his voice, "available even to unchurched heathens such as yourself. My door is always open."

Dugan smiled. "Thank you, Father. I'll remember that."

***

Three hours later, Dugan powered down his laptop and slipped it in his bag. He hadn't accomplished much, but his short foray into the office had been a welcome respite from the apartment. He considered calling either Gillian or Father O'Malley to see how things had gone. If the gathering was still on, he and Ward were going to have to revise their timing for bringing Cassie and Karina to the Kairouz house. He was reaching for the phone when the intercom buzzed.

"Yes, Mrs. Coutts?"

"Mrs. Hogan is holding on line one, sir, and she doesn't sound too happy. Should I tell her you've gone for the day?"

Dugan sighed. "I wish it were that easy, Mrs. Coutts, but she has my mobile number, and if she thinks I'm avoiding her, I expect that may upset her even more."

Dugan pressed the flashing button on the desk phone.

"Yes, Mrs. Hogan, what can I do for you?"

"Well now, you can start by telling me why you're puttin' your oar in the water and preventing us from givin' our Cassie a proper farewell?"

"I'm not sure I'm following you."

"Oh, so it wasn't you that called Father O'Malley and suggested we cancel the gathering after poor Cassie's service?"

"I suggested that neither Gillian nor Alex was up to it and that perhaps he might discuss it with Gillian to find out what she preferred. Until this moment, I didn't know myself what decision she made."

"And how would you be knowin' what state they're in, since you've not bothered to bring yourself round to the house, now have ya'?"

"Mrs. Hogan, you know that's not fair—"

"Fair? Fair, is it? Is it fair our beautiful Cassie's gone and we've not even a body to put in the ground? And who's to blame for that, I ask you? And now we're to say farewell without even the dignity of a funeral feast. Just a few words in a church and no gatherin' to share tales, no relivin' of her life? It's neither fittin' nor proper, I tell you. Even if himself can't bear it, he could be sat in the study with his brandy to help him dull the pain, and there's none that could begrudge him that solace. But what of the rest of us, I ask you. Did you think of that when you decided to go sticking your Yank nose in things that don't concern you?"

"Mrs. Hogan, I know you're upset but—"

"Upset? Oh, aye, I'm upset all right. And know this, Mr. Thomas Dugan, it'll be a cold day in Hell before you set your feet under my table again."

The line went dead, and Dugan sat holding the receiver a moment, then slowly returned it to its cradle. Feelings were obviously running high all around, and after everyone started coming down from the euphoria of Cassie and Karina's survival, he was quite sure the realization that he'd kept the news from them all wasn't going to endear him to anyone, regardless of the justification. The clear implication was that none of them were to be trusted with the secret.

Perhaps things might go better in his absence, but how would he explain that? He hesitated a moment and picked up the phone again, dialing Gillian's mobile phone and hoping she wasn't with Mrs. Hogan when she answered.

"Hello," Gillian said.

"Gillian, this is Tom. Ahh… I just had a call from Mrs. Hogan and—"

"And it didn't go well, I presume? That would account for all the muttered curses and slamming cabinet doors I hear coming from the kitchen."

"Yeah, that's what I'm calling about. I really didn't mean to upset anyone when I called Father O'Malley—"

"No, actually you were right to do that. To be honest, I was already thinking along those lines. I wouldn't have agreed to cancel the gathering otherwise."

"About that. I assumed that even though the larger gathering was canceled that we could come over to the house after the service, but maybe that's not such a good idea."

"Don't be silly, Tom. Of course, you and Anna must come, and Ilya and young Nigel as well. I just assumed that would be the case. Don't even think about not coming. And by the way, since we're forgoing the post-service gathering, I've moved the service to late morning. It will be at ten thirty."

Try as he might, Dugan couldn't think of a way to refuse gracefully.

"Okay. We'll be there."

ST. PETERSBURG
RUSSIAN FEDERATION

Borgdanov was once again sitting in Starbucks, consistency being part and parcel of his cover identity. While a man on the run might skulk in the shadows, Ukrainian textile buyer Vasily Gagarin was conspicuous by his mundane daily routine. In truth, there was little to hide, as he was having less than stellar success with his recruitment mission. He'd already lowered his expectations and begun to consider how best to use his limited resources.

He caught movement from the corner of his eye and glanced casually to the right. It was the man he'd seen come in a bit earlier, expensively dressed and carrying a leather briefcase, but it was his face rather than his clothing that caught the eye. He was horribly disfigured, thick ropes of burn scar extending up out of his collar and across the right side of his face. His body was twisted, one shoulder and hip higher than the other, and his ruined face bore the lines of constant pain as he shuffled toward the exit, dragging his right leg. Poor bastard. Borgdanov looked away, fighting the urge to stare.

As the man passed Borgdanov's table, he stumbled and grabbed the back of an empty chair and the edge of the table for support, dropping his briefcase in the process.

"Oh! Excuse me," the man said as he regained his balance.

"No problem." Borgdanov stood and reached down to retrieve the briefcase. "Here, let me help."

"Most kind of you." The man took the case from Borgdanov and gave him a twisted smile. "Most kind of you, indeed. Thank you very much."

Borgdanov nodded. There was something familiar about the man. The voice perhaps.

"You're welcome," he said to the man's back as the stranger shuffled for the door, faster now, with an obvious sense of urgency.

Very strange. Borgdanov sat back down and picked up his newspaper. Something fluttered out of it to the floor, and he glanced down to see a folded square of white paper. On the front of it in block letters was printed BORGDANOV.

He stared down at the paper a long moment, willing his heart rate back to normal, then reached down casually, picked it up, and unfolded it.

YOU ARE NOT AS INVISIBLE AS YOU THINK. MEET ME AT 2AM. WHERE YOU FIRST TRIUMPHED. COME ALONE. A FRIEND.

1 AM
KAIROUZ RESIDENCE
LONDON, UK

Fedosov crouched in the shrubbery watching the house, a suitcase on either side of him, eager to get to the task at hand. He'd been nervous when he'd monitored the bugs throughout the day, unsure how the cancellation of the gathering impacted his plan. The last call from the American confirming the presence of all three targets had come as a great relief. The entire thing was working out well, actually much better than he could ever have hoped. He'd been a bit nervous about targeting a gathering where he was unsure about the guest list—it would be just his luck to blow up a Member of Parliament or some other important personage—and identifying the potential victims specifically and reducing the collateral damage was an unexpected boon. The only question now was when the occupants of the house would go to bed.

Finally the lights on the ground floor began to wink out until only the study window showed a light. He heard raised voices muffled by the closed window and saw shadows on the glass indicating movement within, but finally that light was extinguished as well. Twenty minutes later, the lights on the second story went dark, and Fedosov let out a relieved sigh. He waited an additional half hour to allow the occupants time to fall asleep and then crept through the darkness to the small basement window, a suitcase in each hand.

VAVILOVICH STREET
ST. PETERSBURG
RUSSIAN FEDERATION

Borgdanov stood well back in the shadows of a narrow alley, watching the front of the abandoned school building across the street. He'd arrived two hours earlier, casually strolling down the near deserted streets surrounding the old school, walking at least two blocks in every direction. Satisfied, he'd come back to wait in the shadows of the alley, shifting his weight from foot to foot and reliving all of his actions since he'd arrived in the country, racking his brain for what he'd done wrong.

He heard a faint noise and moved cautiously to the entrance to the alley to peer around the corner of the building. Far up the empty street at the edge of one of the few working streetlights, a figure approached, dragging his right foot. Borgdanov reached into his coat pocket and wrapped his hand around the grip of his pistol, then faded back into the alley to wait.

Long minutes later, his quarry limped into view, stopping at the gate in a tall chain-link fence beside the school building. Borgdanov saw the man reach into his pocket and extract something, then heard the metallic rattle of a chain on metal—he had a key and was unlocking the gate.

The man disappeared into the darkened schoolyard, leaving the gate standing open—an invitation. Borgdanov stared at the open gate a long moment, then hurried across the street and into the school yard, his hand still gripping the gun in his pocket. He moved through the darkness of the narrow side yard from memory, sensing rather than seeing when it opened onto the spacious school yard behind the building. He yearned to use the small flashlight in his other pocket, but feared making himself an even better target than he already was. He jumped at a sound to his right and spun in that direction, gun in hand.

"Good evening, Dyusha," said a voice from the darkness. "Thank you for coming. I can't see well, but I assume you are pointing a gun in my direction. If so, please put it away. You have nothing to fear from me, and I doubt you could hit me in the dark anyway."

"Ar-Arkady…Arkady Baikov?"

"Very good, Dyusha, but I am surprised you recognized me. I've changed a bit since last we saw each other as schoolboys."

"It was your voice and the fact that you wanted to meet here. Though I wasn't really sure until you spoke again just now. But wh-what happened to you? Was it an accident?"

The man laughed, but there was no humor in it. "An accident? Hardly. As you may recall, most people here are not so accepting of those of us who are different. Those that view us as anything more than freakish curiosities seem to feel somehow threatened by us. One evening after a drinking session, some of our more intellectually challenged countrymen decided it would be good fun to set a freak on fire. They caught me coming out of a restaurant, dragged me into a nearby alley, then tied me up. Then they poured petrol all over me and lit it. I still remember their drunken laughter before I lost consciousness."

"My God! How could you survive?"

"My screams attracted a crowd, who chased the bastards away and doused me with rain water that had collected in a bunch of discarded buckets in the alley." He paused. "Apparently they didn't know I was a freak."

"But how did the bastards even know about… you know?"

"How does anyone know anything? They observe, they suspect, they guess. How long can one avoid sports and locker room showers with medical excuses? Doctors' offices have nurses, and secretaries, and file clerks, and my condition is just too interesting not to discuss. People always find out somehow. How did you find out about me when we were schoolmates?"

Borgdanov didn't answer right away. "I overheard my aunt tell my mother and warn her not to let me associate with you."

Borgdanov heard the pain in Arkady's laugh. "You never were very obedient, but you see my point, *da*? Gossip is a most efficient means of communication. But I've always been curious. Even after you knew, you were the only one who didn't shun me. Who would have thought, Andrei Nikolaevich Borgdanov, the most popular fellow in school, captain of the wrestling team and city champion, would maintain a friendship with the hermaphrodite freak, the 'he-she.' Why, Dyusha?"

"As you said, Arkady, we were friends. One does not abandon a friend because he has a medical condition beyond his control. I... I was sorry when we lost touch with each other after you moved and changed schools."

"Sorry, Dyusha? Or relieved? I tried to contact you several times, but you never returned my phone calls or answered my letters."

Borgdanov said nothing, and after a long silence Arkady sighed in the darkness.

"It's all right, Dyusha. I know it was difficult to stand by me, and you stood firmly when I most needed you. I cannot fault you if you tired of being my sole support. To be honest, I was a bit tired of myself, and I'm sure my being out of sight made it quite easy for me to be out of mind as well," Arkady said. "But enough of that, I didn't meet you to discuss old times. You are in great danger."

Borgdanov stiffened. "What? How can you know—"

"What you're doing? Quite easily, my old friend. I am the chief of data analysis for the Federal Security Service for St. Petersburg and Leningrad Oblast, and you've apparently made enemies in very high places. I was tasked with finding out everything about you and your friend Sergeant Denosovitch. I have been following your activities for the last two days."

Borgdanov tightened his grip on the gun. "So you intend to denounce me?"

Arkady chuckled. "Hardly. If that was my intent, I would not meet with a fellow your size in a deserted school yard, now would I? No, I came to warn you—and to help you."

Borgdanov weighed the gun in his hand but said nothing. He hadn't seen Arkady in over twenty years. Could he be trusted?

"Some days ago," Arkady continued, "I got a call from Vladimir Glazkov, the Chief of the FSB here in St. Petersburg. He gave me Denosovitch's name, which meant nothing to me, and then added yours as Denosovitch's former commander and known associate. I was to provide him background information on you both—which I did, of course—and also to attempt to track your movements. Of course, I recognized your name, and rather than assign the task to one of my subordinates, I kept it for myself."

"How did you find me? I thought I was being quite careful."

"Remarkably so. I couldn't really watch you out of the country, and since I wasn't sure when, or even if you'd return, I initiated surveillance on all your old comrades. When a rather slovenly Ukrainian textile buyer visited three or four of your ex-*Spetsnaz* comrades in a forty-eight-hour period, that was a bit suspicious. And as clever as your disguise is, it could not fool the facial recognition software."

"Who else knows?"

"No one, Dyusha. Kill me now and your secret is safe. I know that's what you're thinking, old times notwithstanding. But I think you should hear me out first."

Borgdanov considered the alternatives. Nothing pointed to treachery on Arkady's part. He had so far done nothing illegal in Russia, so the FSB had no grounds to pick him up, and if Arkady was supplying intelligence to the *Bratstvo*, the mob would have surely attacked him by now. Whatever the threat, it wasn't Arkady. He slipped the gun into his pocket.

"Go on, then."

"I don't know exactly what you're doing, but my research showed that Denosovitch's niece disappeared some months ago. Also Glazkov directed me to look into a British couple named Kairouz and an American named Dugan, all in London. That led me to news reports of the recent police activities against the Russian mob in the UK." Arkady paused. "My conclusion is that the *Bratstvo* is heavily involved, and that you are somehow attempting to mount some sort of action against them. How am I doing so far?"

Borgdanov said nothing, then flinched as ten feet away, Arkady struck a match, bathing them both momentarily in a circle of light as the flame flared. The flare died to a small flame, illuminating Arkady's twisted face as he held the match between cupped hands to light a cigarette. Borgdanov studied the face, not worried about staring now. Beneath the scars, the face looked drawn and jaundiced.

Arkady shook out the match and took a long drag on the cigarette, causing the tip to burn brightly, and Borgdanov heard him exhale audibly into the night air and smelled the cigarette smoke.

"You're playing a dangerous game, Dyusha," Arkady said. "You probably know the *Bratstvo* has powerful connections to the police and the FSB, but what you may fail to understand is that, here in St. Petersburg at least, the *Bratstvo* IS the FSB. You've no chance against them without my help."

"Forgive me, Arkady, but how can you help me?"

"I already have, because you're not being beaten in some squalid dungeon, nor do you have a bullet in your head. But I can do much more. Hold out your hand."

Borgdanov did as requested, and he saw Arkady dimly, as the man approached out of the deeper shadows. He felt something hit his palm.

"That is a flash drive," Arkady said. "On it you will find complete information on the leadership of the FSB and their complementary ranks in the *Bratstvo*. There are also other things—very powerful things. With this information, who knows, you may even survive."

Borgdanov felt the hair rising on the back of his neck. Things that seemed too good to be true usually were.

"How did you get this information?"

"Is it not obvious? In addition to my FSB duties, I am a member of the *Bratstvo*. They do not like 'freaks' any better than anyone else, but my skills as a data analyst are unsurpassed, and because of this, they tolerate me."

"Arkady, how could you join these murderous pigs? Do you know what they have done? What they continue to do to innocent people?"

"I suppose that's a rhetorical question, Dyusha, since it is obvious I know what they do. As far as how I could join, everyone has their price, and the *Bratstvo* met mine. The four bastards that set me on fire died horrible deaths, and this time I got to light the match."

Borgdanov said nothing for a long time, trying to process what he'd just heard.

"So why give this to me? And why now?"

"I'm giving it to you because you will obviously need it, and other than my parents you are the only human being on the face of the earth who has ever treated me decently. And I'm giving it to you now because it no longer makes any difference to me."

"What do you mean? If I use this information against the *Bratstvo*, it may harm you as well. Or worse, they will suspect you gave it to me. I cannot imagine what they will do to you."

Arkady's laughter seemed genuine this time. "I am afraid God, if he exists, has beaten them to it, old friend. Six months ago I was diagnosed with pancreatic cancer. The doctors give me six weeks to live. But don't worry. The pain is already quite exquisite, and I suspect it will feel like much, much longer." He laughed again. "In any event, I don't intend to wait around and find out. In a few days, I will enjoy a fine meal, drink a toast to my one and only true friend Andrei Nikolaevich Borgdanov, and eat the barrel of my pistol for dessert."

"I… I have some contacts in the West. They have advanced treatments for—"

Borgdanov heard another chuckle, then watched the bright tip of the cigarette fall to the ground and disappear as Arkady crushed it underfoot. He sensed his old friend moving even closer and flinched in surprise as he felt hands on his shoulders, and smoker's breath washed over him.

"Dyusha, do not worry so. I have no place in this world. I never have. My parents are dead, and I have no other family. My life has been nothing but pain with promises of more to come. I joined the *Bratstvo* for revenge, and for a while took some perverse satisfaction in inflicting pain on others. But there was no real solace there—I know that now. I've done much harm, and my soul is as twisted and tortured as this body. But if life was once unfair, it is no longer, for now I have earned this fate." Borgdanov saw him smile in the dim light. "Besides, we are Russian! Tragedy is in our genes, is it not? And you always were one to hog the spotlight. Let me be center stage for once, old friend. Take this gift I give you, and let me die the flawed and tragic hero/villain." Arkady laughed again.

Borgdanov nodded, unable to speak, and Arkady pulled the big man into his embrace and then stood on tiptoe to kiss both his cheeks. Then he pushed Borgdanov away.

"We don't have much time, and I want to make sure you fully appreciate the power of this gift. The *Bratstvo* is a huge organization, and like all such entities, now runs on computers. I was instrumental in managing the development of the systems they use and included on the flash drive is a file with the source code for many of their most critical applications. Buried in the code are multiple 'back doors' to allow undetected access to the systems. There are my notes there as well. This will likely all be gibberish to you, my friend, but I assure you that in skilled hands there is no end to the damage this can do. Wield the weapon sparingly and well. Do you understand?"

Borgdanov bobbed his head in an unseen nod, then muttered a soft, "*Da*."

"Go then. I will wait half an hour before I leave."

"*Do svidaniya*, little brother," Borgdanov said softly. "*Stupay s Bogom*." Go with God.

Arkady's teeth flashed in a smile through the dim light. "*Spasibo*, Dyusha, but I suspect that God would prefer that I travel alone. I haven't done much to please Him of late."

Borgdanov smiled sadly and turned toward the gate.

"Oh, and Dyusha, I don't know how well you know these people in the UK, but if they are friends, you should warn them. The *Bratstvo* plans to kill all three of them. Everything I was able to find out is in a file on the flash drive labeled UK."

CHAPTER THIRTY-ONE

Dugan sat next to Anna and glanced down the pew to his left at Alex and Gillian. Gillian was sobbing softly into a handkerchief as on her opposite side Mrs. Hogan was gently rubbing Gillian's back in a vain attempt at consolation. Alex was suitably dressed and shaved for the first time in several days, but he seemed unfocused and near catatonic, staring straight ahead as a single tear leaked down his pallid cheek. Mrs. Hogan peered past the grieving couple at Dugan, and her face turned dark. He quickly looked away.

Gillian had given him a sad smile when they'd arrived, and Alex had offered his hand perfunctorily, his handshake like holding a dead fish, and Dugan caught a whiff of brandy. Ilya and Nigel sat to Dugan's right, on the other side of Anna, the big Russian stone-faced and stoic, while Nigel was visibly struggling to keep it together. But Dugan's discomfort was greater still, knowing that he could have relieved his friends' suffering with a word, and he was struggling with strong second thoughts about having subjected them to this ordeal. This was shaping up to be the longest hour of his life.

The service was not only for Cassie, but also the two Russian women, and Father O'Malley had graciously invited the priest from the nearby Russian Orthodox church to assist him in the service. Dugan was impressed by O'Malley's sensitivity and kindness, but under the circumstances, his greatest concern was that the gesture might double the length of the service and thus his discomfort.

Father O'Malley walked to the pulpit and began to speak.

Unsure as to the exact timing of the day's events, Fedosov decided to take up a position early, to be prepared for any last minute complications. Thus he'd arrived and parked the van on the street in good time to watch the departure of both the Kairouzes, in the company of their driver and the Irish cook. He sat in the back of the van now, with a good view of the driveway through a concealed viewing port. He would be able to observe both the Kairouzes' and Dugan's return, to confirm they were all in place before he detonated the bomb. He was waiting patiently when he got some unexpected visitors.

A taxi pulled to the curb beside the drive, and a rumpled-looking black man got out. He stood a moment, glancing casually around himself. He peered at the van for a long minute and then seemed to mark it in his memory and move on, slowly making an arc as his gaze traversed a full circle around the taxi. Fedosov's sixth sense started sounding an alarm. The man was obviously aware of his surroundings, but what was he doing here. Private security? For who?

He got his answer a short time later, and the man lowered his head and spoke into the taxi. Two dark-haired women exited the cab, and the man motioned them up the drive as he fell in behind them, his head on a swivel. They moved out of sight around the curve in the drive, and Fedosov tensed, trying to assess what impact this latest development might have on his plan. He kept his eye on the house and slipped on the headphones. A short while later, he heard the kitchen door open, and a woman's British-accented voice.

"I'll shut off the alarm."

"Okay," replied a man's voice, undoubtedly the black man, an American by the sound of it. "Then I need to get you two upstairs and out of sight."

"Why?" the woman asked.

"Because I think it would be too much of a shock for your folks to just walk in and find you sitting here. I need to prepare them a bit before I spring you on them," the American said.

"I think for Uncle Ilya it will be no problem," said a second woman, the accent Russian this time.

"Well, maybe," the American said, "but humor me. Let's get you both upstairs for the time being. I'll call up when you can come down."

Fedosov heard murmurs of agreement and then, a moment later, the sound of footsteps on the stairway and cursed the fact that he had no listening devices upstairs. Who were these people, and what were they doing in the house? Should he abort? No, the Chief had already given the green light to some collateral damage as inevitable, and besides, Fedosov had never expected that this Dugan and the Kairouz people would be completely alone.

He sat back in his chair and waited, his patience wearing thin now. He just wanted to finish the job and get the hell away.

ST. PETERSBURG
RUSSIAN FEDERATION

Borgdanov tried Ilya's cell phone again, muttering a curse when the call went to voice mail. He left another message.

"Ilya, I have been trying to reach you. Call me at this number immediately."

He didn't want to communicate in the open, and by doing so he was compromising the strict communication protocol he'd established with Ilya. There were just too many ways communications could be compromised, especially if one end of the call was in Russia, even though both he and Ilya were using burner phones.

The agreed procedure was to leave a draft email message in a dummy Gmail account, to which both men had the user ID and password. Each would log into the account twice a day—Ilya at eleven AM and PM and Borgdanov at noon and midnight—and read any draft message left. Additionally, either could log on at any time with an urgent message, though the sender would know it was unlikely to be received until his correspondent's regular check-in time. Since the messages were never actually sent, they were less likely to attract scrutiny. But despite the low probability of being compromised, the Russians were still circumspect regarding message frequency and content. The only message from Ilya to date, which Borgdanov assumed was sent after the rescue mission, was as heartrending as it was brief. "Regret we failed."

Borgdanov's only message was sent at one in the morning London time, as soon as he'd been able to get to a computer and check the content of the UK file on Arkady's flash drive. His message was equally concise. "Imperative you call me. No. 4." The number four indicated Ilya was to call the fourth number on a list of a dozen numbers Borgdanov had given him, each to a different burner phone that would be discarded immediately after the call.

Ilya should have gotten the message a half hour earlier, and the lack of a call indicated something was seriously wrong, prompting Borgdanov to abandon communications protocol in favor of a direct approach. When Ilya hadn't answered, he'd tried Dugan and then Anna, but both calls went to voice mail. He didn't have numbers for the Kairouzes;, but as a last resort he'd tried Anna's colleagues Lou and Harry, with similar results. Where the hell was everyone?

Borgdanov stood and paced the worn carpet of the shabby hotel room and prayed for Ilya to return his call.

CHAPTER THIRTY-TWO

If anything, the conclusion of the service was the most stressful part. Father O'Malley gave a benediction and, along with the Russian Orthodox priest, moved down the aisle to bid the mourners farewell as they exited the church. The rest of the attendees waited respectfully for the family to file out first, but when they all stood, Alex collapsed. He sank back into the pew, tears streaming down his cheeks and shoulders heaving, as if physically unable to stand. Dugan and Ilya helped him to his feet and along the aisle to the waiting car.

With the family so obviously indisposed, it had fallen to Dugan to return to accept the condolences and well wishes from the exiting mourners—a feat made considerably easier by the presence of both Father O'Malley and the Russian Orthodox priest (whose name he couldn't remember or pronounce) at his side, gently hurrying folks along if they lingered. When the last attendee had shaken hands and moved on, Dugan hurried away before either of the priests could suggest visiting the house to comfort the grieving family.

He glanced at his watch as he rushed to the car park, where Anna waited with Ilya and Nigel. Gillian and Alex would undoubtedly be home by now, and he didn't have a clue as to what was transpiring. Other than bringing the girls to the house, he and Ward didn't have a plan, and Dugan was starting to realize they should have given it a great deal more thought. What exactly were they going to do, say, "Surprise! Your daughter's not dead!" and have her jump out of a fucking cake?

Anna and the others saw him coming and were already sitting in the car by the time he slid behind the wheel, Anna in the front passenger seat, and the two men in the back. Dugan reached for the ignition, then stopped and sat back in his seat. Maybe it was better to break the news to everyone separately. Then maybe Anna could help him figure out the best way to tell Gillian and Alex. Presuming, of course, Ilya and Nigel didn't beat him to death here in the church car park.

"Tom?" Anna asked. "Is something wrong?"

Dugan shook his head and half-turned in his seat so he could see all of them.

"No. But I have something to tell you all. It's going to sound crazy, but I need you to trust me, and you'll understand in a very few minutes." He paused. "Cassie and Karina aren't dead."

No one said anything for a long moment; then Ilya broke the silence.

"*Da, Dyed*. I know. I listened to the sermon. They are with God in Heaven. And maybe is true, and maybe is not. I do not know, but I am not such a strong believer. But… but I like to think the priest is right."

"That's not what I mean. I mean they're both ALIVE. Not in Heaven, but right here in London. I saw them myself yesterday morning, and right now they should be at Alex and Gillian's house."

"What sort of rubbish is that?" Nigel demanded. "We all saw them die. I… I touched her, or one of them, anyway. If this is some sort of cruel Yank funeral humor, it's not amusing."

Dugan shook his head. "The guys on the ship opened the container before they dumped it and rescued Cassie and Karina. Tanya was already dead, and they left her body in the container—that's who you saw, Nigel."

"Why are we just finding this out," Ilya demanded. "Why did the girls not come forward when ship docked?"

"Because they were protecting the guys who saved them. They had no clue we were close by, and the guys on the ship were ordered to dump the container, so the Russian mob would have probably killed their families if they knew any of the girls were rescued—"

"Dugan!" Anna said. "Just drive! You can give us the details on the way."

"*Da*," Ilya said, followed by a 'bloody right' from Nigel.

"I guess that makes it unanimous." Dugan started the car.

OUTSIDE THE KAIROUZ RESIDENCE
LONDON, UK

Fedosov watched the car turn up the drive with the cook and chauffeur in front and the Kairouz couple in the back. So far, so good. Now if this Dugan would just show up, he could finish the job and get out of here—presuming the arrival of the black American and the women didn't complicate matters. He slipped the headphones back on to check out the action inside the house. He heard the back door open and then a surprised gasp.

"Jesse?" he heard the Kairouz woman say. "You startled me. What are you doing here?"

Fedosov heard the hesitation in the man's voice.

"I… I just came to pay my respects," the man said. "I'm so sorry for your loss."

"Thank you," the woman said, "but why didn't you come to the church…and how did you get in? The door was locked and the alarm set."

"I… I just arrived and knew I'd be too late for the service. I called Tom earlier and he told me where the spare key was and gave me the alarm code—"

"I NEED A BLOODY DRINK," said a male British voice, the speech slurred and accompanied by the abrupt sound of chair legs sliding across a tile floor.

"ALEX! Careful! You'll fall," the Kairouz woman again.

"Never you mind," said a woman with an Irish brogue. "I'll get himself sat in the study. Come along, Mr. Kairouz. There's a good fellow." Fedosov heard the sound of stumbling footsteps retreating, then silence.

"Tom said he was taking it hard," the black American's voice again.

"Yes, well, it's difficult for all of us," said the Kairouz woman. "Now about your—"

"Where is Tom?" the black American asked. "I expected him to be with you."

"He'll be along," the Kairouz woman said. "He was detained at the church. And I'm sorry, but we weren't expecting anyone. Can I offer you something? Coffee perhaps? I'll ask Mrs. Hogan to brew a pot."

Fedosov looked up to see a car turning onto the street. As it sped past him, he saw Dugan at the wheel and a red-haired woman in the front passenger seat, along with two men in the back he couldn't see well. The car whipped into the Kairouz drive and disappeared from sight around the curve. Seconds later he heard car doors slamming and then the back door to the kitchen banging open.

"KARINA?" bellowed a deep Russian-accented voice, and then—bedlam.

KAIROUZ RESIDENCE
LONDON, UK

Dugan explained the situation as the car raced toward the Kairouz house, his attempts at soliciting ideas for the best way to break the news to Alex and Gillian overwhelmed by the voices of Nigel and Ilya demanding details of the girls' survival. By the time he pulled into the Kairouzes' drive, he still had no clear idea what to do, and his two back-seat passengers were already opening their doors before he'd brought the car to a complete stop in front of the garage.

"Wait," said Dugan to no avail as the men leaped from the car. He shot a worried look at Anna as she wrestled her crutches from between the seats.

"Go on," Anna said. "Go ahead. You probably need to get in there as soon as possible. I can manage the few steps to the back door on my own."

"You sure—"

Anna smiled. "GO!"

Dugan nodded and jumped out. He entered the kitchen to a scene of chaos. Jesse Ward and Gillian Kairouz stood stock still in the kitchen, puzzled looks on their faces. At the end of the hall, Alex stood in the door to the study, leaning against the door jamb, a glass in his hand. He could see Mrs. Hogan behind Alex, standing ready to offer support. Ilya and Nigel were in the hall, calling the girls' names at the top of their lungs.

Dugan heard answering shouts from up the stairway, and the two men thundered up the steps, while everyone else looked on, obviously confused. And then he heard the unmistakable sound of Cassie's happy laughter, and everything happened at once.

There was the sound of glass breaking on hardwood as Alex dropped the brandy snifter and steadied himself on the door jamb. And then the girls were down the stairs, and the hall was crowded as everyone rushed to them, hugging and kissing and clinging together, consumed with the joy of the return of their loved ones, without regard to the WHY of their particular miracle.

Dugan stood in the kitchen doorway with Ward, hoping some of that goodwill would carry over when they realized he'd delayed the moment of joy. He heard the back door rattle and hurried over to help Anna inside. She grinned at him and thumped down the hall on her crutches toward the happy reunion.

As it turned out, it wasn't much different than having them jump out of a cake, now was it?

Fedosov listened to the melee in his earphones and cursed at the unexpected complication. The noise was general and of sufficient volume to be coming from several of his bugs at once, so he couldn't pinpoint exactly where the targets were in the house. That was a problem.

Despite the fact the Chief had given him discretion in the area of collateral damage, Fedosov was no fool. This was a posh neighborhood, populated with wealthy people who wielded considerable political clout—a Member of Parliament lived only one door down the tree-lined street. A charge large enough to guarantee the complete and utter destruction of the Kairouz residence might also deal death and destruction to influential neighbors, so Fedosov had been selective in his placement of the charges in the basement. He'd placed the heaviest explosives beneath the living room and kitchen, where he might reasonably expect his three targets to congregate at some point. Smaller incendiary charges were spaced throughout the rest of the house and along the perimeter, to ensure the wreckage from the larger blasts was consumed in a raging conflagration. On the off chance any of his targets survived the initial blast, they would surely perish in the fire that followed it. It was a sound plan, all in all, but one predicated on his ability to determine when his three targets were collected together in either the living room or kitchen.

Fedosov scowled as he listened to the confusion coming from his bugs. The addition of additional voices raised in animated conversation completely overwhelmed his ability to tell who was where, and he cursed himself for not having the foresight to plant video cameras. But then again, he'd wanted to keep his footprint as small as possible, and more bugs meant more possibility of discovery.

He considered aborting the hit temporarily, but no, he'd promised the Chief it would happen today—the man expected results, and neither failure nor delay was an option. Besides, he couldn't just leave the charges in place indefinitely. They'd be discovered sooner or later, alerting his targets and making them even more difficult to kill. He settled in to wait and hoped he could discern when his targets were gathered in one of the kill zones.

CHAPTER THIRTY-THREE

Ilya Denosovitch had his right arm tightly around Karina's shoulders as she hugged him around his waist. He hadn't let go of her since she'd bounded down the stairs into his arms moments before. He knew he was grinning like an idiot, yet was unable to stop, and happy tears leaked down his cheeks, which he brushed away with the back of his left hand. *Spetsnaz* do not cry, he reminded himself, then looked at the scene of happy chaos unfolding around him.

Nigel had released Cassie at the bottom of the stairs, and she'd flown into Gillian's waiting arms before reaching out to include a happy but confused Alex in the family embrace. Mrs. Hogan orbited the group, visibly impatient to fold Cassie in a hug of her own, while Nigel stood nearby, beaming but obviously unsure what to do with himself.

Dyed and Anna stood looking on at the end of the hall near the doorway to the kitchen, while beyond them Ilya saw the CIA agent, Jesse Ward. Ward looked relieved, Anna looked happy, and *Dyed* looked uncertain, as if unsure it was all true. The hallway rang with laughter and a confused babble of voices until Mrs. Hogan finally received her expected hug and then pulled away from Cassie, wiping tears from her own eyes before raising her voice to address the group.

"Right then," Mrs. Hogan said. "Into the kitchen, the lot of ya! Maybe if I put some food in your mouths, you'll all be quiet long enough for Cassie and her friend here to tell us how this blessing came to pass. Though I've no doubt it was God's own miracle, it was." And with that, Mrs. Hogan began to shoo the happy milling group toward the sanctity of her kitchen.

Ilya and Karina trailed the crowd, smiling as they filed down the hall. If only the major were here—oh shit, the major. Ilya glanced at his watch, confirming that he was well overdue for his daily 11 AM email check. He stopped in the kitchen doorway and reluctantly released Karina, nodding her into the kitchen as he dug in his pants pocket for his smart phone.

Karina clung to him and looked up at him. "Where are you going, Uncle Ilya?"

Ilya beamed at his niece. "Do not worry, Karina. I will be near. Join the others, and I will be there shortly."

Karina gave him a hesitant smile and joined the celebration in the kitchen while Ilya hung back in the hall, phone in hand. He'd turned his phone off during the memorial service and powered it on now, surprised by the blinking voice mail icon. His surprise grew when he accessed his voice mail and saw multiple messages from what he recognized as burner phone numbers. This couldn't be good news. He glanced at the celebration in the kitchen and moved in the opposite direction, down the hallway and through the front door to take the call in private—unwilling to put a damper on the celebrations. Once outside, he listened to the last message and called the number as instructed.

"Ilya! Thank God," said Borgdanov. "I've been trying for an hour to reach someone."

"I suppose everyone had their phones turned off for the service—"

"Okay. No problem. I have you now. You must—"

"Andrei," Ilya said, "they are alive. Karina and Cassie are both alive."

"What? But you said your mission was unsuccessful."

"It was, but somehow—"

"That's wonderful," Borgdanov said, "and I want to hear about it, but now you must listen closely. The *Bratstvo* bastards have taken out a contract on *Dyed* and the Kairouzes. The hit is already planned, and it will be soon. You must warn them."

"*Da*," Ilya replied. "How? You have details?"

"I know they have the Kairouz house bugged, and that they plan to use a bomb when they are all gathered there, so you must prevent that from happening—&lrquo;

Ilya shoved the phone into his pocket and turned for the door before Borgdanov finished the sentence.

OUTSIDE THE KAIROUZ RESIDENCE
LONDON, UK

Fedosov nodded as the cook's Irish brogue came through his headphones, urging the group into the kitchen. He listened impatiently to the sounds of the happy crowd moving down the hallway, and he switched between his various listening devices to confirm their transit. Sure enough, the volume of their combined chatter rose in the kitchen as it fell in the other rooms. Soon they'd all be exactly where he wanted them.

He tensed and fingered the detonator, but he hesitated, were all three targets in the kill zone? The Chief would be livid if any survived. Should he wait a bit, to ensure everyone was there? He heard chairs being scraped along the floor, and then a woman's voice he didn't recognize. A British accent, youngish, perhaps the redhead on crutches?

"I propose a toast to the safe return of Cassie and Karina," the woman said.

There was a 'hear, hear,' that he recognized as Kairouz, and then a jumble of other responses.

"Wait. Where's Ilya?" a voice said. Clearly an American, probably Dugan. Good. Only the Kairouz woman left to confirm.

"He went out the front to make a phone call," said someone. Female. Russian accent.

"I'll go get him," he heard Dugan respond. "We can't have a toast without Ilya."

Shit! Don't leave, thought Fedosov. And then he smiled. When everyone was gathered for the toast, he'd know with certainty his targets were all there.

He settled back to wait. How accommodating of them to arrange the signal themselves.

***

Ilya reached for the latch just as the door opened to reveal a smiling Dugan.

"Ilya, come in. We're going to toast the girls' return—"

The big Russian grabbed Dugan by the arm and pulled him out onto the front porch.

"What the hell's the matter with you?" Dugan demanded as Ilya dragged him down the walk away from the house.

"*Dyed*, you are in danger. I think there is a bomb in the house. I must get the others out."

"What? Let's go." Dugan turned back to the house.

"*Nyet*." Ilya tightened his grip on Dugan's arm. "The house is bugged, how extensively I do not know, but I think the plan is to kill you and both Alex and Gillian at the same time. I don't know why that has not happened, but I think you must stay separate from them."

"So you go in and get them out, and I stand here with my thumb up my ass?"

Ilya shrugged. "I think is safer for the others also, if you are not close."

Dugan hesitated, then nodded. "Okay. Get them out. I'll stay outside."

Ilya nodded back and ran up the walk and through the front door. He moved down the long hallway and into the kitchen. The group gathered there looked up, everyone smiling.

"Okay, now we have you, but where's Tom?" Anna asked.

"*Dyed* will be in soon," Ilya said. "He is smoking a cigarette."

Anna looked puzzled. "But Tom—" She stopped dead at Ilya's finger in front of his lips.

The group fell silent, but Ward and Anna picked up on Ilya's hand signs and quietly scooted their chairs away from the kitchen table and rose, silently urging the others to do likewise, as they all started moving toward the back door.

***

Dugan watched Ilya disappear into the house, his mind racing. If the Russian mob was intent on killing them all in the house, there was likely someone nearby waiting to pull the trigger. It could all be done very remotely, of course, but if they'd gone to such great lengths to kill them together, they'd likely want a witness on site to confirm the deaths. That meant line of sight, which on these tree-lined streets meant close, very close.

He moved off the sidewalk and crept through the shrubbery to the edge of the expansive front yard. He found a good vantage point behind a boxwood hedge and peered up and down the street. There were a few parked cars, but all were unoccupied, so he kept low behind the hedge and moved to the side of the house. Halfway down the yard, he stopped and slowly raised his eyes above the top of the hedge to check out the side street. Sure enough, a hundred yards beyond the entrance to the driveway, a plumbing repair van sat at the curb.

He started forward in a crouching run, keeping the hedge between himself and the van, with no clear idea what he was going to do when he got there.

***

Fedosov sat listening as the ex-*Spetsnaz* announced his arrival, and then cursed under his breath at the news the American Dugan wasn't with him. Then the conversation seemed to die. Something was wrong, but he couldn't tell what. He sat mentally parsing the possibilities, and then it came to him. He was nothing if not thorough, and he always did his homework on potential targets.

Dugan didn't smoke.

His fingers tightened on the detonator, and he pushed the button.

***

Dugan had just cleared the hedge and turned to exit the driveway into the street when the blast took him full in the back, knocking him off his feet. He fell face first on the drive, momentarily stunned, and then felt the hard cobblestones beneath him as rubble began to rain down, causing him to press himself to the ground and cross his arms over the back of his head for protection.

The last bits of rubble still pattered through the leaves above him when he staggered to his feet and looked toward the ruins of the house. His heart leapt into his throat as secondary explosions engulfed the wreckage in flames, and he took a step toward the house, then stopped. Ilya was there, and he had gotten them out. He HAD to believe that, or otherwise it made no difference. He turned back down the drive and stooped to scoop up a fist-sized chunk of masonry as he raced toward the van, murder in his heart.

The van rocked on its springs as he approached and someone moved about inside. Dugan reached the driver's door and yanked it open just as a small rat-faced man slipped into the driver's seat. The man's surprise was short lived, and he immediately slipped his right hand toward his left armpit, but Dugan was already swinging his rock toward Rat Face's nose. It landed with a satisfying crunch.

The pistol dropped to the floorboard of the van, and Dugan dragged the semi-conscious killer from the vehicle and threw him face down in the street, then knelt on the man's back and raised his rock high, ready to smash the bastard's skull. Then he stopped. He didn't want the little fish, he wanted the boss.

He tossed the rock aside and used his necktie to bind the killer's hands behind his back, and then stood. The man moaned as Dugan pulled him to his feet and pushed him toward the drive of the Kairouz house.

"You'd better hope no one's dead, asshole," Dugan said through clenched teeth, "or you're gonna have a lot more to moan about."

CHAPTER THIRTY-FOUR

Borgdanov paced the worn carpet of his hotel room. It had been over six hours since Ilya terminated their conversation so abruptly, and Borgdanov was worried—no news was definitely not good news. He'd already risked compromising them by contacting Ilya openly in the first place and by continuing to try to reach him since their last call, using the same burner phone on the off chance that Ilya's circumstances were such that he may not have access to the other numbers. He fought the urge to try yet again, then jumped at the muffled buzz of a cell phone, momentarily puzzled until he realized it was not the one he'd been using, but one of the others in his suitcase. He threw the bag on the bed and wrestled with the straps, frantic lest he miss the call.

"*Da!*"

"Andrei, this is Dugan—"

"*Dyed*, is everyone all right? Why are you calling me instead of Ilya?"

"First, everyone is all right, though a bit the worse for wear. The bastards tried to blow up Alex's house with us all inside. Ilya got everyone out in time, but he was the last out when it blew. He stopped a couple of flying bricks, one to the head and another to the torso. He has a concussion and some cracked ribs, but the doctor says he'll be okay in a week or ten days. He—and you—saved all our lives, Andrei. I don't know how to thank you."

"*Nyet.* There is no need for thanks, *Dyed*. I am glad everyone is okay. But tell me of Cassie and Karina. Ilya said they are alive? I do not understand. I thought your rescue mission was unsuccessful."

"So did we. Long story short, the guys on the ship rescued them and smuggled them ashore in the US. From there Cassie contacted Ward. I'll bring you up to speed when we have more time, but for the moment, the *Bratstvo* think the girls are dead, and we'd like to keep it that way. We caught the asshole that planted the bombs, and he has no clue who the girls were, nor did he have time to mention it to his superiors, so we think we're all right there for the moment."

"What of Tanya?"

There was a long pause.

"Tanya didn't make it. She died in the container before the rescue."

"She was a brave young woman," Borgdanov said, "so it seems we have yet another score to settle with these *mafiya* scum. But what is your situation now?"

"Officially, we're all dead. That was Anna's idea to buy us a little time while we figure out what to do. We're all in an MI5 safe house."

"*Da.* Is good idea. And soon, I do not think our *Bratstvo* friends will be a problem. Have Ilya call me when he can. I promised I would not start here without him, and I can give him a week, but then he needs to join me in Prague. I have things in motion here."

"How is the recruitment going?"

"Much better since I got some help from an old friend. So tell Agent Ward I will need that favor as soon as possible."

"How many?"

"Just the families for now."

"How many, Andrei?"

"Fifty-seven."

"Uhh… including your shooters?"

"No. Seventy-two with the operators. Plus, of course, Ilya and myself, Ilya's parents and Karina's family. Eighty-two in all. Is this a problem, *Dyed*?"

"Not financially. Alex and I are committed to making it work, and Hanley bitched a little, but he'll come through as well. But Jesse's gonna shit. That's a lot of people to provide with new identities and slip into the country. I think he normally works in ones and twos."

"I think he will be more than satisfied when he sees the intelligence I have for him, but he will have to trust me for now. We need to get all the families out of Russia as soon as possible. The first of them travel tomorrow from St. Petersburg to Helsinki, Finland. It is a short flight, less than one hour. Also, there are flights to Helsinki from other cities, so the travel pattern won't be so noticeable. If I get them all to Helsinki, how soon can you arrange a charter flight to get them to UK or directly to the US?"

"Probably within twenty-four to forty-eight hours, but I think we should bring them to the UK as tourists first. Jesse may need more time on his end."

"Good. I will have them all in Finland in three days, so plan the charter flight accordingly."

"Will do," Dugan said. "What next?"

"We'll hit the *Bratstvo* in Prague. It is their biggest operation outside of Russia itself, and they have less official protection there. Also, it is the center of their human-trafficking operations. I'm finalizing the operation and the extraction plans now. We should be able to execute within a few days after Ilya arrives."

"We'll be there."

"We? No, *Dyed*, not you—"

"They've attacked me and the people I love. I have every right to be there."

"*Da.* You have the right, but I must be truthful, *Dyed*. You do not have the ability to blend in or the military skills for this mission. You are an asset in many places, and if we were going on a ship, I would want you by my side, but here you would be a liability. Besides, we need someone to arrange things on that end."

"Just a damn minute, Alexei—"

"*Dyed*, I would trust you with my life. I HAVE trusted you with my life. But now I entrust you with something even more precious, the lives of all our families. If something goes wrong or for some reason we do not come back, we need to know there is someone we can trust to take care of them. The others there are our friends, but you are our *brat*—our brother—and someone must remain to guard the family, *da*?"

"I don't know whether to be flattered or pissed off."

"You can be either, or both, as long as we know you are looking after our loved ones."

Dugan sighed. "All right. I'll put up a draft email when I have the flight arrangements out of Helsinki. Keep an eye on the email account."

PRAGUE
CZECH REPUBLIC
1 WEEK LATER

Arsov sat at his old desk, watching a video of the latest whore being seasoned, a nice young brunette from Ekaterinburg in the Sverdlovsk Oblast. She was obviously of Tartar stock, with an exotic look about her that would no doubt make her a moneymaker with the right training. And he had to admit, Beria was doing a good job there. Between brutalizing the girl, and alternating periods of kindness with horrific threats to her family, he already had her broken. The rest would be easy.

Arsov's approval was tempered with caution. Beria was both competent and ambitious, and couldn't conceal his dissatisfaction at the demotion occasioned by Arsov's unexpected return. Arsov had placated him to date with compliments and a bonus paid from his own pocket, but the man had run the Prague operation quite competently during Arsov's absence, and obviously was chafing to do so again. He would bear watching. But that was a worry for another day. Satisfied everything was proceeding as it should, Arsov closed the training video and opened his browser to check out some British news sites.

He'd been elated the previous week to read of the destruction of the Kairouz house and the death of its occupants and assorted guests. He was particularly pleased they'd killed the ex-*Spetsnaz* sergeant, but sorry there had been no mention of Borgdanov. The whereabouts of the Russian former officer was troubling, but not unduly so. Nonetheless, Arzov continued to scout British news reports for any follow-up on the Kairouz bombing or any mention of Borgdanov. He considered contacting the Chief in St. Petersburg directly, to see if he had any information on Borgdanov, but thought better of it. The man frowned on unnecessary contact, and Arsov was doing his best to get back in the Chief's good graces, so perhaps it was best to continue to do a good job here in Prague and to let the memory of the unfortunate situation in London fade. He'd bide his time until another opportunity presented itself.

He glanced at the clock at the bottom of his computer screen—4 PM. He had time to make a run through all the clubs and brothels to keep everyone on their toes. He was sure Beria had everything in hand, but it didn't pay to get sloppy, especially since his own position here was somewhat probationary. He powered down his computer and rose from the desk, just as he heard the distinctive 'sphut' of a suppressed weapon from the living room, followed by a crash.

"Boris?" he called. When his bodyguard failed to answer, he jerked open a desk drawer and retrieved a pistol. "Boris, are you there?" he called again as he moved toward the door.

Arsov burst into the hall, pistol in front of him in a two-handed grip. He swung the weapon right and then quickly back to the left before continuing down the hall toward the living room. He studied the living room over the sights of the pistol, the room deserted except for the very dead body of Boris lying on his back over the smashed glass coffee table, a perfectly round hole between his eyes leaking blood down the side of his face. He felt the stun gun pressed to the back of his skull and stiffened a split second before thousands of volts overwhelmed his nervous system.

***

Arsov's eyes flew open, and he jerked his head back as the acrid smell of ammonia filled his nose. He glimpsed retreating hands in front of his face and struggled to make sense of his surroundings. He was in the 'training' bedroom in the apartment, but the bed had been disassembled and pushed up against the wall. More disconcerting still, he was naked and stretched spread eagle, face up in a half-reclining position, his wrists and ankles tightly bound to something immovable. His genitals rested slightly elevated on a flat piece of concrete shoved into his crotch. He heard movement behind him and tried to turn.

"Careful, Arsov," a voice said. "You might strain your neck, and that can be very painful. We wouldn't want that, now would we?"

The disembodied voice gained a face as a tall man moved into view and stood over him.

"But forgive me. Where are my manners? I am Major Andrei Borgdanov, and this gentleman"—he nodded at another large man that appeared at Arsov's other side—"is Sergeant Ilya Denosovitch."

"Yo-you're supposed to be dead," Arsov said to Denosovitch.

"Sorry to disappoint you," Denosovitch said.

"Wh-what do you want?" Arsov asked, and Borgdanov shrugged.

"Nothing too difficult. Just a little cooperation for now."

"You are insane! Cooperate with you? Do you know what the *Bratstvo* would do to me? And no matter what you do to me, do you think they will let you get away with this? You are already dead, as are your families. But if you release me at once and leave, I will make sure that you are the only ones to die. This is your last chance to save your loved ones."

Borgdanov nodded. "Thank you for your kind and generous offer, but we have already seen to the safety of our loved ones."

"You fool! My men are undoubtedly on the way here now. I suggest you leave while you can."

"Ah yes, your men. By that I presume you mean the forty-three *Bratstvo* thugs that make up your little 'army' here in Prague, spread out to guard your clubs and whorehouses? If so, I regret to inform you that they are all very dead and as we speak are being stacked on the floor of the central warehouse from which you distribute your porn and drugs." Borgdanov looked thoughtful. "It really is amazing how easy it is to take out unsuspecting targets with relatively few trained men and suppressed weapons. Even the former *Spetsnaz* among your soldiers presented little challenge. Surprise really is key, *da*?"

"You're bluffing."

"Oh, but I'm not." Borgdanov glanced at his watch. "And in exactly thirty minutes, their bodies, along with all your porn and drugs, will disappear in a raging warehouse fire."

"You'll never get away with—"

"Yes, I think we will, but before you so predictably threaten me next with the tame policemen the *Bratstvo* has in their pocket, let me save you the trouble. Eight hours ago, Chief Inspector Pavel Makovec was killed by a sniper, and shortly thereafter the other eighteen Prague policemen on your payroll received anonymous phone calls informing them they would be next, should they decide to assist you. They were also provided with details of their involvement with *Bratstvo* and a link and password to a website with full documentation of that involvement, and warned that should they provide any further assistance to your organization, the documentation would be sent to the international news media. Finally, we assured them their 'compensation' would continue to be funded if they would instead cooperate with us. All agreed."

Borgdanov smiled. "So you see, Arsov, your tame policemen now work for me, and I don't think the *Bratstvo* will be back in Prague for a long, long time. Perhaps you should consider cooperation, *da*?"

Arsov studied Borgdanov. The ex-*Spetsnaz* man didn't appear to be bluffing, so perhaps it was time to hedge bets. He'd think of a way to spin it to the *Bratstvo* later, but for the moment his goal was survival.

"Very well," Arsov said. "What do you want to know?"

"Nothing too difficult. Let's begin with the passports. We rescued over a hundred women and children from your little operation. Where are their passports?"

"The passports for the women are in my safe in the office. I… I don't have passports for all the kids. Most were taken on the streets. We normally arrange false papers when we need to move them."

"Very well. Give us the combination." Borgdanov nodded at Denosovitch, who produced a pad and pencil.

Arsov recited the combination as Denosovitch wrote it down and left the room. He returned a short time later and nodded at Borgdanov.

"There are about eighty passports," Denosovitch said.

Borgdanov looked down at Arsov.

"So. That was not so difficult, now was it, Arsov?"

Arsov shook his head. "What more do you want to know?"

Borgdanov looked puzzled. "Know? Nothing. We have all the information we need from you. Now we merely want you to die—slowly and painfully. Unfortunately, it will likely be a bit noisy as well, but given the former use of this room, I suspect it is soundproofed." Borgdanov shrugged. "And if not, I'm sure the neighbors are accustomed to hearing screams and know to mind their own business, *da*?"

Arsov sat, stunned, as Borgdanov nodded to Denosovitch again and the man left the room.

"Wait," said Arsov. "You should not kill me. I can help you. I know things, many things."

"I'm sure you do, but we have much better sources. And besides, WE are not going to kill you. Someone else has claimed that right."

"Hello, Arsov," said a voice to his right, and he twisted his head to see a woman with short black hair enter the room at Denosovitch's side. He recognized the voice, but not the—Karina. Of course, Denosovitch's niece.

"K-Karina? What are you doing here?"

"Oh, it's 'Karina,' now, is it, Arsov? Not 'whore' or 'slut' or any of the other little pet names you called us. I'm so honored you remembered my name. But how about what you called me at first when I could still fight back? Do you remember what you used to say when you beat me and raped me and watched while the others did as well. Because I remember it very well. What was it now? Oh, yes. You would shout, 'That will teach you, you little slut. That will teach you to be a ball breaker.'"

Arsov had been so fixated on the face and the voice, he'd noticed little else, but he flinched now as Karina looked down at his exposed genitals and smiled before she lifted a sledgehammer she'd kept down at her side.

"So finally, Arsov, it seems I really am to become a ball breaker," Karina said as she took the handle of the hammer in a two-handed grip and raised it above her head.

"This is for me and Tanya and all the others," Karina said, and she started toward him.

***

Ilya sat on the sofa in the living room, holding Karina close as she sobbed. Slowly she regained control of herself.

"I-I am sorry, Uncle Ilya."

"Shhh… little Karinka," Ilya said. "Do you think I WANTED you to do this horrible thing? It is only because you insisted that I let you try. But it broke my heart, and I am GLAD you could not. It means the monsters have not conquered you and stolen your humanity. You are our little Karinka still. Brave beyond measure, yes, but not hard. Not brittle and bitter."

Karina pulled back and looked at her uncle. "But what do you mean?"

"I mean that when you take another life, no matter how justified, you lose a bit of yourself. You cannot understand until you do it, and I cannot explain. Sometimes, if you are very angry, it is a good feeling, like a toothache when it stops, but then it becomes an empty feeling. It uses up a little of your soul, I think."

"But, Uncle Ilya, you are a soldier, so—"

"I am not immune, Karinka, but soldiers have tricks. We deceive ourselves and count our enemies only as 'targets,' but in a case like this where the fight is very personal, yes, we pay the price when we kill. It is a price worth paying to protect those we love, but I am glad you did not have to pay it. You have suffered enough, and this is my job, *da*?"

Karina fell silent and hugged him tightly, and Ilya returned her embrace and kissed the top of her head, then gently disengaged himself.

"Stay here now. I must go see the major. It will all be over soon." Ilya stood up.

He walked down the hall and through the door into the training room, closing the door behind him. Arsov lost control of his bodily functions when Karina had started toward him with the hammer, and the stench in the room was almost overpowering. Arsov slumped in the mess, whimpering as the major leaned against the far wall, his arms crossed. Borgdanov looked up.

"I considered finishing him, but I think his fate belongs to you. What do you want to do with him, Ilya?"

Ilya shook his head. "I intended to make him suffer, but he is not worth it. He is only a cockroach, and I will not let him steal anymore of my humanity than he already has."

Borgdanov nodded. "*Da*, you are right. Then step on him quickly, and let's get out of here."

Ilya drew his pistol and shot the cockroach between the eyes.

REGIONAL HQ
FEDERAL SECURITY SERVICE (FSB)
ST. PETERSBURG
RUSSIAN FEDERATION

Vladimir Glazkov looked down, both surprised and annoyed as the cell phone buzzed in the desk drawer. The phone was meant for one-way communication only except in extreme emergencies, so an incoming call couldn't be anything but bad news—or an idiot that would live to regret disturbing him. He yanked open the drawer and looked at the incoming number. Arsov! He should have guessed. He stifled a curse and answered the phone.

"*Da*?"

"Ah. Comrade Glazkov. Good afternoon. Sorry to disturb you," a cheerful voice said.

Glazkov's blood ran cold. No one except those in the highest circles knew his real identity, certainly not Arsov, and that wasn't the fool's voice anyway. He hesitated, torn between hanging up and the need to know more.

"You have the wrong number. There is no one here by that name."

There was an audible sigh. "Very well, then. I will call you 'Chief' if you prefer. It really doesn't matter to me."

"Who is this?"

"Oh, forgive me. I am Major Andrei Borgdanov, formerly of the *Spetsnaz*, but I think you know that. And as you can see, I'm calling from the phone of your late associate, Sergei Arsov."

"I know no one of that name, Major—Borgdanov, is it? I'm sorry, but once again, I believe you have the wrong number."

"And yet, we continue to chat. But perhaps we can end this charade. I presume you're sitting in your office at the FSB, so may I ask you to check your email—not your FSB address, but the 'secret' encrypted one you use to correspond with the rest of the *Bratstvo* leadership."

"Again, Major, I believe you are misinformed." Glazkov struggled to keep the fear from his voice as his fingers flew over the keyboard. In seconds he'd found the single email from an anonymous sender and opened it. He scrolled through it with a growing sense of alarm.

"I think you should have it open by now," Borgdanov said. "And you will see the organizational chart that shows your true identity, along with the identities of the other top *Bratstvo* leaders, along with the positions they occupy in government or legitimate businesses. I emphasize that this is just a small sample of the information I have."

"What do you want?"

"It is not a question of what I want, Glazkov, because what I want, I will take. This is more a matter of an exchange of information to prevent you from making a mistake. A matter of courtesy, so to speak."

"Go on."

"A few hours ago, we destroyed your Prague operation. All of your men there, including Mr. Arsov, are dead. All of your victims have been released and taken to a place of safety, and your warehouse full of drugs, porn, and illegal weapons is presently burning brightly. Additionally, you will no longer enjoy the protection of the Prague police, and should you attempt to make new inroads there, I believe you will find your overtures most unwelcome. Do you understand?"

"You are playing a dangerous game, Borgdanov. You understand, of course, that you are a dead man?"

"Ah, but we are all dead men the moment we are born, are we not, Glazkov? Only the timing and manner of our deaths is in question, and I believe mine will be both peaceful and some time away."

"Believe what you want. You are not a match for the *Bratstvo*. How can you possibly hope to stand against us?"

"Because Glazkov, the information in that email and much, much more is hidden on encrypted servers in several locations worldwide, and in the event of my untimely death by any means, it will be transmitted to every major law enforcement organization as well as to every major news outlet within a matter of hours. The world will know who you really are, what you do, and how you do it, all in sufficient detail to bring your operations to a halt."

"So what? Of course it will be an inconvenience to be so identified, but we are untouchable here in Russia, and do you really think we care about world opinion?"

"No, but I think you care about the money that buys the influence and power you enjoy in Russia, and if I'm reading the data correctly, over 75 percent of that revenue—76.73 percent to quote your latest cash flow report—comes from operations outside of Russia. How long do you think your empire can last even in Russia without the cash to buy the influence you currently enjoy?"

Glazkov sat stunned, imagining the dissolution of all he'd built, until Borgdanov spoke again.

"Glazkov?"

"All right, Borgdanov. What do you want? Part of our operations, I presume?"

"We do not want to play your filthy games, Glazkov. We wish to be neither competitors nor partners. For the moment, we will settle for a truce. Accept that your operations in Prague are finished, withdraw from the UK, and make no attempt to retaliate against anyone connected with this affair, and we will leave you alone."

"For the moment?"

"Nothing lasts forever, Glazkov," Borgdanov replied. "I have no doubt you will begin maneuvering to eliminate us as soon as this call is finished, regardless of what you agree to now. I suggest that if you are so inclined that you first test us in a limited manner, so when I crush your attempts, it will be less painful for you. Remember that I can release information selectively, making sure the damage it does to you is more than proportionate to any harm you might do to me. However, be aware that if any of your actions results in harm to any of my people or their families, the truce is over, and it will be all-out war."

"You are an arrogant bastard, Borgdanov."

"I prefer to think of it as confident."

"And only time will tell if that confidence is justified. Now. Is there anything else we need to discuss?"

"One minor detail. In the email I sent you is the account information for one of *Bratstvo*'s bank accounts in Liechtenstein. As noted in the email, I took the liberty of making a small withdrawal to cover our expenses."

Glazkov turned back to his computer screen and moved his mouse, his blood pressure spiking as he read the note.

"You took it ALL! THERE WAS FIFTY MILLION DOLLARS IN THAT ACCOUNT!"

"A part of which will be used to relocate your victims and their families, as well as to provide counseling. And the rest, well, the rest we'll need to fund ongoing operations. We'll try to get by with what's left, but I suspect mounting a defense against potential attacks will be expensive. A great deal of that depends on you, of course."

Glazkov struggled to compose himself as the silence grew.

"You are a dead man, Borgdanov," he said at last.

"Without doubt. But not tomorrow."

Glazkov sighed. "No. Not tomorrow."

"And may I presume we have an agreement for the moment?"

"*Da*. For the moment."

"Wonderful. It was very nice talking to you, Comrade Glazkov, and do try to keep things in perspective, *da*?" Borgdanov said just before Glazkov heard the click of the disconnect.

He rested his elbows on his desk and buried his face in his hands.

EPILOGUE

Dugan raised his head as the Orthodox priest finished the Russian prayer, and everyone joined in the collective amen. There was a gentle breeze moving across the swim platform on the stern of the large yacht, and he looked out over the blue sky and bluer sea with a sad smile. It was a beautiful day to say goodbye to a beautiful person.

The priest murmured something to Tanya's parents, and they stepped to the stern rail, Tanya's fiancé, Ivan, at their side. Tanya's father tossed a huge floral wreath onto the surface of the sea, and everyone else in the small group stood silently for a long moment and then began to fade back, leaving Tanya's parents and Ivan some time alone with their grief. The charter captain and his five-man crew had manned the rail nearby, all in crisp white uniforms and standing at attention, but the captain left his position now and moved quietly to Dugan's side, his eyebrows raised in an unspoken question.

"Let her drift here as long as they want," Dugan said quietly. "If they look like they're ready to go, check with me first, and I'll confirm it with them."

The captain nodded and dismissed his crew, who moved away quietly to resume their duties. The captain remained nearby looking over the side but keeping a discreet eye on the grieving family, as Dugan followed the rest of the small group of mourners inside.

The crew had prepared a bountiful buffet lunch in the yacht's spacious salon, and the mourners gathered there in small groups as the steward circulated, taking drink orders. Nigel and Cassie stood in one corner, talking quietly with Ilya, Karina and the priest, while Dugan stood with Alex and Gillian, chatting with Borgdanov. Mrs. Hogan had declined the invitation, on the grounds that she got seasick standing on the dock and didn't feel up to an ocean voyage, no matter how short.

"Alex," Borgdanov said, "it was very generous of you to charter this beautiful boat and fly Tanya's people here all the way from Russia. I know that they appreciate it. It is wonderful gesture, and I thank you for it."

Alex shook his head. "It was the least we could do. I hope it gives them some closure."

Beside him, Gillian nodded and brushed away a tear. She started to speak but then shook her head and smiled sadly, as if she didn't trust her own voice.

"Well, I know it means a great deal to them, and to young Ivan too," Borgdanov said. "Evidently he has been going crazy searching for Tanya. He seems like good boy."

The others nodded agreement, and the conversation drifted towards silence, continuing in fits and starts until the captain appeared at the door to the salon and caught Dugan's eye.

"I think they're ready, Mr. Dugan," the captain said as Dugan reached the door.

Dugan nodded and looked over to where Borgdanov now stood with Karina, and beckoned them over to join him as translators.

They found Ivan and Tanya's parents standing together on the swim platform, looking unsure what to do. Karina hurried to their side, and after confirming that they were ready to leave, gently urged the trio inside to get something to eat. Dugan turned to the captain.

"How long back to Jacksonville?"

The captain looked out at the sea. "Sea's like a mill pond. Four hours maybe, four and a half tops."

"Okay. Let's head back."

The captain nodded and left, and less than two minutes later the engine speed began to slowly increase as the bow of the vessel swung due west. Dugan stood at the stern rail with Borgdanov and looked aft as the breeze washed over them.

"So how is Texas?" Dugan asked.

Borgdanov chuckled. "Odessa, Texas, is very different from Odessa in the Ukraine, so I think whoever chose this name has vivid imagination or strange sense of humor."

Dugan laughed. "I thought it might be a bit of an adjustment. But seriously, are all your people okay? Handley's treating you all right?"

"*Da*. Better than all right, and Mr. Ray Handley's ranch is far from town in middle of nowhere, and we can see anyone coming for a very long way." He moved his arms in a sweeping gesture. "It is like being here, in middle of ocean, so security is very easy."

Borgdanov nodded. "No, we could not ask for more, *Dyed*. He brought in many of the houses on wheels—how you call them, mobile homes? But they are very big! Woody tells me they are called 'double times,' I think."

Dugan grinned. "I think you mean double-wides."

"*Da*, double-wides. Anyway they are much bigger than anyone's old apartment in Russia. He laid them all out with streets, and somewhere he even found Russian teacher, so we also have school for the children. We have regular Russian village," Borgdanov said. "Of course, is temporary, but everyone is learning English, and the children are learning very fast. We will move in time, but there is no hurry, I think."

"No regrets?"

Borgdanov gave him a sad smile. "Our hearts are Russian, *Dyed*, so there will always be regrets. But we appreciate the opportunity you have all given us to safeguard our families, so we will try to be good Americans too. The children are very happy, especially the younger ones."

"And," Borgdanov continued, "I am happy that thanks to Arkady, we can repay you, Alex, and Mr. Ray Handley for the money you have spent."

"About your friend Arkady—you do know Ward's lusting after that intelligence, right?"

Borgdanov nodded. "I understand, and we will do anything Ward requires of us, as agreed. I will also give him anything he needs to support an operation, or if he wants specific information about something in Russia or elsewhere, I will help him all I can. But I will not turn over everything I got from Arkady, because when we are not working for Ward, we will work on our own." He smiled. "We are Americans now, and I believe in free enterprise, *da*? Also, I am reminded of what Archimedes said about levers."

Dugan thought a moment. "With a lever and a place to stand, I'll move the world?"

"*Da*," Borgdanov nodded. "Arkady gave me a very great lever, and you and the others have given us a safe place to stand. And I don't want to move the world, just Russia."

"So it's not over between you and the *Bratstvo*?"

Borgdanov's face hardened, and he looked at the eastern horizon.

"Oh no, *Dyed*. It has only just begun."

Author's Notes

As readers of my other work know, while my stories are fictional, they are based on real (or at least plausible) events. That wasn't too difficult in the past; both *Deadly Straits* and *Deadly Coasts* are set in an industry I know quite well and (for the most part) in geographical settings with which I'm familiar. However, when I decided to tackle the issue of human trafficking, that required a lot more research, and what I found wasn't pleasant.

The events in *Deadly Crossing* are fictional, but the cruelty of human trafficking and the methods depicted to control its victims are all too real. And while Russia and the countries of the former Soviet Bloc provide the victims for the story (as they often do in real life), human trafficking takes place in every country and every city in the world, including those of North America and Western Europe. Wherever you're reading this, it's likely that there are hidden victims of this horrible crime within a few hours' (or even a few minutes') journey.

Thank You

Time is a precious commodity. None of us truly knows quite how much we'll have, and most of us are compelled to spend large blocks of it earning a living, making our leisure time more precious still. I am honored that you've chosen to spend some of your precious leisure time reading my work, and sincerely hope you found it enjoyable.

If you enjoyed this book, I do hope you'll spread the word to friends and family. I also hope you'll consider writing a review on Amazon, Goodreads, or one of the many sites dedicated to book reviews. A review need not be lengthy, and it will be most appreciated. Honest reader reviews are the single most effective means for a new author to build a following, and I need all I can get.

If you enjoyed these books of the Dugan series, I invite you to try the three books of my *Disruption Trilogy* listed on the following page. It's a post-apocalyptic tale, set in the near future, and a bit of a departure from the Dugan stories. That said, I personally feel it's some of my best work to date, and based on feedback, almost all of my Dugan readers who've given it a try seem to agree.

And speaking of feedback, I'd love to hear yours, good or bad, so please drop me an email via my website at **www.remcdermott.com**. I respond personally to all emails, though it may take me a while, depending on workload.

While you're on my site (and if you're so inclined) please consider joining my Reader Group so I can alert you to each new book when it becomes available.

That's all for now. Thanks once again for reading my work.

Fair Winds and Following Seas,
R.E. (Bob) McDermott

The Disruption Trilogy
By R.E. McDermott

"McDermott turns the post-apocalyptic genre on its head, with an absolutely stunning look at a terrifyingly realistic, near-future collapse scenario. Leveraging his real-life background and experience as a backdrop, McDermott delivers an unforgettable, fast-paced tale of heroism and survival in a post-apocalyptic world."

USA Today Best-Selling Author - Steve Konkoly

Under a Tell-Tale Sky - When a massive solar flare fries the electrical grid, Captain Jordan Hughes' problems are just starting. Stranded far from home with a now-priceless cargo of fuel and a restless crew, Hughes weighs his options as violence worsens ashore and the world crumbles around the secure haven of his ship, the Pecos Trader. 'Wait and see,' isn't an option. Hughes must get his ship and crew home – but the government arrives with other plans. Book 1 of a sprawling epic that stretches from the bayous of Louisiana's Cajun Country to the deep woods of Maine and all points between. Start the journey.

Push Back – Earth reels in the aftermath of a savage solar storm. Without electrical power or the means to restore it, chaos spreads, and isolated pockets of survivors unite to survive, fending for themselves rather than relying on an overwhelmed government. When that same government morphs into a dictatorship, survivors face another difficult decision; do they knuckle under, or to they PUSH BACK?

Promises To Keep – Survivor resistance stiffens as an increasingly corrupt and tyrannical president clamps down on dissent and seeks to eliminate anyone who might expose his perfidy. Only one man has the credibility and the stature to turn the situation around and fulfill a promise to himself — and the nation. Simon Tremble, fugitive Speaker of the House of Representatives, and the last lawmaker not under control of the corrupt president, climbs out of his hidden hollow and starts south along the Appalachian Trail. He has promises to keep.

30000238R00344

Printed in Great Britain
by Amazon